The Butterflies, Yero and Boca

Allen (Pud) Deters

2020 Tetralogy Edition

Rev 730

The Tetralogy

The Butterflies, Yero and Boca

Part 1: Tales of the Rasha La
Part 2: Beyond the Moonwalk
Part 3: Byways of the Butterfly
Part 4: The Lure of the Dragon Range

...and since it was their turn the monarchs told their own story: A tale of lost children who return to earth as butterflies on the wings of the Fyrstellia, the falling stars.

For when the Lord of Light granted men a mortal life span He founded a halfway house in the nearby heavens as well, the Halls of Waiting, where angels could bring the fallen and tend their spirits until they were ready to go further into the Light. For most it was only a short stay, but not for the children.

"They don't want to go on", reported the Keeper of the Halls. "They want to go back".

Here are two that did – together with an account of their journey into Mexico, caught up along the way in the fortunes of the fairy people on earth.

"It gets worse before it gets better!"

So goes the joke amongst migrators, cheering each other on, laughing at harsh reality.

The jest speaks to an unspoken truth. Some of them will never see the part where it gets better. Those are the odds. But odds are for losers, not migrators!

So journey with them fearlessly! Yes, there are horrible dangers just ahead, but against that you will have a guide – a hummingbird with skill in the arts of light – and for lighter company a pair of brash young monarch butterflies beginning to learn the ways of the wild.

What could go wrong?

Dedication

To all the Lost Children.
May you fulfill your Quests.

Acknowledgements

Special thanks to David and Jan Kapanke for their editing.
—and—
The book cover was drawn by Katheryn Grace Deters.

Contents

Part 1
Tales of the Rasha La

Synopsis

Here you will meet monarch butterflies of the little-known subspecies *Rasha La*, recently arrived in the wildwood: Yero and Boca, a girl and a boy.

You'll find them sheltering overnight in a thorn bush and awaken early with them to an awareness of predators in the trees above – a roost of hungry crows – some wary of the monarch toxicity, some not. Debate ensues about the butterflies' edibility and the Top Crow calls for a review of the old 'Warnings' about food.

They'll escape this time, but a greater danger is about to overtake them. They are the last monarchs of Northern Autumn. They have delayed their migration to enjoy a warm Indian Summer, but this will be the last idyllic day. By late evening snow will fly unexpectedly in a fierce onset of winter. This, with a 2000-mile journey still ahead of them.

Very soon they will need all the willpower of their wild side.

They will need the unquenchable humor of their human side, too. Luckily, that is in surplus.

And they will find themselves desperately in need of a guide to get through the bad weather. But pressing issues must wait, even as the blizzard approaches.

First, they must deal with tribbits!

Chapter 1

Storm Clouds

A thorn bush was perfect. It was already dark in the woods and the wandering monarchs knew that a veil of thorns was better protection overnight than their own reputation. They couldn't have chosen a worse perch, as we shall see. But they were young, just passing through, and unaware of local customs. A brisk shower awoke them in the wee hours, but otherwise the night passed quietly until early dawn when...

Splat!

A drop hit one of the butterflies, jarring her awake. She fumbled around in the gloom and poked her companion.

"Boca! Wake up. It's raining again."

He tried to ignore her. "Lemme be, Yero. Fold your wings."

Splat!

Before she could do so the next drop landed on her back and dribbled down her leg. That was the end of her patience. She folded her wings tight and poked him harder.

"It's raining! I'm moving!"

That brought him awake, bewildered. He felt perfectly dry.

Splat!

The third drop split on her neatly folded wings and trickled down both sides. She yelped and tip-toed away through the thorns in search of leaves to perch under. Boca followed in the dim light.

By good chance there was a canopy of leaves close by. The tough buckthorn bush had thus far ignored the frosts of autumn, retaining most of its green leaves even now on the doorstep of winter.

The new perch was much better. Occasional drops splashed harmlessly off the canopy now and all would have been well, except for a strong, fetid odor. Yero made a face.

"Yuck! What's that *smell?*"

Boca, now wide awake and downwind of his companion, also wrinkled his nose. "I think it's *you*, Yero."

This brought a chuckle, but not from Yero. A rustle of feathers commenced above them followed by more drops. The butterflies peeked up through the leaves and caught the glint of an eye and the shape of a large, dark bird against the dawning sky. A crow was watching them from a perch on a low tree branch just above. The bird leaned down and issued a loud *Caw!* which immediately drew a sharp reply from high above. Obviously, no one liked an extra-early bird.

The noisy one shuffled back and forth on his branch chafing at the rebuke but finally settled down. A minute passed, no more, until Yero poked her companion again.

"What are you trying to *say*, Boca?"

But he was spared answering when the crow interrupted from above, "Haw! You're sitting under the *Roost!"*

We must turn away for a few moments while the pretty girl butterfly adds this up and wishes she could subtract a few 'raindrops' from the total. A little sympathy from her companion would have helped but he grinned and backed away, out from under the leafy canopy.

A butterfly--even a *monarch* butterfly--should be more careful! It was light enough now that the crow could see movement and he lunged murderously for Boca, who barely ducked behind a long spine. The young crow got the spine in his cheek and flipped headlong, squawking, underneath his branch. When the squawking subsided and the crow uprighted himself more scolding, and worse, rained down from higher up. It was still early dawn and the First Rule of the Roost was: "Silence until sunrise!"

No one defended the young bird. He was youngest of all the Roost and therefore lowest in the pecking order - relegated to the dirtiest, bottommost perch. It was up to him to better himself, to move up, which isn't easy since someone above would have to move down.

An old crow just above him squinted and tossed down the final insult: "You are stupid, like the *Yaccaw!* They aren't safe to eat."

That was insulting to the butterflies as well, who certainly got the drift. 'Yaccaw' means 'not us' in the crow dialect but translates as 'dope' or 'oaf' in the common woodland speech.

The old bird should have kept his beak shut. 'Not safe to eat'? That invited argument and the young bird called for a challenge. To move up in the Roost a crow must either win an argument or have a louder "Caw." This one went right for the "Caw" with youthful energy and won. Nearby crows enforced the decision, cocking their heads and peering closely to be sure of it.

As they traded perches, old 'Craw', the loser, pecked the winner on the toe - a mistake when taking up position directly below. Poop rained down immediately, splattering on Craw's head. Changes in the pecking order have consequences. The young winner threw his head back and laughed, "Caw—haw— haw—haw!"

With a sudden rush of wind, a huge owl grabbed the noisy one right off his perch and disappeared into the darker woods.

After that, peace and quiet returned until the sun rose above the hills. When it illuminated the upper reaches of the Roost the daily quarrel broke out, the yakking and cawing that everyone can hear a mile away. Part of the uproar is because they're hungry, but if that were all they could simply fly off and find breakfast. The bigger problem is, crows wake up dissatisfied with the pecking order and no one eats until a new order is settled. Never mind that it was settled just yesterday and every other day. It's never settled with crows.

The quarrel usually breaks out over grudges and complaints, but it can erupt over anything. On this day, a question had been raised about eating - or not eating - certain *Yaccaw*. The crows had thought about it and come to their usual disagreement. Opinions flew in all directions. The monarchs soon felt on trial.

"Speak up!" came a loud voice from the Top Crow, high above. "What's the flap down there?"

"*Yaccaw*. What's edible and what's not."

"Which *Yaccaw*?"

"Can't tell. Brown...something or other."

This drew mocking laughter and a muffled reply from Yero. The Top Crow saw a chance to cut the quarrel short before the usual grievances came up.

"Caw! Get it right or we're outta here!"

Old Craw hopped down to the bush for a better look. A bottom bird can't afford to be wrong about anything or they'll be driven from the Roost entirely. The butterflies had retreated deeper into the bush, but there was no mistaking their kind.

"*Yaccaw,*" crowed the old bird, but it sounded different this time. Higher pitched. Crow speech is like that. A "Caw" can mean many things in different tones.

That settled one question, but not the other. *Monarchs*, was it? Traditionally they were avoided, but the younger crows weren't big on tradition. The free-for-all resumed. Everyone's opinion was welcome if it was loud enough, and lots of them were. There seemed no end. Finally, the Top Crow with the loudest voice of all called for the 'Warnings', and the Roost hushed.

This was unusual. All crows learn something about this in the nest, but not many can tell the story. Old Craw could. He was failing of body but not of mind and welcomed the chance to be important again. He strutted on gimpy legs and quoted from memory:

— The Crow-Mother —

In the Beginning, there was nothing until the Great Spirit made the sun to drive back the darkness. When that was done, He put the earth nearby to be a place for the living. He gave it a gentle spin, so it didn't get too hot or too cold, and set the moon above to provide light in the dark nights. In time the earth bloomed and produced a wonderful bounty, awaiting only someone to eat it. Then Great Spirit called forth children from the Light - all the creatures who would fill up the new world - and gathered them together in the sky.

"Behold the earth, which will be your new home," He announced. "There is room for all and to spare. In a moment, I will send you down. But first there are some things you need to know."

He explained the cycle of day and night, which would be new to them, and the circle of the seasons. He pointed out the seas and the lands and described the varying climates. He spoke at length about social order and good manners (which bored his audience, but they had to listen), and finished up with a few tips about the weather.

"Now you know enough to go on with," He said. "Any questions?"

Being mortals, they had come into the world hungry and they all spoke up at once. "What about *food?*" trumpeted the elephant. He was loudest, but many voices echoed the same question.

"The food is ripening as we speak," replied Great Spirit. "Find what you like. Eat whatever you wish."

This satisfied most of the creatures and Great Spirit was about to send them down when the owl voiced concern.

"What about safety?" she hooted. "Is everything *safe* to eat?"

Great Spirit paused. It was a natural question from a mortal creature, but He hadn't given it much thought. The world was new, after all, and the food clean and pure. But the question deserved consideration. Food can certainly spoil, and mortal stomachs were sure to be unpredictable.

"It's a fair question," He concluded. "Let's find out."

Great Spirit didn't want to risk any of His own children for such a quest, so He summoned a free spirit from that sliver of the world between light and darkness - a huge bird, black as the night.

"I name you 'Utu', the crow," said Great Spirit. "If you wish, you may be first to visit the living world below and taste the food. What do you say?"

Now, Utu was no fool. She guessed immediately that it would be a risky mission but couldn't resist showing up the others. She accepted.

First, she ate all the nuts and berries and the seeds of the plants and grasses, suffering no ill effects; then every last fruit and vegetable, even the edible roots. No problem.

Great Spirit became concerned by such gluttony but reminded Himself that a new season would bring another crop.

Then Utu ate the leaves off all the plants, the bark off the trees, and finally the trees themselves. She ate everything on the face of the earth and grew larger than the moon. Great Spirit frowned but determined to repair it all later.

Then Utu decided to swallow the moon.

"Don't do it!" warned Great Spirit. "It's too cold." Utu did it anyway and suffered indigestion.

"I warned you," reminded Great Spirit.

But Utu had another idea. She decided to fix the problem by swallowing the sun.

"Don't do it!" warned Great Spirit. "It's too hot." Utu did it anyway and suffered worse.

"I warned you," reminded Great Spirit.

But again, Utu ignored Him. There was still one thing left to eat that might settle her stomach: The earth itself.

"Don't do it!" warned Great Spirit. "It's too much."

The Butterflies, Yero and Boca

Utu did it anyway, and it helped to begin with; but then she over-ate, swallowing the whole thing. That was her undoing. She laid an egg but fell mortally ill soon after and fled back to the twilight.

Of course, the egg contained everything she had eaten. It hatched eventually and the world was restored, with something extra: A flock of crows emerged claiming ownership of all the food since Utu was here first.

They still own the food and take what they want because their mother's thought is in them. But her last thought was regret, so they heed the Warnings: *Too cold, too hot,* and *too much.*

***

...Craw finished and turned an eye toward the monarchs. "So! Which warning will save you, little *Yaccaw?* What makes *you* unsafe to eat?"

"Too *HOT!*" protested Yero.

This caused more confusion. The upper Roost couldn't hear well, and lower birds seized on the idea to issue new challenges.

As the unrest rose up toward him the Top Crow worried that even *he* might be challenged. That was the last thing he needed! He crowed loud enough to pause the disturbance and ruled the question out of order.

"The *Yaccaw* are *too small* to be too hot!" he declared. "Anything else?"

Craw sneered. "There's a smaller warning!" he crowed. "They're too *yucky!* One is covered with *yuck.*"

This drew considerable laughter from the Roost. Craw chuckled at his own joke. He was fast becoming a celebrity.

"You tell 'em Mr. Yucky!" shouted Yero when the laughter died down. "You've got it all over your *face!*"

So much for celebrity. The Roost exploded in laughter and began to break up, flying off in search of breakfast. Soon only Craw remained - old, stiff and humiliated. Long minutes passed as the butterflies waited, hoping he would leave as well. It was unnerving the way he cocked his head, listening and watching them. By midday clouds moved in, obscuring the sun. It began to rain again, a passing shower that was welcomed by all.

Yero spread her dirty wings. It felt wonderful to be washed clean! Smelled better too, as Boca thoughtfully pointed out.

Craw shook himself off and noted the fresher smell also. It reminded him that he was hungry. Which reminded him that he was unable to forage the countryside for food, as he once did. Which reminded him that *clean* monarchs were near at hand looking very appetizing, regardless of tradition. When the rain stopped, he began to poke around the thorn bush in search of an opening.

There were avenues to get at the butterflies if the old bird was determined, and a deadly game of keep-away began. It didn't last long. Craw got careless, got poked, and panicked. He shrieked and flapped wildly, flushing the butterflies out of the bush in the confusion. They made a dash toward the brambly edge of the woods some distance away, as straight as butterflies can fly, and ducked into a little tree for cover. Craw landed hard on their heels, roughly grabbing a branch and jabbing at them with his beak.

***

The young tree - a *tribbit,* by lucky chance - didn't offer much protection to begin with, but that soon changed: A minor cuss word split the air. Twiggy fingers reached for the bird's tail and jerked hard. The crow escaped but left a big tailfeather behind. The tribbit, now wide-awake, turned his attention to one of the monarchs still clinging to a twig.

"*Beat it.* I'm not your lunch!"

"Oh, don't worry!" said the butterfly. "We don't eat grass."

16

That irked the tribbit. "It's not grass - it's *leaves!*" he said, and he rustled them vigorously to make his point.

"Leaves, then," said the butterfly airily. "It's all the same."

She somehow hung on, perched upon one of them, while she carried on conversation with the young tree. It was an oak leaf she perched on - burr oak to be exact - and she had no intention of nibbling it.

Neither did the other monarch who fluttered close by, hesitating to land. "We drink nectar," he said. "We're not moths."

"Okay - butterflies then," grumbled the tribbit, still suspicious. "Do itty-bitty butterflies have names?"

The first butterfly folded her arms peevishly. "I'm Yero," she said, "and he's Boca. Do itty-bitty trees have names?"

That surprised the tribbit, but only for a moment. "I'm Yesac," he replied in a huff. "And I can whip any butterfly!"

"If you could catch us!" challenged Yero, lifting off to flutter in his face. "But we're looking for flowers today. Not fights."

"Oh yeah? Well, it's late for flowers," answered Yesac truthfully. "There's still a few, but winter's coming on. What do you eat in winter?"

"Don't be silly," laughed Yero. "We'll be gone before winter."

"We're travelers," said Boca. "We're the journeying Rasha La."

The tribbit was impressed. Here was a name new to him in the wildwood: *Rasha La.* He had thought he knew everything.

"Do you travel far," he asked.

"Yes," bragged Yero. "Just now we've come from that forest way over yonder!" She pointed across an open valley to where wooded hills resumed, perhaps a quarter mile away. She smiled smugly.

But the tribbit was no longer impressed. "That's nothing," he said. "We do that all the time."

The butterflies were amused. They hadn't been around long, perhaps. But they knew a tree when they saw one (even one this small) and trees stayed put exactly where they were. Everyone knows that. Yero confidently took her perch again and Boca joined her.

"Who's 'we'?" they asked, ready for more jokes.

"Itsirk!" said a voice to one side.

"Noiro!" said a voice behind them.

Two more young trees introduced themselves. Noiro was a boy like Yesac, but larger: A young burr oak with deep green eyes that opened along the lines of his bark and flickered when he spoke.

Itsirk was a red oak, rather slimmer than the boys, yet taller than either. She had a certain gracefulness of limb and her eyes were acorn brown.

"We're *tribbits*," they said. Then, astonishingly, all three stepped up out of the ground and danced a little jig on feet that were much like human ones, except they were bigger and had lots more toes.

"We're travelers too," said Noiro.

"High kickers!" said Yesac.

"I'm more of a dancer," laughed Itsirk.

Now it was the butterflies who were impressed. They clung to their perches and rode it out.

"Are all trees like this?" asked Yero when things had settled down again. It was quite an eye-opener, though the tribbits didn't seem dangerous.

"No," shrugged Noiro. "The big ones are rooted solid. They're sleepyheads."

"Only tribbits have *these*," said Yesac, and wiggled his toes.

"But we're the only tribbits and I'm the only girl," said Itsirk. "I'm glad to meet you!"

"We could be friends," offered Noiro. "What do you say to that?"

The Butterflies, Yero and Boca

The butterflies considered this and whispered to each other so softly even the tribbits couldn't hear, and they were known for hearing things they shouldn't.

"All right," said Yero after a bit. "Friends it is! But we can't stay long."

"Why not?" asked the Three.

Yero seemed self-conscious. "The season *is* getting late," she admitted, with a sidelong glance at Yesac. "Soon we must leave." Boca nodded.

"Where to?" asked the Three.

"On the Journey," answered Yero. "That is the way of the Rasha La. We journey to Manino, land of our kind. Do you journey also?"

The tribbits looked at each other, feeling quaint and local.

"No," said Noiro. "We stay here."

"This is our land," said Itsirk. She waved her twiggy fingers toward the wooded hills all around.

"We guard the forest!" declared Yesac. "Do you guard anything?"

The butterflies exchanged a glance. "Just each other," replied Yero. "Does that count?"

It did, except with Yesac.

"You'll have to argue with him," laughed Itsirk. "But the weather is turning out so nice this morning! Could you at least stay for the day?"

"You can meet Nanny," promised Noiro.

"I wouldn't mind," said Yesac.

"Stay for a while!" said the Three.

So they did. Because that is also the way of butterflies, even the Rasha La. They enjoy fine weather, and friendship, and dillydallying in the warm sunshine. These are their main concerns; and now they had all of them at once.

"What do tribbits eat?" asked Yero, after a few minutes of basking. She and Boca hadn't eaten since crossing the valley an hour earlier and were beginning to feel hungry.

"Oh, nothing," said Yesac. He was relaxing, enjoying the fine afternoon, and showed no sign of moving. In fact, all three tribbits had slipped their feet back into the ground and apparently settled down for a while.

"What do you mean 'nothing'?" said Yero. "If you don't eat anything how do you grow?"

"We drink water sometimes," said Yesac.

"Well, that's not 'nothing'."

"I suppose not," replied Yesac with a little yawn.

"Don't you get hungry?"

"Not now. Winter is coming."

This was a ridiculous answer and Yero said so. Everyone in the Northland knows about winter. You need to eat heartily ahead of it and put on fat, or else migrate south to warmer lands. And nobody could live on just water!

But Yesac didn't answer. He had fallen asleep and begun snoring. With tribbits this usually sounds like wind in their branches. With Yesac it sounded like wind and little birds chirping.

The butterflies left in some alarm and flew over to Itsirk. "Yesac is being weird," they reported.

Then Noiro also began to snore. With him it sounded like gusts through a knothole followed by brief periods of lull, and then suddenly more gusts.

The butterflies ducked inside Itsirk's leaves, out of sight.

Itsirk reassured them about the phenomenon which she saw every day. "They're napping. They wake up early and make a racket when others want to sleep, but they peter out in the afternoon sun. So they're conked out, but I can answer your questions." And with that, she was peppered by them.

First, she had to explain why tribbits lose their appetites in autumn and aren't hungry again until the next spring. That one was easy. It's just the way of trees: When their leaves fall, their sap falls too, so they need less and less water as autumn progresses and none at all during winter. If this is done properly winter holds less danger for them. But there are still dangers. Some years snow may not come, and frost can seek out shallow roots and break them. Nothing would please the North Wind more! Or that Witch might send ice to make the whole forest bow before her, such is her power. The wildwood shivers in her presence.

But tribbits have 'foots', not yet stiffened into roots. If the frost pinches their toes *here*, they can move over *there*. They step up out of the ground and go where they please. And when their toes get cold, they can slip back into the ground again because tribbits are great diggers. A few inches of frozen earth are like nothing to them. They go right through it.

Then Itsirk had to explain about her leaves, which were no longer summer-green but iridescent pink, and she talked about the Fall Fest, the festival of colors, and old Master Jack Frost who oversees it with his flock of imps who do the leaf-painting.

"We met him," she confided. "He's very old, older than the eldest trees. He wrote us down in his book, which is good luck. But we're pretty lucky anyway."

The butterflies laughed and began to feel knowledgeable about trees and tribbits and such. But Itsirk's leaves were a different shape than the boys. Was that because she was a girl? It was not.

"Tribbit girls have brown eyes", she explained, "while boys have eyes in shades of green. But leaves show the *kind* of tree. We're oak trees but there are lots of kinds. The Oldster taught us the trees in this wood, but Mister Frost keeps the big list. He has a rhyme for it."

> 'Leaf will tell us,
> They remind us, Of the many, What the kind is:
> Elm is toothy,
> Cherry oval,
> Beech is pointed,
> Walnut fronded,
> Willow thinnest,
> Elder rankest,
> Maple biggest,
> Basswood fattest,
> Red oak sharpest,
> Burr oak rounded...'

"... That's just some of the big ones. It goes on and on. Mr. Frost knows them quite well of course, since it's his business."

A sudden breeze rustled Itsirk's leaves just then and dislodged one. It fluttered to the ground where many leaves already lay from the trees around them. Indeed, many trees were already bare.

"Did that hurt?" asked Yero.

"No," replied Itsirk. "I hardly felt it. I hardly feel my leaves at all since the frost. That part is no fun. It pinches!"

The sudden breeze woke up the boys who yawned slowly. Yesac made little snacking noises to finish up the yawn, and the butterflies remembered they were hungry.

"We're going to have *mallasha*," announced Yero as she lifted off. "There's a nice patch beyond the far edge of the woods. Do you care to join us?"

"I'm full," said Yesac, who was suspicious of new things to try.

"What's *mallasha*?" asked Noiro, who wasn't.

"The butterfly plant," said Yero. "I thought everyone knew that. We drink the nectar."

"What does it look like?"

"Tall, with flowers in big clusters," said Boca. "They like sunshine."

"*Very* fragrant," added Yero. "With fluffy seed pods later."

"White sap in the stems?" inquired Yesac.

"Yes! You've got it!" said the butterflies and clapped their forefeet, which are like hands to them.

Yesac made a face. "That's just milkweed."

"Call it what you want," sniffed Yero. "It's our favorite."

"But it's *poisonous*!" warned Itsirk.

"Naturally!" giggled the butterflies.

The tribbits were flabbergasted.

"You're asking for it!" blurted Yesac. "It's your own fault if you get a stomach-ache."

The butterflies were much amused. "We know it's poisonous," answered Yero with a superior glance at the littlest tribbit. "Only the fierce *Rasha La* dare to dine on it."

"It doesn't hurt us," laughed Boca. "It helps us!"

The tribbits leaned back, narrowing their eyes. It was common knowledge that the plant was a *No-No*.

"Helps you…*how?*" asked Noiro doubtfully.

So Yero revealed the bond between the butterfly plant and the monarchs which is unique and rather frightful. For the Rasha La do partake of the poison, which does not hurt them in the slightest and satisfies all their desire in food. To them it has a delightful taste. In turn the butterflies pollinate the plants as they skip from blossom to blossom, and there is a lasting bonus: The diet instills a toxicity quite deadly to hungry predators that might be looking for a quick meal. Hunting birds and most ravenous creatures know it and leave them alone.

Now the tribbits had an eye-opener. They studied the butterflies with new interest and respect - especially Yesac, who measured toughness in every way.

"Would a nighthawk die if they ate you?" he asked.

"Yes," replied Yero, "and they know it. They don't hunt us."

"How about a big red-tailed hawk?"

"I think so. At least they seem to think so."

"How about an eagle?"

"Oh, don't be silly! We're too small for their meal anyway."

"What if two big hawks each ate half?"

"They don't share like that, silly!"

"What if they did? What if three big hawks shared up the two of you? Would they die?"

Yero made a flustered little noise. "Yes! Unless dummies like you keep talking and make us miss our dinner! Goodbye!"

"Right. We're off to eat poison", laughed Boca. "Then we'll come back and touch you!"

"Do you think it'll *sting?*" asked Yero.

"What if we *drool?*"

"What if we *breathe* on you?"

"Would you get a tummy-ache?"

"Will you faint?"

The butterflies flew off laughing and promising to return as soon as may be, leaving Yesac huffing and puffing. He had met his match.

No sooner had they gone than Atel the hummingbird appeared out of nowhere and hovered before them.

"Nanny!" they cried, and snapped their fingers gladly - even Yesac, though he still frowned.

She laughed. "Well! Two happy faces and one not. What's the trouble, Yesac?" All three burst into explanation.

"Some big-mouth butterflies…" began Yesac.

"*Rasha La,*" corrected Noiro.

"They're nice," put in Itsirk, "He just got into an argument over who's tougher, and all that."

"*They* started it!" said Yesac flatly. "Bragging about eating poison. Now they're coming back to *touch* me". He glanced swiftly at the others. "You heard them!" He got little sympathy.

"They were just teasing," explained Itsirk. "He took it to heart. You know Yesac."

Indeed, she did. Atel the Renewer, white as snow in the autumn sunshine, remembered the tribbits' earliest days and beyond them into histories now mostly forgotten. She knew the Three probably better than they knew themselves, as a good nanny should. Right now, she knew that some one-on-one (and *only* one) talk might soothe the little tribbit.

"I know of the Rasha La," she said. "What have they told you about themselves?" She looked at Yesac.

"They're travelers," he reported. "But they don't travel far—only across the valley. And they eat poison. And then they want to *touch* everybody!"

An odd look passed across Atel's face, but she didn't laugh. A nanny knows when to laugh and when not to.

"It wouldn't hurt you," she explained. "The poison doesn't work that way so you can laugh at them if they do. But the name itself means 'Children of the Journey' for they *are* long journeyers, whatever they may say in fun. I'm surprised any still linger in this late season. They should be far to the south by now."

"Are they really poisonous - or not?"

"They certainly are! It's meant to scare away enemies and it works very well. All the hungry creatures know it, even if tribbits hadn't heard."

"How far do they journey?"

"They go *way* south for the winter like I do. We can't all be as tough as tribbits in the snow."

Yesac smiled broadly and relaxed. "We never met them before. Have they been around long?'

The hummingbird didn't answer right away, and when she finally did, she began exasperatingly in riddles.

"If you mean 'Have *these two* been around long?' I will leave it to them to say - or not say. And if you mean Rasha La in general, there are many answers. Each has a different story. But I can tell you that most folks help them on their journey if they can. It's said they come from the stars; that they are lost children returned to earth. That is what I believe."

"Children like us?"

"Maybe. But more likely children of another Free People; this is the Age of Mankind. Just don't bring up the subject to the Rasha La. They will tell you in their own good time what they want you to know. Be polite! For that matter, be polite to *all* strangers."

"But they aren't strangers anymore. We're friends!"

"That's not what you were saying a little while ago," commented Noiro.

"Friends can fight too!" retorted Yesac, and he would've said more but Atel put a stop to it with an announcement. She was leaving on her own winter's journey, quite soon. Whatever else she might be, Atel was truly a hummingbird in the flesh. Very soon she must fly south, following the flowers and the nectar. It was a sad moment for the tribbits who were old enough to remember other autumns and other departures.

"Tomorrow at the latest, maybe sooner," she told them firmly. "I feel a change in the air."

Then she lectured them sternly on important things to remember over the winter and added a fair amount of her usual good advice.

"Don't forget" (she finished up) "when in doubt about anything, ask the Oldster!" She rolled her eyes slightly. "If he can be *awakened*, that is. If not, ask Owl. If neither is available, put your feet back in the ground and keep them there!" She turned to leave.

"Wait!" called the Three. "You should meet the butterflies!"

"I'll be back. I want to see those dawdlers."

The Butterflies, Yero and Boca

Then she was off, away east to a secluded dell where a burr oak of immense age had napped for centuries - still occasionally waking but become undependable in old age.

***

It was the butterflies who returned first, however, very perturbed about 'brutes' they had encountered beyond the west edge of the woods.

"They ruined our mallasha before we ever got there!" grouched Yero. "Dug it up and trampled it. We scolded them!"

"They're coming this way!" said Boca. "We wanted to warn you."

"What do they look like?" asked Itsirk.

"We don't know...umm, completely," replied Yero, "but one is very huge."

"What do you mean, 'not completely'?" asked Noiro, puzzled.

"Well...umm, they were pushing into thick brambles. We only saw just part of them."

"Oh? Which part?"

"The part that isn't up front."

The tribbits looked at each other. Their eyes flickered playfully.

"You only saw their *rears*?" asked Itsirk.

The butterflies didn't like to admit it, but yes.

"So, you scolded their *rear ends*?" asked Noiro. "That's different. We only talk to front ends."

"Did they answer you?" laughed Yesac. "If you know what I mean."

Oh, yes. The butterflies knew. But they were spared answering the question when menacing noises awoke nearby.

Everyone turned to where the 'brutes' were obviously approaching. A briar patch blocked visibility so it was impossible to see more than a few feet, but noises were coming from the thicket: Queer grunting, snuffling noises mixed with the sounds of twigs snapping and brush and briar being forced aside, as if some large animal were slowly smashing a path through it and perhaps eating something as it came.

"*Now* do you believe us?" said Yero. She landed and hid under Itsirk's top leaves. Boca hid in Noiro's.

Momentarily, a very large animal with floppy ears, a long blunt nose, and short muscular legs roughly shouldered aside a section of blackberry brambles and peered belligerently into the clearing. As it did so a second, much smaller animal appeared beneath, peeking out between the larger animal's front legs - a miniature version of the first in every way except that its ears stood straight up. It was chewing something.

"Grunt!" said the larger one in a deep voice, obviously warning everyone to get out of the way.

"Grunt," said the smaller one, obviously imitating the larger, but it came out high-pitched and squeaky and sounded more like "runt."

To the dismay of the butterflies who remained hidden under their leaves, the tribbits made no attempt to flee or hide. Instead they waved and hailed the intruders.

"It's the pigs!"

"They still haven't been caught!"

"Look how fat they are!"

The larger animal ignored them and fell to digging up the soft earth with its big snout, though it did keep one eye on them and turned its body sideways, the better to show off its ample stomach. But the smaller one came trotting right up to the tribbits as though they were old acquaintances, and that was exactly the case. The larger one was 'Sow', mother to young 'Poo-ig', her brassy offspring. They belonged to a farmer in the neighborhood but had been on-the-loose all summer. They had escaped their pen and were living very well on their own, foraging through the countryside.

"Look, Ma!" called Poo-ig over his shoulder. "It's the talking trees." Sow merely grunted.

"Just look at me now," he said proudly, addressing the tribbits. "Haven't I put on weight?" Poo-ig sauntered in a little circle thrusting his belly downward until he arched swayback. Rolls of baby fat wiggled everywhere. Impressively, his tail had not one but two complete curls. "Well?" he said.

"That's chubby," said Itsirk honestly.

"Never saw a pig so fat," agreed Noiro.

"Or so dumb," said a small voice.

Poo-ig immediately suspected Yesac. "What did you say?" he demanded.

"Nothing, Fatso."

"Yes, you did! I heard you!" He glared but smiled inwardly at 'Fatso'. In case anyone doesn't know, pigs are quite sensitive about their appearance. If a pig is judged to be less than fat, that's a source of embarrassment. So 'Fatso' was a compliment and Yesac knew it. He was trying to be nice. It just didn't work out that way.

"You've got skinny ears!" chirped the small voice.

Poo-ig snorted. "I'll tell Ma!" he threatened.

"What's the use?" chirped the small voice. "She's too fat to fight."

Poo-ig paused and worked that over in his mind to see if it added up to another compliment. It was difficult to say. He abruptly changed the subject.

"Knock it off!" he warned. "And don't call us *pigs*! We're the *Wild Sweena!* Remember??" He thrust his wet snout up at Yesac. "See? No ring!"

That of course separates them from ordinary farm pigs. Wild Sweena have no metal rings in their noses to prevent them from digging up the ground, or 'rooting' as they call it. They also run free, answering only to the *Lure of the Wild Root* which still affects all pigs going back to Old Ripper - worst wild boar of them all - who plowed up the pretty flower gardens of the Elf Queen in the First Age of the world.

It wasn't the first time Poo-ig had thrust his busy nose up at them. Noiro and Yesac secretly admired it and wished for one like it. Tribbits, although spectacular diggers, do not have big, fun noses to do it with.

Itsirk harbored no such thoughts and noticed instead the coating of dirt and... *other things*... around the sides. She looked closely at the mouth, which was still chewing vigorously, half expecting to see the ends of worms. She shivered in disgust and her leaves rustled from it.

"Why don't you blow your nose?" she suggested.

Poo-ig stopped chewing, puzzled. "Why?" he said.

"It's running."

Poo-ig ran his tongue experimentally under his nostrils. It was true! He licked the surface clean, opening and closing his mouth several times in satisfaction as pigs will do when they've tasted a choice morsel.

"Mmmmm," he said.

"Yuck!" said Itsirk.

"Double yuck!" said a small voice.

Poo-ig was offended. He was no longer a baby, perhaps, but he wasn't half-grown yet either. He considered himself to be still in the adorable stage. He recited an old barnyard rhyme:

"Calf is bigger,
Lamb is cuter,
But best of all
Is Pig the Rooter!"

To show what he meant he attacked the leaf-mold vigorously with his snout and was soon throwing up showers of the black dirt underneath.

"I'm rooting," he declared, knowing it would cause a quarrel.

He wasn't disappointed.

"No, you're *not!*" argued Noiro. "Trees do that!"

"I'm rooting!" insisted Poo-ig.

"You're *snooting!*" retorted Itsirk.

"Rooting!" shouted Poo-ig gleefully.

"*Snooting!*" hollered Yesac.

"ROOTING!" Poo-ig scooped dirt from his hole with such exuberance that it flew wildly into the air. Some splattered Itsirk's topmost leaves with unforeseen results: A small voice uttered objections, and Yero fluttered out.

"Who are you?" asked Poo-ig in surprise.

"Yero the butterfly," said she, all ruffled.

"No, you're not. You're a leaf."

"Don't be silly!"

"You're a leaf! I saw you fall." She had fluttered up from other leaves, hadn't she? So, she was a leaf. Poo-ig refused stubbornly to see it any other way.

"Dummy! Leaves don't talk!"

"Yes, they do! You're talking right now."

Yero appealed to Itsirk. "Tell him! He'll listen to you."

She did, but he didn't. Like any young pig, he totally ignored advice from anyone but his mother, and even that was unlikely.

"You're a talking leaf from a talking tree," he snortled. "You can't fool me!"

Boca emerged to take up the debate. "Then what about me? Look! I'm flying - not falling!"

"The wind is doing it," said Poo-ig.

Boca actually landed on Poo-ig's nose. The pig looked cross-eyed at him and wrinkled his lip. Boca started up at the movement and Poo-ig sneezed, sending him tumbling through the air.

Poo-ig grinned triumphantly. "That's what leaves do in a big wind. And *I'm* a big wind!" He went back rooting happily and resumed his argument with the tribbits. It had been a point of dispute all summer.

The tribbits figured trees had first claim to the word, having 'rooted' in the ground since before pigs ever appeared on earth.

Poo-ig didn't give an 'oink' about history.

"We're better at it!" he boasted. "Just look at all this!"

It was hard to disagree. An awful mess had been made in a short time. Sow, never taking an eye off her baby, had plowed a considerable patch of ground near a great hollow log nearby. There stood the last green plants of the year, the jewel flowers: Tall and burnt a bit by frost, but still bearing proudly their little trumpet blossoms, the favorite delicacy of Atel the hummingbird.

Not caring a whit, Sow waded into them with her snout seeking grubs and beetles in the soft earth underneath. Near at hand, Poo-ig was expanding his own mess at a rapid pace. His legs strained as he pushed his eager face through the leaf-mold like a plowshare. From time to time he would pause and scoop dirt left or right, and his rump would flip in the opposite direction to maintain his balance. It was then that Atel retuned. She buzzed Sow like an angry bee.

"Stop!" she ordered. "You are messing up my garden!"

Sow flipped an ear but otherwise took no notice at all. Near the tribbits Poo-ig was digging a deep hole, apparently in pursuit of a worm. Only his wiggling rump stuck out with its curly tail.

Once more Atel ordered them to stop. It was hopeless. Down in his hole Poo-ig couldn't hear and Sow ignored her as she turned over a huge clod of earth, burying most of what remained of the jewel flowers.

Atel got the message and resolved to deliver one of her own. She zipped over to Poo-ig, considered his tail briefly, and selected a single white hair. She gripped it tightly with her feet and pulled like everything. Several things happened immediately:

Part 1: Tales of the Rasha La

Poo-ig flinched and backed out of his hole squealing, twisting the poor tail this way and that, but Atel hung on.

Sow heard and came on the run, abandoning her diggings. Mothers are like that.

The hair gave way and ripped loose. Poo-ig spun around snapping angrily at the hummingbird with his teeth, whereupon Atel darted in and pulled a hair out of his ear as well. She was small, but more than a match for young Poo-ig. Sow arrived then, and Atel zipped up higher to wait for the uproar to subside.

It was some time before things did subside, however. Sows are terribly upset when their babies squeal and this sow had only one piglet of whom she was overprotective. She woofed and made false charges in several directions before finally spotting Atel up above. She paused then, and her eyes narrowed to slits, "So--it's *you*, is it?" she rumbled.

"Certainly," said Atel.

"Attack my little Poo-ig, did you?"

"Certainly," said Atel.

"I don't hear very well," said Sow. "Speak directly into my ear if it's not too much trouble." She flipped one forward helpfully.

Atel knew better than that and remained at altitude. "Are we ready to bargain?" she asked.

But Sow, pigheaded to the last, refused to abandon her trick. "Can't hear," she repeated.

As she stood there shaking her head stupidly Poo-ig dashed underneath for cover, twitching his injured tail. "Get her, Ma!" he squeaked.

Atel pretended to fall for the trick and came closer, but still out of range. "Can you hear me now?" she asked.

Sow judged the distance and shook her head again, cocking it politely. "No, still nothing."

Atel came even closer to where Sow could almost snatch her out of the air, but not quite. Down below Poo-ig was running in circles around his mother's front legs squealing "Now, Ma! Do it now!"

Sow tried to cheat by leaning toward the hummingbird, but Atel reversed a few inches and kept the distance exactly the same. Sow relaxed to her original position. Atel came closer again. This little minuet was performed several times with Sow varying the angle and subtleness of the lean, feeling out her quarry. After about the third feint she felt sure of herself and relaxed for the real lunge soon to follow. Abruptly, Atel zipped in, catching Sow at her ease, and plucked out an eyelash.

Sow squealed and staggered backwards, biting at the air. Underneath, Poo-ig was half-trampled by his mother's feet and kicked sprawling off to one side. He got up slowly and stood shaking, eyes rolling.

Sow was now ready to bargain and inquired concerning Atel's wishes. Pigs are like that, especially the wild ones - totally contrary until it becomes unprofitable. Only then will they consider another point of view. But if this seems dumb, we must remember they've survived quite nicely for Ages doing things their way.

"I want you to leave," directed Atel.

Sow considered and took stock. It was true she'd been bested. That rankled, but the hummingbird had proved quicker than she ever imagined. If she planned to stick around it would be tough to protect her piglet. She had failed so far.

On the other hand, she was tremendously powerful compared to the bird. Why, even little Poo-ig - runt that he was - must be ten times as strong as the pesky hummer! Sow flexed her muscles and tossed her head grandly, feeling much better about herself. "What if we don't?" she grunted.

"Then I will have you evicted."

It was too much. Sow began giggling, setting off a great wheezing motion in her belly. Poo-ig, underneath again, also began giggling - more from a rattled brain and to mimic his mother probably, than from anything Atel said.

"Ah, me!" responded Sow presently. "Do you realize how strong I am? It would take hundreds of you little hummers to move me if I decide to stay. What do you say to that?"

"You will leave soon, and you'll be happy to leave," Atel predicted.

Sow giggled again. Soon her whole belly was heaving from the effort. She wheezed and smacked her chops with pleasure. Down below Poo-ig smacked his chops and giggled.

"What do you think you're going to do?" asked Sow, now brimming with confidence. "Pull out another hair? Surprised me the first time, but I've got lots of hair!" She smirked and wiggled her rump contentedly. It was quite true. Covering her entire body and Poo-ig's too was a thick coating of bristly white hair that would take months to pluck, one by one.

"Don't believe me, do you?" said Atel.

"No," grunted Sow, and switched her tail. She was beginning to be bored and inclined to go back to her business with the jewel flowers.

"I made you quit digging once," said Atel. "I can do it again."

Sow didn't like to be reminded. She felt uncomfortable being shown up in front of Poo-ig. "Anything can happen once," she snapped. "But now I'm ready for you. It won't happen twice."

"Because you're so strong?"

"Exactly!" replied Sow. "Now you're getting it. You are small and weak while the Sweena are large and powerful!" She resumed rooting where she had left off but kept both eyes on the pesky hummingbird who refused to go away. After some preliminary maneuvers with her nose, Sow flipped over a heavy piece of sod with ease. She was beginning to feel cocky.

"There!" she bragged. "You see how easy that was for me?"

Atel seemed impressed. "I certainly did. Can you flip even larger chunks - or is that your limit?"

Sow was annoyed. "Of course I can flip larger chunks! That was just to give you some idea."

"What about stones?" asked Atel.

"No problem," replied Sow. "I do it all the time."

"Big stones?"

"Absolutely!"

"How big? What's your limit?"

"I never found a stone I couldn't turn over," boasted Sow.

"Oh, my! You must be *very* strong!"

"I am. It's been quite an advantage over the years."

"Do you think you could roll that log?" Atel indicated the great hollow log that had been exposed.

Sow looked and recoiled ever so slightly. It was a huge log, nearly three feet thick and almost twenty feet long with a small hollow through the center, settled firmly into several inches of earth. The entire log was plainly visible owing to Sow's earlier rooting which had cleared away most of the jewel flowers.

"Any day!" declared Sow. But she had her doubts, and they came through in her tone of voice which was less than her usual bluster.

"Show me," said Atel sweetly.

Sow winced visibly, and then tried to pass it off. "Don't know why I should," she said offhand. "I might hurt my neck."

"Can't, can you?"

Sow didn't answer. She was too busy thinking. Underneath, Poo-ig spouted unwelcome encouragement: "You can do it, Ma! Show her, Ma!" (Until Sow reached down quickly and nipped his ear.)

"What's in it for me?" Sow wondered out loud. Then, hearing her own voice, she repeated it to the hummingbird. "What's in it for me if I do?"

"Satisfaction," replied Atel. "The satisfaction of living up to your own wild boasts."

Sow bristled. She hadn't been taunted like that since...well, never. "It ain't bragging if you can do it!" she snorted.

"It is if you can't."

Right there most pigs would have rushed blindly over to the log and attacked it, but not Sow.

"Satisfaction is nice," she said. "But it won't fill my belly. What else will you promise me?"

Atel mentally shifted up a gear. The old sow was crafty. "I'll leave your runt alone," she offered.

Sow nodded. That would help, she admitted to herself. It was really impossible to look after Poo-ig under any circumstances. Like a lot of youngsters, he didn't mind very well.

"...As for food, I haven't any to offer," Atel went on. "At least not on the scale you require. That's a shame. I can see you need it."

Sow stiffened. *Need it*? That sounded like an insult. What was the dratted bird up to now? Sow waited, but Atel said no more.

The comment hung in the air, festering.

"Whatever are you talking about?" asked Sow finally, nonchalantly, as though she cared less and was merely making polite conversation.

"Your ribs are showing. You're getting skinny."

In spite of herself Sow glanced back along her flanks. One side looked plump enough. So did the other. "Where?" she demanded.

"Oh, halfway back or a little more. Several are sticking out."

"I don't see any," muttered Sow. She twisted as far as she could and walked in a circle like a dog chasing its tail.

Atel laughed. "Ribs sticking out. Skinny. Getting weak. Signs of advancing age! How old are you?"

Sow was mortified. Even Poo-ig was mortified. He backed up some distance and looked for the telltale ribs. That did it. Sow lost her temper and stomped over to the log with fire in her eyes.

The first tentative shove yielded nothing. Then Sow went to work in earnest. She got down on her knees and began to undermine it in the middle. Soon she had worked her snout underneath and began a vigorous rocking motion with her body, lifting mightily with her nose and straining forward with her legs, then rocking backwards - only to push again suddenly. She developed a rhythm. The log actually began to rock and quickly picked up the tempo. Lurch--plop! Lurch--plop! The old log took on a life of its own. Unbelievably, Sow seemed on the verge of victory when a funny thing happened: A most revolting smell began to fill the air. Each time Sow heaved the log part way over and let it fall back - plop! - the odor intensified.

Sow stepped back and stood panting, testing the air. Little Poo-ig darted under her belly and held his breath. He glared suspiciously at the tribbits, then at Atel hovering safely above the stench.

"Give up, madam?" asked the hummingbird.

Sow shook her head cussedly and redoubled her efforts against the log; but the harder she rocked it the worse the smell became, and it seemed to come from the log itself. Yet for all her strenuous lifting and shoving Sow was unable to roll the log completely over. With a final, futile effort Sow fell back exhausted. Plop! The log slammed down to its original position. The smell was oppressive.

A noise awoke inside the log, a scratching noise that began in the center and proceeded toward the larger end. Sow moved back nervously to watch the opening, guessing correctly that whatever smelled so bad must be on its way out. Poo-ig scurried after, trying to stay underneath.

A face appeared in the hollow and blinked in the afternoon sun; then it yawned. It had whiskers and a long nose with a shiny black tip, and lots of black hair - except for a bold white stripe that began on top of the nose and ran back between the eyes and up over the forehead.

It was a skunk, of course. A young one. And the old hollow log was a 'skagaboom', which is what these creatures call their dens if they happen to occur in a hollow log like this one.

He was not in the best mood. Nor would you be if you were awakened several hours before the usual time by someone shaking the dickens out of your bed. The skunk stepped down out of the log with sleepy eyes and looked around at the mess.

Then he looked accusingly at Sow.

"What you do to my doorstep?" he asked.

Sow had never met a skunk before, face to face, and now she had she was less than awed. Here was a little critter smaller than Poo-ig, hardly a threat to a powerful animal like herself. She shrugged and went back to her digging, expecting the skunk to wander off and take his smell with him.

"I'm rooting," she said. "Don't bother me."

The skunk's dander went up, but not yet his tail. He had never met pigs before either. He wrinkled his nose in disgust. "You do skedaddle," he warned. "You stink!"

Sow snorted, inadvertently blowing her nose. "Little smarty!" she hissed, "It's *you* who are smelly!"

Poo-ig, emboldened by his mother's temper, blew his own nose enthusiastically at the skunk with disastrous results.

All in one motion the skunk spun around and arched his beautiful tail - then charged in reverse, stamping his feet as he came.

The pigs stared stupidly just that little bit too long. When the skunk was perhaps five feet away, he let fly with his secret weapon, catching the Mighty Sweena full in the face with a heavy mist.

Sow squealed and fled back into the briar patch. Poo-ig followed as best he could with eyes closed and tail between his legs.

In no time the pigs disappeared. Atel followed. Soon all sounds of their retreat dwindled into the distance. Whether they were happy to be gone as Atel had foretold was uncertain, but they should have been. Everyone else remained trapped in the smell even after the skunk put down his tail; unfortunately, the tribbits and butterflies were sitting downwind and dare not move lest they get it next.

To make matters worse the young skunk vented his temper over the mess, spraying the overturned earth in several places. Maybe he was marking his territory against further intrusions, maybe just trying get even with the pigs, but for neighbors downwind it became intolerable. It was bad enough for the butterflies high up on top. It was even worse for the tribbits down lower, and especially bad for Yesac, the shortest, right next to the unpleasantness.

"Stop that!" he protested. "The pigs are gone, and the stink is terrible!"

Up went the skunk's tail and he shuffled backward toward the voice, looking for targets. Seeing none he stopped within pointblank range of Yesac and looked to both sides, tail erect and quivering. It was a tense moment.

"Who say that?" he demanded.

Yesac remained silent. Yet the very silence unnerved the skunk. "Come out or I shoot!" he warned.

"No! Wait!" yelped Itsirk to one side.

The skunk shifted his aim.

"Easy! Take it *easy*," cautioned Noiro.

The skunk shifted again, bewildered, and then realized the little trees themselves were speaking. He was amazed. "What do you talking?" he demanded. "Trees don't do that!" To punctuate the message, he twitched his tail. He knew how to get results.

"*Some* do," replied Itsirk quickly.

"We're tribbits," said Noiro.

"Tribbits are *friendly*," added Itsirk, and smiled as best she could. So did Noiro. But Yesac frowned.

It was an impasse. The tribbits dare not up and move lest the skunk let fly. He seemed to have a hair trigger. But the skunk dare not let down his guard lest the tribbits turn dangerous. He was rather timid at heart and very unpracticed in the art of making friends. The standoff stretched on for a minute or more, until Yesac broke the silence.

"Well, that settles it," he bragged. "*I'm* the toughest one in the woods!"

"How that?" said the skunk in surprise, and some annoyance.

"By weeding out the losers. I used to think Sow was toughest, but you showed her up."

"That right. So why you?"

"Because you're scared of me."

The skunk arched higher and started shuffling. "How do say *that??*"

Yesac sneered. "Because all this time you could've sprayed me - but you didn't dare!"

At this very fortuitous moment Atel showed up again.

"Kagu!" she said quickly. "Put your tail down! They won't hurt you." She was well-acquainted with the young stinker.

"Do they your friends?"

Atel smiled. "Yes. *Friends!* Don't shoot."

On that promising note, the butterflies re-emerged from the leaves and said hello. The skunk licked his lips greedily and reached for them. Skunks do have one thing in common with pigs: They'll eat almost anything.

"No, no, no," warned Atel. "Butterflies are just to look at, not to touch!" To even up the discipline she introduced Kagu to the tribbits and instructed them to behave nicely. "Kagu is an orphan," she explained, "and deserves extra consideration."

The young skunk finally relaxed and Atel turned to the butterflies. "We haven't formally met, I believe. I'm Atel."

The butterflies introduced themselves and bowed politely to her, and also to Kagu.

"Now maybe we can all be friends!" said Yero in relief. But the skunk wasn't so sure. For his part he was willing, but he worried that it wouldn't last.

"We be friends *now*," he reasoned. "But what if Kagu spray again? Then friends leave. It always that way."

"But you'll be careful, won't you?" asked Yero.

"Oh, sure."

"You won't spray *us*, will you?"

"Oh, no."

"You won't spray without *warning*, will you?"

Kagu pussyfooted. "Oh, I don't know..."

"You don't *know??*"

The skunk grinned bashfully. "Sometime I do that," he said.

***

At that moment, a great horned owl hooted back around the hill. Kagu froze in fear, covering his face with his tail. "*Owl!*" he whispered hoarsely. But the owl didn't appear, and the call faded away. Atel used the moment to remind the skunk of his lessons.

"Yes, it's owl," she warned. "He's only waking up now, but he will be out later- -he and others. All will be hunting you, except one. Do you remember what I taught you?" Kagu nodded, a bit doubtfully.

"Listen carefully to their call," she prompted. "Most owls say, *Whooo-ooo-ooo! Our* owl will say, *Kagu-ooo-ooo!* ...and you need not fear him. Remember the difference!"

Kagu mimicked the call and regained some courage. He sauntered over to his doorstep and inspected the damage again, spraying a little here and there more as a confidence-builder than anything. It put him in a fine mood and his tail went way down. Yero applauded and everyone else did likewise. It was a smart move. An appreciated skunk is a happy skunk, and a happy skunk is a better-smelling skunk. But not to push their luck, the tribbits stepped quietly up out of the ground and moved upwind. Kagu only grinned. He didn't mind. All his friends were 'upwind' friends.

"How did he become an orphan?" whispered Yero as the skunk continued his out-housekeeping.

Atel rolled her eyes to the heavens. Clouds had swallowed the sunset. It was very dark in the west. Faint, early stars twinkled above them. "Our friend, *our* owl, did that. Can't blame him. It's survival of the fittest out in the Wild. We all know it. But I made him promise to let little Kagu grow up."

"He ate the mother skunk?"

"He certainly did. I don't believe owls have any sense of smell."

"Did Kagu see it?"

"Yes. I told him his mother is one of the stars now. That comforts him. He likes to talk about it, so you needn't be shy if it comes up."

Kagu scratched a little dirt over the sprayed ground to make the smell last longer and approached again in excellent spirits.

"If you don't mind," said Yero after a bit of small talk, "How do skunks come by such an 'exotic' aroma?" It seemed a fair question, though possibly a little embarrassing, but Kagu took no offense.

"Cabbage," he said. "Cabbage do that."

"Oh," said Yero. She had heard of cabbage. "Does it give you gas?"

It didn't. In fact, as Kagu went on to explain, it was rather more complicated.

The skunk had for once found a stationary audience and they soon found themselves listening to a story about the origins of skunks, a strange tale passed down from their ancestors. Atel helped a bit with the older history but Kagu (and all young skunks) know the story well. Things had been different once upon a time. The skunk - or 'Skagon' as they called themselves - had not always possessed their 'exotic' aroma.

—The Miracle of the Kagnabag—

Long ago in the First Age of the World, in the Negoro Assur, the mountains of eternal snow at the top of the world, dwelt the evil North Wind in her stronghold of sorcery and ice.

Great was her power. Lofty was her crystal throne. But barren was that land for the North Wind did not love life as others do. Indeed, she loved desolation and death and little else, unless it was the wolf-servants, or her dread soldiers - the imperishable Chillbanes of the north.

It pleased her to look down from that high place at all the icy ruin and waste which she had wrought, which mirrored the emptiness of her soul. But if her gaze passed far to the south she beheld green things growing, and birds singing, and free creatures living in warm lands where winter came not. They bowed to no one, which annoyed her; but worst of all the green lands were a reminder that her power had limits - great though it may be - and there were other Powers in the world, undaunted.

Long time the North Wind brooded upon these thoughts. Ever her malice grew, and she gathered forces in secret. When all was ready, she sent for her captains and said to them, "Go south with your legions and swallow up the lands of the living, for your Queen desires dominion over all others. Go now and return with tokens of victory!"

Then the captains, masters of shifting shape, transformed themselves into shrieking gales among the mountain peaks and stormed southward in driving blizzards.

Thus began the terrible Winter of the North Wind, of which many tales are told, and which is still remembered in the legends of the forest.

Nowhere did that winter strike harder than the Forest of Greenwood and the meadowlands of the Skagon, the skunks, who dwelt in harmony in those days with other creatures of the forest; in harmony and close companionship, for the skunks smelled better when the world was young.

Sadly, the Skagon suffered great loss in that winter despite rich fur and a knack for scrounging, for while they found dens or made burrows they didn't put away a supply of food like the gopher or squirrel; and though they slept for periods, they couldn't hibernate like the woodchuck or bear. Winter was not yet old when they were forced out into the snow by empty bellies.

By mid-winter, alas, the ranks of the Skagon began to thin. As they grew colder and hungrier, they became easy prey for the soldiers of the North Wind who patrolled vigilantly in the white meadows.

Yet ever the cold deepened and blizzard followed blizzard. Fresh legions of the North Wind passed endlessly southward to conquer new lands. In their wake foundered the last of the Skagon - a pitiful remnant huddled in a deep valley where marsh flowers bloomed in happier days. Time came when they also faced starvation for all trace of food had long vanished.

Then the improbable happened: In a rift between great snowbanks on the valley floor the snow began to melt. Unbelievably, small circles of bare earth appeared, followed shortly by unique (but foul-smelling) whorls of green leaves thrusting upward with abandon into the cold air. It was the "Kagnabag," familiar but well-avoided plant of the damp forest, so putrid and stinky that it produced its own heat and ignored the weather.

Thereupon the Skagon were faced with a choice: Were they willing to approach the plant and nibble its leaves? Skunks claim they hesitated with dignity. History records otherwise. At any rate, the nourishment and warmth of the plant proved irresistible and, after a bite or two, the Skagon discovered that the taste was better than the smell. Thus began the long relationship between the animal and the plant, without which skunks would amount to no more than a small footnote to ancient tales. The Skagon were saved - for the moment.

Then the captains of the North Wind ordered specimens collected of this and of that, to be taken back to their Queen as proof of victory in the warm lands. Dead birds were gathered from the forest floor; dead leaves from plants and trees were selected; and much other evidence, both live and un-live, was amassed and sent to the Negoro Assur for the North Wind to gloat over.

The Witch was pleased and nodded in satisfaction as the tokens of victory were paraded before her - until live specimens were displayed. Then she was wroth.

"What is this?" she roared. "I did not desire prisoners!"

"As you wish, Majesty," said Azo, greatest of captains. "These were sent for your amusement only. They are the last of their kinds, intended to please Your Majesty as curiosities."

"They do not amuse me," said the North Wind.

The captains bowed low.

One after another the prisoners were marched into oblivion until the Skagon were brought forth, still smelling to high heaven from hanging around the Kagnabag. Then even the North Wind was curious and asked questions concerning the animals, and the captains told what they knew. The Witch considered this at length.

"Let them live," she decided. "And since they love the plant so much, I will entwine their destinies". She spoke words in a strange, harsh tongue and laughed a stony laugh.

Then the Skagon were sent back to their meadows, which remained in the grip of winter, and they deemed themselves unchanged. But it was not so.

For though the North Wind was defeated at last by Greater Powers and Spring came to the ravaged lands, the baby skunks did not appear as before in the dens of their mothers, and a great sadness fell upon the Skagon.

Until one among them remembered the words of the North Wind and counselled that they should return to the marsh of the Kagnabag, and the Skagon did so.

And lo! Within the whorl of each plant was a ripe baby skunk, ready for the picking.

From that time onward baby skunks have always appeared inside the warm but awful-smelling Kagnabag, which itself is now commonly called 'skunk cabbage'.

That is how the babies get their smell, which they do not outgrow; and it's there in late winter or early spring where the mother skunks find their young: Plump and happy - but reeking like the Kagnabag. And there they pick them, like the fruit of the plant.

But smelly or no, the mothers are glad to have them. And the babies are none the wiser, for they were born that way.

***

Kagu ended his tale. The wind had picked up. Storm clouds had deepened and approached relentlessly from the west. Atel took note and noticed also the butterflies stealing glances at the sky. The tribbits watched the clouds as well, but with only passing concern. Whatever came they would have to weather it as usual. And Yesac had other things on his mind.

"Did it hurt?" he asked.

"What hurt?" said Kagu.

"When they picked you. Did that hurt?"

"Oh, no. Not if he ripe."

"Were you ripe?"

"Mother said I *really* ripe. She picks me. See?" Kagu sat up on his haunches and displayed his belly button.

There was general approval at that point. Everyone accepted the proof of the belly button as ample testimony. Then it was Kagu's turn to be curious. He addressed the tribbits. "Do come from cabbage too?"

The Three looked at each other and made faces. The butterflies giggled.

"They came from acorns," answered Atel.

Kagu brightened and licked his lips. "New acorns best," he said. "No worms." The tribbits scowled.

"A lot of folks eat acorns, it's true," said Atel quickly. "Only the lucky ones survive. Squirrel forgot where he hid theirs, just over in the briar patch."

"We grew up from the ground like regular trees," said Noiro.

"We don't *stink*," muttered Yesac, looking for an argument. He didn't get it.

"That too bad," said Kagu in obvious sympathy. "But how do walk? Cabbage stay put."

"Nanny taught us," said Itsirk. "She sang when we sprouted and woke us up. Sing to him, Nanny! Sing him the story."

Atel didn't sing, but recited a woodland rhyme:

At the end of the day
When the light fades away
But you wouldn't quite say it was night,

Trees of very small size
Yawn and open their eyes
And they watch the moonrise and starlight.

They aren't yet root-bound
So, with hardly a sound
They step out of the ground, and they smile.

Then they romp in delight
Through the woods in plain sight
Until way past midnight. But meanwhile--

The night's getting old.
And no matter how bold,
When your tosies get cold, it's no fun.

Then our brave tenderfeet
Leave the woods; they retreat
To the meadows to greet the new sun.

Ah! The warmth of the day
Makes them sleepy. They stay,
And soak up every ray of the dawn.

But if you (or if we)
Ever saw such a tree
About all we'd see is a yawn.

They are small. Never big.
Just a shrub or a sprig.
But their twigs are surprisingly strong.

And the smallest of these,
The wee children of trees,
Are the tribbits of story and song!

Atel finished and excused herself. She didn't say why, but it wasn't hard for the tribbits to guess. A final lecture to Owl about the orphan skunk was doubtless on her mind. Kagu watched her go and noticed the sky. He sat up again eagerly. Clouds had overtaken most of the stars, but some still twinkled in the southeast. He pointed to the brightest one. "Mother! She there," he said confidently. "She come back now soon."

No one said anything. No one had time. In the midst of his happy moment a darker cloud passed overhead and blotted out the heavens. A shadow fell upon them all and his dream was dashed. Kagu cast his eyes to the ground and covered his ears.

"Owl!" he wailed. "Owl do it again!"

"No. Not owl," reassured Noiro. "It's just a cloud. She'll come back out."

Kagu took heart enough to peek up at the tribbits, but not any higher.

"You can help," suggested Itsirk. She touched her trunk where the heartwood was thickest. "Keep her safe here, *inside you*, where owl can't reach!"

In a show of truth, the cloud passed on and the star reappeared, bright as ever. Kagu grinned ear-to-ear and suddenly announced he was hungry. He stuck out his pink tongue, which is considered a friendly gesture with his kind, and ambled off into the evening.

***

As though their time had come, leaves began to fall regularly from the tribbits, drifting daintily downward to alight with a faint rustle on the forest floor. Once or twice the butterflies were caught by surprise and had to bail off their perch as it fell away beneath them, until Itsirk showed them a firm leaf they could depend on. In the deepening gloom a nip and *bite* stole into the air, but at least the wind had calmed. It was the lull before a storm.

The talk turned to the butterflies whose story had not yet been told. The tribbits were curious. Yesac especially was skeptical of their 'long-journeying'. He pointed to the nearby hill where they had come from.

"Where were you before that?" he asked.

Yero waved vaguely at the heavens. "Up *there*," she said. "Though you probably won't believe it."

Clearly Yesac didn't, and began to say so, but Boca interrupted him, pointing suddenly to the far southern sky. A falling star appeared briefly, spectacularly, before disappearing beneath the horizon.

"There!" he exclaimed. "There is a Rasha La, come to earth! Thus we came also."

***

And since it was their turn the monarchs told their own story: A tale of lost children who do indeed return to earth as butterflies on the wings of the Fyrstellia, the falling stars.

For when the Lord of Light granted men a mortal life span He founded a halfway house in the nearby heavens as well, the Halls of Waiting, where angels could bring the fallen and tend their spirits until they were ready to go further into the Light. For most it was only a short stay, but not for the children.

"They don't want to go on," reported the Keeper of the Halls. "They want to go back."

The Lord considered this. "Since they are mortal they cannot go back as they were," He answered. "But offer them a choice: Let them return as monarch butterflies if they wish to attempt the Quest - the great migration of their kind. Offer them that."

"Yes, Lord. But such a journey will be difficult - *too* difficult, I fear, for many small butterflies."

"Indeed. Very difficult. But those who complete the journey will return with triumph in their eyes and peace in their hearts."

"And those who don't?"

"They will not remember, and I will bring them to you again and yet again until they do. I need to know their hearts are at peace, Keeper. And I want to see that look in their eyes."

***

The butterflies finished their tale and fell silent. Far to the southeast only one or two stars remained. Overhead the advancing weather front had devoured the rest. The air turned chill and raw and the tribbits' leaves fell steadily, but not yet the leaf where the butterflies perched. That held firm.

The tale was new to the tribbits but as children themselves, with a child's eye for the truth, they accepted it - except the part about riding the Falling Stars. That part wanted some evidence.

"Kagu has his belly button and we have Nanny to tell our story," said Noiro. "What proof do you have?"

In answer, Yero reached back and carefully picked a tiny orange speck from one wing, the tiniest of specks, and let it fall. It sparkled.

"Esporellia," she said softly.

"Stardust," said Boca. "From the fiery tail."

"We need it on our wings," said Yero. "We can't fly without it."

Quite so. It is the warm stardust which the Rasha La are endowed with, and which they must replenish on their wings, that allows them to fly. Without it their wings work poorly if at all. They must keep the dust in good repair for by their wings alone can they ever reach their goal.

Should they lose it, they must hide up by day and climb as best they can to a high place by night to catch the little sparkles as they fall and try to regain what was lost. It is a slow process and unlikely to succeed, for there are many perils in the world, even for the Rasha La.

Atel returned and together they talked on into the night, sometimes boisterously, but more and more in hushed tones. Overhead the vanguard of darker, thicker clouds passed beyond them into the east.

Frequently now, Atel caught glimpses as the butterflies glanced furtively toward the threatening skies. Purposely she steered the conversation toward the farewells that must be made and journeys which lay ahead. But the butterflies seemed unwilling to talk about it now the time had come and changed the subject quickly back to more sociable topics, until finally the hummingbird announced that she must leave, at once.

"The weather has changed," she said pointedly. "Winter is at hand. Even now I have tarried overlong. So have you."

Having said that she made no move to go but waited for the butterflies to speak plainly. In that brief moment Itsirk's last leaf fell but one. A pathetic sight presented itself: The last monarchs of autumn perched on the last oak leaf of the year.

"We should be gone by now," said Boca at last, realizing fully the danger that loomed so near.

Yero turned to the tribbits to make her goodbyes. It was harder, leaving them now. "We go to Manino," she said seriously.

The tribbits nodded, disappointed.

"Tell me, where is Manino?" asked Atel.

Yero looked at her feet. "Far, far away," she said miserably.

Boca cast another worried look at the sky. Yero stretched her wings in the cold air and made as if to say a polite nothing, but words gushed forth before she could stop them.

"They told us to follow the summer," she said, waving vaguely toward the south. "*Turn left at the setting sun*," they said. "*That is all the direction you need, and you will find friends along the way.*"

"Who are 'they'," asked Atel.

Yero looked wistfully to the heavens. "Angels," she answered. "Angels of the Light. But they can't help us now." Boca shook his head.

"They warned us," he said. "All the other Rasha La are gone. Gone before we ever came. We're the last of the year, this far north."

Atel was beginning to be very worried for them. She knew storm clouds well. In the gloom these gleamed like snowdrifts. "Are you afraid?" she asked. She doubted now that they would ever find what they were seeking.

The butterflies didn't reply right away. A cold wind came out of the north and they edged closer together on Itsirk's last leaf. Finally, Yero answered.

"Yes," she said in a small voice. "We've been afraid to leave because we're alone."

"What are your plans?" asked Atel.

Yero looked fearfully at the advancing storm. "We thought we might ride the North Wind," she whispered, "Since we don't know the way."

Atel looked sharply at her, and again at the storm which promised imminent snow. Soon it would be too late. She made up her mind.

"You must leave immediately," she advised. "But you shouldn't travel alone. And you should *never* trust the North Wind!"

"But how else can we pass through the storm?" asked Boca. "With no stars to guide by?"

All paths suddenly seemed blocked to them and their Quest doomed before it ever began. The wind increased.

"Go where the East Wind goes and the North wind follows," said Atel. "And put your faith in friends, as was foretold. I will go with you."

Chapter 2

Shaggara

While Atel disappeared briefly on an errand the butterflies made their farewells, much relieved and promising to return in the spring sunshine.

"After all, we have a guide now!" said Yero. "The rest should be easy."

"Easy?" said Noiro, surprised. "You said it was a very long way."

"Oh, for sure! But I expect we'll be stopping quite often for nectar and naps, and other things. That's how butterflies travel."

Noiro had strong doubts. "Don't count on it. Nanny means business. She'll go fast."

"No problem," assured Yero, full of confidence again. "We can go fast, too. We're much faster than you'd ever expect. We might even go ahead sometimes! But we like to stop fairly often. I'm sure she'll understand."

The tribbits looked round at each other, barely believing their ears. They knew their own Nanny and how much patience she had for dawdling. Well, Nanny said she was going with them. She must know what she was in for. There was very little she didn't know.

"Just don't be surprised when she gets tough," warned Noiro.

"She looks sweet as sugar, pure white and all," put in Itsirk, "But you saw what she did to the pigs."

"Oh, we can follow orders!" pledged Yero. "Butterflies are good at that too. The only thing that might go wrong would be if it snows, and we couldn't see her."

"You'll *hear* her," promised Itsirk. "You'll hear her loud and clear if you goof up; and there are worse things than pigs out in the wild. Do what she says!"

The butterflies nodded, serious for a moment.

"She does tricks," volunteered Yesac. "Wait til you see---" But he didn't finish.

"They're not waiting for anything!" announced the hummingbird, suddenly reappearing. "And the only trick will be: We're leaving right *now.* I've been up for a look at the weather and it's not good."

"Look after each other and don't freeze your toes!" she reminded the tribbits.

"We will!" they chimed. "We won't!"

"Goodbye then - and really goodbye!" She turned back to the butterflies who immediately fluttered up from Itsirk's last leaf.

At that moment several things happened, none of them good omens: The leaf dislodged and fell, signaling the end of autumn, and a frost mite bit Yesac on the toe. He kicked at it and uttered a bad word, but Atel didn't scold or even notice. Her attention was still on the leaf. As it hit the ground, another smaller object landed beside it - very pretty, very white: The first snowflake of the season. Winter had begun.

"Fly!" she urged in alarm.

Gradually, the slowpoke butterflies did. Their aimless circling motions became purposeful swoops and soars as they warmed up cold wings in the night air. When the tribbits thought they had seen the last of them they reappeared one more time, hurtling down right under their noses and laughing as if on a runaway roller coaster - with Atel on their heels, eyes glinting angrily.

"Goodbye!" they shouted. "See you in the spring!" Then they were gone for good into the dark sky and the tribbits were alone.

Yesac kicked at a weed.

"Well, they're gone," he said. "Now what are we going to do?" A second snowflake came down and landed by the first one. Noiro picked them both up with twiggy fingers and handed them to Yesac.

"Make a snowman," he yawned. "I'm going to take a nap."

A hundred feet above, it was a very different story. The butterflies were having difficulty gaining altitude or even maintaining what they had. The higher they climbed the harder the wind blew, which was fine usually; but this wind was a biting downdraft, colder even than the chilly air in the woods. It swirled down repeatedly, drawing the butterflies with it into near collisions with branches and coarse undergrowth near the ground. There, finally, the hurtling descent eased, and they could begin the climb again, but when they were swept down and right through a barbed wire fence - amazingly missing the wires - Atel called a halt. They were getting nowhere.

"This is no good," she declared as thick snow suddenly burst into the air around them. "There is just no traveling in this weather. We can't fight the wind."

"But we need to get up high," insisted the butterflies. "We can't flutter all the way."

"Another day," replied Atel. "But not *this* day. We must seek shelter somewhere."

"But where *is* any shelter?" complained Yero, trying to dodge the sharp flakes and getting cranky about it. And what use was a guide anyway, who couldn't find a safe direction? It was so hopeless!

Another burst of snow filled the air, blotting out any view. A huge snowflake blew past, just missing Boca who uttered the same word Yesac had used.

Their guide ignored all of it, quickly re-calculating and changing her plan on the go.

"Follow me closely," she ordered. "There is some protection in my wake. I will lead you to a place I know. A place nearby. Follow as closely as you can!"

It wasn't far as the crow flies, though there were no crows to show the way. Like most sensible creatures, they were in their deepest roosts now. But the burst of snow didn't confuse the hummingbird. Not here in her summer range. The butterflies were knocked off course, but she rounded them up and carried them on her back to a hole in a big cherry tree. It was a raccoon's den, very much occupied. Atel knew the occupant and ventured in alone to inquire about temporary accommodations. It didn't take long.

"I've told her who you are, and you're allowed to come in," said the hummingbird, re-emerging shortly. "But this is upsetting to her when she's trying to get to sleep. Go in but be courteous. Be *silent*, if that's possible. I am going to look for overnight shelter and will return soon. She has work for you, so expect some. Be nice!" Atel turned quickly to leave.

"Wait! -- " called Yero. "What's her name? Who is she?"

"'Bumble' - a fine, gluttonous old sow of many summers - but don't call her that. She prefers 'Joo-Ool, Queen of Thieves'. They are a proud race."

"Proud of thievery?"

"Certainly. It's their time-honored livelihood. Just leave it at that. Be polite! Wait for me here!"

With that, she was gone in a new flurry of snow that pelted the butterflies as it swirled around the trunk.

"You go first," said Boca. "You're better at talking."

They crept inside and found relief at once. The snow didn't come in and they could walk on dry fur that got warmer as they tiptoed up the coon's back and onto the top of her head. Yero felt a need to say something nice and spoke politely into an ear.

"Very generous of you, ma'am, to share your home. It's stormy outside."

"Don't mention it," mumbled the coon.

"Well it *is* nice of you. Did you steal this place?"

The coon opened her eyes and actually chuckled. "Don't mention *that* either, if you know what I mean."

Yero laughed. The coon was boss here and it's always wise to laugh at the boss's jokes.

"I won't say a thing. Good job, though! It's very cozy."

The coon relaxed and closed her eyes again. "Yes, it's warm," she yawned. "I always steal my winter's den. It's 'hot' property then, when the snow flies - get it?" She laughed again at her own joke, but it was quite true. She had 'appropriated' the place very recently from a big Pileated Woodpecker. More like piracy, really, than ordinary theft.

"Our guide says you're famous," added Yero, on a roll now. "Is it true you are the one-and-only 'Joo-Ool', Queen of Thieves?"

"I am. But I like to keep that quiet too. Throw off suspicion, see? Makes my job easier. By the way, your job is to scratch my back! Didn't the hummingbird tell you?"

"Sort of, I guess." Yero understood now why Atel had left out the details. "Umm...where does it itch?"

"Between the shoulders where I can't reach. Just start scratching. I'll tell you where. It's driving me crazy!"

It's not much fun, scratching someone else's back if they have fur and you don't know what might be causing the itch. Yero wasn't eager to find out. Worse yet, the itch was a long way down from the top of her head, which the butterflies had found to be the warm spot. Heat rises, there's just no stopping it, and in mammals a lot comes out the top. Well, goodbye to the warm toes. Yero tiptoed down the bristly mane to the trouble spot and parted the hair a bit to have a look.

"Oh, my! You have dandruff!" she exclaimed. "That's bound to itch."

"I do not!" asserted the coon. "What's dandruff?"

"Little flaky stuff from not washing."

The Queen of Thieves flinched, nearly tossing the butterflies from their seats.

"Don't get smart with me!" she barked. "For your information, I wash everything I eat. I practically live in the water! Don't tell me I don't wash!"

"Sorry, sorry! It must be dust then."

"Yes - *dust,* and it itches. Scratch it!"

"Sorry, again! *Very* sorry! Look, I'm not good at this. Boca is better. Just a moment. He'll do it."

Yero smiled sweetly as she traded places. "I'm doing the talking," she whispered in passing. "You need a job too."

Boca grumbled and began picking away, guitar-style, on the stiff outer hairs.

The coon shifted position impatiently. "Deeper!" she growled. "Just get down in there."

Boca parted the hair a bit more and peered inside. The light wasn't very good. He reached in and fumbled around for the bottom. He didn't find it, but he found *something* - or rather, something found him.

"Ouch!"

He jerked his hand back and examined it for blood. There wasn't any, but he could see a bite mark on it. It made him mad and he pulled the bristles apart to see what bit him, expecting a big fight. He was deflated to discover only a very small bug busily chewing at the coon's skin. It seemed to have forgotten about him already, until he reached down to smack it. The bug saw the movement instantly and scurried behind a bristle, snapping its little jaws at him.

"Lice!" Boca shouted, unfortunately.

The coon was indignant, insisting it must be a tick. "Ladies don't have lice!" she informed him heatedly, and Yero up on top benefited as the anger and warmth rose up through the fur.

"Get it out of there! Get rid of it!" ordered Joo-Ool.

Boca demanded help and Yero couldn't refuse. They found a broken bristle to prod the thing but didn't have to do it. Luck turned in their favor. The louse was about done for. It was a stray bird louse, left behind by the woodpecker as she departed in a rush, and lice don't survive well from one species to the next. Bird lice can chew through bird skin but not tough animal hide. This one was about finished, having used its last strength to fight off Boca. It lay on its back now, feebly kicking the air.

"Is it better now?" hollered Yero.

Joo-Ool sighed and relaxed. "Much better," she said. The itch was gone. The butterflies went back up top where it was warmer but unfortunately, the warmth was evaporating too, along with the coon's anxiety. Before long, she was making contented noises and going to sleep. All too soon, Yero's feet were getting cold. But she figured out a solution.

"That louse, or whatever, was a pretty good thief, wasn't he?" she said to Boca, loud enough for the coon to overhear. "Just think! Stealing a few bites from the Queen herself!"

Joo-Ool recoiled so sharply she passed gas and that rose, too, along with her temper. She scolded the butterflies severely, as if they were her own naughty babies. It was quite a lecture and the butterflies ignored all of it, luxuriating instead in the warmth that lasted well beyond the gas and the tongue-lashing.

When she finally cooled down Yero could hardly wait to do it again.

"Please excuse me for that last," she began. "I should be more careful what I say. We met another sow lately who rooted up the ground, and *she* was touchy too."

Joo-Ool gasped, dumbfounded. "Are you calling me a *pig?*" Her temperature shot back up immediately. The butterflies grinned at each other.

"Just a sow," giggled Yero. "Why? Do you have piglets also?"

In the tumult that followed, the butterflies were lucky to escape with their lives, fleeing out the door as Joo-Ool's canines snapped just behind (and would have chomped them if her furious hot breath hadn't pushed them ahead). The Queen of Thieves actually climbed part way out of the den to give chase, but snow was thickening again, and she lost sight of her little guests.

As for the foolish pair, they were blown onto a boxelder tree nearby and crawled around to the leeward side in humiliation - there to perch upside-down under a small branch where it was still dry and ponder in silence the wisdom of insulting a Queen in her own castle.

For some time neither spoke, but simply listened to the wind and shook sticky flakes from their wings. The stuff wanted to melt against the esporellia and cling irritatingly, and there seemed no escaping it even under the protective branch. The butterflies edged closer together trying to avoid it until the space between them closed. There was a margin of safety under the branch for one butterfly perhaps, but not enough for two.

"You'll have to move over a little," said Yero. "The snow is getting on me over here."

"I can't. It's getting on me too"

"Most boys - if they were heroes - would do it anyway."

"Most girls, if they were polite, wouldn't get us thrown out of that coon's den."

Yero hung her head. "Oh, Boca - I'm sorry! I did go over the line, didn't I? I sure wouldn't do that again."

"Don't feel bad. I laughed too."

"I know, but *I'm* more to blame. And Joo-Ool will be mad at Atel too, and it's all my fault!"

Silence fell again, except for the wind. But butterflies don't mope and fret very long. They set about improving their fortunes almost immediately. It was with this in mind that Yero returned to the question of the weather and especially the wind, which had strengthened.

"I don't expect sympathy," she said, "But it's blowing harder again over here. What's it like on your side?"

"Pretty bad."

"I know that, Boca, but *how* bad? Move over a tiny step and see if it's any worse. You can always move back."

Boca finally budged just enough to prove her wrong. The weather hit him, and he stepped right back, getting his feet tangled with Yero's. When he got untangled, he felt more exposed to the weather than he had been but couldn't be sure. They clung to the branch in silence for a while longer. Yero was very serene.

"The wind is *swirling* over here now," she said after a few minutes. "It's something to do with the shape of the tree, I think, or the wind is shifting. Can't you move over just a teeny little bit?"

"No." Boca was sure he had lost ground already and determined not to let it happen again.

"At least lean out a little and test the wind. There's no harm in that."

Boca leaned out a little, then back. "It's no good, Yero."

"That wasn't much. Lean out as far as you dare."

That presented a dilemma. Boys hate to back down from a dare, even when they know better. He leaned out as far as he could while keeping a good grip with his feet.

"It's bad, like I said."

"Is that all you can go? Can't you lean farther?"

The dare made him do it. He lifted his inside legs and leaned further. A snowflake whacked him right in the face and he jerked back.

"Ouch!" yelped Yero. "Please be careful. That's my foot."

Either she had shifted over very smoothly or he had overreacted getting back, and he was pretty sure which was which. He fumed.

"It's better over here now," reported Yero. "The wind must've changed again, or something."

Boca opened his mouth to object but Yero quickly changed the subject.

"Look!" she said excitedly. "Another den!"

Boca peered through the snow. It had let up somewhat. They were on a hillside crowded with boxelder trees like their own. Not far downhill the woods thinned, and boxelders gave way to huge elms along a washout gully, very tall trees except one. The biggest of all had lost its entire top but still dominated everything around it: A giant stump twenty feet tall, roots partly exposed, rearing up to a mass of vegetation on the broken top that fed on rotting wood. Right in the middle of the massive trunk, facing the butterflies enticingly, was a knothole, doorway to the interior.

"I see it," said Boca, "But our guide might not. She said to stay here - in the coon's den, that is - but at least she'll see us here."

"We could make it right now," said Yero, ignoring his misgivings. "We'll stay by the opening, so we don't miss her."

That made sense. But they waited a moment too long. A new squall blew into the woods catching them from the side. Boca turned and came face-to-face with a wall of snowflakes. He ducked the first and that slapped into Yero, breaking her grip on the branch. She tumbled sideways into the air in the general direction of the knothole. The next flake hit Boca square in the flank, and he went tumbling after. By some sixth sense they righted themselves and found the safe haven, landing only inches from the opening. Eagerly they looked inside.

The interior was hollow and very large. A rough path led inward. Boca stepped forward but Yero reached out an arm to restrain him.

"We'd better announce ourselves first," she said. She leaned into the doorway and called out, "Hello! Is anyone home?"

Silence greeted her voice, yet not the silence of a vacant room or an empty barn. Moments passed awkwardly.

"Well? Is there?" she repeated after a decent interval, her tone suggesting manners and patience, but not without end. It was drier at least just inside the threshold, a welcome respite from the swirling snow, but the draft was uncomfortable in the doorway.

Boca shivered.

"Can we come in?" he called hopefully.

As though someone had waited for him to speak, and not Yero, a sudden hiss and exhale of breath came from unknown depths below.

"Yesss...ahh!" rasped a voice. "Please do."

Whether it was the voice or because of a sudden rush of cold air through the opening, both butterflies shivered. They stepped forward several paces to where the draft was more bearable, but no further just yet.

"Thank you," said Yero, and she meant it, sinister voice or no.

"Ahhh!" came the reply. Or perhaps it was only the breath of the owner of the voice. It was difficult to guess. Meager light from the opening cast an arc of illumination against the far wall of the hollow stump, enough so the butterflies saw that their entryway 'path' was just an inner remnant of an old branch. Outside, it had broken off and weathered away, but inside the tough knot had resisted rotting. It now formed a jutting precipice into the void. Above, all was dark, yet the echo of their voices told them that emptiness stretched upward. Below, intermittent glimmers gave faint illumination at odd moments, but few and very faint. From that darkness the voice beckoned sweetly.

"Ahh! Sss...My pretties. Come in, yesss!"

The butterflies took another step, just one. A rush of warmth came over them. Below, the voice trailed off into a soothing series of hisses and exhalations, as if the owner was pleased with the progression of events.

No way could the butterflies guess who that owner was or grasp the awful trap into which they were being maneuvered.

They couldn't know. No one ever did until the last moment. And no one ever escaped old Whissah, Grande Dame of Shaggara, as the stump was named by the brood within.

Hideous she was in appearance; evil and cunning of purpose. Deadly was her venom. Aye, deadly she was in every way, but especially in the black arts of bewitchment. Even now as she hung upside-down in the bowels of Shaggara it was strands of deceit - and not silk - that she wove in the darkness. She was mortally hungry.

"Ahhh...yesss!" she sympathized. "Tha be ssso cold? Sssss...Come in... yesss...Tha be no foes here, jussst...friends...ahhhhhhhh!"

It wasn't a nice voice, though Whissah had done what she could to refine it in the long years of her reign, the years of waiting when food was often hard to come by. She spoke in measured tones and though the sound was coarse and unseemly, which she couldn't improve, the words were fair and pleasing to the ear. Such is the way of all spiders of the web who entice their prey. It is a mistake to listen.

"Where are you?" asked Yero curiously, leaning far over one side of the jutting walkway. Her eyes couldn't fathom the darkness, nor could Boca's, who peered down from the other side. The voice droned on reassuringly.

"Ssss...Down...down, my pretties! Ahhh...What be thy wissshes?"

"It's cold and it's snowing," explained Yero reasonably. "We're only looking for safety and shelter overnight."

"We'll be gone tomorrow," said Boca.

From far below came swift intake of breath as if the owner was displeased, then long, slow exhale and a sigh of understanding.

"Ahhh...sssss...quite natural...yesss...and tha be safe here, yessss. Ahhhhh...safe and snug from the storm."

The butterflies relaxed slowly. Why not? They were high above the voice, whatever it was. High and safe and dry. If worse came to worse the open door would provide an easy exit. They began the ritual of opening and closing their wings slowly to dry them, which all butterflies do. And they listened.

The voice kept up a steady, rhythmic conversation of its own, rising and falling, sometimes fading away entirely only to recapture its audience with a new intake or exhale of breath. On it droned, promising trust and fellowship until inevitably the butterflies began to fall under the spider-charm, which affects all who listen.

"Warm, yesss," the voice was saying. "And tha be friends, yesss? Ahhh...tha be guessst here...ssss...and snug, yesss...soft, yessss...art ressstful now?"

The Butterflies, Yero and Boca

"Yesss," mumbled Boca, more than half-asleep already. It had been a dangerous evening and a long day. He was tired and weary and rightfully so. He closed one eye and slouched over the edge of the walkway as though a magnet were drawing him.

Yero gave him a dig and laughed nervously.

"Straighten up!" she said. "Don't hiss!"

Boca blinked, little comprehending. Below, the voice coaxed and beguiled with sugary phrases.

"Step forward, yessss...proceed, yessss...Come! Come in trusssty friendship...ssss...ahhhhh!"

Yero felt her own eyes grow heavy. An unpleasant urge to run to the voice gripped her. She fought it wildly, not really knowing why. Her antennae drooped against her will. In spite of herself, she took a step forward, then another. Beside her Boca suddenly scrambled madly toward the very point of the walkway. With all her remaining will Yero reached ahead and grabbed hold of his leg, then held on tightly as he struggled like an idiot. Below, the voice prodded them.

"Run, yesss...Come now, *yesss*... Ahhh...Tha be safe and warm with us, yesss... and *juicy*... yesss...and *tassssty*...Yesss! Yesss!"

Yero's head swam as the voice washed over her hypnotically. Her limbs numbed. Her grip weakened on Boca's leg.

"Ahhhh...release, yessss...Come sleepy to usss! Yesss...ahhhhhh!"

Warning bells rang furiously in her mind. 'Sleepy?' 'Tasty?' What was that about? Suddenly Boca jerked free and began to roll off the edge. She grabbed with both arms, barely preventing it, and pinched as hard as she could. Boca yelped and awakened. The spell faltered.

"The door! The door!" cried Yero and ran for it. Boca followed, angry and bewildered. Behind them dark shapes swept downward and landed on the walkway. In front of them a large body suddenly blocked the door, shutting out most of the light. The butterflies stopped in their tracks. A great spider squatted there.

"Tha be nah free!" it sputtered, and bared terrible fangs.

There was no escape. It would have needed a hundred butterflies to win the doorway. Behind, rustling noises warned of other dangers. The butterflies lifted off, avoiding immediate calamity, only to discover the awful secret of the shadows: Great sticky webs hung everywhere. Voices awoke in spaces around them.

"Tha be juicy...yesss."

"Sweet...yesss."

"Toothsome..."

"Tender..."

"Savory!"

"Da thee kill now, mother?"

The butterflies dodged clumsily among the webs finding little room to fly. Wherever their wings bumped into the hairy strands, bits of esporellia rubbed off and clung there, shimmering in the darkness, affording some illumination at a price. But when they tried to alight, grasping the webs with their feet, the strands were sharp and biting, and hard to let loose from.

"Leave us alone!" shouted Yero, but the voices jeered.

"Come to usss! Yesss...ahhh!"

"Don't you know who we are?" Yero warned. "We're the poisonous Rasha La! Eat us and you'll die!" There followed a moment of silence, then raucous laughter.

"Dossst hear, girls?" snickered the original voice below. "Tha be *poison* to thee...sssss!"

Clamorous bubbling and reveling noises erupted as if boiling mud pots had been unlidded.

"Yesss...*Poison*...*Yesss!*" hissed many voices.

"Give usss!"

"Give usss some!"

"Come to usss!"

"Yesss...ahhhhh!"

***

Ahhh - *Rasspinsah!* Fabled widow-spiders of yore! Heiresses of the hourglass with which they taunt their victims. Little did they fear poison, having legendary store of it themselves.

As the butterflies fluttered forlornly, a blood-red glow awoke way down below: The hourglass of Whissah as she hung belly upward from her great web. Instantly the voices stilled around them. Silence enveloped Shaggara. Then the evil voice wafted up from the depths.

"Tha be the *time*...aaahhhhh!"

From dark shadows came swift answer: "The *time*...yesss!"

With it came a flurry of activity as black spiders leaped downward from hidden perches trailing new strands of gooey web, then climbed nimbly back up and did it again. Each time, they passed alarmingly close to the dodging butterflies, whether by accident or design, and sailed by with hissing noises.

Yero soon suspected the near misses were intentional, meant to terrify and sow panic. Nor was she far wrong. She shuddered at the way the clumsy-looking creatures could scamper up their prickly ropes, agile and swift. Her own feet were still sore as if from burning nettles, but the widows gripped the webs gleefully, as if their feet were all scales and claws. She wasn't far wrong about that either.

Unerringly, they always landed on the entryway path, there to anchor their webs. There were many strands already--an impassable picket fence walling them off from the doorway. That part didn't really matter. The Doorward remained. They could see her watching them, front legs casually folded, rubbing her chin.

All too soon, the spiders finished a curtain from the path to the webbing above and began constructing radial spokes from it to the walls of the stump, starting up high and working downward, forcing the butterflies helplessly toward the monstrosity who awaited them at the bottom. A peek showed that her hourglass was nearly empty already. They had precious little time left.

"What can we do?" cried Boca. But Yero could see nothing that offered any hope either. There were no other exits - not the tiniest hint of the tiniest hole. Her heart sank.

"Let's just keep flying as long as we can," she answered. "That's all we can do. I'm sorry that I brought us here! So sorry!"

"We came together, Yero!"

Yero couldn't resist another peek below and wished she hadn't. "If it's the end I hope it's quick," she whispered. Boca nodded silently.

The widows had forced them well below the pathway by now and were tightening what little room remained, mocking them in their helplessness, mimicking their words.

"Tha mussst fly...yesss!"

"Sorry, yesss...."

"Die quickly - Sssss!"

"Come, now… "

"Come to usss!"

"Yesss...ahhh!"

"Da thee now, mother?"

Underneath, very close now, the last drops were draining from the hourglass. The bottom half glowed brightly and bulged, the top gleamed but faintly.

The brood had worked themselves into a frenzy. Little discipline remained save a common fear of the great spider at the bottom. Even the largest of her daughters didn't dare approach her too closely, but there was no need. The Grande Dame would dine first, naturally, but everyone would get a chance for scraps. 'Mother' always left some for her daughters.

Whissah knew that her horrible life must end in time, but the ancient race of Arachne must live on. Against that day she groomed and prepared the most promising of her daughters: The largest, the strongest, the cruelest. All the daughters were pitted in competition for the leavings from her meals. How she loved the spectacle! The weakest daughters disappeared along with the scraps. She enjoyed that, too. Good riddance!

Only a few feet above her now, the daughters clustered thickly on drooping webs, scurrying back and forth, the better to be in position when the moment came. That time was only a heartbeat away.

Sandwiched between mother and daughters the butterflies flapped wildly, eyeing now the hourglass as it finished out, now the frothing daughters barely inches above them. The whole interior of Shaggara reverberated to grotesque noises. At that hopeless moment, a small voice called to them from the shadows off to one side.

"Ya, ya," it said. "You better come with me, eh?"

The Two didn't hesitate. They veered desperately toward the friendly voice. In that instant things began to happen very fast: The butterflies perceived a darker crack in the dark wall, several inches high and perhaps wide enough to slip through; below, the hourglass winked out; from above the bloodthirsty daughters leaped down for the kill.

Yero struck the crack stomach-first, knocking the wind out of her. She found herself stuck momentarily, then burst through with a surge of energy. The wall was no more than half an inch thick. Boca was not as fortunate. He landed next to the crack and wedged himself into it but could budge no further.

"Help! Yero! They're coming!" he cried.

She pulled his arm for all she was worth. He still didn't budge. Then the obvious dawned on her.

"Exhale!" she shouted. "Go limp!"

Unfortunately, it wasn't the sort of thing Boca was in the mood for. Strong limbs were grabbing for him. Claws clutched at his wings. He thrashed frantically. Then he turned and looked directly into the face of a huge spider, mouth crookedly agape, fangs dripping, and he remembered no more.

Half an inch away on the safe side Yero found a new burst of energy. She braced her legs on either side of the crack and pulled with a strength she never knew she had. All at once, the limp, unconscious Boca popped through, cheating the surprised spiders. Both butterflies tumbled into a heap on a damp floor beyond. The last thing Yero remembered was peeking past Boca who lay sprawled on top of her, watching spider limbs groping through the crack. Then she, too, blacked out.

***

When she awakened, it was quiet. The groping limbs were gone. It was still dark, but her eyes were getting used to it. She found herself lying on her side. Somehow, Boca must have rolled off because there he was, millimeters from her nose, still sleeping. She waggled her wings a little, experimentally. Everything seemed in order. She sat up and looked around. Then she saw it - or more to the point she saw *them*: Long spider legs outlined against the crack, not on the other side. She gasped and gave Boca a dig with her foot. It looked like a fight after all.

The legs moved slowly, deliberately, toward her. They were very long. The spider connected to them must be huge indeed.

She gave Boca another dig, finally rousing him.

"Get up!" she whispered urgently. "We're being attacked!"

"I know," groaned Boca. "They have my wings! One has my leg! Pull harder, Yero, pull harder!" he wriggled feebly, unable to shake off his nightmare. How the spiders clawed at him! The more he struggled the more they clawed! Yero reached out and pulled his nose.

"Wake up, silly," she whispered. "Those spiders are gone, but another one is here right now. Wake up!"

Boca finally awakened - and bounced upright. The tall, menacing legs came very close and stopped. They still couldn't make out the spider's body in the poor light. Then high-pitched nasal laughter tinkled down at them.

"Nay! No spider, no!" said a friendly voice. "I'm Poppy."

Yero liked the voice - the same that had called to them in their desperation. But it just didn't add up. She knew spider legs by now.

"If you aren't a spider...what *are* you?" she asked. "You have spider legs, at least. I can see that."

"Ya. No spider, no! I am Host," said the voice.

"I thought you said you were 'Poppy'."

"Ya, ya. Poppy, ya. Poppy the Host. Ya-hoo-ya!"

It was a daddylonglegs, slightly daft by all indications. Having introduced himself to his own satisfaction he lapsed into an odd ritual, shuffling slowly from side to side and tapping his feet in a pattern. He struck up conversation with himself and began discussing the butterflies.

"Ya, ya: One, two. One, two. One, two. Six, ya. Nay! No spiders, no. What *is* it then, Poppy? No spiders, no. What then? Is it Host? Nay! *Six legs*, eh? Not Host, no. What then, Poppy?"

On it went like that. Poppy posed questions to himself and attempted to answer them. He didn't know what the butterflies were and was rapidly running out of guesses. He ruled out spiders because they had eight legs and the butterflies had only six. He ruled out his own kind for the same reason. Then he talked in circles for a while, trying to dredge up memories of things other than himself and the widows for comparison. Sadly, he was unable to. Poppy had been alone in his little side-chamber for a long, long time. Finally, he stood still.

"I think I can help you," offered Yero. "We're a kind of butterfly. We're the Rasha La."

"Ah, ya! Dat's right!" said Poppy happily. He resumed shuffling.

"So, you've heard about us? That's nice. It seems like a lot of folks have."

"Have you spoken with others like us?" asked Boca.

Poppy didn't answer right away. He shuffled as close as he dared and allowed his body to droop way down within all those legs, the better to observe the butterflies. It worked the other way around, too: The butterflies now saw that his body was tiny. They had expected much more. He was mostly face and jowls and drooping whiskers, really no body at all to speak of. Just now Poppy was slightly embarrassed. He had been bluffing. He had no idea what they were talking about.

"Ya, ya. Never saw any," he admitted. "What's butterflies, eh?"

Yero explained a few things. Poppy was surprised about wings and flying. His own experience was strictly pedestrian. He imagined the butterflies jumping down from on high much like the spiders, using their wings for rudders. He knew there were tall places outside. He still remembered looking up, up, as a lad, beholding the awesome tower of Shaggara. *There* was a place to go, he had decided (against the advice of his mother). Up, up, he had climbed and entered the front door. That was a mistake as he soon learned the hard way, but at the time it didn't seem dangerous. He had been so light of foot, so creepsy and quiet, that he was halfway down the inner wall before the Rasspinsah had discovered him. Hoo! How they had come leaping and hissing! Only to be disappointed. A lone daddylonglegs was hardly a mouthful for the smallest of them. In their rage they had torn him apart, limb from limb. He, himself, was accidentally flung legless to the damp, rotting floor far below. That had been his introduction to Shaggara. A small footnote to greater matters for the Rasspinsah. But he had survived and gone on to become their worst irritation.

For weeks, Poppy had laid exactly where he rolled from his tumble, in a tiny crevasse between decaying chips of wood, hungry and thirsty but unable to move. In desperation, he began to chew the damp wood rot and found it to impart sustenance - and strange sensations. Poppy would hesitate to admit it, but the stuff made him 'high', and still did. He had become addicted to it long ago in the pit of Shaggara while he grew new legs.

The Butterflies, Yero and Boca

One day he had discovered he could walk again and faced a choice: Should he attempt to escape - or stay where he was, out of sight? It wasn't an easy choice. In the end, with a last chew of the putrefying floor material, he started upwards past the great web of the old she-spider, and then he made a second mistake. He touched the web.

Again came the spiders, none faster than old Whissah. Poppy did not realize until that moment, but spiders know instantly when anything touches their web, especially if that thing is alive. And Poppy was alive, though not for long. He made a slow daddylonglegs dash for the door, but as Whissah rushed up after him he had come upon the crack in the wall and slipped through. Presto! He had escaped the widows whose bellies were too fat to follow, and when they glared angrily through the crack, he had spit juice in their eyes. That stopped them - even Whissah, though she had plenty of other tricks.

She put spells on him: Commands of obedience that had served her well, and her ancestors, for generations. They had no effect on Poppy.

Probably it was his diet. Though she didn't know it, Whissah was opposed by an unbalanced mind. Charms didn't stick to him, simply amused him and washed off him. He laughed at her and walked away to explore the little side-chamber. He found great store of the damp chewing material in an attic, high above. It was all he wanted out of life. There was no exit, but he no longer cared.

That's how he came to be here, he explained to the butterflies. He told them the whole story, ignoring their impatience. He liked them. They were pals now!

"Ya, ya. You stay with me. Hoo! Und we chew together! So! We be good friends, eh?" Poppy beamed.

Yero smiled but shook her head slowly. She didn't want to hurt his feelings but there were big obstacles.

"I wish we could," she said, "but we have to find a way out. We're expected outside. And I'm really sorry about your, um... *food*... but butterflies can't chew very well. We only drink."

"Ya, ya. Yust try it. You'll like it," encouraged Poppy.

The butterflies looked helplessly at each other. Poppy prattled on. "Hoo! Dat's good for 'em, eh Poppy? Ya, und *feel* good too, eh? Hoo-de-hoo! Dat be fine for butterflies. No other food, no."

Off went Poppy on another soliloquy, tapping his toes and promising happy days ahead if they would 'yust try' his favorite dish. For a fellow who moved so slowly he jabbered with great speed and few pauses. Obviously, he did a lot of this in his side chamber. Even Yero found it almost impossible to break in and found her attention straying, sizing up the room.

It was utterly dark except for some illumination through the crack, and about a hop, skip, and jump across the floor. But it extended upward; how far, she couldn't tell. The walls were smooth except for the face opposite the crack. There, a rough stairway had been worn into the wall from much use. She edged toward it. Poppy beamed.

"Oh, ya! Dat's the way, ya. Smart butterflies, eh Poppy? Und go for lunch? Hoo! Up we go!"

With measured tread he led the way, babbling about food and steps - and something unexpectedly hopeful that he called his 'window'. Yero and Boca followed eagerly, feeling for the steps as they went.

By a quirk of nature, the old tree had developed a double trunk in earlier years--an overgrown sucker, really. At some point the sucker had died and been enveloped by the tree. Little trace of it remained outside, but within it had rotted and gone hollow just like the big trunk. Up, up the hollow continued, to where it opened into a larger, oozy-smelling room filled with the dangling roots of small shrubs and parasitic plants above the great stump. The climbers had not got halfway up, however, when Poppy called a halt.

"Hoo! Ya, ya. Und rest now, eh? Poppy rest, ya. Rest up now und go more later. Oof da!"

Poppy was tired. He had those great long legs but only an itty-bitty body to supply power for them. Then too, his diet was at fault. Whatever bonus might be in it, the rot was something less than nutritious. And Poppy wasn't as young as he used to be. It all added up.

The butterflies on the other hand were full of energy and anxious at any delay, with hopes now of finding a way out at the top. Surely, their guide must be at her wit's end outside! How long had they been in the stump? It might be hours. How long had they been unconscious? Who knew! Even the stairway seemed designed to hinder progress. It was fine for a slow old geezer with eight legs but for butterflies the steps were too close, and when Yero took two at a time she quickly found herself caught up to Poppy. And there was no rushing Poppy.

"Are you rested now?" she asked after a minute or two.

He wasn't. Far from it. He looked more interested in taking a nap than taking up the climb again.

"Dat Host must rest," he said, and closed his eyes. The butterflies didn't like the looks of that and asked questions to keep him awake, but they were losing the battle. The daddylonglegs would answer politely, but only after a long pause. And the pauses were getting longer. Finally, Yero suggested contentiously that he really *was* a spider after all, which worked wonderfully well. Poppy's eyes opened immediately.

"Eh? What's dat you say, eh? Nay hoo-da! No webs, no sticky ropes, no nothing! No, no! What's dat, eh?"

"Well, you have those eight legs and everything..." continued Yero, secretly delighted at his reaction.

"Oof Da! Nay! No, no! Ya, und what do you know, eh? Hooda! So, Poppy knows best. Ya! He is Host, ya. He is Poppy. Hoo! Poppy the Host. Ya-hoo-ya!"

He was indignant. He also looked totally out of the mood for naps. Yero kept the conversation going.

"Okay, I believe you," she said. "But if you aren't related to spiders, who are you related to? Or are you a kind of your own?"

"Ya. Host is yust Host, eh? No spider, no. Ha-ha, silly."

"Why do you call yourself *Host*, if I may ask? Is it because you are nice to your guests?"

Poppy brightened. "Ya, dat's it!" he said.

Yero was pleased. Just a lucky guess, probably, but it's always nice to be a step ahead in any conversation. Gave one a feeling of being in control of the situation. She needed that just now. And Poppy *was* nice to his guests. He had certainly saved them from the widows. She thanked him properly. So did Boca. They were in his debt. Poppy blushed.

"You really *are* nice!" said Yero. "You're a perfect host."

"It's a perfect name too," added Boca. "It fits so well! Are all Hosts like you?"

Poppy squirmed a little bit. "Oh ya, sure - well, no."

"Yes *and* no? What do you mean?" asked Yero.

"Ya, ya. Nice. Oh, ya! Plenty nice. But dat's not it, no."

"Not *what*?"

"Not *why*. I am *Host*, ya. But not for that."

"That's not the reason for the name?"

Poppy shook his head ruefully. The more he thought about it, he knew it wasn't the real reason after all.

"Well, then - why *do* you call yourself Host?" asked Boca curiously. "Is it because there are lots of you, somewhere? Is it that kind of host, with large numbers?"

"Ya, dat's it!" Poppy was smiling again.

The butterflies applauded but glanced at each other carefully. Poppy certainly was a different sort. And Poppy clapped too, all caught up in the fellowship of the moment.

"You must excuse me," admitted Yero. "There's so much I don't know about Hosts. Do you gather in throngs, then? Do you have armies and such?"

Poppy blinked and shook his head in several directions. He wasn't very sure anymore. The memories were hazy. Oh, he remembered others of his kind, sometimes quite well: His mother, some

47

sisters and brothers, but that was about it. Is that what she meant? He doubted it. As for 'throngs and armies' - what's that, eh? He was totally at a loss. His smile began to turn down at the edges. He considered saying 'yes' again, but the butterflies were sure to inquire further. They were so full of questions and he had no answers. He admitted another mistake. That seemed best.

"Ya, ya. Well, no. Dat's not it either."

"It's not?" Yero was confused. "Then why did you say it was?"

"Ya, ya. Because butterflies said so, eh? Ya. Poppy is yust agreeing. Ha-ha. Guess again."

They weren't about to. This was getting ridiculous. And wasn't Poppy soon rested? How about moving on? Yero was as polite as possible under the circumstances but Poppy refused to budge. He had found a game and friends to play it with.

"Ya, ya. Yust guess first, eh? Ha-ha! Then we go."

He chewed his rot with relish and grinned without spilling. Ya, this was great! All too soon, maybe, the butterflies would be gone and the fun over with. So, while it lasted, let them guess away! They soon did.

"Is it because you're a 'host-age' here, and the spiders won't let you out?" asked Boca. "Is that it?"

"Ya, dat's it! No! It's not." Poppy was getting confused. He wanted to agree with his friends, but they were guessing all wrong. He wished they would understand but they didn't.

Boca demanded a straight answer. "Is it - or isn't it? It can't be both!"

But it could! Poppy saw a loophole. Shucks, why couldn't he have it both ways? There were two butterflies asking, eh? So, he should be allowed extra answers.

"Ya, ya. But *no*. Nay! Guess again."

"Is it because you have lice or something?" asked Yero quickly. It caught Poppy off-guard. He was insulted. Of course, he didn't have lice! He knew about lice. They were as big as he was. How could he have that? Gross! They must guess again and be nicer this time! That's what he wanted to say, but he stubbornly refused to say it.

"Did we guess?" the butterflies giggled.

Poppy refused to talk. Even refused to spit his juice. Refused to do anything! Regrettably, he felt his chew trickling back into his throat with a burning sensation. He hoped the whole dilemma could be cleared up quickly, but it wasn't. He was too stubborn.

First Yero, then Boca tried to patch things up. They wheedled and cajoled. They soothed and comforted. Yero asked Poppy for a hint, just a little hint. Then the butterflies would guess again and be nicer this time.

Poppy allowed himself to be cheered up. He didn't think he could stop himself from hinting anyway or he would soon choke on his chewy juice. He cleared his throat vigorously, making a vulgar noise..."HOST!"

Poppy smiled shyly and spat expertly into a niche in the wall.

Little doubt remained about the origin of the name.

"Is dat it?" said Yero.

"Dat's it! Ya-hoo-ya! We go now," said Poppy. It had been a fun game, almost as much fun as the games he played with the widows. Oh ya! So! He would take his friends to the attic where his best chewing material was aging. They couldn't say no to that! Stiffly, he set off again up the stairs with the butterflies close behind.

Poppy moved faster on this leg up, mindful of fresh reward waiting at the top. Maybe he was a doddering Geezer earlier, but soon he displayed a spry shuffle, and finally a bounce. He hummed a spritely tune.

As the climbers approached the top, light appeared above them, flickering and irregular. Now it lit up the entire stairway; now it disappeared entirely. But if the butterflies inquired hopefully, Poppy brushed it off.

"Ya, ya. It yust glows. Nice lights."

The stairway went around a corner and up one last flight to a landing, then more steps - old crumbling tree rings arranged in a half-circle. Beyond these the climbers entered a room with a domed ceiling festooned with dangling roots that formed living curtains. From unexpected directions will-o-wisp vapors glowed, much stronger here than in the spider's pit. They winked out, only to pop up in a new corner. When the butterflies turned to look it was always too late; the lights were already somewhere else. Sometimes when they flickered it seemed the curtains moved, and Boca worried they might be webs closing in on them. Even the air was close and stuffy, and reeked of decaying matter.

Poppy slipped through the hanging roots with the ease of long practice and made for a place near the far wall. The butterflies followed looking eagerly for the window, but there was none in evidence. The best that could be said for the place so far was that the roots at least weren't sharp or sticky like real spider webs.

"Hoo! Yee ha! Now try this!" said Poppy up ahead. He picked pieces of wet rot off the floor and popped them into his mouth. Even as he did so, a drop of water fell...*splash!* ...behind him. Poppy ignored it but the butterflies gladly helped themselves to a drink. It was then, in a moment when the lights were out, that they found themselves leaning over an amber skylight. They were yet on solid footing, but in front of them a patch of floor was paper-thin. Below, quite visible, stretched the great webs of the main chamber. It was Poppy's window, but it led nowhere. Their last hope was dashed.

"Ha-ha!" laughed Poppy softly, unaware of their despair, "Now is fun, eh? We watch!"

He savored everything up here: The fresh chew, the soap opera below, and the life-giving moisture that dripped from the ceiling. Even in winter the huge stump didn't freeze inside but remained a constant temperature much like a cave, cool but livable, and the water continued to drip, always in the same spot. This was his home proper, where he spent most of his time - not counting frequent treks below to annoy and bedevil the mighty Rasspinsah.

Time was, he had found himself peeking down unexpectedly at the widows and realized he had nearly eaten through their ceiling. Since that happy day he had spent contented hours widening the window, peeling it ever thinner, and mostly enjoying the show. He loved to spy on his archenemies. For their part, the spiders showed interest at first in the strange glows that appeared, but never caught on to Poppy watching. In so doing, he had learned much about them.

"Hoo! Watch now. Whissah kill, eh? Oh ya! Because butterflies escape."

Not daring to move lest the widows spot their movement, Yero and Boca watched a grisly scene unfold.

Isstah the Doorward remained stoically at her post ("Oh ya. Dat's her, dat Isstah, ya. Very patient," explained Poppy). The rest of them skittered about in a state of great excitement. Dangling from the point of the entryway path was the source of all the excitement and the prey of the moment: One of their own, squirming and frothing desperately, still un-caught. From the pathway, her largest, most treacherous sisters leered down, relishing the moment. Glowing again far below was the bloody hourglass of Whissah, put to new use and running out fast.

"See?" whispered Poppy. "They hunger now, und no butterflies to eat, eh? No, no butterflies. Ha-ha! Und empty tummies, eh? Ya, ya. Und then sisters say, 'Ahhh...thisss one isss fault!' Oh ya. Watch now!"

Time suddenly ran out for the unlucky spider at the end of the rope. Hungry sisters clambered down after her. The first received a nasty bite and tumbled perilously toward Whissah below, but others swarmed over the chosen victim faster than she could defend herself. Then the rope broke and the whole flailing mass fell, smashing through webs that recoiled like whips. Excepting Isstah, the whole brood rushed down after.

It was too dark to see what transpired in the murky depths, and that was just as well to Yero's way of thinking; but it was easy to guess when the spiders reappeared climbing up the walls, chewing and slavering. The noise level subsided. One last, smallish sister appeared, lugging a stump of fresh leg which she flung to Isstah, and then hastily retreated. Isstah wolfed it down. It was no more than an appetizer, really, for a spider her size. The last Yero saw was the Doorward spitting a claw out the door, into the storm.

Silence reigned in the attic for long minutes. Poppy was occupied adding small bits to his chew. It was surprising how much he could pack in there. But the butterflies scarcely noticed as they stared mesmerized through the window. Thoughts of escape, which had seemed possible a short while ago, vanished absolutely. They could well imagine clinging to the end of their own rope. Yet they were together at least, and with a friend (however daft). Then the lights failed altogether for a while, and the butterflies found each other and clasped hands in the darkness.

"Ya, ya, then," said Poppy when the will-o-wisps returned. He was still nibbling happily. "Dat's good, eh? Ya, butterflies eat too. Mustn't be silly. Then we go. Ya. Down we go. Ya! Und tease widows! Ya-hoo-ya! Dat be fun! You'll see."

"I don't think so," said Yero. "If there is no other window..." (Here she paused hopefully but Poppy shook his head) ..."then I'd rather stay here and watch. Maybe they'll leave, or go to sleep, or something. If there's any chance we must be ready to make a dash for the door."

Poppy wouldn't listen to such talk. It was 'yust silly'. The Widows never went anywhere – *ever* - and if they slept, they slept lightly. Oh, ya. He knew! Worse yet, they kept watchers. *Always* watchers. The butterflies would never escape. They would be caught. So sad. Why not stay with Poppy instead? Much more sensible.

"We'll have fun, eh? Ya-hoo-ya! Dat's so fun! We go down. Ya. Und stir 'em up. Ya. Ha-ha! You'll see."

As Poppy continued to coax, vague glimmerings of a plan arose in Yero's mind and would not go away.

"What happens when you tease them?" she asked suddenly.

"Eh? Come on, then. We go down. You'll see."

"Just a moment. When you tease them, do they come running? Do they hiss and try to reach you through the crack?"

Poppy was tickled. The butterflies were catching on! Oh ya! You betcha. Und spit in their eye! Dat's right.

"What about Isstah? Would she leave the doorway? Would she come running with the rest?"

Poppy wasn't sure. How could he know that? Did he look like twins? He couldn't be up *here* watching and down *there* teasing all at the same time, eh? Nay-hoo-da! He couldn't do that, silly!

"Yust come along," he insisted. "We'll tease 'em now. Dat's good fun. You'll see."

"You go first," suggested Yero. "We'll come later."

No way! Poppy had a plan and was sticking to it. He refused to leave his new friends. "Nay! No, no. We be pals now, eh? Und pals come with Poppy. Ya. So! Don't be silly!" He shuffled down the shallow steps to the wide landing, then came right back.

"Ya, ya! Come on now. Poppy show you. You'll see."

Poppy got his way. After all, he was indispensable. No plan could work without his help. Boca gave it up and followed, and Yero too, after a last peek through the window.

The trip back down was much faster. Gravity helped, and so did Poppy. He was in a hurry now and his normal shuffle was forgotten. He cleared his throat with anticipation and glee.

"HOST!"

The butterflies had to scramble or be left behind. There were no rests and Poppy chattered non-stop. Actually, he was thinking in snatches of verse, trying out new insults and rehearsing old favorites. Like a good Maestro, he was warming up:

"Ah, Missah-Pie! Ya, ya. Und Lassah too, eh? Oh ya, dat's good. Hoo-ya! Und yust those? Nay! Ha-ha! Lots more, you betcha! Dat whole bunch! Ha-ha! Oh, ya!"

As they approached the bottom, Poppy began to gesture with two (and sometimes four) legs as he talked. There was a consequent loss of speed, and a few anxious moments when Yero worried that he might lose his footing and fall, but it didn't happen.

Soon, dim light materialized, seeping through the crack in the wall. Abruptly the stair ended. They had arrived at Poppy's 'foyer', as it should properly be called. Poppy was raring to go and wasted no time. He scampered to the crack and leaned dangerously far out.

"Ya-hoo-ya!" he whinnied. "Where's Old Maids?"

Quicker than you could say 'ropes and dopes', outraged widows appeared at the opening, reaching with crooked limbs into the foyer. Poppy ducked back giggling, escaping the claws by the thinnest of margins. Right there, almost within their grasp, he went into his risky act. The butterflies were appalled and climbed back up several steps, but Poppy had done this many times. He knew exactly how far the Widows could reach. He knew which ones had the longest, quickest, deftest legs. He knew everything.

"Ya, you betcha! Und pitty-pat too, eh? Oh ya. Yust watch now! You'll see."

Poppy launched into his shuffling routine with three pairs of legs, but with the front pair he began pitty-patting the back of each claw as they lunged toward him, keeping in perfect time with his shuffle. It was very entertaining from his point of view, but it drove the spiders wild. "Stir 'em up," Poppy had promised, and they went stir-crazy. Such a venomous din awoke that snakes and lizards would have backed off. Boca climbed another step and called for Poppy to be more careful; things were getting out of hand, but the Maestro only laughed. He was going to have his fun. "Hoo! Yust watch now!" He began to tickle with the pittypats.

When the Widows were stirred up to his satisfaction, he commenced to whistle a happy tune along with it. Presently an extra-large and wicked pair of eyes pressed against the opening, forcing lesser sisters aside. Poppy was delighted and sang a little ditty especially for her:

> Ah, Missah-Pie! Got evil eye.
> Lean closer now und don't be shy.
> 'Cause Poppy chew---
> Ya, yust for you---
> Dat rotty, yummy, gummy goo!
> It sting a bit When Poppy spit!
> HOS-TA!
> Yee-Ha!

When he came to 'HOS-TA!' he let her have it right in the eye. Obviously, it did sting - enough to discourage most spiders probably - but Missah hung in there, cursing him in epithets specially reserved for males; but when she got it in the other eye too, she disappeared. Another large sister with vile eyes and jabbing legs quickly took her place.

Lord knows how many times the daddylonglegs had performed this routine, or variations of it; but he was such a thorn in their flesh they couldn't resist even when they knew better. And they paid dearly for a chance to curse and grab at him. It stung more than a 'bit'.

> Und Lassah too? Ya, how are you?
> You stink, my lovely poopsy-doo!
> What awful smell, I know so well.
> Back off, you mucky ma'moiselle!
> But, yust a bit...
> I need to spit!
> HOS-TA!

Hoo Ya!

Lassah, every bit as big and strong as Missah, fared exactly the same: A few curses, a few futile lunges, all bought at the price of humiliation and sore eyes. She disappeared in her turn and was instantly replaced by Isstah, the Doorward. The butterflies could scarcely believe their eyes. Maybe the maddened Widows *did* leave the door unguarded during such free-for-alls! Boca, with Yero right behind, headed back up the stairs to try the window. If they could somehow get through it, perhaps they might still make a dash to escape! Poppy never noticed. He launched into a new jingle:

Hoo! Isstah, dear. So mad, I fear.
Und poke your silly nose so near.
What ugly nose!
So big it grows!
Till stupid Isstah hardly shows
Behind dat beak.
Ha! She's a freak!
HOS-TA!
Oh, ya!

Isstah sputtered and bedamned, and nearly hooked Poppy with a surprising uppercut motion that had him for an instant, until he gave her the old 'limp-leg'. That was the highlight of her turn. Then she got it in the eye too and exhaled long and loudly. Halfway up the stairs the butterflies kept climbing, hearing everything, worried their friend would be caught by some widow with a tricky move and their last chance of escape die with him. They were right to worry. Poppy, always a daredevil, was taking unusual chances and didn't care. He'd never had so much fun.

Somehow the Grande Dame sensed it in her web and took a rare turn at the crack. Poppy never moved back an inch. Here was the best possible sport: Dat Old Bag Herself! Oh, ya! Pittypat!

"Now Whissah lass; so fun to sass!
I know you hiss from too much gas.
What ugly hag!
Dat fat old bag
She kiss the boys und make 'em gag!
Now peek-a-boo...
Ya! Here's for you!
HOS-TA!
Oh, ya! HOS-TA! HOS-TA!"

Very unfortunately, Poppy leaned forward at a bad moment to deliver an extra *HOS-TA*, just as wily old Whissah executed a double-pincer tactic. She caught him by both front legs. He knew it when it happened. She cackled.

High up the stairway the butterflies heard that cackle, then another, more dreadful sound. Poppy wailed in anguish. Boca stopped, but Yero pulled him upward.

"I'm sorry too," she said, "but there's nothing we can do! It was bound to happen. Hurry!"

Then they were in the attic, brushing through hanging roots in the dark, losing precious dust from their wings. That couldn't be helped either. The fickle lights awoke brighter than ever just as they arrived at the window so they couldn't see anything but their own reflections; but when they pressed their faces close the lights went out again, leaving them with night-blindness.

"Darn it! Darn it...wait a minute," said Yero. "My gosh! Poppy thought of everything." Her fingers had slipped into a crack around the edge. She lifted carefully. The window came up a little. They both lifted hard; now was no time for half-measures. The window swung up like a trapdoor. Bracing it open with their arms, they peered down through the hole.

There wasn't a spider to be seen, anywhere. The entryway path was deserted. The door was unguarded. There was nothing to stop them - except the webs.

The webs! Who could have guessed that Shaggara was so abominably full of them up in the dark ceiling? Funnel-shaped webs pointed in all directions, and in-between were dusty cobwebs. The way looked impassable. Butterfly wings slip nicely through a crack, maybe. But spider tunnels need a round spider body, alas. Yero slumped in despair.

"Let's go anyway," said Boca wearily.

First one, then the other dropped through, carefully shutting the window behind them. Click. It locked. Poppy had made sure it couldn't be opened from below. Instantly all noises paused down by the foyer. The spiders were aware of them.

"Follow me!" said Boca. He dashed into the nearest web tunnel with some size to it, wishing perversely that they were all big enough for Whissah. Yero followed. There was no going back.

All the tunnels started wide, like the mouth of a brass horn, but rapidly narrowed to a bottleneck. If one could squeeze through the small part the tunnels flared out again, and there was usually a choice of several new directions. Right now, that was a bigger problem than the tight places. They could squeeze through those by contorting their wings painfully, but the choices! How should they choose? There was no map, only a maze. And then it was too late.

A large Widow appeared on the entryway path and skittered to the doorway. It was Isstah. Half-blind or not she knew where the door was and set about spinning webbing across the opening. Others came into view, madly climbing the webbing that festooned the walls. One - the largest and swiftest - ducked into the ceiling maze first. The rest followed single file, nipping at each other's heels. Clearly, they meant to cut off any approach to the door. But when the butterflies reversed and made for open spaces instead, the Widows split and cut them off from that too.

Soon there were no more possibilities. Everywhere they went they came face-to-face with ugly spiders; yet if they retreated, they found less room to maneuver. Finally, they chose a place to make their stand, wide enough to use their wings a little. They had only moments before a widow showed her ugly face in the nearest bottleneck. It was Missah, a favorite of the Grande Dame. She exhaled with much pleasure.

"Ahhhhhh...Trapped, yesss..." she breathed, and made a queer clicking noise with her beak. The others stopped where they were. Missah giggled (if one could call it that), a gravelly, frothing sound. Unnerving. The butterflies trembled but stood their ground.

"Unhappy, yesss...Ahhhh! ...Ssso sad---"

Boca spit at her, right in the face. By her look of revulsion, she would make him pay for it.

"Haaaah! *Grasssp*...yessss! *Soon! Yesss!*"

"Yesss! Yesss!" echoed the others. "Da thee now, Mother?"

Involuntarily Yero glanced down, expecting to see the infernal hourglass again. It was not in evidence. Instead, there was the blubbery bulk of Whissah herself ponderously climbing the wall. Yero looked away.

Presently they heard her labored breathing as she approached the dense tangle of webs and felt them sag and stretch as she put her full weight onto them. Her daughters anxiously awaited her arrival. Here was a rare treat: 'Mother' would administer the coup-de-grace! They knew what was expected of them.

They rushed the butterflies, slinging sticky webs like lassoes. A short but terrific scuffle ensued. Before Yero and Boca were trussed one spider was blinded and another had a broken leg; but the butterflies had been bitten to tame them and were feeling the effects. Another scuffle broke out as the brood tore apart a wounded sister and scrapped over the pieces.

Then Whissah arrived and poked her face through the last bottleneck. Boca couldn't imagine how she would ever get through with her fat body. Did it even matter? He was slipping into numbness.

At that moment, beyond hope, a clear voice called up from below. The voice was unmistakable. Yero rolled sideways to look.

"Hold it there, madam! Those are my friends. I'll be taking them with me."

It was Atel, perched boldly on the entryway path. Somehow, she had burst Isstah's web and now held that daughter by the neck at the end of her beak. She made sure Isstah was dead for all to see and tossed her into the abyss.

There was a collective exhale at Isstah's fate. A few opportunists scurried down after fresh meat. But not Whissah. The Grande Dame saw better fare. She snarled and issued curt orders to regroup.

"Widow Spiders, come and see!

What isss?

Widow Spiders come to me!

All hissssss!"

Chapter 3

Spell and Counterspell

They hissed, and it was the sound of wind rising and darkness falling. On the entryway path Atel felt the breath of the Rasspinsah rush past her cheeks, heavy and bitter. With it came clear warning: The prisoners would not be handed over. There would be a fight.

But first Whissah intended to measure her adversary. She had met many in her time but never such as this, and she was prudent by habit. Not that it mattered much. The Grande Dame possessed deadly skills, as the bothersome hummingbird would soon find out, and felt secure enough to toy with her foe.

"Ahhh, come now...sss! The Pretties are mine, yesss...But what of *thyssself*, Dearie? Shall we discuss *businesss*...? Ahhh! Dah thee offer a *swap?*"

"No. We'll be leaving together. I have stated my purpose, madam. Hand over my companions or suffer the consequences."

"Ahhh! *Stated*, yesss...*purpose*, yesss...but talk is cheap, Dearie. Give usss *thyssself* in their place...and the Pretties go free!"

"No thanks. I'll stick with my own plan."

Sssss! So polite, yesss...So *proper*...ssssss...But shall we discuss *murder*, Dearie? ...Ahhh! Poor Isstah, dear daughter...Dah thee nah crussssh her and slassssh her?"

"That was the cost of admission, as you well know. And this is a *den* of murderers, or I'm a dingbat."

"Sss! S*ave usss!* Save usss from *liars!* Tha be no murderers here unlesss they be outsiders!" (Here Whissah checked her temper.) "But come, come...The Pretties are safe for now, yessss...But what of thyssself, Dearie? Art cold and weary? Sssss? Be welcome then...and sssnug...from the ssstorm."

"*Welcome and snug?* I guess that's how you tempted my companions, near enough. No thanks. I won't be staying any longer than I have to."

"Yesss...mossst naturally, Dearie...And tha be free to leave, nah? But dah thee nah *cozy* and... *pleasssant?* Cassst away our troubles!... sss...Shall we rather have peace and truces? Yessss...and *trusssty friendship?* Just *say* so...yesss...and it shall *be.*"

So great was the lulling power of the voice that Atel relaxed ever so slightly, a minute downward tilt of the beak that was carefully noted by the brood above. Imperceptibly, the deadliest of the daughters began to edge through their tunnels to where they could leap swiftly down when the time was right. How simple! They had every confidence in the Grande Dame. And lo! What sumptuous feast beckoned! Enough to go around, maybe. The first time in memory for the youngest.

On droned Whissah, assuring, mollifying. It was an uncomplicated spell. A charm, really. In the realm of spiders there are many variations of this particular charm, the most widely used of all: 'Atzb', the allurement of flying insects, taught by the magician Sihir to Attrap himself, first of spiders, in the depths of Time. Now the Grande Dame of Shaggara wove similar promises in the ear of her prey. None ever lied more skillfully than she.

Atel's beak drooped further. High above, creeping daughters edged into their staging areas. On her belly, the hourglass of Whissah began to gleam. Close at hand, trussed tightly, the butterflies lost consciousness. Small wonder with poison, webbing, and the breath of spiders.

Then, when things were getting dangerous indeed, the white hummingbird raised her head and shook off the spell as if it were a minor thing.

Cocking her head back she sang softly, almost sighing, as when cold grasses in a meadow bend eastward in the night, longing for the morning. As if in answer, the howling wind slackened outside. A hush fell upon the woodlands. Somewhere in the dark sky above, the clouds thinned. A glimmer of predawn brightened the doorway. Shards of webbing hung loosely there, where Isstah had done her last duty.

From above came faint creaking noises as hungry daughters retreated toward their mother, unsure of themselves at this new turn of events. For the first time in their experience Whissah had slipped, however temporarily.

As the hummingbird sang, more and more pale light stole through the doorway, met the resisting darkness and overcame it. Against the will of the Grande Dame, her shield of darkness diminished until half the chamber was filled with an eerie glow; yet Whissah did nothing. Daughters clustered thickly around her, wary of her appetite, but warier still of the uncanny light; yet still Whissah did nothing, unwilling or unable.

Atel sang on. Outside, dawn grew noticeably. The snow dwindled to flurries. Inside, the light reached up to the bottommost strands of the great canopy. The strands shrank, became taut, threatened to break, for that is the way of the Rasspinsah and all their crafts: They cannot endure the sun or the broad light of day. It is their great weakness.

In that moment of vulnerability, the daughters gasped with many voices, for just as they are instantly aware of footsteps on their web, they are also aware of light touching it. It hurts them. And this light, though still wan and feeble, was no ordinary light it seemed.

At the sound of their labored breathing Whissah awoke from her trance and gasped in her turn, realizing in an instant that she herself had been charmed. Never in her abhorrent life had such a thing happened! Her wrath knew no bounds. Great bubbling noises escaped her. Vile droplets spewed from her mouth, landing like acid on the backs of her daughters. Then she cursed instinctively against the dreaded light, invoking 'Uzlm', the Gathering Darkness.

Long have the Rasspinsah cherished and profited from that curse. Now in her hour of need Whissah wielded it as a powerful spell and regained the initiative. From the roots of Shaggara - indeed, from the roots of the earth - came darkness in answer, boiling up from the depths to engulf the invading light and swallow it. It parted as it reached the entryway path, leaving Atel and the pathway untouched, then ascended all around her and came together again above, cloaking all else in deep shadow: Pungent, unsavory shadow, remindful of ashes and cinders. Most creatures that lurk in dark holes would flee from it, for they have some virtue and are merely unpleasant to behold. Not so the Rasspinsah who serve a forbidden Master. Oh, yesss! It is *He* who allots shadow according to 'Uzlm'.

Atel felt a collective exhale of breath. Creepsy noises awoke as the emboldened daughters advanced again. She felt her own spell succumb. Outside, the growing dawn faded away. The storm regained strength. Worse, snowflakes pelted the doorway, clinging to the broken web and restricting available light. The pathway dimmed.

By some trick of shifting shadows or an anxious mind, Atel glimpsed the hourglass of Whissah high above - the hourglass and two trussed bundles close by. Then the vision faded, and more. All vision blurred and faded. Had her eyes been robbed of sight - or had darkness triumphed altogether in the stump?

She passed into a dream world. In her dream she saw spiders crawling in a dark pit, many of them, searching for something. For a while she watched curiously, wondering what it might be. Then a raspy voice called down to the spiders, "Tha be the time!" Sticky ropes dangled for them. Slavering spiders gave up their search and climbed the ropes eagerly to some better reward.

In her dream, Atel realized they had been looking for *her*, was much relieved. But soon anguished cries came from up above. They troubled her terribly, though she couldn't remember why, or who might be crying out.

Another vision passed before her of hungry spiders crowding around lashed bundles, squabbling over them. A hint of orange appeared through the lashings and she guessed what must be inside. She cried out but her voice was pathetically weak, too weak to be heard.

"Here!" she whispered. "I am here! I'll make the swap!"

But the spiders did hear. They had been toying with her all the while. Now they laughed. They were going to devour the orange bundles anyway. They just wanted to hear her beg mercy. Now that she groveled, they were satisfied and bent deliciously to their meal.

Atel screamed in her nightmare but it made no noise. She tried to fly, only to discover she had somehow got tangled in the sticky ropes and the more she struggled the worse she became entangled. A large spider dangled just above, directing others to slip the ropes round and round her. The spider relished her struggle.

"Isss fasssstened? Yesss!" she exulted.

Atel awakened to discover the dream was true. Spiders were indeed trussing her! Others were repairing the web in the doorway. Missah, eldest daughter of the Grande Dame, hovered languidly just above, directing operations. She hissed long and low as the hummingbird came to.

"Dah thee dissssturb?" she exclaimed venomously and attacked headlong with gaping jaws.

Atel lowered her beak in greeting, upon which Missah impaled herself with a shriek and a grunt. The force of the collision ripped loose her bonds and Atel extracted her beak from the struggling spider with a sharp tug. The gaping wound bubbled with green juices, opening and closing in regular time with the spider's mouth. Then Missah curled into a fetal ball and toppled off the entryway path, dead - no longer Mother's 'favorite'.

She wasn't the last to be thus greeted. Several others attacked immediately, hoping to deliver a fatal bite before Atel slipped entirely loose of the webbing. They met exactly the same fate. The rest fled up into shadow.

Then again Atel began to sing, but this time it was the sound of birds stirring at daybreak. Crows raised a ruckus in the distance. Somewhere a rooster crowed. Outside, the storm commenced to break up. Unseen from within, patches of blue sky appeared. Inevitably, one coincided with the rising sun. A ray or two passed over the woodlands like the glint of eagles, pausing at Shaggara to melt through snowflakes and webbing before moving on.

Inside, Atel caught the light in her breast feathers and reflected it back in a tight beam to melt away the remaining mess in the doorway. Morning light entered; not much at first, but enough to energize the mirror of Atel, and more than was good for Black Widows.

Now they crouched in their tunnels or hung cowering beneath them, fearful of what might happen next. Whissah cowered most of all in the heart of the tunnels where darkness clung thickest. But for the Widows there was worse to come. Atel sang on.

An eerie glow spread downward from the mirror. Wherever it touched webbing, it flared brightly. As it penetrated the depths all webbing stretched and snapped. Loose ends writhed like the tails of bats put to hot fire. The light reached the great web near the bottom. There was a bright flash, diminishing to smaller flashes and crackles. The larger part of the web disappeared. Acrid smoke wafted upwards. The Brood watched it all, fascinated, though it hurt their eyes.

Atel sang on. In her hiding place, Whissah succumbed to visions in her turn, visions of despair. She saw bright eyes below, searching for her. She knew they must not find her. As she watched, the eyes grew suddenly brighter, blazing like fire. Ahhhh...Ssssss! They knew where she was! Whissah shuddered and the canopy of webbing jiggled. Then voices called to her, requesting permission to go quench the lights that hurt them so.

Her daughters!

"Dah thee kill, Mother? And desssstroy?"

"Yesss!" answered Whissah, much relieved. Ahhh, yesss...let them do it! About time they earned their keep, the sluggards!

She leaned forward to watch the fun - but what was this? The daughters weren't attacking. They were scurrying and hiding. Scurrying and hiding! What was *this*? Dah thee nah *kill*?

With a twinge in her black heart she realized they were asking *her* to do the dirty work. The whelps! They had no stomach for battle with uncanny lights.

Then the bright eyes searched her out and fixed on her. By some acoustical trick or echo, her own voice intoned from below, "Tha be the time!" A very bright flash accompanied her voice and more smoke wafted up to her. Another twinge gripped her heart: She had forgotten her precious egg-mass! Doubtless, it too was now destroyed. Her maternal instincts revolted at the thought. Her lovely egg-mass, destroyed! It was perhaps the only thing that could have jolted her out of the trance.

She awoke cursing, limbs flailing, rending the very webbing of her tunnel. The horrible bright eyes winked out. Outside, a final, nasty squall blew into the woods. Fresh wind howled through the doorway. Whissah shook off remnants of bleariness and took stock. Then she laughed. A silly dream! Ssssss! So much for that! Now she would crussssh the little bird who perched so insolently! Once more she invoked 'Uzlm', to gain time for that which would follow.

From odd corners, her daughters emerged. One had taken shelter quite near Mother. Impudently near! So *that* was it, was it? One little slip and the brat thought Mother was beaten? The snot! Whissah popped the brat into her maw and glared at the rest of her brood. At the mere glance, they backed further away. Worthless bunch! So, the best two were dead: Missah and Isstah. Of the rest, only Lassah showed real promise. Only Lassah! Ssss!

As shadow rose up again from below the Grande Dame made signs to her daughter, signs long rehearsed, telling what was expected of her: Before the coming onslaught she must leave Shaggara. Confident or not, Whissah had obligations to her race. The Rasspinsah must not fail! To this end, she must send a daughter to found a new colony. It would be Lassah, now. She was quite ready, having long since been instructed in the Arts with her sisters.

Next, Whissah performed obeisance to That-which-eats-light, beyond the stars. Lifting her face, she croaked a greeting, punctuated with many subservient hisses. Words she spoke that were poison of themselves. Slowly at first, but then swiftly, a pocket of impenetrable blackness formed around her and organized into fingers. The fingers moved through the spider tunnels at her behest, snake-like, seeking the living hummingbird below - the fingers of 'Mawt', the Black Death.

"Yessss...Now we shall see!" breathed Whissah eagerly. "Oh yesss!" Just once before had she conjured up the spell of death - to clean out the bat colony when she took over Shaggara. The Master hadn't liked that, had he? Oh, no. Bats were also his friends; but he had gone along with it. Ssss! How the fingers had throttled the squeaky things! Ssss! How she had gloated! But she hadn't dared to use the spell since.

Now she needed it, and she hadn't forgotten. But it was very difficult, very tiring. She licked froth from her beak and concentrated harder. Nothing less would do, not this time. She was very much aware now of the hummingbird's strength, which equaled her own. But the struggle should soon be ended if the squall could hold together outside. That was the only risk and it couldn't be helped. Curse the bird, and her skill with light!

But Whissah needn't worry. Everything was turning in her favor: The hummingbird was again blinded and held fast, and this time she did not dream. Oh, no. This time she perched mindlessly, though it required supreme effort by the Grande Dame. And the doorway was rapidly filling with snow! So much for the bird's puny chances.

Out that door slipped Lassah, unnecessarily it seemed now. Whissah nearly lost her grip as she glanced after, found herself slipping, struggling to hold the bird motionless. Beads of sweat broke out like pustules on her forehead, ran down her face and dripped onto the webbed floor. A drop splashed right onto Yero's face as she lay sleeping under the great spider.

It stung. Yero opened her eyes. Directly above her was the Grande Dame, breathing heavily, focusing beyond her, ignoring her. The last good light from below reflected off the spider's clustered eyes. Yero tried to turn away but couldn't. Something prevented her from rolling to her left, the only direction her trussed wings would allow. Something lumpy and warm. Boca! He was still with her but also wrapped securely. With one free leg she gave him a sharp dig. She was rewarded with a cross, muffled reply. Good! He was alive.

She made herself relax and glanced downward. All in a rush she remembered everything up to the moment she passed out.

Atel was here! She had found them! There she was now, on the path below. But something was wrong, terribly wrong. Black fingers were moving down toward her, obviously up to no good. Even as she watched, the fingers paused and joined to form a groping hand, then moved stealthily onward.

But Atel did nothing! Surely, she must see the danger - why didn't she *do* something? Yero shouted a warning as loud as she dared. It wasn't easy with webbing across her mouth, nor did Atel seem to hear. She called louder, as loud as she was able, but her voice responded poorly, and the effort weakened her.

Then Atel shifted her eyes and looked directly at her. As from a great distance, Yero heard the hummingbird's voice calling urgently: "Do something - quick!"

Yero reached up to do 'something' to Whissah but could barely touch her bulky abdomen. She tickled, lightly, which was all she could do. Whissah scarcely noticed. The only effect Yero could see was a tightening of her facial lines.

Below, however, even this little bit was paying off. Though Yero couldn't watch, the Black Hand was having as difficult a time as she was. Deprived of the last ounce of Whissah's strength due to Yero's small distraction, it groped for the hummingbird's throat...but fell just short.

Panic welled up in Yero's throat. Try as she might there was nothing more she could do. Her fingers too, fell just short. She spoke directly to the spider, boldly insulting her, but to no avail. Then she thought once more of Boca.

She gave him another kick and was rewarded with a minor cuss word, which she overlooked.

"Boca, do you have a free arm or leg?"

"I don't know, Yero. I'm numb."

"You're dumb?"

"Don't tease me, Yero!"

"Boca, there's no need to be critical of yourself. Even if you *are* dumb you can still do a small job I have in mind."

Exactly as she hoped, Boca lost his temper and squirmed strenuously in his wrappings, overcoming the numbness by so doing. Suddenly he popped an arm free and groped for Yero, pinching at her wrappings. She was thrilled.

"That's perfect!" she told him. "Now - pinch Fatso in the belly back there! Hurry!"

Something in the way she said it got through to him and he transferred his anger to the spider crouched above. It was easy where he was, farther to her rear. The big abdomen puffed down invitingly close. He pinched with all his strength - a minor blow surely, at the edge of a real battle, but it was enough and more than enough. Whissah lost her concentration and her last chance of victory. Atel sang a clear note of command. Rudderless, the Black Hand clenched once, twice, and dissipated.

In her lair, the Grande Dame sensed disaster. Spitefully, she determined to kill the butterflies anyway to dash the hummingbird's hopes, but as she reached for the troublesome pair events passed beyond her control.

In the sky above Shaggara the clouds parted completely. Sunlight dazzled the winter woodlands. Scintillating rays poked through the last gap in the frosty doorway, met Atel's mirror at just the right angle, and reflected upward. Shadows vanished in an instant. Webs smoldered and broke apart. Unthinkable light struck Whissah, blinding her, and she fell, crashing heavily against the entryway path on her way to the bottom. Atel let her go to attend more pressing errands. Two of them. Yero and Boca also fell.

Their bonds had loosened but their wings were in no condition to fly at all, nor were their bodies. Atel caught them and set them on the pathway in a warm sunbeam. There they rested well into the morning while their guide finished the job on the spiders, some of whom still skittered about the walls grasping at the loose ends of webs. For a while her mirror had work aplenty, directing the light of day where it had never gone before. One by one, light discovered the stragglers, and they fell. Most were dead before they hit bottom. Others succumbed to the fall. Atel herself went down to make sure while the butterflies talked quietly.

"I take back what I said," giggled Yero. "You're not so dumb after all."

"Thank you. That's more praise than usual."

"You deserve some. And who knows? Maybe the worst of the journey is behind us now. I can't imagine anything worse than spiders."

"I'm not so sure. It'll be cold out in the snow."

"The snow won't *eat* us, Boca."

"It might, if it's deep enough."

"Piffle! We're butterflies. We'll float over it with the greatest of ease." Yero tried to demonstrate, waggling her wings and stepping lightly along the path. She had to give it up. Her wings were still wrinkled and very sore.

Boca grinned ruefully. "I don't think I could do any better. But you know, we might be able to walk on *top* of the snow and not sink in."

"Do you think so?" said Yero seriously. "Could we walk on top?"

"Sure, if we had slippers."

"What difference would that make?"

"We would have warm feet."

Yero laughed. Good old Boca! And bless Atel too! Sitting there in the warm sunbeam she felt good about their chances. Maybe it was the warmth, or maybe just the swifter recovery common to creatures of the wild, but her wings, and Boca's too, were already beginning to straighten out, and the pain of the spider bites was a little less.

Atel returned from her work and perched beside them. For a few moments she studied them keenly, taking note of their wings which had lost nearly all their dust, but more so their mood, which surprised her. She hadn't expected good cheer. That would make her job easier. But right now there was a mystery to clear up.

"The spiders are all dead, including Boss-Lady," she reported.

The butterflies clapped their hands. They expected no less.

"Was it much of a battle to finish her off?" asked Boca. He wanted details because "…If we see the tribbits again, I want to tell the story."

Atel smiled and made a mental note. "It wasn't really a *battle*…" she began, but when the butterflies looked disappointed, she added a bit of color, "…It was more like a *duel*. Of course, Madam Spider wasn't in the best shape by that time. Her fat body had splattered from the fall and she was dying…"

"Good! Good!" cheered the butterflies. "Now *she* is the juicy one!"

"Well…ahem…it did make quite a mess. I left her for last, and when I returned she had dug herself into a hole in the damp sawdust. Only her mouth showed out. Very defiant. Rather than take unnecessary chances I simply stuffed a good-sized chunk of dry rot into her mouth. She choked on it."

The butterflies were grimly pleased with the payback.

"She murdered a friend of ours," said Yero. "A good friend."

"Murdered?" Atel looked surprised. "When was that?"

"Oh, before you came. A funny little fellow with long legs. Not a spider."

Boca cleared his throat: "*HOST!* That's what he called his kind. We called him 'Poppy', but Whissah caught him. He's gone."

Atel chuckled. "Not completely! But there isn't much left. He was hiding under the chunk I stuffed into Boss-Lady's mouth. Your friend thought that was very funny, that she should die from it. He claims to like the stuff."

"He does, silly fellow! So, he's alive?"

"Certainly. He wants to see you. Shall we go down?"

It was Poppy, all right. Atel's question was answered, but the butterflies had many of their own, and Poppy too. She let them talk. The afternoon was getting on, anyway. It would be best to spend the night in the old stump where it would be warm. They could resume their journey in the morning. It would be difficult now. Food would be hard to come by and they would need warm lodging every night.

Poppy was his usual talkative self except that his legs were gone. All that remained was his tiny body, but that didn't seem to bother him at all. He was happy to see his friends - the only friends he could remember.

"Ya, ya!" he beamed. "So! Tha be safe, eh? Und Poppy too, eh? Und no more spiders? Hoo! Dat be fine for pals. Ya-hoo-ya!"

The 'pals' were amazed. How did he ever manage to escape - if that was the proper word --? Poppy was more than happy to explain.

"Hoo! Tha be clever Old Bag, dat Whissah, eh? Oh ya. Und Poppy slips, ya. Too bad for Poppy. Too bad! She grabs him - Oof! So! Old Bag is happy, oh ya. Und she be eating Poppy, you betcha, legs first. Then sisters say, 'Give usss some!' But she won't share. No! Just gobble, eh? So, sisters grab Poppy too! Dat's right. Grab und run! Oof! Legs here, legs there, und all fight. But Poppy falls down, down. Very sneaky. So! He hides, eh? Like before. Ya! Und grow new legs. Ha-ha! Dat's good for Poppy."

It seemed incredible. The Widows had hated him so! But when they finally got him all they got was his legs. It only went to show that being small can be a blessing.

"Didn't they look for you?" asked Boca. "They must have known that, umm ...*one* part of you went missing."

"Nah. Tha be all jealous, eh? So! Who got Poppy's best part? Nobody knows. Ha-ha! They don't know what happened. Und then Isstah says, 'Juicy ones essssscape!' Ah, dat be too bad for butterflies."

It sure was, but all's well that ends well. The Four shared a good laugh, well earned. Each had played a key part: Take away any one of them and Black Widows would still rule Shaggara, fatter and more secure than ever.

They talked on into the evening discussing spiders, *HOSTS*, butterflies and hummingbirds. Night fell and the temperature outside dropped drastically. A frigid wind came out of the northwest. Soldiers of the North Wind patrolled the countryside. Butterflies had better be indoors.

When the others went to sleep, Atel flew up to have a look outside. The sky was absolutely clear and ablaze with stars. She borrowed some of the starlight and made a final inspection of Shaggara lest any Widows were still alive and hiding, meaning to have their revenge during the night. There were none. All was quiet. She introduced a spell of forewarning into the doorway and dozed off on the entryway path.

Next morning Poppy was up early, a habit he had picked up to annoy the Widows who preferred to sleep late. Since there were none to annoy, he rustled up breakfast instead. The lack of legs didn't slow him down at all. He rolled this way and that, using the natural bulging motion of his jowls for propulsion; so, the more he talked - and the faster he talked - the quicker he moved. If he wished to turn left or right, he simply talked out the other side of his mouth. Even his mustache, which could well have been a hindrance, was employed as a brake. Now that the Widows were gone and he had nothing to occupy him, he was full of questions (all the better to move around with).

Were the butterflies awake yet? He made sure of it. Time was a-wasting! Mustn't be sleepyheads, eh? Did they wish to grab a bite with him, and start the day off proper? Ha-ha. Be careful! Poppy is yust one small bite himself now! Ya, you betcha. Don't eat Poppy!

No one volunteered to share his food, which perplexed him as before, but didn't dampen his enthusiasm. "Ya! Yust watch. Do like this!" He wobbled around the damp, decaying floor, nibbling here and there, sometimes nodding in satisfaction, occasionally spitting something back out. Atel joined the breakfast party and had her chance to decline as well, which she did. By now Poppy expected it and hardly paused, wobbling this way and that but carefully avoiding the loose ends of web that still dangled from the walls, twisting and flopping as if in a light breeze.

"Squirming" was the word Yero used. It didn't take much imagination to see that the loose ends were searching, *reaching* out to each other. The longer ones braided together, then fell apart and reached for others. The great web had been torn asunder but the wall still crawled with the frazzled stubs. Yero shivered in distaste.

"They act like they're alive," she muttered. "*Are* they?"

"In their own way," answered Atel. "Most spiders are solitary, and their webs provide company. They talk to each other, so 'tis said."

"No joke?"

"No joke. Ask Poppy."

Poppy didn't need to be asked. He overheard and was astonished at such ignorance. "Ya! You betcha! Und tell little secrets, eh? Oh ya. Und tattle on strangers too, eh? Oof! Ya, ya. Und talk with little voices? Nay! No voices, no. Dat be yust toesie-talk."

"I believe it," said Boca. "Remember, Yero, when we dropped through the window? I had an awful feeling like we set off an alarm."

"Yeah. But we're not touching them now, so what are they doing? Talking to each other?"

Poppy nodded, accidentally doing a somersault toward the wall. A long 'frazzler' flopped behind him. He calmly maneuvered around it, jabbering all the while. "Oh, ya! Talking und seeking, eh? Ha-ha! Seeking *Dat Old Bag*, ya-hoo-ya! Where *isss*?"

"Don't they know she's dead?"

Poppy didn't think so. But it didn't matter. Soon, all would be lost. He waxed sorrowful. "Gone! *All gone*, eh? Ya, spiders too, oh ya. Poor, poor Poppy! He can't tease sisters now. Dat's too bad. Nay-hoo-da!"

The daddylonglegs was having second thoughts about his future, beginning already to miss the Widows. What would he do for fun?

"When your new legs are grown you could go outside," suggested Yero. "Maybe find others of your kind? I'm sure that would be fun."

The thought didn't comfort Poppy, but Yero couldn't think of anything better and Atel was beginning to be impatient.

As guide, she reminded the butterflies that it was time to leave but was met with reluctance. What about Poppy? They couldn't take him along but how could they leave him in the shape he was in? Atel put the question directly to the daddylonglegs.

Surprisingly, Poppy had anticipated it. He figured they would be leaving. "Oh, ya. Nay! Soon tha be no more pals. Oof da." But would they do Poppy a favor? He rolled onto his back, so to speak, and looked up, up to the high ceiling where his window was. Hoo-ya! Dat was his favorite place. Could they put him up there, eh? Up where the floor tasted better? You see, ha-ha, Widows had lived in this part of Shaggara forever, and the tainted condition of the lower floor showed it.

"Dat be nicer food upstairs," he grinned. "D'nah think?"

Before anyone could answer, Boca shattered the moment with a yelp of distress. Poppy's flopped-out 'frazzler' had wrapped around his leg and was pulling him toward the wall; and before anyone could react, a dozen more loose ends lent a hand, spiraling around his whole body and *jerking* him toward the wall like a rubber band snapping back. Caught off balance, he hit it sideways with enough force to knock the wind out of him as still more 'frazzlers' got into the act, obviously reinforcing each other. A whole wiggling section of the wall braided itself tautly in fleeting moments.

Boca himself was muted after just one yelp. Several rough strands had wrapped around his head, gagging and strangling him, even as Yero tried to pry them loose.

By now Atel's mirror was also at work, burning through the bonds in a circle around Boca as close as she dared; but when she had done all she could he was still held tight and losing consciousness.

"Do these!" shouted Yero, unable to loosen the 'chokers'; but Atel was at a loss. The 'chokers' were anchored behind Boca out of sight and to try and burn them off his neck would be the death of him. Her mirror wasn't that precise. Then Poppy wobbled into the hopeless situation.

"Ya, ya. Try *this*," he suggested, spitting something at Yero that disgusted her when she caught it; but Poppy was serious. "Rub it in - Oof da! Und fool 'em, eh?"

It was - what else? - spider waste in a handy pellet form. Atel caught on right away.

"Pretend it's a bar of soap!" she shouted to Yero. "Scrub his face and neck. The webs will think he's a spider!" To her credit Yero began 'washing' him up immediately without really understanding why, and soon got a gooey 'lather' going from the neck and up. Atel joined in with her own little bar and began 'soaping' the rest of him.

"Webbing too!" she directed, and Yero bent to the task. Suddenly one strand slipped loose, then another. Boca made a gurgling noise as the last 'choker' let go. That one whipped Yero's soap bar up into her face and she backed away, spitting, as Boca pulled free and staggered away from the wall. While he recovered, their guide tidied up all the loose ends, burning them off at the nub.

Boca felt welts on his neck and became aware of the bad smell, but his thoughts were all for his deliverance. "I couldn't have lasted any longer," he said gratefully. "What happened? Did Atel burn the webs?"

"Some," answered Yero, "but not the ones around your neck." She paused a moment, then added, "We were just lucky there. Poppy had soap, and we lathered you up until they slipped loose."

"Wow. Does he have any more? I still smell pretty bad."

"No, we used it all up. But let's take Poppy back upstairs. I'm dirty too and we can wash up in the attic."

No one disagreed. Yero carefully picked Poppy up and Atel gave them all a lift up to Poppy's foyer. There, the passengers disembarked and proceeded through the lucky crack in the wall, and on up the worn stairway: Yero first with Poppy, and Boca just behind in case she dropped him, which was quite possible since Poppy jabbered all the way and was difficult to hold on to. She juggled him, if truth be told, sometimes catching him politely by the backside, sometimes by grabbing his mouth and interrupting a sentence, but they reached the attic without mishap.

They set him near the window and washed up in the water drip. A real bar of soap would've been nice there, but the shower helped a lot. Then, much against Poppy's wishes, they gathered chips and made a barrier across the shallow stairs so he couldn't roll out of the attic and fall all the way to the bottom. He would have to grow reasonably long legs to cross it. With legs like that, he should be able to negotiate the stairs. Then he could get down to his foyer or anywhere else without hurting himself. They thanked him again, but Poppy wouldn't hear of it. As he saw it, he was right back where he started, so everyone came out even.

"Dat's good fun!" he grinned, and wished them luck, but he didn't seem quite the Poppy of old. Boca opened the window and they dropped through onto the back of their guide, waiting for them. Yero closed the window behind. Click! It locked. It was all they could do.

Atel took them down to the doorway, pausing in the opening. Before them lay a strange landscape, unrecognizable from days past. It had been a great storm.

"Could you put a spell of some kind on this knothole?" asked Yero. "To make him a little safer? He's so defenseless right now."

"Spiders--or who knows what--will come right in if it's left open," predicted Boca.

But Atel didn't see things their way. "I think your daddylonglegs would welcome that," she replied. "If he were to peek through his window one day and see new webs below and the whole stump full of nasty spiders again, I'm sure he would love it. He would hurry down to that foyer of his and get his game up, risking his fool neck and loving every minute of it." She frowned at the thought of it but continued. "In the end we can't protect folks from themselves. Certainly not Poppy. He wouldn't want it. He'd be very unhappy if he couldn't take risks. Since he puts only himself at risk, he should be allowed to do so. We'll leave the door open."

They left Shaggara behind, the hummingbird and her passengers, and were soon cruising along above the highest treetops. There, free of any shadow, the morning sun warmed them a little, but only a little. And it didn't warm the Earth at all.

Below, and as far as the eye could see, stretched a vast whiteness broken only by small woodlands and fencerows. Everywhere, huge drifts had piled up. There was no sign of flowers or green plants, or life of any kind.

By mid-morning the butterflies were chilled even in the sunshine - a chill made worse by the lack of esporellia on their wings - and hinted broadly about putting down somewhere out of the wind.

"It can't be easy hauling a couple of bums," said Yero. "At least you should take *breaks*. We're easy to please!" Her voice shook a little.

"Then I'll please you by going on, and not stopping. We'll all live much longer if we can escape the snow. But go ahead and shiver. Don't fight it. It'll help to keep you warm."

"We can't help it anyway. How much farther does it go?"

"The snow? Farther south than I expected. Maybe a lot farther. How long can butterflies go without food?"

"Who knows? We aren't much for experimenting like that, but we *can* stand some cold. We just don't like it. And it gets on the nerves watching endless snowfields. It's like a curse."

"It is. But it's a temporary curse compared to the Widows'. Ours should be ended in a few days. Theirs has plagued them for Ages and may never end."

"Oh, great. Now we're to feel *sorry* for them about something? Well, they deserve it, whatever it was!"

"By now they do, yes. There are lots of such broods today - folks would be shocked if they knew how many - and the Widows are quite pleased with themselves. If their curse could be lifted, I'm sure they would refuse the offer. But it was a curse that *led* to such wickedness. It will never change now."

"What happened? Where did they come from?"

"The Widows are descended from the human race. Do you want to hear more?"

"Why not? The human race is lucky to be rid of them. There are still a few other stinkers left though, so we've heard."

Atel laughed. "So I've heard, too! There are a few stinkers in every kind, unfortunately. But with the Rasspinsah it's all of them."

"Rasspinsah?" asked Boca. "What's that? Poppy called them 'Old Maids'."

"He would. They hate it. *Rasspinsah - Spinsters* in our language - was their ancient name, but they call themselves 'Widows' now, for respectability. The truth is, they're widows by their own hands. It's called 'murder' in more civilized societies, but tradition evolved differently with them. They preferred darkness for good reason, but it corrupted them. Before long, they saw nothing wrong with killing and eating each other, especially if the victim was a male - the lowest, most miserable caste.

Only one or two males are allowed to live from each brood - the meekest, most docile and servile - until the Grand Dame tires of them. When her patience begins to run short, the whole brood gathers to watch the red hourglass on her belly. The unlucky males see it too and beg for mercy, but the hourglass is their Law. When it runs out everyone turns on them. Mercy in their society means being ripped into bite-sized pieces quickly. It's their tradition, but there was a cause for such wickedness. That part goes back to the old 'gods' and 'goddesses' of an earlier Age."

—The Rasspinsah—

In the First Age of the World aboriginal spirits awoke with the heating of the Earth - rogue offshoots of creation, no doubt, and trouble for the future, but imbued with strength from the molten interior. Little is recorded of them before the human race appeared, but they were amused by humankind and took human shapes to themselves for vanity and mischief. Men were awed by them and called them *gods* - a fair description of their powers, but not their behavior which was often sinful and selfish.

One well-known story has the goddess Athena showing mercy on a mortal girl, Arachne, following a weaving contest in which the girl lost and promptly hanged herself in despair. Athena usually gets credit in the story for bringing the girl mercifully back to life as a spider by changing the rope to a strand of web. But like so many historical accounts, the winner cleaned up the story to look better.

In truth, the incident was all about a young man betrothed to Arachne but desired by Athena. The young man witnessed the event and it was no weaving contest. The girl was quite accomplished and would have won that. Nor was there any suicide - just a cruel make-over done to the girl by Athena in a jealous rage. (Oh, *yesss!* That part is true.)

All who witnessed it fled in horror save the young man; but Athena remained also for a while to gloat over the spider-girl who groveled among the stones.

"Tha be a natural artiste," Athena taunted. "Can tha weave a tapestry of happiness now? I think nah, but tha be free to try."

Arachne saw the doom that stretched before her and made a final plea. In horrible hissing voice, loathsome as the spider's body in which she found herself, she begged Athena to turn her betrothed into like form so they could have a life together. But the young man fled at the repulsive voice, little understanding the words. Grief overwhelmed the spider-girl and she cried bitterly, "How long, Oh Goddesss, mussst I remain like *thisss*?"

Then Athena traced an hourglass on the spider-girl's belly and pricked her finger above it - and Lo! A drop of blood turned the glass half-full, as though hope of mercy remained and some limit be placed on the penitence.

"Tha be the time!" said Athena with a hint of a smile. "Art happier now?"

Arachne bowed awkwardly in gratitude. Already the blood was flowing to the empty half. Athena made as if to leave, adding that she would catch up to the young man and explain, but when she had gone a few steps she turned back with a wicked leer.

"Ah, yes," she said. "Tha be one thing more: When the glass is empty tha must turn around, nah? And tha must start over again."

Thenceforth through all Ages the daughters of Arachne have dwelt hidden, loathing their gross appearance but loathing even more the male of the species, for they call all males faithless. They have not forgotten.

The hourglass they keep, and like the poison in their hearts it has been put to practical use. When they have cornered their prey they love to gloat, like Athena long ago. It heightens their pleasure. Counting down the hourglass is their greatest pleasure. Don't be around when it runs out.

As Atel hoped, the story kept her passengers from dwelling on their own miseries and even prompted a few questions rather than complaints about the weather. Boca didn't mind the gruesome parts and wanted to know more about the poison, having gotten a dose of it himself. In fact, owing to inactivity, both butterflies were stiffening up again, partly from the cold but also from their bites.

"We were lucky," said Boca. "I think we were being saved for Boss-Lady, and she was to finish us off. We didn't get a full dose."

"I agree. You are both proving tougher than I expected, but you wouldn't survive a strong widow-bite. Neither would I. We were lucky."

"But we're still pretty stiff and sore. Do you think we got a half-dose"?

"No. It would've been less than that. Boss-Lady would've been very upset if you couldn't struggle for her amusement."

"But we must've gotten at least a quarter-dose."

"I doubt that too. They can kill animals as large as a full-grown raccoon, or even larger. Are you a fourth as big as a coon?"

The question hung there a little while before Boca answered, "No," and then *that* hung in the air a while too, until Yero finally spoke up.

"We aren't a fourth as smart, either. At least I'm not. I wondered when *that* would get brought up."

Atel had to admire the honesty. "No lasting harm done if you learned from it," she said. "Joo-Ool didn't take it out on me."

"That's a relief. Why not?"

"I complimented her. *They called me a sow!* she bellowed. *I can see why, as fat as you are!* I replied. That took the edge off her temper. They're a lot more like pigs than they'd ever admit."

The butterflies laughed. That warmed them as much as anything on a cold day and put them in a jolly mood for a while thinking up other such 'compliments' they might use, and who they might use them on.

Miles passed beneath them with no end of snow. In late afternoon, as the sunshine weakened, doubt grew in the hummingbird's mind. The snow if anything was becoming deeper. They all needed food, not to mention shelter, and there was nothing in sight but vast snowfields with less and less trees.

"We are f-f-freezing," said Yero finally. "The wind is f-freezing us solid." It was time.

Atel put down in a lonely grove of burr oak trees (if three trees can make up a grove), on the flat stump of a fourth that had once stood with them. She immediately saw something inviting, but Boca discovered something else even sooner, or thought he did. He leaped off Atel's back and hopped around the stump like a bird dog, sniffing the air, not frozen solid after all.

"He thinks there is 'mallasha'," interpreted Yero. "Thinks he can smell it. I don't smell anything, but there's no stopping him."

"It's here!" declared Boca. "Pretty close, I'm sure of it, but it's hard to pinpoint in the wind." He leaned way out, teetering over the edge of the stump.

The wind had shifted around to the southwest by now. It had blown the stump-top clear of snow and carved a hollow on that side. Using his imagination freely Boca declared *that* to be the source of the aroma - somewhere in the hollow, under the snow. He leaped into the hollow forthwith, followed by Yero, and began to dig.

Atel let them dig. What could it hurt for a few minutes? She had hoped they could get some exercise somehow. But less than a minute passed before they found treasure.

"Come! Help us dig!" called Yero. "He's right for once." Boca ignored that, busily brushing off a blossom. It was frozen or nearly so, but there were others under it.

Their guide did better than just dig, reflecting the rays of the setting sun with her mirror, concentrating them onto the flowers. A whole cluster appeared before long and then - bonanza! The remaining snow fell away into a void beneath, leaving the whole cluster exposed like a buffet for the butterflies. They wasted no time about it.

Atel went hungry, of course, but she had another thought in mind. High in one of the burr oaks was a beehive, almost certainly deserted now: A large hive of the type that hang from branches. A hornet's nest. She called down to the butterflies to excuse herself.

"Ahoy down there! I think I'll buzz up to that thing in the tree - see it? - and investigate. Want to come along when you're finished?"

Yero politely declined. "This will take until dark, unless the flowers freeze, and they're starting to. Is it too late to warm them again?"

"It is. The sun has gone."

"Okay. See you later." She wanted no part of the nest. Neither did Boca. They knew about hornets. Almost everyone does. Bald-faced hornets and their big paper hives are notorious.

Regardless, Atel went up to see what could be seen. As she got closer it appeared even more obvious that it was empty, as it should be by now. No bees were coming or going. The entrance was partly filled with snow. On the windward side there was some damage. A bird, probably, had ripped through several outer layers but stopped at that point. The hive was still weatherproof by all appearances.

She went back and studied the entrance more closely, whisking away snow with the draft from her beating wings. There had been no traffic since the storm at least. As a final measure, she moved laterally around the fattest part of the hive giving it a brisk drumming with her wing feathers. Nothing stirred inside. It was empty. She returned to the stump in fine spirits.

"Good news!" she said. "I've reserved accommodations for three."

"In *that?*" asked Yero.

"Certainly. It should be nice and cozy. The entrance is smallish, but big enough for butterflies used to cramped spider tunnels." Atel smiled.

"Oh, great. Did you...um...inquire about vacancy?"

"I haven't actually been inside, but the place seems to be empty."

"*Seems* to be?"

"Yes. I'll go in first and assume all the risk. Let's go."

The weather left little choice. The wind was picking up again, and though it was out of the south it could be days before it warmed up much. Anyway, their dinner table had folded up tightly for the night.

The butterflies spread their wings helplessly and looked to the sky. A moon was rising. Stars were coming out. Some esporellia would fall, but they would freeze to death long before they caught much of it. When Atel hopped down alongside they willingly came aboard.

Curiously, the butterflies felt much braver when they got to the entrance. Probably it was the effect of food in their bellies.

Whatever, they insisted on coming along in.

"We must be there in case of trouble," said Yero.

Atel didn't answer. She poked her head inside, paused to listen, then squeezed all the way in. The butterflies followed. A faintly sweetish aroma greeted them. There was no sound except their own breathing. It was very dark. Atel whispered in a language unknown to them - once, twice, three times - and waited. Presently an aura of moonbeams followed inside. In that light the explorers saw a winding tunnel ahead, much larger than the narrow opening, all made of the same papery material as the outside walls. It climbed away upward and to their right. Judging by the position of the entrance, which was down low, they were heading for the center of the hive.

Atel moved forward. The moonbeams followed her like a shawl.

Chapter 4

Night Lodgings

The butterflies hurried after single file but were soon obliged to crouch as the ceiling lowered. Yero in the middle worried that Atel would get stuck up ahead of her. She inquired repeatedly voicing her concern, but never got an answer. Boca, bringing up the rear, worried that hornets were sneaking up behind him and voiced his anxiety to Yero. He didn't get any answer either. Then Atel stopped, so everyone stopped. It seemed obvious to Yero that the worst had happened - that Atel was now stuck in the narrow tunnel with no way to get her loose. She watched for telltale signs of a struggle, but the hummingbird didn't move.

Each was left with their own thoughts. Boca was more convinced than ever about hornets on his heels. Far behind, wind whistled in the doorway. To Boca it sounded like angry buzzing. He waggled his wings, the little bit that he could, to fend them off.

Yero noticed the warmth of the tunnel for the first time. Combined with fresh nectar in her stomach she suddenly felt very sleepy. Put simply, she'd had enough fresh air for one day. She tried vainly to keep her eyes open, nodded off for a few moments, then re-awakened to a hollow, booming noise. A strong gust of wind swirling through the trees had swung the hive like a pendulum. On the backswing it bumped into a sturdy limb, causing the sound, but to Yero it was baffling and terrifying. She tried to imagine what could make such a noise. Surely it had awakened every last hornet! All thought of sleep left her.

Atel stepped forward and disappeared, moonbeams and all. Yero scrambled to catch up and bumped her nose, then realized the tunnel turned sharply. She felt her way carefully around the corner and promptly stepped off the edge into the dark interior.

Nimbly, she spun around in mid-air and grabbed the edge to pull herself back up. As she did so, something passed by her face. There was a muffled 'thud' and sharp exclamation. Boca had found the corner with his nose too.

"Shhh!" she warned him. "Stand still! Don't step on my fingers."

"Oh...is that you, Yero?"

"Yes. There's a drop-off here. I don't know where Atel has gone."

"Not taken prisoner, I hope."

"I don't know. She disappeared."

As if in answer there came a loud buzzing from the depths of the hive, rising up toward them. The butterflies backed up together to make a stand, resisting the urge to flee. Woe and misery! Surely this was the Queen Bee herself coming to deal with intruders! The buzzing grew quickly louder. Air stirred in their faces. Without warning, a ghostly light sprang up in front of them. A stinger jabbed toward them. Yero did the only thing she could think of in self-defense, but the buzzing increased. She was hard-pressed to hold on. Then a nasal voice scolded her.

"Yero! Let go my beak!"

It was their guide. Yero let go with great relief. "Where have you been? We were worried!"

"I don't know why!" replied Atel irritably. She rubbed her beak with a feather and sneezed. The motion propelled her backward an inch or two but somehow dispelled her irritation. She looked around proudly.

"Well, this is it!" she said. "Abandoned at least a month ago. How do you like it?"

The butterflies glanced nervously around. The light was quite dim. Near at hand were honeycomb formations. Beyond were half-imagined shadows and pits.

"Could you...umm...turn up your light a bit?" said Yero.

"A little. Not much. I didn't bring much along, I'm afraid."

Gradually the light improved, or their eyes got used to the dimness. They found they were able to see better than in the spider's lair. Near at hand indeed were combs, anchored to the ceiling, openings pointing downward. All were empty. Little papery caps dangled from some of the cells, still attached by an odd corner, but nothing was in them.

Withal, the hive consisted of many levels or tiers of comb formations arranged one above the other with ample space between for comings and goings. Each tier was fastened securely to the outside wall and to the level above by means of tough stems. Everything - floor, combs and wall - was fashioned of the same spongy stuff as the outside shell and seemed flimsy to the touch but taken as a whole, the hive was very sturdy.

As the cramped entry tunnel turned the sharp corner, it opened into a larger hallway high up in the hive, with ample wing space. Yero now saw that her 'drop-off' amounted to no more than an inch, and hopped down, feeling rather silly. Boca joined her and they walked gingerly to the center of the hive. There the short hallway ended abruptly, and a real drop-off yawned: A spacious central shaft more than four inches in diameter penetrated all levels from top to bottom. Atel joined them at the brink. Above were several tiers. Perhaps five. Below were many more. It looked a long way down.

"It's warm enough here in the hallway," said Atel. "Also, there is extra room for our wings. I think we'll stay right here for the night."

The butterflies didn't answer right away. Now that comfort and security were assured, they entertained bolder thoughts. For example, was there honey in the hive? Were hornets like honeybees that way? Were there other secret treasures? Were there (and here Boca was more curious than Yero) any dead hornets to be found? He wouldn't mind a peep at one of those. No, the butterflies wouldn't mind a look around. Atel expected it.

"I suppose a quick look won't hurt," she sighed, "but the truth is, there's not much to see. I scouted the place out. That's where I disappeared to."

"Yes, I'm sure you're right," said Yero politely. "But if we could just climb down a level or two..."

"And if you could sort of light things up..."

"And pick us up again at the bottom..."

Wasn't that the sort of thing guides were for? Of course! Atel had little choice. Sleep was totally forgotten.

With a squeal and a whoop they were off, going headfirst over the edge and swinging back into the tier below like monkeys with orange wings. While Atel hovered in the main shaftway Yero struck off in one direction, Boca in another, poking into empty cells and dark corners. There was no honey. No treasure. The tier was deserted and empty; but that did not discourage the explorers.

The next tier was much the same - unoccupied and bare - as were the half-dozen after that. But in the eighth tier down from the hallway were many cells with a jelly-like filling. Here was the source of the elusive sweet odor they had noticed earlier. Yero was tempted to taste it. The meal by the stump had whetted her appetite.

"Let's stay here for a bit," she said. "The bees have left a banquet! Try some, Boca."

He demurred, on advice of their guide.

"I wouldn't, if I were you," she cautioned. "It doesn't smell right. Anyway, I thought you only dined on your mallasha."

"Well, yes--*usually*," explained Yero. "But in great need some honey would be fine. Maybe jelly too, if it's soft enough."

"Then you are doubly advised against it. This isn't honey at all, nor ordinary jelly either. It's bee-jelly, and it's gone stale. Probably left for that reason."

"Maybe, but suppose the bees were just full? Maybe they ate all they could but were in a hurry to leave, so they left some for hungry travelers that might come along."

"And maybe they will now return, taking you for their queen, and attend to your every wish," laughed Atel. "But I doubt it. I will try some before we leave because I need it. I haven't eaten today.

But my stomach is bigger and stronger than yours so I can gamble a little. Do you still wish to test your luck?"

Yero folded her arms and tapped a foot stubbornly.

"She isn't about to," interpreted Boca, "unless one of us does it first. Yero is just being Yero. She is testing her mouth and it's working fine, as usual."

Yero proved him right, and they went on to the next tier, and the one after that. It was becoming noticeably colder as they approached the bottom. The hive, which was very wide at the top, was tapering rapidly. The exploration of the lower parts was nearly complete. It was down there on the 19th level below the hall, the bottommost level of all, that they discovered Inezz the hornet. Boca was first to see her.

She was dead by all appearances, attached stiffly to the underside of a comb. Her un-seeing eyes were fixed on the shaftway in a baleful stare. It seemed odd to Boca that she could cling there without falling to the floor. He stepped closer, whistling for Yero. She gasped.

"Get back, dummy! Atel - come quick! There's one in here!"

Boca didn't back off at all. "Wow"! He marveled. "She's bigger than we are, not counting our wings! I had almost given up hope of finding one."

"Given up *hope*? You *hoped* for this? Wish her away again! She makes me nervous."

"Oh, Yero!" he laughed, "It's not dangerous. She's a stiff! Don't be sissy now, just because you're a girl."

Yero frowned. "I'm not sissy!"

"Come closer, then."

"I will. When I'm ready. I'm not ready yet."

"Sissy."

"Listen, you! I'm playing it safe, that's all. You should too, if you're smart." She folded her arms again. "Besides, I just think we should consult our guide."

"Yero is right," said Atel who had been watching closely. "One shouldn't tempt fate (or dead hornets) without good reason. If you've had a look, we'll go back upstairs where it's warmer."

"But I *do* have a good reason," grumbled Boca. "I want to see her stinger. I'm sure she doesn't mind. Why should anyone else?"

"Don't touch her," warned Atel. Yero smirked.

"Now it's girls against boys, and I'm the only boy!"

"Wrong again," corrected Atel. "I'm speaking as your guide."

"Then couldn't you sort of...*guide* her rear end down so I can see the stinger? That's all I want. I promise."

"No. Let's go. Or I'll put out the light."

Yero looked very smug. Atel turned to leave. In that moment, Boca reached up and tugged at the hornet's abdomen. Several unlucky things happened very quickly:

The hornet came unstuck and fell on top of him.

The temperature on that level reached a critical point.

The hornet's eyes focused. She rattled her wings.

"Save me!" cried Boca, scrambling madly to disengage. That he did get out from under was only because the hornet remained a bit disoriented, but moments later the Travelers faced an angry hornet in her own home.

"Bzzzzzz!"

It was difficult to say if the buzz came from her mouth or her wings, or both. In the confines of Level 19 it was intimidating. The butterflies took shelter behind Atel, expecting her to do something.

After a few preliminary movements, the hornet adopted a threatening posture, approaching them half-sideways, bobbing and weaving, abdomen at the ready. Yero found herself wondering which end was more intelligent; they were both so active. Boca never took his eyes from the stinger end.

"Bzzzzzz!"

The hornet advanced to within an inch of the hummingbird's beak and continued to make menacing movements, backing slowly away and rushing forward again.

"Bzzzzzz!"

The noise was deafening. The butterflies clambered onto Atel's back. They were ready to go! What was keeping their guide? Then Atel spoke in a kindly voice. Not to them.

"So. You were only sleeping. The rest are gone."

The hornet paused briefly. Her body temperature was still rising. Had it not been for the strange visitors warming the Level she never would have awakened until spring - if she lived that long. Alazz! Probably not. But for her there had been no other choice.

"Bzzzzzz!"

Yezz, she was alone! Idiot bird! Of course, Inezz knew that. Hazards, yezz! But she would do her duty. She would defend the Kozza, the great nest. Oh yezz, the strangers would fear her!

Warming to the idea she half-flew, half-skipped three quarters of the way around the Level to frighten them. It was working! The bird and her fluzzers fearfully turned about-face, lest Inezz get behind them. Bzzz! Good! They were afraid! Afraid she would *zing* them. Yezzz! *Zing* them!

She performed an encore like a maniac, all the way around this time, zipping ominously close to the intruders. She noted the unnerving effect upon the fluzzers and felt proud. Proud and worthy! Zzz! The swarm should see her now. Muzz! Buzz!

But she was tiring. She had not eaten in a long time. Why didn't the pezzky intruders leave? Hadn't she frightened them silly? Had they lost their wits? Bzzz! Why didn't they leave?

"Buzz off!" she said in her sternest tone.

"Certainly," replied Atel. "We shall retire to the front hall and spend the night. That's all we ask. Tomorrow we'll be gone."

"Nezz! You muzz leave now! I say *now!* Bzzz! Inezz am I!"

Atel shrugged, unimpressed, making no move to retreat.

The hornet went on another tear, a full-blown razzmatazz. The butterflies cringed. Inezz was quick to notice. Soon the bird would panic also! Yezz! The request was out of the question anyway. Out of the question! She feinted expertly at the bird, knowing the terror her skill could inspire. Bzzz! Why wasn't it working?

Inezz had to stop. She was very weak and had pretty much used up her bag of tricks. Alazz! She muzz speak with the intruders, outsmart them. But she muzz be careful!

"Bzzz! Ruzz!" she fussed. "Why don't you leave?"

"You can't make us," said Atel.

Inezz bristled. "Zing izz death! Duzz she want that? Duzz? Buzz?"

"Go ahead. Sting us," said Atel. The butterflies could scarcely believe their ears.

Inezz tried to fly again, but it was a poor effort and she knew it. Even the fluzzers knew it. The bluff had failed. She landed clumsily. Her abdomen drooped.

"Can't do it, can you?" said Atel.

Inezz shook her head miserably. She now expected to be killed without mercy. Had she been able to carry out her own threats she most certainly would have. Oh, yezz! It was part of the upbringing of every hornet: Fight to the death! Protect the Kozza!

But she had failed. Now she must submit and accept punishment. She closed her eyes and folded back her antennae to await the blow. Almost, she welcomed it. She was surprised the blow didn't come quickly. Atel broke the silence. "Relax. If that's settled, maybe we can talk."

Inezz opened her eyes with trepidation. What was this? Foolish bird! Foolish fluzzers. They should strike! Why didn't they strike? But now the fluzzers were speaking to her, saying alarming things.

"You can be our prisoner," teased Yero.

"We'll interrogate you," said Boca.

"Tell us your secrets!" giggled the butterflies. They were well recovered from their fright.

Inezz flinched visibly. Prizzoner? Secrets? It was unheard of. Hornets never took prizzoners. It was not the wazzpish way. And... *secrets?* Bzzz! Inezz shuddered. It was not a pleasant thought, not pleasant. Was that their game - torture and secrets? If so, they would find her most difficult. *Most* difficult! Uzzz!

On the other hand, if they wanted talk - *plain talk* - Inezz wouldn't mind at all. That was her style.

"Say what?" she asked, confused.

"Pay no attention to *them*," replied Atel impatiently. "They mean no harm. But if you like, we can visit together. We have news."

"Nooz?"

"Yes. Tidings of the world outside. Are you interested?"

"Why, yezz," said the hornet sociably. "I am always interested in nooz! You should have mentioned thizz sooner."

"I would have, but there were distractions."

"Don't let that stop you. Fuzza! When there's nooz, the swarm izz always ready to listen. Always!" At this, Inezz moved closer, but the light bothered her eyes after her long nap. Atel let it grow dim.

"What would you like to hear about?"

"What about ...*seazons*, and all that? Where are the leafhoppers and midges? What are folks up to that they...zzzzzz... *shouldn't be?* The swarm loves nooz!"

"Okay. First, I'm sorry to say, you are the only hornet we've seen."

It was an innocent remark, but one that Inezz didn't like. Her eyes went opaque. Her voice grew surly.

"That izz unimportant. Boring! Tell us real nooz. It's my bizzness, you might say. Tell me something I don't know!"

"I'm getting to that. We haven't seen any of the Inzis - the small flying folk - because of the weather. There's been a blizzard."

"You don't say!"

"Yes, I do. A big storm. The snow is very deep."

"You don't say!"

"I certainly do. You asked, and I told you."

"Oh yezz, I realize that. But go on! What else izz happening? Do you know any...zzz...embarrassing incidents?"

"Embarrassing? Why would you want to know?"

"Don't be zilly! That's the best kind. Nooz izz just nooz unless it's...shall we say...rumors and whizzpers?"

"You mean gossip? Is that what hornets do? Gossip?"

"Bzzzzz!" Inezz was insulted. She went opaque, waspish and sullen.

"I'll apologize for that one," said Atel. "But there are very few folks to be found at all right now. There's hardly any gossi--er, I meant *news*. It's the weather, that's all."

Inezz turned in a huff and looked the other way. There was an awkward moment. Then Yero grinned playfully.

"Boca here said he was *dumb*. How do you like that?"

"I never did!"

He took a swipe at her, which she ducked. She jumped to the floor, laughing. The hornet resumed interest, peering closely at Boca.

"I muzz say, he looks bright enough. What a surprise!" Inezz shook her head reprovingly. "Reminds me of a young buzzer up on 4th, one time..." she began, and launched into a story about... "a nephew, you know. Young brat up on Zelda's Level..." while Yero smiled serenely and Boca scowled.

"Yezz, the young buzzer was a pezzimist," Inezz recalled. "Can't imagine why. A boy mind you! No work ahead of him, juzz fun and games. Uzzz! Well, my girls straightened out that little zipher - and hizz nursemaid!" She winked meaningfully at Atel. "They want to pamper 'em, you know. Especially the boys. What rot! They need dizzzipline!" Inezz was not a gentle soul.

"Whatever happened to the little fellow?" asked Yero.

"Izz knows," shrugged Inezz. "Can't keep track of them all. Grew up lazy, shiftless and happy, I suppose."

"I 'spose," giggled Yero.

Boca couldn't take any more. He pointed to Yero. "She's a blabbermouth! How do you like that?"

Inezz studied her for a moment, nodded approvingly. "Why, that's juzz fine. Juzz fine! One always hopes they'll grow up like their mother. Reminds me of a hatchling on 11th one time..." Inezz launched into another gossipy story, this one about..."a nosy little thing in the care of mizz-what's-her-name up there. Cutest little bizzy-body you ever saw, always telling tales on her cellmates." Inezz sighed. "Even the Nanzies, the nursemaids, had to watch out for that one. Kept them on their toes! 'What can we do with her?' they asked, 'she tattles on everyone!' 'Oh, juzz nurse her along', we told them. 'She hazz a nose for nooz! She'll go far someday'."

Yero frowned, but Boca felt much better.

"Whatever happened to the little busybody?" he asked.

"Well, zad to say, her jaws wore out prematurely. What a shame, with such potential. What a shame."

"I 'spose that's what happens," giggled Boca.

"Not nezzessarily. Why, I remember a young thing on 7th tier - a servant girl, I think she was - who never stopped talking from the day she hatched. What a marvel! Her jaws held up juzz fine. Unfortunately, she was a scatterbrain. Her head was full of words, but nothing was in them."

"I 'spose that happens too," giggled Boca.

"Yezz, all too often. We had a strange hatch right up here on 18th last summer where they were all like that: Chattery little buzzers with empty heads. Anzy, the Tierward, blamed it on hot weather. Bzzz! You never saw such a noizy bunch!"

"That's girls for you," giggled Boca.

Inezz shook her head. "No, it izzn't. Not on 18th. Those were boys."

It was Yero's turn to smile again. "Do you mean to say boys are shiftless---and *blabby* too?"

"Abzzolutely!"

"Why didn't you just throw them out?"

"Bzzz! Nezzz! That izzn't allowed. Her Majesty is fond of them."

"Whatever for?"

"Oh, little boys become big boys, you know. Zoon they become dashing gentlemen in Her Majesty's Court. Very important. Everyone curtsies to her favorites."

"So, they're like Kings, then?"

Inezz was scandalized. "Bzzz! Nezza! There are no silly Kings! There is only the Great Izz, whom none approach without permission!"

"So, it's all girls in charge here, too?" grumbled Boca. "That's baloney."

Inezz almost choked on her buzz. "Dizzy fluzzer! He duzzn't know! Duzzn't know! Buzzwahh! Say nezza!" She chanted:

"Hail to the Izz!

Rise all abuzz!

The Queen just izz!

She always wazz!"

She cast a withering look at Boca and hammered home the message. "Huzza! Long live the Queen! There are *no silly Kings*! Buzzwahh!"

"What do the boys think about that?" asked Boca defiantly.

Inezz laughed at him with much satisfaction. "I muzz say, some are very disappointed. Hazza! There wazz a sassy one down on 22nd last summer with, you know, *delusions* like that. Sazzha told me about it, I believe. That was her Level. Cheeky little buzzer! Wanted to order her girls around even before he hatched! Came to a bad end that one did - sooner rather than later, if you know what I mean!"

Atel shook her head. "I only count 19 levels. How do you get 22?"

Inezz backed away, eyes shifting rapidly, then stepped belligerently forward. "Huzz! So Inezz izz *stupid*? Izz that what you say? Buzzzwah! Bug out with your fluzzers! The Kozza izz *my* bizzness. *My* bizzness! Not yours!" Having said that, she backed off again and would say no more.

To be sure, Inezz was difficult to get along with. This could be said of any hornet. Moods struck her unpredictably, allowing scant warning. But where most hornets stung swiftly when riled and relieved their anger, she had no such outlet. Instead, she pouted. Soon she surrendered to self-pity and began to weep.

Yero felt sorry for the ugly thing.

"Are you lonesome?" she asked. Inezz nodded, still weeping.

"Yezz. Oh, yezz! Hazards and lizards! *Cast out*, I was! Helpless I was against so many. Uzzz!"

Without preamble she poured out her sad story - a tale of injustice and woe - with many a razzle and bustle.

She had lost her stinger defending the Kozza. For that, she was branded useless and banished from the hive. Never mind that she had lost it heroically, in mortal combat with a large hairy animal. There was no witnezz. No witnezz! That had sealed her fate.

Inezz sobbed uncontrollably, a pathetic noise lost between a buzz and a rustle. Boca was surprised to discover he felt sorry for her too.

"Why would they banish you for that?" he asked. "In a big hive like this there must've been plenty of stingers. Couldn't you do some other work?"

"No! Alazz, that izz not permitted. Not for one of my exalted status. 'Stazzha', I was: Superior of the Guard. Superior! I could not accept a lezzer post."

"You'd rather get tossed out than do something else?"

"Bzzz! Dizzy fluzzer! He has no idea. No idea! In the Kozza, one must progress! Always! Never slip back. Nezza!"

"Well, then, couldn't you move *up*?" suggested Yero. "Take a higher job? You must've had some pull."

"Zzz! No! Nezz! There is no place *up* for the Stazzha. There is only the Queen above. Only the Queen! Huzza! Long live the Glorious Izz!"

"But if that's true," pointed out Atel, "then it must have been the Queen who had you cast out."

"Nezza! Long live the Izz!"

"Had to be. Why do you defend her now?"

"Long live the Izz!"

"Oh, stop it! You'll have to start thinking for yourself now."

***

A troubled look passed over the hornet's face. Conflicts raged within her. Part of her mind knew very well that the Queen had done her dirty, but her conscious mind couldn't accept it. Since she couldn't face the truth, her mind turned inward seeking escape from the paradox.

Inezz no longer saw the 'intruders'. She only saw a clear path to the sun. Other hornets, old friends of hers, were flying within the well-marked borders of the path. Inezz joined them and reveled in the companionship of her kind which she had lately been denied.

But Inezz found herself stealing furtive glances outside the path, knowing she shouldn't. Her friends saw and drew away from her. Then Inezz looked only toward the sun, never to the side, hoping to repair her mistake.

The scene changed. Inezz still flew the pathway, still was shunned, but now she approached the sun: A feat unheard-of! The others fell far behind. A wicked, naughty feeling leapt into her heart. Knowing the others couldn't see her, she boldly looked left and right at forbidden things! Then she looked forward and terror gripped her. The sun revealed itself to be the Glorious Izz who was aware of her sins. Inezz fled.

Once more the scene changed. Inezz found herself in the Kozza entry tunnel. She cast her eyes down to avoid unfriendly faces, aware that she was no longer welcome. It was hard, struggling up the tunnel against the combined will of the swarm, but worse was still to come unless she could find a place of safety. Finally, darkness took her, and her dream ended.

***

Watching it all, Yero thought it ridiculous that a full-grown hornet would wedge herself into a brood cell like a baby, but that's what Inezz had done at the end, and it was a tight fit. She even pulled the loose, papery cap over her eyes so only her mouth was left showing. She made infant noises.

"She has returned to the egg," said Atel.

***

For Inezz, a new dream began. Her adult life had faded away and she awoke to thought once more as a pre-hatchling. She took comfort in the darkness and confines of the cell walls. Voices washed over her, the pleasant deliberations of a busy hive. She tested her strength. Yezz! It was increasing. Soon the time would come to emerge from her cell and join the voices. All her cellmates had hatched. She felt the emptiness of their cells next to hers.

She grew impatient. It should be her turn! It *was* her turn! She threw open the cap and crawled out to take up her life's work. Yezz! Oh yezz, she knew what was expected of her and bent to the task.

Still in her dream, Inezz went right to work cleaning a cell. She didn't respond to questions but kept her eyes obediently on her work, repeating instructions from her superiors of years gone by.

Before the very eyes of the Travelers she progressed through the caste system of the hive, parroting her old training lessons about the social order that she had been so familiar with.

***

A strict order was enforced, as in all beehives. Oddly enough the very youngest, the pre-hatchlings in their cells, were the most privileged, excepting only the Queen. Grown-ups fed and tended them. The little ones were constantly pampered - until they hatched.

That came as a jolt for the young ones. One minute they were receiving jelly or juicy insects, courtesy of the nursemaids. The next minute they might get the urge to hatch and, presto: It was the real world, baby! No more free meals. No more idle loafing. Orders were issued to them. Work was expected of them. And, hey! They better get busy or punishment was in store for them! Some tried to back up into their cells again, bewildered, only to find them already occupied: A Bozo, a cleaner of the lowest caste, was already preparing the cell for Her Majesty's egg. All the new hatchlings started out as Bozos.

Thus, the first weeks of a hornet's life were spent doing menial tasks that no one else liked. If they were cheerful about it and made no trouble they were promoted to the 'Nanzies', the large class of nursemaids who tended the little buzzers in their cells. If they were cheerful about *that*, and made no trouble, they could expect to graduate to repair and maintenance at about six to eight weeks. If they were incompetent or lazy it took longer, and a bad attitude stalled all progress. It was not unheard-of that a sourpuss spent her whole life as a Bozo.

Maintenance was a big step up in class. The 'Nezzers' as they were called, repaired clean cells after the Bozos were finished and escaped the slavish nursemaid duty. They also built new combs and worked on the many-layered Kozza itself which must be expanded constantly as summer went on, and a Nezzer 1st/Class could leave the hive on work detail to fetch building materials. It was every hornet's first taste of fresh air and weather.

Most Nezzers were anxious to progress to the next caste, but a fair number liked carpenter work and chose to make a career of it. These were the 'Vizers' and were easy to spot because they gave most of the orders. Similar Vizers were to be found in every caste and rather resembled sergeants in an army.

The Nezzers who did go on faced a choice: Did they want to be 'Browzzers'? Or 'Rowzzers? It marked a fork in the career path.

The Browzzers gathered nectar and other sweet juices for jelly and fetched it back to their superiors, the 'Cuizziniers', who put it up in combs for future consumption. The Cuizziniers, though, were a finicky lot, as apt to reject fresh nectar as accept it. They zealously preserved the secret of the Royal Jelly and kept it from all others (even the Queen). They were a small, haughty caste who only rarely accepted a new apprentice.

The Rowzzers, while roughly equal to the Gatherers, followed a different calling. These were hunters of other insects, fierce types who welcomed battle. The Rowzzers caught meat for the table, which provided the other half of the diet for the young and the hive-bound castes. It was a dangerous occupation and no few of them came to grief, but those who survived earned the right to join the 'Stazzi' - the *Security Guards* - a job no less dangerous but more privileged and feared. A Stazzi could order anyone around except the Queen, so even the uppity Cuizziniers and the hoity-toity 'Zervahs' (special attendants to the Queen) thought twice before sassing a Guard.

It also followed that 'security' meant guarding against dangers from within as well as from without, so the Stazzi - particularly the Boss, the 'Stazzha' herself - were the official sifters of gossip about the hive.

***

Inezz fell silent. From her most recent remarks, the Travelers knew she had found her way back to the present. They sensed her eyes upon them. For her part, Inezz remembered the 'intruders' clearly again. She wondered idly if she had talked more than she ought to but dismissed the thought. Buzzwah! So what? She felt much better about herself now. Suppose she let a few things 'slip'...Hzzz? She owed nothing to the Queen. Buzzzwah!

"Are you all right now?" asked Atel.

Inezz nodded. "Fine! Juzz fine. Never better!" She shook her head to clear it more. What a fool she had been all her life! Always she had risked everything to please the Queen, and for what? She saw now that the Glorious Izz had been selfish and depraved. Why hadn't she seen it long ago? She shook her head again and her sight cleared perfectly. "Have I got nooz for you!" she began...

***

Inezz had made 'Stazzha' the previous year when the Old Stazzha disappeared. Her claim, which involved an interview with the Queen, was accepted, but it had been a shock. From afar the Queen had always looked lovely. Up close she was not, and her persona was even uglier. She was neurotic, convinced that someone was plotting against her. It was the Stazzha's job to find answers.

For the rest of that summer, and the whole summer just past, Inezz briefed the Queen thrice daily about all the latest 'nooz'. Incidents abounded, but that was to be expected in a large hive, and many a conversation turned to just that: The *size* of the hive. It had become phenomenal. In fact, the swarm hadn't divided in more than three years - since the Glorification of the present Queen - and wasn't about to any time soon. Sadly, there had been bad luck with the Daughters-In-Waiting.

Certainly, it wasn't Her Majesty's fault. She had laid eggs and everything, all as it should be. And the Royal Daughters grew well, even displayed an endearing snobbishness. But none ever hatched. It was unclear why this should be so. Morale suffered.

Withal, the Glorious One neared her dotage and grew rancorous. She demanded loyalty but no longer inspired it. Life became drudgery, especially for the hive bound. More Zervahs were called for to attend Her Majesty's whims. More Hozos were called for also. These were handsome boys who - by edict of the Queen - mostly just laid around and became fat. They were the only lazy caste in the Kozza, resented by everyone except the Queen. Discontent festered, which made Inezz' job increasingly busy.

Summer waned and autumn arrived with more unhappy tidings: The new Daughters-In-Waiting had once again withered in their cells and the Queen had stopped laying Royal Eggs entirely. At the same time, she kept very busy laying ordinary eggs and took to cavorting outside with her boyfriends until all hours of the afternoons. By now she was grossly fat and in serious danger of a flying accident.

One day while she was gone a-frolicking a strange bit of news came to Inezz by way of an unhappy Zervah. The frightened girl had seen something she shouldn't and feared for her life. But before Inezz could act on the nooz, grave emergency called.

The Queen indeed had suffered an accident. She had run aground, sustaining minor bruises (mostly to her ego) and now refused to attempt the return trip. The Hozos were no help at all, but a few Guards 'happened by' and organized a rescue. Soon the Stazzi arrived in large numbers and carried Her Majesty back to the hive, ignoring her protests. Things went downhill fast after that.

The Glorious One vowed to root out 'usurpers', which meant almost anyone. Hundreds were executed and dumped out. Then the Royal Jelly ran out owing to a shortage of workers. She even ordered the Hozos put to the sting since she could no longer fly with them in the meadows. Things became so chaotic that Inezz confronted the Queen with the young Zervah and her story. That was a disaster.

The Queen stung the girl forthwith, killing her, and would have stung Inezz too, but decided to use finesse instead.

"You're a good girl, Inezz," she cooed. "Do you believe the silly Zervah, hzzz? Say nezza, hzz? Say nezza!"

With no witness to back her up, Inezz had acquiesced, dropping any accusation that may have been implied. But one day soon when a raccoon was reported in the tree, the Queen sent Inezz alone to drive it away.

***

"Uzzz!" groaned Inezz, dredging up the memory. "Alone I was against the hairy fienzz! But Inezz am I! I zing - zz! And zing - zzt! Ruzz! Huzza! Inezz is victorious! But alazz! She has lost her zinger."

Alas, indeed. For now, the Queen had an excuse to get rid of her. Without a zinger, she was the butt of all jokes. She could no longer be "Stazzha." The plan was to fire her one moment and have her executed the next, but Inezz had escaped like a common criminal.

"What did the servant girl see?" asked Yero.

The hornet's voice dropped to a whisper. "Zzzz, something *strange*, hzz? The Zervah didn't lie, nezz. Nezza! Inezz too, has seen."

"What did you see?"

"Zzz! Hush! There are ghozztly ears, hzz? Inezz will show you."

She took off erratically into the main shaftway, glancing off outcroppings of combs as she went. Atel waited until the noises ceased, far above.

"Wherever she is, she has landed."

"Wherever she is, I doubt it's where she planned on," said Yero. "What's the matter? Is she sick?'

"No, just weak. She's been sleeping in the cold for - who knows? A month, maybe. We'll excuse her."

"How did you know she had no stinger?" asked Boca.

"Simple. Anyone who's tangled with hornets will tell you they sting first and talk later. If Inezz *could* have, she already *would* have. She bluffed, and it gave her away. But you underestimate your guide. Inezz was lucky. Hop aboard. We'll go up where it's warmer."

They found Inezz in the 5th Level down from the top, just above the hallway, quietly waiting for them. It was different, this Level. A different smell. Richer. Exotic. There were fewer combs, so the ceiling was high and the surroundings spacious. In the corner where Inezz waited were no combs at all, just a few large brood cells. The caps were transparent, not yet open. Boca put his nose up to one and peered through. Staring back at him with unseeing eyes was the bald face of a hornet.

"There's one in here," he said. "It's sleeping."

Inezz rustled her wings. "Nezza. She's dead. All of them, dead: The 'Dozzhdat', Daughters-In-Waiting."

There were seven Royal Cells, one in the middle and six around the outside, configured neatly in a hexagon. All were occupied. All were dead. With trembling hand Inezz reached toward them. Her forearm didn't like it, jerking away as it approached the caps. Inezz spoke solemnly.

"See *there*...zzzzz...the *deed!*"

Her hand, still squinching, pointed to a hole near the edge of a cap; then, by turns in perfect silence, she pointed to similar holes in the other six.

"Sting holes?' asked Atel.

"Yezz. Oh *yezz*."

"The Queen did this?"

Inezz stood mute, unable to utter the final indictment.

"That was a dirty trick, even for a hornet!" whistled Boca.

Inezz didn't hear. What turmoil now embroiled her mind was impossible to guess. Her eyes went opaque and she sagged against the wall, unresponsive.

"I think we can take that as a 'Yes'," said Atel.

"What a witch!" said Yero. "She killed her own daughters?"

"To keep the throne, sure."

"It's hard to feel sorry for hornets," muttered Boca, "But these were like sitting ducks."

Yero studied the faces behind the caps. "They look exactly like Inezz," she said, mildly surprised. "What makes them special, or whatever? That word she said."

"'Dozzhdat'? The Royal Jelly, of course." Atel pointed to the combs around the level. They were fewer, but the cells were larger. She inhaled the aroma; even empty they smelled delicious. "That's the only difference. Any girl could become Queen if she was raised on this stuff. Most do get a taste, so I've heard; but after that it's plain jelly and insects for them. But for the Queen and her growing daughters it's Royal Jelly - morning, noon and night! Do you know what happens when a Daughter-In-Waiting comes of age? Grows up?"

"I think she goes away and a bunch of bees follow her."

"Precisely. But it didn't happen here. The Old Queen was greedy and ruthless. So, she took matters into her own...umm, *rear end!* There, that's the tale. If Inezz reawakens I think she would agree."

"There's just one more thing..." began Boca.

Atel felt a tiny twinge of irritation. The butterflies were *so* like the tribbits that way! "Well? What has been left out?"

"Where has the Queen gone, and the rest of the hornets?"

Atel laughed. "Of course, they've gone where all wild bees go in the winter."

"And where is that?"

"No one knows, usually."

"That's not any answer."

"It'll have to do. You might ask Inezz if you get a chance. In the meantime, let's take a clue from her. Get some sleep! We'll need it."

There were no complaints. The evening was late, and it was warmer up at this level, especially inside the Royal Tier. Outside, the south wind gusted anew, causing the hive to sway on its mooring. In spite of the motion, sleep came quickly.

***

In the middle of the night the wind increased to a gale. The hive swung dangerously, bumping repeatedly into the nearby branch. Eerie noises awoke. Yero stirred, as did Boca, but remained in that transcendental state between sound sleep and half wakefulness. Atel was wide-awake.

Driven snow caught up high by the wind peppered the walls of the Kozza. Once or twice chunks of ice, dislodged from somewhere, thumped hollowly against it. Then the wind swung around more to the southeast and several chunks in a row thudded into the hive. Atel worried that a shard striking the mooring would send the hive plummeting and debated waking her companions.

Imperceptibly a new sound awoke, strengthening each time the hive swung...*Bump*...into the branch: A humming, droning sound. A 'buzzing' sound that seemed to come from all around them, from the combs and even the walls. The butterflies heard it and came fully awake. Yero stole a glance at Inezz, but she was stone-still.

"If it isn't her, what *is* it?" she whispered.

No one answered except the sound itself. The wind swirled almost violently. Bump...Bump...Bump! Buzzz! The noise level increased with each bump. Inezz stirred finally.

"The Kozza remembers," she intoned. "Hear now the Sezz!"

"What's tha-a-at?" stammered Boca. "Friends of yours?"

"Shuzzz! Do not interrupt ghozztly voices! Day is coming. Work is at hand. Worship now the Queen!"

In rhapsody she began to chant, her voice rising and falling with the wind. She watched the Travelers closely, expecting them to join in, but they did not! Idiots! *Everyone* must chant! What was *thizz*?

"Blazzphemy!" she snarled.

Inezz had reverted once more to another time and saw a group of hatchlings in front of her - hatchlings in need of a tongue-lashing! She knew how to administer one. Bzzz! Bozos muzz learn! Bozos muzz chant! The Sezz speaks to the hive at the break of day. Lizzzen up, young fools! As Stazzha, she would make an example of them later!

Inezz invoked a sharp reminder about the Sezz, the Historian of the Swarm, who began each workday by reciting the List of Queens all the way back to the beginning. It was a long list and the Sezz must begin in the dark of night for proper timing. "Huzza: Glory to the Izz of 'Hrazzt', Queen of the oak tree! Huzza: Glory to the Izz of 'Sazzna', the tall pine! Huzza: Glory to the Izz of 'Allfullz', the thicket of thorns! Huzza!"

So it went. The Historian guided the swarm in unbroken sequence through strange lands, across great waters, to a time much revered but now only dimly remembered when the Great Izz tasted the first bouquet.

But now the wind was calming down. The hive bumped and banged less often. The ghozztly voices diminished, disappeared altogether. Ah! The Sezz was finishing! Glory to the Izz! Inezz bided her time.

In the wee hours of morning when even the hummingbird was asleep, Inezz moved. Creepsy and secretly she made her way to the central shaft; thence downward hand over hand, Level to Level, she descended with nary a sound.

In her mind, all the shadows fell away and the sun came out: The light of a new day promised by the Sezz! Yezz, oh yezz! Day was dawning! Huzza! She must get on with her life's work. Into the dark regions of the hive she disappeared. Time passed slowly. Undisturbed, the Travelers slept on - until awakened by an anguished cry they, bolted to attention.

"Where's Inezz?" said Yero. "She's gone."

"I just heard her!" said Boca. "From down below!"

"She must have fallen!"

The butterflies crowded the brink, peering into the dark shaft, guessing away and jumping to conclusions.

"Excuse me! Coming through!" interrupted Atel. "I'm going down to investigate and you can both come along. That was a cry of distress."

They found her at the very bottom again, on Level 19, but she didn't cling stiffly to the comb this time. Instead, she lay curled up in a corner. Atel leaned close thinking extra body heat might revitalize her once more. It didn't. Even warm hands on her cheek did nothing.

"She's gone. Really gone, this time," said Atel.

"What from?" muttered Yero. "The fall?"

"No. There would be bruises."

"The cold, then?" It was noticeably colder this time, down on the bottom level.

"Not that either. Not so suddenly. It would only put her to sleep again. Something else."

Nevertheless, it was hard to ignore the colder air. It seeped through the wall now, on the side that had banged into the branch. It wasn't hard to imagine the damage that had been done. Carefully, Atel turned the hornet over, seeking a clue. Boca shuffled his feet and waggled his wings to stay warm. It occurred to him that his feet were warmer than the rest of him. Yero turned to help Atel.

Boca reached down with one hand and felt the floor. It was warm to the touch, but when he tried another spot it was cold. Puzzled, he scrabbled around with his fingers and found a crack. It formed a neat oval about an inch across. Outside the oval it was cold, but within it was noticeably warm. Without thinking, he slipped deft fingers into the crack and lifted. Something shifted. He let go but the oval didn't fall back into place; it swung upward inexorably. He gasped. Behind him, Yero gasped.

"Boca...Inezz was stung! Here's the wound!"

Boca didn't answer but leaned forward with desolate curiosity, realizing he beheld a doorway into the unknown. At that moment Atel moved slightly. Her moonbeams swept past. In the light, many dark arms threw open the trapdoor. In front of Boca's very nose appeared the bald faces of angry hornets.

"No," he croaked, unsure if he actually made any noise.

Hornets began to climb out of the 'Secrezza', the hidden sanctum-within-the-hive. "Bzzz!" The swarm hated to be disturbed. First the fugitive Inezz - now thizzz! "Bzzz! Say nezzza!" The ugliest hornet Boca ever saw came right up at him.

If the swarm had any weakness, it was a tendency to buzz prematurely. Normally that didn't matter in such an agile race, but normally they didn't face hummingbirds in battle. Now, they did.

Atel turned and saw. In a flurry of motion, she slammed the door, holding it shut by main weight. Those hornets that were partly out were caught in the crack. She speared them mercilessly as they struggled. Boca grabbed a threatening arm to restrain it but felt himself losing the contest. He yelped again, this time loudly. Yero pitched in and together they pinned the maverick limb while the hummingbird snipped it off cleanly.

"Holy moly!" shouted Yero. "What did you get into?"

"I don't know!"

The butterflies worked feverishly, stomping at groping fingers that squeezed up through the crack. It only made the hornets angrier. An awful racket came up through the floor. Boca yelped again. He had been bitten on the toe; the hornets were chewing through the trapdoor! Atel began to sing.

The moonbeams gathered beneath her, converging intensely. The hornets cursed the light and drew back, underneath the door. Only for a while. Hornets can abide light perfectly well once their eyes get used to it. The respite would be short.

"What about a spell of closing!" suggested Yero.

"Hush! I'm thinking about it," whispered Atel with some loss of patience, "but it's tricky! There are many spells that will lock a door, but few that can prevent breaking it down - or chewing through! Those take more time. Hush!"

Atel sang a lullaby like a cool breeze in the oak branches with autumn leaves falling. As she sang, the wind outside finally ceased. Tranquility came to the winter landscape. The hive hung still. In the Secrezza, hornets felt the tranquility and became less angry. Those who were angriest near the door heard the lullaby clearest and were soothed against their wishes.

Still singing, Atel allowed the moonbeams to soften and dispel. Night returned to the 19th Level. When the serenity was strong enough, the Travelers left that place and returned to the front hall. It was taking a chance, since there was no proper spell on the Secrezza door at all, just upon the hornets. But Atel felt this was as good as they could get.

"Obstruction is a delicate thing," she said. "Difficult to set up under good conditions. Foolish in the face of opposition. I'm glad I didn't try it. They're soothed now. Maybe they'll forget us."

"Just *maybe*? What about some extra spell? They wouldn't fight it now."

"Yes, they would. When they perceived a new spell growing, the other would collapse. Trust me! This is not an easy business."

"So, what do we do? Just wait here and hope it works?"

"Yes. Get some sleep. I'll watch."

The butterflies wanted no part of it. The lullaby had done nothing to them. Boca, especially, had been spooked by the trapdoor. For a while they talked quietly between themselves but grew no sleepier. Bees were on their minds.

"Why did they come out and sting Inezz?" asked Yero after a while. "She wasn't doing any harm."

"That depends on your point of view," replied Atel. "Hornets think different thoughts than other folk."

"But why didn't they do it before we came? She was here."

"Maybe they didn't know it."

"Then how did they find out?"

"I don't know. Maybe she opened the door. Maybe she hoped to regain favor by betraying us."

"Oh, it couldn't be that! Not Inezz."

"You explain it then."

Yero folded her arms in front of her. "We think hornets were coming to get us. Inezz saw them coming and fought without a stinger, and the Queen killed her."

Atel smiled. "Maybe. The Queen certainly hated her."

"That's another thing," said Yero, warming to the subject. "First she said there was only ever *one* Queen. Then she talked about many Queens in a long line. Which is true?"

"Many Queens, but each is believed to be a reincarnation of the First. 'Tis said that wild bees still remember her - but not the tame ones."

"Tame ones? Is there such a thing?"

"Sure. Honeybees, mostly. Men keep them and share the profits - the honey, that is."

"Bees just give it up?"

"Reluctantly, I'm sure. But in exchange for nice homes."

"I still wouldn't trust them."

"A wise thought. Bees are very independent, especially wasps and hornets. But men don't want those anyway. They don't make honey."

"I don't think they would have time. Inezz liked to talk, mostly."

Atel laughed. "How true! That was always a problem. If you two aren't going to sleep, I'll tell you a story about that."

"Fine," said Boca. "Just put some boys in there."

"I will," said Atel. "But just one, and not among the bees. History is what it is."

—The Tale of Izz—

Long ago in the First Age of the World, in the sweet-scented valley that men called Kypso (but few dared enter), dwelt all the bees in the world together with their Queen, the immortal Izz.

They called even themselves that - the *Izz* - but their Queen was *The* Izz - upon which all agreed, for she was fabulous - and the valley they named Izz in her honor since She, Herself, dwelt there. Yea: Loyal were her subjects though utterly different in appearance, a most unlikely alliance, yet perfectly united in the service of Izz.

What then of this Queen? Several accounts survive the Ages: Each perfectly true in their own way, but not any other way. History just is that way. It boils down to whom you ask.

Men tell the tale of Yassel, beekeeper of Kypso, and take most of the credit for the way things turned out. It was the man Yassel they say (and no elf), who finally conquered that land; and if 'conquer' is rather a brash term for events in those far-off days, men use it anyway. Who's to stop them?

Elves tell it differently, casting themselves more importantly and relegating Yassel to a minor role. They are quick to contrast their own noble motives with the 'coarse greed' of mortal men. Yassel (they say) was after honey. Nothing more.

Bees - especially wasps and their close relatives, the hornets - tell their own tale, full of treachery on the part of both men and elves. They do not speak kindly of any who walk the earth but bear a special grudge against Yassel and the human race. It has been so since the world was young, but not in the very beginning.

Little is known of those first bees on earth, save that the Lord put them everywhere to pollinate the flowers. As the lands bloomed, bees found the blossoms and all was well, so the Lord busied Himself elsewhere. But when next He looked upon earth, things had changed.

A Queen Bee had emerged - the *Glorious Izz* - who weaved enthrallment into the winds of the world. Her charm was irresistible. Bees of every stripe and strain swarmed to her idyllic valley, and there they stayed because of the magnificent flowers that bloomed year-round. Oh, how the rest of the world coveted the flowers! But they could not have them by decree of Her Glorious Self - a hornet of colossal vanity; nor would she permit visitors, on a Royal Whim.

Unfortunately, flowers did poorly in other lands save for those pollinated by lesser insects, certainly not what the Lord had intended. But the bees stayed where they were and kept their border closed. Any who would enter risked death.

The Lord preferred to let the Free Peoples sort out their own problems and left well enough alone, but nothing was done. Without bees to pollinate, fruitage and yield withered in forest and field. Trees grew old and there were few seedlings. The Free Peoples grew hungry. Finally, the Lord appeared in their dreams asking unsettling questions: "Who will speak with the bees? Who will tame them?"

Who indeed could open the land of Izz? More to the point, who could entice the bees out of their valley? Because until that was settled, nothing was settled.

Elves bestirred themselves first, seeking peaceful solutions. They sent emissaries to the mouth of the valley where encircling cliffs sheered abruptly at the banks of the wide valley stream. There, where the stream issued southward into other lands, elves came in their boats bearing gifts and flattery. They were rebuffed every time.

Always it was the same story: The sentinels of Izz came buzzing to the boats, barring the way. Warrior bees - large wasps and hornets, and powerful bristle-bees patrolled the borders. They listened to a few fair words but quickly lost patience and resorted to their stingers. At that dire moment, the elves always jumped into the water. Most got stung anyway and the delegation became a laughingstock. Afterward, an account of the fun was sent to the Queen, who delighted in these little stories.

It mystified the bees why elves kept coming back, but that's elves for you. They have patience. They live for Ages, remember, and can afford a lofty perspective. But their approach was too subtle. Noble purpose means nothing to mad bees.

But if elves were bothersome, bees found men to be ten times worse. Like elves, men were persistent, but they never tried the same trick twice. They swam underwater to get into the valley, they scaled the high cliffs and shinnied down tall trees, they came with smoke and fire, and they fashioned suits of netting to serve as armor. A fair number did get into the valley, but most of them wished they hadn't.

One man in particular, a cabinetmaker named Yassel, had great success. Like most men, it wasn't flowers or abstract motives that inspired him, but simply honey for his family and a few jars to sell. Taxes were lower then, so a bit of profit meant a better life. Raiding bee trees was worth the risk.

Ah! The honey trees of Kypso! Within the valley were ancient, hollow lindens of the most cavernous sort, sheltered from all but the gentlest breezes. The trees provided homes for the Izz and harbored the secret of the marvelous white honey for which they were famous: When the lindens bloomed, bees attended those fragrant blossoms only, making honey day and night.

So it went. Men stole a little honey, which infuriated the bees; but in truth, the bees produced prodigious quantities and could afford some loss. Then the unexpected happened.

The land of Izz and many other lands were overwhelmed by the Winter of the North Wind. Gales came unexpectedly out of that region, roaring into the valley from its least protected quarter. Down went most of the trees like matchsticks before the storm.

Many bees perished. Those that survived swarmed to a few remaining trees and cleaved to the boles in great masses, huddling to stay warm in the crackling cold.

In the depths of that winter the man Yassel conceived a plan and began building cabinets with many drawers, leaving holes where the drawer handles might have been. When he had finished several in his shop, he took them by sled into the valley and spoke to the bees, who were pretty tame in that weather.

"Greetings from 'Chazza': He-who-is-stronger-than-you!" said Yassel in the bee language. He felt many eyes upon him.

"Sizz," came the answer. "Hello, thief."

Yassel smiled and patted a cabinet, opening a few drawers for exhibit. Inside was honey, salvaged from downed lindens.

"I see that many of you are stuck outside in the bad weather," he went on, "so I offer a deal: Any who wish may take these cabinets for lodging. Much warmer, I'm sure! In return, I expect a share of new honey when summer returns. What say you?"

There was no answer, but when Yassel returned next day the swarm wasn't on the tree anymore. All had taken refuge in the warm cabinets. Yassel whistled happily on the way home.

All that winter, as ice and snow and frigid gales brought down the remaining trees, Yassel kept busy in his shop and fetched more cabinets out to the valley where bees were happy to move into them. At last only the Royal Grove remained standing. He decided to pay a visit.

Rising majestically in a sheltered dell where the frozen stream looped northward in the middle of the valley stood three trees together, greater than any others. Perhaps 60 feet above the sawdusty ground their separate trunks came together to form one immense bole, fraught with seams and cracks through which bees trafficked on summery days, mainly to satisfy the whims of Herself, the All-Glorious, who resided within. Refugees now swelled the great hive far beyond its usual numbers, overflowing underneath in a mass that sagged near to the ground.

"Greetings from' Chazza'!" hailed the man, as he had hailed other, lesser bee trees. But this time the Queen, Herself, answered.

"Don't be obnoxious, thief! You are just a man, and your reputation precedes you."

Yassel knew by this that he was expected. For weeks he had worked on three special cabinets. On this day he brought the first to tempt the Queen. It was impressive as bee cabinets go, spacious and very ornately finished.

"Whatever you say, Majesty," he replied. "But times change, and so have I. Once I stole honey, I admit. Today I return it."

He opened several drawers, dripping with honeycombs. "This is for you; in case your own reserve is running low. Also the cabinet, which you'll find warm, not drafty."

The Queen buzzed irritably but stayed well hidden within the swarm. "So! The thief returnzz my own and... *Szzz*...calls himself generous? My, my! And now I'm to live in hizz...what do you call it? Hizz *thing*. Bzzz! Go away, thief! I have a palace already."

Yassel shook his head, eyeing the overloaded trees. "Not for long, I think." But the Queen spoke no more that day.

The following morning Yassel returned with the second cabinet, larger and finer than the first, and noted that bees had occupied the other overnight as he expected, but not the Queen; for when he hailed the Royal Kozza she answered forthwith.

"So. The thief returnzz again! What have you brought me today?"

Obligingly, Yassel showed off the new cabinet, opening many drawers. One was larger than the rest and lined not with honey, but plush velvet. He left that one open, guessing correctly that the Queen was watching. Immediately, like a great arm, the swarm extended itself down to inspect the pretty furnishings.

Yassel smiled.

"This I offer today," he said.

"Tizz *smallish*," sniffed the Queen. "Ezzpecially the nicer quarters. Good enough for servants, perhaps."

With that, the swarm gathered itself up to its previous configuration and the Queen pouted. Yassel stood silent for some while, listening to the creaking and groaning of the lindens under their heavy load.

"I'll leave it anyway, by the other," he announced loudly, "in case you change your mind. Your trees are about to collapse. I hope you know that."

There was no answer, unless it was a shiver that began inside the swarm and caused the trees to groan dangerously. It began to snow.

That night the snowfall increased and Yassel worried for his plan. The Queen must be alive for it to succeed. Early next morning he set off with the third cabinet on his sled and found heavy going in the drifts. It was afternoon when he finally arrived and found the Royal Grove still standing. A glance at the second cabinet told him it was full of bees. Once again, he hailed the Kozza.

"Greetings, Majesty! Are you there?"

"Naturally, thief. Do you bear gifts?"

"Yes, but this is the last. The snow is becoming too deep."

It was deluxe. On one side many drawers opened, lined with whitest honey. He showed these first. As before, the swarm extended itself down for a closer look. Yassel turned the sled around and showed the other side, which had only one compartment. He opened the door slowly to reveal a plush interior with combs of Royal Jelly, and mirrors.

The swarm was intrigued with those, craning itself like a gangly neck to peer inside. That's what Yassel was waiting for. When the Queen stuck her vain neck out to admire herself in the mirrors, he grabbed her with a gloved hand and shoved her all the way in, locking the door behind. Several things happened very quickly:

The Queen voiced her displeasure and tried to squeeze out the drilled opening. It was far too small.

The swarm shuddered. The Royal Grove shook ominously, making noises like popcorn.

Yassel heaved the sled away, knowing what was coming. He made some progress.

The great trees groaned for the last time and collapsed in a heap, spilling honeycomb and crushing the greater part of the swarm - but not Yassel or the cabinets, safely off to the side.

***

That is how the bees were finally tamed and beekeeping introduced. But of course, the story didn't end there. Spring eventually came again. Snow melted and the bees got busy. Or rather, Yassel discovered that some got busy, and some didn't. Some put up honey, but others went off hunting. Some were bossy, some loafed, and some gossiped.

Of the latter, the worst were wasps and hornets. They were also inclined to be bossy, being a warrior race. Unfortunately, The Glorious Izz was one of them so they dominated, occupying most of the cabinets. Since there were no other suitable hives the honeybees couldn't increase. Production looked un-promising. Yassel suspected the Queen's mischief and went to have a talk with her, the first since her capture.

"Greetings, Majesty," he announced, tapping loudly at her door. "Are you still pouting?" Angry hornets buzzed everywhere trying to sting through his netting.

"Nizz! Go away. I am receiving nooz!"

"News?"

"Yezz. Nooz. Don't interrupt!"

"You mean 'gossip', I'll wager."

There was a heavy pause. The Glorious One was getting cross. "Zomeone's gossip is zomeone else's Nooz!" she snapped.

"Maybe. I'll be the judge of that! Here's fair warning: Knock off the gossip and make honey, or I'll kick you out."

"Do you hear, girls?" came the Queen's voice. "'He' will be judge. A *boy*." Laughter erupted within, a wicked buzzing sound, and then died away. "Judge this, then," said the Queen in sly tones. "Zzzz! Lean close."

Against his better judgment, Yassel bent an ear to the hole. Soon his cheeks turned bright pink and he straightened up, embarrassed.

"Oh yezz! I know about *that*," laughed the Queen. "But there's more! Lizzen to *this*..."

Yassel knew better by now but couldn't resist. He had his faults and wondered how much she knew. He put an ear to the hole again, but blushed and jerked away almost immediately. "That's not true!" he protested.

"Oh, but it is! That's what my girls tell me, anyway. So, let's have no more talk of...*Szzz*...'eviction' or we'll spread the nooz around, Hzzz?"

That was the Queen's game. Gossip and blackmail. It had served her well. Now she had an inconvenient tidbit on the Beekeeper or thought she did. Unfortunately for Her Majesty this particular story was false, and Yassel knew he could prove it. He grinned deliciously and gave her a taste of her own medicine.

"Hear all ye Izz!" he announced loudly. "The Glorious Queen has whiskers!"

He never meant it to happen, but the Queen died of embarrassment on the spot. Wasps and hornets - especially the bald-faced ones - have never forgotten, though other bees were relieved. Much scandalous information passed away with her and good riddance. But none of the bees left the valley. They still loved the land of flowers, now more than ever.

Yassel fulfilled his threat and kicked the wasps and hornets out of his cabinets. It came as a blow, on top of the Queen's death. "Where will we live?" they buzzed.

Yassel shrugged. "Chew on rotten wood, for all I care. Make hives out of that. It'll give your busy mouths something better to do!"

***

Atel finished her tale. She tossed up a bit of loose paper from the floor and watched it flutter down the central shaft.

"That's how they make this stuff," she explained. "Mouthful by mouthful out of weeds and such. It must be tiring work. But it never stopped their gossiping."

"How did the bees ever get out of that valley?" asked Yero. "Did they finally leave on their own?"

"And what about the elves?" asked Boca. "They thought they were pretty important. Did they ever *do* anything important?"

"To answer both questions at once, the bees did leave - though not entirely on their own. Elves had something to do with that. They talked to the trees."

"Well? What good is that?"

"Lots. You've met the tribbits. All trees were free in those days. Great hollow trees went into the valley and became bee trees. When the bees got comfortable, the trees just moseyed out of there and carried their passengers to the far corners of the earth."

The butterflies laughed.

"You should teach the tribbits that trick," said Yero. "I'd love to watch Yesac eat a hornet!"

"I don't think so! But it *was* a clever trick. It's all ancient history now of course, except with the hornets. They still carry the grudge."

The butterflies looked nervously toward the central shaft.

"Come! We'll leave them behind," suggested Atel. "It's morning outside."

Following their guide in the same order they came in, the butterflies set off into the tunnel and soon emerged into bright sunshine.

Chapter 5

The Brothers Rupl

Atel stepped out first and disappeared; then Yero and Boca emerged, shading their eyes against the sun. Quickly, they climbed to the top of the nest for a look around. The wind, now directly out of the east, was cold but the grey nest soaked up the sun and felt warm under their feet. Soon their guide returned, anxious to start.

"I hadn't expected the wind shift," she said, worried. "Not this soon. We must be off! More snow is on the way."

"Oh, I doubt it," replied Yero, unconcerned. "See? There isn't a cloud in the sky!"

She laughed. So did Boca. Butterflies do, whenever they can. What was the rush? The sun was shining! Surely there was time for a bit of relaxation after such a harrowing adventure? Hummingbirds were so busy! They should take time to warm their feet.

"We can spend the whole morning here!" declared Yero grandly.

"We can always leave quickly if bad weather comes up," said Boca.

"Don't worry so much!" they sang.

"Someone has to, or nobody will!" replied Atel impatiently. "You didn't take weather notes obviously, but our blizzard blew in on a northeast wind. It's back to the east again now. That's a big clue to our future. As I read it, we have this day to cover a lot of ground and find some food. One day! Not to mention we must find shelter this evening. Come! Off we go!"

Off they went, the butterflies again hitching a ride. The scenery was boring. As endless white fields passed beneath them, they quietly discussed Inezz and the events of the night. Of particular interest to Yero was the question of the 'Secrezza', and what Boca could possibly have been thinking by opening it.

"I was going to ask about that when it was all behind us. I never would've opened it, Boca."

He knew it was coming. Yero wasn't the type to just put such things away and never touch them again.

"It all started with a 'knock-knock'," he explained.

"A *what*?"

"A 'knock-knock' sound. While you were busy with Inezz I was on guard, watching and listening for trouble! Well, I put my ear to the floor and heard a sound like 'knock-knock'."

"Really?"

"Yeah, like someone knocking at the door. So, I answered, 'Who's there?' *'We are'*, said a voice on the other side. 'We?' I asked, opening it a crack - 'We *who?'* Then they threw open the door as if I had invited them and said, *'We who are going to sting you!'* It was risky, Yero. I know that now. But I believe it was the right thing. We should always answer the door, don't you think?"

Yero laughed. "I guess so. It would be a sad world if nobody answered their door."

"That's a relief. I'm glad you agree."

"I do. Sort of."

"What does that mean?"

"I would've done it differently."

"Yeah? How?"

"When I heard the *knocking,* I would've knocked back."

"What good would that do?"

"The hornets would be confused! Then *they* would say, 'Who's there?' Get it? Things would turn out different: 'Nobody', I would answer. *'Nobody who?'* 'Nobody at all'."

Yero smiled at the thought. "That's what *I* would've said, and they never would have opened the door."

"Maybe. Or instead of, *'Who's there?'* they would've said, *'Come in!'*, and just opened the door and grabbed you."

"They wouldn't have done that, Boca. Knock-knocks don't work that way, not if they're done properly."

"I know that, and you know it. But do hornets know it?"

"They seem to know a lot about a lot of things. But it's funny, with hornets. I never felt like they were *dreadful*. Not like the spiders, I mean. Just regular folks with dreadful *tempers*. I'll miss Inezz and her girl-talk."

"I bet you will. And I'm glad to know what girl-talk *is*. Boy hornets don't amount to much, maybe, but I bet they don't gossip like the girls."

"I wouldn't know! I've never met one. But if they don't exchange news, they must be a stupid bunch!"

"Now you're talking like them," chuckled Boca. "Hearing 'nooz' and exchanging 'nooz'. That's just girls gossiping."

"Boys are as bad as anyone! Don't deny it."

"But I do deny it. Take Poppy now. Mostly, he talked to himself. That's not gossip. And he stuck to the facts."

"So do girls! We state the facts exactly as we see them."

"Put it any way you want, but girls are famous for it."

"Girls are famous for a lot of things," sniffed Yero. "Another thing more or less won't make much difference."

"This one's 'lesser', that's for sure."

"Soon I'm going to lose my temper, Boca!"

"Ha! There you go - just like the hornets!"

Boca laughed longer and harder than was good for him. His sides began to ache from it; but when he let go of Atel to hold his sides, the wind took him. He went end-over-end into the winter sky. Yero let him go for a satisfying moment before sounding the alarm. They caught him only inches above the snow. Atel wasn't pleased about the delay, but Boca was still happy. Even happier.

"You didn't have to catch me," he exclaimed. "I was flying!" He waggled his bare wings, still in some surprise.

"You were flying straight down," said Yero.

"I was?"

"Yes. When everything's white I suppose it's hard to tell. But I must confess, we were gossiping about you, Boca."

"That isn't nice."

"Well, we did. I was a busybody. 'Boca fell off and went tumbling', I told Atel. *'Where?'* she asked. *'We must catch him!'*

'Oh, some ways behind', I said, 'but if we catch him, he'll know we've been gossiping about him'. *'What can we do?'* said Atel. *'We can't just let him fall!'* In the end, we decided to save you and let *you* decide, Boca. Should we have gossiped? Or not?"

"That wasn't gossip! That was important!"

"Call it whatever you want. The hornets call it 'nooz'."

***

The day wore on with little change in scenery. The butterflies talked less and less, and Atel hardly at all. Noon skipped past, and with it another meal that couldn't be made up. The snow lay ever deeper, the whiteness ever more complete, the terrain broken only by an occasional ice-covered stream or small river. By afternoon, clouds appeared in the west and southwest in front of them, still far-off but darkening. Atel changed course and flew straight south hoping the new weather might bypass them to the north.

"Now you see why I was worried," she said openly.

"Is it another big storm?" asked Boca.

"I can't tell, but I'm trying to avoid it altogether as you can see. We've been fairly lucky so far about shelter, but this land is unfriendly to folk who live in the wild. Not much wild land at all, is there? No trees, hardly even fencerows." She cocked her head in dismay. She who had been a steward for so long had misgivings about the stewardship that unfolded beneath them. In such inhospitable regions, where would they find shelter?

"What lives in a place like this?" said Yero.

"Men, mostly," replied the hummingbird. "Not much else."

"Why do they make it like this - where nothing grows?"

"Oh, I didn't mean it like that. It's not wasteland. This is very green all summer. Men raise crops here - for themselves and their animals. It's the Age of Men and their families, as you know. That must be respected and not begrudged. We'll just fly over it."

"Does anyone live here besides them?"

"Certainly. In summer there are quite a few birds and butterflies; also rodents, worms, grasshoppers, gnats, various flies - *lots* of the Inzis. At night there would be bats, oodles of mosquitoes, bugs of all kinds, and fireflies. Also moths, *lots* of moths."

"Yuck! What is it about moths, anyway? We've met a few and they were downright rude. We didn't like them."

"Nor I. They are creatures of the dark. Keep your distance."

"So, they're all nasty?"

"Not all. Some would simply ignore you. But others could be very dangerous to the Rasha La."

"You better tell us about the dangerous ones."

"Not now. You would waste energy stewing about it. I will only tell you that they are legendary enemies of trees and many other green plants."

"Yesac didn't like them. Do they bite?"

"Not *they*, so much as their caterpillars. But you don't need to worry in the winter."

"Do they go south too?"

"No. Some hibernate. Others die after laying their eggs."

Yero laughed. "Where do they hibernate? In the snow?"

"Not *in* it. *Under* it. They burrow into the ground, or into grass or stubble. And the eggs are everywhere. When summer returns so will they, in greater numbers than ever, or so it will seem."

"Even after all this deep snow?"

"Because of the deep snow. It protects them from the cold.

"I doubt that. Snow is awfully cold."

"To butterflies and hummingbirds, yes. But that's *our* point of view. Others welcome the stuff and spend a nice, comfy winter beneath it. Trees appreciate it. It keeps their roots warm. With warm toes they can sleep better."

"Is that what the tribbits are doing?"

Atel shook her head. "I greatly doubt it. It's what they *should* be doing; therefore, they're probably doing something else. Since there is plenty of snow, I'm not going to worry about them romping about."

The butterflies found it hard to believe that tribbits could frolic through drifts with bare feet. What about frostbite? "Did you warn them enough?" worried Yero. The idea of a snow blanket seemed nutty to her.

"I certainly did. I spend half of the summer warning them about things. But don't worry about snow, at least. You'd be surprised how tough their little toes are."

The butterflies laughed. "Spare us! Spare us! We already know how tough they *think* they are."

"Some of that boasting is true," cautioned Atel. "And more will become true every year, though I'm sure there are odd moments when the talk runs out ahead of the truth."

"And of course, they don't have a big journey like we do," said Yero loftily, "or those tough little toes would soon be lagging, not running out ahead."

"And butterflies never lag?"

"Never!" declared Yero. "Unless we fall off."

***

By mid-afternoon the sun was swallowed by oncoming clouds. Plainly, another big storm was brewing. Atel shifted course to the southeast but the storm advanced very quickly, threatening to overtake them in the open lands.

She flew lower now, searching for any kind of sturdy cover to hole up in. Mercifully the snow held off, but any sign of decent shelter held off too.

An hour before nightfall they came to another frozen river, wider than earlier ones and swift enough along the north bank to maintain some open water. There, where current lapped at the shore as it swept around a bend, the tall riverbank had been undermined and overhung a narrow shoreline. Into that narrow space winter had not yet come. Green plants stood there next to the water, still free of snow. Boca spotted them as they swooped over the bank and headed across the water. Had he not glanced behind they would have missed it. The hummingbird made an abrupt U-turn to investigate.

There was no mallasha but there were swamp thistles, mint and even jewel flowers still in bloom to some degree. An accidental buffet, all the more welcome for being unexpected.

The butterflies asked to be set on the thistle blossoms, which aren't their favorite nectar but much sweeter than one would ever guess. Atel went to the Jewel flowers. For half an hour or more the only sounds were the lapping of water against the bank, the hum of the hummingbird, and the leisurely rustle of the northeast wind as it sifted old snow off the top of the riverbank. Most of the snow fell harmlessly into the water and disappeared, but some clung to the lip of the overhang above, forming an awning of sorts that gradually built outward. Chunks frequently broke off, but the awning re-made itself continually from the drifting snow.

The butterflies watched as they dined. When the awning made progress they took heart and smiled at each other, imagining that it would continue to build. When large pieces broke off, they frowned and didn't exchange glances; but it seemed possible that the awning could extend itself well out over the water if it would behave, affording lots more protection from the weather.

During this time the temperature rose several degrees to near the thawing point ahead of the new storm, which helped the progress of the awning considerably. The snow became stickier and clung better. The awning built itself out several feet from the edge of the bank, much to the delight of the young audience.

Then the whole works broke off with a mighty "Whump!" all along the bend of the river. It was more than could easily be dissolved in the water. The slush was forced against the shore where it piled up and remained. This development, which was at first disappointing, offered its own possibilities: If more snow collected at the shoreline building upward, perhaps it could meet the awning as that built out and downward. With any luck, the butterflies figured, a whole wall might form as a shield against the storm.

Near dark the wind picked up and the awning began to show very good progress. The Travelers all knew by now - as wild things know without saying - that they must pass the night where they were as best they could. Anything else was too much of a risk. Here at least was food, one wall, and part of a roof. But 'making the best of it' was enjoyable so far.

The thistles were many-branched and less spiny than, say, bull thistles (but still spiny enough to discourage climbing), and nearly mature with many heads already gone to down; yet, so numerous were the branches that a fair number of fresh flowers persisted even at this late date. The flower heads were wide and upright, making convenient banquet tables, and the flowers themselves weren't prickly at all, but soft and sweet-smelling.

Since they couldn't fly and were eager to try as many as possible, the butterflies jumped from one head to another. Sometimes this meant bouncing off fluffy thistledown to reach the next flower, but no matter. Butterflies have marvelous balance and dexterity. They bounced around almost like grasshoppers.

When Yero found herself at the bottom of the thistle she stepped onto a fuzzy mint leaf nearby and used the single stemmed plant as a ladder back up. The mint flowers were pink and clustered around the stem so conveniently that she tasted them too and found the nectar passable if a bit strong for her liking. Boca followed her example and found a mint stem of his own to climb, and so they regained enough altitude to do it all over again.

Twilight crept over the river. The wind picked up another notch, as did the drifting. Snow sifted over the bank constantly now with scarcely a pause, falling mostly into the river, but with the stronger breeze a swirling effect became evident. A drift began to rise up along the slush-line, all up and down the shore, exactly as the butterflies had hoped. They exchanged broad grins.

With evening, too, came new snow out of the dark sky, and more wind. The storm had arrived in force. Visibility dwindled to the blowing snow, the white awning above them, and the growing drift atop the slush in front of them. The temperature by now had lost the several degrees again. In the colder air the awning stiffened and solidified its gains of the past hour. The new snow drifted more readily. Sheets of it came over the riverbank into the eddying air and were deposited along the shore. The slush line bulged gradually into the river and turned to ice. More snow piled on top of that, creating a wider drift. As the base widened, the ridge of the drift grew taller, intensifying the swirl and speeding the process. But the process was still slow, for all of that.

The butterflies paused in their meal and sat on a thistle flower to watch the snow. Atel joined them on a nearby one. By some trick of the air currents a few flakes constantly swept in toward them, not quite reaching them, although some landed at their feet. There they sat, unmelting, where they couldn't be ignored.

"Look at that one," said Yero, pointing to the nearest. "It's like a triangle with holes punched out. I didn't know snowflakes could be shaped like that."

"Look at that one, then," said Boca. "It's like a bloodroot flower with the six points, but more feathery."

"It is, isn't it? And there's one sort of like an anemone: Fatter in the middle and with stubbier petals."

Soon they had classified every flake and hoped more would come in. Several soon did, much to their delight.

"Here's one like a trillium."

"This one's like a star flower."

"Here's another trillium!"

"It is, isn't it? It's just like the other one."

"Can't be," commented Atel, not bothering to look. "No two are alike. Not *those* two, anyway."

"Well, they are," said Yero stubbornly. "Three long points with crystally edges."

"Look closer," said Atel.

On closer inspection tiny differences did turn up. Minor ones, but still differences. They weren't identical at all. Another flake, and then another landed. These were way different except that (like all of them) they were made up of tiny hexagonal crystals. Very pretty.

"Why does it snow?" asked Yero.

Atel didn't answer right away but cocked an eye out at the storm and listened. Maybe a minute went by, maybe more. The butterflies also listened, but there was nothing to hear except the wind.

"It snows because of the North Wind of course," answered Atel presently. "But she doesn't make the snowflakes. The *Snogg* does that. And the *Hoo* keeps watch to make sure no two are alike."

"The 'Snogg' and the 'Hoo'?"

"Certainly. That's never been any secret."

"I didn't know it," said Yero. "Do you hear them?"

"Yes. I know what to listen for. The Hoo is counting."

"And what is she counting?"

"Snowflakes, of course. But the 'Hoo' is a 'He', or so they always say."

"Why does he bother counting? And how could he know anyway, if two were the same? There must be millions coming down right now."

"Yes, millions. But he knows. He *always* knows."

"You better tell us about it. Butterflies should know too."

"I would argue that. If butterflies did what was good for them, they would never learn about snow or blizzards, or *anything* about winter. But since we're stuck in the middle of it, I suppose it's only fair you should know what's happening."

—The Snogg and the Hoo—

There was a time Ages ago when the Four Winds spoke to each other and didn't quarrel - a remarkable period of good weather not likely to be repeated while the world lasts. So long ago was this that only the Winds themselves now remember - and the Lord of Light who created them - but others have learned much about the wind just by listening to it.

Trees especially are well acquainted with the wind since they are out in it every day and have taken the trouble to learn the language. Not that they set out to learn it, maybe. A thing like that happens naturally, and we should be thankful. Thus have been preserved many tales otherwise long forgotten.

And how may we learn this history - so well preserved by the trees? Not by asking them, sad to say, unless by rare fortune you find one unsleeping, and by even rarer luck the tree is sociable. Such trees were once common in the woods but nowadays are downright hard to find. Any that still remember the tales are enormously old. *And* sleepy. *And* grumpy when awakened.

But sometimes on a breezy day in the lucky month of May, when the warmth has seeped well into the heartwood, they will speak with polite strangers who greet them properly, and the proper approach is with a cheery disposition and a keen remark about the weather. That will rouse them if anything will; but come prepared if you are a big person! Trees like young children and will talk to them at great length, but they won't put up with a stupid adult for one minute.

Remarks about the wind are the most likely to elicit response. For example, if the morning is sunny with wind in the south you might say, "Beg your pardon..." and go on to inquire about..."a bit of shade later, against the heat." Chances are an old tree might bestir itself at that. If an east wind is blowing, rain might be in the offing; a west wind portends fair weather; a north breeze is cooler. But these are only general. In some parts of the world the rules are reversed, and local weather everywhere is unusual. When in doubt, ask a farmer for advice.

But suppose a casual wanderer fell into such a conversation, being possessed of sufficient weather-lore and proper demeanor. What kind of tale should they request that might hold the tree's attention? That's easy. If you have a chance, ask about the Snogg and the Hoo. No tree could resist that, and you'll find yourself comfortably entertained for hours.

It all started (if you'll permit an abridged version), soon after the Beginning, when the Lord of Light raised the lands above the sea. As the lands slowly dried in the quiet atmosphere, He pondered improvements. Indeed, He had many in mind, but such things aren't simple. An 'improvement' might produce exactly the desired result - or set off unintended consequences.

In His wisdom, He introduced the Kingdom of Plants and stirred the atmosphere to produce weather, awakening the Four Winds. Mighty progeny were they, the Four Sisters, but not identical. Owing to the tilt of the earth and different angles of the sun they had different attitudes - especially at different latitudes. The Lord acquainted them with each other and set tasks for them to act in harmony or mild discord to produce gentle showers and fair weather.

When he had done this much, He was pleased. For a while He left it at that and turned to other Works throughout the heavens, leaving the Winds to work their magic and encourage life in His absence.

The Temperate Sisters had been given charge of the West wind and the East, so that moist air from the oceans would drift over dry land, and they faithfully discharged their task. But the others, the cold wind of the poles and the hot wind of the tropics-the North Wind and the South--were given to decide where the rain should fall, and when. The responsibility was great, but the task was simple: They need only note where deficiency existed and go there. The resulting clash of hot and cold air does the rest. Unfortunately, they fell into disagreement, with dire results upon the weather.

Each accused the other of stretching their influence. Both were correct. But regardless who may have started it, the argument quickly became polarized and led to hostilities.

Most living things side with the South Wind in this war, especially trees and plants who can't escape the ice and frigid gales. That Wind offers a strong case against her enemy, pointing to the advance of glaciers and the freezing of great waters - evidence that cannot be denied.

But the North Wind also has supporters who warn of excesses from the South. In truth, given free rein the South Wind would be the undoing of her own friends; for although she brings warmth, she often bringeth too much, and stayeth too long.

So, the Intemperate Two cheated and squabbled and their thought, which should have gone to the needs of others, degenerated into plans of conquest. Much harm was wrought in the Lord's absence.

Wherever the North Wind prevailed, gargantuan snowfalls and ice storms were unleashed. Unbearable cold followed.

Where the South Wind advanced, horrendous rainstorms inundated the lands. Searing temperatures melted the ice in calamitous floods, yet deserts arose in their wake.

When again the Lord looked upon earth little remained of the Kingdom of Plants. He was angered and lectured the wayward winds, asking why they had not done as He directed; but the Intemperate Sisters only blamed each other in loud voices. The Lord judged them equally at fault and sternly repeated His earlier instructions, knowing that the harm could be repaired if the winds behaved. Then He went away, allowing them a second chance.

But the North Wind felt abused in the scolding, thinking she had been unfairly charged. She pouted in her icy stronghold, refusing to speak to her sisters or visit them. The South Wind also pouted and loitered, reasoning that if great activity brought only rebuke, then she would do nothing.

Of course, their idleness made matters worse; for though the temperate sisters provided as moist an atmosphere as plants could want, little rain fell without the clash of winds. Clouds could not form in the stable air. Then again the Lord returned, not a moment too soon.

"So be it!" said He, "If you won't cooperate, I issue this injunction: You will both go back to work *now* or be fired!"

"Moreover, since some compromise *must* be reached, you will each appoint a negotiator to bargain your side of the dispute. *They* will settle the weather!"

Thus, the antagonists were brought to mediation and thus began the longest, most drawn-out haggling in history, haggling that has never been resolved and continues to this day. The North Wind sent Snogg. The South Wind sent Hoo. Both proved worthy choices, but long-winded.

The Snogg (as he prefers) was an important wind in his own right, an expert in ice making and veteran of many battles in the disputed territories. The North Wind hesitated to pull such a Captain out of the wars but chose him anyway for his experience.

The Hoo was unheard-of: A minor updraft from a remote jungle. Eyebrows were raised when this unknown took his place opposite the celebrated Snogg. The Snogg wasted no time.

"Let's get it on, little fellow!" he boomed. "As senior officer I will outline certain facts and areas of *mutual agreemen*t. You may challenge specific points. Feel free to do so! But speak up or I won't hear you."

Ignoring objections, the Snogg launched into a blustery harangue lasting for weeks. When the Hoo tried to protest, Snogg simply inflated his bluster and drowned him out. The Snogg was used to making vast plans and giving orders.

It was obvious to onlookers that the Snogg would simply overwhelm his puny opponent and that would be that. In her stronghold, the North Wind snickered at reports and ramped up plans to freeze the world.

But when the Snogg finished and thrust pen and ink at the Hoo to sign the document, a funny thing happened. The Hoo refused to sign. Instead, he took the opportunity to voice objection. Observers were stunned. The Snogg was incredulous.

Specifically, *what* do you object to?" he demanded.

"Only one thing," replied the Hoo.

"Name it," said the Snogg expansively, "and I will compromise. We cannot permit a small detail to stand between us."

"Your position on everything," replied the Hoo. "I object to that."

The Snogg hissed ice fog and eyed his opponent anew. The Hoo pressed his advantage.

"What concessions will you now offer to address the variance?" he asked. "For surely the great Snogg remembers his own words."

The Two might have come to blows then, were it not for Arbiters posted by the Lord, and now the South Wind snickered at reports in her turn. She had picked her negotiator for one quality only: The Hoo was easily the stubbornest little rain cloud in her employ.

Negotiations settled into a pattern. Naturally the Snogg wanted all precipitation to fall in some form of ice. The Hoo wanted rain. Neither would budge. The talks came to an early impasse.

After years of fruitless quibbling the Arbiters pointed to the natural seasons. Surely those were beyond dispute? The North Wind could have her way in winter, perhaps - and the South Wind in summer? That would leave only half the year to argue about. Yet even this utter reality was rejected by both sides.

"What is to prevent him from cheating?" argued the Hoo. "He may pile up more snow in one season than can be melted in the next."

"That's perfectly natural," said the Snogg. "Whoever works hardest, wins."

"Up to a point," ruled the Arbiters. "The question of rain or snow is for you to decide. But some limit must be placed on each."

"It will be easy with rain," laughed the Snogg. "A few drops and this little fellow will be pooped out."

"We shall see," answered the Hoo politely. "But you do have quite a reputation for snow-making. That is well known."

"Why, yes I do," replied the Snogg, flattered. "I make snowflakes by the zillions."

"That many?"

"Sure! And snowflakes require *art*, unlike your drippy-drops."

"Oh, fluff to that! If you've seen one snowflake you've seen 'em all."

"That's where you're wrong! Most snowflakes are completely different from each other. *Unique.*"

"Most? Not *all*?"

"Make it *all*, then! No two are alike!" boasted the Snogg.

"I agree!" shouted the Hoo in delight. It was the first point of agreement, so ruled by the Arbiters, despite vehement protest from the North.

So it went. The Hoo had never done anything of note and so was not tempted to boast. The Snogg had done remarkable deeds and itched to brag about them, but he underestimated his rival.

Some progress was therefore made. The Snogg in his vanity pledged that if ever two snowflakes were found to be identical, a storm must end. Upon further baiting he arrogantly offered to let the Hoo watch for duplicates. The North Wind had a word with Snogg after that and bargaining slowed way down.

To even things up, the Arbiters ruled that raindrops in a storm could not exceed the number of flakes in the biggest snowfall. It pained the Hoo to lose points that way, but something really had to be done. Naturally, both sides tried hard to bend the rules.

'Storms by night' was a sticking point. Inspection was impossible. It was finally agreed that all such flakes or drops be examined in advance, but as anyone knows, there are no sure things after dark.

'Height of Storms' presented similar problems. Each side piled up clouds as high as possible to make visibility bad for the other inspector. The proud Snogg eventually agreed to 'No Limit'. His bad luck: Storms pile up higher in warm air. Then Snogg curses like thunder and sends bolts of light to make counting easier.

'Size of flakes or drops' was a sore point. De facto agreement permits 'whatever will hang together'.

A lot of weather is yet to be settled, such as Simultaneous Storms, Hail, Sleet, Frost, Fog, Unruly Winds, and other disruptions still too numerous to itemize.

Ages have passed with lots of debate, but no new agreements. Since the North and South Winds give little thought to the Plant Kingdom the Temperate Sisters have learned do it for them, delivering moisture and low pressure as best they can to where it's needed. They know the others will then race to fill the voids. Wherever those two meet the clash produces storms, and whoever gets there first with the most has their way. It's not perfect, but weather never is.

They're up there still, a-bargaining, the Snogg and the Hoo. A careful listener can pick up snatches of it during any storm, and even on quiet evenings when there's no particular weather. That's when they like to sit at their table and jaw, rehashing all the old arguments. It has become a game to them.

***

Atel finished. For a while the butterflies were silent, listening to the storm. Try as they might, they couldn't pick out voices from all the moans and whistles. They were getting a bit sleepy anyway. The gap had closed considerably between the awning and the drift rising up from below. They could no longer see the open water beyond. In their hollow it felt almost cozy and they fancied the temperature to have warmed somewhat. Beside her Boca nodded off, but Yero remained awake, marveling about the snow.

"Are snowflakes *really* all-different?" she asked.

"They have to be. Those are the rules of the game."

"Then I think the Hoo has the hardest part, making sure of it."

"No. He has a trick up his sleeve."

"He'd have to. What is it?"

"It happens like this: The Snogg, depending on his mood, can come up with almost infinite designs. No trick there. He really does it. Naturally, he finds it easy at first and harder as he goes along. Toward the end of a storm he invents them slower and slower. The snowfall dwindles to just flurries. Finally, he is stumped. After a pause, he cheats. Inevitably, the Hoo catches him. Then the storm ends."

"Yes. But *how* does he catch him?"

The Butterflies, Yero and Boca

"In some ways the Snogg isn't too smart, then?"

"No, and let's be thankful for his little quirk. His storms last long enough as it is."

Yero also fell asleep, and finally the hummingbird. But not the Snogg or the Hoo. Far into the night they played their game while the North Wind drifted the snow over the riverbank. Shortly after dawn the Snogg cheated, and the Hoo caught him. Snow stopped falling but it still drifted with the wind. There is no limit on that.

Sometime earlier, in the wee hours of the night, the gap between awning and drift had closed completely. The Travelers were shut in. Yet still more snow sifted over the bank, thickening the drift, which now became a wall. The butterflies awoke around mid-morning and were delighted with the development.

"We can stay here until the storm ends," said Boca. "What could be better?"

When they looked for their guide to share the news, she wasn't there; but it didn't dampen their spirits. Boca noted that the drift had risen to the very edge of their thistle flower, nearly to their toes, and they laughed about it. Yero noted that some light came through the wall where it must be thinnest, at the seam where the gap had closed, and they laughed about that too. Then they both remembered that some nectar remained in some of the flowers, and the laughter was quickly replaced by sipping noises.

Soon Atel returned, without explanation, and resumed her own meal, but she toyed with her food, drinking very little.

"There you go worrying again," said Yero. "Don't worry! Soon the storm will end."

"The storm has ended already," said Atel.

"So much the better! We can finish here and then leave."

"It isn't that simple. I've had a look around. We're in a cave now, a tunnel along the riverbank. I've found no way out."

"There's always a way out," said Yero confidently.

"Something will turn up," agreed Boca.

"Why rush anyway? We have everything we need right now."

For once their guide agreed. If there was no obvious way out, they might as well have breakfast. They could explore more later. She went after the flowers with renewed appetite.

The storm had indeed come to an end. Outside, the sun shone brilliantly. It was cold, well below freezing, but the wind had tamed down. Drifting had stopped. As the sun climbed toward midday the Travelers could see more thin spots in the wall where light filtered through. Atel zipped here and there marking the spots just in case, but she held no real hope of digging out. Even at its thinnest, she estimated the wall to be almost a foot thick.

Equally disturbing, she noticed ice crystals on the flowers and plants, and even on protuberances of the dirt bank itself. If they were to be trapped here for any length of time, it wouldn't be in a land of plenty. It would be in a dark ice cave with frozen flowers. Sooner or later the frost would seek them out too - first the butterflies, then herself. Atel shivered.

"Can't you melt a way out?" asked Boca.

"No, I tried earlier. The light's too weak. If we can find a tiny hole, I could enlarge it. But I'm afraid we're snowed in for the day."

"Ouch!" yelped Boca and swatted Yero on the arm. "Don't pinch!"

"I'm not! Don't slap!"

"Well, I didn't pinch myself! So, who was it?"

"Move your wings!" said Atel quickly.

The Two looked at her in mild surprise but began to do it. Boca yelped again and plucked something from the edge of a wing. It was a frost crystal, trying to form.

"You'll have to move your wings constantly to keep that from happening," said Atel. "Also, we'd better drink all the nectar we can before it freezes. Some has frozen already."

Indeed, it had. But not all. For another hour there was some to be found. Then the plants were played out. The sun was now at its zenith outside.

"Come with me," said Atel. "We'll follow the tunnel and see what there is to see. The light will never be better. If there is a hole somewhere - or *almost* a hole - we'll find it."

Carrying the butterflies again on her back, the hummingbird struck off westward. The tunnel grew dark and narrow immediately, then opened into a room nearly as large as the first. There were no flowers or plants of any kind, just bare riverbank and semi-frozen slush-floor. There were thin spots in the wall, but not quite as thin. The Travelers moved on, through new narrows and into other large, empty rooms. Each time they came into a new room it seemed bright after the darkness of the narrows, but it was just illusionary and disappointing. At last they came to a narrows that was a dead end and turned back only to see a mink appear in the last open narrows behind them, blocking what had suddenly become their exit. The animal stopped right in the doorway and sniffed the air, then spotted the hummingbird and her passengers at the other end of the room. She promptly laid down on the snowy threshold and made herself comfortable in her nice fur coat, barring the door.

She was a fish eater by preference, but with the change in weather they had migrated downstream to deeper holes. She had planned to follow them now, taking her departure through a hole in the slush-floor of this very room. But just now she had discovered lunch - small, but sure. Obviously, there was no other way out for *them*.

Such were the Travelers' unspoken thoughts as well. Underwater exits were for swimmers, not fliers; and now the empty room looked even less hospitable. There were no convenient perches at all. Perhaps they could all cling to meager footholds on the dirt wall when their guide tired, and perhaps the mink might finally give up and leave, hopefully down the hole. But time would pass that couldn't be made up. The sun would sink, and with it the last chance of finding some escape that had been overlooked. Atel saw no better idea than to go and talk things over.

She left the butterflies clinging to shreds of roots near the top of the bank and went to parley, but as she approached the mink something caught her eye.

The narrows in that area was high up between the riverbank and the drift wall, and the doorway was small. The mink, at her ease on the threshold would be impossible to get past. But the 'doorstep' in front of her formed a snow shelf jutting out into the room, a fragile-looking shelf high above the slush-floor. Maybe the mink sensed the fragility in front of her, maybe not.

"Good day, madam," said Atel. "May I be of help?"

"Yes. I'm hungry, so you can help me with that."

"Sorry, but I've no fish to offer."

"No? Well, they're scarce right now. But I eat other things too."

"I've no frogs, clams, or muskrats either. I do apologize."

"I'll just wait. I'm sure you'll think of something."

"I'll try. Will you excuse me for a moment? Perhaps the butterflies have ideas."

"Tell them I love butterflies, fresh *or* frozen!"

"You're not familiar with their kind, then? These are very poisonous. It's all over their wings."

"Ha-ha. Look - I wasn't born yesterday, birdie."

"Just a fair warning. If you'll excuse me then..."

"It's what we thought," reported Atel. "She's hungry."

"Too bad," said Yero. "She looks pretty comfortable there."

"Yes. Any ideas?"

"We're poisonous. Doesn't she know that?"

"She's young. She never heard of it."

"You told her?"

"Certainly, but she didn't believe it. You may have to show her." Atel smiled at the blank looks and continued. "I'll do the talking. Just play along." She collected them on her back once more and approached the shelf.

"The butterflies do have a suggestion," she announced politely. "They can show you where to find spiders and hornets. Good enough for a stinky weasel."

The mink growled.

"Now, don't be upset; they're only trying to help. Remember: You can't eat *them* because they're poisonous."

Boca laughed.

Yero waved.

The mink showed her teeth.

"Still don't believe it? Okay - *smell* the poison." The hummingbird moved closer, tilting her back so the creature could come get a good whiff.

The mink came all right. Getting a 'whiff' was the last thing on her mind, but the snow shelf broke off and she tumbled down with it. Atel darted through the door and kept going all the way to the original room - there to pause on a tall thistle and listen for pursuit. Tracks on the floor showed the mink had come from the east and probably been through all the rooms.

"Bear in mind," Atel pointed out, "the mink came *in* somewhere. Maybe even the roof, hmm? But more likely the floor. So, she might be *waiting* for us up ahead, even as we sit here looking back. We'll stay put for a few minutes."

The minutes passed uneventfully and the tension lessened, at least for the butterflies.

"I've been thinking," said Boca finally. "What about a spell of blasting? Are there any like that?"

"One or two. But I'm not going to try them."

"I suppose you have your reasons," said Yero.

"I do."

"I suppose you'll tell us, sooner or later."

"I suppose."

"Why not sooner? Butterflies get itchy when we have to wait."

"They do? I didn't know! You should scratch that."

"Not that kind! You know what I mean."

"Oh yes. If you must know, I've been going over those, and others, in my mind all morning. I'm sorry, but I simply need more light to make anything work. A bit of *direct* light. Even a ray or two would help. I can't make something out of nothing and trying would just wear me out. Let's just proceed with caution."

Going east there were fewer narrows, and the rooms were longer with less slush and deeper snow. In the first room were flowers, but they were frozen, already enveloped in white frost. In the second room were stinging nettles, brown but still potent. In both rooms, there were brighter areas on the wall, but they were only tantalizing like the others. Then the tunnel ended in breathtaking fashion at a place where spring water seeped out of the riverbank. Icicles and frozen flowage blocked the way ahead, glimmering faintly in hues of blue and green.

The icicles were wet and still growing. Water leaked from somewhere above, forming a thin film on the ice that exuded slowly downward. Most froze on the way down to produce pretty waves and ripples, but some moisture oozed all the way down to the tip. Occasionally a drip fell and landed on a nub of ice growing up from below; but more often a drip half-formed, then froze in the cold air, extending the icicle.

In one place water dripped steadily, almost a trickle, falling into a melt-hole where the mink tracks came up out of. Here is where the animal had entered the snow tunnels. Splashing noises arose from water beneath, no doubt the shallow edge of the river. Atel backed away and reversed course, thinking to go back, but her passengers had other ideas. Sure, the mink *had* been here, but she wasn't here now; and they weren't afraid of a little ice. Not pretty ice like this.

"Can we explore the icicles a little?" asked Yero. "At least until our feet get cold? There's nothing else to do."

"I guess so, if that makes you happy," sighed Atel. "But walk where it's most frozen and dry, not in any slush that might suddenly freeze around your feet. We don't want to get stuck, do we?"

She set them down where it was driest and went off to perch on a nettle where she could keep one eye on them and one on the melt-hole. 'Exploring' lasted all of a couple minutes until the more promising passages quickly played out, then gave way to a game of 'hide and seek'.

All at once Boca yelped and disappeared behind a row of icicles overhanging a shelf. When he didn't pop out again at the other end of the row, Yero went in after him. When she didn't reappear, Atel went looking and found them both gone. Behind the icicles were several side-passages leading inward. The ice floor was quite hard. There were no tracks or any other sign of the butterflies. Where had they gone? She listened at the mouth of each passage and fancied hearing them faintly in all of them. She was about to plunge into the middle passage when Yero burst out from the next one in a panic and bumped right into her.

"Another frost crystal is attacking him!" she blurted out. "It wants to form on his nose! He keeps going farther into the tunnels trying to escape it."

A thing like that might seem trivial to big folk but it's not trifling at all to a butterfly. The dratted things can be persistent. If you've ever been chased by an angry bee, it will give you some idea. Yero plunged back in with Atel close behind.

The passage grew darker, but not altogether dark. A faint glow emanated from the ice around them so that the passage itself appeared darker than the surrounding walls. In places, Yero glimpsed *things* in the ice. Illusions. Shadows that looked like faces. But when she looked again, they were gone; she had been mistaken. The passage opened into a small chamber studded with ice-pillars, but there was no sign of Boca. Beyond the largest pillar the passage continued, but now there were obstacles.

The ice flow had invaded shrubbery. Stiff twigs poked into the passage from the most inconvenient angles. The light was shrouded from all this, so they must wiggle and feel their way forward in near darkness. Finally, light returned and they left the twiggy maze behind. Slush appeared on the floor of the passage. Atel, up front now, was relieved to see tracks in it - obviously Boca's - and said so. Yero didn't answer.

She had been seeing *things* again. The ice was less blue now, and more yellow, as if real sunlight was getting into it. At the same moment Atel saw tracks, Yero looked to one side and found herself face-to-face with a butterfly.

It wasn't Boca, or any Rasha La. It was a common yellow of the type men call 'Sulphurs'. Its eyes were open, a dream-like expression on its face. It perched on a twig of shrubbery, all encased in clear ice several inches thick. Atel turned and saw it too.

"What's she doing?" whispered Yero in amazement. "She shouldn't be in there!"

"No, she shouldn't. She was unlucky."

"She's frozen solid! Why didn't she move before it got so bad?"

"Because she was already cold and asleep, in hibernation until spring. I think she is dreaming and may awaken from it again."

"She's not dead?"

"No. Strange as it may seem."

"I'm not so sure," whispered Yero. "It seems pretty strange."

"Some butterflies just are that way. So are big trees, if you remember. When the ice melts next spring she may actually awaken and be no worse for the wear. Let's hope we're not still here with her."

Yero waggled her wings more vigorously at the thought. Fascinated, she watched until Atel moved on, and only slowly followed. They passed through a dip in the tunnel where slush had collected in some depth but were able to creep along the very edge where it was firmer. There followed several sharp corners and then a slippery stretch tilting downhill, leading to another row of hanging icicles. They stepped through a gap onto a broad ledge and emerged into a new snow cave beyond the ice flow. Boca was waiting there, no longer bothered by the pesky frost-crystal. He gestured around him.

"Look at them all," he said in wonder. "There must be hundreds."

The room was full of shrubbery like what they had come through. In places, entire shrubs stood in the open. In other places they were mostly buried in the snowbank. On twigs and branches everywhere were a host of Sulphur butterflies like the one Yero had seen. Twigs, butterflies, and all were coated with thick white frost - tragic, yet beautiful at the same time. But even as they gazed upon the scene, a horribly revolting thing happened.

Erupting from the floor in a spray of snow came a shrew, nose wiggling and legs churning. It sniffed out the nearest Sulphurs--a group of fifty or more on a half-buried shrub--and proceeded to make a meal of them in shrew fashion, tearing and slavering like a starving animal. Plainly the creature ate here regularly. In the immediate area and throughout the room were shreds of yellow wings in the trampled snow. The shrew was a frequent visitor.

"No!" hollered Boca. "Atel! Stop him!"

At the sound, the shrew grabbed a Sulphur in his mouth and vanished with it into the snowy floor. Just like that, the ugly scene was over with in only a few seconds. Yero and Boca both started across the floor to see about survivors. Atel shouted a warning but they ignored her, so caught up were they in the misfortune of the Sulphurs. Then it happened again.

The shrew burst up through the snow in front of them, whether by accident or design, and came straight for them, mouth wide open. It was only by millimeters that Atel saved them, knocking them out of the path. The shrew, never even slowing, continued on its way and was soon gorging on more Sulphurs. Atel collected her passengers and deposited them on a tall shrub while she went after the thing, gathering what light was available and reflecting it at the hungry creature. It worked, but the shrew took a yellow butterfly with him when he retreated down under.

Minutes later, up he came again as voracious as ever and grabbed another. This time he was gone again before Atel could do anything, down under the snow where lights and unwelcome noises couldn't hurt him.

The shrew couldn't tolerate much light. That's just how shrews are. Nor could he stand certain high-pitched noises. They made his head hurt and affected his equilibrium in unpleasant ways. Except for touch and smell, he didn't fully understand things around him. But if the shrew couldn't see his claws in front of his face or hear very well, his nose made up for it. Right now, as he gobbled the Sulphur in his tunnel-beneath-the-snow, his nose was telling him that new butterflies and a *bird* had entered his larder. The idea made him very angry and his appetite soared.

Such anger was common with him (and all shrews) and manifested itself in crude gluttony. Worse yet, the angrier he became the more energy he wasted, and the sooner he became hungry again. And shrews are easily angered so they eat all the time.

He wolfed the Sulphur and struck off at a shrewd angle, planning to surface at a particular shrub in such a way that the bird would have difficulty attacking him. Already, only days after the first big snow, he had numerous runways. Some he had made himself; some had been made by a certain helpful mouse (He slavered, recalling *that* feast), and some were simply voids in the buried shrubbery. He now made good use of them. A sixth sense guided him.

Yero was first to see him the next time. The disgusting thing had climbed onto a low branch and was eating his way along, taking a bite out of each Sulphur, then shoving the remains off the branch and tearing into the next one. Yero stepped forward, breaking off an ice crystal, and fired it at the shrew. It just missed his bristly nose but struck the Sulphur in front of him, one of only four left on the branch. Ping! The crystal made a ringing sound glancing off a frosty wing. For some reason the shrew stopped what he was doing. Yero threw another crystal. It also missed, regrettably striking another Sulphur. But this time there was no 'ping'. This time the whole room reverberated to a sharp cuss word - quite unmentionable - that could only have come from Yero.

Boca stared at her. Atel frowned severely. Yero hardly noticed. A glimmer of – *something* - seized her. She threw another crystal, this time aiming for the Sulphurs, though she couldn't have said why.

Bingo! The first Sulphur got hit again. Piercing curses echoed throughout the room, lasting longer than an echo ought to. Inspiration took Yero and she started firing crystal after crystal. One missed everything, one struck the shrew with no effect, and several more hit Sulphurs. The civility of the chamber was assaulted by high-pitched oaths. The shrew reacted defensively, uttering shrill noises of his own and backing unsteadily along the branch.

Boca began throwing crystals too. More cuss-*ing* erupted; but amidst all the noise the open question was: Who was the cuss-*er*? Could ricocheting crystals produce profanity? It seemed unlikely. It was unlike Yero too, but nobody else was doing it. Suddenly the shrew sat upright on the branch and rubbed his head helplessly. Atel flew down behind him and touched him lightly on the shoulder. The shrew jumped and turned in surprise.

"Boo!" shouted the hummingbird.

It was too much for the shrew. He fell off the branch and landed in the snow, feet up in the air, dead. That's how shrews are too. They can dish it out, but they can't take it. When he lay still, they all went down to the branch of the four Sulphurs and Atel expected a straight answer about the bad language.

"It wasn't me," insisted Yero. "It was *them!*" She pointed to the remaining Sulphurs; but now the excitement had evaporated, she wasn't very sure what had happened. Boca just shook his head, baffled.

"All's well that *ends* well," said Atel disapprovingly. "The shrew *is* dead and that's the main thing. I just wonder it couldn't have been done in better taste!"

Yero studied the Sulphurs. They remained perfectly still, giving no hint. Clearly, they were frozen stiff. Trying hard to recapture her earlier confidence, Yero reached out and touched a wing. Nothing happened. She stepped back, glancing sheepishly at her companions. Boca giggled. Atel sniffed critically.

Perturbed, Yero stepped forward again and tweaked a Sulphur in the nose, sharply.

"*Thank-ee hee!*" trilled the Sulphur, without moving so much as an eyebrow.

"You're welcome," replied Yero, stepping quickly back again.

A few moments of silence followed. Giggling and critical sniffing evaporated. This was indisputable. Experimentally, Yero tweaked the 2nd Sulphur in the line.

"*Ee most kind-lee!*" it reverberated.

"Thank you, too!" said Yero, and tweaked the nose again.

"*Ee welcome bee,*" said the Sulphur.

Yero turned to her friends triumphantly. "You see? They can't speak on their own. We have to help them."

It was true. Somehow their minds were alert even though they were trapped solidly in frost. When tapped sharply they spoke through the ringing vibrations. Usually the one talked that was tapped, but not always. Because of their frost connection to each other it was like an old telephone party line. Occasionally, if #1 was tapped, #4 answered. Sometimes it was a different combination. This made no difference when they agreed on things, but when Yero asked for names it got all jumbled. No matter which one she tapped (By now, to be polite, she tweaked antennae, not noses), the result was gibberish. At best, it rhymed roughly with 'pupil' or 'scruple', which couldn't be right. When Boca tweaked, the result was the same: All four seemed to answer, but inconveniently at the same time.

"We'll call you '*Rupl*', if you don't mind," decided Yero. "That means all of you together. If we mean just one of you, we'll say a number. She counted them off: 1-2-3-4, being very careful not to touch them while counting. That way there was no argument.

The Sulphurs were cordial and gave the impression they would like to talk at greater length but a few words at a time were all that could be managed. Then the vibrations weakened, and the voice was lost. When Yero tweaked harder it didn't help and even caused a bit of frost to flake away.

Atel showed how to tweak correctly. Like most tests of skill, it didn't matter so much how strongly one tweaked, but rather that the tweaking was done at the proper angle.

Usually, since #1 was handiest, and because that one seemed a natural spokesperson, they addressed their questions to it. By stepping sideways onto a twig, however, it was easy enough to tweak any of them, and they often did.

"Are you boys or girls?" Boca asked of #1.

"*Narra-hee, see? We are brothers.*"

"Oh good! Four boys? No girls?"

"*No girls. No Hurra-shee. Can't you tell?*"

"Well...no," admitted Boca lamely. "Is that hard to do?" He almost forgot, then remembered and tweaked #1. But #4 answered.

"*Ee are kind-lee, but stupid — Hee? Don't insult mee!*"

"I wasn't! And I didn't ask you, anyway. We just don't know!" Deliberately, Boca didn't tweak anyone. To be polite, Yero finally called on #1, but #4 answered and continued lecturing.

"*Girls are prett-ee-hee? Boys are dashing - see? Like mee!*"

"That doesn't tell me anything. Are boys stronger, then?"

"*Stronger-lee? What's that bee?*"

"You're strong if you have muscles, if you can lift heavy stuff. You don't look very strong."

"*Ha-ha-hee! Who cares? We dashing bee — especially mee!*"

"That sounds pretty stuck-up," commented Yero. "What about your brothers? They look dashing too."

"*Oh, not bad-hee? Not bad-lee. But not like mee.*"

To be fair, Yero conducted a poll of the brothers. Surprisingly, they all agreed with #4: "*Tru-lee*"; "*Exact-lee*"; "*Precise-lee!*"

"Okay, but just remember we gave you all a chance to object.

What is it that makes #4 so dashing, then?"

#4 was now content to let others sing his praises. The Travelers could almost hear his conceited sigh as they did so with no jealousy whatever.

#1 gushed over the exceptional yellow on his brother's wings. It was very rich, almost a shade of orange, definitely deeper than the others.

#2 admired the dots on #4's wings. The black dots on the forewings were a darker, deeper black than anyone else's, and the white dots on the hindwings less conspicuous.

#3 liked #4's black fringe. Here was the biggest difference among the Sulphurs: Numbers 1 & 3 had a good bit of black on the outer edges - considerably more than #2 - but nothing like #4. His black fringe was half-again as wide and twice as black.

"So - just because #4 has a darker complexion he's more 'dashing'?" asked Yero. "Is that all there is to it?"

"*Nah-wee!*" protested #1. "*Also modesty, see? No boasting-hee?*"

"Well, good grief! You're doing it *for* him!"

"*Ah-wee! Yessir-eee! He is the 'Shurra-hee', O-leee!*"

"The 'Shurra-hee'? What's that?"

"O-leee! The most dashing of ALL, see?"

Yero rolled her eyes in disgust. "Okay, I can see he's the darkest of you. Is that a big deal?"

"Ya-weee! Look around. You'll see. Our brother is most dashing of ALL! Of the whole flock! Heee?"

#4, befitting of such a rare and handsome creature, stayed aloof.

Yero and Boca indulged the Sulphurs a little longer, mostly listening, but the unending praise grew boring. Yero first, and then Boca quit tweaking them altogether.

"Seems dumb, doesn't it?" whispered Yero. "He looks plain to me. Even homely. The brighter ones are more handsome."

"Shhh," said Boca. "I think they can hear you."

"Well? So what? Let #4 get his nose out of joint. I'm a girl, and I don't think he's handsome at all!"

"They are not Rasha La," cautioned Atel. "Be open-minded. They think what they want to think, not what *you* think. Let it go."

Yero thought about it. She considered herself open-minded, but she'd had her fill of #4's ego. "I just wish we could change the subject," she said.

"Change it then. Ask a different question."

Yero thought some more. There was one thing in particular she was curious about, but it was along the same lines.

"How do you rate girls, then?" she asked, turning slightly to advantage so the orange of her wings was most evident. She hesitated, then reached out and tweaked #4, but the handsome one ignored her. #1 answered for him.

"If ee excuse mee, the Shurra-hee can't be bothered now."

"Well! I couldn't care less! But I still want an answer, see? And you can give it to me, *see?*"

Boca chuckled. "You're starting to talk like them now. Just don't pick up any bad language."

Yero ignored him and tweaked #1, wishing now she hadn't brought up the subject. But since she *had*, she was going to pursue it! It surprised her when #1 wasn't rude at all.

"Ah-wee! Girls are more White-lee, more Bright-lee! And pret-tee noses, hee? Ooo-la! Love-lee! Love-lee!"

Yero felt much better, almost flattered. She allowed her wings to fan slowly, dazzlingly in the glow of many crystals. This was more like it. When she asked a delicate question, she expected a nice answer. So that was it, hmm? The brighter, more radiant girls were loveliest. Just as it should be! She couldn't resist glancing at her own wings, comparing them to what must be a lot of girls in the shrubbery all around. The sulphurs simply lacked flair. Anyone could see that. #1 certainly did. She smiled coyly and fished for more compliments.

"What a nice thing to say! Thank you! I suppose you have girlfriends, then?"

"Oooo-ee!" *"Pret-tee!"* *"Shimmer-ee!"* Numbers 1, 2, and 3 all answered, nearly at once. The sulphurs were a very romantic bunch. Yero was kept busy for a while just tweaking, to allow full answers. Yes, they had girlfriends. Yes, they loved to talk about them!

#1 gushed silly rhapsodies. He had a special sweetheart of his very own. Naturally, she didn't know it yet. She was one of the best, a white wing. Doubtless, other boys coveted her also. It would all be resolved next spring at the 'Herra-thee', the Bridal Pool, when the lovely lass made her choice. Her reflection would smile at someone, possibly himself! Bliss would automatically follow. The other suitors would have to scramble after lesser lasses, *"He-he-hee!"*

Yero took note of a few white wings here and there about the shrubbery. There weren't many. *These* were special? She almost laughed.

"You should set your sights higher," she advised. "The yellows are better. Not as good as orange, of course. But pretty."

"Nah-wee! Orange might be great for boys, hee? But not girls! Nahzee!"

"I beg your pardon!"

Orange be too dark, hee? Not bright-lee! Not white-lee!"

"All you care about in girls is *light complexion*?"

"*Most-lee. But don't be angry. Eee teeny bit pret-tee be, and cute nose, zee? But dark edges! Oh-feee!*"

"Oh-*feee*?? Look at *this*!" She waggled a wing in front of his nose, showing off the dazzling white and orange spots within the black fringe. Just as quickly she stepped back, offended and mad. So! Sparkles and radiant colors counted for nothing? Ha! Still, she was curious.

"Which girl is prettiest then? Prettiest of all?"

"*Oo-la-zee! That's easy: The Hurra-shee!*"

"Which one is that?"

"*Up, up, see? Highest of all! Ooo-leee!*"

The Travelers looked up, following the frozen gaze of the Brothers Rupl. They hadn't noticed before, but all the Sulphurs (except #4) were gazing in the same direction, toward a shrub that grew out near the top of the bank. There, within inches of the snow-awning on the tip-top branch, were a dozen or so white wings and one pale yellow. The yellow had four white spots and not a speck of black anywhere. Quite striking, actually. The whites faced the yellow to their left.

"Is that her? The yellow out on the end?" asked Yero.

"*Oo-lee! Oo-lee!*" replied #1.

"*Love-lee!*" said #2.

"*Exquisite-lee!*" agreed #3.

"*Not bad-lee,*" commented #4. "*Do you think she deserves me?*"

"I wouldn't know," retorted Yero. "She'd have to be pretty snooty!"

"*Ah, me! She'd better be!*" said the Shurra-hee. "*Extremely fussee, hee? If she be, she'll pick me.*"

"Oh, great. Then you'll have lots of snooty kids."

"*Prob-lee. And deserved-lee, if they take after me.*"

"What if she smiles at #3 instead?"

The Shurra-hee emitted an odd tinkling sound, amused.

"*Ee funn-ee! Very! My average brother stands no chance, hee? Nahwee! Only me.*"

#1 took it from there: "*Yea! Oh-yee! It is preordained,*" he intoned. "*The Hurra-shee shall smile upon the Shurra-hee at the Bridal Pool in the days of Spring, Oh-yee! For they are the 'Beau-see', the Prettiest Ones. It is their destiny!*"

"What if she likes someone else? That could happen."

"*Nah-feee! Nah-feee! It would bring bad luck, see?*"

"Why? Butterflies should be free to choose."

"*We are, most-lee. But not the Beau-see!*"

He went on (with extra tweaks) to explain why. In summer, the Sulphurs spent most of their time lolling around puddles of water, admiring themselves and each other. This is part of their birthright and vital to the self-assurance of the flock. All are deemed 'pretty' (or 'dashing') by universal acclaim. Sulphur butterflies are unselfish that way, generous in their praise.

Naturally, as summer wears on, some are deemed even prettier or more dashing than usual. This doesn't cause jealousy in a well-adjusted flock and is a normal winnowing process toward choosing the *Prettiest Ones*. These are important decisions, for winter will come again. When it comes, the flock looks to the Hurra-shee for leadership. Under her guidance they will overwinter.

"You mean *she brought* you here?" asked Boca. "You followed her?"

The brothers agreed immediately. Of course! Naturally! That was her job. Yero and Boca looked at each other in astonishment but let it go. It was beyond comment anyway.

The ways of Sulphurs were not unknown to their guide, but it surprised Atel that the Hurra-shee was a yellow. She knew it was unusual since whites are nearly always lighter in overall tone. That's what counted. Pure white was best, but rare. All these white attendants had minor blemishes while the yellow was as perfect as a yellow could be. But there had to be doubts about it. It couldn't have been good for morale.

"Why is the Hurra-shee out on the end, and not surrounded by her 'Court'?" asked Yero. That's what seemed strange to her: Why have a beauty contest and then push the winner off to the side?

"*The Hurra-shee likes it, a-hee? So others approach correct-lee. Never from her left, nah-wee!*"

"She can only be approached from her right?"

"*Oo-lee! It's her best side, hee?*"

"Oh. Does the flock decide that also?"

"*Eee! Nah-wee! No one tells a girl that, hee? Very personal, see?*"

"Okay, fine. But why take it so seriously? If she's that pretty, it shouldn't matter."

"*Well, dumb-dee-dee! It's all the difference, hee? Between overwintering under her wise guidance - or perishing utter-leee!*"

"Begging your pardon, but this set-up doesn't seem very well planned. What does anyone's 'best side' have to do with it?"

It had a lot to do with it. The Sulphurs found themselves here because the Hurra-shee had fancied facing west across the water puddles to admire her reflection in the sunset. Her best side, then, faced north. Owing to that quirk of fate, they had migrated north. It was unfortunate, perhaps. Still, the Hurra-shee knew best.

"You trust her on *that* - just because she's prettiest?"

"*Oh yea! Oh Yee!*" said #1 with conviction.

"Do you think you'll be safe here until spring?"

The vibrations fell out of tune. Became twangy. Crystals shook loose here and there. Yero tried each of the brothers again but the voices were jumbled.

She stepped back. "They don't agree, do they?"

"No. At least one is very worried," replied Atel.

"Ask again," said Boca. "Do like this." He reached out and put a hand on #4 to keep him quiet. Yero and Atel each hushed a Brother as well. In this way #1 was allowed to answer by himself. His voice was very faint, but he wasn't worried. Nor was #3. But #2 was. Very much so.

Maybe it's because he was ugliest that he had doubts. Maybe he was just smarter than his 'betters'. But doubts he had, and claimed he wasn't the only one in the roost. Many had been worried since it became obvious that a yellow was prettiest. It had caused trouble right away. It was *uncustomary!* Anything uncustomary was frowned upon. It raised unsettling questions: Would the Shurra-hee *go* for a yellow? Would the doubters *follow* a yellow? Would a yellow possess leadership qualities? Within memory, the Hurra-shee of the flock had always been white. There were no old tales to go by.

Only days before the first snow the flock had finally rallied behind her, but bad luck followed immediately as some had predicted. Now it had come to this.

"Maybe your bad luck is ended now the shrew is dead," suggested Yero. It was certainly a bright spot. She wished now that she could cheer them up. She let them all answer.

"*Curse that---!!*" (There followed several epithets which need not be reported here.) The tone was loud and clear. On the shrew, Rupl was in perfect agreement. Regrettably, the extra-loud burst caused more frost to slough away. At the same time, their remaining frost showed signs of melting. Maybe this was due to the bodily warmth of the Travelers, or maybe memories of the shrew stirred up something hot inside the Sulphurs, but Atel called a halt to the visit. She loaded up her passengers and moved back.

"One never knows about these things," she said, "but it can't be good to thaw them out. They would only freeze again, so let them stay frozen until the time is right."

"But I have more questions," objected Yero.

"So do I. I should like to ask about the way south where they have lately come from, silly creatures. But, alas! We have a bit of escaping to do or we aren't going anywhere."

***

105

The Butterflies, Yero and Boca

The way east ended there, in the room of the Sulphurs. No tunnel led beyond. The river went straight southward from that point, after the bend. The bank was less undermined and lay open to the west so that instead of forming a snow cave the wind had scoured the bank bare.

They turned back, passing through the shrubbery again. They shouted their farewells to Rupl from a distance and re-entered Boca's ice tunnel. They were nearly too late. Slush had been collecting in the low spot. Yero and Boca were able to skitter through on top of the slush. It barely supported them. Their guide wasn't as fortunate and had to force a way through, half swimming, half-crawling. In a few minutes the passage would be impassable. No one spoke. The way was now shut behind them.

When they reemerged into the room of nettles the sound of water greeted them. At the place where it dripped into a melt hole, the noise was a little louder. Moving water could be seen just below. Even as they watched, a small piece of the floor broke off and fell *splash!* into it. Fresh mink tracks also led down into the hole. The animal had followed them after all but missed them while they were beyond the ice flow. They hurried on. The next room hadn't changed one bit, and then they found themselves back where they started, among the frozen thistle flowers. The floor was trampled in this room. Obviously, the mink had found their old scent and searched the place. Atel regretted calling her a 'weasel' now. That must have struck a nerve.

The butterflies perched on a thistle, on a blossom gone to down, while Atel continued to the west, double-checking every possible light source. But possibilities were running out for them. They could probably pass another night in the cave, and maybe another day after that. It just depended on when the frost crystals attacked in force.

"Will we be like Rupl then?" wondered Yero. "Speaking only when we're called upon?" The prospect of holding her tongue so obediently didn't thrill her.

"If it does happen let's touch wings, Yero. Like they did. I think we could at least talk to each other that way, don't you?"

"We might. We could hold hands too. If the Sulphurs can hibernate, maybe we can. Maybe all butterflies can."

"Maybe so. But I like the journey better. We have a good start now."

"We did, but we need a *jump-start*, Boca. Oh, well. That's what guides are for! Let's watch."

"And listen."

"Sure! Listen away! Why? Do you hear Atel coming?"

"I hear water below us. I could hear it better if you were quiet."

"Oh, that. It's only the river, silly."

"I know. But it's louder, don't you think?"

The sound of the river current, ever-present in the cave, was a bit louder - at least to butterfly ears. For several minutes the Two listened, wondering what it could mean. Atel returned in fair spirits to announce that evening had come and there was no sign of the mink. Offering no reason, she moved the butterflies to another thistle, well under the riverbank. The cave grew dark.

"I was thinking..." began Yero after a while, "What about a spell for doors? If you made a small one, we could open it."

"I can imagine that," laughed Atel. "And if I could make flowers, we would never go hungry! But I will leave the imagining to you. I've been told lately not to worry so much, and I think I'll take that advice. 'Something will turn up', so I've been told. I'm just going to relax. I think we're due for a turn of luck." They fell silent, listening to the sound of water hurrying by beneath the snow. The cave grew very dark. Late in the evening when only Atel was awake the floor turned to slush on the river side. The drift wall sagged slowly. As it did so, the current ate into it more swiftly. Late in the evening their guide finally joined the butterflies in slumber, but about midnight the stench of mink entered their dreams.

Atel awoke, instantly aware that the smell was real. The animal was prowling near the thistle they so recently had perched on. Stealthy noises infiltrated the darkness as the mink stood up tall, following

106

her nose to the very flower the butterflies had sat on, and chomped right where they should be with an audible 'snap', followed by dry hacking and the spitting out of thistledown. Then silence returned while the mink's nose zeroed in on their new location.

Atel decided to awaken the butterflies, but a moment later that job fell to Mother Nature when the drift wall collapsed into the river. Everything went that wasn't rooted into the riverbank, including the mink. The butterflies were awakened by a splash and a roar!

"We beat the North Wind!" said Yero in amazement as remnants of the drift-wall swept downstream.

"Yes, a victory!" agreed Atel. "And we may live to tell the tale. But we won't defeat her. That task must fall to a Greater Power. Our job is still survival, or escape".

"But we have survived. We're free!"

"For now. But how far south do the new snowfields reach? Maybe farther than we can go without food".

The butterflies said nothing. The chill of their recent journey still hung like icicles in the back of their minds.

"What about 'escape', then?" said Boca finally. "What did you mean by that?"

Atel directed their gaze to the heavens. "We leave all this behind and go up there, into the Night Sky. There must be a better way forward."

This was met by sullen silence. The butterflies plainly did not want to return to the heavens at all - to abandon their journey, as they saw it.

Presently the air stirred again as a new wind, a noisy one, approached from the North. As it drew near voices emerged clearly, for they made up most of the noise. There was no doubt of them. The Snogg was touring the battlefield, gloating, but the Hoo was with him, poo-pooing all of it.

"See now what I can do, little fellow?" the Snogg bragged as they passed overhead, and the wind gusted wildly when he spoke. But it calmed as the Hoo replied. "Is that all?" he chuckled. "I should let you cheat, maybe. This is nothing".

The wind gusted anew as the Snogg roared, "No, it's *not* all! And I'll do it again just to shut you up!"

They passed southwards, arguing, and the wind followed. But the Snogg wasn't just taking a tour. He was leading an army of chillbanes, soldiers of the North Wind, to occupy the newly conquered lands. When the air became still again the Travelers felt a deeper cold and became aware of whispers in the air around them. It was different than with the ice crystals. This cold reached for their hearts. Yero shivered, couldn't stop shivering. She glanced up again at the starry sky.

"What are our chances up there?" she asked suddenly.

"Better", replied their guide. "Pretty good, maybe. If there is stardust enough to repair your wings, I plan to put you back to work".

"There's lots", laughed Yero. "But of course, we'll have to hitch a ride"

Part 2
Beyond the Moonwalk

Synopsis

Wherein the monarchs with their guide enter the Night Sky to renew the stardust on their wings. There, in a kingdom behind the Aurora, they are drawn into a long-awaited uprising of the lesser fairy lasses against their slave masters. The cause celebre is Boca, nicknamed *Ombomba* – 'The boy who lit the fuse' – by his pixie admirers. He is the first boy ever to turn up in Nyo, an event that upsets the status quo.

The 'burning fuse' inevitably leads to an explosion. War and cataclysm engulf the Night Sky, hidden from earthly eyes by the great curtain of the Aurora.

Chapter 6

Nyo

In that hour the Travelers entered the Night Sky, realm of secrets beyond the ken of mortal men. Ascending high on shifting paths among the moonbeams they came at last to Nyo, uttermost region of air, where fairies are. But they saw no fairies. There were only the stars in their thousands.

Esporellia appeared above them helter-skelter, entering the atmosphere like small fireworks, mostly yellow and orange. It was easy to catch as it floated down past them. Atel need only circle slowly beneath the showers while the butterflies spread their wings, and it was enough to gather the precious dust which did not dim when it touched them but continued to twinkle brightly. Before long the butterflies glowed with the light of stars that was on them, and the light of angels that was in them, and they slipped softly from the back of their guide and flew unaided in the elixir and serenity of that place.

"You see?" said Yero after a while, "There's lots, isn't there? A shame most of this goes to waste".

"A shame if it really did", said Atel. "But nothing is lost. It becomes part of the earth. And also, the fairies collect it".

"What are fairies like?" asked Boca. "We've never actually met any".

"Most folk haven't nowadays. But surely you've heard stories? Fairies were once common on earth. Fairy lore still is, I hope".

"Sure, we've heard stories", said Yero. "I guess everyone has. But that's not like meeting someone. Are they friendly? Do you know any?"

"I have known them; and yes, most are quite friendly if you can put up with a bit of mischief. You would like them, and they would like you".

"What do they do with the esporellia?"

"Well, for one thing they put it on their wings. Just like you do".

"Really?" said Yero. "Then we are related?"

"You have something in common. No one is related to fairies directly. They are a kind of their own. Very independent, if I may say so".

"Do they live here?"

Atel nodded. "This is fairyland, if you like. Is it what you expected?"

The butterflies shook their heads slowly.

"Not at all", said Yero. "I always thought fairyland would be more, umm...well, I mean..."

"...Down to earth?"

"Yes! With trees and flowers. You know, very pretty".

"Isn't this pretty?"

Yero gazed at the stars. Many more were visible up here where the air was thin and clear. It was beautiful but reminded her not at all of any fairyland. Something was missing.

"Is this where you met fairies?" she asked.

"No, although I was here long ago. That's how I know the way. I came with friends".

"Fairies?"

"Yes. Well - *pixies*, actually. That's what they called themselves".

"What's the difference?"

"Size. And temperament. Most fairies are larger and a bit more serious. Pixies are small. Some aren't much bigger than we are. There is quite a variety of fairy-folk".

"Where are they? The ones up here, I mean?" It suddenly occurred to Yero what was missing from fairyland: The fairies themselves.

"I don't know", replied Atel. "I expected to see them. I hope to speak with their Queen".

"Do we have to?" groaned Boca.

"Yes. She won't hurt you".

"Scared of the girls?" chirped Yero.

"Easy for you to say!" retorted Boca. "I'm outnumbered now, and she'll make it *three* to one. I get the worst of it because I'm the only boy!"

"If you get the worst of it, it's because you're *Boca*. You shouldn't ask for so much trouble".

"I'm not asking for any now!"

"That won't last long".

"Please!" interjected Atel. "We may not even see them! There are (or were) quite a few, but Nyo is vast. This is just a small corner".

"Do all the fairies live here?" asked Yero.

Their guide hesitated, then spit it out: "No. Only the *Nara*, the girls - except for a few lasses who still remain on the earth".

"No boys?"

"No. They don't come here. Never did".

"What did I tell you?" groaned Boca. "It's worse than I thought: *All* girls!""

"Don't be silly", laughed Yero. "This will be nice."

"Someday you'll be the underdog, Yero. Then we'll see!"

"Maybe I'll like that!" said she and turned to Atel again. "But where are the boy fairies if they aren't here?"

"No one knows precisely".

"Even the girls don't know?"

"Least of all, the girls".

"Not even you?"

"I have my own thoughts".

"You could share them, so we'd all know".

"Not now. It's a long story that hasn't ended yet. I only know the beginning. I can't guess the ending".

"I can", grumbled Boca. "That's when the boys will be marched up in front of the High Queen to be punished".

"Do them good," sniffed Yero. "Stubborn bunch, the way it sounds. Honestly, boys are all the same!"

"At least we're smart enough to stay away from bossy girls, if we can help it".

"Well, *I'm* a girl. *Atel's* a girl".

"Can't help it if you hang around me all the time".

"—!"

"Stop right there!" said the hummingbird. "Not another word! We're here to heal your wings. Heal them! There's no rush about it. Then we'll worry about later".

A peculiar thing happened as they gathered more and more of the esporellia. They began to fade, and the light went to their eyes. Even the hummingbird, who made no effort to do so, accumulated a lot and began to fade, and her eyes grew brighter; but the change came slowly, and for a long time they noticed nothing. For a while, they watched the moon above them and listened to faint music that had begun nearby. Flutes were playing somewhere, and something else about an octave higher. Piccolos, possibly.

At first the music came from below, and they looked down, but saw no one playing. The next moment it came from one side, but there wasn't anyone there either. Then it came from the other side. Then it faded away, only to come floating down with the esporellia, like a gift from the stars.

"Who is playing?" asked Yero. "Are they playing for us?"

"No. Not for you", smiled Atel. "It's fairy music, and that lingers".

"Like an echo?"

"Yes. An echo that keeps going for quite a long time, but very softly. We hear it because of the quiet in the night sky".

"That's neat! But how can it do that up here? There's nothing for it to echo off".

"Yes, there is. You just don't see it yet".

"I see the moon. I see the stars. There's nothing else".

"But there is. I'm confident now that we are near the Moonwalk, as I had hoped."

"What's that? I don't see anything".

"You will. It's a pathway in the sky, made by girl fairies long ago in case the boys should ever come this way. It leads to their city - or used to. It appears only under a full moon, like this one".

"And the music comes from that?"

"Certainly. As I said, fairy music lingers. It lingers longest in places the girls loved best - like the Moonwalk, or their ayas, their old dwelling places in the woodlands down below. I have known many an abandoned aya by the music that lingered long after the fairy was gone. There are such places even within the cities of men, where fairies once lived in forgotten forests".

"Wow. That's a long echo".

"It is. Men used to call it fairy magic, but it never was. It came from the trees, who were fond of them; or if the trees were gone, then from the earth itself that the trees were rooted in".

As they loitered, the moon rose to a zenith in the night sky. Suddenly, perhaps triggered by a certain angle of moonlight, the esporellia showers increased above them and came together all around them with a dizzying, spiraling, mixing motion that ended almost as soon as it began with breathtaking results: A pathway appeared out of nowhere, miles above the surface of the earth.

"I wasn't expecting *trees*", blurted Boca.

Yero, for once, was speechless.

It was a woodland path, meandering off indefinitely east and west. The path itself was paved of precious and semi-precious stones, comfortably wide enough for a child but perhaps a bit narrow for a big person, had there been any. Forest flora crowded the path and leaned out into it, the better to display autumn flowers and foliage. Along the shoulders of the path were great trees, very girthy, very tall. In places their limbs overspread the path so that orange and golden leaves fell right down onto it. The smell of late flowers and turning leaves came to the Travelers as they hovered at treetop level. It looked very real, yet all had been woven of stardust in a twinkling. How could it be?

"Wow!" said Yero finally. "What next?"

"We land", said Atel. "Aren't you hungry?"

*****

So it happened that the butterflies found supper where they least expected it. Yet even here in the celestial kingdom of fairies the seasons do pass, and the phantasmal leaves must fall, so there was not a smorgasbord of fresh blossoms to choose from. But (like the music) flowers linger in that kingdom, so a fair number of autumn blossoms were still about, and even some summer varieties that are finished at that latitude, down below on solid earth.

Of course, the moonwalk is not quite like solid earth. How could it be, made of insubstantial matter? But to hummingbirds or butterflies it was firm beneath their feet. And the nectar was real, if a bit weak, which they made up for by drinking extra.

"What a blessing!" said Yero after a while (for Boca had found mallasha and she was sharing it with him) "It's a lucky thing we came by. When the fairies set up a banquet, I'm sure they want someone to enjoy it".

Boca nodded but kept drinking. He figured Yero would talk enough for both of them, so an occasional nod or grunt on his part would be sufficient. This proved correct. Yero went on for some time with only short pauses, marveling at one thing after another until it occurred to her that the music was receding into the distance.

"Boca, do you realize it's running away from us?" she said.

"What is?"

"The music. Don't you hear? It's running away over there and leaving us." She pointed, but Boca was only mildly interested.

"It's going to do whatever it wants, Yero. We can't stop it".

"But we could follow".

"And skip supper?"

"Skip supper? Do you know how long you've been eating?"

"Not long enough. There's still some left".

"There's bound to be more as we go along".

"Can't be too sure. Can't be too careful".

"Well, we're going to lose it then and maybe our chance to see fairies along with it. The music is probably lonesome and going off to look for them".

"Exactly so", commented Atel. "But I doubt if the fairies have been gone long. They come here often or used to. If we follow, we may very well come upon them".

"Well, Boca! Do you hear?" said Yero. "If you'll quit stuffing yourself for a minute we can go and see fairies".

"Why hurry? They'll only be doing silly things anyway".

"And what makes you say that?"

"They're girls. Atel said so".

"She never said *silly*."

"Didn't have to. They're *girls*, she said".

"You'll see, Boca! If you think fairies are silly - just wait! They'll have magic, and lots of stuff you won't even understand. You'll see!"

"Maybe. But I bet they won't be doing anything important".

"Just wait, Boca. Just you wait!"

***

The Travelers moved off down the path in the direction where the music had disappeared, for so it had by now. As a compromise with Boca they went slowly, sampling a lot of celestial blossoms as they went.

There were several varieties of mallasha. Besides the common pink there were yellows, and also a bright orange type they'd not seen before. Boca tasted them all and pronounced them "good, but a lot weaker than down below".

Along the border of the path were purple columbines too, and bee balm, but in the shadow of the trees they saw red fuchsias and even a tall cardinal flower which Atel could not resist.

The path made many turns. Around every turn some new gastronomical possibility presented itself so that even Boca gained confidence the food wouldn't run out. Then the Travelers moved along at a brisker pace, trying something here or there, but quickly hurrying on to see what new delights awaited beyond the next turn. In their excitement, they failed to realize they had caught up again to the music and don't you know they flitted right around a big tree whose roots bulged out into the path - and blundered onto a group of fairies. This is what they saw:

The moonwalk opened into a wide space after the tree. The path split and circled a small lawn dotted with white clover, coming together again on the opposite side. The full moon shone very brightly into the natural opening and esporellia arrived in coordinated bursts, keeping time with the music, which was happy now. In the midst of this, a dozen young lasses of various sizes were playing and frolicking. They were obviously fairies. Anyone would guess that from their wings, which were filmy and transparent - rather like double dragonfly wings, except larger. They had to be larger because fairies - even the smallest pixies - are much larger than dragonflies. The wings moved constantly and Yero couldn't decide if this was necessary to keep the fairies from falling through the pathway, or if the pathway was firm beneath them and they just moved their wings for pleasure like butterflies often do. The truth is, the fairies of Nyo are featherweights despite their appearance (which runs to chubby). Gravity hardly affects them at all.

Their dresses were woven of autumn leaves and flowers, with sprigs of ripe berries in their hair, or circlets of the moonseed vine. One plump little maid wore white thistledown and tended to rise when talking. Then she was obliged to use her wings to arrest her altitude. Her name was Airy, and she was coaxing her friends into a favorite game. It didn't take much coaxing. The Travelers settled themselves behind the roots of the tree and peeked out to watch.

Airy and another named Lolly and one other fairy produced artist's brushes and set to work at imaginary easels. But these were no mortal artists working with ordinary paint. They worked with the glittering stardust which came to them as they needed it. Viola! A few bold strokes, a swirl of esporellia, and it was done: Three pictures had been painted. Or rather, three stout figures stood there - very lifelike, if a bit fuzzy.

Yero guessed right away these must be boys because of their beards, and that's what they were: Boy fairies, as perfect as the lasses could remember them. They were fuzzy because the lasses hadn't seen the boys in a very long time and the memory was fading; but the other lasses cheerfully overlooked this.

"Ah! Not bad, not bad", they laughed. "Come! Th'must join hands now".

All the lasses joined hands then and danced in a ring around the lawn while the music raced gaily, and the fuzzy boy fairies looked round and round in bewilderment. Now the music changed, and the lasses reversed direction with giggles and squeals. So it went. First one way, then back the other way they danced as their laughter and the music together rose toward a crescendo. Then - Boom! - a gong sounded, and everyone stopped breathlessly to see how it matched up. Of the dozen lasses, three were exactly facing boys: Airy, Lolly, and a blushing maid named Poo.

The way the game was played these three lasses had 'won' the boys (or were stuck with them, depending on your point of view), and a formal dance now commenced. Cheerful Airy and romantic Lolly stepped quickly into the lawn and pretended to dance with their 'sweethearts'. Blushing Poo took a few bashful steps forward. It now became clear that the boys actually had some life to them and did not approve of this but were rather a captive crew. The rest of the fairies resumed dancing around the circle and sang:

> "Lolly and Airy loves Noggin and Nary,
> Everyone kno-o-o-o-ws it's true!
> Pixie or fairy, someday they will marry.
> Surely! But what about Boo?

Indeed, what about Boo? The third boy fairy grew suddenly fuzzier and winked out, as if he had a mind of his own. The fairies around the circle enjoyed this immensely and offered light-hearted suggestions.

"Oh, foo! D'thu see, Poo? He's gone. Th'must fetch him back again!"

Alternating expressions of relief and annoyance struggled for control of Poo's face. Annoyance won. She stepped forward and waved her brush with a purpose. Esporellia rushed into the void. There now! Boo, a much slenderer boy, was 'fetched' back and looked none too happy about it. Poo immediately reverted to being bashful, but the other lasses cheered and the music struck up once more. The fairies sang:

"Boo is so skinny and he's such a ninny,
Not like the o-o-o-o-ther two!
Who would take *that* one, and not a nice fat one?
Don't anybody want Boo?

At that, Poo's heart seemed to melt, and she took another step forward, very shy.

"I'll take him", she managed to say. "I think he's nice".

It was a special moment as she reached to take his sort-of-fuzzy hand. The other lasses 'O-o-oh-ed' and 'Ah-h-h-ed'. It was all just too mushy for Boca and he laughed out loud.

Of course, the fairies hadn't noticed they were being watched. When he laughed, they disappeared in a twinkling along with the music and the boys, but the Moonwalk remained.

***

"What did you go and do *that* for?" whispered Yero. "Now you've ruined everything!"

"I couldn't help it. They were being so dumb".

"It wasn't dumb. It was beautiful!"

Boca only giggled. This didn't help. Their guide had to step in.

"It was both", she ruled. "And now, Boca, curb your tongue! Maybe they'll return".

"Just answer me one thing", grinned Boca. "Were those boys real or fake? It's even sillier if they were fake".

Atel frowned. "Fuzzy, yes. Fake? I don't think so. It seemed to me they were alive somewhere else and *partly* here". This did not satisfy Boca at all.

"If they were only *partly* here that means they *weren't* here", he insisted. "That's the same as fake". He shook his head, much amused. "And the girls were *dancing* with them!" he added for Yero's benefit.

"Tell him some more, so he stops!" she beseeched Atel. "There must be more to it!"

Atel explained briefly about the magic of the Nara, the girl fairies of Nyo, who paint with the dust of the heavens and are everything human artists would like to be (but can't) for they can create anew anything they ever saw. Would you like a forest pathway with great beech trees and a lush understory? Would you like jack-in-the-pulpit and sweet columbine and bright marigolds crowding the path, and all of it up in the night sky simply miles and miles from anywhere? Easy! A few guiding brush strokes and - Poof! - esporellia does the rest. Minor repairs may be necessary as years go by, owing to the eroding effects of gravity and so forth, but the pictures are real. The fairies of Nyo step right into them and have adventures.

But the memory must be perfect, or the magic doesn't work well. If the fairies don't remember a thing clearly from below, then it cannot be brought up to Nyo, and is lost forever. So it is with the boy fairies, alas. The memory is no longer clear, and that's how they turn out; but this does not stop the girls from trying and so they carry on as if their romance was brand-new, and not thousands of years old. To them, it seems like only yesterday.

Atel fell silent, expecting a barrage of questions; but at that very moment the fairies came back suddenly, acting like nothing unusual had happened.

Laughing, they raced to the lawn and fell to searching for four-leaf clovers. In fairyland there's a good chance of finding them, and soon Airy had one. A very small lass named Florry found the next one, then Lolly, and then a sweet little maid named Flossie who smiled around at everyone. Four girls were enough for the next game, and that made the lucky four. The others were good sports and backed off and began to dance the Ring again. With only eight to make the Ring, they couldn't quite hold hands now and link up the circle, but they made a comical try at it. First someone would lose their grip over *here* (and everyone would laugh); then they would re-join but the Ring would pull apart over *there*.

But the lucky four stepped to the center of the lawn and, reaching up, touched their clovers together. The four clovers became one, and the one stayed up in the air all by itself. Then the lucky lasses stepped back and went to work with their brushes. A hush fell upon the Moonwalk. Even the music waited to see what would happen.

Esporellia went to the clover and it grew larger until each leaf was big and paunchy and drooped like a fat boy's stomach, and then with a swirl and flourish that's what they became: Four boy fairies sitting back to back with ample stomachs drooping over their crossed legs. They were fuzzy, like before. Noggin and Nary were among them along with two new boys, all unwashed and unkempt. Their shirts rode up over their tummies, exposing belly buttons, and they didn't care. That's boy fairies for you. With no female influence in their lives, they have very little manners.

Yero studied them critically. The boys sort of came and went, becoming clearer, then fuzzier again. At their fuzziest, it was hard to see them at all. At their best, it seemed to Yero that they were aware of the girls. Perhaps not to see them, but to hear them, because whenever the girls said anything mushy (especially Lolly) the boys scowled and fidgeted (especially Noggin). But they never stood up, nor spoke a word.

Now the girls dancing the Ring winked out and made voices for the silent boys: "Oh Lolly, you are so-o-o-o lovely!" said a voice pretending to be Noggin's. Other voices imitated the two new boys, reciting romantic messages to Florrie and Flossie who eagerly awaited them. Nary seemed to catch on to this and clapped his hands over his mouth. It didn't save him. A loud kissing noise was ventriloquized behind his hands. It surprised him and he threw his hands open, which made it look like he was throwing the kiss to Airy.

"Th'was *so sweet*, Sugarplum!" she sang. Nary quickly covered his mouth again.

The music played tenderly now, expectantly. There was a bit of an awkward silence. The four girls waited serenely for... *something*. Then it came.

"Dearest darlings, we love you!" said voices pretending to be the boys. "Will you marry us?"

The girls clasped hands to their bosoms.

"Gosh - I don't know!" gasped Airy.

"This is so sudden!" exclaimed Lolly.

"Please, we need time to consider!" said Florrie and Flossie.

The music struck up a livelier tune and the four lasses made a half-circle. They hummed a bit, as if 'considering', then did this:

(4 fairies speak) "Maybe we will, and maybe we won't!
(Lolly sings) But, you really aren't bad looking,
(Florrie sings) So if *you* will do the cooking,
(Flossie sings) And attend to all our wishes,
(Airy sings) And do all the dirty dishes,
(All sing) ...We'll be surprised if we don't".

(4 fairies speak) "Maybe we will, and maybe we won't!
(Lolly sings) But, if *you* will do the sweeping,
(Florrie sings) And the rest of the housekeeping,
(Flossie sings) Like the washing and the sewing,
(Airy sings) ...Also gardening and hoeing...
(All sing) ...We'll be surprised if we don't".

(4 fairies speak) "Maybe we will, and maybe we won't!
(Lolly sings) So, right now the answer's 'maybe',
(Florrie sings) But if *you* will feed the baby,

(Flossie sings) And fetch all his nosey wipers,
(Airy sings) And be there to change his diapers,
(All sing) ...We'll be surprised if we don't!"

The lasses laughed and giggled. It was plain to Yero that this was all in good fun. Boca didn't think so. Neither did the boy fairies, who seemed to pick up on certain lines. 'Diapers' and 'nosey wipers' obviously pained them, though by now the reception was going very fuzzy and it was hard to see their faces at all. Nevertheless, it was time for one last game.

The four girls quieted down and waited for the boys to 'speak up' again. Sure enough, they did.

"We have made beautiful rings", said the 'boys'. "These are for you".

The girls picked up gems from the pathway and set them on their fingers, holding them high to catch the light of stars. Airy held hers up to a blue star and the gem magnified the light. The others aligned theirs with different stars, which accentuated the gems prettily in several colors.

"It's so-o-o beautiful", breathed Airy.

"They're *all* beautiful", said Lolly, nearly swooning.

"Then with these rings let us plight our troth", intoned the 'boys'. Noggin scowled and Nary shook his head vigorously, but Lolly advanced upon them with arms wide.

"My honeybunch", she crooned. "I could just kiss you!" She meant Noggin alone, but 'honeybunch' shook them all up. That's when the boys winked out for good and there was no fetching them back. The other girls all reappeared and shared a happy moment together. Boca snorted loudly in disgust.

Poof! The lasses disappeared once more in the blink of an eye.

"You did it *again!*" blurted Yero. "I can't believe this! We should stuff flowers in your mouth".

Boca snorted even louder. "Sure! You'd fit right in around here. Boys don't get to talk at all! Girls talk for them - or make kissing noises like that. It's not fair and I wouldn't stand for it either! They sure didn't".

"Oh, don't be so grouchy! It was beautiful and there's no harm done".

"No harm to any girls! But how would you like it if you weren't allowed to talk and someone put words in *your* mouth?"

"It wasn't like that, Boca. The boys just weren't *able* to talk, so the girls supplied the words that the boys probably would've said if they *were* able to".

"Baloney! They wouldn't have said that mush!"

"Well! If they wouldn't say anything nice then it's better if they couldn't talk at all. Honestly, girls should do the talking most of the time and things would go a whole lot better".

"You're doing most of the talking now, and things are getting a whole lot worse!"

"Then try this, Boca: Be silent and I'll supply the words! I'll put you in a better mood in no time".

Boca turned and sulked, but Yero went merrily on exploring her new idea. Gee, what possibilities! "Now say this, Boca: 'I've been thinking about all our arguments, Yero, and I realize I was wrong every time. Please accept my most sincere humble apologies!'" She laughed, but Boca spun around quick as a flea. There would have been real trouble, but their guide hurriedly hushed them. Something was happening.

A gong sounded somewhere, and the Moonwalk faded into nothing. Yero felt the tree root softening underneath her. Moments later, root and tree were gone, and she was glad she had wings, for she needed them. Looking around quickly she saw the last traces of the Moonwalk wink out. The night sky returned and she was alone, and a little frightened.

"Boca, where are you?"

"Over here, Yero. But we've disappeared like everything else".

He turned then and saw her eyes shining, and she saw his, and a small fear left her; but when Yero approached too closely they bumped noses, for they were still butterflies.

"Oof! Boca—that's *you*, isn't it?"

"Yeah. Me and my nose".

"Good. Well, we'll have to talk more now so we don't lose each other".

"You can be in charge of that".

"Yes. It's important that someone keeps up the conversation. Can you see me at all?"

"Just your eyes. They're like blue-green stars".

"Do they twinkle like real ones?"

"Sure. And there is Atel above you. I see her eyes too".

"You're seeing stars. Atel is right behind you".

"Don't always correct me, Yero!"

"Someone has to. It might as well be me".

"Tell her, Atel! This time she's wrong".

"Yes, she's wrong", said Atel, unexpectedly from below. "But so are you".

"Then who...?" began Yero, but her voice trailed away.

"A fairy lass", said Atel quietly. "A pixie. See? They are back".

Pairs of eyes appeared all around them. Half-imagined laughter permeated the air.

"They are curious", said Atel. "They don't get visitors often. Look at them. Let them see your eyes. It's important".

The butterflies watched with wide eyes. The lasses approached closely, sprinkling esporellia as they came. It settled on the Travelers giving them outline against the night sky. In this way, their whereabouts and kind were revealed. The pixies marveled at the butterflies and touched them softly on their faces and along the edge of their wings. Boca kept turning stubbornly away, but Yero let them do this and watched their eyes, trying to guess the location of their invisible bodies. Sometimes when the eyes were aligned against a darker patch of sky she saw, or thought she saw, shapes that flashed like silver fish turning in deep water. It was the wings she glimpsed, for fairy wings shun darkness. Light easily finds them.

Now the one named Airy took shape again, satisfied of the visitors' intentions. One by one, beginning with Lolly, the others did likewise.

"We have come to you as friends and ask your favor", said Atel. "I was here long ago. Do any remember?"

"Yes", said Airy without hesitation. "We remember thee well, Lady. Th'were in the Founding, when lasses were leaving the forests and coming up in large numbers. Thu are welcome now more than ever, and always have the Queen's favor".

"Thank you", said Atel. "You are very gracious".

The lass brightened, for they love compliments. She snapped her fingers and the Moonwalk also came out of hiding, in full, as if it had never gone away.

"We are glad to see thee", she continued. "But who are these?"

"My companions, and the main reason I am here. They have recently escaped ill-treatment by spiders. This one is Yero".

"A pretty name for a pretty girl. We are pleased to meet thee, Yero, and to offer our help. Girls must stick together whenever we can".

Atel hurried on. "The season is late for them. I'm sure you recognize their kind".

"Assuredly so. How long wilt thu be staying?"

"A little while, and then we must leave. Their journey awaits. It cannot wait overlong".

The pixies turned to the butterflies seriously. "Thy journey is well-known to us", said Airy. "Always we have aided the Rasha La and we'll help again if we can. But we cannot grant the Queen's favor to new guests. Only she can do that".

"Very well", said Atel. "I had hoped to speak with her anyway".

Airy frowned. "'Tis easier said than done these days, I must tell you. But we are getting ahead of ourselves. We've met Yero. Who is the other?"

"That's Boca", said Atel with some hesitation.

"*Boca*? An odd name for a girl. Less musical. Less delicate, if I may say so".

"With reason. He is a boy".

"A *boy*??" The pixies gasped and took three steps back, then two steps forward again.

"I should have noticed", breathed Airy. "The radiance is *opposite*".

"He's cute!" blurted Lolly.

"Bodacious!" giggled Florry.

"It's such a shame he can't stay!" complained Poo.

"Can't stay? What do you mean?" asked Atel.

"It's because of the rules", apologized Airy. "Th'are strict rules now, especially about boys".

"What about them?"

The pixies glanced nervously at each other. An awkward silence hatched. Atel let it grow, waiting for an answer. Yero ran out of patience first.

"Well?" she asked. "What *about* boys? I know they can be a pain..." (here Boca rewarded her with an elbow) ...but they aren't all *that* bad!"

"Oh, we agree!" said Airy. "Boca is welcome here on the Moonwalk always! And the Queen would welcome him, beyond doubt. 'Tis *in-between* where the trouble lies: Th'Anya are stronger than ever. *They* make the rules."

Atel tilted her beak a few degrees. "They were always trouble. What are they up to now?"

Airy rolled her eyes. "Th'rule *everything*, that's what. An' the strictest rule of all is: *No boys allowed!*"

"But you weren't worried about breaking that rule a little while ago", reminded Yero. "We did see you".

The pixies blushed and laughed.

"We are so illegal!" giggled Poo. "We break that rule all the time, out here".

"We're the criminals of the heavens", laughed Lolly, "But we can get away with it on the Moonwalk".

"That's because th'Anya don't know where it *is* anymore", explained Airy. "They abolished the Moonwalk long ago - or meant to. Th'would be a terrible punishment now if they discovered it still *here*, and us *on* it an' all".

"Why?" asked Yero. "It's pretty!"

"Thank you!" replied Airy. "But you saw *why* we like it, and *that's* the problem. D'thu see? We think there is yet some chance the boys will come one day and see it — and take a liking to the jeweled path an' all, even as we originally hoped. This happy thought d'not please th'Anya, so they outlaw it".

"Just *being* here is against the rules?"

"Big time!" laughed Airy. "But we volunteer for maintenance duty on the official road, just to get away. Then we sneak out here and have a little fun. There's no fun anywhere else. Nyo is all drudgery now".

"What's the penalty if you're caught?" asked Atel.

Airy shuddered and lost altitude. So did others. "We don't know exactly. We don't want to know. Rule-breakers sometimes disappear, an' we never see them again".

"The Queen permits this to happen?"

"The Queen is removed from us. 'Held prisoner', you might say. We cannot look to her for help".

"The Anya are cruel. I knew them well, long ago. But this is worse than I expected. Do any fairies resist these days?"

"A few, so they say, but th'rest of us live under the whip. We can't fight them. Th'Anya are big girls, understand. Many on our side are just pixies, like us. And th'Anya grow stronger: They woo the largest of us to be their apprentices. Sadly, some accept. There are rewards for so doing".

"What of the girls who still remain down on the earth? I know several and there are others. Could they help?"

Airy shrugged. "There aren't many. An' those who remain below do so mostly because th'Anya are up *here* ".

"Then go back down. Join them. Leave the Anya to themselves".

"'Tis strictly *not* permitted. Where would we go, anyway? We came up because our homes were destroyed down there".

"Make new ones. It wouldn't be the first time. There are still many beautiful places".

The pixies shook their heads sadly. "No, Lady. We cannot", replied Airy. "Or I should say: A few of us could, but th'would make the rest suffer for it. We couldn't do that to our friends".

"And the Nar? The boys? Do you get news of them? *Real* news, aside from your games?"

"We've had none at all. We hoped thu might".

"I know a few. They haven't changed one bit".

There was a collective gasp. Lolly caught her breath first.

"Th'*will*!" she said excitedly. "We're sure of it!"

"Good luck with *that*. Anything's possible, I suppose".

Airy laughed. "We know! We *do* know how difficult they are. A 'few', you say?"

Atel nodded.

"Which ones?" asked Poo.

It was the question they all wanted to ask but were afraid to. Chances were very small that one might be their own special favorite; and now the question was asked, most had second thoughts.

"Oh, Poo! D'thu want to be disappointed?" said Airy. "Let's each think they're our own. That's enough for now".

"How many, at least?" pressed Poo. "Are there many?"

"A few that I know well, and they know others", replied Atel. "They've had plenty of their own troubles, mind you. That's all I can say".

The pixies saw they would get no more out of her for now, and little did it matter. Here was news about the boys! Real news! The first good bit of hearsay in Ages. Girl talk bubbled up and kept bubbling for some time.

"What do you think of fairies now, Boca?" whispered Yero after a minute or two. "Have you changed your mind?"

"A little. These pixies seem okay. Goofy about boys maybe, but they'd never be mean to one".

"Oh, I'm proud of you! You're going to behave then?"

"Unless they try to kiss me, or stuff like that. But it's interesting how they act just like other girls".

"In what way?" Yero's guard went up.

"They gossip. Listen".

"There you go *again* and it's not true! Don't you get it? They maybe just received news about their very own boyfriends! If it's like it sounds, it must be the first news in a long, long time. That's important to girls and it should be important to boys, too!"

"Well, it's nice to learn they're up to something important, and that boys are what's important. But it's full of 'if's and 'maybe's, so that makes it gossip".

"Those words are for the boys, Boca! 'If' the boys are sociable, 'maybe' they'll be considered important".

"These boys weren't sociable at all, remember? But just listen to the girls talk about them. Oh, yeah! Boys are important up here".

Yero laughed. "Okay. I'll admit boys are important when you say 'talk', and not 'gossip'. But listen, Boca, the boys could be a lot *more* important if they came up and helped throw out those 'Onions', or whatever they call themselves".

"Maybe the boys don't know about any trouble. But you're right about those 'Onions'. They should be rooted out and some tough boys would be just the ones to do it".

"I'll admit that too—but what if they never come? That leaves only you. Is one boy enough, do you think?" Yero smiled.

"Sure. One boy to lead them all into trouble".

Yero laughed again. "That's what I'm afraid of. You should say, 'lead them into battle', or, 'lead them to war'. It would sound better".

"What I'd really like is to lead them to lunch, Yero. After going hungry so much I just can't get enough".

"I know. I feel a little bit the same way. And begging their pardon if any fairies might be listening, but this nectar up here doesn't stick to your ribs, does it? It's sweet and tasty and all that, but sort of 'thin'".

"Yeah. Not very filling. I wouldn't mind living here, but I would have to eat almost all the time".

"Then please have extra helpings", invited Airy, who had come over quietly and heard the last few words. "Thu are guests and we must keep thy tummies full! D'thu like sweet clover?"

The butterflies didn't mind at all, but Airy soon learned that a meal in progress didn't hush Yero much.

"Why do the 'Onions' have all the power?" she wanted to know.

"Th'just have it. Th'have *always* had it, except for the Queen".

"But how did it start?"

"Because th'were bigger and stronger—and especially *meaner*. And the *meaner* part has gotten worse this past Age." She sighed, and then laughed quietly. "But, 'tis spelled A-n-y-a, not O-n-i-o-n".

"But they're very strong, you said".

"Yes. *Very* strong".

"Do they make you cry?"

"Sometimes, when they are wicked".

"Onions do that when they're too strong. So that's what Boca and I will call them".

"Thu are funny, Yero, but don't let *them* hear such, or 'twill be the Dark Pits for you!"

"Oh, I doubt it. Atel would never stand for that".

"She might have to, if you get into big trouble. So, mind thy manners! Let her do the talking if you meet them".

"Okay. But why do they hate the boys? That seems silly".

"A while ago—thu would say *Ages* ago—their pride was hurt when the boys ignored them. We were all hurt, I suppose, but how do you stay mad at a boy you like? Most of us got over it pretty soon. Th'Anya never will".

"I still don't get it".

"Their vanity won't allow it. Th'keep their grudge to the bitter, bitter end".

"And they won't allow Boca now because of that old argument?"

"Exactly".

"But he's not a fairy".

"Doesn't matter. 'Boys are boys', that's what they think".

"That's sort of true. But why did they ignore you anyway, in the first place? Most boys would at least pull your hair or shove slimy frogs in your face. A lot of boys do that stuff".

"Oh yes", said Airy. "Th'*did* happen! Are all boys like that? But it irritated th'Anya, who considered themselves quite sophisticated. 'Grow up!' they scolded, and their pretty faces began to harden. 'Not yet', laughed the boys. 'There's plenty of time for that later!'" Airy sighed wistfully. "That's when we began to grow apart, and we've been apart ever since. Our romance makes a sad tale".

"Will you tell the story? We have plenty of time".

Airy glanced at the moon. "You do, maybe, but we're going to be late returning from work detail. We should be getting back".

"Oh, foo to that!" said Lolly, joining them. "We're always late so it won't make much difference". All the pixies gathered around.

"Yes!" exulted Yero. "A romantic fairy tale told by a real fairy! Pay attention, Boca. This should be good". He ignored her and occupied himself with the sweet clover nearby.

"Maybe", said Airy. "But probably not what you expect".

"That's okay. Stories are always more fun when you don't know the ending!"

"More *interesting*, let's say. But we don't know the ending either. We like to think there are chapters yet to be written, and therein lie our hopes"

"And your romance?"

"That is our hope. As to the story, 'tis best to start at th'beginning".

—The Fairy Folk—

In the Beginning, after the great works of creation, there remained the dust from those works scattered throughout the heavens. It was untidy and the Lord of Light pondered the tidying up, but for a long while the tidying was put off.

There were good reasons. The great works still demanded much attention and always will. Indeed, there was no end to His universe or to His labor, nor is there still; but He lavished many spare moments upon the green earth where He put the offspring of His thought: The Children of the Creation. In those early days the Lord was pleased with His children, who were yet few, and thought of them often while He was away. One thought only nagged at him: Had He introduced enough to populate the entire earth? Maybe not, for there was obviously a lot room to spare.

About that time, He turned reluctantly to the stardust, which really ought to be cleaned up, and a solution occurred to Him.

From the dust He brought forth the Fairy People, that myriad of winged folk who have since haunted and enchanted this world. Made as they were from leftovers, they were a sundry lot - ranging from downright ugly to stunningly beautiful. In each of them originally was a spark of good—that surely from His light which is in the dust.

When He had brought forth as many as seemed prudent, He spoke to them, revealing their origin and purpose: "Thou art the Nar and the Nara, sons and daughters of the stars, for thou art born of them and their light is in thee. But ye shall dwell on earth for a while and be named many names. Go now and dwell in the empty quarters and make those your own. But do not love the green earth overmuch, for a time will come when it seemeth crowded to thee and unpleasant. Then ye shall return to the deep heavens, to places appointed for thee, for as long as the dust shall last".

"How long might that be?" asked a bold fairy.

The Lord paused a moment. "Quite a while, I'm thinking. Unless someone unforeseen sweeps it up".

Thus, fairies appeared on earth as an afterthought and settled themselves in, and that was about the last thing fairies ever did in accordance with His wishes.

Airy paused and sighed. "That's about the last the boys ever had to do with the girls, too. Hindsight is clear but in those days we never really faced up to the truth. Not for a long time. We just said the boys were 'lost'; but the truth is we grew apart for lack of common interest. That part showed up right away".

"Boys and girls *are* different", commented Yero. "That's nothing new. But you can still be friends, can't you?"

"True. But one must see another occasionally for friendship to prosper. We rarely saw them even in the early days. It was a big new world, and we lost them right away".

***

The Butterflies, Yero and Boca

From the first, the Nara loved open woodlands with herbs and flowers and bright pools under the stars. All growing things interested them, from toadstools to towering trees. In enchanted places, often a pretty dell or glen with water, fairy lasses found homes to their liking. These were their 'ayas', the special places on earth they loved best, and they seldom strayed far from them. But always in their minds were the stars from whence they came, to which they must someday return. Thenceward toward the heavens they gazed frequently, and even today in some parts of the world they can be seen thus in moonlit meadows, if folks knew what to look for.

But the Nar were enamored of gold and earthly treasure and cast their eyes toward the streambed, the outcropping of rock, and the roots of mountains. They ignored wildflowers and morning dew, and finally the heavens.

But though their paths diverged from the start, neither side was willing to wholly abandon the other. Not for a long time. Estrangement happened only gradually.

It's true the Nar found treasure and hoarded it like misers. It was true they avoided the beautiful ayas which did not appeal to their adventurous spirit. But it was also true in early years that they fashioned jewelry and pretty ornaments for the Nara, hoping to please them and win their favor. This part has been rather overlooked by the girls.

One day the Nar came to them offering amulets of gold, gleaming in the morning sun.

"Take these for your own", they said. "Do they not gleam more brightly than buttercups in a meadow?"

But the girls demurred, for the gold was cold to touch. "These are pretty", they replied, "but we like buttercups better". Their idea of ornaments and décor ran more into the natural and stayed there.

The boys were annoyed and returned to their mines and smithies. Their hope of enticing the Nara thither was dashed, and so opportunity was lost for that time.

Yet eventually they came again to the girls, offering bracelets of silver inlaid with names against a background of silver trees.

"Take these as a token of our friendship", they said. "Do they not gleam brighter than beech-boles in the moonlight?"

But the girls spurned the bracelets, which were cold to the touch. "These are well-made", they answered. "But we like real trees better".

Thus, the rift widened. The Nar were chagrined and didn't return again.

Centuries passed since the Nar had come calling. Into the ayas a loneliness came creeping. Questions occurred to the Nara and were debated in their councils. Had they been unreasonable? Abrupt? Some said yes, some argued no. Yet over them all, like a pall, hung this: There were no fairy children, and always the population of men increased. Already there were many crowded places that fairies could not abide. Ages might yet pass, but the future was no longer in doubt. Others would overrun the earth exactly as the Lord had foretold. Then the Nara must leave regardless, their purpose ended. It seemed unlikely there could be any children later.

The Lady Yoyonneh, acclaimed Queen by then (but not by all) urged conciliation: "We're comfortable in our ayas, maybe, but I hear no rejoicing. The quiet wears on the soul. For myself, I would gladly gamble all I have for a chance at joy. What say thee? Let us seek out the Nar in our turn. I guess their hearts have hardened, but we must find a way into them before it's too late".

The girls followed her lead, but they didn't find the Nar easily, who lived now entirely underground; yet eventually they did, at the yawning mouth of the Subterraneum — vast caverns beneath the Mountains of Moor.

To this reunion the Nara brought gifts of their own: Wreaths of the Luft plant which require only fresh air and sunshine to produce endless blossoms. These they offered in hopes the living plants might awaken something in the hearts of the Nar, but it was not to be. The boys set them aside, explaining that the wreaths would die in the caverns. By now, other possibilities didn't occur to them.

"Leave them outside then", suggested Yoyonneh, "for they are rare, and we would fain see them perish. But come at whiles and look at them and think of us".

The girls left, thinking not to overstay their welcome but to return another day, and Yoyonneh urged them to find new homes in those mountains, as close to the caverns as may be, for it seemed to her that if they dwelt nearby friendship could blossom anew.

And lo! Goodwill blossomed swiftly, like the remarkable wreaths, for when the Nara returned in a fortnight the Nar awaited them, loitering in the shade of trees by the entrance. The wreaths had been placed with care on branches where sunlight would find them.

Now the boys brought forth gifts also: Delicate rings of gold set with precious gems the like of which had never been seen, for these were the tinted diamonds of Toonda, obtained at great risk from deep troll-halls while the trolls slept. The boys held them up to the sunlight.

"See now!" they said. "Do not the stones glitter more brightly than stars of an evening? These are for you".

Many of the girls might have accepted them and learned their real magic: When a girl looked through one, she beheld the boy who gave it to her—alive—on the other side. It worked the other way around too, or would have, but for the coldhearted Anya—those pompous ladies who by now formed the most dominant class.

"D'thu forget?" they lectured the boys haughtily, "The stars live truly, and we are of them. Compare us not to lifeless stones!"

"Not true", countered the Nar. "For even as He made starlight the Lord also made the earth and these mountains. Judge not His works lest ye know them well. Behold, the stones live! His light is in them". They held up the rings in the shadow of the cavern mouth. Light welled up from the stones and the shadow was removed.

But the Anya belittled them. Acrimony boiled over and the reunion failed. The girls went away and abandoned those mountains for a thousand years. They never saw the Nar again and pride is to blame for that. The last they ever heard was a disturbing rumor. The boys (so it went) had bartered their wings to the trolls for gold.

Ages went by. The time of the Elves passed. Men multiplied. Time came when the Lord called upon the Fairy Folk to leave and return to the heavens. That's when problems arose.

The Nar remained hidden, lending truth to the old rumor. Certainly, without wings, they could hardly answer the call.

But the Nara also refused it, being unwilling at the end to abandon their kin. Doubtless, Yoyonneh and the multitude of ordinary fairy lasses had their way in this, and not the Anya. So, the matter rested for many years.

Yet always Men increased, in time overspreading the better part of the earth. Many a fairy lass fled her aya before them, never to return. With no place else to go they became secretive spirits of the upper atmosphere. Children of the twilight.

For now, the Lord has relented and given to them the Night Sky nearest the earth for their own, that they might not perish utterly. Not yet. But when the last girl fairy has grown weary of the crowded earth, and their music is gone, then the Nara shall pass away forever from the world and be no more.

***

Airy ended her tale wistfully. "There it is", she said. "Now th'know more than most. Did thu ever hear of the fabled mouse 'Moustoffal' who lived on with just his eyes and his tail? 'Twas the price he paid to live beyond his time, and 'tis our fate too: We're left with only our eyes and a sad tale. We are all ghosts".

"You seem pretty lively for ghosts", said Yero. "Are you sure of that?" The pixies all laughed in good nature and crowded close with their merry faces.

"Does it matter?" asked Lolly. "If we are, 'twas not without warning. If nay, we soon shall be. You can say 'faded' or 'fading' if you like. We don't mind".

"We'll say 'fading', since you're still here".

"A good choice. And we shan't fade altogether so long as we retain clear memory of real things below, d'thu see? But we are only as real as the pictures we paint. If we begin to forget, then our pictures will grow fuzzy. Th'will lose reality, and so shall we. But th'Anya forbid returning below to refresh our memories so we gradually *do* forget, and we fade along with our artwork".

"But your Moonwalk is good! We don't know all the plants, but the ones we know look fine".

"Thank you! But th'must remember, 'twas made in the very early days when we trafficked freely up and down. To the practiced eye there are...weak spots now".

"Like the nectar?" said Boca, matter-of-factly. "It tastes as good as any, but it's not as thick as we're used to. Know what I mean?"

"It's *thin*?"

"Yeah. I'm sorry to have to say so".

"Say away, and we'll fix it! Thy recollection is fresh and thu can help us in this way! Is there anything else?" The pixies were anxious to make repairs, though very careful about it.

The Travelers busied themselves sampling all their favorite flowers, and for a while there was pleasant work to be done. It was at this point that the pixies surprised the butterflies by turning into butterflies themselves—magnificent yellow swallowtails—and joined in the nectar tasting, for (as Airy explained) they also drew sustenance from the flowers. Almost from the beginning the Nara possessed the ability to change shape—a trick the Nar never learned or cared to learn—and it is partly because of this that the girls are able to survive in Nyo where celestial flowers are common, but fruit is rare.

The taste differences proved fairly minor but Yero, and especially Boca, were fussy about the mallasha.

"It's more like *candy* now", said he, when they adjusted it.

After a lot of hemming and hawing, the pixies took something out.

"Now it's flat", said Boca.

More discussion. Finally, something else was added.

"Too sugary", said Boca.

Further adjustments ensued; then, "No fragrance"; followed by, "Too perfumy"; followed by, "Needs honey"; followed by, "Just right, but it's still too thin".

This produced consternation and prolonged discussion among the pixies.

Yero whispered, "Boca! Cool it. They're doing the best they can".

"I'm only trying to help. We *are* experts, Yero".

"Yes, but...well, what I'm trying to say is, call it *good* now! They mustn't get the idea that boys are never satisfied, see? It would ruin their romance".

"Well, that's not true. I'll be perfectly happy when they get it right".

"They *do* have it right. You even admitted it, except it's thin. And maybe that's a good thing, Boca".

"I don't know why".

"I do. That's so hungry guests don't get so fat they fall back down to earth".

Boca stopped sipping and patted his tummy happily. "Save me if I do fall", he said. "Fat boys can't fly". Then he went right back to the tasting.

In the end, the pixies were unable to thicken the nectar, which upset them very much. They changed from swallowtails back to fairies and stamped their feet and pouted with their pretty little faces.

"I'm sorry", said Boca, at Yero's prodding. "It's no big deal".

"But it *is!*" said Airy. "We're fading faster than we thought. We're losing our strength. We've been away from solid ground too long".

"You used to return at whiles to dance the Ring", said Atel. "Couldn't you sneak down for that?"

"Alas, no. We would not get away with it. We could *do* it, but th'would *know* when we checked back in. The green earth hath a fresh smell that 'stinks' to their upturned noses. We ha' learned this the hard way, long ago".

"And that is making me mad!" said Poo. She stamped her foot hard. Everyone looked at her in surprise because Poo hardly ever got mad—and then she stamped again, even harder. "It's so hopeless!" she wailed. "Th'Anya stop all our fun—and now we can't even thicken up the nectar!" Poo burst into tears.

Something changed in the pixies at that moment. They all frowned and stamped their feet, which jiggled the entire Moonwalk, which caused them to laugh, but the fierce feeling did not go away. Instead, it grew: A feeling of righteous stubbornness. Even the music, which had been in the background, joined in now with a stirring tune.

"We must *do* something!" the pixies exclaimed. "We *will* do something!"

"But what?" sobbed Poo.

"We must fight!" said Lolly, "Or soon we'll disappear forever".

"But how?" sobbed Poo.

"We'll raise the alarm!" vowed Airy. "We've got Boca now and news of the boys down below, too. That'll stir things up! But most important of all, we must reach the Queen!"

"You can come with us", offered Yero. "We're going to see her".

"Thu are *guests* here", laughed Airy, "so please accompany *us*, instead! But our paths do go together now, come what may".

"Onward!" shouted the pixies.

"To the Queen!"

Chapter 7

The Dais

'Twas a merry party that marched off down the Moonwalk, stepping lightly to a stirring tune. The music was eager and raced ahead of them, beckoning them. Rather too fast, perhaps. The pixies were no marchers. Being as light as they are, every purposeful step propelled them into the air; but this didn't interrupt their rhythm as they simply stayed in step during the big bounces and landed again smoothly some distance ahead. It looked comical to the butterflies bringing up the rear but Yero noticed something else too: When the pixies touched the firm pathway they showed up better, and when they bounced for a long way they faded again, noticeably. She studied Boca critically for a moment.

"You're like the mallasha right now", she informed him. "It's thin and weak and so is your shape".

"It is?"

"Yes. The color is going to your eyes again. The rest of you is going dark".

"Darker is richer where I come from. You could use more of that".

"It depends who you ask. Rupl didn't like my dark edges, and up here I agree. We should try to be brighter, so we don't disappear".

"Our eyes would still shine, so it's no big deal".

"Not if we're sleeping".

"Everyone will hear you snoring, Yero".

"That will just mean I'm getting my beauty rest. *You* could use more of *that*, Boca".

"Boys aren't into that stuff".

Yero laughed. "I guess not. But listen, I feel more *real* when people can see me—okay? So, let's touch the path like the pixies do and take a hop, skip, and jump. I think it'll keep us from fading".

They tried this and quickly fell way behind since their steps were so small, but they brightened exactly as Yero expected.

"You see, Boca? Touching down is important up here. It helps our complexion. We won't disappear so long as there's a firm path to walk on. I think that's what's saving the pixies".

"Maybe so. But when we go back down into daylight, darker will be better. Be careful then, Yero, or you'll disappear in the sunshine".

"Or maybe I'll just dazzle everyone like a fairy princess!"

"I'll stick close to you. If you start to disappear, I'll smear mud on your nose. Then people will say, 'See the plum? Let's squeeze it for the juice!', and they'll find you. But they won't call you a princess".

"Yuck! Maybe I do stick my nose out sometimes, but only a boy would squeeze a runny one!" Yero wiped hers irritably, whether it needed it or not.

Boca smiled proudly.

Far ahead, the pixies began to sing as they marched, and the butterflies flew to catch up. It was a rebellious little tune, and the music changed to fifes and rolling drums. The pixies were in fine fettle:

> "Th'Anya say,
> *'Do this! Do that!*
> *An' hustle up you little brat!*
> *No time for play!'*
> That's what they say.
> Well, phew to them!
> And drat!

Th'Anya say,
'No boys allowed!
No one! No way!
Be strong and proud until doomsday!'
That's what they say.
Well, *BOO!* To that old crowd!

Th'Anya say,
'You cannot go!
You cannot visit down below!
Don't disobey!'
That's what they say.
Well, *FOO!* To the old crows!

We say, *pooh-pooh!*
And *toodle-oo!*
We'll show them what small fry can do!
We'll break taboo,
And other stuff!
We've had enough!
WE'VE HAD ENOUGH!"

Yero was surprised how fierce the pixies had suddenly become until, at their loudest, fiercest moment one of them giggled at such an idea and the fierceness dissolved. They were quite an undisciplined little army and they knew it. Even the music knew it and now faded reluctantly into the background.

"It's no sense wasting our strength here anyway", reasoned Lolly. "Better to save it for later".

"Aye to that", agreed Airy. "Mustn't get too hot under the collar or we shall float away like th'pretty balloons that men send up".

"Oh, yes", teased another. "Especially Airy. She's such a windbag already".

"All the better!" laughed Airy, floating higher again in spite of herself. "So, when trouble comes at th'Dais I shall rise above the fight — perhaps even above the Curtain! — to carry news of victory to the Queen".

"Perhaps to float off into space", said another quietly. "No one can fly over the Northern Lights where the solar wind blows in. And th'Anya guard the door".

A hush fell. For all the bravado, they well knew what lay ahead. There would be trouble indeed. Most likely they would all be thrown into the Lockups or worse. The hush deepened and the pixies slowed finally to a stop. No one spoke. For long moments there was no sound at all. Then the music called to them from up ahead with chimes — or an attempt at chimes, as if it too had a fuzzy memory.

Someone, maybe Poo, took a small step forward, then another. Someone else took a step, then Airy did, and Lolly too. The butterflies watched the bravest steps ever taken in Nyo. Steps that could still be retraced but wouldn't be. Steps toward their own doom, very likely. Soon every pixie was walking again in silence.

"What will happen?" asked Yero of their guide.

"A fight", answered Atel quietly. "One they cannot win".

"Can we help?"

"We had better try. We stirred this up".

The silence stretched on and on, but not the trees. They came to a last grove of burr oaks with wide sweeping limbs where the path twisted through the crowded trunks. It was far too narrow (thought

Yero) for paunchy boys to squeeze through, should they ever come this way, but when she mentioned it to Boca he pointed to a weedy, neglected detour. The pixies had provided for such a possibility. Almost hidden under tall grass off to one side was a bypass and a sign: 'Pudgy Path'.

After the burr oaks, all trees diminished into smaller varieties and scrub. Here were staghorn sumac, plum, and hawthorns, along with sweetshrubs, hazel, and berry brambles unfamiliar to the butterflies. These gave way in turn to blue-stemmed grasses and prairie flowers. There were purple coneflowers, minty bee balm, patches of goldenrod, and lots of blue sage, quite fragrant for this late date. Boca would have loitered at the sage bushes but there wasn't time. The moon would soon wane, and the pixies were anxious to reach something—some *place*—just ahead, while it was still bright.

They approached a hillock clothed in short grasses, now grown out into lacy seed-heads in late autumn. On top of the hillock, surrounded by a low rock wall was a courtyard. On either side of the entrance were short pillars of stone scarcely higher than the wall. Brass lamps were set atop the pillars, shuttered so their light was cast down onto the walk. As they entered the courtyard, Yero saw an identical entrance across the way (or exit, if it came to that) and still another to her right—that one built in grand style with a colonnade and enclosed archway.

But the pixies broke gleefully toward a roofed cistern in the center of the courtyard. Off they raced across a lawn of white clover and crowded around it, kneeling on the flat stone rim and peering down inside. Atel joined them. Airy politely gave her own space to another and turned to the butterflies.

"Come with me", she said. "Let's have a look out the other gate, where the North Loop enters". As she allowed herself to rise to their level, she explained that the Moonwalk formed a great curve in the night sky. They had arrived on the South Loop, but further out the Moonwalk bent northward to return at higher latitude to this same place. "Like a lasso to catch the boys", she smiled. "That's what we used to say. In those days another Walk led off through the Grand Arch toward the Aurora and our city beyond, but we destroyed that part ourselves, to keep th'Anya away from this".

The North entrance looked just like the South, maybe, but the lamps lit up a far different picture. It was snowing outside and piling up, already covering the Walk several inches deep and turning the hillock white on that side, but no flakes came through the entrance yet. Visibility was poor but Boca thought he could see drifts across the path not far out.

"D'thu see?" said Airy. "Already it's winter here. Th'wouldn't be very nice for butterflies".

Yero gawked. Boca alighted next to the lamp.

"Sit here, Yero", he said. "It's warm and we can watch it snow with no worries".

"Safe for *now*", cautioned Airy. "But in a few days th'first snows will blow in and come to the South Walk too. Th'will soon be deep where we just entered. Then we come here seldom until next spring. Thu were taking a big chance at this late date".

"Oh, we weren't worried", replied Yero bravely. "Atel would never guide us into trouble we couldn't get out of. We just came through a big snowstorm down below".

"Yes? Thu are doubly lucky then. The Lady Aleta can do much. We are glad to see her. It gives us hope".

"The Lady *who?*"

"Aleta. Whom you know as Atel. Did you not know she was once a fairy?"

"No. I guess that was before we met her".

"Yes. Long before. She was one of the first in Nyo, one of the founding sisters, and her beauty matched even the Queen's. All the founders were murdered or exiled when th'Anya took over. But hummingbird or fairy, Aleta's radiance is still the same. She is very radiant".

"Can she change? Like you changed into swallowtails?"

Airy frowned. "I don't think so. We change all the time to dine, or just for fun, but always to butterflies and back again. She is...different now. I don't think so".

The sound of laughter interrupted them from the direction of the cistern. "Come", said Airy. "Th'must see this!"

Boca frowned, suspicious. "You go", he told Yero. "You're a girl. You like that stuff. I'm staying here".

It was a wishing well and the pixies, forgetting their cares for a moment, were making wishes. Taking turns, they rubbed cloverleaves in their fingers, closing their eyes to make a wish. Just now, a pretty green-eyed pixie named Fetchfern was opening her eyes to see if her wish would come true. Yero fluttered lower for a better look. There was water in the well and its reflection in the moonlight was just changing. A picture emerged of rocks and trees. Sitting in the shade, leaning back against a trunk was a boy fairy, a little fuzzy like the others had been, sleeping and snoring with his mouth open. A fat spider had just begun to spin a web from the curly hair on the boy's head down to his curly beard and was encountering difficulty. The first strand of webbing had been easy to play out when the spider had jumped downhill to the beard. Now the spider was attempting to climb back up the 'rope' to make another jump. But each time he got halfway the boy snored with gusto, knocking spiderman off balance to almost fall onto the boy's tongue, which stuck out after each snore to make licking motions. The pixies loved that part and enjoyed one more close call before Atel intervened.

"You'd better hurry", she warned. "The moon is going down".

"Yes! Save him, Fetch!" urged someone. "The poor spider, I mean".

More laughter. Then Fetchfern tossed one cloverleaf into the well. 'Plink'. It hit the water with a musical sound that startled the little spider and he did fall onto the tip of Tobin's tongue (for that was the boy's name), awakening Tobin who spat him out and looked around, sensing more trouble. He would not be disappointed. The hair on his neck stood up and he looked up instinctively to see who was watching. That's when 'Fetch' dropped the other leaves. 'Plink-itty-plink...Wee-ooo!' A wolf whistle arose from below, as if from Tobin. It was great fun for everyone but him. He promptly scuttled into a hole in the ground.

Atel groaned. "You're making things worse, not better, if they *are* alive somewhere".

"If they *are*, at least th'haven't started eating spiders", said someone else.

The pixies all laughed, except Fetchfern. "They're all we have", she said wistfully. "Our wishy-washy boyfriends".

"I wish they *would* wash", said Flossie honestly.

"They will!" promised Lolly. "Th'will change after we marry them! I'm *sure* th'will!"

"Just be careful what you wish here", cautioned Atel. "Remember, this of all the Moonwalk is the Queen's own handiwork. But quickly—if you're going to do it, do it now!"

Yero wondered what 'it' meant. She doubted it had anything to do with soap. The mood turned fierce again unexpectedly. Everyone looked up. Above the old windlass and wooden bucket, hanging motionless from the rafters, were chimes and a gong wrapped in cloth. Airy floated up and began to unwrap them. As each slipcover came off, the silver chime underneath became restless. When the last of six was uncovered, she gave the gong a little twirl and a music was re-born that had bided its time since the Founding. Round and round went the gong, bouncing eagerly from one chime to the next, and for all the harps in Nyo the music was the sweetest ever heard in that place. Long had it waited to announce the arrival of the boys (for that was its purpose) and it exaggerated now, but no matter. The pixies were serious about raising a revolt against the Anya. It started with this.

When enough music had collected in the courtyard, it moved quickly off through the archway and disappeared into the night sky. Boca, exploring the archway on his own, looked up in surprise.

"We've done it now", said Lolly, speaking for everyone, and they moved off toward the archway following the chimes. Passing through, Atel paused a moment to look back. Most of the archway and colonnade to their right was overgrown by a venerable Moonseed vine.

"Behold", she said to the butterflies, "The history of Nyo in the living plant. Here are the names of all who came before".

There were many. The old vine had described them in the twists and curls of its natural growth with larger writing closest to the massive stem and roots.

The pixies gathered round. Airy parted loops of drooping vine and pointed to the first name, gnarly and encrusted, that had once sprouted forth: 'Yoyonneh'. From there the vine branched three ways, naming 'Aleta', 'Hydia', and 'Lorelei'.

"The Three", said Airy.

In answer (or no answer), Atel zipped suddenly to the top of the arch where a small movement caught her eye. "See?" she said. "It is vigilant still."

Even as they watched, new growth appeared—first a small shoot, then a leaf, then another, and finally a runner growing at about the speed of a deliberate calligrapher wrote: 'Yero of the Rasha La'. Yero was thrilled and clapped her hands. The pixies laughed and clapped with her.

"See? The name is larger than the girl", pointed out Lolly.

"But more silent", said another.

"Much more silent", laughed still another. "D'thu think it has the right girl?"

"At least your watering hasn't been for nothing", said Yero graciously, spotting an old sprinkler can set neatly by the arch.

Boca had wandered off, bored by girl talk, to the other side of the archway, there to poke around an old stump that had once sprouted but withered. Naturally, he found a boy thing.

"Look!" he shouted. "A bug! There's a bug in here".

The scaly bark flaked off as the bug uncovered itself to reveal—not a bug after all, but a green shoot. It advanced eagerly, produced one big leaf, and scrawled: 'Boca of the Rasha La, first of boys'. The penmanship was messy but legible. Everyone clapped and there were hoots and hollers. Boca grinned and waved, and Yero even admitted later that it seemed like a pretty big deal; but as they took heart in this good omen the moon went down and the Moonwalk with it. The vine did not disappear, nor the Wishing Well, but the archway dimmed. Yero looked back and all that remained of the lawn were the clover blossoms—or were they just the stars? It was hard to tell at a glance, and that's all she got.

"Oh no!" said Poo. "We're late! Th'will punish us!"

"'Twill be worse than that, Poo", said someone quietly. "Let us hope everyone hears the chimes".

Away they all flew into an empty sky, steering now toward the Northern Lights in the distance, and the butterflies had their guide to themselves for a while.

"You never told us you were so important", said Yero.

"No. Because I'm not".

But Airy said you were, and your fairy name is right next to the Queen's".

"So that makes me special?"

"Sure. It's a big deal, isn't it?"

"No. Nor does the Queen consider herself 'special'. That's for such as the Anya, who think only of themselves. It's not my way, nor should it be yours".

"But I'll bet there isn't another 'Aleta' up here—or 'Atel' the hummingbird either".

"True, but only because each fairy has their own unique name. I suppose we're all special that way". She recited:

> "I feel I'm no one special,
> Though I'm the only one I've got,
> So, I guess that makes me special—
> Even though I'm sure I'm not!"

Yero laughed. "I like that. Did you make it up?"

"No. But it's a good reminder to be humble".

"But we *are* each special that way. There's no one else like us".

"Don't dwell on it".

"But we can say *you're* special because you help us, can't we? That makes you special to us".

"That makes us friends. Friends help each other out of friendship. That's another difference between us and *them*".

"But if we spend *all* our time helping others..."

"Enough, please! There is something up ahead that I have no memory of".

The pixies were debating something. They had come to another pathway, of sorts.

"The 'Official Road', if you please", said Airy, gesturing with disgust. "'Tis their Big Project, but we do all the work. Th'Anya, who do not fly, hope in this way to discover what remains of the Moonwalk and destroy it forever". She smiled. "We ha' told them many times that th'Moonwalk is gone, but they suspect we lie".

"We're not trusted", grinned Lolly, and went into a pantomime. She cast an arm over her head like a hood and waved vaguely at the sky. "We know it's still out there somewhere!" she scolded. "We know the small fry have been untruthful! We *know!*"

The pixies enjoyed it, but it usually wasn't any laughing matter. The Anya recruited an apprentice now and then, with flattery and bribes. From them they learned the fresh gossip, and no few 'small fry' had gone to the Lockups for truths, half-truths, and prattle tattled by a 'turncoat'.

Thus, rumors persisted about the Moonwalk, and hence the blacktop road begun many years earlier but progressing very, very slowly. The material was similar to asphalt, dark and not easy to follow in the night sky without a moon. The Anya, clever ones, had devised a way of collecting the buoyant smog and oily soot that drifted up from below and used it—not esporellia—as the building material for their dirty empire. How they gummed it together and retained the buoyancy was their secret, but the pixies suspected that a lot of pure esporellia was robbed from the beauty of Nyo and mixed with the gook. Where they found the heat to do this was their secret too; but the stuff was mined or collected somewhere and the Anya themselves escorted steaming shipments of it to the outpost at the Aurora—the 'Curtain', as it was called. From there, small fry were sent out with wheelbarrows to do the actual work. An apprentice was sometimes sent along to act important, and the Anya themselves occasionally ventured out a way to inspect, but not often, and never under a full moon because they aren't fond of the light.

The problem just now for the pixies was the wheelbarrows, parked here where they had left them earlier.

"Th'will be angry if we don't bring them back", worried Poo.

"Th'will be angry anyway", said Lolly.

"But it might help a *little*".

"When they find out what we're up to, th'won't care about wheelbarrows", said Florrie. "They'll wring our necks!"

"That they will", agreed Airy. "And anyhow Poo, pushing these things all the way back will make us later still".

It was decided to dump the still-warm gook over the edge, as usual, and also to let the air out of the tires. That put them all in a better mood.

"I hope no one is underneath when that lands", whistled Yero.

"Oh, it never does", assured Airy. "It's not packed, so it scatters into the air". She turned serious. "It'll be collected anew one day and end up in th'wheelbarrows again if we fail in our purpose now. Th'work parties will be much larger if we *do* fail, an' th'*will* find the courtyard. All will be destroyed".

Nothing more was said or needed to be, and no one walked on the tacky road. For a long way there was nothing to break the monotony of the blacktop—not even a dirty gravel shoulder—unless it was the dreary mile-markers, and they hurried past those because of the crows, ugly tar sculptures set atop the posts like gargoyles. It seemed to Yero when she peeked at them that the eyes shifted and followed, but she said nothing.

The Butterflies, Yero and Boca

Ahead, things began to look more promising. The great Aurora drew ever closer. Yero marveled at the sight. At the far ends, left and right, danced shapes of pink, constantly fading and re-inventing themselves, but always pink. In between the pinks hung a great tapestry, a flowing green Curtain looming very large now, as the road drew near. Yero could see the folds billowing gracefully in a teasing, rippling motion. The Curtain was shut, yet the road made straight for the center as if expecting it to part at the last moment.

When they drew nearer, however, they saw that the road didn't lead directly to the Curtain but to an imposing natural bluff in front of it and appeared to end in a cul-de-sac where a tall stump reared up in the middle. From there a short walkway led across a gap to steps going up to an overlook—a Dais—or possibly to a smaller shelf below. Yero couldn't be sure. On the Dais itself, black specks stood out.

"There's more crows", she whispered to Boca. "Unless it's those Onions".

"I almost hope it is Onions", he replied. "I don't like the crows at all. They've been watching us".

"Creepy, aren't they? I don't know where they flew in from, but we don't want to go there".

"Th'Anya set them out", said Airy, overhearing. "Th'can't fly, but th'*caw* to each other and tell tattle-tales on us when we shirk, so the Big Shots can be lazy and sit in th'chairs back here, an' still oversee the roadbuilding. Or so th'*think*". Humor flitted across Airy's face but disappeared again almost as quickly. "They don't make anything pretty, th'Anya—just ugly structures, an' creepy stuff like th'crows. That's what they like. See now th'masterpiece: 'Gorda the Great'".

The 'stump' in the cul-de-sac came into closer focus. It was, or soon would be, a large gook sculpture: A hooded figure in flowing black robes rising up thirty feet or more. Threatening arms extended towards them—toward any who approached on the road—palms out in the universal sign: 'Stop! Do not pass!' Pixies labored there under the watchful eye of a tall fairy in similar robes, but with hood thrown back revealing a pretty face and short, dark hair.

"'Nasha the nitpicker'", warned Airy. "Get ready for it".

"An Onion?" asked Yero.

"An apprentice. Right now, she's just a know-it-all. We used to be friends".

Nasha saw them from a distance and waited with a scowl that looked wrong on such a pretty face, until she spoke. Then the scowl fit much better.

"So! The little ones return at last, an hour late and three wheelbarrows short. What say thee, brats?"

"Th'wheelbarrows broke down an' all", shrugged Airy. "Flat tires".

"On all *three*?"

"Sure. Go look for yourself. You load them too heavy".

"Smarty britches! You'll pay for that".

"We always pay anyway, Nasha".

Nasha drew herself up as tall and menacing as a pretty girl could. "Thu are forgetting with whom th'speak! 'Tis *Sister* Nasha to you now. Remember that!"

"It's hard not to. Th'were our friend, once".

"No more!" Nasha was getting the hang of the 'ugly' part. "But if th'*would* be my friend just shape up and follow the rules! Because now it's trouble for me an' I must report everything to the Big Sisters. Let's see th'hands!"

Out of habit, the pixies turned palms up for inspection. Nasha spat in disgust.

"Not much work, did thee? Thu ought to work harder—like Glinterglow here!" She laughed over her shoulder at the pixies laboring on the statue. The smallest and dirtiest of them shot Nasha a look but said nothing.

"But surely we have a more pressing issue", continued Nasha. "D'thu expect to smuggle trespassers by me? Who are the tag-a-longs? Bring forth the urchins and ankle-biters!" Nasha had spied Atel and Yero from a distance but hadn't known what to do about them. She still wasn't sure but dared not hesitate any longer.

Atel who was most visible came forward, followed by Yero who had faded again except for her eyes. Boca shut his eyes and was overlooked for the moment.

"Urchins?" said Atel. "Tsk, tsk. Courtesy here is a lot less than it once was".

"Courtesy can wait. Not I. Name th'selves!"

"Certainly. I am Atel. Are weary travelers unwelcome then?"

"We shall see. Big Sisters will decide that". Nasha relaxed a bit, having thus managed to pass the buck off to her seniors. But the hummingbird unnerved her. She was more than she seemed although Nasha couldn't put her finger on it. She was less worried about the other, probably a butterfly, though it was hard to tell. She reached up for esporellia. A little came to her hand, but not much. That trick had become trickier since she had donned the black robe! However, the little should suffice. She advanced, sprinkling it as she came. It went right to Yero, settling on her wings, confirming her outline.

"And who is this?"

"My companion. Her name is Yero. I'm sure you recognize her kind".

"I do", said Nasha more quietly. "I will indulge her for my part". (Here Nasha bit her tongue for being 'soft'.) "Come along then, if th'have no sly purpose — or turn back now! Tis still thy choice".

"We're going that way anyway", shrugged Atel. "We'll go with you".

"Th'will be questions!" blustered Nasha, struggling to stay in control. "Hard labor awaits any who lie!" She reached up again and attracted enough esporellia to brighten Yero a little more, but a small amount found Boca who was thus exposed. Nasha took a step back, startled.

"What is this?" she demanded. "A stowaway? Are there others?"

"No others. That is Boca, also of the Rasha La. A boy".

Nasha backed several more steps, saying nothing. The pixies giggled. Nasha blushed and ran.

"That was bad", said Yero. "Girls don't like to be surprised like that. Now there'll be trouble".

"There was going to be trouble anyway", grumbled Boca.

"He is right", said Atel. "The statue tells us that much. There is no welcome here for any visitors".

There was a stir on the High Dais as Nasha reported up to her seniors from the shelf below. The black spots Yero had seen from a distance were figures exactly like the huge statue, but life-size. A dozen of them arose from recliners and easy chairs to cluster near the top of the stair. Together like that, with flowing black robes, they reminded her of stuff pouring out the back end of a dump truck. Then her attention turned to the statue close at hand, to several pixies peeking out from behind it. The one named Glinterglow had a smudged nose and was very dirty, but they were all smudged badly with the gook. Airy and the others were calling to them, telling about the Moonseed vines and the chimes, and teasing 'Glinter' about her nose.

"They always put you here", said Lolly, "though I can't imagine why. Thu are no good at mud sculpture".

"If only it *was* mud", said Glinter, "I could wash it off. They put me here because of my name. Th'find it amusing". She came out from behind the sculpture to some 'ooh's (but no 'ahh's) and stood there for all to see, a little muckamuffin.

"We rang the chimes", Airy was saying. "Did you hear the music?"

"So, it *was* you!" whispered Glinter. "Oh, yes! The music came right by and circled us twice. It scared the dickens out of Nasha. Then it went straight to th'Dais and th'was a hullaballoo! Afterward, everyone sat down an' pretended nothing happened — until you came. Be careful! Th'have cooked up a nasty surprise, we think".

"Why not come with us? We could use the help".

"I don't know, Airy. Working here under th'whips and all, an' them staring down at us...well, we feel th'whips a lot. We're scared".

"Can't blame you for that. But we're going on. Something feels good about this, Glinter. We've got help. We may have a trick or two they won't expect". She nodded toward Atel, who was lost in thought, studying the Dais.

Hope flickered in Glinter's eyes for a brief moment, until a loud wail from the Dais sobered her up. "*Th'Chorus!*" she whispered, folding a dirty wing over her eyes. "The second time today! Oh me!"

Nasha returned with another, a much less pretty apprentice: A loner in the Anya ranks. Once in another Age she had a beautiful singing voice reminiscent of the Whip-poor-will, but she had turned bitter and remained an apprentice with no further ambition except a wicked urge to use her whip. Now they called her the 'Whipper-will' and let her do their dirty work. Her eyes reflected red in the starlight as Nasha gave the word. Everyone was to approach the Dais immediately—but *not* the smudge-fairies who had been consorting with felons. They would stay. The Whipper-will loosened her leather to punish them.

Atel said something to Airy, who summoned a shower of esporellia. As the 'Whipper' drew a practiced backstroke, Atel drew the light to her breast and reflected it harshly into the mean red eyes. The ugly one yelled in pain and dropped her weapon, clutching at her face. Nasha, bewildered, covered her own eyes. Glinter blinked, not yet believing she was spared. The Whipper staggered and sat down. Up on the Dais, the Chorus changed to a lower note. Nasha risked a peep.

"Lead on", Atel ordered her. "Bring the whip".

Nasha bent to fetch it, flinched from it twice, and then picked it up with one finger and her thumb, looking like a fool.

"Don't worry, I won't hurt you", said Atel. "It's obvious you don't know how to use that thing". (Muffled laughter). Atel gave the pixies a stern look, and a last glance at the 'Whipper' who looked harmless enough, rocking back and forth with her head in her hands.

Excepting only the hummingbird and Nasha, it was quite a confident party that approached the Dais. Nasha signaled to stop at the walkway and climbed up alone to the small landing a few steps below the Dais where she knelt down. The 'Chorus of the Crows' (as the small fry called it) diminished to a single voice and then other voices rejoined it. Something was decided quickly. Nasha motioned for all to come up.

The small landing was designed like a place of worship. There were no pews, but there were kneelers. Looming above and leaning over the edge of the Dais were the Anya, black hoods pulled way forward so nothing but shadow was visible beneath.

In practice, it was supposed to work like this: Small fry knelt and began a ritual chanting that would eventually lead to an audience with the Great Ones. Or it might not. All depended on the attitude of 'prayer' and the tone of supplication. The Great Ones didn't recognize just anyone. They liked to be toadied up to. It made them purr.

They purred now, or hummed softly, out of habit. Nasha, still holding the whip between thumb and forefinger, motioned everyone to kneel. No one did. Fear crossed her face. Atel rose up to an even level with the Chorus with Yero and Boca tagging behind. The humming dropped almost below the range of hearing and the Chorus spoke in a forbidding baritone voice.

"Kneel, wanderers! You have wandered into our domain now!"

"I would kneel before the Queen if she asked, but no other", answered Atel.

In reply the humming dropped even further in tone, coming more from the bottom of the Chorus than the top, producing a vibration in the stone (for stone it was), loosening pieces that tumbled down among the pixies. Worse, the light on their wings began to be drawn to the black robes and swallowed up. They went pale, then dimmed.

Yero expected the pixies to do something, but they didn't. Then she saw her own light drawn away toward the robes, and Boca's as well. She bent her will to stem the flow and discovered that she could, barely.

Part 2: Beyond the Moonwalk

The Chorus was less than pleased with its composition. It had put down insolence before on occasion. The pixies were no match for it at all. But the wanderers were different, more obstinate. There was a light in the butterflies that did not easily come away, and the bird was very difficult. Just now as the pixies were darkening up nicely the bird played a dirty trick, drawing light from the Aurora and giving it to the brats, reversing the nice progression. The Chorus lowered its tone still more. The robes billowed out, soaking up light greedily, but the mirror of Atel kept the landing well lit.

Now the Chorus made its greatest effort. The steps trembled and split. Stone shards flew dangerously. But the light could not be put out. The Aurora has a life of its own. It was here long before the Anya. The humming stopped suddenly, and the Chorus spoke in a low voice to the trembling Nasha. She turned to the others.

"They are satisfied", she said in awe. "Thu are permitted to come up". She herself did so immediately, taking a long step up the cracked stair. Everyone else took wing.

The Chorus broke up. The hooded ones melted back to stand on either side of the road, which resumed at the top of the steps going toward the Curtain. Altogether, the blufftop was much larger than Yero expected — a good-sized meadow, all grown up in browning meadow grass except the blacktop road. Off to the right some distance was a black stone building or barracks from which more Big Sisters now emerged. Thataway, the grass was beaten into the dirt. To the left was a more open space and a large cistern — plainly the source of water for the garrison judging by a trodden path and a huge Anya who sat on the stone parapet of the cistern drinking out of a bucket with a dipper. This thirsty one was Gorda, Boss of the Dais. Now she thrust the empty bucket at an apprentice for a refill and the old rope crank was put to use. Now she deigned to notice the troublemakers and motioned to them.

"You thirsty?" she boomed. "Everyone's thirsty! Come, we're not uncivilized here".

For the pixies, the cistern was a usual stop on the way to their smaller barracks after work detail, but today they hesitated. Not so the Big Sisters who promptly queued up around the far side, jostling roughly for position and joking about it. The apprentice became fully occupied with them and Nasha was ordered to ladle out cupfuls to the pixies, who approached now because of the novelty. Nasha? Serving *them*? It was too delicious to pass up. Oddly, she didn't seem to mind and even offered refills. A small bowl was set out for Atel and the butterflies, but they stayed up out of reach. This didn't seem to bother Gorda at all.

"So, what's your business, exactly?" she asked Atel. "I didn't catch that part".

"My companions were in need of the stardust", answered the hummingbird. "In dire need. Would you deny them?"

"Of course not, of course not! As I said, we're not uncivilized. So! That's why you are in Nyo. But why have you come *here*, to our poor outpost — and in cahoots with our small fry?"

"As to the pixies, it was a chance meeting and a happy one. I would not see them punished for this. As to the other, I hope to see the Queen and ask favor for my companions. Where is she?"

"Well, now. Her Highness is difficult to approach these days. Perhaps I could send word..."

"No. We wish to see her personally".

"If only it were that simple!" mused Gorda. "But she has isolated herself. She sees no one".

"I don't believe it".

"Oh, it's true! Ask anyone. Ask the small fry if you wish. No one sees her anymore".

"We can't see her because of th —," said Airy before Nasha shoved a cup in her mouth. A few drops spilled, landing at her feet with little tinkles.

"Because of the 'water' she was about to say", finished Gorda. "The small fry can't handle the boats, and that's how we travel now inside the Curtain where the river flows. Didn't they mention? There are rules now. Everyone checks their wings here, and so there is order within where there wasn't any before. Quite a lot of improvements have been made, actually. We have fine artwork too. You may have noticed". She gestured grandly to her sculpture, below.

"But come!" Gorda went on. "Drink up! Surely you have a thirst after that unfortunate business a moment ago? The Sisters sure worked up some".

Gorda laughed—a big belly laugh—and called for another round for everyone, herself included. The Sisters all thought this very amusing. They cranked up their own buckets now, freeing the other apprentice to help serve the pixies—who seemed about to speak but got cups pushed in their mouths instead. More drops spilled with little tinkles.

"Is there much left?" Gorda called over her shoulder.

"A bucket or two", came the answer, along with hilarious laughter. Then things happened quickly. As Gorda turned to the front again her robe billowed out, tripping Nasha who spilled an entire cup on the ground. The splashing sound gave way to the music of free chimes leaping up from the spill.

"The chimes!" shouted Lolly. "Th'drownded 'em in the well! We've been drinking them up!"

Boca chose that moment to look into the well and Gorda grabbed for him as he fluttered past. She missed, lost her balance, and fell in with a horrible shriek, hitting what water was left with her oversized backside. More than a couple buckets splashed up out, onto everyone and everything. The Big Sisters dabbed at the ground with their robes to soak it up, but it was too late. The music had escaped. *Chimes, chimes, chimes* filled the air with a sweet sound and drifted off toward the Curtain. Guards were posted there, where it was tied, but it didn't matter. The music sailed right through, right past them, because it had no body. The pixies cheered, and then were heard no more. Black robes curled around them and dragged them inside with their nice Big Sisters. Atel drew bright light from the Curtain, but the Anya laughed at her behind their deep hoods where light couldn't find them.

A bit of a stalemate ensued while some of the largest Sisters worked at getting Gorda out of the cistern. The rope broke twice, and more rope was fetched. All the while Gorda hollered and cussed. Atel moved the butterflies away some distance, but they still heard every word.

"What is she saying?" asked Yero. "Is it orders?"

"Yes. She is upset", explained Atel. "She wishes them to hurry".

"And they sure do, don't they? But I don't understand half of the words".

"Nothing wrong with that. Ignorance can be a virtue".

"But I do understand *some* of them".

"Well, at least you know it's the language of bad people".

"But Boca knows some that I don't".

"Well, that's not enough to make him bad, Yero".

Her face lit up. "Then *use* the words, Boca", she whispered. "Give them orders to let our friends loose!"

At that moment the rope broke again but they had hold of Gorda and rolled her out, sputtering. Boca was thus spared a small dilemma, but none of them from the much larger one.

Gorda glared. "Stay up there as long as you want", she fumed at the Travelers. "We have plenty to chew on while we wait, if you get my meaning!" As if to underscore this, muffled cries came from under the black robes. Boca did use a cuss word then, but the Sisters laughed at him.

"Come down! Come down!" they called. "We'll let you in with your friends!"

"We'll see about that", said Atel under her breath, and drew more of the Aurora to herself, reflecting it in a narrow beam. She turned slowly until the beam found a black robe. In a few moments the robe smoldered where the beam touched it and burst into a small flame. It was Gorda's robe, and she didn't notice until a hole opened up and she smelled smoke. She expelled more bad words then, and lesser Anya rushed to put out the flame, but it was a stubborn little fire. Some ran for water, but of course the rope was broken and the bucket down at the bottom. Meanwhile Atel shifted her beam to another robe, and then another. Lolly and another pixie clambered out the holes.

"Now *that* one!" said Yero, pointing. "I think she's got Airy!"

Atel obliged, but amid the confusion a voice suddenly bellowed, "To the Guardhouse!"

It was a comical race. Their robes flowed well out around the Sisters and trailed unfortunately behind so that the whole mob constantly stepped on each other's train causing tripping and falling, and thereby more pixies escaped including Airy. Now it was the butterflies' turn to laugh.

"Come up, come up!" they called. "Or can't you fly?"

One Sister shook a fist at them and promptly stepped on someone else's robe. That Sister jerked loose, pulling the angry one's feet out from under right near the doorway. There was a scramble to get inside and two more pixies slipped out of the melee. One was Flossie. Wisps of smoke wafted out the door for several minutes.

"Wow", said Lolly, and fell to shivering. Six out of twelve had escaped and all were shivering.

"What happened?" asked Atel.

"Cold", said Lolly. "Bitter cold".

"*Pinching* cold!" said another.

"*Biting* cold!" said Flossie and showed marks. Blood had been drawn. None of them would say any more.

At length, Gorda's voice came from the shadow of the doorway, addressing Atel and speaking callously of the prisoners she held and her plans for them. "You and your butterflies can still scram with no hard feelings", she growled, "But I want your small fry. They belong to this Post!"

Atel hesitated. Boca whispered something that made her smile. "Yes", she agreed quietly. "Let's see how vain our hostess is!" She flew off and came back a few minutes later, together with Glinterglow and the smudge fairies. Soon a plume of smoke arose from below, where the big statue would be, and drifted across to the Guardhouse. "Now we'll bargain", predicted Atel.

Shortly several Anya emerged to investigate, seeming more worried about their own robes than the origin of the smoke, but there was no danger of that. Atel let them go. When they started shouting about the statue up in flames, however, things got lively really quick.

"Look!" said Yero. "The sack race is on again".

She was surprised how many Big Sisters came piling out to save the sculpture. Even the Curtain guards ran to help. Then Gorda's voice came again from the barracks and chased the good feeling away.

"Clever girl. Very clever! But Gorda is babysitting now!" A sharp cry came from within, then another. "Oh, clumsy me!" Gorda continued, "I must be poking the brats with the diaper pins—but they struggle so! Tsk, tsk. Can't be helped, I'm afraid. What say you now, clever bird?"

"That a woman's work is never done", replied Atel. She went back to the top of the broken stairway and surveyed the hysteria below. The Anya were crowded around the statue, trying to smother the fire with their robes. Sometimes it helped; sometimes it just fanned the flames. They were so preoccupied they didn't notice the hummingbird setting fire to the short walkway below the stair, cutting off their retreat.

"Gorda!" she called upon her return. "I have given your girls more work. The walk is afire behind them now. Perhaps they can fly back? Or perhaps not. What say thee?"

Regrettably, Gorda had a little temper then, or more likely it was calculated, but pixies suffered for this. Fresh cries pierced the air. After a decent interval Gorda spoke, ready to bargain.

"I know who you are—or *were*! What do you really want?"

"The pixies, unhurt, and the Queen's favor for my young friends, as I have said".

"It's a little late for that first part. What'll you give up for the brats?"

"We'll leave and follow the chimes. You'll be rid of us".

"For all the good it'll do you!"

"It might. By now, the music has reached the city. Things may turn against your kind very quickly."

Gorda laughed another belly laugh. "Ah, me!" she sniggered. "It's long indeed since we threw you out, isn't it? Things have changed up here! Where once there was a city there is now a swamp and a few miserable swamp rats. Your precious chimes will drown again and *stay* drowned this time!"

"I don't believe it".

"Oh, I speak true. Quite true. Ask the brats".

Lolly shrugged helplessly, nodding her head. Gorda chuckled away.

"So! They hadn't told you everything? That's been a problem for me too. They simply can't be trusted! But one so clever must have foreseen that". She paused long enough to cause a few more wails of anguish. Gorda was on a roll and knew how to keep it going.

"There's also the matter of the wings, as I mentioned earlier", she went on, as the wails began to subside. "Rules are: Everyone checks their wings. You will too".

This was rather a shock to the butterflies but not to their guide. Fairies can take off their wings of course, and often do, to brush and groom them. It was the truth behind the old rumor about the boys trading theirs for gold. Of course, hummingbirds can't, nor can butterflies.

"Don't be silly", said Atel.

"I'm not. It's the rules. But you don't have to believe poor Gorda. We'll ask the small fry. Here! Talk to them, brat!"

A big, gloved hand reached out, dangling a pixie by the hair. It was Poo, and it was hard to look at her. Sores covered her face. Poo was not up to talking, which Gorda found amusing. "Eh? Something got your tongue, brat? Dear me! Another safety pin maybe. Tsk!" Poo was jerked back inside.

"Well?" taunted Gorda. "The wings are a problem, I suppose. Can't take 'em off anymore? Ho-ho! I won't even ask what happened. It's quite a comedown from the Big Shot you were to just an itty-bitty bird! But that's the deal: The brats check their wings, as always. I'll have it no other way; but I'm at a loss what to do about you and your flutterbugs." There was another pause. Poo screamed somewhere inside the barracks. Gorda chuckled.

"We'll sit in the boats", said Atel.

"What assurance do you give?"

"I have only my word".

"That's nothing!" sneered Gorda. "What else?"

A howl went up just then, down below. The firefighters had saved Gorda's statue only to turn around and discover a wall of flames separating them from home.

"The more I think about it, we can do business", said Gorda quickly. "But someone must *escort* you. I can't come, naturally, and I'm short-handed just now...Hmm, let's see..." (Moments later Nasha got the heave-ho out the door.) "*She* will be in charge and I will send a pet crow..." (The glove reached out and plopped a sticky crow into Nasha's hands. It squawked) ..."and bird and butterflies will be chained to the crow..." (Lengths of fine chain flew out the door and wrapped around Nasha's arm like bolas. The crow settled down, looking pleased.) ..."and that's my final offer. Take it or leave it".

"I'll leave it. We'll sit, but only voluntarily".

There was a pause in the haggling. The howling from below grew shriller. Gorda quickly changed tactics.

"Nasha gives orders and you promise to obey them?"

"She can order all she wants but nobody's going to listen".

"Sit—and NOT fly?"

"Agreed. Now let the pixies go".

"Gladly!" growled Gorda. "They stink like mildew, little rats!"

"That's honest sweat", reproved Atel, "which your kind is unfamiliar with".

Gorda ignored that and threw them out. Poo had to be helped, but Atel showed surprisingly little patience.

"Hurry! To the Curtain! Check your wings and let's go!"

Up close, Yero saw that the Great Curtain had substance and even sewn seams with tiny stitches. *Very* tiny stitches. An expert seamstress did those.

There was an updraft near the Curtain, which was fortunate since that's where the pixies must go: High up on the Aurora itself to hang their wings among many, many others. Poo needed help with this and some, like Glinter, carried so much tar smudge that it was a struggle. Everyone ignored Nasha as she shouted orders about forming lines and taking turns.

Atel used the time to have another look below the Dais, from where smoke and noise was still arising. She half-smiled, half-frowned. The Big Sisters were breaking chunks off Gorda's statue and hurling them at the burning walkway, snuffing the flames. She returned in alarm to urge haste, but when the last pixie had hung her wings and it was time to come down, there was simply no hurrying them.

For one thing, they needed a good billow of the curtain, much like a surfer needs a good wave. Then they can ride it down like a slide. Even Poo enjoyed this. They squealed in delight; little caring what cares awaited at the bottom.

But others cared. Gorda half-emerged from the Guardhouse, looking and listening. Less smoke arose now from below, much less. Nasha also showed keen interest.

In almost a festive mood, the pixies regrouped and skipped toward the Part in the Curtain, which was unguarded but closed. It could be opened by simply pulling a rope, like most curtains, but it was tied up high where only Nasha could reach it. She smirked and walked away, leaving them to their dilemma.

The rope had always been tied up high and never made any difference to winged fairies. Now they had none, but they were in a playful mood and it easily occurred to them to make a pyramid; but the doing was found to be harder than the supposing, because of the giggling. Atel had to be sharp with them, and then another problem popped up: The tallest pyramid they could make was 3-high, which left the top girl still inches short of the rope. Try as she might, she couldn't reach, and the pyramid was tiring. Finally, Yero alighted on her fingertip and reached up with bigger ideas than she was capable of. Yet when she touched the rope it loosened by itself and the Curtain parted, because some pixies are very small and the Seamstresses of Yore meant for all to be welcome, even the smallest; and so they marched through, carrying Poo, who was crying again—not because of her painful wounds, but only because she wasn't able be part of the pyramid.

Chapter 8

The Rowah

When they had all gone through, the Curtain shut behind them on its own. Atel stayed there, the butterflies lingering also, while the others went on. It was springtime on this side and a marshy waterway attracted them just ahead, downhill from the curtain. Nasha barked orders. The pixies were to follow her! She marched off importantly to the left, along the blacktop service road that curved around a long bend in the marsh toward a distant quay where the Anya docked their sleek boats. No one followed. The pixies were veterans now and the fresh air only fed their insubordination. Nasha was ignored.

The pixies went skipping off the road straight into the weeds and the weeds parted to reveal a path, an old shortcut down to the water, to the young *Rowah* trickling down from higher ground where it siphoned off the Aurora itself.

Airy, first to reach the water, splashed with her feet and laughed about it. They all did, especially Poo when they set her on a large lily pad, because the water felt cool on her sores. Then they went about rounding up lily pads for everyone.

Nasha stopped up on the road finally when no one followed. "No, no!" she shouted back. "Th'must follow to the *boats*! Th'must honor the agreement!" She looked ridiculous with the tarbaby crow in one arm, scolding and gesturing with the other, and the pixies down by the creek no longer in sight.

"We're going that way too", Airy called up to her. "But why walk?"

"She needs the exercise", suggested Glinter. "Th'get fat with no work to do!"

Everyone laughed. Nasha saw she was beaten and changed tactics, following down the pathway to join them. Conveniently for her purpose, Airy and Lolly had just boarded a lily pad by the water's edge. These were large pads, easily big enough to accommodate a fairy like Nasha.

"Wait for me!" she exclaimed, but somehow managed to step on the edge of their pad — submerging that corner, and then the rest of it, in a mad scramble to get aboard. The water was shallow, and no one was in danger of drowning, but a mess and a hindrance resulted because the other pixies had found lily pads upstream and now Nasha sat in the middle blocking traffic.

"Oh, clumsy!" she sputtered. "I'm out of practice at this sort of thing".

"Get your own!" said Lolly, shaking off water. Airy stood waist-deep and just glared.

"Maybe I'm too heavy with th'crow" an' all", said Nasha. She turned quickly and plopped the nasty thing on a lily pad with Flossie who was just managing to drift past. The crow flapped one wing, more in an effort to smear Flossie than to keep its own balance. She saw it coming and rolled off into the water, tilting the pad so the crow rolled off the other side. Then there was trouble.

The water didn't like the crow, being naturally clean and pure from the Aurora, and the bird exactly opposite. The crow was burned, and squawked.

Nasha scooped the thing up and started dabbing with her dry sleeves, managing at the same time to sink another lily pad floating past, spilling two more pixies into the stream. The crow attempted to shake itself off but couldn't, being more a collection of goo than muscle, and the only result was an unclean dribble down Nasha's arm and off her elbow. Very amusing and served her right.

"Th'must put diapers on thy pet", suggested Airy. "T'would save thy sleeve".

Nasha shifted the crow to her other arm and the upset creature dribbled on that sleeve too, upsetting Nasha. She was an Anya apprentice and proud of it but hadn't yet lost the urge to be clean and pretty.

"Shame th'have nothing to use for diapers", said Lolly. "D'have anything at all?"

"Use thy *hood*, apprentice!" called another. "Th'have no other use for it!"

It was such fun; but when the laughter subsided there stood Nasha still, blocking the creek and spoiling for a fight. She held the crow at arm's length and marched upstream shaking it at everyone. The pixies had to bail off their lily pads or be splattered and fouled.

Nasha laughed now in her turn, knowing she was gaining valuable time. She glanced up the path toward the Curtain. The hummingbird still lingered there and the bothersome butterflies with her. Good! She must be having trouble. Just now she would be discovering that her spells didn't work! The Anya had 'fixed' it so the curtain couldn't be shut against them.

This was true, as Atel was quickly learning. She had tried several spells of closing with no effect at all. Now a shadow fell on the Curtain, and more shadows. The Anya were on the other side. Atel said something softly, so softly the butterflies couldn't hear, and waited.

The rope jerked. The Curtain quivered. A bit of smoke, a smell of charred flesh, and a blood-curdling yelp came through. The Curtain stayed shut. Atel turned to leave and saw the butterflies still there. "Skedaddle, ninnies!" she whispered angrily, "We don't have much time".

"But what was *that* about?" asked Yero. "Did you lock the door?"

"No! Spells don't work. I asked a favor of the rope".

"You asked the *rope?*"

"Yes! Go! We're wasting precious time. If you must know, the rope is friendly to us and promised to burn their fingers. Now fly! To the water!"

They found the mess in the creek and Nasha stalling all progress, but she was frightened of the hummingbird and backed off. Atel shouted orders. Quickly now everyone found new lily pads, the pixies mostly doubling up on them with room to spare. Even Nasha found one big enough to hold her and proved quite nimble about it now, as the others were moving out.

In short order a small flotilla got under way, drifting and paddling out into the current of the young stream. Faithful to her promise, Atel also took a seat on a lily pad and the butterflies joined her. Boca was more than willing.

He took up position on the very curl of the forward lip of the pad to look for fish in the water. Yero alighted next to him, eager for a boat ride, but scoffed at the notion of fish.

"Are there fish in here?" she asked their guide. "Boca thinks so".

"No", replied Atel, and left it at that. The undulating lily pad was giving her an odd feeling in the stomach.

"See Boca? There aren't any. She would know".

"I'll find some. A good fisherman can find fish anywhere".

"That's just being silly. You don't even have a fishing pole".

"Don't bother a fisherman when he's on the water".

"No hook, no line, no sinkers, no bait", Yero ticked off.

"I'll worry about that when I spot the fish".

"Also, we're too small and the fish would be too big if there *were* any".

"She's right", said a cool voice nearby. "There are no fish in these waters".

They had drifted close to Nasha. Too close.

"No, no fish at all. But you can have this!" With a fierce grin, she plopped the sticky crow on their pad.

"Caw", it said in its croaking voice. It pecked at Yero, missing, but leaving her indignant.

"What'd you do *that* for?"

The crow didn't answer but pecked again, closer this time. He was getting the range. Yero moved. So did Boca. Luckily there was some room, enough to keep a safe distance. Nasha had plopped it just on the edge, the furthest she could reach, and not in the middle where she intended. Also, by luck, the crow wasn't able to walk or move much at all, except to lean disgustingly toward them, trying to smear them. For the moment they were safe — and Atel too, on the opposite side of the pad.

Luck was beginning to work against all of them, however, back at the Curtain. A cloud of smoke grew and loomed huge there, dimming a whole section of the Aurora and throwing the stream and all the nearby landscape into shadow. The smell came down to the water and they heard the crackle of fire. The Anya were burning the Curtain! Flames burst through near the rope and spread upward. A hole opened up and through the gap poured the Big Sisters, cursing and shouting. The mob set off around toward the quay where they would intercept the pixies. It was a race now.

At least the lily pads had caught the current and speeded up, but eddies often snagged and slowed them down again, requiring time-consuming hand paddling to get free of them; but when they did pull free they usually had to wait for the next pad to get out of their own trouble. Anyone could see that the Anya would beat them to the quay, get in their boats, and simply round up the lily-paddlers. Certainly, the Anya could see it, and their cruel laughter boomed out across the marsh. But an unlikely thing happened, against all the rules of the heavens.

High above, the smoky shadow was parted. Yero looked up and saw the face of a lady, very large, almost ghostly, peering down at them. Using her hands, she parted the shadow wider and held it open. Light streamed through and illuminated the smoldering Curtain. A scowl creased her kindly face. She licked her thumb, reached down and pinched out the fire where it still burned, then licked the thumb again and produced needle and thread to repair the damage, but paused, undecided. What was the use? The wars of mortals were unending! At that moment the Anya, who did not see her as they hurried along the service road, caught sight of the hapless lily pads again, still caught in the eddies, and erupted with laughter.

Seemingly, that was the final straw for the Seamstress as she surveyed the whole scene and identified the arsonists. Her scowl deepened as she sized up the situation and decided to deal out a bit of justice. She produced a small sewing scissors with which she reached down and snipped the mooring lines at the quay. Before the Big Sisters ever came around the last bend and saw it happen, their sleek black boats drifted off into the current. The Great Lady nodded with satisfaction and withdrew, for she had overstepped her bounds by such interference; but before the opening closed it seemed to Yero that the Lady winked at them, and Atel rose into the air for a moment to return the greeting.

"Who was *that?*" said Yero in awe.

"An Artisan", replied Atel in great relief. "One of the Artisans of Evermore, the Ladies who assist the Lord in the never-ending ordering of the world. I met her once, long ago. She's nice, probably *too* nice. She wasn't supposed to do that".

"Wow, I'm glad she did".

"So am I. I've had enough battle for one day".

"Why wasn't she supposed to? Anyone could see we needed help. She saw it".

"Yes, but there are rules—especially in the Evermore. The Immortals are not allowed to interfere in mortal matters".

"But fairies are immortal, more or less".

"Less, not more, and certainly not forever. And like men, fairies were given a charge along with our mortality: To learn and grow, each of us and together as free people. If we aren't allowed our mistakes, we won't learn from them. We won't grow. We would diminish".

"Then what about those Anya? They've been around for ages too, and they haven't learned anything. Nothing nice, anyway".

"I don't know the answer, Yero. It doesn't seem fair, does it? But I can't imagine any reward will come of it".

A roar went up from the quay, not far ahead now. This time the Anya weren't laughing. They had won the race only to see their boats drifting off, disappearing downstream. They stood staring helplessly for they can't swim. Big Sisters sink in these celestial waters.

142

But now the lily pad flotilla came into view upstream. A more optimistic roar went up. Nasha on her lily pad arose with it, drawing herself up to her full height. Visions of glory occurred to her and she made quick plans to herd the small fry into the grateful arms of her superiors. At last! She would be appreciated! Probably promoted. Possibly even allowed to pull up her hood like a real Anya! She reveled in these thoughts and positioned her pad for the roundup, or tried to, but a curse twisted her pretty mouth. The stupid pad didn't respond like a proper boat! The black boats *listened*! One only had to *lean* this way or that. The fool lily pad didn't listen!

The Rowah was already wider, deeper, and faster here at the quay from many trickling tributaries in the marsh, and apprentice Nasha found herself hopelessly out of position to round up anyone. Just now, she was floating toward the dock while the small fry hugged the opposite shore, paddling hard with their disobedient little fingers! Desperately she sat down and paddled too, splashing away, but felt foolish doing so in front of the Bosses and stood up again. That was a mistake.

"Seize them!" ordered Gorda, and Nasha made a valiant effort, leaning dangerously far to try and grab the nearest pixies. Too far! Unused to such an unresponsive craft, she lost her balance and fell in—splash!

Nasha bobbed up several times before going down for keeps. Each time up, she heard the Anya cursing her failure (which she expected) but offering no help at all (which was utterly devastating). Her heart sank, and she sank with it. Time passed, and soon she didn't really care anymore.

But what was this? Someone had her by the hair! Were not embarrassing failure, despair, and an untimely end bad enough? Now humiliation! Dragged by the hair! Ouch! It hurt! Leave me alone! Such were her thoughts as pixies pulled her to the surface and somehow onto her own lily pad where she lay waterlogged and unconscious. There she heard voices from the world she had so nearly left, vaguely familiar. She listened with the detached curiosity of one caught between two worlds. The loudest voices, oddly, seemed from far away:

"Ha! Little fools! You have saved your own slavemaster! How dumb is that?"

"You'll *always* be slaves, and *we* the masters, little fools!"

"Apprentice Nasha! Get your unprofessional act together! Resume command or be punished!"

Something re-focused in the blur of Nasha's mind. *Nasha*? That's my name! An urgency gripped her, and she tried to move, but couldn't.

That soon changed. Something landed *thump* on her stomach and she spit up water. Then it happened again—thump! More water. Nasha opened her eyes, still but half-conscious. The pixies were using her for a trampoline, one after another, and skipping back across several lily pads to get in line for another turn. Oof! More water. Nasha coughed and gasped for air. Yes! *Air*! That's what she needed! And she was getting it. Thump! Gasp! Thump! Gasp!

Nasha came wide-awake just as Pursy, the fattest pixie, landed—Whump! Nasha gasped and grabbed for her, but even a fat pixie was too quick for her just now.

"Whoa! Enough!" shouted Airy. "The slavemaster waketh!"

Much laughter commenced, and a quick pixie getaway. Everyone hopscotched to their own lily pads and paddled off a safe distance.

Nasha sat up and looked around. The current was taking them swiftly downstream now. Way behind, she could still see the quay and the Big Sisters, arms waving threateningly in the air, fists shaking. She could no longer make out their words but could easily imagine. She shivered in her wet robe and closed her eyes.

In the absence of Nasha's authority the tarbaby crow tried to assume command, cawing and croaking and flapping its heavy wings a little. It was pathetically weak about that, being only able to lift them an inch or so; but flying was never its intention. When it dropped the wings, air was expelled from underneath smelling of sulphur and accompanied by rude noises. Again and again it flapped, like a naughty student in class, causing the lily pad to lurch and bob and unsettling Atel's stomach until she became seasick, but the crow still wouldn't quit. Yero tried to reason with it, or at least get its attention. Their guide didn't need any more problems just now.

"Look", she addressed the bird politely, "We're all stuck here together whether we like it or not, so why don't we try to get along?"

In answer, the crow leaned toward the butterflies as far as it could and coughed—a smutty, hacking cough from lungs that had never been clean, never would be. Bits and crumbles flew. One landed on Yero's elbow and stuck there. When she tried to pick it off it got stuck in her fingers. When Boca tried to help, his fingers got stuck in the tacky mess too.

The crow pulled itself upright and watched, enjoying the spectacle. Unable to even separate their fingers the butterflies finally dipped their hands in the water. That helped. The stuff melted off and bubbled to the surface.

"Maybe you shouldn't have said 'stuck together'", whispered Boca. "Try something else".

Yero stepped forward again and folded her arms firmly. "See here, now", she said. "We don't have enough room over here on our side. You can have *half* the pad, but we need the other half. It's only fair, and I'll mark a line". She proceeded to the middle and began stepping off a border, only barely eluding disaster when the crow did a belly flop trying to squash her. When it missed, the crow wiggled its wings and twisted its head side to side trying at least to dirty as much of the pad as it could, but the meanness was its undoing. It got stuck there face down on the pad and couldn't even move its head. All it could do was give dirty looks and cough, but the cough was directed now and easy to avoid.

"You learn about sharing awful slowly, but at least you're learning", scolded Yero. "Okay, we'll use your rules. You can have the part you're stuck to and we get everything else. There! Now everyone's happy and we can be friends".

"Yeah!" chuckled Boca. "You *need* friends now, stuck down like that. You need someone to feed you!"

"I hadn't thought of that", said Yero. "Boca is right. You must eat a lot, as fat as you are. What do they feed you? Flies? Beetles?"

"Maybe coal", suggested Boca. "Naughty children get coal in their Christmas stockings. Now I know where they get rid of it. These crows eat it".

"Oh, Boca, it's behaving so well now. We should feed it something nicer! If you *do* catch a fish, we could shove that down its beak".

"Good idea! It could cough up its own seasonings, too, and sprinkle them on top".

"That would be nice, Boca. I'm sure spices would be delicious!"

The crow coughed angrily, expelling more shreds and speckles.

Boca threw up his hands. "*Now* what? It's wasted the spices!"

"Well, a lot of meals start with a salad. That would be better than nothing—and there's some right now, in the water!"

Together the butterflies got hold of a small leaf floating by and hauled it aboard, so when next the crow opened its beak it got the salad shoved in there and began to choke, exactly as planned; but they underestimated the thing. With a terrific effort it tore itself loose and bolted upright, spitting out the leaf. It would've gone over backwards too, right into the stream and a well-deserved finish, but unfortunately its bottom was still stuck to the pad. As it was, water came aboard during the disturbance and began to melt the bottom loose. Worse yet, the crow squirmed in the water and discovered it could move a little. The ugly thing had regained the advantage and knew it.

If it had any legs or feet they couldn't be seen, but that didn't matter. It could move! It began to wriggle toward the middle. From there, it could flop on anyone! The red eyes gleamed.

Yero worried for Atel, in the throes of seasickness, and cast about for ideas. Water had freed the ghoulish thing, but it was still their only hope. The stream was narrowing now, the current increasing, as the Rowah sped downhill into a winding channel. Inspiration seized her.

"Boca!" she whispered urgently, "Can you think up a rhyme to upset the crow? Something rude?"

"Maybe. What for?"

"Watch. You'll see."

She fluttered up in front of the crow, wary of its filthy beak, and set about harassing it—sticking out her tongue, making faces, even darting around from behind to spit in its eye. The thing lunged and pecked but was too slow for any moving target. When she had its full attention, she sang:

> "Blackbird Lumpkin
> Fat as a pumpkin!
> He can't fly
> From tree to tree!
> He can't fly
> And he can't catch me!"

She laughed and the crow lost its temper. Then it was Boca's turn:

> "Face all gook,
> Just look! Just look!
> He just 'caw',
> Dumb bird! Dumb bird!
> He just 'caw'. Can't say one word".

The crow pecked wildly and missed. Both butterflies laughed, and Yero sang:

> "Nope. Can't talk.
> Just squawk. Just squawk.
> Can't even walk,
> Just fuss. Just fuss.
> Wings all mud—and he can't catch us!"

The crow was frantic, pecking at them, sputtering, lunging, and missing. Yero spotted a sharp turn just ahead.

"Now, Boca!" she shouted.

They both fluttered way too close and hung in the air at the point of the crow's beak in that tantalizing way that only butterflies have. Everyone thinks they can reach out and touch them, but nobody can. The crow thought so and pecked with all his might at just the wrong moment as the lily pad careened sharply the opposite way around the turn. Oops! The devilish thing did a neat forward summersault off the pad and disappeared under the water with hardly a splash.

The butterflies grabbed perches on either side of their guide to ride out the rough water ahead. It got wild. The lily pad spun through corner after corner in foam and spray until a steep chute funneled them into a narrow tunnel and finally—Spalooosh! They came to rest in a calm, dark pool at the bottom, last of the lily-paddlers to arrive. Miraculously, no one had been lost. When Yero opened her eyes, Nasha was on the nearest pad, smiling at her.

"You can join me if you like", said the apprentice. "There's plenty of room on my pad—and no grease". Everyone looked at her. Nobody said a word. She blushed. "Th'don't have to, of course. I'm done giving orders". She slipped out of her black robe and went to throw it into the pool, but Atel stirred and asked her not to.

"Not yet, please! Keep the robe. And thank you for the kind offer. We'll gladly join you, as soon as my stomach tells me I can move".

Nasha smiled gratefully and tried to fluff her old outfit that she still wore underneath: A sundress of soft rushes, cleverly pleated, but now matted down from the heavy robe.

"You're pretty as ever now", said Airy.

"Thank you, but I don't deserve that. I'm sorry, especially for Poo. Th'can be very cruel, th'Big Sisters".

"We want you back", said Poo. "Especially now".

The flotilla had drifted away from the splashing chute, toward tranquil water in the center of the pool. Off to the side a bucket and rope lift dangled along the sheer wall, a dirty bucket the pixies were more than familiar with. It was for the hot gook from the big boats that hauled it upriver. The freight runs ended here, cargo was offloaded, and everything humped the rest of the way by slave labor. Their labor.

Glinter frowned and looked away but reminders of their slave masters were everywhere. Even the pretty pool reflected her soiled likeness back up at her. She bore all the marks of a 'smudge-fairy', as Gorda enjoyed calling them. Glinter uttered a subdued oath and commenced washing up. The other 'smudgers' followed suit with resentful glances at Nasha, who averted her eyes. Boca suddenly burst the awkward moment.

"Fish!" he exclaimed. "There *are* fish. Two of them!"

The ugly moment was gone. Several pixies even laughed. "There aren't any fish in these waters", said Airy. "Thu are mistaken".

"Well, here they are anyway", insisted Boca. "I see them".

Everyone looked out of curiosity. No one else saw the fish. Then Airy suddenly laughed. "Oh yes! *Those* fish. We don't see them often now, since the waters are dirtier."

Everyone spotted them then, except Yero.

"Look *there*", said Boca, pointing. "One is higher, the other down lower, facing opposite directions. Just sitting there".

Yero tried. Visibility was good in the sheltered pool and she could even see stars through the water, but no fish.

It was Nasha who reached over and traced an outline on the surface of the water. There! The fish appeared. Nasha finished by drawing a line from the mouth of the upper fish down to the mouth of the lower one.

"'Tis illusion that they're just under th'water", she said. "They are far away. We only see them because of the stars that outline them. Men call things like that 'constellations'".

"See, Boca? They're not real", said Yero smugly.

"Oh, but they are!" said Airy. "They're the Fish of Eternity, who swim together in th'heavens, never to return to the seas".

Yero remained skeptical. "What do they eat then? Are they nibbling a noodle there?"

"Nay. 'Tis a fisherman's line".

"And where is the fisherman?"

"Th'have eaten him, fishing pole an' all. But it's a blessing they're gone from this earth".

"So they don't eat all the fishermen?"

"So they don't eat all the *fish*. Th'were gluttonous in the old days an' ate everything — even their own babies".

"Yikes! Boca - pay attention. Fishing is dangerous!"

Boca grinned and clapped his hands. "Tell us more", he said. "Tell us a fishing story!"

"Very well", agreed Airy. "'Twill take a few minutes, time for tummies to settle, hmm?" (Here Atel nodded and closed her eyes.)

—The Fish of Eternity—

In the Beginning the Lord breathed air upon the earth, and poured the waters, and raised up the lands; and so there were three parts to the whole, of which two were given to the Free Peoples: The air and the lands. But the waters remained empty for drinking and for making the weather, and for a while it was good. Then men got bored.

Being who they are they made war, and between wars they hunted the great beasts of the earth. They took pride in vanquishing the largest and fiercest, stuffing them afterwards to hang on their dining room walls for bragging rights.

There were many wars. Yet from the beasts' point of view entirely too much idle time in-between, and too many hunters; and so the great beasts dwindled. That's when men *really* got bored and grumpy. They hung around their homes with nothing to do and it irritated their pretty wives. A group of womenfolk finally called upon the Lord to address the problem.

"The guys have run out of adventures", they complained. "Now they sit at home and tell us how to run the house and garden. Swell fellows, mind you, but having them around all day is too much. Could you please think up something for them to do?"

The Lord had become concerned watching the great beasts dwindle, so the time was ripe for action—but what, exactly?

There remained one vast possibility: The waters. Weeds and squiggly things had gotten into them by now, but nothing big enough to interest men.

About that time the men cornered the last pair of giant slugs that once oozed so terrifyingly over the earth—a pair named Kala and Riba—and certainly would've finished them off, for although they were huge (much bigger than whales) they were ponderous and slow. Here the Lord intervened, asking, "What next after this, sons of men? When the great beasts are gone, they'll be gone forever. What then?" While the men thought about this, He put a suggestion to the slugs, asking if they would agree to live in the seas.

"I'll give you breath under the waters", He offered, "and also...rudders and so forth, to help you swim".

It was an easy choice for the slugs, but the men were reluctant to give up their quarry.

"There will be sport *later*", promised the Lord. "A new sport! It shouldn't take long. Just let these two populate the waters".

"But these are *trophies, and* we've got 'em *now!*" retorted one rude fellow. "How will we get 'em back once they're loose?"

"Oafish!" muttered the Lord under his breath, but the womenfolk overheard and thought He said, *Go fish!* They seized on the phrase and that's what it came to be called: 'Fishing', even leading to 'Fishing Trips!'

The giant slugs seemed a good choice at first, as they were already slimy and possessed of an efficient shape to glide through the water. But they frustrated the Lord, for though they were fruitful and multiplied as He intended, they were gluttonous and ate everything in the ocean—even their own young—so the seas did not fill up with sport fish as promised. Men with their new fishing poles caught pitifully few. Truth be told, Kala and Riba probably caught and ate more fishermen than the other way around. The sport proved unrewarding. Men lost interest. They went home skunked and disgruntled and caused trouble around the house. No one was happy.

The Lord scolded the great fishes, but by now they savored the forbidden tastes and there was no changing their bad habits; yet a solution had to be found. The Lord pondered a bit.

One evening He rearranged the stars above the ocean into an outline of a mighty fisherman and awakened him, directing him to cast his hook into the waters and catch out the troublesome pair. Men saw and called him 'Angill', Angler of the Evening, and learned to recognize his constellation in the heavens; but they shook their heads about his timing. Being close to the water they had learned that the great fishes fed mostly during the day.

Now, if one of the two could be called greediest, it was Kala. She would eat anything that fit into her mouth. When her own babies were scarce, she would prowl busy harbors swallowing small boats, sailors and all. Or she might snack on careless fishermen, or even small children on the beach, coming upon them in a great rush of water and retreating again to the deeps with her prize.

One day Kala saw a most delightful morsel up on the beach, a plump lad of perhaps ten summers, and called to him, beckoning him closer to the surf where she could snatch him. But the lad was no fool. In fact, it was the Lord Himself, as he chose to appear to the mother of fishes.

"No thank you", He called down to her. "The sun is warm! 'Tis pleasant up here".

"As you please", said Kala. "I only wanted to play. There are so few fishes to swim with". She left then, but not very fast, nor very far. There was something irresistible about the lad. Yummy!

"Art warm and tanned by now?" she inquired sweetly, returning in a little while. "Ready for a nice swim? Come join me!"

The lad took a few tantalizing steps toward the water but stopped, remembering that he had only recently eaten, and of course the age-old advice: Don't go in swimming for at least a half-hour afterward. He retraced his steps and lay down, yawning and stretching delectably.

The big fish left again, but only a short distance, and bided her time. She was obsessed now with devouring the lad and returned in less than half an hour.

"Art digestible now — er, I mean, is thy tummy settled?" she asked eagerly.

But no, it wasn't yet. The lad decided that a nap might help, and went to sleep on the sand, just out of reach.

Kala hung around impatiently. The sun went down, but the boy held her attention. She was become ravenously hungry.

Sunset faded. The stars appeared. Angill the Fisherman sprang into the sky and cast his hook in front of her nose, baited with corn. The boy watched secretly but nothing happened. Kala ignored the bait and moved her nose away.

The boy pretended to awaken, stretching enticingly. At this signal Angill reeled in his line and changed the bait. He put a wriggling worm on the hook and cast that in front of her nose. Still no luck.

The boy stretched again, lusciously, and struck up conversation to stoke her appetite, noting that the air had turned cool. He approached the water unexpectedly and dipped a teasing toe. "Oh, it's warm!" he observed. "This might be a fine time to swim".

"Yes, yes!" slobbered Kala. "'Tis most appetiz — er, I mean 'comfy' out here. Do come in!"

The lad dawdled and tiptoed, but Kala had crowded too close into the shallows to mount a rush onto the beach. Angill dangled another bait, this time a lively grasshopper. Kala gave it a passing glance, no more. A squiggly crawfish fared no better.

"Come, come!" urged Kala, venturing so shallow her jaw scraped bottom, "What is stopping thee? The water is so morsel — er, I meant to say, 'mild'".

"To be honest", confessed the lad, "I fear thou wilt devour me".

"Oh, drivel", protested Kala piously. "Why wouldst ever think so?"

"There are many stories in the villages".

"Oh, the gossip. Okay, I cannot tell a lie. I have eaten a few people in my time, but only the old and the lame. The weak ones. This helps to make mankind stronger".

"That doesn't sound so bad", conceded the boy. "What is thy favorite food of all, if I may ask?"

"You may. We're friends now. I prefer smaller fish, usually. In fact, I recently ate my own offspring, and I'm not particularly hungry. The new eggs will hatch in a few days and that is soon enough for my next meal. So, join me! You are perfectly savory — er, I meant to say, 'safe'".

Acting on this tip, Angill cast a silver minnow. Kala nibbled on it but felt the hook and spit it out. Angill quickly changed bait one last time.

Kala feigned to lose interest and moved off toward deep water. The boy took a dangerous step or two into the surf and called to her. She smiled inwardly and prepared to rush him. Angill dangled the new offering. Whatever it was, it caught Kala's eye at the last instant and she lunged for it instead of the boy. The Great Fisherman set the hook and the fight was on.

Great was that battle between fisherman and fish—the greatest that ever was. Into the darkest depths she fled, but this only served the fisherman's purpose; for the harder she pulled, the deeper the hook bit into her lip until she learned her lesson.

Then followed a duel of wits as Kala tried to gain enough slack to spit the hook, but no matter how cleverly she tangled and snagged the line it stayed taut because it embodied the purpose of the Lord. And when she tried to cut the line on coral reefs or break it by main strength it proved unbreakable, for it was woven from eternal strands of the Lord's will. In a fit of anger Kala leaped high into the air, splashing spectacularly from ocean to ocean, deluging the lands with spray. In this way, many lakes were formed that still remain; but for Kala there was no escape. In the end, Angill reeled in his catch and reached for the fish to hold up his trophy, but he never did. At that moment Riba, Father of Fishes, leaped into the sky and swallowed the Fisherman, pole and all.

***

Airy finished her tale. The Constellation of the Fishes was harder to see as they drifted toward the lower end of the pool. Here the high banks leaned back allowing more starlight and a glare to form on the surface.

"So that's why there are two fishes but no fisherman, Boca", said Airy. "Would you still like to try your luck with them?"

"Yeah, if I could use his pole".

"Those fish are much bigger than you are".

"Shouldn't matter. I think it's all in the pole and the bait— especially the bait", reasoned Boca, and began to act out the historic duel fancying himself as Angill, mightiest of anglers! He stomped about and jerked on the imaginary pole, grunting as loud as a butterfly can grunt and setting the lily pad a-wobble, much to Atel's discomfort.

"One thing, though. What was that bait she finally bit on?"

"No one knows", shrugged Airy. "Great Fishermen usually keep th'secrets, so I've heard. That's why th'catch fish when nobody else does".

"Could it have been a spider?" said Boca, bouncing away. "Or maybe a fat tadpole?"

"Maybe".

"How about a jumping cricket?" He showed how a cricket could jump, and land, and jump again.

"Possibly. It must have been quite lively".

That was enough for the seasick hummingbird. "I'm sure it was a butterfly", she protested. "Because even when they're jumping and flapping their wings, they can't stop flapping their mouths!"

She also guessed it was as good a time as any to abandon the greasy pad and join Nasha, and that was about as far as she felt like flying. But Nasha's pad was larger and considerably more stable, and a slow improvement set in with her seasickness.

To encourage this, each lass plucked something soft from their dress: A leaf or blade of grass, some thistledown or flower petals, and made a pillow to cushion her from the movements. But the worst was behind them now—the whitewater, the chutes, and the crow too, for that matter. Downstream a broad valley opened before them. The Rowah slowed and meandered through a maze of twisting turns and oxbows. The water turned darker, the current slower and unpredictable. There were dead-end channels and channels choked with weeds that had to be avoided.

Nasha 'officially' released Atel and the butterflies from their pledge to sit, so they could scout ahead for open water. It made a good joke but she was serious, and Atel took it seriously too and sent the butterflies out. This helped, at times. None of the pixies had been down this way in half an age.

They were long-time 'out-posters' at the Curtain. That's where they lived and stayed, unless they caused serious trouble and got sent downriver to some special punishment. Nasha had been the last to pass this way as a new apprentice destined for Gorda's command. That was on a regular tarboat loaded with gook for the 'outgoing' road. But there'd been trouble that day, and some fast maneuvering. Her memory wasn't clear either.

Nor were the latest reports brought back by the butterflies, unfortunately. There was little or no open water ahead anywhere, no obvious channel at all. Just shore weeds and seaweeds.

"*And* mosquitoes", reported Boca.

The lily-paddlers had to feel their way along, sounding for depth with cattail stems and going on Nasha's best recollections which were often wrong. Tall rushes and sedges rose from anything resembling firm ground and leaned over the clogged channels, obscuring the view. They came to a place where pickerelweed overgrew the channel but a slow current trickled through and they did their best to follow, pushing stems aside and lifting the big leaves out of the way. It was wet, sweaty work and the mosquitoes were becoming intolerable. Finally, all progress came to a halt and everyone swatted at them with leaves.

"Who brought these things up here, anyway? That was just dumb!" griped Yero as she fluttered and dodged among them. She wasn't sure if they meant to bite her or fight her.

"Th'Anya, of course", replied Airy. "To make life miserable for us".

"Well, it worked. But why are they so loud? They're just ordinary mosquitoes!"

"'Tis amusing, that. Th'Sister who fetched them up is fat and lazy, accustomed to long naps. Down below in her old aya-by-a-river the mosquitoes often wakened her, a-buzzing loudly in her ear, so that's how she remembered them and fetched them up. Unhappily, th'haven't faded like some nicer things".

"I hope they annoy her up here too"!

"Not much", said Nasha. "Th'hoods protect them. But it's more than the mosquitoes. It's all these weeds! After they flooded the City th'brought up invasive, nuisance stuff to choke th'backwaters an' force everyone out into their camps. But it makes river traffic difficult for them too. Th'didn't think about *that* part".

They finally just ignored the mosquitoes and pushed on through the tangle toward what looked like open water but proved to be an illusion. Burr-reed grew there with its strappy leaves floating flat on the surface, pointing in every direction. The burrs themselves poked a few inches above the water on little stalks. Patience was needed and no one had much of that left.

The only way forward was to scoop up the tangled leaves one at a time and flop them downstream, trying to cover over as many burrs as possible so the pads wouldn't get snagged. With practice they got better, but it was sloppy, scratchy work, and they were so busy with the burr-reed they were surprised when the channel opened out beyond the last rushes into a small estuary. That's where the boats were.

It was a stagnant pool, backed up against a thick growth of brush that prevented through-traffic downriver. Trash and garbage floated everywhere, bobbing about in the duckweed scum. Gorda's bunch were litterers.

"I heard th'mess was getting worse", muttered Lolly.

"Much worse," said Nasha. "All up and down the river. Gossip is probably short of the truth".

"Gossip is hard to come by, at th'Outpost. We don't get to talk to the 'muckers' often. But we've heard about the mess down here".

"The Swamp is even slimier than this. The *City,* I suppose I should say, but there's no resemblance anymore. Tar boats have spread th'algae everywhere. The whole City is infested with it now".

"And how do we get through this brush an' down *into* the City?" asked Airy. "What is that stuff, anyway?"

Part 2: Beyond the Moonwalk

"Sumac", said Laca, a little pixie who hadn't spoken much before. "Th'poison kind. Don't touch it. I learned the hard way".

It looked impossible to proceed without touching it. The whole lower part of the estuary was a regular thicket of it, and no way around that could be seen.

"'Tis a job for th'boats", said Nasha cheerfully. "*That* boat, I should say. We'll borrow Gorda's".

It wasn't hard to guess which that was. They were all the usual swiftboats but one. Gorda's personal craft was quite impressive. All the comforts of home for her and the Big Sisters! But not for prisoners.

That was one of Gorda's favorite things, escorting prisoners. There were small fry needing punishment all along the river, all the time. Transporting them was a hobby of Gorda's. The usual thing was to ship offenders to a different post and give them a taste of the worst jobs the new post had to offer. The system worked well. There was a surplus of dirty jobs in the Anya Empire. Still, it was a problem for the Bosses to deal with. But Gorda had figured long ago how to deal with it in style.

Her boat was much larger than the swiftboats but retained the same shallow draft and sleek design, a craft suitable for swift water or calm, but with amenities. Except for the chauffeur's post on the very prow, the forward section was enclosed, the better to pamper Gorda and a few guests and keep the 'skeeters' off their upturned noses. Astern from the cabin were narrow benches along the gunwales with leg-irons and manacles of various sizes, and oars with metal spikes stowed underneath. A buffet table took up the middle and it was clear from the length of the shackle chains that the buffet was not meant for the prisoners.

The lily-paddlers worked their way through the floating refuse and approached the boat but Laca warned against touching it with wet hands. It was good advice for the butterflies but most of the others knew this. They'd all had a ride in this boat before, when they were shipped out to the Dais outpost; but little Laca had toiled at the Boatworks itself for almost half an Age before that. It was drudgery there, manufacturing the Anya craft out of the abominable tar-gook, but the dangerous part was rubbing in the finish. She explained how the shiny black boats got their shine.

On every return trip downriver, the 'mucker-fairy' crews harvested sumac for the sap and resins it contained. The muckers had to be allowed gloves for the job or they would absorb a lethal dose of poison (leading to an unfortunate shortage of slaves), but at least the muckers got rid of the sumac at the Boatworks. There, it was handled every day and gloves were only partial protection against the sticky sap. The boatworkers even smeared tar all over their arms and legs for protection, but still suffered rashes and sores.

The sap was squeezed out of the sumac stems and smeared on the gunwales and sides to waterproof and (hopefully) to fireproof the finished boats, and to impart the glossy finish the Anya were fond of. The boatworkers suspected the poisonous stuff was responsible for the way the craft responded to the Anya, but to no one else.

"Excellent advice—don't touch!" agreed Nasha. "'Twill burn unwary hands severely. But Gorda and th'Sisters never *climbed* aboard. They *walked*, very dignified, and so will we".

She touched the keel here and there with a stick, experimentally. On the third try, a ramp extended itself out to welcome them, a long wooden ramp with an easy incline and an unglossed handrail. This was for the Boss.

They pirated the vessel and all the pixies immediately pointed out where they had been chained years earlier 'on the way up'. Everyone remembered their irons, except one.

"Where were you then, Laca?" asked Poo. "I hope th'didn't have you rubbing in varnish all the way".

"Nay. I was locked up as well".

"Forgive me", teased Lolly, "but I don't see any irons that small".

"No. No irons for little Laca!" said she. "I was special".

151

Just then, Nasha figured out the spell to open the cabin door. She grinned. "No one knows the password except Gorda, and she always whispers it. But it's not hard to guess: 'Gorda the Great', same as her sculpture".

That opened the front door also, so Nasha passed through to reach the small forward deck and pilot's perch. Everyone went inside out of curiosity, even Atel, who was beginning to feel herself again.

There wasn't a whole lot inside the cabin but there were nice cushioned chairs (One, doubtless Gorda's, included armrests and an ornate bullwhip coiled neatly on the cushion.) There was also a cupboard with dishes and bottles of greenish goo labeled 'Dressing', a drawer of silverware, and a utility cabinet with brooms, extra chains and irons, and a birdcage.

"That's where th'kept me", said Laca in a small voice. "In the cage. I might as well admit it".

"Me too", confessed Poo, "after I slipped out of the irons. But I had to! I'm allergic to irons".

"Aren't we all!" agreed Glinter. "I guess everybody is".

When the truth came out, most of the pixies admitted to spending some time in the birdcage. Gorda did enjoy pixies in irons, but she was getting lazier. These days she liked to just put her feet up and be entertained in the cabin. There was always a pixie or two in the cage for her to tease.

Up front, Nasha took a deep breath and assumed the pilot's post but backed away immediately. "The craft will not heed lest I put on my robe", she said distastefully.

It had been dumped in the aft cargo hold still wet and had to be wrung out. Nasha shivered when she put it on.

"Take it off again", suggested Atel. "I'll try to dry it".

"It's only partly the water", said Nasha. "You wouldn't believe how cold these things are". But she gladly slipped out of it. She hung it on the cabin door and Atel went to work. Soon steam was rising, but it was a sickly green steam. The pixies looked away, beginning to be bored.

"Come, little servants", suggested Nasha cheerfully. "Th'can do some cleaning in the meanwhile — and I will join thee".

The boat needed it. The deck was littered with shriveled, trampled 'salad greens', the everyday food of the Anya. They had always been big, leaning toward fat, even in the old days down below. Somehow, they remained as fat as ever up here in Nyo but made a show of being on diets. "No thank you! No nectar for us! We're on diets", was a timeworn excuse. The small fry suspected the Anya had lost the trick of shape shifting — could no longer turn into butterflies — and the diet talk was just to cover up their weakness.

"'Tis funny how things work out", said Airy, wrinkling her nose near the dirty floor. "If not for Aleta we would surely be prisoners now, on this very boat, an' Nasha would be making us clean up. Now we're doing it anyway!"

"'Tis good practice", replied Nasha. "If thy side ever wins, th'will be lots of clean-up to be done".

"If *we* win, Nasha. You're with us again now".

"Yes, I am", said Nasha quietly. "But I don't think I'll be around for the clean-up afterward. I'm a *double* traitor now, d'thu see? I'll be marked special".

Everyone knew it was true, and they just left it at that. To change the subject Nasha set about cleaning the buffet table, using a cattail spike to scrub it. The table was smeared with the same green goo they had seen in the bottles. It was salad dressing, of course, which probably accounted for the extra calories in the Big Sister's diets.

"Where do they get salad dressing?" asked Yero. "I thought they never made anything nice".

"Nothing pretty", said Airy. "But they used to tend gardens, downriver. For the greens, I suppose".

"Th'still do", said Nasha. "They tend it th'selves, actually, some of them. The dressing is what collects in the pitcher plants".

"Bugs and all?" said Yero, gagging.

"Do not eat the dressing!" said Nasha, frowning. She put on the dry robe and made her way forward again to the pilot's perch. This time the boat heeded. She leaned backward and to one side. The boat reversed and turned. She leaned forward slowly, carefully. The boat edged ahead through the trash. Nasha studied the sumac thicket closely.

"There!" she pointed. "The channel. D'thu see?"

Nobody saw anything but sumac. Yero offered her services again, and Boca's, to scout ahead, worried that Nasha's memory was off, but she wasn't even listening.

"Look for boat scrapes on the bark", she said. "I see them! This is it, I'm sure." She reversed the boat some ways into the trash and squared it around, aiming it precisely, then leaned sharply forward. The boat lurched ahead directly at the thicket. Atel and the butterflies took to the air. Everyone else ducked and braced themselves. For nothing. The boat easily parted the brush, even pushed over the top of some of it with hardly a bump. The tough stems seemed purposely to give way, a reminder of the power of the Anya. Whoever ruled the Rowah ruled fairyland.

Beyond was a channel bordered by flooded trees, mostly willows that drooped overhead, rooted in some forgotten riverbank down under. Water lapped against the mossy trunks; or rather, the scummy duckweed did. Their lily pads would've been stuck in it, but the scum didn't affect Gorda's boat at all. Yero and Boca, perched on the front of the cabin felt a breeze in their faces as they picked up speed, and the mosquitoes quit bothering.

They passed from the upper marshes into the 'Swamp' proper. The boundary was still marked with Sweet Flag, and the crew was welcomed by the aroma, as travelers had been welcomed since the Founding. They paused at Airy's urging and Nasha reached down through the scum and pinched off a bit of the root for Atel.

"The aroma is good for anyone", Airy explained. "But th'root is good for queasiness. 'Tis gingery".

"We've entered the Old City", she said to the butterflies. "'Twas named 'Ah' in happier days. Now we call it 'Blah'".

"Are all the buildings underwater then?" asked Boca.

Airy smiled. "Th'never were any. Fairies have no need of such things, except th'Anya. But the City wasn't a forest, nor an open picnic park like men prefer either. 'Twas something in-between: Something *fairyish* with many waterways winding through a wood, and many open glades with flowers and exotic plants—room enough for all of us and all had some part in th'making. The ayas were so blended that the beauty of Ah flowed like the water. Many lived here, but to the untrained eye it might have seemed like none at all, for we dress in the trappings of the wildwood as you see. I wonder how they dress now...if th'still are fugitives—*rebels*—on the loose here".

"Everyone says there are", put in Lolly. "But th'Anya are tight-lipped. Th'hate to admit it, we think".

"There still *are*," called Nasha from her perch. "You can believe that! Th'Anya curse them terribly! Every loaded tar boat comes up through here, remember, and despite heavy precautions there are losses. All too often a boat is actually sunk by the 'rebels'. Th'Anya call them 'Rats'. *Swamp* Rats".

She hardly got the words out when a racket and jangle broke out right underneath her.

"Alarm!" she shouted, almost pitching into the water as the boat bumped and slid sideways against a thick rope rigged with a variety of metal objects. They clanked and banged and rattled against the boat and each other and included even toots and whistles as swamp gasses were disturbed and bubbled to the surface. It went on and on, as the boat jostled and bumped, until Nasha regained her balance and wits and leaned back properly. The boat reversed a few feet and held there. Silence settled for a long moment, no more. Then the fireworks started. Flaming arrows rained overhead from several directions. The Swamp Rats struck hard.

They meant business and the arrows were meant for the pilot first, and for the boat itself, especially the cabin. Their bows were strong with strings of wire salvaged from the harps—real harps brought up in the Founding—but the arrows, like everything else up here, were forged of stardust and disintegrated at speed. Nevertheless, they were very effective in two ways: The Big Sisters hated the bright light, and the arrows arrived as a hail of sparks, eager to start fires.

Nasha leapt into the scummy water, her robe flickering with little flames. All the lasses jumped for it. Ploop! Ploop! They submerged for protection under the scum. Yero and Boca hid under the buffet table. Atel disappeared.

Quickly, the one-sided battle was over. A lively fire danced on Gorda's cabin roof, the boat drifted into the alarm rope again, and the pixies bobbed up and down shouting, "Friends! Friends!" trying to make themselves heard above the clatter and din.

Out of the shadows came the 'Rats on what looked like water skis and threw a thick mat over the gunwale to board the vessel. They were all over the boat in moments, spoiling for a fight and looking disappointed at the lack of resistance.

"Hoy up there!" shouted Nasha. "Put out that fire! We'll be needing the boat".

"Hoy down there!" retorted one of the 'Rats. "The boat hath new Masters! Put thy request in writing an' send it through proper channels". The 'Rats aboard laughed.

Another 'Rat had found Gorda's personal whip and now cracked it at Nasha, missing barely but splattering duckweed in her face. "Come up an' fight!" this one taunted. "Th'must be fearsome indeed if thu were the lone escort". The 'fearsome' one went under, clearly in trouble.

"We're friends!" insisted Nasha, bobbing up again.

"Some are. We shall save those. As for thee, cling to thy black hood, Turncoat. See if that keeps thee afloat!"

They all laughed again, up on the boat deck, a dozen or more of them. Now they threw ropes and lassoed the pixies, pulling them boatside where they too could scramble aboard over the mat. There followed animated discussion but still delay about Nasha until finally an empty salad dressing bottle tied to a rope smacked her in the face, cracking her nose. The 'Rat on the other end flicked the rope and the bottle jumped and smacked her nose again.

"Grab quick, Anya!" shouted the roper. "The good girls here ask that we fish thee out".

Another 'Rat approached over the water at a much slower pace. "Carefully, Jibber", she cautioned. "We mustn't drown that one. Ha' thee got the fire under control?"

"We're getting to that", replied Jib. She glanced briefly at Lorelei, the late arrival. "You've got something on your shoulder there".

"D'thu hear?" said Lorelei to whatever-it-was on her shoulder. "You're a 'something' now. You've come up in the world".

"Better than nothing", laughed Atel. "Shall we go aboard?"

They did, and Lorelei introduced her old friend to the other 'Rats. 'Re-introduced', rather. Everyone had known the fairy Aleta once upon a time. Jib was a bit embarrassed about her comment.

"I meant no insult", she apologized. "It's just—well, you know Lorelei. Something is always stuck in her hair".

"I would've perched there myself", replied the hummingbird, "but she already had the bat".

In the moment of silence that followed, Lorelei reached back to see if it was true. It was. The creature took fright and flew away when she disturbed it. Everyone laughed, even Lorelei finally.

"But where are your guests?" she asked the pixies. "Where are the Rasha La?"

Everyone shrugged. Yero's voice came from under the table. "Is the bat gone?"

"It better be!" said Lorelei. "Come out. Your guide has been talking about you".

"And once you're acquainted you might find a perch in Lorelei's hair", suggested Atel. "She has a vacancy now".

The butterflies came out and danced in the air.

"This is Yero", said Atel. "She will explain everything. And this is Boca. He caused the stir up at Gorda's camp. Big trouble, if I may say so".

"A *boy*?" A dozen tough Swamp Rats took a step back. There were giggles.

"Yes, a boy. A lot of the trouble can be traced straight to him, but some goes to her as well".

"Then let's hear what happened", said Lorelei. "I like them already. Rebels fit in well with our bunch".

Yero didn't need any more prompting. "Airy let loose the chimes", she began. "But old Gorda caught the music and drowned it in her cistern, and then everyone was drinking it! But we didn't know it until she fell in and made a huge splash because she's so fat, and *that's* how the music escaped..." she paused in front of Lorelei's nose..."Um, is it all right if we *do* take a seat?" There was something about her hair that just looked welcoming. How could she refuse? Lorelei nodded. The butterflies settled in and Yero went on, bringing everything up to the moment — spending more time than necessary, perhaps, on the tarbaby crow episode because the 'Rats were much amused by that. Everyone agreed she had been clever and Yero decided that was a good place to stop and just enjoy the attention.

"Th'Anya perched crows all through th'swamp once, to spy us out", recalled one of the 'Rats. "We did much th'same with poles — plopped them into th'water".

"Oh", said Yero, and dropped the subject.

The Swamp Rats, although large like Nasha, were otherwise nearly identical to the Outpost pixies except for dress. They were 'dressed' in duckweed and algae, but it was on purpose, and at least the stuff was dry. This group was part of the 'upper' band. Another, larger group made up the 'lower' band down near the locks and dam. They had quick, elusive names like 'Flurry', 'Lightfoot', and 'Ski', and seemed to possess these very traits, which is probably why they escaped captivity in the first place and ended up here. Lorelei was definitely their leader.

"She's our 'thinker'", said Flit respectfully, and then laughed. "We had to find some job for her. She's too slow to be a raider".

Lorelei smiled absent-mindedly while talking to herself: "The Music — so *that's* how it got spooked. We wondered!" She turned to the hummingbird on her shoulder. "The Music was frightened and discouraged to find a dismal swamp here and not th'happy City it expected. It kept going, looking for the Queen naturally. But something bad must've happened down at th'locks, and it went into hiding — we didn't know where".

Putting a finger to her lips, she reached over the gunwale and caught the alarm rope. Flit and Jibber lent a hand, carefully pulling it closer until Lorelei was able to take an odd piece of metal in each hand and bump them softly together. "Clink" ("ping, pong, ping..."); a pretty echo, much prettier than it ought to have been, kept echoing. They set the alarms back in the water and the echo stopped. "Long time since we had music in the City", said Lorelei.

"'Twas taken from us", she told the butterflies. "We managed to save some and kept it safe in th'chimes. Your guide had a hand in that. But my, it's grown! We heard it from afar, coming downriver. It reminded us of th'jazzy parades we used to throw, welcoming lasses coming up from below".

"The boats were prettier then", said Atel. "I don't suppose the Anya throw parades".

"But they do!" smiled Jibber. "They parade through th'city exactly once a week, on business. Our population is small now, but we welcome them as best we can":

— Big Girls on Parade —

On schedule, every Saturday
Downriver, at some grimy quay,
A tarboat lowers the ol' gangway-
An' up the ol' gangplank they toil:
Th'Muckers, loading mucky oil

An' mucky grime onto the ship.
Th'Muckers toil beneath th'whip.

An' this is *right* we're told, 'cause all
— All *mucker fairies* — are quite small
Compared to those who wield th'whips.
One must be tall to snap a whip!
To be th'Master of a ship!
So little girls wield th'spades
While Big Girls go on parades!

Th'Biggest ride up on a float,
A decorated transport boat,
All polished up with creosote.
Grand Marshalls perch there, fore and aft,
While all around, the smaller craft —
So sleek and black! (Some burnt or charred)
Maneuver like a color guard.

Then Flitter twirls her baton
An' skates out front to lure them on:
'Le escort ala water-ski'
To our reception jamboree —
Where our welcoming committee
Known as 'Swamp Rats' or 'Banditti',
Waits to drown 'em, more's th'pity.

--- But first: Parades deserve huzzah!
So we bring music back to Ah
In tangled rope-alarms (Ha-ha!)
It's just an off-key 'clink' or 'clunk'
Because, of course, it's all space junk.
As Big Bands go, it's not so hot.
We'd give 'em more, but it's all we've got.

This tangles oars and slows th'galley,
Makes th'tarboat shillyshally,
So *then* we play the grand finale.
Our Chief Firebug has a chance to
Make some music they can *dance* to:
Something light, like sparks an' rockets
That find Anya hoods an' pockets.
(An' with luck, th'*underpants* too!).

"Swamp life is boring, between raids", said Jibber. "So, we joke around an' make up stuff like that. Raiding was more exciting in the bad old days when th'Anya first threw up th'dam an' flooded the City. Th'were stupid about fighting us back then. We sank boats an' drowned Blackcoats almost at will. But they didn't stay stupid very long. Now th'have escort vessels with extra whips and pikes, an' we have losses too. Lorelei invents new tricks to bother them but we're more a nuisance now than a real threat".

"But it's still fun", said Flit. "They must soak th'selves down when they come now, to protect against the fireworks; an' the water stinks, as you know. Ha-ha! So th'*hate* their job an' that makes it all worthwhile. I only wish we could see th'scowls under their hoods!"

"I wish I could've seen Gorda scowl, back at th'Dais", mused Lorelei. "She always scowled when th'talk turned to boys; but just so you know, young mister Boca—most of the girls *don't*".

There was a moment of silence. The 'Rats were nervous about a boy in their midst, but way too curious to back off.

"Here they go again", whispered Yero with some annoyance. "Don't do anything dumb!"

Boca closed his eyes but didn't wink out, or even dim. Not here in the very heart of the old realm, and he knew it from their talk.

"Th'radiance is...*different*", whispered one of the "Rats.

"*Fetching!*" whispered another. "Or even *dashing!* Not pretty, like a girl, but *handsome!* Oh my!"

"But a boy of so few words!" complained a third, a lass called 'Scamp'. "I want a boy who will flatter me".

"With compliments?" suggested the first 'Rat.

"Yes. All girls like that".

"About your cleverness and your beauty?"

"Why, yes! Sparingly, of course. I would do most of the talking—especially about th'*wedding!* I want a *big* wedding! You're all invited an' I plan on eleven bridesmaids with—"

"Whoa, Scamp! Practice on Boca then, for th'boy of your dreams will need to be a boy of few words also!"

Everyone laughed, including the third 'Rat (Properly named 'Scamper'). "Maybe so", said she, "but my beau will think up a pet name for me, an' *we* ought to think up one for Boca! Something sweet, of course".

Several mushy suggestions were put forth right away. Yero giggled. Boca blushed. Lorelei intervened.

"Girls, please! Boys are shy of that stuff if you didn't know. How about something noble? Why not *Ombomba*: 'The boy who lit the fuse'?"

It was a popular choice. Everyone liked it. Even Boca liked it. He opened his eyes and took to the air to do a 'fly-by' curtain call, and then another. It drew enthusiastic applause.

"Was that really necessary?" sniffed Yero when the great Ombomba landed again (a little higher up in Lorelei's hair, now, than where she was). "I'm sure she only thought about that because boys like to play with matches".

"Maybe, but someone has to", said Boca importantly. "There's a war on".

"Yes, yes. But do you have to carry on quite that much?"

"Can't help it, Yero. I'm a boy of few words. I have to make up for it with deeds". (Even so, Boca did find a few gallant words for his new admirers, but the story cannot pause for all of them. There *was* a war on, after all.)

"...Which brings us to the question: What next?" said Lorelei. "At least now we have the key". She reached down and jangled the rope again. Music rose above the clanking of the junk and filled the air around them, regaining courage from what it had overheard.

"Half the key", reminded Atel. "The Queen being the other half—and we must bring them together somehow".

"Yes. Somehow. 'Twill need deception. Th'Anya are very powerful between here and there".

"So I gather. Where is she?"

"On an island. Alone. In the Hole".

"The what?"

"The *Hole*. The *sinkhole* where th'Rowah disappears now. Th'Anya opened it up in the bad old days. It likely would have swallowed us all but the Queen stopped it, temporarily".

"That's a long 'temporary'".

"Poor word. I should've said: 'Ever since, for the whole Age'. Time flies, doesn't it? But so long as her island is still there, and her on it, the sinkhole is plugged. That's how we know she's still there; but no one ever sees her. Even th'mucker-fairies who slave in the Hole every day never see her because of the fog." She turned to the 'Rats. "How many have worked in the Hole?" At least half raised their hands, including Jibber, who only shrugged.

"We've all worked with th'muck one place or another", she said, "except *her*, maybe!" She pointed an accusing finger at Nasha, who blushed in embarrassment but answered the challenge.

"I worked with it", she responded. "Down in that Hole." She turned to Atel. "That's where th'muck collects", she explained. "It bubbles up to th'surface of the sinkhole pool an' smears onto shore. Th'seems no end to it. A long Age of that dirty job was finally enough for me, so I 'joined up'". She looked Jibber in the eye. "I wish I hadn't", she said. "Now I'm trying to make up for it".

"Just don't expect us to believe you".

"Leave it there", warned Lorelei. "That's more than enough".

It wasn't enough for the 'Rats by the looks on their faces, but the Outpost pixies rallied around Nasha. A testy truce ensued.

"I don't like the idea of fog", said Atel. "The Music will be wary of the Big Sisters now, but it could get lost in the fog and recaptured. Are the Anya strong down in there?"

Nasha shook her head. "No worries on that point. Th'Anya themselves seldom venture into the Hole. Too dirty! But th'fog never lifts. There's something hot under that pool, an' it steams. Maybe the Rowah leaks away down under, or maybe it just evaporates into the fog. No one knows. Either way, the river ends; but there'll be big trouble before you ever get that far".

"*Way* before", agreed Lorelei. "The first problem will be the Locks, down at the dam. There's always a garrison of Blackcoats there, an' if they don't like what th'see they'll set th'crows a-cawing all downstream to the Big Camp. That's where the Bosses are: Th'*Big* Bosses. If *they* suspect trouble, they'll stop all river traffic and you'll never get anywhere near the Queen. We need ideas. Anybody?"

"I have one", said Nasha, standing up tall in her soggy black robe. "I think I can bluff past them. But you'll have to trust me".

That was more than the 'Rats could swallow. The mood turned icy between the two groups. Atel hovered in the middle trying to prevent mutiny.

"If there are better ideas, let's hear them! We'll gladly listen. If not, we'll need *her*. None of *us* could fool them. Any better ideas?"

There weren't any, but the 'Rats plainly wanted no part of Nasha. The pixies all took a step forward. The 'Rats stepped back, scowling. Lorelei groaned. Atel refused to foresee any conflict.

"Keep your girls here, Lorelei. We'll attempt the bluff. Fewer are better anyway for deception; and you'll be working overtime, if you mean to go ahead with your own plan".

Lorelei nodded. "A flood would be useful at th'proper moment, hmm? Even better if th'smell trouble an' gather along the river! We've wanted to do this for a long time, but the time hasn't been right. We're ready now, except for final touches. But the timing must be up to you. Make some music. We'll hear it".

"There'll be muckers down in the Hole", warned Nasha. "There are always muckers down there". Lorelei nodded silently.

"The Queen, too", said Atel. "It'll be a somber victory if she is drowned along with her music".

"But still a victory and freedom hath a music of its own. We all know—the slave girls downriver know it too—that our side will only get one chance. This is it, I think".

No one disagreed, neither pixie nor 'Rat. But that's all they agreed on.

"Okay, then" —said Atel after a moment—"about your Blackcoats down at the Locks. Will they have news from Gorda?"

"No. Th'Anya can't fly and th'crows can't either. Any news must pass through here on a boat".

"The last 'Parade' went up an' back five days ago", put in Jibber. "The only news they took back was, th'Swamp Rats are alive an' well".

"Th'will suspect nothing at the Locks", said Nasha.

"Who would know better?" sneered Jibber. "But down at the Big Camp th'*will* suspect. *They'll* stop you! If you slip up, girl, an' they get th'music—it's *over*. We're *done for*. Don't fail us!"

"I can only do my best".

That didn't impress the 'Rats, and there was trouble when Nasha asked for archery gear and wanted to bundle up the rope alarm too and stow everything in Gorda's cargo box. Even the music didn't like that. Lorelei had to explain the plan twice and they had to take extra care not to bump the metal pieces while they did this, lest the music flee.

"I wouldn't want to be locked up like that either", whispered Yero. "Music should always be free".

"At least we still are", replied Boca. "We can fly if we have to".

"Not for long", Atel informed them. "You'll be joining me in the birdcage".

"*There*? Why?"

"Because you're too small for leg irons. Come along".

Another near mutiny erupted at the sight of Nasha locking up the pixies all along the benches. Lorelei somehow kept order and made sure the pixies got something to eat. The 'Rats shared their lunch out of small bags that hung on their belts. It was liquid and tasted like honey.

"'Tisn't, of course", Flitter admitted to the butterflies, "since there are no flowers here in th'Swamp. 'Tis mostly sour tree sap an' we improve th'flavor...artificially".

"What does that mean?" asked Yero doubtfully.

"It's mind over matter, girl. 'Tis only sour if you think about it, so don't".

"I can't *stop* thinking about it now", whispered Boca, sipping half-heartedly from a few drops set aside for them.

"Me either", admitted Yero. "I'm glad for the lunch, but next time I won't ask how it's made".

Nasha locked the cage then and started another quarrel by refusing the food. That didn't help anything and led to an angry parting. She took up her post in front and leaned into it. The black boat moved off downstream.

"Don't fail, girl!" Jib shouted after them. Nasha never looked back. The last the butterflies saw was Lorelei talking to them and the 'Rats hardly listening. Then the boat swept around a corner of the channel, out of sight.

"You'll see them again soon", said Atel, as if reading the butterflies' minds. "They're coming to council and they are faster than any black boat. Just enjoy the ride while you can".

To be fair, it wasn't all that bad in the cage if one could overlook the smell. Yero grumbled about that.

"Ignore it", said Atel shortly.

"One thing at a time, I wish! We're still ignoring the food!"

"Then take a really good whiff, and this will help you forget the other!"

Yero turned away in disgust, which was exactly what the hummingbird wanted so she could think in peace. Very soon the Swamp Rats did reappear and passed them by, skimming along on their 'batts'. Several shouted insults and barely veiled threats at Nasha. The butterflies could see tears trickling down past her swollen nose when she looked the other way, for the cage was inside the open door just behind her.

"Don't listen!" shouted Yero. "They don't know you".

"No, but th'have seen me in my robe more than once. I've been through here before on this very boat".

The Butterflies, Yero and Boca

"Well, Boca and I are ignoring two things already for stink and bad taste. Let's ignore those 'Rats for the same reasons".

That bucked up Nasha's spirits. She kept her eyes on the channel ahead, but she smiled.

The channel opened into a small lake after a while, and she slowed the boat. A big crowd of 'Rats were there, waiting. Nasha whispered that this was once the 'town square', the very center of Ah, where the channels all came together. "I didn't know there were so many rebels", she whistled. "I have much to ignore".

There were several hundred with grim, impatient faces. Lorelei seemed to be number one here also, but another girl was at her elbow. Yero looked around as best she could from the cage. If all channels merged here, there was no sign of them. The poison sumac grew solidly around the pool, except where the sawgrass stood tall. If happy memories lingered, they were well hidden.

Nasha held out the birdcage to Lorelei and a growl went up from the crowd. Lorelei ignored it and engaged Atel in urgent conversation. The lass at her elbow, a pretty blonde, raised a hand and the growl subsided. Moonlight seemed to find her face wherever she looked, but mostly she stared curiously at the butterflies. Yero felt comfortable under her gaze. The lass winked and smiled at them, not even listening. Whatever Lorelei and Atel were discussing she already knew, apparently. Then the short meeting was over, the lass joined them on the boat, and Nasha clapped her in irons as well. Then they were off again.

"Her name is 'Catchbeam'", said Atel. "She has volunteered to be the 'whipping girl' for the entertainment of the guards down at the Locks. Someone has to, or we all will be, and that would be disastrous. We'll need our strength further downriver. We can't afford to be weakened too soon".

"She's gonna *ask* for it?"

"Yes".

Atel said no more, but it wasn't hard to imagine the rest. Yero shuddered.

The Swamp Rats melted into the shadows between one backward glance and the next. Soon the boat came to places that were more open. The channel pools deepened and only the tops of old trees stuck up above the water. They were dead, these trees, having died untimely. Their leaves hadn't colored properly and still stuck to their twigs as if aware that something was wrong and waiting for it to be put right again.

Atel was in a solemn mood and gave only one-word answers, so mostly the butterflies listened to talk from the back of the boat where things were more cheerful. It was like a party back there. Everyone knew Catchbeam and she was a very bad criminal by the sounds of it, but the sounds were mostly laughter. Nasha glanced back once or twice through the open door and shook her head, but if Yero asked about trouble ahead she gave even shorter answers than their guide did.

The channel gave way finally to a wide-open pool with no treetops at all, and the pool ended at an earthen embankment overgrown with coarse grasses. Nasha relaxed and let a slow current take them toward the left shore where the pool narrowed and spilled over steep rubble into a churning pool below. To the left of that again were locks where boats could pass through. A number of hooded Anya lounged there on a bench in front of the Lock Shack. Nasha steered directly for the lock gate, expecting it to open. An apprentice scurried to the big wheel and began cranking furiously.

"More speed, Azi!" Nasha hollered. "Special cargo for downriver". It was partly in jest. They knew each other well.

"Keep thy hood down!" shouted the other with a grin. "You know how slow this thing is".

The gate gradually opened and Nasha nosed the boat into the lock. Just as slowly, the hooded ones bestirred themselves from their bench and came to stand on the lock wall only a few feet away.

"Tie 'er up for now!" barked one of them—shorter and fatter, *much* fatter—than the others. The apprentice abandoned the gate wheel in haste and tossed a rope. Nasha caught it and made it fast, and the boat was pulled up tight to the wall. The Fat One stepped carelessly aboard, narrowly missing Lolly on the bench, and looked around.

"What have we here now?" she wheezed, breathing heavily from her exertion. Nasha quickly presented herself front and center, bowing correctly to the fat one.

"Apprentice Nasha reporting—" she began but was interrupted.

"I know who you are and where you're *supposed* to be! I know all that. I wanna know what you're doing *here*. Who are these?"

"The usual. Petty criminals for re-assignment".

"Sure, sure". The Fat One looked up and down the benches. "Typical delinquents—except *this* one!" She stomped hard on Catchbeam's foot, didn't get the reaction she expected, and stomped again. Catchbeam just smiled, but the effort had winded the fat Anya.

"You...just wait...'Rat! We'll...make you squeak!" She puffed and took a minute to catch her breath. "What else you got?"

"A trophy for the Triad!" said Nasha proudly. "One of the cursed rope alarms". She pointed toward the cargo hold. The Fat One barely glanced.

"Junk. Those things are a dime a dozen. What else?"

"Something special. *Very special*. But you're to keep your fingers *off!* —That's Gorda's exact words". This bordered on insubordination and Nasha well knew it. "*Very special*", she repeated stubbornly.

"Show me!" hissed the Fat One.

"Will you keep your fingers off? I'm under orders".

"Sure, sure! Now hop quick, girl, or we'll chain you to a door right alongside this one!" She stomped at Catchbeam's foot again but missed. This time she didn't have the wind to try again. Nasha hurried inside the cabin and came back with the birdcage, holding it high. All the Anya leaned back, even the Fat One, at the sight.

"Oooo!" she cooed, recognizing the hummingbird's radiance. "How'd Gorda snatch *that* one?"

"Th'small fry are her pals. We used them for bait an' caught a big fish".

"Never thought I'd see it!" said the Fat One deliciously. "She used to be quite the Big Shot. Here, gimme that!"

Nasha pulled the cage away quickly. "Not for you! She's for the Triad. Let us pass".

"Not so fast, not so fast! Somethin' stinks here. Whatta you doin' all by yourself with such important cargo? Gorda woulda sent a riot squad along on this trip".

"She did. I'm all that's left! The others drowned", lied Nasha. "Where are your patrols when they're needed? That's what Gorda will be asking". Nasha pointed to several swift boats bumping idly against their moorings near the Lock Shack. Nasha knew how it was, up and down the river. The Anya were lazy and lived in dread of the Swamp Rats. The duty schedule here at the locks always called for regular patrols through the Swamp but patrols seldom ventured out. The weekly convoys were more than enough excitement for the Big Sisters.

Nasha pointed to the fire-charred cabin roof. "That's the only stink, Madame, not counting th'dirty criminals. There was an ambush. A big fight. I should be commended for not losing the prisoners". It was a convincing act, especially with the broken nose and ugly bruises up into her eyes. Nasha didn't have to act that part. The Fat One seemed to buy it, but obviously itched to get her fingers on Atel.

"Sure, sure—but I wanna play with the bird a bit, before the Big Bosses get her. An old score to settle, you might say". She grabbed for the cage again; Nasha backed away.

"Not for you, Madame—that's *orders!* I'm calling ahead". Before anyone could stop her, Nasha shouted a few guttural syllables to the local crow perched on the gable end of the Shack. The thing was more obese even than the Lock Boss and seemed very interested in the goings-on. Now it raised its ugly voice and initiated a 'caw', passing the news downriver from one crow to the next. In a few minutes, it would reach the Big Camp and the news would make them smile. They would be expecting the prize very soon, unspoiled.

The Fat One was enraged. It was *her* job, and not any snot-nosed apprentice's, to manage the crows! Her fingers that had so wanted to pinch the bird twitched in their gloves impotently. Then it occurred to her that the unauthorized 'caw' was just a notice about the prized prisoner—not her own shortcomings. She quickly turned the whole episode to her advantage, ordering the crow to send a follow-up message granting herself full credit.

That taken care of, she turned her attention to revenge. Hmm! Who best to take it out on? It couldn't be the bird now, and it couldn't be the snotty apprentice, not today; but it could be anyone else. Her gaze fell immediately on Catchbeam, the smiling one.

At a word, the other Blackcoats boarded. At another word, Catchbeam was unshackled and dragged to the cabin doors where she was clapped into irons hanging there for just this purpose.

"Now then", said the Fat One unexpectedly to Nasha, "Let's see what a Big Girl you are!" She thrust a bullwhip into her hand and gestured toward Catchbeam. "Entertain us", she ordered, and sat herself down—half on the bench, half on top of poor little Poo, never even noticing.

This is what Catchbeam had volunteered for—but not Nasha. The Fat One sensed her reluctance and was thrilled. "Do it!" she commanded. Nasha did but wasn't very good with the whip and was soon ordered out of the way as professionals took over. Catchbeam finally did close her eyes but never quit smiling, so the whipping went on and on. At last the Fat One got bored and had to be helped up out of the boat, and that needed all of the others, so the whipping came to a halt. But once ashore, she ordered them back aboard to serve as extra guards down the river and to "Pass the *sting* around to the small fry".

The Lock Boss felt mighty clever, but Nasha thanked her sincerely with a worried glance at the treetops upstream. "There are 300 whacko rebels right up there!" she said nervously. "They almost killed me already. There's no telling what th'might do next".

Fatty hesitated. Her arrogance evaporated. Trouble right here at the Locks wasn't unheard-of. The last thing she needed was some crazy assault when she was short-handed. Certainly not today! She was eager to work the crows and send more glowing messages. Why, this could be her finest moment! But she needed security. She pulled three Sisters off the boat again, leaving the fourth partly because (like herself) that one was too fat to help anyway if the 'Rats attacked.

"Put 'em through!" she barked at Azi, "Then jump in a boat and scout the trees up there!" She waved upstream and ducked inside the Lock Shack with her Sisters on her heels. Azi bent to the task obediently, cranking the gate wheel. Two thoughts came to her mind immediately: She wasn't going to scout very far, and the bosses wouldn't be outside watching anyway.

***

The fourth Anya was a bad one, unfortunately. Nasha knew her reputation. Her official title was 'Madame Eve', but in her own mind she liked to add an 'L' to the end of it. Her thing was details, playing with them until she ferreted out liars and cheats among her superiors, and then using the little scandals to her advantage. Thus, she had worked her way up to Second Lock Officer by blackmail, grabbing promotions that would have gone to her victims. That was the other reason the Lock Boss left her on the boat—to get snoopy Madame Eve out of her own hair.

Now she sat atop the rear cargo hold, using the bundled rope alarm as a seat cushion, and asked harmless questions—almost friendly ones, at least in tone. She was curious and very sympathetic about the manacles and leg irons. Did they chafe? She wished folks would understand that not all Anya were cruel like the Lock Boss. Some like herself were willing to grant consideration—even clemency, on occasion—to ordinary prisoners. So, the irons were not too tight? Good! That was a relief to her. It was so stupid was it not, to mistreat prisoners? Some of the Bosses just didn't understand. The *detainees* (she preferred this less-harsh term) were always expected to go straight to work at their new post, and how could they do so if they were beaten? Eve sighed and gestured sympathetically. It would've been more convincing if she showed a sympathetic face too, but like all the Big Sisters that was hidden under the deep hood. Still, it was a good act.

"Really, the irons aren't bad at all", replied Flossie. "See? Th'don't even hold me". She pulled her arms out to demonstrate.

"My, my", said Madame Eve, "You can't be much of a criminal or they'd lock you up tighter! What minor offense are you charged with?"

"Oh, the usual stuff", said Flossie more evasively. "You know. Smarting off an' whatnot".

"What about the other girls?"

"Same thing, mostly. Just sassing".

"That doesn't sound serious. Is that all?"

"Well, we fibbed about flat tires on th'wheelbarrows". It still bothered Flossie to have told a fib. She glanced sidelong at Lolly next to her. Lolly gave her an elbow in the ribs to quiet her down.

"But that still doesn't seem like much", crooned Eve. "If I were Gorda I wouldn't make any big deal about that. I wish she were here right now! I'd tell her so! Where is she anyway? She usually rides along on these little trips".

Flossie kept quiet this time, but Eve let the question hang in the air until another pixie finally spoke up. Some of the pixies were just very sweet lasses willing to be nice if only someone would be nice to them. And Eve was good at acting nice.

"She fell into th'cistern an' got all wet", said Poo. There were giggles up and down the benches at this.

Eve giggled too. "That's so amusing! I'm not fond of her, you know. How did it happen?"

"Trying to grab th'butterflies", said another lass.

"An' missing", said another. More giggles.

"Oh my, I wish I had seen that! She is so clumsy, isn't she? No wonder she missed the boat then. It takes time to dry wet robes. Build a fire and all that..."

"Oh, th'was plenty of fire!" laughed Florry. "Not that it did *her* any good".

"That would be the bird at work!" growled Eve, unable to keep the edge out of her voice. She barked and Nasha came back to see what was wanted, letting the boat drift slowly with the current. The river was wide and easy to navigate below the locks anyway—just follow the buoys upon which the crows were perched. Madame Eve pulled out a large, dirty handkerchief and threw it at her. "Cover the cage!" she ordered. "Tie it tight. I don't want any trouble aboard". Then she settled back and tried to get into her nice character again.

"The bird has much to answer for", she sighed. "It's unfair of her—*selfish!*—to involve the little ones in criminal activity. She ought to be ashamed!"

"She's very nice!" scolded Poo. "You don't know her".

"Well, that's partly true", replied Eve agreeably. "I knew her long ago, but I suppose we've both changed. All we know now is what the Big Bosses tell us, and they don't like her. But perhaps there are two sides to the story?"

"For sure! Your bunch is so mean, it's no wonder you get trouble!"

"Don't give me that sob story!" snapped Eve. "I'm sure it was because of *her* this boat was attacked and innocent guards lost, the little *witch*!" Atel really irked her and it showed. The pixies were on their guard now, even Poo and Flossie. Eve saw it, took a deep breath, and smiled again.

"Please, make allowance for that last. We had words once, nothing more. I have *long* forgiven her! Unknown to me some prejudice lingered, but I cast it out now! My heart has changed greatly, turning more toward the light. I wish I could open it and show you. I wish *all* the Sisters could change as I have and perhaps find peace. I live to forgive now. I could even forgive *that* one..."(Pointing to Catchbeam, still dangling from her chains) "...who has harmed so many of us! You must have noticed when the others were whipping the poor creature, that I didn't lift a finger against her".

"Not to help her either", pointed out Airy.

"But, to *not hurt her* was something, don't you agree? Be fair, please. I can't be blamed for what my superiors do. In all honesty, I have come gradually to admire the rebels. I yearn for a day when we set aside our differences and work together again for the greater good!"

"Oh, you'd put them to work, all right!" jeered Lolly.

"Peace! Peace be with you, girl! I only revealed what's in my heart. Have I not bared my soul here? To be ridiculed, perhaps, but opened it nonetheless? In the same spirit of honesty, I ask, how did the rebels fail to capture this vessel? I would have bet on them".

Her voice was beginning to lull a few of them again. Flossie opened her mouth to speak but Airy beat her to it.

"You can thank *that* one!" she said bitterly, jerking a thumb up front at Nasha. "When everyone else jumped ship she took th'helm an' outran the rebels. Then she made *us* put out th'fire!"

Eve switched tactics, zeroing in more directly on her target. "So heroic of her! But I hate fighting. I've always favored the arts—most of all the old Music! It was so beautiful! Faith, we had thought it lost forever; but lately it wafted down from upstream even as far as the Locks. It brought tears to my eyes, though I don't deny some were displeased. We all know who *they* are. But some of us took heart! Then to our dismay it went away again, and we heard it no more. Have you any news?" No one did. Eve kept her cool and tried again.

"I remember the 'Good Old Days', don't we all? One could spend a whole day just listening to melodies! Oh, some didn't love it, but they grow weary now. Something is missing in their hearts. Maybe just the Music? Had you thought of this? Maybe the Big Bosses are weariest of all and if the Music found their hearts it could begin the healing of Ah! How I wish I could spend my poor life searching for it, for this musical treasure that belongs equally to all! But I fear that misguided souls will lock it away again now and sit on it forever".

The pixies couldn't help laughing at the irony. Madame Eve got a blank look and began to get mad.

"It's right under your big *butt*", giggled Poo, and then clapped a horrified hand over her mouth.

Eve stared at her, putting things together in her mind. Dead silence fell. They approached a buoy and the crow was chuckling from what it overheard. Then Madame Eve chuckled too, and it grew into an evil laugh. It wasn't hard to guess everything now.

"Oh-ho! This was easier than I expected!" she chortled and bestirred her buttocks. She stood up with a grunt, turned around and bent over to grab the rope alarm with its curious noisemakers just as Nasha appeared in the cabin doorway with Gorda's whip. By lucky chance, she snapped it good for once and stung Eve on the rump with a loud report. Madame pitched headfirst over the hold and into the river. She bobbed up again but Nasha grabbed an oar and smacked her on top of the hood. That was the end of Madame Eve and it was very upsetting to the tarbaby crow as they passed by, so Nasha swung the oar again and knocked that ugly creature into the water as well. All the pixies cheered except Poo, who sobbed uncontrollably.

"Don't go blaming yourself", said Airy. "She had to be got rid of somehow." But Poo was inconsolable.

"Let her cry", said Nasha. "'Twill look realistic when we get to the Big Camp. That won't be long now".

She pulled the cloth off the birdcage and set it up where the occupants could see the river, then released Catchbeam from her chains to sit in the cabin. The whipping girl's eyes were open again and she was already beginning to recover, as only fairy folk can. Nasha unlocked the pixie's irons but left them on loosely. Then she dug out the archery gear from the bottom of the hold and stacked it neatly on the buffet table.

"Looks like it was 'captured', I hope", she said. "But we won't fool them for long. You'll know what to do with these when the time comes".

Part 2: Beyond the Moonwalk

The voyage quieted down then, except for the crows, who cawed incessantly. Maybe it was messages coming down from the locks, or maybe the crows had just seen more than they should have, but the boat was now out of favor with them. The only other noises were Poo in back, and Nasha up front whispering with Atel.

All too soon, they came to places where black-robed Anya populated the shores and stared as the boat went by. They passed the gardens where a few Blackcoats were actually working, and then the Boatworks where Little Laca pointed out a few landmarks. The place looked almost abandoned.

"After hours, I guess", she said. "Th'must be only one shift now".

"That's a bit of luck", said Nasha. "Th'good girls will be in th'barracks, higher up. What say thee to music, Aleta? We are nearing the showdown".

"What are our chances there, alone?"

"No chance at all. None ".

"And with Lorelei's help?"

"We probably still die, but they die with us".

"Ask the others. We do this together".

When Nasha turned around the pixies raised their fists, all of them. No word was spoken.

"Send the message", directed Atel.

Nasha smiled fiercely and signaled the pixies, but Catchbeam rose, well-enough recovered, and made her way aft. She banged two pieces of the junk together and a single high note leapt back upstream toward the locks and the swamp above them. She then assumed her position at the 'whipping door' once more, arms loosely in the irons.

Now the river swerved to the left, widening into a bay on that side. The shore hummed with activity. This was the Big Camp and it stretched for a mile or more with its buildings and other construction in progress. At the far, lower end of the bay was a promontory point where the river narrowed again, gathering itself for a swift dash over the falls beyond. Gates stretched across the narrows to collect any wayward craft that would otherwise be lost in the cataract as the Rowah emptied itself into the 'Hole'. Even where they still were, above the Camp, the falls rumbled, and fog shrouded everything below the gates.

On the promontory point was assembled the Grand Chorus, several score of the Blackcoats in echelons, arranged by height like a fine church choir. This was their deadliest weapon, but not turned loose just yet. First, the boat must report to the Big Bosses. Nasha covered the cage again with the black rag.

Without hesitation she steered toward a huge floating wharf, black like their boats, and blacker still with a great crowd of the Anya awaiting them. At the very end of the wharf stood three Anya together, taller than all others.

"Th'Big Bosses are waiting", Nasha whispered to the birdcage. "They call th'selves the 'Triad'. Everything is in their favor here except th'Curtain. The Aurora is very bright above us, even brighter than usual. Here we are then..."

She slowed the boat and stopped just far enough away that the boarding plank didn't seem to reach. "Forgive me!" she cried and reversed the craft awkwardly. The plank still didn't reach.

"I'm just an apprentice!" she shouted. "Never ran th'boat before". The Assemblage remained silent, its patience wearing thin. Nasha clumsily attempted more fits and starts, unable to bring the boat alongside but exposing the rear deck to the crowd, which pressed closer and closer, looking for the advertised 'prize'. Nasha noted what appeared to be the last straggling Blackcoats coming down from barracks up on higher ground.

"Where is Madame Eve?" demanded a spokesmadam.

"Lost", answered Nasha simply. "But I still have *all* th'prisoners! That's Catchbeam on the door".

An appreciative growl went up. The Triad purred at the sight.

"A toy to play with!" trilled the spokesmadam. "Very nice, though overdue. Now summon enough skill to dock the boat. We are most anxious to see the other prize!"

"Here she is!" answered Nasha, acting stupid. She held the cage high and pulled off the rag.

It wasn't proper protocol at all, but the Anya were eager to see the hated Aleta—in any form—delivered to them so neat and tidy. Right there under the Aurora she couldn't hide her radiance if she had wanted to, and everyone recognized it. A huge roar went up, and then Atel gave them more. Much more. With every eye upon her she verily burst with light and blinded them all—for a few moments, at least.

Nasha made use of the respite, swerving away and steering for the narrows gates as fast as she could propel the boat. Their little trick had gained that much. A head start before the Anya shore patrol could blink away the glare and give chase in their swiftboats. But it didn't delay the Grand Chorus as much. Now it raised its great voice, much louder than the Chorus back at the Dais. The first high notes were aimed at the boatmaster and found their mark. Nasha expected it and died instantly but confounded her murderers by falling purposely forward onto the bow so the power of the robe was still directed forward and the boat surged on toward the gates.

Along the wharf, the quickest, meanest patrol goons blinked out the glare and leaped into the fastest skimming craft to pursue. Up ahead at the gates all hands grabbed long-handled gaffs and waited. On Gorda's boat, Catchbeam and the pixies shook off their shackles and opened the birdcage. Then the force really hit. The Chorus shifted focus from Nasha to the rest of the crew and struck them like a physical blow. There were hundreds of Anya by now on or near the Wharf and at least half as many on the promontory point, all acting now as synchronized choirs to the Grand Chorus.

This was the center of the Anya Empire and the Chorus was their instrument of power. The Big Sisters had always been known for shouting down more reasonable voices and had taken that rude social weapon to this extreme. They fancied it as the 'New Music' after they got rid of the other and added a few melodic and rhythmic refinements that worked well to control the servant class. Now in grave emergency they skipped the small stuff and just hit the dominant seventh chords. The pixies were struck with a clash of cymbals in their souls, but not before they unleashed a hail of arrows at the oncoming swiftboats. They broke apart into sparks and cinders of course, but Swamp Rat magic sent most of this into the dark hoods, burning those within and putting them out of action, yet others kept coming.

Atel lay sprawled, insensible, near Nasha's body on the foredeck. The butterflies were beside her, but very much awake. Maybe they had been shielded by Nasha, or maybe their spirits were just different from the fairies, but this Chorus, too, was having trouble with them.

"So! At least *you* heroes are still with it!" said a cheerful voice. It was Catchbeam—she of the unbreakable spirit (or as the Anya called her—'Cuckoo'). "We need pilots! Grab Nasha's robe. *Lean*, like *she* did. Steer for the gates. Steer the boat!"

She grabbed Gorda's whip and headed back aft as cheerful as ever. She had long waited to pay back the Anya for many whippings! What could be more fun than this?

The butterflies did as they were told and found to their great surprise they *could* steer, and even gain a little bit of speed. Touching the robe was the key. They perched atop Nasha's hood to see over the bow and saw nothing but trouble ahead or behind. Things were quickly becoming impossible. Catchbeam was fighting off several boats single-handedly and making them pay dearly. But while she was winning to portside, other patrols were pulling up to the starboard gunwale, and the boat was slowing down, way down, obeying a new command from the Grand Chorus, until they were almost dead in the water.

Then the unthinkable happened.

The Chorus faltered and quit, to be replaced by a less-organized noise: The up-river crows were squawking in panic and behind that a larger noise was growing swiftly, a great hollow roar. The 'Rats had blown the dam with their clever fireworks. A churning wall of water and debris heaved into sight upstream. Lorelei's flood was coming.

Atel and the pixies stirred, awakening quickly once the power of the chorus was removed. The boat regained speed. Several Blackcoats that had got aboard stood dumbstruck at the unfolding catastrophe. Catchbeam simply pushed them overboard.

"Brace yourselves!" shouted Atel. "We're going to hit the gates!" Indeed, they were. The butterflies had steered well; but the gate crew, still following orders, reached with their long gaffs.

Crunch! The boat broke the barricade, only to be snagged by many hooks. Surely, they would've been hauled to one side or the other, but the opposing crews worked against each other in their panic, holding the boat amidstream. Catchbeam laughed in their faces.

"Look!" She pointed to the wall of water just now tossing the big wharf like a toy with all their Sisters. "A nice bath for you pigs, courtesy of the Swamp Rats!"

The gaffers lost their nerve and ran for higher ground, stepping on each other's robes and cursing. Yero could tell from Catchbeam's broad grin that they wouldn't make it. The boat broke through the wreckage dragging the gaffs alongside and the pixies pitched them over. Then fog took them, shutting out everything but the twin roars: The flood behind and the cataracts just ahead.

"Don't go down with the ship", said a voice behind Yero. "You have work to do yet!" She turned around. Airy, Lolly, and all the pixies had come forward. Catchbeam was still busy with something astern.

"Your wings!" remembered Yero suddenly. "They're back on the Curtain!"

Airy nodded. None of the pixies looked unhappy now, as their doom approached. Poo even smiled.

"We win", she said simply.

There were no goodbyes. There wasn't time. The fog parted briefly above the falls. A giant crow rose up on a rock in front of them, a last unsleeping sentinel against trespassers. It pecked viciously down, splintering the boat to pieces. In the instant before it struck Catchbeam held the rope alarm high and shook the music out of it—Clang! Bong! Bang! —and from that racket sweet overtures escaped into the mist. The pixies cheered. Then all reality exploded and Yero was lost, flying into the fog, calling for Boca. They almost bumped nose to nose. Atel appeared out of nowhere. "Follow the music!" she shouted above the roar of the water. Then they lost her, and they lost each other again.

***

A vision appeared to Yero as she hurtled through the fog: A Lady. Yero knew instinctively that it was the Queen. She was tall and splendid, taller than any fairy Yero had seen, dressed in the pleated leaves of purple coneflowers. She wore no crown, but the purple flowers came together like a wreath on her shoulders. Her expression was difficult to read—friendly maybe, but very serious. She beckoned Yero and pointed to a mirror, one of many that now appeared around them. In the mirror— in all the mirrors—Yero saw her own reflection, but differently. She saw herself as she had been in other times and places, beginning as a baby and growing up as a child.

Oddly, she was still at speed and felt wind on her wings, but time slowed down in front of the mirrors. There was time enough to look in all of them, enough even to dawdle before a few. One or two of them embarrassed her. She blushed and hurried past those, but mostly it was fun, and she lingered. Unexpectedly, the mirrors seemed to work both ways and many of the reflections were aware of her, too. Some of the people in them smiled and waved.

The mirrors brought her gradually up to the present and she knew she was getting close when she saw a mirror with Boca in the fog. She paused at that one, shaking her head. What was he doing? Sitting on something. Just sitting. Honestly, boys could be so lazy.

"Don't look at me like that!" said Boca-in-the-mirror. She stuck her tongue out to show him who was real and who was just a reflection. The Boca reached out and tweaked it—Ploop!

"Oh yuck!" she spluttered. "Only a real Boca would do that!" She glared at him.

The Boca laughed obnoxiously. "Come and sit down".

She finally did and her feet tingled. "It's a harp", he explained, tapping one toe. "The Music came here and went right into it. I can feel it in my toes like it's talking to me. I think it wants me to play the strings".

"Don't do it, Boca. It might belong to the Queen, and She ought to play it".

"You're probably right. You know what? I met her already, in the fog".

"Me too. Did you look in the mirrors? I saw my whole life in them".

"No. No mirrors. She showed me a picture book and turned the pages for me, but it was my own story! I was *in* it, along with everyone I ever knew".

"Okay. Same thing, sort of. Would you change any pages—if you could?"

"A few. Yeah. Some were just too silly, the ones with girls in them".

"Oh, Boca. You're sillier than anyone! You should see yourself showing off in front of the fairy lasses".

"They expect that. I can't disappoint them".

Yero rolled her eyes. "That's not what I was getting at! What I *meant* was—did you see the pages where you were naughty? There should've been some".

"Oh yeah. She made sure I saw *those*. How about you?"

"Yes. I felt like I was...on trial, almost, and had to be my own judge." She lowered her voice. "I'll bet that's why she scares the 'Onions': They don't dare look in the mirrors! I know my trial would've been easier if I was, like—a little closer to *perfect*." She frowned and snapped her fingers. "From now on I will be!"

"Don't bother. Girls are never perfect".

"Oh? And boys *are*? You don't think you have any faults?"

"Not many. We're heroes. They call me 'Ombomba'. Hey—where're you going?"

"A safe distance", answered Yero, walking quickly away.

"What's the danger?"

"Your swollen head. It might explode, and I don't want to get hit by flying baloney".

That's how Atel found them. She appeared out of the mist behind them, perched once more on someone's shoulder—not Lorelei's this time but another, taller fairy who greeted them with a weary smile. They turned and recognized the Queen.

The fog was lifting noticeably, letting in more light. But it was hard to guess whether the Queen was young, or old, or even what color her hair was. Her dress, which might once have been pretty leaves, was all mud. She was a mess, but she smiled and sat at the harp and played a little, and the harp music went up and out to the far corners of Nyo, and all who survived the flood knew that the Music was in the Queen's harp once more and she was free. The Artisan heard it too and decided to stitch up the Curtain after all when she got time for it. It would be needed, so long as the Music lived.

***

"Your guide has told me a little about you", said the Queen, "and I would learn more, as time allows. Lorelei named you well, Ombomba! I thank you and Yero for what you have given us!"

Yero and even the great Boca Ombomba were embarrassed to be so greeted by a real Queen. They shuffled their feet and bowed, Yero very properly and the great Ombomba more herky-jerky because he bumped his chin on the harp and mumbled something unfit for a Queen; but Yero said, "I'm afraid we brought a lot of trouble and that's about all".

"Trouble indeed", agreed the Queen seriously. "But trouble long-expected. Much sorrow has befallen, but th'Anya will be broken now. We will be free".

"Come", said Atel. "There is no denying the sorrow".

"I don't think I want to know", said Yero. The last moments above the falls rushed into her mind again.

"Come", said Atel once more. "Before anything else, you must know who to keep in your hearts. Some of our friends did perish, though not all".

The fog had lifted higher now and the butterflies saw they were on an island in a sort of crater. A small lake was all around them, strewn with floating wreckage and rubbish. They perched with Atel on the Queen's shoulder as she walked the shoreline. Other fairies were there, searching through the debris along the shore. There was Catchbeam, and Flossie, and Little Laca! Altogether five of their shipmates had survived and been pulled ashore by the Queen during the cataclysm.

The flood had swept most of the Anya, together with their boats and the greater part of their ugly culture over the falls and down into the pool. Under such pressure the pool had flushed like bathroom plumbing, to somewhere. The Big Sisters and most of their heavier stuff went down. But like bathroom plumbing, too much can be too much. The pool plugged at the bottom and now the water level was beginning to rise. The highest point on the island where the harp stood, the only part with grass, rose only a tall step above the sand, and only a narrow strip of sand now remained. Along that narrow beach had been laid out a long row of dresses salvaged from the flotsam, mostly size small and smaller. Yero recognized Airy's and Lolly's. There were Florrie's and Poo's, and Glinter's too. The butterflies flew down to them, and their friends came and stood with them while Yero wept and Boca kicked the sand and tried not to.

"You need to know", said the Queen, "That these girls did not go down utterly with the Anya, for th'spirits are lighter than water. Lighter than air, too. Th'have perished surely, but with fairy-folk there is some chance of renewal in Ages yet to come. Keep them in thy hearts".

Yero suddenly remembered another friend. She shuddered and looked down the row, but there were no black robes. "What about Nasha?" she asked. "We never would have made it without her!"

The Queen shook her head, uncertain. "I don't know, but I can't believe the Lord of Light would let her slip into the abyss. Pray for her with us"

They did this for her, and for all their friends, and by then the water was lapping at the hems of the dresses. It was time to leave. Catchbeam and the others began quickly to fold the dresses and the Queen went to save her harp.

"These we will keep", said Catchbeam grimly, "and wash them clean, far upstream. Th'will be more of them. See over there."

The fog had lifted almost entirely by now. Across the water were other fairies walking the far shore, also poking about the floating mess. The top of the waterfall came into view, pouring dirty water and more junk into the crater where it disappeared in spray. The pool was rising quickly now. The butterflies took to the air, alarmed. The fairies grabbed up the neatly folded dresses and stepped up to the grassy knoll.

"How will you get out of here?" asked Yero.

Little Laca smiled and pointed to a damaged vessel beached nose-up along the shoreline. "Th'Anya hath provided transportation".

The Queen had commandeered a black boat, a luxury cruiser—still seaworthy, barely. It squatted astern, partly submerging several lounge chairs on the aft deck. They were more than the usual chairs, even at a casual glance. There were three, arranged in a semi-circle facing each other, well cushioned with deep impressions revealing the favored lounging positions of their owners. They were mounted on runners like sleighs with the front and rear tip of each runner curling up and out, ending in the heads of serpents. The runners were underwater, and the water stirred around them. "Keep forward", advised the Queen. "Th'chairs are lashed to the deck. Beware the lashings."

'Curiosity killed the cat', as we all know, and it almost got Yero in the next moment. She flew closer for a better look and was nearly eaten. There were wriggling things in the water. The water boiled and half a dozen heads struck upward, fangs agape. They jerked to a stop just inches beneath her.

Atel zipped into that narrow space and whisked her away. Yero's mouth opened and closed but no words came out.

"Beware the *lashings!*" repeated the Queen more sternly. "They *are* tied, but they're alive!"

She pushed off and jumped aboard, grabbing up a floating stick to guide the craft through the mess. Catchbeam found a board and began to paddle. Everyone pitched in and paddled with some bit of driftwood, although Little Laca's stick didn't actually reach the water.

Boca was spooked by Yero's close call and pumped her for information, but she was still speechless. He finally declared that her speechlessness was more amazing than the lashings. "Did they get your tongue?" he asked seriously.

She stuck it out to prove him wrong.

"That's a relief!" he said. "We'll need it again one day. I can't give all the good advice around here".

"Okay, smarty! Figure this out then: If they're snakes—they *look* like snakes, but she says they're *tied*—what's to stop them from un-tying themselves and coming for us?"

"A good knot would stop them, like round snakes tied in a square knot. Did you see the knots?"

"All I saw was their mouths".

"Probably girls, then. You'd have to look past their mouths to find the real answer".

"*You* go look then! They'll probably kiss the Great Ombomba and tell you their secrets".

"Shouldn't have to. It's about the knots. Has to be".

"He's partly right", said Laca, finally tossing her short oar. "They *are* tied in knots, and th'*never* come loose".

Boca grinned.

"—And what is he partly *wrong* about?"

"Girls, boys—or something else? Nobody knows what they are. They're called 'slurms'— snakes with heads on both ends. Th'Anya use them for handcuffs, tying them on our wrists. The knot is in the middle an' th'could easily *untie* th'selves, but neither end will budge an inch. It makes them short-tempered and rude. Th'know the language and how to hurt your feelings, an' they *do* bite!" She curled her lip with satisfaction. "They'll drown when they go down. Th'can't breathe water".

"Won't they untie themselves even then?"

"Never. 'Tis not in their nature to help anyone. Not even their own rear ends".

Even as they talked, the stern tilted more into the water. The slurms stretched to keep their heads above, looking like rows of infernal tulips.

"Whose are they, anyway? The chairs, I mean?"

"The Triad. The Big Bosses. They enjoyed a cruise now and then to watch th'slaves at work along the river". Laca laughed. "Th'were always together, the three of them, because th'didn't trust each other separately. Th'hated each other for sharing power. Hated even to let each other speak. It's all so dumb. Th'might as well let th'slurms be Boss instead, all these years. 'Twould've been just the same".

But the time of the slurms was ending. The cruiser was sinking fast. The stern tilted and went down for good. The bow lifted and everyone scrambled forward with whatever they could carry; but the tides of fortune, so soon after rescuing her, were not about to drown the Queen in a dirty sinkhole. As the dark water swallowed the boat, she stepped gracefully onto a broken section of the great wharf as it floated past and walked elegantly to shore.

***

So the Queen's exile was ended, and she returned from an Age of lonely service to her people. No one noticed that she had no wings because no one else had any either and she said nothing.

The sinkhole had opened at the beginning of the 'Trouble', and everyone knew it was some mischief of the Anya. The Queen had gone to deal with it, and never came back. 'Exile' became the usual explanation, but it was far more serious.

When she had tried to stop it, she found it to be much stronger than she was, for it was a tear in the fabric of the heavens. When she couldn't even slow it, she appealed to the Artisans, but they were no immediate help.

"Your own kin have opened this", they told her. "Like it or not, you share responsibility".

"That's fair", replied Yoyonneh, "and I would accept it. But this is far beyond me".

The Artisans shook their heads, not because they would withhold help, but because there was no known way to close the hole. It was not the first sinkhole that had appeared and the Lord Himself frowned when asked about them.

"Your kin have opened a way to the Darkness", the Artisans told her. "We cannot stitch it shut. Our threads don't hold. What can you give us to work with?"

"My wings. Myself. That's all I have".

***

They took her wings and crushed them, blowing the dust into the whirlpool with the breath of their own hopes. The whirlpool slowed but didn't stop. The tear still leaked enough to swallow the whole river, but the violence lessened. An island appeared in the middle and the pool rose up around it. Onto the island she went with her harp to be the watcher on the water; but the water was unnaturally warm. Fog closed over everything. Centuries passed. The sands of time formed a beach, and the beach eroded. The island grew smaller. A time would come when the sinkhole would swallow it and reopen. That would be the end of fairyland and probably much more. But as better luck would have it, visitors came to Nyo before the end, a hummingbird and two butterflies. It would all be duly recorded in the Book of Ages eventually, but for now the butterflies were barely noticed.

***

The beach was wider on the outer wall of the sinkhole, wider and uglier. For centuries slave 'mucker' fairies had toiled here, collecting the oily gook as it bubbled up from below and congealed on the surface like soft, slimy flapjacks. It bubbled up no longer, but fairies were there in groups searching for nicer things in the clutter, with urgency now as the water rose faster. There was a somber mood and another long row of dresses laid out neatly. No one bowed to the Queen. She wasn't that kind of Royalty. But they gathered up the raiment of the fallen and welcomed her gladly in the little time at hand. Then everyone made their way to the cliffs and the cargo lift to escape the rising water.

It was a manual lift and the muckers rode in the same greasy buckets with the cargo. The Anya had thought that amusing and made it a rule: No clean buckets and no clean pixies! The rule still held but no one cared. Everyone was dirty anyway and the pool was rising fast. When the Queen had clambered out of the last bucket the muckers tipped the boom structure into the mess below. No one felt up to cheering but it was a good feeling when it went over.

At the Queen's suggestion, they used the lift ropes to make a barricade across the old riverbed where it had been left high and dry by the sinkhole. Dusty and forgotten for a long Age it would soon run with water again, carrying the Rowah back to the Aurora to be recycled and dry-cleaned in the solar wind, but the floating trash would remain here until it all sank, or was sunk.

A number of muckers who had done a tour of duty at the Dais volunteered to raft the river back to the Curtain, hopefully to save the wings before Gorda guessed what was up.

Everyone else marched upstream along the muddy shore, making slow progress and a small start on the cleanup, kicking and tossing trash into the river which still ran high.

Nothing recognizable remained along the banks. The gates, when they came to them, were gone, the levees washed away. The promontory was an island now, the Grand Chorus just a bad dream. The big wharf — except for the lucky piece that ended up in the sinkhole — had washed up onto higher ground and came to rest like a grand walkway to the front door of the only building that escaped serious damage: The Lockups, the dreaded prison of the Anya. Catchbeam led most of the party ahead to scout what remained of the Big Camp while the Queen approached the Lockups with Atel and the butterflies.

A crowd of free fairies milled around the entrance cheering prisoners as they emerged, blinking, into the broad light of the Aurora. Some had been in their cells far too long and needed help, but still smiled. Everyone cheered the Queen. It was like a holiday outside; but inside, down deep, serious trouble remained. The Warden and some of her turnkeys were holed up in the old part of the dungeons.

"Th'have hostages", said someone. "Th'say say they will kill them".

"We will go down", said the Queen. "Who knows the way?"

A grimy fairy named Dat stepped forward. "I was a slave here, a water-bearer. I can show the way but thu will need a light. Th'were never any lights and we worked like the blind, counting our steps. I know the way".

"I can arrange light", said the Queen, "if our young friends will volunteer..." She turned to the butterflies..."D'thu mind?" So saying, she drew as much light down from the Curtain as they could hold, before it went to their eyes, and so they went inside.

The part of the building above ground was the office, a single-story blockhouse with one big room. (Not counting a cupula in the roof for the crows. From the noise, and the mess on the floor, there were several up there still.) Pixies were ransacking the place, going through files, trying to trace missing friends. It was a grim business. Many would never be found.

The Queen's party went down worn steps to the lower levels with the butterflies lighting the way. Dat counted out loud from habit, "...18, 19, 20". That brought them to a landing and a choice of three doors. She pointed to the middle door. "Shovels an' buckets". To the right: "Th'new addition, the Big Jail". To the left: "The Old Lockups; in we go". She took four small steps sideways, grabbed the handle and opened it. Yero saw that she kept her eyes closed. Dat trusted her memory more than the light.

A dank, moldy smell greeted them. There had always been water seepage in the old part. This had been put out as the reason for excavating the new addition, but everyone knew that was baloney. The jailers kept the old part full and soon filled the new one too — 'due to the increase in rule-breaking'. This was unfortunately true, because no one could keep track of all the new rules.

Dat held the door open politely. "There are 4 more levels down to the very bottom, but th'Warden an' her gang are just below us, next level down". Dat intended to go no further so the others went on through. There was a narrow landing beyond the door and a crumbling stair leading down and to the right.

"Watch the steps, Highness", said Yero politely. "Some of them are missing".

They went down part way and stopped. A hooded Anya awaited them at the bottom. Now the hooded one tapped her club rhythmically on the stone and challenged them, as if it were yesterday and she was still posted at the main entrance up above.

"Speak now! Speak now! Who approaches the House of Purification?"

"You're behind the times down here", replied Atel. "The House is under new management. Tell us instead: Who are you?"

"I am Yobba, First Chaperone of Residents", growled the guard. She stubbornly resumed tapping the club and chanting: "None may enter without appointment. State your business".

Atel dismissed her. "Our business is with your boss. Fetch her. Tell her the Queen awaits".

With that bit of news, Yobba disappeared into the gloom. The Queen descended to the bottom of the stair. Presently Yobba returned, skulking behind a much broader figure. This was old Jawl, the Warden. She tramped boldly up to the Queen.

"My!" she drawled. "Whatta we got here? Can't be the same girl I remember! Too skinny. That'sa trouble with vacations. Folks don't eat right. Sorry to see you, old girl. I figured you was retired for keeps".

The Queen ignored it. "Where are the hostages?"

"Whooo! All business? Well, I don't mind doin' honest business. But clean up your language. 'Hostage' is too harsh. Maybe they talk that way upstairs, but down here we've got a 'folksier' atmosphere. We got Big Folks who wanna leave peacefully an' little folks who wouldn't mind that neither". Jawl paused. Right on cue a dreadful choking noise came from the gloomy cells behind her.

The Queen turned to leave, climbed several steps. Jawl said something quiet over her shoulder. The choking noise worsened alarmingly. Yoyonneh reached the door above.

"Where you goin'?" hollered Jawl. "We're just gettin' started!"

"I don't negotiate that way", answered Yoyonneh, and walked out. Atel and the butterflies remained. The hummingbird let Jawl think about things for a minute before resuming negotiations.

"So much for the 'folksy' stuff", she said then. "Now you get me. Do you remember me?"

Jawl snarled and spat on the floor. "Oh yeah, Babe. *Very* disappointed. Word was we'd done you in!"

"Tsk. Clean up your own language, Jawl. If I tire of this, I'll let the pixies have you. There are simply mobs of free fairies outside, in the mood for revenge. They have...creative ideas about settling with you".

"So? Spit out your offer, Babe. Bearing in mind that I've got creative ideas too, for their playmates back here".

"You're free to leave—provided the hostages are alive".

Jawl sneered. "Yeah, and run the gauntlet outside? I'm sure the Dungeon Rats have broken out the whips. I don't think so!"

"There'll be no trouble unless you ask for it. But once outside you must make a choice: To stay on probation and work at the cleanup with the rest of us - or leave Nyo and never return".

Jawl spat in Atel's direction. "That's what I think of your offer, Babe! But supplies'll run low down here, sooner or later. We ain't got much choice, do we?"

"No".

"I want the skinny one's word, not yours".

Atel waited for something more respectful.

Jawl straightened up. "That's your *Queen*", she said sweetly.

Atel went and returned with her.

"Your word?" demanded Jawl. "We're free to go? No reprisals?"

"Correct—on the conditions Aleta spelled out. Unless there are dead or dying hostages. That would complicate matters".

Yobba got an elbow in the ribs and hustled off. Soon the whole turnkey gang emerged and began to line up, acting quite pleased. Atel passed the word to Dat who went up and spread it around. The deal wasn't very popular.

"First, the hostages", said the Queen. "Where are they?"

Jawl gestured carelessly behind, toward the cells. "No sweat. A few bumps and bruises, that's all".

Atel went to check it out. Jawl shrugged. "She'll see. My girls know how to play without leaving marks. Not many, anyway".

Atel returned and nodded angrily. "They'll recover, with time". Hoots and laughter broke out from the gang.

Dat returned to warn of an ugly mood above. "And there is another prisoner, *way* down", she added. "The jailers must be held accountable for her also".

Jawl snickered, overhearing. "Shucks, almost forgot. I'll throw *her* in on the deal. But hey—" (sounds of discontent drifted down the open stairway) —"we want an escort outa here!"

The Queen shook her head. "You're Big Girls. Escort thyselves".

She headed for the cellblock as the line of Black-robed prison guards shuffled upstairs, almost two dozen of them, stumbling on the broken steps. Up front, another step gave way under the Warden. The last guard in line swatted irritably at the butterflies but missed.

Sounds of argument breaking out above faded as they entered the cellblock. Jawl had not lied. The hostages looked better than they were. Dat volunteered to get help for them and gave directions to the lone prisoner, way down. "All th'way to the bottom, th'lowest level. In the last cell where th'water stands. She was always alone".

It was Hydia, their old pal, one of the original Three. She sat on a pile of rubble that Dat and other Dungeon Rats had made for her and stared into the dark with eyes that saw nothing, ears that heard nothing, clothed without knowing it in rags the 'Rats had stolen to keep her warm.

The Anya had been mighty pleased when they captured this one during the Trouble: One of the 'Babes', as they called the Three. They tried lots of tricks to get secrets out of her, but she was a stubborn girl. When nothing worked, they paraded her in a cage for sport, while she lasted. When she ended up like this, they lost interest and left her to rot down here. Her mind was gone but the flesh persisted due to the kindnesses of the slave workers. Yoyonneh carried her up and pixies took her into their care, for the Queen was needed outside. There had been bad trouble only minutes earlier.

Jawl and her bullies had been shaken when the Queen turned up—and not an army of Big Sisters. They had imagined the uprising to be just a local mutiny. But they were shocked at the devastation outside.

They stood on the ruined wharf and gawked. Before them was nothing but the river! Little remained of the Big Camp, and there wasn't another black robe in sight. That's when they had got mean; wrestling whips away from the smaller fairies and laying about in fury.

They had been quickly surrounded, and Jawl's fears proved true. The crowd of free fairies stoned them with bricks from their own blockhouse. Near the end, something disturbing happened. The Gang, all but three, laid down on the ground, as if to surrender maybe, but serpents slithered out of their robes and tried to escape into the river. They were stoned too but melted into an oily liquid that trickled into the water. No one dared touch it, but it didn't make a slick. It sank, like everything else invented by the Anya.

The remaining three surrendered—newer apprentices who had recently been allowed to pull up their hoods. Now they showed why the Anya wore them. They threw open their robes exposing skin riddled with sores, starting to slough off. Skin in the early stages of molting. This sort of thing wasn't advertised when the Anya recruited pretty new apprentices. It came later. The three were horrified at their transformation and eager to quit, if only it wasn't too late.

"Throw th'robes into the river", the Queen directed. "*All* the robes! A lot of garbage must go downstream yet, and good riddance; 'twill help to seal up the sinkhole. After that, you can help care for the weaker prisoners, and for yourselves, by taking in as much light as you can here in the open. See that Hydia gets help too. Show her kindness, whether she feels it or not. And bathe in the river. Each day it should run a little cleaner. If there is hope for you, it is that".

She turned to the crowd. "To everyone else: Show mercy where you can. 'Tis satisfying to slay our enemies and we're not done with that yet - but have a care! We may find ourselves too few to restore Ah. What then, girls? Remember, we are here at the mercy of another. He could change his mind. Look for friends among the enemy. Some will have honest remorse".

"Remorse will be *ours*", shouted an angry fairy, "when we get a knife in th'back for showing mercy!"

"You are hot for battle, Anni-moto", replied Yoyonneh. "You will be much-needed today! And afterward I want *you* to guard the prisoners".

Everyone smiled, even Anni-moto, and turned to what would become a bloody battle in the ruins. Before it was over, they would find quite a few Anya in small groups that had taken cover at the last moments before the flood hit. It was bitter fighting and Anni-moto had plenty of work, for the Anya were hard to slay. Some, when cornered, leaped into the waters and drowned. Others fought to the death, then turned into serpents like the Jailers, and had to be stoned again. Afterward the pixies formed bucket brigades and washed the stains from the banks of the river.

Part 2: Beyond the Moonwalk

The Queen and a small party including Catchbeam and the Travelers continued upstream to the Boatworks. Here, things were better. Few of the senior Anya hung around there anyway, owing to the toxic fumes and liquids. Nearly two dozen apprentices were eager to switch sides if the free fairies would let them, and they were more willing here because the apprentices had it hard too. They were the inspectors and floor bosses right in the middle of the noxious atmosphere and got burns and rashes the same as the slaves. It was a joke among the Bosses that Boatworks apprentices wouldn't become alarmed as others did at their progressive skin decay because (Ha-ha!) *everyone* got it at the Boatworks!

The apprentices had tossed their robes into the floodwaters immediately and begged mercy. To begin making amends, some were already busy smashing up 'tarboats' in various stages of construction and dumping the pieces into the current. Others, assisted by free fairies, were setting up a production line for old-style canoes.

As the Queen's party was about to move on, several Swamp Rats arrived, skating down the river on their 'batts'. They had messages from Lorelei, but the dismantling of brand new tarboats caught their attention right away.

"What is this?" they joked. "No more sport for us?"

"Nay", replied the boatworkers. "Thu've had thy fun. We're shutting down the line due to lack of customers".

"We can understand that", laughed the 'Rats. "Th'were poorly made. Fell apart at th'slightest touch".

"We watered down th'glue!" retorted the boatworkers. "You pesky pirates could never sink a good boat".

"We never had the chance. You saboteurs don't know how to make one!"

"Give us a few days. We're a 'for-profit' enterprise now. Our new canoes will soon be everywhere".

"For some of that profit we might share our knowledge about travel on the water".

"We'll listen, but there's more to sailing than just strapping bread-boards on thy feet".

"Our 'batts' are seaworthy, at least. That's one thing thu could learn!"

"Too small, too small. Big enough to haul th'news, maybe. But that's about it".

"That's the only worthwhile cargo anyway, for th'past Age".

"Quite true. But things are looking up. Soon thu can come down here an' get real jobs!"

That's how it went for a while. These groups knew each other pretty well, but seldom got a chance to talk. Now they did and they'd had lots of time to think up wisecracks.

"Maybe we will", predicted a 'Rat. "A nice soft job so we can look pretty for the boys! *Ombomba* there is the first. More will surely follow".

This is what the boatworkers really wanted to know. The war was going well; that was already old news. But the chimes had promised news of the boys! Boca didn't disappoint. He favored the crowd with 'a few suitable words' and made an audacious loop-de-loop above them, exactly as a hero should.

"I knew it already", whispered one of the boatworkers. "He had such an unusual radiance".

"I saw it too", whispered another, louder.

"I *like* it." said someone else.

"I liked him *first*!"

It was long past whispering by now. Boca enjoyed every moment. Then one of the Swamp Rats noticed the apprentices standing around, listening. "Hey, slackers", she barked, "Back to work!"

They hopped to it, grabbing up mauls and pry bars and bumping into each other. But the Swamp Rats were jesting. They knew what things had been like here for everyone. Now they got out bottles of clean spring water from above the swamp and bathed Catchbeam's welts, and then went among the boatworkers and the amazed apprentices too and bathed their ugly sores.

"Lorelei's idea?" asked Atel. "Or just the rebel way?"

"Both", said a 'Rat named Skip. "We need the help. Always have. We raided this place quite a bit an' never found an apprentice who wouldn't desert, given the chance. Jana over there was an apprentice here once". The 'Rat heard and turned, rolling up her sleeves. There were scars, but they were fading. "These apprentices paid heavy dues", continued Skip. "Anyway, playing with Lorelei's fire all these years, we've learned how to treat burns."

The 'Rats brought news of fighting up at the locks, too. The Fat One and her entire garrison had holed up in the Guard Shack and refused offers to talk, so the 'Rats had smoked them out. The Lock Boss was first up the cellar stairs, whining and blubbering, with the other officers on her heels. They had their whips but couldn't see too well. The 'Rats had fire. Caught between the blazing Shack and the water, the Blackcoats chose water. One by one they jumped in and drowned, except the Fat One who had to be pushed in. There were lots of volunteers for that, and so the battle ended — but where was the rest of the garrison? The 'Rats searched the cellar of the still-smoking Shack and found the Garrison apprentices. The officers had breathed through their hoods, but these five were forbidden to pull theirs up for protection. Two had perished; three others survived, including Azi, and were put to demolishing the empty locks.

"There is likely a big battle yet to be fought", warned Skip. "We used up all our fireworks on the dam, and by the looks of the breach didn't think we'd be needed downriver, so after th'Locks most of us headed upstream with slingshots and light gear, hoping to catch Gorda by surprise — however unlikely".

"Yes, unlikely", agreed Atel. "We'd like to be there for the fight; but it's a slow march for the Queen, and others, in the mud. Do you have extra 'batts'?"

"We don't. We carve them out of wood as we need them. But we brought carving tools for the unemployed bums here, thinking to put them to work. Take ours! We'll make more".

'Batting' looked easy but wasn't. Lessons were needed. The Swamp Rats assisted Catchbeam as instructors, but it was overall a slow learning process.

"The butterflies and I will scout ahead", said Atel diplomatically. I wish to speak with the gardeners. You can catch up with us there".

Neither the Queen, nor any of the rookie 'batters' objected, or hardly even heard. It was all they could do to stay upright; and from the cheers and jeers of the onlookers there were already enough witnesses to spread the gossip about the Queen's spectacular spills.

So the original Travelers came to the Gardens and found several Anya Superiors puttering around, raking up scummy algae and shoveling it into the great pitcher plants. The place stunk and the foulness obviously centered on the pitchers. The rest of the gardens, mostly patches of salad vegetables, were ruined, smothered with mud and slime. Only the big pitchers and the quaint garden house beyond had been uphill enough to escape it. The pitchers were very impressive, twice as tall as the gardeners — and these gardeners were large, even among the Anya.

"You could stuff a whole gardener into one", Yero found herself thinking, "and her feet wouldn't even stick out". It was more than true. There were a half-dozen of the monstrous things slowly wobbling on their fat stems, leaves drooping wetly alongside. The gardeners were using a stepladder to climb up and dump garbage in. Yero peeked inside one, and that cured her curiosity. They were half full of something quite rotten with scummy green algae on top, freshly added, and putrid stuff bubbling up from below.

Two gardeners continued to rake scum into little piles. A third slowly straightened and put a hand on her sore back, her hood gently shaking at the sight of Atel.

"My, my! We haven't seen you in a while. Pray don't add to our troubles. A gardener's life is hard enough".

"I'll agree with that", said Atel. "I also am a gardener".

That sounded promising. The Anya relaxed slightly. "Ah! Wildflowers, one would suppose. No offense, Lady, but we're Big Girls here, and Big Girls need big food. It's a lot of work and it all falls on the poor gardeners. Pray don't be harsh".

"I only need to ask a few questions".

"Go ahead, but you'll find it boring. We don't get into politics here. There simply isn't time".

"Haven't you kept slaves, with all this work?"

"Okay, you caught me there. We *have* requested a bit of help during busy seasons, but we've always done the heavy lifting ourselves. You can ask anyone. There haven't been any complaints".

"I certainly would ask, but I don't see any slaves".

"Well, there *aren't* any. As I said, we do almost all the work ourselves, always have". She bent to it, still clutching her stiff back. "Ohh!" she moaned. "At my age I wouldn't mind slowing down".

"I have good news then. You can cut back on production. There aren't many of your kind left".

The gardeners acted quite bored with the news, but Atel noted their hoods turned silently toward each other. The butterflies wandered off to the pretty garden house.

"That so?" replied the talkative one presently. "It'll be a relief! As I said, we're weary of it. Everyone takes gardeners for granted".

Atel noticed a stack of empty jars behind one of the pitchers and inquired about them.

"For preserves, of course. Some of the ladies tire of fresh salad. But these sat around too long and spoiled, so we emptied them into the pitchers with the other garbage. Yes, yes. We know the plants stink! We don't appreciate it either, but one must have garbage disposal, alas".

"Certainly. And the jars are stacked there now...for what reason?"

"We must empty the pitchers from time to time when they get too full. Here, let me show you! We have no secrets".

She grabbed up several jars and very carefully parted the leaves of the plant to reveal a good-sized drain valve tapped into the base. She proceeded to fill a jar with heavy greenish slop, passed it to a Sister, and went to fill another jar. The Sister trudged down a worn path to what might have been a remnant of a boat dock, there to dump out the jar into the water.

"To be quite honest I don't know what the small fry eat nowadays", said the talkative one sociably. "When they help us here, they have no appetite — quite understandable with the odor. Still, if they take over, we wouldn't mind working for them, would we, Sisters?" The hoods wagged agreeably. "Yes, yes", she continued, "Everyone can use a good gardener".

"You'll soon have your chance to apply for a job. Other visitors will arrive shortly. The Queen will be among them".

That got their attention. The talkative one flinched, spilling the goo on her fingers. Absent-mindedly she licked it off, and then quickly spat it out.

The Queen and her party were already drawing near, gliding fairly smoothly on their batts, except the Queen herself who needed a bit of steadying. The rule seemed to be: The taller the fairy, the easier it was to tip over. Atel went to round up the butterflies who had been snooping.

"They've been burying stuff behind the garden house", said Yero. "And the house is stuffed with jars."

"It looks just like that salad dressing on Gorda's boat", said Boca.

"We'll see if they can explain it all to the Queen", said Atel.

For a Lady who had suffered so much, the Queen was remarkably forgiving; but she was also in a hurry to get upstream and see about Gorda, so she pressed them. The talkative one was very nice, very helpful. Yes, yes, she welcomed questions. As she had already explained to the hummingbird, the pitchers were for garbage disposal; but there was too much now, after the flood, so they were emptying them into the dirty river. What? The jars in the house? Same waste, from the pitchers; but they had saved it up while the river was clean, not wanting to pollute. That would be disgusting! So it piled up. They had begun to bury some behind the house (as the snoopy butterflies had probably seen!) but quit that because landfills are so messy! In all honesty, a flood was a good thing once in a while, was it not? A chance to clean up and start fresh! The talkative one earned her adjective several times over and finished up with a plea to raise nice vegetables for the Queen. All the while, she tapped jar after jar from the pitcher plant and her Sisters dumped them into the river. Finally, the Queen tired of the monotone.

"Just clean the place up. We'll discuss amnesty later. 'Twill be difficult for you, I'm afraid, being Superiors".

The Sisters bowed very low. The Queen turned to leave. The talkative one began out of habit to fill another jar. Something small and metallic came out the tap and made a little 'ping' on the bottom of the jar. The Queen paused and a faraway look came in her eye. Atel zipped back to the busy gardener who continued filling the jar as fast as she could.

"We'll take that one", said Atel.

The talkative one hissed softly but gave it up to the Queen who turned it around half a turn in the light of the Aurora. Something shiny and red was inside, against the glass. A pin. A strawberry pin.

"I knew the girl who wore this, or one just like it", she said. "Her name is Lili".

"*Was*, maybe", said Catchbeam. "Everyone knew her. She never took off the pin".

There was an awful silence as the free fairies guessed the truth. The gardeners shrank back among the pitchers fearfully.

"There was an accident", blubbered the talkative one. "Very sad, very sad! We tried to save her!"

She wasn't fooling anyone. The free fairies pressed in. First one, then another of the gardeners bumped clumsily into the drooping leaves. That was a no-no. The great plants became aware of them. What followed was quite natural between a pitcher plant and its prey, but the noteworthy thing in Yero's mind would always be: "Yes! The big gardeners *did* fit inside, feet and all!"

The Queen put the little pin on her collar and the party moved on upstream. No one spoke of the gardens again, or the heart-wrenching cleanup that awaited in that place. It would have to wait until the war was won.

They came to the locks and passed them by. The river flowed freely through a huge gap, leaving the locks high and dry off to the side. Smoke still rose from where the shack had been, and 'Rats had set fire to the lock walls and their machinery. It burned well. Everything was constructed of the tar gook and hardened alloys of the gook. Freed apprentices tended the fires while the 'Rats themselves lounged on the grass throwing dice, a typical pastime for them and for pirates throughout all Ages.

They waved and shouted greetings as the Queen's party went on through the gap, entering a surreal landscape: The old high-water mark on the dike glared down from thirty feet above and the 'Swamp' ahead was now a skeletal forest of dead trees, no longer submerged. The Rowah flowed in a new channel carved by the flood, and the exposed forest floor was nothing but mud and brush—heaps and snarls of it. Nothing at all was recognizable from long ago and the party kept their gaze on the water ahead, all in total silence except for the constant breaking of dead branches from the weight of seaweed festooned upon them. Thus, they passed through what had once been the most beautiful part of fairyland and were relieved to put it behind them.

They came to the upper marches and the sumac barrier. A rush of water now held the tough stems down where Nasha had crashed the boat through, leaving a gushing channel just wide enough for batts if they dared it. One by one they did. Beyond that, current had forced a way through trash and seaweed, and they were able to follow an organized channel all the way to the pool where Boca saw the fish. It was deserted. They portaged there, employing the old tar bucket lift up to the service road and eventually back to navigable water beyond the chutes but there was no one, anywhere. Urgency gripped them. Maybe a small army of Swamp Rats could overthrow Gorda if they recovered their wings, but she commanded the largest garrison outside the Big Camp.

They came to the Quay, also deserted, and followed the stream around to the little-used shortcut. There they stashed their batts in the weeds and made their way quickly up the slope.

Part 2: Beyond the Moonwalk

The Curtain was still dark and smelled of smoke. A big hole had been burned and loose ends waved slowly in the wind. A wide trail with many footprints led inward through the cold ashes. Swamp Rats had come this way—but where were they? In front of them stretched the trampled grounds of the Dais, the cistern, and the Guardhouse. But there were no fairies.

Then a roar went up from beyond the Dais followed by the crack of a whip, harsh laughter, and another angry roar. They hurried to the precipice. All around on the steep slopes were angry Swamp Rats. Below, on the cul-de-sac, Gorda's whole garrison lounged on the outgoing road or near the ruined statue, which looked like a scarecrow now, trying to shoo birds away. There were 60 or 70 Big Sisters out there, quite safe from retribution. They had chopped off the walkway altogether so no one could get out to them and posted the Whipper-will at the gap. Just now, the 'Whipper' was providing entertainment for the gang with a bit of target practice.

Nearby, Gorda lay on a recliner. Two apprentices held a dark sheet above her, billowing it slowly as a fan, but mostly just to shield their boss from the light of the moon. She was pleased with herself because she held the trumps in a deadly game playing out before them: Stacked and piled high all around her sculpture were fairy wings. She *had* them, so many she allowed the 'Whipper' to play with a few.

And play she did. Selecting a small pair from the stack, she tossed them high in the air and uncoiled her whip to smash them, as she had smashed another pair moments earlier, and another before that. Atel flew into her face this time and threw off her aim, but the wings fluttered downward. The Whipper covered her eyes and let them fall.

"Let's catch them!" whispered Yero, and the butterflies went for it. The free fairies cheered, but the Big Sisters snatched up more whips. As the butterflies struggled under the weight, many whips lashed out. Snap! Crack! Smack! Dust flew off the wings from near misses. Atel's mirror sprang to life but couldn't stop all of them. "Use the wings! Ride them!" she shouted, but they couldn't hear.

No matter. The butterflies, who understand airfoils like few others, had already thought of it. They suddenly laid flat on the wings and surfed out of range, toward the cliffs. There they caught an updraft and soared back up. The Swamp Rats caught them like Frisbees.

Tremendous cheers! The Blackcoats cursed and looked to Gorda who calmly raised an arm, unworried. So. The small fry had won a small victory? So what? They would soon realize they were simply back where they started. She yawned and decided to take a nap.

Atel quickly recognized the balance of power. The morale boost helped, but Gorda remained firmly in control. She went to Lorelei, standing alone with the Queen on the shelf with the kneelers, and alighted on her shoulder. "Thinking again?" she asked.

"Aye. Gorda did the smart thing, collecting all the wings as soon as she lost you. Had them stacked up before we ambushed you in th'swamp, probably. A shame she's on th'wrong side. She's very clever".

The Queen nodded. "Still, I expect you have some sort of plan?"

"Yes. First, we send Aleta to parley".

"That's a start. Aleta?"

"Good idea. We understand each other, Gorda and I. Anything special you want me to find out?"

"Her rock-bottom terms—I doubt th'will have to ask—but more so the *mood* out there in the ranks. They aren't all Superiors".

Gorda was very mellow when Atel arrived. She smiled broadly. "Well, well! The bird returns to the scene of her crime. All criminals do, eventually. And with the little troublemakers still in tow! How cute".

Only now did Atel realize the butterflies had tagged along and shot them an angry look.

"Now, now," reproved Gorda, "They're only following your poor example, flying after you promised not to".

"Things have changed, Gorda, as you must know. But our agreement never included this side of the Curtain".

"Details. I suppose I should've put it in writing, but I trusted you to follow the spirit! Oh well, the Courts will sort it all out as time allows. But I've been worried about my pet. I trust you turned the crow in to proper Authorities downriver?"

"No. The creature was lost overboard".

Gorda became visibly annoyed. "Who was responsible for *that*, may I ask?"

"We were", chirped Yero coming closer, but not too close. "Well, mostly me".

"You aren't big enough to be guilty, little pest! Don't lie to old Gorda".

"Oh, we didn't *push* it in. It tried to peck us and missed. Fell into the water on its own, like you did in the cistern".

Gorda frowned thoughtfully. "I have friends down in the gardens, little pest", she growled. "They have special places for annoying insects like you!"

"The pitcher plants?" piped Boca. "They're not hungry".

Gorda frowned deeper. "That would be news. I've heard they're always hungry".

"They're full of gardeners".

Gorda digested that in silence and decided to ignore the butterflies. She turned back to Atel.

"Times certainly have changed, then! I see Old 'Yo has broken out of jail too. What next, I wonder?"

"We might make peace", suggested Atel.

"Ah. A deal! Let's see...you have —*whatever*—and I have the *wings*. If I give the word, my girls will smear 'em with tar and dump 'em over. We'll see how many of *those* your little pests can save".

The butterflies started to chirp but Atel hushed them. "Be nice! Madame Gorda needs time to adjust. It won't be easy for her now, out here all alone".

"Alone?" Gorda feigned surprise. She could read signs as well as anyone and guessed most of the truth, but it only made her more dangerous. "To be honest, I had entertained the idea of letting the small fry back into servitude under the old rules. But if we're *orphans*..." (She chuckled behind her hood) ..." if we're *orphans* out here, it'll be tougher to keep the servants in line. The wings will have to go. But enough about that for now! We'll chat later. It's time for lunch. Will you join us?"

"Certainly. May we all come?"

"Sorry, no. There ain't enough room, what with all this trash..." She waved at the stacks of wings. "You may bring one guest".

"That will be the Queen".

"Naturally".

Atel sent the butterflies to deliver the message. Yoyonneh waved and descended the stairs.

"We'll need your gangplank across", said Atel.

"Oh? She has no wings either? How common! Well, we're not without pity for the old and the lame." She motioned to the apprentices. It took all ten of them to hoist the plank and extend it across the gap. Atel went to have a word with the Queen as she crossed, but mostly it was a few words for Yero and Boca. A small errand.

***

"Ah! Just look at you—our old friend!" called Gorda, not bothering to rise. "Are you able to navigate there? Do you need a cane?"

"Thank you, no. Better to keep temptation away. I might spank thee with it".

"My, my. Still sassy after all these years? Then I must have your hands bound while you're here. Can't have you reaching into your bag of tricks". The Queen allowed this so long as Atel was on her shoulder. Gorda relaxed visibly.

"Now then", she said more sociably, "Perhaps you didn't get enough to eat this past Age? We're about to have lunch—just a salad, of course. Will you join us?"

"Thank you, but no. I was hoping to reach the Moonwalk and sample a few late flowers. Is this the right road?"

Gorda hesitated a bit. "As far as it goes, yes", she replied. "May I speak plainly on this subject? My intention has always been noble. From the *heart*. I wish to extend the service road right up to the Moonwalk. That'll make easier access for those like yourself who must walk, and for renewed traffic up and down as in the old days. But the small fry doubt my sincerity. They subvert the effort".

"Why? Th'must have a reason".

"Pettiness. It matches their size".

"Had you ever thought of treating them better?"

"I did ask myself that once, but decided I was too benevolent already. Mustn't spoil the working class, you know! They might sit down and never get up".

"Like yourselves?"

"Exactly! Not everyone can be leaders. The small fry don't understand that; but excuse me now! Lunch is served! My girls are hungry. Afterward, we'll walk the road together for a bit of exercise, a bit of Big-Girl talk. Who knows? We may strike a deal".

Gorda waved an arm again. The apprentices hauled back the plank and now busied themselves serving the meal. The Sisters jostled and elbowed until most found places to sit around the cul-de-sac. Some leaned roughly against the stacks of wings. The apprentices fetched bags of greens from a large store that had been piled along the outgoing road, filled bowls generously, and served them. Jars of dressing were passed around and the butterflies watched to see who helped themselves. They all did. Most had seconds. The empty, greasy bowls were passed (or just tossed) back to the apprentices. Not sure what to do with the dirty dishes, they simply stacked them up for now and took clean ones for themselves. Only one of them — the Whipper — took dressing, lapping it up like soup.

Eventually, Gorda heaved herself up from the recliner and made her way to the outbound road where the Queen patiently waited. The Boss of the Dais was amiable with a good meal in her belly.

"I *do* wish we had more timely news out here", she confided. "Perhaps, had we known the *extent* of the calamity...who can say? We might have made peace and avoided this ugly standoff". She was dying to know more details.

"You should have", replied the Queen. "As Aleta implied, you are the only surviving garrison".

"Yes, she mentioned that. So, something quite out of the ordinary happened downriver..."

"Yes".

"Something catastrophic..."

"Yes".

"Well - *what?*"

"A flood".

Gorda snorted. "Everyone knows *that*. The river comes around again! Tell me something I don't know!"

"Th'Grand Chorus was drowned".

"Ah! And the Big Bosses?"

"Gone. Down the sinkhole".

"Well, now! That does put us in a lonely position, if you can be believed".

"Thu don't have to take my word for it. Go see for thyself".

Another snorting noise escaped Gorda's hood. "I don't think so! The small fry would murder me".

"I will accompany and guarantee thy safety. Thu ought to see, Gorda. Nothing is left of thy empire except this little cul-de-sac".

"My, my! Then I suppose you've given thought to terms for *our* surrender".

"Yes. We're offering conditional amnesty".

"Ah! But it would be difficult for us, after all these years, to be under someone else's thumb. You must see that".

"At least consider it", suggested Yoyonneh, then turned quickly and announced it loudly for all to hear: "Amnesty for any who wish it, with a period of probation to make amends!" Everyone heard.

There was a pause in the general chatter that Gorda didn't like. Her amiable pretense fell away. "*Probation!*" she mocked. "*Amends!* Slavery in reverse, that's all!"

"'Twill mean working shoulder to shoulder during cleanup. Thu will be watched closely, but I pledge th'will be treated fairly and decently. Don't confuse it with thy own tyranny".

Gorda made a disgusting noise and spat at the fairy wings. It fell short, hitting an apprentice. Gorda didn't even notice.

"Pledges mean nothing", she growled. "The bird made a pledge too—and look what happened!" Atel felt her dark glance.

"D'thu refuse then? Either way, I think thy crew should make their own choices".

Gorda bellied up to the Queen belligerently, her breath wafting sourly from under her hood. "*I'm* boss here!" she hissed. "*I* decide!"

"And...?"

Gorda didn't answer immediately. Thoughts of grandeur were percolating in her head. So, the Big Bosses were gone? That made room for a new Boss, as she saw it: Gorda the Great! She would've been part of the Triad in the first place, had she been but a few inches taller. Should've been! Now at last a bit of luck had come her way. She grabbed it.

"I *do* refuse!" she said. "Stupid idea. Beneath my dignity. I have a better one".

"Fair enough. I welcome a free exchange of ideas".

"Ain't nothing free in it for you, old girl, but it shouldn't be too traumatic. You're used to being a prisoner. You were stuck at the other end of Ah, and now you're stuck at this end. I'm keeping you for a while".

"I'm disappointed. I don't believe you have any future in Nyo after all".

"For once I agree with you! Come! Let's walk. The girls need their exercise and it's been a while since I inspected the road".

She issued orders. The 'Whipper' would be left in charge for a few minutes to guard the gap. The rest of the Sisters were to bring shovels, brooms and trowels, all the smudge fairies' tools, and do some maintenance on the road. Gorda wanted them to get a taste of slavery so they would fight harder when the fight came. She herself led the way with a wheelbarrow.

Okay, let's be serious. She led the way *in* a wheelbarrow, and several stout Sisters took turns pushing it while the Queen walked alongside.

"As I was saying", continued Gorda, "I *do* agree with you. There's no future up here for my girls or me. Pledges are worthless. The small fry are grudge-holders, vindictive. We would have no peace. But there's a way to satisfy everyone: Take us to your Wishing Well and kick us out of Nyo!"

Gorda talked on. She had no intention of leaving Nyo. Ever. She just had a lot of leverage right now and dearly wished to smash that Well, and with it the Moonwalk. *That* would let the air out of the puffed-up small fry and settle some scores!

"We'll need your help getting down through the Well", she went on. "No wings, y'know. But that also guarantees we ain't coming back".

The Queen said nothing, so Atel said nothing out of deference. Gorda carried on like it was a done deal and ordered her porters to pause at each crow. The crows delighted Gorda. She tousled them and they squirmed and protested.

"I want to take some of them down with me", she said fondly. "The statue is too damaged, alas, but I want to take some of my art along".

They came to the end of the blacktop where the pixies' three wheelbarrows still sat with flat tires. Beyond was nothing except the moon and stars.

"See?" complained Gorda. "The small fry build me a road to nowhere. Is it any wonder I grow impatient? Oh, well. With your help now, it'll soon be finished properly".

"You expect me to order this?"

"Of course. They'll do anything for you. I must keep you prisoner till then, naturally, but not one moment longer! Then you'll be rid of us. You don't mind, do ya? For such a worthy cause?"

"I do mind. I dislike being a prisoner".

"I apologize then, but I *must* do this. I don't understand your stubbornness".

"I don't trust thee. Th'would destroy the Well".

Gorda acted sad, aggrieved. Her hood leaned onto a sleeve for support. "Oh, for heaven's sake", she muttered, "I thought we had put *that* sort of thing behind us!"

A moment later she didn't have to fake distress. The crows went off at the Dais and each one could be heard as the 'caw' grew closer. All the Big Sisters grew agitated.

"Bad news?" inquired the Queen.

Gorda listened intently until the nearest crow squawked, to be sure, and then heaved herself up from the wheelbarrow in a frenzy. "Bad news for *you!*" she screamed and shoved Yoyonneh off the end of the road to certain death below. Unfortunately for her, the Queen had a fistful of black robe and dragged the Boss with her.

In the instant of silence that followed, the first pixies appeared in the sky around them. There had been a mutiny back at the cul-de-sac, the one thing Gorda hadn't accounted for. Lorelei had been talking to nine apprentices who didn't like salad dressing, and suddenly the Queen's doom wasn't so imminent after all. She was caught in free fall by free fairies and carried back to the Dais in triumph. Gorda's Gang stampeded back along the road without their boss, but no happy future awaited them.

The nine apprentices had overcome the 'Whipper' and extended the plank over the gap. Free fairies had skipped across to claim their wings while the nine chopped away with pickaxes at the outbound road beyond the cul-de-sac. The crows cawed and squawked at the traitors and were ignored. By the time the Gang returned, a wide gap had been chopped. The gang was marooned on the wrong side. Their last chance was to bridge the gap and fight it out for a piece of their crumbling empire.

They had nothing to work with except themselves, but as the pixies had thought of making a pyramid these bullies imagined a living bridge. It would take only two of them. While their pals threw chunks of blacktop and cracked whips to keep the apprentices at bay, a big strong Sister climbed on another's shoulders and the 'double-decker dame' tramped confidently toward the gap. Anyone could see they would easily bridge it. Fierce laughter rumbled up out on the road, but then the gap began to widen. A flock of winged fairies had tied ropes to the distant end of the roadway and were pulling steadily. Now the road was moving of its own momentum. Laughter was replaced by panic. The 'double-decker' was having second thoughts. Someone gave the 'dame' a push finally, but too late. The living bridge missed its moorings and headed toward the green earth below and a hard landing. The rest of the Gang stood dumbfounded.

The free fairies laughed and waved to them

"Goodbye!"

"Lucky thing th'packed a lunch out there!"

"Th'will be dieting for a few years!"

"Or a few hundred!"

"'Twill help thy waistlines!"

That's a fair sampling. There was much more. Of course, the Big Sisters had a few things to say, too, but we won't repeat those. There are enough bad words floating about the atmosphere already.

***

Most of Swamp Rats had found their wings. Other wings were taken downriver to known survivors. Still others were claimed later by fairies who unexpectedly turned up alive. Some dozens were hung back up on the Curtain to be re-earned by apprentices, over time. And some wings were gone because the 'Whipper' had used them for sport. That one paid with her life — hung at the end of her own whip.

But many wings would never be reclaimed, for no few lasses had perished in the flood and during the long Age of Slavery. Under the Queen's direction, they broke up Gorda's statue and threw it over the edge. In its place they arranged the Wings of the Lost as a memorial. Altogether there were nearly as many lost wings as found ones, for it had been a terrible Age.

But it was over.

Atel and the butterflies lingered for days, as time is counted below where the earth spins under the Night Sky. Old friends had much to catch up on. Atel, along with the Queen and Lorelei on their batts, made a trip downriver. The butterflies accompanied them into the heart of the Swamp and excused themselves there to hang out with Catchbeam and Flossie and Little Laca, and other friends they had made among the Swamp Rats. The cleanup was getting into full swing and everyone pitched in, Yero and Boca included.

"We wish we could be of more help", they said in a weary moment. "But cleanup isn't our best talent". They were picking tiny leaves of scummy duckweed off the sweet flag plants and tossing them like Frisbees at trash floating by in the water. All junk and garbage went into the river now, destined for 'The Hole'. No one knew how deep it was, but it was hoped there would be room for all the Anya trash.

"If thu clean enough so we *notice*, we might put up a sign here to remember you by", teased the Pixies.

"We'll probably have to leave before then", said Yero wearily. "But feel free to put up a sign later".

Boca was more interested. "You could write: 'Here Ombomba began the cleanup of the city. Yero helped a little'".

"Maybe it should just say, 'Look closely or you'll miss this!'" suggested Catchbeam.

"There already is a memorial", said a voice. It was Lorelei, returning from downriver in one of her thoughtful moods. "They are recorded in the Silver Vine, as we all are".

But no one else was serious. "C'mon, Lorelei!" laughed Catchbeam, "At least we should post their pictures on a traffic sign. Then everyone would know to expect some delay ahead".

"I like that. A traffic sign", agreed Yoyonneh, arriving in a canoe with Atel on her shoulder. She brought it to a stop with a flick of an oar. It was the first of the new style from the Free Boatworks, covered with overlapping strips of bark salvaged from the dead trees. If the design worked well there would be plenty of raw material.

The Queen reached toward the Aurora and drew a flourish of esporellia. It swirled around, curious, until it saw her idea and swooshed into it. A stout wooden post took shape, anchoring itself firmly into the riverbank. A large sign — a billboard — coalesced, attaching itself to the post, showing Yero and Boca as they were at that very moment, leaning lazily on their shovels. In beautiful calligraphy it warned: SLOW BUTTERFLIES WORKING.

It was an immediate hit and looked sturdy enough to last for Ages. The butterflies just smiled and tossed more Frisbees.

"Aleta says th'must leave soon", said Yoyonneh. "So, ride with me now. We'll be test pilots together of this canoe. They plan to produce lots of boats. Th'will be needed now for free trade, and for those who lost their wings. Come, ride on my shoulder! 'Tis pretty smooth. Even Aleta rode, for a while".

"Then we'll risk it", said the butterflies solemnly, "because everyone knows she's no sailor".

Atel bowed to laughter all around, and they went upstream with their friends and quite a large party altogether. They were going to visit the Wishing Well. A new Age was come. A Free Age. Thought was awakening to use the Well again and re-visit the green earth. Romance beckoned many, and some held out hope of finding their wings down below. There would be traffic again as soon as cleanup allowed, and the Queen encouraged this idea. But today she meant to see that her instrument was in good working order, good enough to send the Travelers off.

Part 2: Beyond the Moonwalk

All the way through the Swamp free fairies waved and greeted them with good cheer and jests, mostly aimed at Ombomba. Everyone wanted to flirt with him; and this did not fall on deaf ears. Boca flirted right back. More than once he whispered to the Queen to..."Take it easy, Your Highness. There's no big hurry, is there?"

When they arrived at the Dais there was another, smaller marker waiting for them, fashioned by Gorda's apprentices who were barred from passing through the Curtain until the Dais was restored. Now they bowed low, hoping no one would disapprove. They had made dazzling replicas of the butterflies and perched them on the charred Curtain rope. But even as everyone watched, one lifted off and fluttered frivolously around the general area, to no apparent purpose. It dimmed somewhat and the light went to its eyes.

"Thu have refreshed our memory of butterflies", smiled the apprentices. "Two are just right for this job, to go dilly-dallying by turns". Everyone laughed, but the apprentices bowed again, very humbly. "Thu will be Greeters in th'New Age", they said more seriously. "'Twill give us hope that sometime soon we also may pass through".

"Thank you" ...Yero replied graciously, and she would have said more but the apprentices (very pretty girls in Nasha's mold, behind their scars) began fawning over Boca.

"The *aura*! So handsome!"

"Dashing!"

"Are *all* boys so dashing?"

"So courageous?"

"So gallant...?"

"I can only speak for myself ---" began Ombomba, but The Queen moved on out of necessity. Time was pressing.

"This is getting out of hand, Boca," whispered Yero irritably. "It really *is* time you got hauled back to earth!"

Perhaps so, but Ombomba felt the need to perform a few loops out of gallantry. The apprentices naturally blew kisses, and it was only natural that Ombomba blew them back.

When the moon rose in its fullness, a bevy of lasses launched into the Night Sky in the direction of the Moonwalk, or where they guessed it must be. They carried the Queen in a silk hammock, holding up the corners by turns with Yoyonneh managing somehow to look dignified among the folds and billows. Only a true Queen could do that.

The blacktop road with Gorda's Gang still on it had drifted slowly off in the direction of the sunrise. The black-robed ones could look forward to a bright morning, bright and hot. The road would soften and give way beneath them. Silhouetted against the faint dawn they looked to Boca like a row of bad teeth in a crocodile jaw.

When they arrived at the Courtyard, everyone took time to read the vines, especially the upstart one with Boca's name. It had grown a bit, sprouting an extra leaf, and this was widely thought to be a good omen.

But there would be no fresh nectar for the Queen or anyone else. Winter had come with a vengeance to the South Loop also. Snow was drifting in through both gateways onto the lawn. The Courtyard itself was charmed, meant to stay open even during winter, but it couldn't withstand the worst storms, and one was raging now.

Gusts through the south gate blew clear across the Courtyard. A drift had formed from the gate to the Wishing Well and beyond. Most of the lawn was covered and a snowcap had formed on the roof of the Well, but a bare margin encircled the well due to swirling winds.

Spirits fell. This had always been the most fun part, searching for fairy lads through the well (which did indeed see things below) and failing that, at least *wish* some lads into the picture. It was great fun. But there was no joy in getting snow down one's neck.

They crowded around anyway and peered into the well. All was white. The water had frozen and a coverlet of snow settled on top of the ice.

"Somehow, we must use this", said Atel. "Paths among the moonbeams will not get us back down in this weather".

"Aye to that", agreed Lorelei. "And where might those paths take thee, anyway? The earth spins beneath us. Let's try something here. Back up just a bit".

Reaching over to the windlass, she loosened the brake lever. Rope spun freely off the drum. The wooden bucket plunged down from the ceiling. It cracked the ice and jarred snow off the roof, onto her head. That lightened the mood and the fairies made a game of it, cranking the bucket back up while the Queen wrote a number in the snow. Everyone guessed at it and Catchbeam won the first turn at tripping the brake lever: Whrrr...Crunch! The bucket busted halfway through the ice. Willing hands cranked it up again. Flit tripped it next. Everyone wanted a turn and the 'lucky' ones all got snow down their necks. Lots of it. The storm outside was worsening. Squalls blew regularly through the gate now.

"'Tis open enough, I think", said Yoyonneh finally. "Thu better leave now an' *we'd* better too! We mustn't get snowed in here—right, girls? I'm sure everyone wants to get back to work!" She was rewarded with patient smiles.

"Cleanup will take longer now, without us", commented Yero.

"Doubtless. But for inspiration we can look at your sign".

Yero just grinned. "Yes, yes. But I do wish we had our shovels now. Just look at the slushy mess down there".

Little Laca smiled and produced them. She had brought them along.

"We were worried", explained Catchbeam, "that without these you would have nothing to lean on".

"We'll miss you, Yero", said Flossie when the laughter calmed down. "A lot. And the girls will *really* miss Ombomba".

He waved and flew around the well, dipping and waggling his wings at all the girls, braving the snow. Boca was getting used to the life of a celebrity.

Yoyonneh cast a spell, moving her hands over the well. A light began to emerge in the dark water. Floating ice chunks appeared as shadows. She waited. Yero fidgeted.

"There's just one thing..." she began. The Queen turned to her. "Well, I mean...we know this is a secret place up here. Can we talk about you down below?"

"I don't see why not", replied Yoyonneh. "The only folk down there who could harm us are men, and they wouldn't believe you anyway. Th'would wink and laugh at such fairy tales".

"Oh-oh!" interrupted the pixies.

All had turned white again, down in the well.

"Is it broken?" asked Flossie.

"I don't think so!" answered Yoyonneh. She frowned. "I believe we're looking straight down, *way* down. But it's snowing there too. That's not good! Give me a moment. I'll move the picture". She changed the spell slightly. There seemed to be no movement until suddenly brown grass appeared, sticking above the snow. The scene moved rapidly across the grass until the snow disappeared and stark trees came into the edge of the picture, late autumn trees with no leaves.

"There. Is this okay?" she asked Atel. "It's not far south of the river where you last were, but far enough that winter hasn't quite arrived".

"Ask her if she can move the picture all the way to Manino", whispered Yero.

"I could, maybe", smiled Yoyonneh, overhearing. "But it wouldn't be my place to do so. Besides, your guide would then be out of work. Would'st want that, I wonder?"

"I guess not. We wouldn't want her to be unemployed. She likes being busy".

"So thoughtful," replied Atel. "Say goodbye! Don't forget your shovels!"

Into the well they went, landing on a small ice floe. Atel directed them to push ice chunks aside with their shovels and clear as much open water as they could.

"We're going to dive", she warned.

That didn't sound very promising but they followed orders, employing the shovels as poles.

"That's enough", said Atel almost immediately. "Climb on my back and hang on tight! Ready?"

"I think so", said Yero nervously.

Boca didn't hear. He was stealing one last look at his admirers up above. The last thing he remembered was the lasses waving to him and blowing kisses. He started to blow a kiss back, but something grabbed his ankle and dragged him under.

Part 3
Byways of the Butterfly

Synopsis

Wherein the travelers return to the green earth below only to find it much as they had left it: Snow covered and icy. Rogues and rascals lie in ambush ahead of them, everywhere along the migratory route: A pitiable hitchhiker, a Mugwump and his Toady Court, a den of virtuous sidewinders, a bleached cattle skull seeking rehabilitation, a packrat with a ferris wheel, and others – each with their own style of robbery or murder. Excellent liars, all of them. But migrators aren't easily caught. Always their journey calls to them. While they still live, they will heed the call.

"Turn left at the setting sun", so they had been told. Prophetic words, for the Rio Grande River and a turning point in their journey await in that direction. But the Great American Desert lies between.

Chapter 9

Yero And the Gypsy Moth

When he went under, Boca looked down expecting to see Yero pulling his foot but was shocked instead to see a fish swallowing him. It had his foot between huge lips and looked him in the eye for a terrifying moment, then opened wide and lunged upward, swallowing him all in one gulp. It happened so fast he never thought about screaming until darkness closed over him; then he realized he was already screaming. From somewhere a voice was shouting at him, "Follow me! Follow me!"

Well, how dumb was that? He couldn't follow anyone in the dark and tried to explain. "I can't!" he shouted back. "Didn't you see? I've been swallowed by a fish!"

"Open your eyes", said the voice.

Of course! How could he have forgotten? But when he opened them, he saw only hallucinations—the moon and stars—and quickly shut them again, fearful that digestive gasses were overcoming him. He decided to hold his breath and pinch his nose, but the fish's stomach muscles were pinching it already and shaking it!

"Open your eyes!" the voice demanded.

"Id's too lade!" he lamented. "Da vish is already digestig me!"

The fish's stomach suddenly pinched very hard. Boca yelped and opened his eyes involuntarily. There was Atel, fiercely gripping his schnozz.

"You've been fooled!" she informed him, releasing his nose. "The pixies are teasing you, that's all! A little prank. There's no fish, and you're *falling*. Your shovel is just above you. Reach up and grab it. Don't let it go! Do you hear me?"

Boca grabbed it, even though it seemed dumb. Relief washed over him. He wasn't being swallowed after all! With a new lease on life he stretched his wings to dry in the rushing air and realized it was very cold. Brrr!

Atel turned her attention to Yero who was also having a bad dream by the signs: Eyes pinched shut, face screwed into wrinkles, holding her nose just like Boca. What was it with the noses all of a sudden? It was even harder to pull Yero out of her pixie charm.

"No, no!" she kept shouting, and when Atel pulled her hand away from her nose she pinched it shut again with the other. The hummingbird finally brought her out of the spell by tickling her, and even then Yero was unsure which vision was real.

"Kagu was waiting for me under the water!" she finally explained in a rush of words. "I don't know how he could be, but he was! He said I laughed at him. I tried to tell him it wasn't me. It was those tribbits, especially that littlest one! But Kagu just said, 'Now you do pay for it!' And he sprayed a big cloud, and there was just no *stopping*! I fell right *into* it! Smell me. Do I stink?"

Atel laughed but went through the motions to satisfy Yero and calm her down. She promised herself to get even someday with the mischievous pixies. They had tricked her too. Very realistic. She wiggled her tail again, in spite of herself, to make sure there were no injuries. She felt embarrassed, being fooled so easily.

When she went under her thought was all with the butterflies, to be sure they came along, and she had been surprised to look down and discover she was falling right into a quilting party! The Artisans were there, busily working away with bags of needles next to them—open bags with *sharps* sticking up—and it was too late to slow her descent! Ouch!

She shook her head to be rid of the silly dream and resolved to keep it to herself. She glanced at Yero who was holding her nose again and shivering. Boca was too. But their eyes were open, and they had their shovels. Good!

"Now - *shake* those shovels!" she ordered. "Shake hard!"

The butterflies looked baffled and skeptical.

"*Shake* them, ninnies!" she repeated. "I'm not joking! You'll see why".

When they finally did, the shovels fell apart in a sparkling shower of esporellia. The butterflies knew what to do with that. A lot of their own had rubbed off against the icy slush in the Well. Now they spent the rest of the descent catching the new dust on their wings. The pixies had made a joke of sending the shovels, but they knew the esporellia would be needed.

Thus, the Travelers returned to the Green Earth but found it much as they had left it, depressingly snow-covered and cold. The weather was against them down here too, not snowing but something even more hazardous. It was sleeting. There were trees nearby if they could buck the headwind and get to them.

"Follow in my wake!" directed Atel. The wind drowned out her voice, but the butterflies caught on, and so they reached the leeward side of a large tree, an old burr oak. The trees were all big and bare of leaves, but this one on the very edge of the forest was especially girthy. Atel landed on an outthrust spur of bark. There were lots of spurs and ridges, with deep crevices cutting between them, all up and down the huge trunk. Here at least was protection from flying ice and the worst of the wind, and here they would have to stay for now.

"The Wishing Well must be broken after all", complained Yero. "There wasn't supposed to be snow".

"No, there wasn't", said Atel. "But the Well hadn't been used in centuries. It might be just a little *slow*, a little behind the times. Maybe what we saw in the Well was yesterday, or the day before".

"Or last week", said Boca, disgusted. "Or last *year*. We're way too far north, don't you think?"

"No. I think we're right where we want to be, but the Well is sluggish and hasn't kept up with the weather".

"Where we *want* to be?" Boca shivered in spite of the fresh esporellia. "Pardon my saying, but who would ever want to be here if they had any choice?"

"The bees, at least. This is a honeybee tree if you hadn't noticed. That should interest you".

"Not that again! I'm not going into another hive".

"You won't have to. We'll ask for some honey. They usually listen to folks who ask nicely, but they insist on good manners".

"Couldn't you just get carry-outs?"

"It doesn't work that way, Boca. Now, brush up your manners! Their front door is down there, just below. See it? The Doorward is studying you right now. Act *nice*".

The butterflies looked. It was true. About ten or twelve 'shovel-lengths' down the guard glared up at them from another spur of bark — the front porch of an entrance in the crevice behind.

"Bow toward her, both of you", instructed Atel. "Slowly! And don't eyeball her while you do it. You are lowly beggars asking for alms. Don't worry. She sees the weather. She knows things are tough. She won't sting anybody".

The Travelers bowed politely. The Doorward went through an odd, slow dance, moving this way and that, and finally disappeared inside. Atel seemed pleased but said nothing. Minutes passed and nothing happened. Boca uttered something impatient just as the Doorward reappeared. She stopped to glare up at them again, and Boca put on his best innocent look. After a minute or so the warder seemed to buy it, or at least excuse it, and went into another dance while other bees came and went. Finally, she resumed her post and ignored them altogether. Boca exhaled. So did Atel. But Yero whistled softly, admiringly.

"It's like 'interpretive dance', isn't it?" she asked. "What was she telling us?"

"That dinner is served. Shall we go down?"

Portions had been arranged way out on the very lip of the porch: One larger for the hummingbird, two much smaller, with golden comb honey on 'plates' of wax. The warder paid them no further attention and no other bees appeared, but a low, steady hum — the conference of thousands of bees winding down into hibernation — drifted up to them from unguessed depths in the hollow tree.

"Delicious!" pronounced Boca with a smile. "Although I still like mallasha better".

Atel gave him a sharp look. It was lucky that he smiled when he said it, probably. The warder was paying close attention even if it didn't seem like it. Bees don't always understand other woodland languages well, but they read expressions and body language *very* well, and take offense quickly.

All too soon the meal was over before anyone was quite full. Atel whispered instructions about stacking the 'plates' and turned to Yero who was eager to try some of the dance.

"Yes, we must show our gratitude. Do like this..." she said and began the correct movement but never finished. The Doorward suddenly grew agitated at Boca who hadn't stacked his plate after all but held it out for 'seconds'. This was bad form and the news spread fast, even in a hive that was half-asleep. All Atel could do was hustle the butterflies away into the stinging sleet to another tree nearby, out of sight. Boca didn't understand the hubbub.

"What's wrong with 'seconds'?" he asked. "It's like a compliment!"

"No, it's ingratitude in their eyes — all the more since we hadn't thanked them yet for the first helping".

"Well, I'm sorry. I was still hungry. Could we go back and apologize when they calm down?"

"And ask for another helping? Sorry, no. Unless we had something to trade maybe. Some bit of helpful information about nectar flowers, or a tip about some animal nearby that might threaten the hive. Something useful to them. Some favor. Do you have anything?"

"No".

"Then don't hang around where they can see you. They work hard, these bees. They earn every drop of their honey with long, long hours, and they're generous to those in real need. But they hate bums and loafers. I don't blame them".

"And you ruined the dance lesson too!" complained Yero.

"Get over it!" said Atel. "I'm leaving, and I don't want to leave you arguing. I may return tomorrow, maybe the day after, but I need to scout ahead. There are several routes south from here, each with their own hazards. The risks are worrisome. I want to spy them out".

"What are we supposed to do in the meantime — if we're not allowed to go begging?" said Yero irritably. Boca kicked at a piece of loose bark.

"Keep going!" said Atel brightly. "Take a southerly course as soon as the weather allows. This is only the beginning of a large wood. At the far southern end it marches up to a wide river and stops, since trees don't swim or have wings. You should make it to the river by the time I get back if you don't dawdle. I'll meet you there!"

With no further delay she left, and the butterflies were alone. Boca took a few steps around the trunk into the wind, to watch her go, and was rewarded with a last warning.

"Stay out of the sleet! Don't be foolish!"

He went back and the two of them, not speaking to each other just now, huddled in a deep fold of the bark. A raw, drafty breeze found them there and they backed deeper into the fold until a wailing noise commenced behind them. Turning, Yero beheld a piteous creature shivering there, wings all askew, trying to shelter in a crevasse. It was a moth. To be frank, it was the rear end of one wagging in the cold air while the front end tried to burrow deeper into the crevasse. The moth was smaller than Yero judging by the wings, which were white with zigzag black markings, but the creature's body was substantial.

"Leave me! Leave me to my misery!" blubbered the moth without even looking back. Boca wondered how the moth was aware of them, but Yero felt a pang of sympathy and stepped forward.

"What is it?" she asked. "Are you cold?"

"Yes, cold. But that's not important".

"It's not?"

"No. I will starve to death before I freeze", said the moth, still trying to burrow in, still not looking.

"Oh, you poor thing! How long since you've eaten?"

"How long? Too long! I don't remember".

Boca couldn't help it. "You're *fat*", he said matter-of-factly.

There was an embarrassing silence. Yero gave him a disapproving look. The moth, haggard and misunderstood, turned slowly to face the unfair criticism.

"So it might seem", she admitted (for she was a girl), "but it's only a last reserve. It will go quickly now in the cold nights and there is nothing more, nothing but dry bark to eat. I will perish and no one will care".

"Well, fly away then and find food", said Boca.

"There it is! There it *always* is: The male chauvinism. Our boys, our *Gennoot*, fly away too, leaving the poor girls behind. You must be a boy".

"I am, and I don't feel sorry for lazy girls. You're just fat and lazy".

Yero opened her mouth to protest, edging a step or two toward the poor thing, but the moth whimpered, "We girls *can't* fly. Hardly at all. I would go down into the snow before I ever got to the next tree".

"Go on a diet then", shrugged Boca. "Starve off a few pounds. It'll do you good".

"That's enough, Boca!" interrupted Yero. "I'm sure she has her reasons. Just let her talk. You're being very rude!"

Boca shrugged again. Anyone could see how fat the moth was. But the creature looked gratefully at Yero and moved closer, soaking up moral support.

"Thank you! Oh, thank you! Boys don't understand. Our girls—we *Zaza*—have very small wings. Too small to fly with, alas!" The moth burst into tears. Boca didn't buy it for a moment.

"That's just another way of saying you're too fat".

"Boca!" scolded Yero, "Those who *can* fly shouldn't make fun of those who *can't*".

The two girls edged closer, farther away from Boca. The moth let the tears run on the outside but smiled on the inside. This was going to be easier than she expected! She curtsied to the nice butterfly.

"What's your name, if I may ask?" she inquired politely.

"I'm Yero, and of course *that*..."(She pointed with some aggravation) ..."is Boca, as you heard. What's your name?"

"I don't have one", said the moth. "I come from a poor family and we only went by our last name". She made a guttural sound: "Romm...rom... rommm..." then smiled shyly. "That's our old family name. Some yokels—excuse me! —some folks call us Gypsies".

Boca scoffed. "Too poor to have a *name?* That's even more stupid! Names are free".

Yero folded her forearms and scowled, but the gypsy showed only patience and humility to gain more of Yero's sympathy. It was working great.

"Unusual, yes. Silly, yes. Even stupid maybe, yes. But still true. We were very, very poor, living hand-to-mouth, just trying to stay alive. Some of us did starve. Poor sisters! Poor brothers too, alas! We had no food. We were given no names. What good are names when you are starving?"

"Good grief..." mumbled Boca and turned away. It was the dumbest story he ever heard, but it was only half a lie, so she was able to tell it sincerely. Sometimes her family *was* hard-pressed to stay alive. Some did starve, as she said. But the dark secret behind it was, there were hordes of them—a plague of them—especially the young, the caterpillars. Her entire family history was a scandal of gluttony, not 'struggling to survive' (although that happened too, when they had devoured every green leaf and starvation set in of their own doing). As for not having names, that was both true and untrue. There might be thousands of them in the caterpillar stage from only a few mothers, so the mothers didn't bother. There weren't enough names to go around anyway. But the young took names to themselves if they reached the adult moth stage. They grew up very talented and clever. Entertaining. Especially the girls. But the girls couldn't fly well. She spoke the truth about that part. And they could hardly fly at all when their bellies were fat with eggs. They needed help to reach the next forest where the little hatchlings would find a fresh buffet.

The gypsy moths took names of things they were good at, things they aspired to. These names were only known among themselves, the Romm, never whispered to dumb 'yokels' as they call the rest of us. This particular gypsy fancied herself as the 'Hitcher' and dreamed of becoming the 'Phurri-Dai', the leader who escapes a dead forest to start a colony in a new one.

So Boca stepped away, being unpopular now, glad to put a little distance between himself and the girls. When he looked back, the gypsy was chanting rhythmically and teaching Yero a bit of folk dance:

> "Romm...omminy...rommm
> *Felony* romm
> *Gluttony* romm
> Omminy...romminy
> *Sly*-minny
> *Lie*-minny
> *Crime*-inny
> Romm!"

Boca stopped and listened again, surprised. *What?* It sounded the same the second time. He called to Yero but failed to get her attention. He went closer and shouted. She finally looked at him.

"Don't you hear what she's saying?" Boca shouted. He had to shout because the gypsy was. She was chanting louder and louder. "She's talking about lying, cheating and stealing!" Boca shouted. "Listen!"

But Yero was having fun, paying attention only to the beat and the movements. She just laughed. "Don't be so suspicious about everything!" she replied as she swung nicely into a rhythm. Boca saw the hint of a smile on the gypsy's face and noted dryly that the 'shivering, starving' thing showed no effects of that anymore. He gave it up in disgust and moved away around the trunk.

As he turned the corner, Boca came face to face again with the weather. It was improving slowly. The sleet had let up at least, if not the wind. He leaned into it and moved around the tree across the rough ridges of bark. This may not sound difficult, but you probably don't have huge sails attached to your back that could grab a gale and send you tumbling. Even Boca, an expert with airfoils, found it tricky where the wind glanced hard off the tree. Once past that point it was better, but a lot of bark was missing on the windward side and more was still flaking off. Boca realized suddenly that the tree was dead and resolved to retrace his steps quickly before a chunk blew away right underneath him and took him with it.

As he backed carefully, step by step, he came upon the remains of a papery shell tucked into a fold of the bark, the usual cheap moth imitation of the pretty butterfly chrysalis. It had buff-colored hair clinging to it that matched the gypsy, and it wasn't hard to guess that she'd hatched right *here*—the lazy thing! —and in her whole adult life had only ventured as far as the other side of the tree. But here was another shell, and another. Lots of them! There were dozens of the shells, or remnants of them, in the deep grooves of the bark. The gypsy might've hatched from any of them. Boca disapproved greatly of all this. It was just like moths, always way more of them than there should be. If he had his way, he would put the 'should be' figure at about zero. But where were all the other moths?

He didn't have time to think about it. A gust of wind broke loose another chunk of dead bark and sent it tumbling wildly through the air. Boca retreated back around the tree. Yero and the gypsy were still into folk dance and enjoying it immensely. He was not very welcome, nor did they particularly listen when he spoke. He found a place off to one side and considered the situation. It was mid-morning and Atel wouldn't be back until tomorrow or even the next day, so there was after all no dire need to go on while the headwind was blowing so hard.

Or was it?

It dawned on him that the wind was lessening. The storm seemed to have blown itself out with that last wild gust. Ice coated almost everything but that shouldn't matter to them. They were only passing through. He finally got Yero off to the side, but she didn't want to leave.

"Don't get lazy like your friend", he warned her. "We have a long way to go!" Yero didn't even take offense; she was in such a great mood.

"Who's lazy?" she laughed. "We've been dancing the whole while! Oh, Boca! She even told my fortune! She said I'm romantic, but realistic too. She looked into an ice-crystal, Boca, and saw Atel! She described her almost perfectly. And she knew about our journey and everything".

Boca stuck out his tongue, "Blebbbth! Do you believe that stuff?"

Yero ignored that and lowered her voice. "She even said our guide would leave us soon and we would have to make our way without her. She said that, and that part's already true! And she said there is mercy in my eyes, that one day when I least expect it, I'll help someone in great need. Isn't that neat?"

"Oh, Yero, that's *so* hokie! I'm sure she was hiding right here when we came and eavesdropped. It would be easy then to tell your future".

"No, it's more than that! She says she hears voices".

"Ours, I suppose. What did she say about me?"

"She doesn't like you. She says you'll try to stop a good deed from happening".

Boca laughed. "You call that fortune-telling? I told her fortune right away. She's lazy!"

"She didn't like *you* from the start either".

"That's because I saw through her act. She's never done anything in her whole life! I found where she was hatched, just around the tree, and this is as far as she ever travelled. She's a slug!"

The gypsy had come closer to listen. Her eyes flashed at this, but she held her tongue. Boca challenged her.

"A *lot* of you hatched, by the signs! Where are the others? Did they fly away? Maybe they weren't as fat as you?"

The gypsy was careful not to show her temper. That wouldn't do. Everything depended on sympathy. She worked up another whimper and cast her eyes down.

"Gone, all gone", she said sorrowfully. "Birds ate them. Sisters, yes, brothers too. All of them. Everyone but me. Why me? Why just me? I'm all that's left!" She buried her face in one wing and sobbed, "I wish they had eaten me too! Eaten me — and left someone *else*. The loneliness is the worst part!"

Yero looked accusingly at Boca and tried to comfort the gypsy, but to no avail. The poor thing was inconsolable. Her awful memories were flooding back. "Yi-yee! The birds! The birds!" she shrieked and trembled all over.

It was a very good act and it was working, as she saw discreetly peeking out from under the wing. The girl was completely on her side now, and with any luck the nasty boy would go away again. She almost laughed. Excellent!

Boca's suspicions were justified, of course. Behind her tearful act, she was the last survivor in a survival-of-the-fittest struggle. Sure, birds had gotten their share when she was growing up, but the family numbered millions and every little muncher knew what lay ahead when the forest was laid bare, when every green leaf was gone: The youngest and weakest would starve and no tears would be shed for them.

The older munchers went on to fashion pupal shells and hatch out as moths. The boys — lucky boys! — flew off to seek their fortunes then, leaving their girlfriends in the lurch. If any girls were to survive — if the family itself was to survive — at least one girl would have to beg, borrow or steal a ride out of here, because this forest was dead.

Most of the females had tried to ride the wind, but it hadn't been in their favor this year. It only carried them back where the family had come from. That was no good. Those woods were chewed over. Some girls waited for the right winds, but they were weak. Those girls didn't get far. When there were only a dozen left in the tree, a thought occurred to this girl that twelve was too many — that if a ride came along and just one gypsy remained, her chances of being picked up might be better. So she murdered the other eleven one night and bided her time while the eggs inside her grew larger. Very soon now, she would have to lay them. She couldn't hold them much longer. She had almost despaired before the butterflies turned up. Now she smiled inwardly, pleased with her performance. Getting her eggs to a new forest was worth any amount of murder and mayhem. She would be hailed as the 'Phurri-Dai'! Besides, she rather enjoyed murder. Now she deliberately eased off the sobbing to just sniffles and trembles.

"Don't worry about me", she snuffled. "I'll make do".

"Oh, I doubt it!" said Yero. "I don't like to leave you like this".

"You're leaving? So soon?"

"Well, not this very moment..." Yero glanced at Boca who obviously was ready and getting impatient about it..."but we *do* have to leave soon. The storm is over. We only stopped because of the weather. We couldn't make headway into it".

"So that's the direction you're going?" pined the gypsy wistfully, pointing to the southwest where the bad weather had blown in from.

"Yes, quite a long way hopefully".

Boca was already airborne, fluttering about, testing the breeze, and waiting. It was nearly calm.

"That's where I'd go too, if I could", sniffled the gypsy. "That's where the boys went...especially the one I like".

"You have a boyfriend?"

"Oh, yes! He went scouting, looking for a... a *Honeymoon Home* for us, but it's been so long! I'm afraid something's happened to him".

"Well...what does he look like? We could take a message in case we see him. We'll keep an eye out".

"Oh, I wish! But that won't work. He looks just like the other gypsy boys to everyone except me. I can't explain it any better. It's true love, that's all".

She buried her face in her wing again and wept for her lost love, gambling that this stuff would tug at Yero's heartstrings. It did. She went and pleaded with Boca.

"There must be *something* we can do for her. It's just so sad!"

"Do something like *what?*" scoffed Boca. "Some things are just impossible. And it's always the girl things!"

"Don't talk like that! You're loud and she'll hear, and she's sad enough already".

"Well, if you can think of anything, think it up quick because I'm leaving. You know we're supposed to press on".

"Yes — okay! Go ahead then. But I'm at least going to say goodbye. I owe her that".

"You don't owe her anything".

"Yes, I do. She offered friendship when she didn't have to. I'm going to cheer her up a bit and wish her luck".

Boca left. Yero settled down again by the gypsy who was still sobbing. "We really have to leave", she said, "but I wish you the best. It was so nice of you to teach me the dance. I wish there was more I could do, but..."

The unfinished sentence didn't hang in the air long. "I'll *try*", whimpered the gypsy, then she raised her voice bravely: "Let me try to come with you! It's my only hope".

The Butterflies, Yero and Boca

With that, she launched herself into the air in the general direction Boca had gone, beating her wings hopelessly. She went down at a steep angle and struck the icy crust headfirst.

"Oh, my gosh! Are you hurt?" Yero landed quickly to offer help but the moth was unresponsive for a while. Yero berated herself, fearing the worst. But the gypsy wasn't dead, and when she came to she was more determined than ever.

"I'll try again", she vowed. "I'll keep trying. Please don't leave yet!"

"But how? You need to start from a tall tree".

"I'll climb! Please—just wait! Just a few minutes".

"Well...you'll have to hurry. I don't want to lose Boca".

The gypsy scurried across the ice, lost control, and slid into a tussock. She got out of that, only to flounder.

"Listen", said Yero. "I'm going to give you one good chance. That's all I have time for. Climb on my back and I'll carry you up".

"You will? You'll give me a ride?"

"Yes, but hurry!"

That's how Boca found them when he returned looking for Yero. The gypsy was on board and Yero was struggling to launch under the considerable weight. He said a bad word under his breath. He'd gotten quite some distance into the forest before he decided to backtrack and found it totally empty. There were no birds, no squirrels, nothing moving around. Even the trees seemed lifeless. Many were losing their bark. It was a ghostly place, but it wasn't small. It appeared to go on for miles. No way could Yero carry the dratted gypsy that far.

"What do you think you're doing?" he shouted. "You can't carry her. She's too heavy!"

That was all the inspiration Yero needed. *Couldn't?* She sure *could!* With an effort she got up, only to learn there were issues with balance and freedom of movement. The gypsy did her best to stay in the middle and not interfere, but there was no ignoring the weight. Yero just had to shift into a lower gear and lug it. Remarkably, they made it back up and Yero even went to the next higher branch to give the gypsy a better chance.

"There!" she said. "Try it from here".

"I beg your pardon?" said the moth.

"Fly from here. It's higher. It's a better chance".

"You want me to do that *again*?"

"Well—yes. That's why I carried you up here".

"Oh! I'm so embarrassed. I misunderstood! When you said you would 'give me a ride', I thought...I *hoped*...Oh, forgive me!"

"What did you think I meant? How far..."

"Please, it was only a fool's hope! When I read your fortune and saw how good-hearted you are, I hoped—Oh! Don't mind me! Thank you for just being my friend!"

Before Yero could answer, the gypsy leaped into the air once more with a terrified shriek, flapped wildly, and hit the ice at an even steeper angle, being sure to scratch her face this time. When Yero reached her, she was bleeding all down her cheek and there was blood on the ice. She tried to speak but it was hard. Yero leaned close.

"Thank you", the gypsy finally whispered. "I never could have made it this far without you". And with that, she closed her eyes and went limp.

"Leave her!" said Boca. "Let's go".

"I can't leave her like *this*!"

"Why not? Looks like she's a goner anyway".

"I can't help it if I'm good-hearted, Boca!"

"Do something good-hearted for *us* then!"

"That's not the meaning of 'good-hearted'—Oh, look! She's moving. She's still alive!"

Part 3: Byways of the Butterfly

The gypsy moaned, turning to show off her wound to best advantage. "If only...to see my lost love..." she mumbled, reaching feebly toward Yero who decided to help just once more.

"Climb on", she said. "I'll give you one more lift, but that's it. Then I'm going".

For someone in such tough shape the gypsy jumped aboard easily. "Take me to the highest branch", she whispered hoarsely, "Please don't drop me".

"I won't. Just help me balance".

"You'll take me to the highest branch?"

"Yes!" said Yero, a bit exasperated. Talking was a bother as she struggled to gain altitude. She reached the top branch and landed on it. "This is it then", she puffed. "Goodbye and good luck!"

"Wait—I'm scared! Wait just a moment...please!"

"I'm sorry, but I have to go".

The gypsy burst into tears. "I'm still going to follow!" she blubbered. "You're my only friend". She dismounted to make what was likely a suicide dive. Yero didn't know what to do.

"Good!" shouted Boca. "Let's go now!"

The gypsy leaped to her death with barely a sigh. She was pretty confident of being saved and Yero didn't disappoint. Bare inches above the ground she swooped underneath, caught her, and plunged laboriously through the cold air into the ghostly wood.

"Bless you!" said the gypsy. "I would have perished".

Yero grunted. This was hard labor.

"Just one thing to calm my fears", continued the gypsy. "Are you my truest, best friend? Will you ever abandon me?"

"I'll carry you as far as I can. I can't promise any more".

The gypsy snickered to herself, but outwardly she thanked Yero several times over and burst into a Gypsy travelling song:

> "I'm sure they'll say they *need* us,
> When we come!
> They'll prob'ly even *feed* us,
> When we come!
> 'Cause it'll be just *me* to dine,
> An' maybe one or two *pals* o' mine.
> Goodwill is guaranteed us
> When we come!"

It did lighten the mood for a few minutes, but they hadn't gone far before Yero began to lose altitude and had to stop on a low branch to catch her breath. The gypsy, very confident now, dismounted politely to allow Yero's aching muscles to recuperate and to put off the time when the butterfly could go no further; but that ugly moment would come sooner or later.

"Thanks", said Yero, stretching her stiff back. "I need a break".

"Glad to help any way I can", replied the gypsy.

Boca, hovering nearby, said something under his breath again. It was now well past noon and the sun was peeking through the storm clouds as they thinned and cracked apart in the cold air high above. The wood brightened and was revealed to be absolutely bare. There should have been autumn leaves yet, at least some, Boca noted in surprise; but there were none. There wasn't a single leaf clinging anywhere. They had fallen and been covered by the snow, so it seemed. That was a lucky deception for the gypsy, for there were no leaves beneath the snow. The gypsy family had eaten all of them. But no one would suspect until spring.

Yero caught her breath and they went on. After the break she was able to gain some altitude and Boca began to hope she had gotten her second wind, as often happens. But no such luck. It wasn't long before she had to land again. The gypsy was very considerate and climbed down once more. Boca circled, fuming. The break needed to be a little longer this time, and after a few minutes the gypsy began to shift from one foot to the other standing on the icy branch. Yero didn't notice but Boca did.

"What's with you?" he demanded. "Getting cold feet, you pampered thing?"

"Well, yes", the gypsy admitted, and shot him a dirty look. "I wasn't going to say anything".

"You better *not*, freeloader!"

Yero bestirred. "It's okay Boca. The ice *is* cold on the branch and her feet were warm on my back. It's a big temperature change".

Boca made a face. "Don't apologize for her! She can do that herself".

"I have nothing to apologize for", said the moth. "I wasn't complaining".

"Then stand still and quit dancing!"

"Gypsies can't help dancing. It's in our hearts. Anyway, dancing is a joyful thing, isn't it Yero?"

"Yes, but I'd rather not talk just now".

"See?" The gypsy looked accusingly up at Boca. "Leave us alone. Let her rest!"

To stop the argument Yero took a deep breath and embarked on the next leg through the woods. So the afternoon passed, a leg at a time, and the legs became shorter while the breaks became longer. All the while, the woods went on with no end in sight. Boca lost patience and began to wander during the breaks.

The gypsy, too, began to lose patience and offer little criticisms instead of support. She was starting to get her cramps. Soon now, her eggs must be laid. She wouldn't be able to hold them in when the cramps grew strong. She had a few hours, perhaps. She couldn't be sure. Gypsy females only do this once and then perish, but she remembered stories and advice from older females in her youth.

"Thirsty", muttered Yero during one rest. It was her first actual complaint, long overdue.

"If it isn't one thing it's another", grumbled the gypsy, dancing back and forth again on an icy branch. Her drooping abdomen bounced on the branch in time with her step, and that wasn't good at all. It brought on cramps. She really needed a better ride. Something bigger and faster. But she was stuck with this pooping-out butterfly and it would have to do.

"Chew on some ice", she suggested unkindly.

Yero was so tired she didn't even take offense. Then the gypsy complained about her cramps. Yero did hear that.

"I'm getting cramps too, in my wings", she advised the gypsy. "I won't be able to carry you much longer". There was an edge to her voice that got the moth's attention. Oops! This *was* her only ride. The boy sure wouldn't help.

"I'm so sorry, so sorry!" she gushed, all friendly again. "Yes, back spasms. Let me help. I can help".

To be sure, it was partly to get her own cold feet up again, but she climbed onto Yero's back and proceeded to do a nice massage while warming them. Boca didn't return during that rest and they made it quite a way before the next one. 'No Boca' suited the gypsy just fine and she was busy giving another massage in hopes they could lose him for good when he found them again. He'd been looking for some end to the woods—east, west or south. He'd found none and told Yero so.

"You've gotta dump this bum!" he said urgently. "Or we'll never get out of here. It's a long, long ways yet!"

"I... can't. I... promised", answered Yero. The gypsy was busily massaging, rubbing away the soreness and with it any urgency to pay much attention to Boca.

"Now we see it, don't we?" whispered the gypsy. "As was foretold! That one will try to undo a good deed! He talks and talks, and makes trouble, but does he help? Does he give nice back rubs? No, he doesn't help at all".

Yero said nothing. She was fatigued and the back rub was so welcome she hardly paid attention to the argument. Boca was disappointed and angry. When the moth flashed a snide grin at him, it was too much.

"Alright! You two deserve each other!" he shouted, and flew away south, intending to go on alone. However, later in the afternoon when his temper cooled he turned back, at a loss what he could do to bring Yero to her senses but knowing he had to keep trying. It was on the way back, going north, that he found evidence he could use.

The ice storm had blown through in the direction he was now going, so the trees were coated in ice as he approached them. It glared with the sun behind, so he zigzagged forward at angles to avoid the blinding glare. From these angles, he could see through the ice as if looking through a window, and there it was: The answer to the riddle, or millions of answers. On the south face of all the trees — except where the bark was entirely gone — were hundreds and thousands of the empty pupal shells like those on the tree where they met the gypsy. The whole forest had been simply swarming with gypsies! They had killed this forest - or had done so growing up as caterpillars. Boca shuddered at the thought of entire trees crawling with munching worms.

But there was more. In places, the ice acted as a magnifying glass and he saw egg-clusters tucked into the cracks. They fooled him at first, being covered over with the belly hairs of the moths, but where bark had broken off the underlying egg-masses were easy to identify: New eggs for *next year*!

The rest wasn't hard to guess from hints the gypsy herself had let out. The boys had gone on to other forests, but they laid no eggs. The girls were left, unable to fly, and had perished in many ways. Most had laid their eggs anyway on exposed south sides of their trees where early spring sunshine could hatch them. But these would hatch in a leafless forest and die.

Boca suddenly guessed the final part of the riddle. The dratted gypsy! The dratted *fat* gypsy! What was she so fat with? What else but eggs? She was the cleverest of them all, not laying her eggs but instead plotting escape! Now she had cast her spell on Yero and hitched a ride. Boca shuddered again and backtracked as fast as he could, hoping to find the others before dark.

He found them, and they had come further than he expected. They were perched on another icy branch but Yero was easy to spot in a winter woods of white and brown. Or rather, Yero was perched on the branch and the gypsy was sitting on her back keeping her feet warm. She had decided Boca was gone for good and dropped the friendly pretense. No more girl talk, no more back rubs. She did nag Yero to chew ice against dehydration, but otherwise drove her impatiently. A few more flights, a few more stupid rests, and then the river crossing. Oh, yes. The cursed river! The natural barrier. Except for *that* her family would never have been stopped! She gave Yero a kick in the side, like a rodeo rider, to get her going again, but her timing was bad. Boca returned just when Yero was angry at her passenger.

"Sorry! So sorry!" the moth blurted as Boca approached. "I was trying to climb down, to give you relief. Please forgive my clumsiness!"

"Don't forgive anything!" said Boca fiercely. "She's a criminal and I can prove it".

Yero looked up with the old fire in her eyes. "I'm listening".

Before the gypsy could make a distraction, Boca pointed out the eggs under the ice of the tree trunk, still illuminated by the last rays of afternoon sun, and spilled out the story.

"The trees are all dead, Yero. She murdered them! Her and 'one or two' zillion little 'pals' of hers — an army of caterpillars! They ate every leaf. Then they turned into moths like her and laid eggs. See? Look at them all! They're everywhere. But not *her* eggs. She wants to lay those in a new forest and kill more trees!"

But the gypsy broke off an ice-shard and held it to Yero's throat, to show who was still boss. "So what!" she jeered at Boca. "So, you guessed? So what! It took you long enough, yokel! Sure, I'm a murderer, and I'll murder this slowpoke too if I have to!"

"If you do", replied Boca, "You'll never get where you want to go".

"No, so sad. But neither will *she*. Ha-ha! So, don't get any ideas. Are you sissies up to night travel, like real moths?"

"We've done our share".

"Well, you'll do your share tonight and my share too, since I'm riding! And we'll be going faster. *Much* faster!" She spurred Yero in the sides again, hard this time. The gangster was coming out in her. She needed speed and no longer cared how she got it.

"You'll pay for that", said Boca.

"I don't think so!" crowed the gypsy. She kicked again and they were off.

The sun had set now, but a bright moon coming up in the east would help to light the way. Yero was thankful for that. If she hit a stray branch in the dark, the gypsy would probably carry out her threat. She could feel the shard against her neck every time she beat her wings, but if she complained the gypsy just laughed, "I like it this way! You give a smoother ride when you feel the edge".

"It would be stupid to cut her throat by accident", warned Boca. "If it happens, I'll make sure you don't get another ride. You'll die in the snow".

In spite of the pleasure it gave her, the gypsy pulled the shard back a little. The concession galled her, but it did make sense.

"Is that better, faintheart?" she taunted. "Then show it!" She dug her heels in again to make sure everyone knew who was still in charge.

Yero did fly better without the shard scraping her throat and nosed upward into the fresh moonlight. That's when it happened, and her throat likely would've been cut a minute earlier.

There was a musical hum in the air followed suddenly by a hollow BOOM! —the sound of a nighthawk's wings, audible only at the last instant as he struck his prey, too late for evasive action.

The nighthawk would have swerved, had he noticed Yero under the gypsy, but as it happened the collision was a surprise to everyone involved. Owing to the confusion, the hawk didn't get the whole moth, but he did get most of one wing.

"Sorry about that", he apologized to Yero as he wolfed down the wing. "Didn't see you under there".

"Ha! Goatsucker!" shrilled the gypsy. "You missed!" She had managed to hang on still clutching her ice-shard, even as Yero crash-landed on a branch. The nighthawk ended up on the branch below.

"I got part of you, Vandal", answered the hawk. "You're lopsided now".

"So? I don't care about the wing. Don't use 'em, y'know".

"Then give me the other as well. I'm still hungry".

"Goon!" The gypsy scratched the shard against Yero's neck. "Thug! But I'm glad to see you pity these brats. Makes it easy to get rid of you! Vamoose with your big yap, or I'll spill her blood, see?"

"Yes, I see everything. I just wish I saw it a minute ago when I had you by surprise. Gypsy and eggs! My favorite. Very rare on the wing".

"It only takes one of us", mocked the gypsy. "And I'll be the one!"

"You'll be a dead one. I'll watch where you go".

"Stinking murderers! You and all your buddy-buddies!"

The hawk laughed at her, expelling a puff of gypsy-wing dust. He much preferred other moths but made a special point to eat gypsies wherever he found them. It was invariably the 'Gennoot', the boys. This was the first 'flying Zaza' he'd come across.

"Call us anything you want", replied the hawk, "but we know who the *real* murderers are. You murder whole forests! Do the butterflies know?"

"Sure", laughed the gypsy. "They were slow to figure it out, but they finally did. So, blab away with your big yap! They know everything and it don't matter, 'cause *I've* got the knife!" With that, she broke off a new shard and tested it against Yero's throat.

The hawk left without another word, but loitered, usually within sight or hearing. The gypsy didn't like that at all, and for a while was so preoccupied she eased up on Yero.

The respite didn't last long. At the end of the next leg the Gypsy had no patience at all. Boca volunteered to take a turn but was refused; nor was he allowed to do back rubs or even approach, and the abuse got worse. A routine developed where they flew as far as Yero could be kicked and lashed, then they landed on a new icy branch where she was allowed a few short minutes to catch her breath while the moth grew impatient. Usually the gypsy broke off a new shard as the other began to melt in her grip, being sure to test it for sharpness against Yero's neck.

To pry the creature's mind away from abuse Boca asked questions and had success when he inquired about her family business (outlawry) and their specialty (hitching a ride to the scene of the next crime). Her family was proud of their talents and long history of surviving in a world hostile to them.

They had turned up in an earlier Age, in a distant land, having bummed a ride from somewhere else, and overstepped their bounds immediately. They ignored all rules of good behavior, taking what they wanted and going where they weren't welcome, always using as an excuse the poverty of their poor, huge family.

"We were so needy", lamented the gypsy, fondly reciting her version of history (and allowing Yero an extra minute of rest without intending to) ..."so truly needy! Naturally we had to beg, borrow and steal. But it was for the children, always for the children. Who could refuse food for little children? But some folk did refuse. Selfish folk who wouldn't share! We know them even today. Jerks!"

She suddenly realized the rest period had run long and kicked Yero into action, breaking off a new shard to tease her with. The moon was setting but she pushed Yero all the harder, even when the night grew dark, lit only by stars. When she was finally allowed to stop, Yero had trouble landing and nearly slipped off, drawing the gypsy's wrath, but Boca got her bragging again about her family.

The gypsy spoke of a time of persecution when the family had been jailed — banished to a small woodlot, an isolated stand of bitter thorn bushes. Unfairly so! Yet this was done, and they were guarded and made to stay. But worse was to come: The wardens slaughtered them, massacred the children! Yes, the Family learned murder because it was done to them during the purges. They learned other tricks also, to fool their enemies and win their escape. The cleverest female, the 'Phurri-Dai' had masterminded it, duping some yokels into a ride out of there, and the family had been free ever since.

"You wouldn't believe how easy it is", crowed the gypsy. "Fools and yokels are everywhere! A new one always comes along, it never fails. Just look at yourselves! Ha-ha!" It was hard to swallow, especially for Yero who knew it was her own fault.

But as the cocky gypsy broke off a new shard and tested it against her neck (It cut in a bit, making her yelp), a shadow of an idea fell upon her; so when next the gypsy whipped her it didn't sting as bad. That's how it is with slaves when they see a glimmer of hope.

But Boca didn't see it. It was getting too dark to see much at all, and he worried Yero would crash into something. Ignoring threats and warnings, he went down and led the way just in front of her.

So the dead of night passed, and the dark hour before dawn. Rest stops became frequent out of necessity and Yero paid dearly for them. The gypsy was getting serious cramps, urgent egg-laying cramps with less and less time between them. Now she who had been so cruel turned unexpectedly calm as dawn grew in the eastern sky, worried that any movement might trigger the egg-laying process. But her voice rang out as sharply as ever, just now cursing Yero for an overlong break. It had little effect without the physical abuse, and so the break stretched on for long minutes until the sun poked above the eastern hills and fell brightly upon the highest treetops. Then Yero stirred and spoke for the first time in hours.

"How much farther?"

"*How much farther? Are we there yet*?" The gypsy mocked her.

"You don't know, do you?" Boca shot back.

"Oh, yes! Not far now, as the crow flies. I wish you *were* crows, with some real speed!"

"Just tell me", said Yero quietly.

"Suck it up, faintheart! It's still two flights, probably three as hopeless as you've become. Don't worry, I'll tell you when we're there. Then you can let me off and go your own way".

Oh, she wished she could rake her heels along Yero's flank! But she hardly dared move. She consoled herself in the knowledge that both butterflies were headed for a bad end if she could manage it. She had to murder them, of course, to preserve secrecy. The new neighbors mustn't know! Neighbors were always unfriendly. They would search for her eggs, if word got out. No one *ever* gave her family a break! Aargh! Her cramps came again. She grimaced but passed it off as impatience.

"Let's go, sluggards!" she taunted. "I've been too lenient of late". She broke off a new shard to prod with but didn't have to. Yero was pumped, determined to finish.

It promised to be a nice morning, but cold down under the shadow of the trees. Yero surprised the gypsy with a burst of energy that carried them above the treetops, up where the sun felt good on her wings, and so they made remarkable progress for a while before she inevitably began to tire.

"There it is!" exclaimed the gypsy just as they were slipping below the treetops again. "The river! Did you see it? Take me across to the woods beyond, and your job is finished".

"How far?" asked Yero, underneath, on another icy branch. She hadn't gotten to see. It's hard to see much while someone is stepping on your head.

"Two more flights. It should be only one, but you're a wimp".

That did it. Yero took off with little rest and soared above the trees once more. The gypsy was ecstatic. Her cramps were almost continuous now, but the river was right there! Her thoughts turned to the double-murder soon to come. The girl would be easy of course, but the boy might be too! She intended to do the deed unexpectedly, just as they were safely across. The girl would shriek when it happened and that should bring the snotty boy within knife range. He would be careless, eager to help. She really looked forward to stabbing *that* one!

"Soon you'll be rid of me!" she urged.

She became almost giddy as the river approached. Maybe the silly butterfly could make it in one flight after all! She relaxed just a bit. The sun felt good on her injured back. The warmth soaked in, energizing her muscles. Now they passed over the last trees and approached the water. The river was wide-open with only a little ice along the shoreline. Now they were past the shoreline and still going! The butterfly had lost altitude, but enough remained for the crossing. Now they were halfway! She could see branches on the trees ahead—and *buds* on the twigs. Hallelujah! The Promised Land! A deadly sneer curled her mouth as she pondered the precise timing of the murder—but what was *this*?

A shadow flitted across her brow and she glanced up. The confounded Goatsucker! Some of these jerks—they just never gave up! No matter, maybe. The hawk wouldn't strike so long as she had a death-grip on the butterfly. The plan should still work. She gripped the shard tighter to be ready, but it slipped in her grip. It had been melting in the sunshine. A glance told her the cutting edge was soft. Bad luck! But she could change the plan, get a nice ride down into thick, concealing brush and let the deal work out honestly, just as she had promised. She almost laughed. That would be something new in family history!

Unfortunately for the gypsy, Yero was anticipating the melting shard, having planned for this exact circumstance. Directly above the middle of the river she did a summersault and dumped the gypsy to her choice of fates below: She could choose to simply drown in the rushing water, or she could flap her one wing and try to fly, which might give the nighthawk time to snatch her out of the air. But as the gypsy couldn't decide on such short notice how she preferred to perish, the matter was decided for her. A large fish leaped out of the water and swallowed her.

"It was a bass!" exulted Boca. "Did you hear? *'You bass'*, she said, and then it swallowed her. But she had a good, close look. It must have been one of those largemouths."

Yero just smiled. "I'm tired", she said. The nighthawk gave her a lift the rest of the way and stayed with them until mid-afternoon.

"I never flew in broad daylight", he said. "*Ever*. Until today. But I couldn't let the gypsy get away with it. She would've murdered you. That was clever, allowing her 'knife' melt in the sun".

"It's all I could think of. She was sure I'd have to rest again, so she didn't bother to break off a new one that last time".

"She liked to talk about murder", said Boca. "She said her family learned murder because it was done to *them*, when they were in jail somewhere".

"That old sob story? Sounds pretty innocent when they tell it, doesn't it?"

"We knew better by then. But were they really in jail? They should be".

The nighthawk gazed back across the river at the dead forest. "Yes, they were, but they escaped. They were a terrible scourge, killing trees and then hitching a ride to greener pastures. Finally, decent folk cornered their 'Family' and confined them to a lonely patch of brush. Pixies guarded them by day, we nighthawks by night; but the only murder was what they did to each other when they overpopulated the place—murder by starvation.

I'm not sure how they escaped. Hitched a ride with starlings, according to one story. Promised to pick lice in exchange for the ride. But I'd be surprised if they did any real work.

They're very cunning about starting a new colony now, laying low for a couple years until their population is ready to explode. When it does it's too late to stop them, and the new forest is doomed. The river was all that stopped this bunch".

"That's where we'd be, maybe in that same fish's belly, if the sun wasn't out this morning", said Yero. "I'm really tired".

"It surprised me that you could carry her so far. You're tougher than you look".

Yero smiled. "I'm not sure if that's a compliment, but I was ashamed of being fooled and wanted to make up for it".

"You did, girl. And made up for *our* mistake too! We patrol the river and the dead wood, but we missed that moth. I was expecting you; did you know? It was only by chance that she was with you". The hawk's eyes flashed angrily. "If we missed *her*, we may have missed others! I will speak with my kin tonight. We will go hunting again".

"Can any of the trees come back next spring?" asked Boca.

"No. Some will try, but you must have seen all the eggs. The forest is doomed. Our hope is that all the gypsies die with it".

"What about the smallest trees?" asked Yero. "There are some that wake up. They call themselves 'tribbits'".

The hawk looked surprised. "You know them? I'm sorry, but it was *those* the caterpillars went after first. We knew them. Nighthawks have always known them".

"Did they die then?" Yero waved back across the water.

"We don't know. We told them to leave, but they didn't want to hear that at all. They were trying to wake up the old trees. They kept trying until—well, until we didn't see them anymore. Our hope is that they left before the end".

"When the moths are gone, new tribbits should sprout, shouldn't they?" asked Boca. "But if none are left from before—who will wake up the first one?"

"Nighthawks, maybe", said a familiar voice. It was Atel, returning in the morning sunshine. She was no stranger to the hawk.

"Here they are then, ma'am", he reported. "Safe and sound, as you requested. They did play some part in that themselves. I'm sure they'll explain".

"Thank you! I'm sure they will. You'll keep an eye out for new seedlings, then? I also am concerned".

The nighthawk laughed wryly. "Be assured that we'll awaken them! My kin once hunted by day; did you know? Like normal folk! But we're light sleepers and the little trees kept us awake at night.

We finally adopted their upside-down schedule. Don't worry; we'll be happy to wake *them* up for a change!" The hawk bid goodbye and went hunting.

Atel was not pleased about the business with the gypsy but hadn't been there herself, so she didn't offer criticism. Instead, she complimented them on how it all worked out. Naturally, that was followed by her inevitable question: "What did you learn from this?"

Quite a bit of education had taken place. Yero put it this way: "Just because someone asks for help doesn't mean they deserve it".

"Excellent! My goodness, I think I should leave you two alone more often. Experience is a better teacher than I am".

"But she doesn't know where our next meal is coming from. We're hoping you do".

"I do. It's in our future and is even now approaching from that direction".

"And what direction is that, exactly?"

"The one that we'll be taking. You have a choice of three".

"Not counting behind us, I suppose".

"Correct. There is no dinner back there, as you have seen".

"But we know nothing of the other three".

"I can help you there. We'll narrow the choices to two—south or west—because neither Manino nor anything else of interest lies east just now".

"And? What are the others like?"

"To the west are mountains. There are safe routes through the passes some years, but winter has come on strong this year. We would probably starve in the mountain valleys, unless we froze to death first".

The butterflies edged together. This was getting a whole lot more serious than they expected.

"Which leaves...." ventured Yero.

"The southern route. More direct. Warmer. Plenty of food. I recommend it".

"I suppose there's a catch".

"Certainly. There's always a catch. Life is just one catch after another! I'm glad to see you expect it".

"Will you be giving any hints about *this* catch?"

"Yes. The 'catch' is, we ourselves might be caught, and that would take all the fun out of it. Shall we get started?"

"Might as well, if there's no other way".

"There isn't. Not this year. The trouble will begin about a day's journey south when we come to the marsh".

"Can't we just fly over it?"

"We'll try, but our timing is bad. The moon is full and the skies over the marsh will be swarming with the 'Fuzz', as these moths call themselves. They're very territorial. In summer the marsh can be crossed in daytime, but with cooler weather they patrol *all* the time".

"So, when can we cross?"

"I don't know. We'll see how it is and make our plans then".

"But why not go around?'

"The marshes stretch on and on. To the west, we would run up against the mountains, to the east they turn north again, and I worry about the next snowstorm. The North Wind is strong this year. I don't want to take that chance".

"At least her blizzards haven't crossed this river yet", said Boca.

It was true. There was a bit of ice on the banks and small patches of white in the shadows below, but very little, and as they made their way into the new forest all sign of snow disappeared. In the understory there were even green leaves—a few hardy bushes still sheltered from the weather—but no flowers for famished butterflies.

Part 3: Byways of the Butterfly

The flat river valley gave way to rolling hills, and the trees changed. They came to places where maples dominated, whole hillsides of them, and the forest floor was thick with their orange leaves.

"Sugar maples", said Atel. "If this were late winter instead of early, men would be tapping them for the sweet sap, and we could ask for some. Wouldn't that be nice?"

The Two frowned and tried not to listen.

"I suppose I shouldn't talk about food", laughed Atel, "but I'm hungry! Aren't you?"

The butterflies saw no humor.

"Come then, see what I found this morning".

It was an old wooden bucket hanging on a tree back around the bend of a hill, forgotten by the sap-gatherers.

"See?" said their Guide. "Your next meal approacheth from the future, as I predicted". She flew right up and landed on the rim of the bucket. It was overflowing but hung crookedly enough so that the rim was dry and un-sticky on one side. The butterflies landed eagerly, and then made faces, very un-eagerly.

"We're supposed to drink *that*?" asked Yero.

"Sure". Atel brushed away a bug or two and other floating bits of who-knows-what, enough to make an opening, and dipped her tongue in without delay. Yero grimaced.

There was an occasional drip, drip from a rusty metal spigot tapped into the trunk. A few squiggly bugs under it seemed to be enjoying lunch as much as the hummingbird. Yero nearly gagged.

"Better drink", said Atel. "It's not real high class, but if you scrape the bugs away, you'll be surprised how good it is".

Boca smiled and did so, carefully pushing stuff toward Yero, and tasted the sap. "Like the Moonwalk nectar", he decided. "Good, but thin".

Yero got over her squeamishness after a minute or two, remembering that she had shared flowers with bugs before. She dipped a finger and licked it off. It *was* good; so she had her dinner that way, inspecting her finger each time because (as she confided to Boca later) "The bugs acted like it was their swimming pool, and you never know what happens in a swimming pool".

The forest on this side of the river was much smaller and they soon came to country that was more open, first scrub and then pasturelands with unbroken breezes. They entered a hill country with cattle, lots of cattle in small herds everywhere — a grazing paradise with ponds and natural springs in every ravine.

Darkness fell and the thirsty Travelers stopped at a pond for a drink of plain water, choosing a pool they had to share with only one critter, a yearling Hereford. It barely noticed them. Boca was curious and asked if it had a name.

"*Steer*", replied the critter haughtily.

"I thought steers were bigger", said Boca. The comment wasn't well received.

"You gotcher nerve, little twit!" said the steer, and swished his tail at the Travellers, narrowly missing. They scattered and regrouped over the water a safe distance in front of the steer. Atel approached closer, carefully.

"The butterfly wishes to apologize", she said, annoyed, and summoned Boca front and center. He didn't want to but did as told.

"I beg your pardon", he said. "You really *are* a big steer. I guess I was thinking about bulls".

That was even worse. No steer ever wants to be reminded of that. This one snorted and shook his head in a fit of temper. Mucous flew from his nose and the gob walloped Atel in spite of her quick reflexes. The steer was much amused by that and even became sociable while the hummingbird took a bath.

"No use me takin' offense", he remarked. "You little twitterbugs don't know nuthin' anyways".

"That's where you're wrong!" replied Yero, taking offense in her turn. "We fly, so we've seen more country than you have".

"Sure, you fly over all the best grass in the hill country. If you were smart, you'd come down an' eat some".

"We don't eat grass".

"I know. That's why yer such runts".

"Now *you're* doing the insulting".

"Don't matter! Gotta go by what I see. Cute little brand y'all got there, though".

"What do you mean?"

"Yer *brand*, twit. Them marks on yer wings. Don't recognize 'em. What herd do y'all belong to?"

The butterflies looked at each other. "We're a *herd* now, Boca", Yero giggled. "How do you like that?"

"Speak up!" boomed the steer. "Every herd has its own brand. Mine is the coolest of all". He swung his rump around and showed off a big scar on his hip in the shape of a 4-leaf clover. "I'm from the 'Lucky-4' herd. What's yers?"

"I guess the cowboys would call us 'Monarchs'", said Yero.

"That's pretty stupid", replied the steer. "Dull! You need a better name, something catchy. Where's your ranch?"

"That way", said Yero, pointing south. "But it's quite a ways".

"So's mine", said the steer knowingly. "I got m'self lost, sort of on purpose. I ain't goin' to no corral again! But it does get lonesome".

"Why don't you hang out with some of the others? There are cattle everywhere".

The young steer tossed his horns and stamped. "No way! They're just run-of-the-mill cattle. Everyday brands. Rooty-poot".

"Rooty-poot?"

"That's what the mushy 'pies' are made of that folks step in out here".

"Oh! We aren't supposed to talk about things like that".

"Well! *Be* tenderfoots then! We talk about it all the time out on the range, and watch where we *step*, too! See, it's no big deal steppin' in your *own*, just don't step in someone *else's*, get it?"

They got it, but that wasn't all. Cattle school continued for a while as their guide washed and washed. They learned one or two more things they didn't need to, but also got a peek into the ways of an earthbound creature who looked up, and the steer had a glimpse into life up above looking down. As they 'shot the breeze', and Atel washed and washed, the Northern Lights sprang into the sky, the great billowing Curtain that the butterflies knew so well. The steer wasn't impressed.

"Comes an' goes. Seen it before".

"We've been there", said Boca. "Way up there! We just came back. Do you think it's brighter tonight?"

"Might be. Sure, I guess so. But it's no biggie if you were there. Cows do that too".

"Do what? Go up *there*?"

"Sure! See that moon? You know what the moon *is*, don't you? That big round thing up there?"

"Naturally! Everybody does!"

"Simmer down, pardner! Well, a cow jumped *over* it. The cowboys sing about that all the time. How does it go again? Oh, yeah... 'the little dog laughed...yadda-yadda...and the cow jumped over the moon!' I've heard it a dozen times. So them lights, the moon, all that stuff up there—it's no big deal to range cattle".

"Ready to go?" asked Atel from a distance.

"I guess so", said Boca. "We've learned a lot".

Atel narrowed her eyes. The young steer turned to leave too, and the sudden movement loosened bubbles in his digestive tract that escaped noisily into the fresh air.

"So long, pardners", he called back over his shoulder. But Atel had hustled the butterflies out of earshot in a hurry and they didn't answer. The steer was insulted.

"Well!" he belched. "That was rude!"

Half a mile away Boca thought so too.

"We never said goodbye!"

"No!" said Atel brusquely. "Why? Do you want to go back?"

"We ended up being pals. It would be good manners".

"That critter wouldn't know good manners if they smacked him on the nose!"

Yero smiled. "Good manners wouldn't do that, would they?"

"Unfortunately, no. But someone ought to!"

"His mother should, since she never taught him any manners".

"I'm sure she tried, Yero. But with range cattle, the boys just don't care about manners".

"What's the use?" said Boca admiringly. "Those boys grow up to be big fighters! All boys are born to be fighters".

"Born to cause trouble, let's say", laughed Yero. "I admit, you did start a war all by yourself".

"One war is enough", said Atel. "We're not going back. But I'll tell you a story about range cattle. There's a reason why the boys are so ornery and difficult".

— The Bull —

All in all, according to old cowboy tales, the Great Creation went smoothly until The Lord drew forth the children from His Light – all the creatures who were to inhabit the new world. Being mortals, they were an unruly lot, very impatient to get on with it, but the Lord assembled them in the sky first to give instructions and smooth out a few of their rough edges before turning them loose on the earth below.

The lecture ran longer than planned, owing to their unruliness, but He made sure each species learned exactly what was expected of them. He demanded promises and got them, but it wasn't easy. Some species simply didn't like to take orders. Range cattle fell into that group.

To introduce that species the Lord had brought forth a majestic specimen equal to the task of defending a herd against fearsome predators.

"I name you Taurus, the bull", the Lord told him, and began to outline his purpose. But the bull snorted and raked violently with his hooves, as he would soon paw and tear up the green grass below in a typical fit of temper.

"I know what I want!" he bellowed. "I want to *fight* - with someone who doesn't run away!"

"You won't be disappointed", promised the Lord. "You'll meet plenty of vicious opponents".

Taurus hooked his great horns toward the earth below. "Good! Send me down!"

The Lord breathed patience upon him, to no effect; then reason, then sociality. Nothing worked.

"Cool it!" He replied finally - and blew frost up the bull's nose. That worked, and the Lord drew forth a group of cows from the Light. "This is your herd which you must protect", He explained. "Say hello!"

"Lucky girls!" boomed Taurus. "I'm your hero!"

The cows weren't much impressed and called him *Insuffera*-bull amongst themselves. The Lord sent them all down anyway. Taurus soon wandered off looking for trouble and the cows didn't follow him, so the Lord sent down a couple other bulls, making sure they were a more sociable type.

Bad came to worse, however, as often happens in the mortal world. The nice bulls couldn't fight off the beasts, so the herd all but disappeared the first year. It would've been wiped out entirely, but Taurus happened upon the last cow as she fought off lions to protect her calves, a baby bull and heifer.

Hey! This was what Taurus liked! He routed the lions and actually gained a few admirers. He taught the baby bull to snort, to fight, and to boast - to be an *insuffera*-bull like himself! The rest is history. Range cattle survived, but they are hard to handle. It takes a cowboy.

Boca grinned. "So, the bull was the big hero! I knew it".

"He certainly was", agreed Atel. "One of two".

"Two bulls?"

"No. The cow was also a hero. No one fights harder for her babies than their mother. She gets half the credit".

Yero laughed. "That's good! Mister 'Insuffera-bull', huh? I like that".

"Excellent! You'll meet a different kind of insufferables tomorrow morning. Come, let's hurry".

Chapter 10

The Mugwump of Nassump

It was dark when the Travelers came to the bluffs above the marsh. The moon had gone down and the Aurora shifted off somewhere to the west, following the night sky around the world. Starlight hinted at a great valley before them, but all was obscured by fog.

"We might as well try it right now", said Atel. "It's the only way to find out. Stay close!"

She headed directly for the fog bank below and leveled off just above it, hoping it would provide some cover. They needed it immediately. Dark-bellied moths came down at them out of the dark sky and were upon them almost before they knew it. Broad-shouldered, stubby-winged and heavy-bodied, they packed a wallop when they slammed into their target, as even Atel learned the hard way; but their main weapon was grotesque legs with sharp spurs on the inner side for rasping and ripping.

"Into the fog!" shouted Atel, and for once the butterflies were ahead of her; but even inside the fog they didn't slip away easily. The moths--the 'Fuzz' that Atel had warned about--came right in after them and might have separated them in the confusion had not the hummingbird scooped up her friends and escaped to the rear, back up the bluff, keeping very close to the ground. They took cover in an alcove, a shallow cave near their starting point.

"Well!" she said, breathing hard. "Now that you've been introduced, what do you think of your new neighbors?"

"They don't ask questions, do they?" replied Yero. She had lost some dust from a collision but escaped real injury. Boca had been raked painfully all the way up his neck and across his cheek, and a small hole poked in one wing. The Fuzz had gone for Atel's eyes but missed. In retaliation she had speared several, but there were dozens.

"No, they don't bother with niceties", said Atel, remembering other skirmishes. "And though Boca may doubt this, they don't kill if they can help it. They try to capture trespassers alive, not drive them off. I don't know why and don't plan to find out."

"So now what?"

"We wait for daylight and try again".

"Won't they be waiting for us?"

"Not this squadron, at least. They have night fighters and day fighters. I don't know how organized they are. Maybe they file reports for the next shift, maybe not. We'll find out".

Prophetic words. By dawn the moths were gathering, and by full light they were everywhere, searching high and low, but mostly up high. Any crossing attempt at altitude was out of the question.

"We wait", whispered Atel. "They'll thin out sooner or later. Then maybe we'll slip down unnoticed and fly in the fog just above the marsh grass. I can guide by that".

The Fuzz did thin out above them, but only to approach and search the face of the bluff, rock by rock. Presently one idled past the alcove, then circled back and landed right at the entrance. He spoke into the opening while the Travelers pressed against the wall, barely out of sight.

"Maybe you *were* here and left again, or maybe you're still in there, but I smell you!"

The words were strong and bold, but the voice was nervous.

"Orders are: Just take prisoners. Don't hurt 'em", came the voice. "Nobody gets hurt, that's the deal".

The moth took a step inside and called again. "You're to be escorted--just *escorted*". The Fuzzer was torn between rumor of the hummingbird's sharp beak and a rare opportunity for reward if he could deliver the fugitives to his flight leader. He was pretty sure they were inside because the scent was getting stronger. He took another step and paused.

"You'll be given a *fair hearing*", he continued, searching the dim nooks and corners with his moth eyes. Oddly for a moth he didn't see very well in the dark. He'd been on day shift so long he'd gotten used to it.

"Everyone gets a fair hearing if they give themselves up", he went on. "You'll be treated decent. If you have an honorable reason for trespass, you'll be found innocent".

Another step forward. One more step and he would surely see them.

"A speaker can be appointed for you at the hearing if you wish", offered the moth hopefully. "That's to help those who are bashful before the Great Mugwump". His eyes were gradually getting accustomed. He still didn't see anyone, but he was sure now the fugitives were there. He tossed out his last bait: "Lucky for you, the Mugwump is forgiving. Admit your guilt and you'll be released. He lets everyone go after their hearing, and that's the truth".

The moth took one step too many. Atel lunged swiftly and snipped his head clean off, but not quite swiftly enough. The Fuzzer passed gas--or rather *pheromones*--that spread quickly into the air.

"Now! Straight down into the fog!" ordered Atel. There followed a mad scramble as the Travelers winged down the bluff and hundreds of the Fuzz rushed to the source of the pheromones. A rear-guard battle broke out between the hummingbird and angry moths pressing closely behind. Somehow, they escaped into the fog and hid up in marsh grass. The fog had settled right to the 'ground', using the term loosely. Beneath them was water, actually. They had found shelter in a tussock, though they didn't yet know it because the fog was so thick.

The Fuzz undertook a pattern search, but moths aren't fond of thick fog. It collects on their hairy bodies and especially on their feathery antennae, very annoying. Being soldiers they followed orders, but the poor visibility didn't help and soon they were just going through the motions, expecting that word would come down to wait until the fog lifted.

It would lift of course, as the day went on. It always thinned and lifted some in sunny weather, but never burned off completely this time of year when the air was cool and the marsh waters comparatively warm.

Yero watched one of the searchers idle past as close as the next tussock without spotting them, there to become tangled in the grass rather comically. She started to giggle, then put a hand over her mouth. Boca gave her an elbow and a frown. As they watched, the Fuzzer slipped down a wet stem and had to extricate himself dripping from the water. He shook himself, looked around to be sure no one had observed his clumsiness, and took off upwards.

"Okay, we should be safe now", said Yero.

"Safe until the fog lifts", corrected Atel. "Which it will. But until then--if we're quiet--we can move".

In addition to the fog, the Travelers had another advantage. They were migrators, so even in a place like this they retained a fair sense of direction. But the fog was thick and got even thicker as they went forward. The humor went out of it for Yero when she herself flew into a tussock that just appeared out of nowhere in the gloom and was showered with cold drops.

Then the marsh changed abruptly. The water and tussock islands all disappeared, replaced by cattails and other reeds. It became a bog with some firm ground but thick with vegetation, much too thick to fly through, so they had to go up over the tops of the reeds. And there they quickly found trouble.

The fog had lifted enough for the Fuzz to resume the search and the Travelers almost bumped right into one. He released the pheromone gas with a little 'pop' and dodged away, up into thicker fog above.

"You know, when it comes to passing gas, I'll take that steer any day over these Fuzzers", said Boca. "At least with him, if nothing hit you, that was the end of the trouble".

"Boca!" said Atel sternly, "Some lessons aren't worth learning! Fly now, while we can!"

They kicked it into high gear but didn't get far at all before more moths appeared out of the fog. The Travelers did the only thing they could. They folded wings and dropped into the tangle of stems, broken crowns and brown leaves, all propped up by newer growth underneath. The Fuzz quickly pinpointed where they had disappeared and clustered above the general area. They could be heard clearly, shouting orders and sending reports up their chain of command.

Squads of them smeared mud on their faces and lighter parts of their bodies and slipped into the tangle to ferret out the fugitives. In all honesty, it looked like the jig was up; but Boca, being a boy, found another 'boy' thing--a dirty hole mostly covered over with fallen stems. He accidentally stepped into it and whispered the news. "I was poking around..." he began, but their guide ducked into the hole immediately and pulled him after. Yero slipped in last and began to arrange the covering from underneath but Atel stopped her.

The stems directly above sank downward, almost imperceptibly. Someone was stepping on them, standing right above them. Soon there were more steps, separate from the first. All this in perfect silence. The Fuzz commandos were meeting exactly where they expected to make the capture but finding nothing. They would figure it out soon enough, Atel guessed, and quietly led the way further into the hole.

She was wrong in that. The Fuzz, being creatures of the air, didn't easily suspect anything subterranean. They were boys, it was true, but they just didn't have a Boca among them. They wriggled through and infiltrated the reeds throughout the area, but the search came up empty. The Higher-Ups didn't like to hear that, and prisoners were taken of their own ranks who had 'slipped up'. These were led away to their own 'fair hearings' at the court of the Great Mugwump. That part was true, as the unlucky moth in the cave had promised. Every prisoner did get a legal hearing.

Meanwhile, the fugitives were learning about travel in a mucky tunnel. That's what it turned out to be: A runway of sorts made by some animal. By good luck it led off generally southwards, the exact direction they wished to go. They enjoyed their escape, as anyone would, and didn't stay quiet for too long.

"Whatever animal made this, I could just kiss them", said Yero in relief.

"Be careful what you wish for", replied Atel when a sliver of decent light filtered in. "It looks 'muskrat-ish' to me". She pointed to a groove in the mud where the animal had dragged something. "That's the tail", she explained. "The usual mark of a muskrat".

"Do they eat butterflies?" asked Yero.

"Sorry to say, yes. They'll eat most anything if they're hungry. Butterfly finger-food would suit them just fine".

"Oh, great--and we're stuck in its tunnel! Will it be catching up to us, then? Or the other way around?"

"We're catching up, at the moment, but that's assuming a lot. We're probably slower than *it* is, which would be fine, but there will surely be side tunnels to complicate things. We may not even see the animal and so you won't get your chance to kiss it. Don't get your hopes up".

She turned to Boca, bringing up the rear. "If we *do* meet the muskrat, try not to insult it! Anything might happen and there's no clean water to wash up afterwards".

They climbed gradually to higher ground--just a few feet above water level still--but the reeds of the tunnel changed to coarse sedges, becoming almost like a thatched roof. Side tunnels did appear, leading off downward into darkness. They found themselves on an elevated wrinkle of ground that meandered through the bog and were happy at least to walk on something dry, since neither butterflies nor hummingbirds are great walkers at all. But walk they did, for although the tunnel was just big enough and sometimes light enough to fly in, it was mostly dark and dangerous, riddled with the sharp ends of sedges. It appeared, when a beam of light fell into the runway, that the muskrat had chewed and eaten its way along, and that's how the passage had been made in the first place.

A noise came from somewhere up ahead and they paused. Atel went to investigate and returned in good spirits.

211

"It's a lady muskrat but she's pointed the other way and would not be able to turn around in the narrow passage. I spoke with her and she has agreed to let us follow, and so use her property. There is one problem. She's busy eating her way along, widening the runway as she goes, because she is going to have babies. She is very fat just now and her progress is slow, so ours will be too. She made it clear that she is normally 'slim and trim', so don't call her 'fat' when we speak with her! That will be soon because she wants to meet you".

"Do we have to?" asked Yero. "Couldn't we take one of these side-tunnels and detour around her?"

"Which one? And where would it go? I think we should just respect her wishes. It's not too much to ask. This *is* her property".

As they made their way forward, the noises grew louder. Crunching and chewing noises. It was very dark. Then Yero tripped over something and the noises stopped.

"Who is it?" said a booming voice up ahead of them. The voice would've been even louder, but the muskrat was talking with her mouth full and continuing to chew and swallow. She didn't stop eating just because a conversation had started, but she did shift her weight to one side allowing a bit of light to slip past. In this light Yero saw what she had tripped on--a snake! --and shrieked.

Silence fell. The muskrat stopped chewing, a rare moment.

"What's going on?" boomed the voice.

"Not a problem", answered Atel quickly. "One of the butterflies I described has taken fright in the dark, silly thing".

The muskrat shifted her weight further, allowing a bit more light past. "Is that better, little weenie?"

In the new light Yero saw that it wasn't a snake at all but only the muskrat's tail moving around.

"Step forward. Talk to the tail", whispered Atel, and gave Yero a little push.

"I am Yero the butterfly--not any weenie!" she answered angrily. She tried to address the tail, but the muskrat was agitated, and the tail was a moving target. She finally grabbed the tip and held it like a microphone with both hands as it wiggled and waved about. "Thank you for letting us use your tunnel", she managed to say. "If I was up in front of you, I would bow politely".

"Don't bother", said the muskrat, taking time to snap off a new stem and begin munching it. "Actually, you're lucky to be where you are. I'm hungry. I wouldn't mind some butterfly right now. Dry, though. Moth is better. Juicier".

This was more information than Yero cared for. She let go the tail and backed off. Atel nudged Boca forward. His job looked easier. The tail had calmed down and seemed to be awaiting the next speaker like some sort of back-door receptionist.

Muskrats depend a lot on their tails, for those who don't know. The tails look bare and scaly, even slimy when wet, but they have a surprising store of natural intelligence and a direct link to the front. Their tails have evolved like this because of the need for some wits behind them in their runways. The more northerly muskrats--being fatter and furrier in the cold climate--are least able to see behind, so their tails have developed the highest intelligence. The Travelers were dealing with a tail of above-average IQ, and it sensed trouble with Boca. He announced his name and got as far as..."Thank you, Mrs. Rat..." when the tail slapped him and sent him tumbling. The rest of the animal munched away up front giving no indication that it knew anything of this.

"You insulted her", whispered Atel. "They are sometimes called 'rats', but they resent it! Try again. Be nicer".

Boca hesitated. The tail thought it had delivered only a soft cuff, but it smarted.

"Thank you, Mrs. Musk..." he began once more, leaning forward more than actually stepping ahead. Whap! The tail took offense again, this time tattling about it to the main brain up front.

"I am *not* married!" boomed the voice. "I wouldn't marry that run-around liar if he was the last male in the marsh!"

"Try 'Musquash'", whispered Atel. "We need to get back in her good graces to ask directions".

Boca didn't want to. After a little while, the tail started tapping impatiently.

"Go on! Remember: 'Musquash'. She'll like that".

She did. At least the tail did. Boca offered a nice apology, apparently accepted because the tail reached up playfully, tweaking his nose and tickling his cheeks. When it pulled one of his antennae back and let it spring into the other, *bonk,* he called it enough and backed away. Atel was as pleased as the tail, but as she considered how to frame a polite question about directions the tail raised and curled happily like a pig's tail, exposing a lot of what it usually covered up. Boca couldn't resist.

"There's your chance, Yero", he chuckled. "You wanted to kiss whoever made the tunnel. There's your chance". He pointed at the general area under the tail.

"*You* kiss her!" shouted Yero, and a squabble broke out. The tail was so insulted that it personally went up front and spilled the whole disgusting story, finishing up by beating its own master over the nose.

Atel grabbed the quarrelling pair and beat a retreat as the animal began backing up, swinging its tail and discharging a stench of musk. They passed by the first side-tunnel, and then another, in case the muskrat was mad enough to pursue that far, but it was a good bet she would soon remember how hungry she was and get on with dinner. Backing up through the tunnel was difficult anyway, against the grain of chewed and broken stems, and she soon gave it up. The Travelers could've taken the very first turnoff. Maybe that would've been better--who knows? But they took another and soon found themselves in a confusing maize of branch tunnels and forks. They chose one and it came to an end. They tried another and it looped back to the same place. Then Yero saw her.

Up ahead in the main branch passageway was a silk moth, very beautiful, standing at a fork of the tunnel. She glowed, or maybe a ray of light illuminated her, accentuating her fabulous wings as they gracefully opened and closed. She beckoned to them.

"Beautiful", whispered Boca.

"For a *moth*", said Yero shortly. "Anyway, she already has a suitor. See?"

A large butterfly emerged from one of the forks and bowed on bended knee before her. She ignored him and beckoned again to the Travelers, who went forward out of curiosity and to inquire about directions. As they approached, the new butterfly turned to face them as if he would defend the pretty silk moth.

"Halt! Who approacheth?" he demanded. "The Oo will not see anyone".

Atel ignored him. The butterfly, a snobbish Regal Fritillary, drew himself up to his full height--a bit taller than the Rasha La--and challenged them again in superior tones.

"The Oo will not see you! I am her spokesman. State your business or begone!"

"Sure", said Atel reasonably. "We're seeking an exit from these runways".

"Very well, madam. I will take that under advisement. Good day!"

"Ask *her*", said Atel, ignoring the rudeness. "Is she the Oo?"

"She is *of* the Royal Oo's", corrected the Fritillary. "But she does not speak. She allows me speak for her".

"If she doesn't talk, how do you know what she wants to say?"

The Fritillary lifted his nose so high he could no longer see beneath him. "I know what I *want* her to say, and that's answer enough for a commoner!" He puffed himself up. "I can trace my ancestry through 70 generations of Royalty!"

"What a waste", muttered Atel. "All that pedigree, and it can't even produce a spokesman who knows something. That's just annoying!"

"I shall pass on your comments at an appropriate time, madam", said the Fritillary stiffly. "Be advised that you are wearing out our patience. That is all. You are dismissed".

Atel laughed. "In a moment, I will ask the Oo myself. But first, I'm curious. Where did *you* come from? What's a pompous Fop like you doing in a rough place like this?"

"*Foppish*, if you please. That is my full, noble name. I do not shorten it like the little folk". His nose went up another tick. "As to my itinerary, it was Court Business; but alas, I was pursued in the fog by anarchists! The moths ran me aground".

"I had guessed that much", said Atel dryly. "How did you escape them and end up *here*, with her?"

"The fog parted at the last moment to reveal her Royal Family", marveled Foppish. "The ruffians saw them too. 'The *Oo!* The *Oo!*' they shouted and went for them instead! I crashed and wandered alone in dark tunnels until Royal Destiny brought me here. Now *she* will show the way, and I shall marry a Princess worthy of me!"

"And? Which way to your Princess?"

It was hard for him, but Foppish swallowed his pride. "I can't decide", he admitted. "*You* ask her".

So she did. The silk moth curtsied elegantly and gestured to the left-hand tunnel. Atel turned back to Foppish. "Lead the way!"

"I can't go in *there*!" protested Foppish. "I'll wait here".

"Why? Something wrong?"

"A vulgar noise, madam! Remindful of the lower classes".

Boca took a few steps into the passage and came back. "Snoring", he reported. "Something snoring in there". Yero and Atel took a listen also. There was no doubt, except what kind of animal. It didn't sound small.

Through all of this, the silk moth continued to smile and curtsy, urging them left. The high-strung Fritillary was fast reaching his cracking point. He knelt again on one knee and begged for directions more deserving of his noble station. She ignored him and he groveled. Atel decided to end the charade. She stepped forward and swung her beak like a sword right through the beautiful moth. Yero and Boca were startled. Foppish was aghast. The silk moth didn't even notice.

"She's not real", said Atel. "She's an apparition. A will-o-wisp, I think. I don't know what's behind this, but we ought to make our own choice here".

The silk moth faded and winked out as if she couldn't keep her form when everyone saw through her. But Foppish leaped desperately to a different conclusion.

"It's my Royal Destiny that you exposed this *fake!*" he raved. "She was trying to lead me astray!" With a maniacal look of understanding, he rushed into the right-hand tunnel.

"We'll follow at a safe distance", said the hummingbird. "He's flipped his lid, but we may learn something. I'm sure he has a point about the choice here. It's fateful. The apparition was here for a purpose".

They had to hurry. The Fritillary, recklessly shouting, was already far ahead. The tunnel slanted downward taking on a hint of mustiness and a faint odor of clamshells. It got stuffy, then oozy. Their feet stepped *splash* into puddles between chips and bits of cattail stems. Low dirt banks appeared on both sides. They were hurrying down a sunken road and it was still sinking. Far ahead, they could hear Foppish splashing along, still shouting wildly.

A bad smell assaulted them, rotten but unlike vegetation. The butterflies stopped and covered their noses. That's when they realized they didn't hear Foppish anymore.

"Back!" said Atel. "Swamp gas".

The butterflies were already in full retreat. Luckily, all three made it back to the fork with only light headaches to show for their close call. Atel went back up to the main passageway to see about other possible routes, leaving the Two to recover and rest a bit.

Maybe it was the light-headedness from the gas, but the butterflies became giddy. They had no pity at all for the Fritillary.

"It's a lesson to remember", giggled Yero. "Even Royal Snobs can be good for something".

Boca grinned. "Yeah. Just throw away the Royal stuff and keep what's left. The only good thing was rushing in like a fool so common folk could learn from his mistake".

"We shouldn't laugh, Boca. Royals could make good scouts--if we had *enough* of them."

But she did laugh, and Boca too. He puffed himself up like Foppish and tilted his nose.

"Those silk moths are crazy for me!" he crowed.

"You look ridiculous", said Yero honestly.

"I shall choose a Royal Princess worthy of me---"

Yero had to laugh. Boca strutted.

"Don't try our patience, commoner! I have 70 generations---"

"---But have you kept up the paperwork?"

"I'm a Royal. I can't be bothered."

"You'll need proof to show the Royal Mother-in-Law".

"Piffle. Either one is Royal, or one is *not*. Obviously, I *am!*" Boca managed to elevate his nose still higher.

"But what if they want documents? Royal Weddings are grand events. There would be papers and stuff to sign".

"I have *people* to do that. Little bitty people. My people will talk to their people---"

"Here's one of *my* people", said Yero, waving cheerfully. Their guide re-joined them, having overheard some of the silliness.

"So, you have little bitty people, Boca? I do too. Marsh mites. So does Yero, I'm sure. That's what you were talking about, I suppose? Let's pick them off".

It's a long way down the ladder of evolution from Royalty to sitting around in a circle picking mites off each other, but Boca managed to climb down.

"We have a choice of two animals, it seems", announced their guide presently. "Our muskrat, or another like her, is munching its way down the side-passage toward us, blocking it. We can go meet her - or take a chance on the left-hand tunnel and whatever's snoring in there".

No one spoke for a few minutes. Each had their own thoughts--and mites--to occupy them. Each drew a mental picture of what might be snoring in the left-hand tunnel.

Boca figured muskrat. There seemed to be lots and it was a muskrat tunnel after all, so what else? It frightened him. What could be worse than an animal with a brain on both ends? It could be snoring up front but wide-awake behind. Still, there was some chance of getting along provided this one hadn't spoken with 'Musquash'. He made up his mind to go forward but bring up the rear and let the others do the talking.

Yero repeated to herself over and over: "Let it be a rabbit. Let it be a rabbit". But in her mind, a sinister shape moved into the nice picture: A mink, all snapping teeth and bloodthirsty. It leaped for the rabbit's throat! Yero shivered and pushed the picture away.

Atel hoped it was a turtle, any kind of turtle. They were usually slower. They also stunk pretty badly, so she would know for sure when they got closer.

None of the guesses were even close; but then, the marsh was large and unexplored. Life had evolved on its own here, isolated from the outside world.

They started into the tunnel and gained hope. The snoring had subsided and a faint glow appeared up ahead, possibly an open door. But when they rounded a corner it wasn't a door at all but just another gleaming silk moth, this one a pastel yellow, at another fork in the passage. She waited for the inevitable question and invited them to take another left turn. Boca at the rear couldn't resist brushing her with a wing tip to see if she was real. She wasn't, and the touch upset her delicate balance of animation. She faded and fell apart exactly as the other had.

The snoring started up again, low at first, then building to a growl. It paused suddenly, only to return at full blast. It took courage to keep going. Obviously, some large beast lay in wait.

They came to another fork, and another, both attended by the apparitions. They barely glanced at them anymore except to ask the way, and then hurried on. Atel didn't believe in postponing trouble that was sure to come.

Abruptly the snoring ceased, and a murmur of many voices came to them from somewhere ahead. A glow appeared beyond the next corner, another silk moth probably. But this time it wasn't. This time the light was the end of the tunnel. Then the light flickered. There was a hush and a sharp 'snap' followed by roars of approval, cheering, and finally a huge rumbling laugh.

Atel slowed. The rumbling voice was wicked, familiar yet not familiar. A pretty silk moth appeared at the mouth of the tunnel beckoning them forward, then more silk moths. Yero peeked past their guide and saw them. These seemed livelier. They moved more quickly. They had bracelets. They entered the tunnel with smiles to greet the Travelers. Atel blamed herself later for letting her guard down, but she was taken aback by the sight of the owner of the voice: A huge bullfrog.

While her eyes were fixed on him and a veritable air force of the Fuzz, the beautiful smiling silk moths slipped past her and slipped 'bracelets' on the butterflies--one cuff on them, one cuff on their own wrists. It all happened very quickly as they emerged from the tunnel at water's edge. More silk moths crowded around and hustled the butterflies across floating reeds to an island--and just like that, the bullfrog had hostages. Atel had little choice but to follow in hopes of freeing them.

The water surrounding the island was a small bay connected by a narrow tidewater to the river that watered the marsh. The bullfrog squatted on the island. He was boss here. He was the Mugwump. His fiefdom included nearly the entire area, locally called 'Nassump'. Time had passed while they were in the tunnels. The sky was darkening from fog above and evening above that, but Nassump was well lit: The bullfrog's belly gleamed brightly.

Even as Atel pried her eyes off him, silk moths slipped tethers and fetters on the butterflies and crowded them tightly with knives--teeth of some kind--long and sharp. Fish teeth.

A squad of Fuzz afoot marched up. Everyone seemed to be armed with the long fish teeth. An officer swaggered forward.

"We knew you'd turn up, they all do", he informed Atel. "You are wanted for murder and mayhem. Naturally, you'll be given a fair trial. Will you come peacefully, or do we have to play rough with your pals?"

It had happened too fast. There wasn't much she could do immediately without putting them all at risk. She hadn't expected such efficiency. She would soon get used to it. Everything was very efficient in the Mugwump's fiefdom to answer the challenge from across the water. That's where the Mugwump mostly fixed his attention. He always kept at least one eye on the other island across the way to make sure the Lady Oo didn't pull any tricks.

It was true, what Foppish had glimpsed. The Lady Oo was Matriarch of the silk moths, Queen and Mother. Her island was much different from the Mugwump's bare sandbar. Hers--though smaller-- was lush with vegetation, even including a little tree. There was no bridge to her island. She had no police force, no slaves. The Lady Oo didn't like the Mugwump's noise and whoop-de-do. But she also had lights: Many of the will-o-wisps, her apparition offspring, floated just on the surface of the water luring unwary Fuzz down close where the fishes could reach them.

When her real daughters came of age they flew low, scattering above the will-o-wisps for camouflage, and some escaped thereby into the greater marsh. But the Fuzz caught most and held them as concubines, offering them to the Great Mugwump whom they worshipped as a god. He liked to make the daughters dance in his Court as cheap showgirls, knowing this infuriated the Oo. All in all, the rivalry was a standoff and a boon to the local economy because it provided lots of jobs. But beneath the fanfare and razzle-dazzle a drama was unfolding. The islands hated each other in general but a truly deadly duel was playing out between the Mugwump and the Lady.

All frogs are equipped with a secret weapon besides their strong legs and jaws, a weapon that makes them extra-dangerous--namely their tongue. This frightening appendage can lash out like lightning, latch onto flying insects (or anything else) and snap back into their mouths with the goodies in a split second. The Mugwump, due to his tremendous size and long practice, could almost nab the Lady Oo right off her perch 20 feet away in the little tree if she wasn't careful.

She was very careful but loved to torment him, always putting her best will-o-wisp creations right on the shore, letting them flutter about and play peekaboo among the sedges and rushes. Often, he would lash his terrible tongue across the water aiming for a flicker of movement, only to hit nothing (which was embarrassing) or even to snag on a burr. Then a hush would fall on the sandbar and the Oo would laugh sweetly as the big bullfrog jerked his tongue loose, adding scratches and injury to the insult.

She perched mostly in the little plum tree where his tongue couldn't quite reach, raising her daughters there and plotting the downfall of her enemy. To this purpose, she had made acquaintance with the catfish, probably the only creature in the marsh with a mouth bigger than the Mugwump's. Morning and night the catfish came up the side-channel from the river and cruised the little bay looking for supper. There were always smaller fish, attracted to floundering Fuzz, who were in turn lured by the will-o-wisps, so the catfish was assured of some snacks. But what brought him back day after day was the sight of the Great Mugwump, so sumptuously fat, so temptingly close to shore!

That was the Oo's fond dream and reasonably practical plan. When she riled him up the Mugwump edged closer to the water, the better to bring the Lady into range. But he was her equal in cleverness. He knew where she was in her tree just beyond his reach. Oh, he knew! He knew about the catfish too and saw him lurking under the water when the surface was calm. He knew this pig of a fish wanted him and delighted in staying just out of its reach. He even boasted across the water that it was a stupid idea anyway, that he was too big for any fish to swallow.

His own plan was to practice, practice, move back a bit and practice some more. It was simply a matter of applied mathematics in his view. If he could stretch out his tongue just a few more feet, he could take the Lady right out of her tree. His range was a bit short yet, maybe, but her silly will-o-wisps made wonderful practice, if she only knew!

Right now, however, the Mugwump turned to his most important chore, the nightly meal. Everything else could wait--the Lady Oo, the catfish, all the usual hoopla on his sandbar, even the new prisoners who looked so sporting. Everything. The fireflies were coming out!

He picked off the first ten or twelve and felt them wiggle and struggle in his fat jowls wondering what happened to them. In their excitement, they flashed like crazy. The light shone out through the thin skin. He tilted his head back to show off the flashes, drawing oohs and ahs from the admiring Fuzz.

You can laugh if you want at the foolish Fuzz who call themselves warrior moths and yet bow down to the glowing Mugwump, falling for this simple trick, but that's how moths are about lights. It's just in their blood, and the bullfrog knew it.

His favorite food had always been lightning bugs. They were such easy targets. What could be easier? He had searched out where they were thickest and found this place, Nassump. He immediately staked his claim, devouring several amphibians who dared to loiter. Then he gorged on the fireflies.

A funny thing happened as he grew larger and larger. His skin had to stretch to cover his stomach and the flashes came through. Some of the bugs stayed alive in there until the next evening, so he became illuminated permanently. Then the moths came to the light. He ate them too, but as time passed and his ego grew, he hatched a plan: If they wanted to worship him and take orders, he would be glad to give them! It had come down to this: He ruled the entire marsh - but not the other island. That last part irritated, so he focused hard on the thing that always cheered him up: Eating!

Meanwhile, directly in front of Atel, the sand heaved up revealing the head and shoulders of a toad. He'd been watching her with one eye and the Mugwump with the other while dug into the ground as toads like to do. All around the sandbar more toads emerged, even as the warrior moths abandoned their police duties and gathered around the Mugwump to worship.

"That's it now", grumped the toad, half to himself, half to Atel. "The stupid Fuzz will be useless for a while. Lucky for Big Boy he's got his Toady bodyguards to pick up the slack". He stuck his warty nose right up to the hummingbird's beak.

"Not so lucky for you, Toots. Don't get any dumb ideas. Your itty-bitty beak won't even prick me. Now, let's get a nice halter on you...hmmm...odd size..." Here the Toady beckoned to the silk moth slave girls who carried a selection. "I'm sure you realize", he mentioned as he went to put one on, "these dolls will stick your little pals if you make a fuss. Ah, very good! Smart girl! You know the score".

Everyone knew the score on the sandbar. The Toady gave an order. The Travelers were marched off to the back of the island, to a rusty old minnow trap partly buried there, and shoved through the minnow inlet where sharp wires allowed incoming prisoners but not outgoing ones. There was an outlet door on the top side of the trap, but it was shut tight. A Toady jailor sat on it and glared down, eyeing his new inmates. Two more strong-arm toadies were stationed inside to keep order. Surprisingly, they now unhooked the cuffs, halter, and other restraints leaving the new prisoners free to roam the jail, had there been any room. There wasn't much. There already was a bewildered mob of fish flies milling around, a little skipper butterfly who whimpered and wept in a corner, and a gorgeous silk moth girl, angry and defiant.

"What are you in for?" the silk moth asked Yero. "We get oddballs, but I never saw your kind".

Yero explained as best she could in the short time that might be available. Preparations of some kind were swiftly being made outside the jail. A large group of Toadies was coming together, jawing and arguing theatrically.

"Journey, huh? Well, it ends here", said the silk moth. "This is their Kangaroo Court. We'll be given a 'fair trial', and then we'll all be frog food. I wish I had better news. You look like a decent girl, maybe even a bit goody-goody. You don't deserve this".

"Do you?"

"Maybe. They'll say so". She jerked a thumb at the Toady crew. "I don't take orders well".

"What about her?" Yero pointed to the skipper.

The silk moth shrugged. "The usual sad story, I suppose. At least she'll soon be out of her misery".

A couple of Toadies approached by themselves, mildly interested in the prisoners. They had jewelry--lengths of fine chain and metal circlets draped on their warts.

"Got anything of value?" inquired one, hopefully. No one answered. "What about you, Toots?" he addressed Atel rudely. She simply looked the other way. "Nobody? Too bad. Good luck defending yourselves, then". The pair chuckled and waddled off.

"Lawyers", said the silk moth, and made a rude gesture to them. "Here's something of value!" she shouted. Just as she hoped, they looked back and scowled.

"Was that wise?" asked Atel.

"Doesn't matter. I've seen this dozens of times. Nobody gets off the hook. It would ruin the fun".

The preliminaries were about to begin. An extra-warty Toady assumed a perch on a teeter-totter rock. ("The 'Scale of Justice'", sneered the silk moth.) The extra-warty one was Chief Justice, very solemn. A dozen others squatted on the sand in a loose group as jury. One of the bedazzled lawyers hopped forward importantly: The Prosecutor.

"Bring forth the crybaby", he ordered. The strong-arm Toadies dragged the terrified skipper up to the wire mesh to receive her fair trial. The wretch was too demoralized to give her name or even open her eyes.

"You are charged with trespass", sneered the Prosecutor. "Do you have anything to say in your defense?"

Of course not. Anyone could see that. The Prosecutor looked to the jury (But under Toady law 'j' is pronounced 'h', so *jury* means *hurry*, and that was the main idea because there were always lots of defendants to be condemned.) The jury turned thumbs down. The Chief Justice took this under advisement. The final verdict depended on the rock itself. If it tipped forward, the defendant was guilty as charged; if it tipped backward, they were innocent. The warty one hopped forward to get a guilty verdict quickly and get on to the next case.

Taking them in their order of imprisonment, the strong-arms next ordered the flock of fish flies into ranks facing the mesh wall. Right. Good luck with that. The flock was unorganized and never would be organized. They had hatched that very morning and would live only until tomorrow; such is their life span. They have no time for marching or ranks. They were upset that half their life span had been wasted already.

"The charge is hatching during the Mugwump's nap. Terribly unthoughtful! How do you plead?"

The fish flies had no idea whom they had offended or why and just reverted to mutual complaining: "I didn't know about any rule like that--did you? No! Nobody told me! Did they tell you? No! What's a Mugwump? I don't know, do you? No clue! What are *rules*, then? I don't know - how should *I* know? Well, someone should ask! Okay--*you* do it. Oh, no--not me! *You* do it!"

It went on even when the Prosecutor shouted and the Chief Justice pounded on the rock. Nothing got their attention until the strong-arms knocked some heads together. Finally, there was silence.

"So! You plead ignorance of the law", the Prosecutor concluded correctly. "But ignorance is no defense. Most fish flies hatch while he's awake. *They* know how to do it! You should too!" He turned to the jury and waved his arms indignantly. "Waste of the Court's time! Should've been a 'fait accompli'. Had they hatched more conveniently, the Mugwump would already have eaten them". The jury gave thumbs down and the Scale of Justice banged forward. Guilty!

Next, the bullies grabbed for the silk moth, but she leaped forward on her own to the 'witness stand'.

"Name!" hissed the Prosecutor. The silk moth laughed at him.

"Lulu, as you know very well, Fatso. The same Lulu who's been carrying messages for you".

"Not germane! Strike that from the record!" shouted the Prosecutor. The jury plugged their ears. The silk moth laughed at them too, enjoying her little bit of revenge.

"*Secret* messages!" she shouted. "The lot of you are planning to shove Big Boy into the---"

The strong-arms gagged her quickly, before she could say more. Lulu was a rebellious type.

"Incorrigible!" the Chief Justice ruled. "Counsel will be appointed for you". The other bedazzled one assumed the defense. It took only moments after that to find her guilty, but there were worried glances among the Toadies. The proceedings had caught the attention of the Mugwump.

"Next!" bellowed the Prosecutor, hoping to move on quickly before the Mugwump asked any questions. At that moment, fortunately for the Toadies, there was a disturbance outside the jail. A dragonfly chasing a damselfly innocently crashed into the Mugwump's ear, right in the middle of worship. The Fuzz caught them and they were thrown into jail too, but even inside they only had eyes for each other.

Atel stepped up to the mesh next, on her own like Lulu had done.

"Name!"

"Atel".

"Whatever. You are charged with trespass, murder, attempted murder and, umm...oh my! (A loyal silk moth slave whispered case history into his ear) ...a whole list of other crimes and misdemeanors. How do you plead?"

"Self-defense. I will represent my friends here also. They are innocent for the same reason: Self-defense".

"That's cute", snickered the Prosecutor. "You been to Law School or what?" The jury laughed. So did the Chief Justice.

"Self-taught".

"Ah. That explains the gap in your education, which I will now remedy". The Prosecutor loved to show off his knowledge. It was the only thing he would allow extra time for. "The concept of self-defense doesn't exist for criminals like yourself who attack the Law or agents of the Law", he explained. "In layman's terms this means that when you got into a scrape with the Fuzz it was your own fault". He turned to the Chief Justice. "I ask the Court to deny the plea".

"Denied". The warty one was bored.

"Any other defense, Toots?"

"Your Scale of Justice is rigged. There's a block under the back end there. Take it out".

"Reckless endangerment!" belched the Prosecutor. "The block *supports* justice. Without it, the Chief Justice could be overturned! The block stays where it is. Anything else? Quickly!"

"Insanity, then".

"You admit it? Good! That'll work: Guilty, insane, plus a confession. Okay, that wraps it up..."

"I meant *innocent* by reason of insanity".

"Look, around here we find it's the guilty who do the most insane things, but it's up to the jury now".

"I wasn't finished. I meant insanity on *your* part".

"*Very* cute, Toots. We'll call that a 'theoretical concept'. It has no reality and soon neither will you!" He turned to the jury, but they had already turned thumbs down. *Bonk!* went the Scale of Justice. The Travelers were found guilty and promptly ignored.

"Next", droned the Chief Justice.

The strong-arms slapped the damselfly on the rear and her admirer too. Startled, they darted forward, stopping just short of the wire.

"Names!" bawled the Prosecutor.

They had none, except the romantic nicknames they had given each other, and they declined to reveal those. It annoyed the Prosecutor that they were stubborn about it. Pet names were so amusing! Oh, well: "Names will be appointed for you". He turned to the stenographer, another silk moth. "For the record, they will be called 'Flutter' and 'Strutter'..." The silk moth quickly chewed holes in a leaf. (Silk moths do have such a written language and are useful for this, but no one ever reads them, so the Court records just collect dust.) "...charged with trespass and ignoring official orders. How do you plead?"

"Guilty, sir", admitted Strutter, "But with mitigating circumstances".

"Oh, great. Another country lawyer".

"I am referring to this girl, sir! Isn't she beautiful? She's gorgeous! I couldn't take my eyes off her. That's why it happened".

Flutter looked gratefully at her sweetheart. They commenced whispering again. The Prosecutor was appalled at the lack of decorum and decided to just skip to the end with these ninnies.

"The penalty for trespass near the Mugwump is death by ingestion--Chapter 1, page 1".

The jury was growing impatient too and the Scale clanked down before he even finished. Behind them the Great Mugwump was nodding off again, exactly what the Prosecutor was waiting for. He grinned at the Chief Justice. "Request lunch recess!"

The Toadies flicked their tongues around to loosen them up. The warty one cast a worried look over his shoulder, but the Mugwump had fallen asleep and was beginning to snore.

"Granted", he whispered. All the Toadies headed for the cage. The quickest and nimblest hopped up on top, others crowded as closely as they could. The jailors knew what to do. When 'Big Boy' dozed off the Toadies feasted on food that was supposed to be reserved for him, in this case the fish flies. The guard up top threw open the hatch and guards inside stirred up the fish flies, who saw their chance and went for the exit.

None escaped, not with all those sticky tongues stabbing into the flock. In half a minute an entire class of defendants was eliminated, and the Toadies were commending each other for expediting sentence and saving valuable Court time.

"Fat pigs", shouted Lulu. "Do you think he won't notice? The cage was full, and when he wakes up--nearly empty. He'll be mad!"

"Nah, he's getting old and forgetful", rebutted the Prosecutor, still swallowing his lunch. "He won't say nuthin'. Don't wanna let on he's slippin'. We're not worried".

As if to prove that last, one of the strong-arm guards snapped up the terrified little skipper from her corner too and snuffed out one more life.

But there was no end to life in Nassump and everyone knew it. That's why it had become so cheap. The marsh was rich with the elements of life, and Nassump--the very heart of the marsh--was overflowing with the richness, enough cheap life to support banquets, parties, and all the rich tastes of the Mugwump's Court. It's tough to be stuck at the bottom of the food chain like the fish flies, but someone has to be. Anyway, with all these well-fed bigger folk lounging around, job opportunities open up for lesser folk too, especially in entertainment. Even now the Mugwump was waking up from his nap and calling for the dancing girls.

The Fuzz handled this for the Mugwump. Worship was over and they hurried to get the show on the road; but it was the senior slave girls, really, who organized the troupe, trained them, and defended them from the many scoundrels on the sandbar.

Yero recognized one of the dancers who had slipped the cuffs on her.

"Really, you shouldn't blame her", said Lulu. "They do what they're told, or they're turned over to some officer of the Fuzz as a personal attendant, or to the Toadies, like me, as an errand girl".

"You were a dancer?"

"Not for long. It's good work for a slave, mind you, but I didn't keep my mouth shut. Hey! These girls are pretty good".

A chorus line of silk moths sallied forth onto the open sand to the Mugwump's right. He watched them with one eye, mildly interested. In his younger years he would turn and watch with both eyes, or even jump up and join the chorus line. Whew! That turned out badly. He lacked rhythm and trampled many of the girls; but he was Mugwump and he liked it, so he kept it up until he was too fat to enjoy it. It had put a strain on the Fuzz to capture enough girls. The performances were sometimes reduced to solos. It was better now, in his older age. The chorus lines were long, often several lines, and the fun went on and on.

It was his greatest delight to capture the Oo's daughters and force them into tawdry performances in plain sight of her. The Fuzz and assorted scalawags in his service enjoyed the shows too. Warrior moths flocked to the spectacle by the hundreds, and tonight a pair of crayfish scuttled up along shore and snapped their pincers at the dancers. The Mugwump tolerated crayfish to clean up the garbage that his crowd generated which would otherwise begin to stink. He preferred pristine swamp stink--not landfill.

There was a disturbance. The dancers near the water broke ranks. The senior choreographer shouted for order. The crowd booed, and then hooted when they saw what was happening. A lizard-like creature had come partly out of the water and got the last girl in the line. It was a siren, something like an eel but with small front legs and huge external gills that gave it an alien appearance. Now it backed slowly into the water with its prize, daring anyone to interfere. The poor silk moth flapped helplessly and that's probably what attracted an even bigger predator.

In a rush of frothing water, the siren shrieked, let go the dancer, and was sucked under into the catfish's mouth. He had to eat too. It's hungry work coming up from the river twice a day, hoping for a chance at the Mugwump.

Everyone including the Mugwump edged back from shore, but the worst danger was over. The catfish headed back for the river with a squirmy siren in his maw.

The Butterflies, Yero and Boca

The dancer, nearly gone anyway, suddenly disappeared too as the next biggest eater-under-the-water served himself. Even from their cage the butterflies saw the big splashes and were spooked by all the gluttony.

"What was *that* one?" asked Boca.

"Another fish probably--who knows?" answered Lulu. "Just don't get too close to the water".

The Mugwump stirred, raised his arms and clapped once, loudly. It wasn't applause. It was the signal to move on with the evening's entertainment. Normally he liked to watch the girls until they were exhausted and stumbling. Then he would turn to his Toadies and nit-pick the performance, recalling a higher level of skill years ago. But tonight he was edgy. When the catfish showed up it made him nervous. And when he got nervous there was only one remedy: Food!

"This is it, then", said Lulu. "Been nice knowin' you".

"What's happening?" asked Yero.

"We're to be released, as promised", said Lulu sarcastically. "I'll go first. I think I can still get the Toadies into trouble".

"Released? Isn't that good news?"

"Released for target practice", replied Lulu bitterly. "We're to be his midnight snack. The Toadies enjoy this, but I'm going to spoil their fun". She cast a nasty glance at the guards.

There was a breathtaking bustle to clear away dancers and a few stage props. When the Mugwump got impatient, everyone knew to run for their lives. Not all made it. The almighty tongue lashed out two, three times and cleaned up that many stragglers. One was the chief choreographer trying to hustle her girls offstage. Future performances would suffer from this and some excuse would have to be invented. No one would dare tell him it was his own fault.

Now the Mugwump turned the other way, toward the cage, to see what had been collected for his evening's sport. He blinked. The cage was almost empty. How could that be? Wasn't it full only a little while ago? He narrowed his eyes. One...Two...Three...Four...Five...Six, counting the bird. A pitiful group, and himself as hungry as an alligator! He croaked loudly, the signal to release the first prisoner: "Jugga Rumm!"

The strong-arms opened the hatch and grabbed for Lulu but she eluded them again and flew out the opening. There was a hush as everyone expected her to do the usual thing, namely skedaddle as fast as possible away from the Mugwump. To everyone's surprise, she flew directly at him and tattled into his ear a couple things about his thugs that made him angry. She paid for her fun of course. He zapped her out of the air just in front of his nose, but she went out (or 'in') laughing. Then he actually rose up on all fours and turned to face his Toadies. They scattered.

He had never trusted them much. Who could trust a toad? They did keep order on the sandbar, but the Fuzz were his favorites. They patrolled the whole marsh and captured prisoners. Without them, his fun would come to an end. However, on the sandbar itself some real muscle was needed. He'd taken on various servants over the years with mixed success--other amphibians, a crow, even rats. The Toadies were the best help for the least trouble--until now! He believed Lulu's last words. Push *him* into the bay? For catfish food? *How dare they!*"

Most of the Toadies were furiously digging into the sand hoping to escape the wrath. A few just stood dumbstruck. The Mugwump guessed correctly that the fastest diggers were the guiltiest - but blast it, he didn't like sand on his tongue! He went for one who was probably innocent to make an example. Zap! The tongue latched onto one of the strong-arms, the one sitting on the hatch atop the cage. The tongue got good traction on all the warts and jerked reflexively back, pulling the toad off his perch despite a strong grip on the trapdoor. It swung open behind him as he sailed through the air and into the Mugwump's mouth. Everyone watched the big gulp except the damselfly and her sweetheart who weren't paying attention. They saw the open door and simply zipped out, escaping into the marsh when no one was looking with the blind luck of the blissful.

In their wake the Travelers also escaped, but it was only the start of any real getaway. There would be a few moments of grace while the Mugwump was swallowing his jailor - not enough to get out of his range, Atel figured, but enough to make mischief since the Fuzz were absent from the sky. They knew not to be up when Big Boy was having sport.

Yero and Boca instinctively dashed for the island across the water, the nearest place not under the Mugwump's control, willing to take a chance with the Lady Oo. Atel made a dash for the Mugwump hoping to distract him for a few moments by reflecting light into his eyes, using his own belly for a light source; but she underestimated the bullfrog.

Before she got close enough, he finished gulping the Toady and his jaw muscles flexed. That's when she flashed him as best she could, and dodged. The tongue barely missed her, overshot and hit the jail cage beyond, sticking to the wires. Seeing this, the hummingbird took off after the butterflies with some hope of making it; but the Mugwump wasn't beaten yet. He retracted the errant tongue, jerking the partly buried minnow trap free. The tongue broke loose and snapped back instantly, ready for the next shot. The rusty trap rolled into the water with the strong-arm Toadies still inside and disappeared.

As fast as she was, Atel wasn't fast enough or yet far enough away. The Mugwump stepped forward, leaning as far as he dared, and let fly with pure rage over things lately gone wrong. The sticky tongue easily caught up to her just as she neared safety but passed her by - the first time in memory that he had missed a fleeing target.

There is a clever mechanism in the eye of a bullfrog, a quirk that gives them advantage over their prey: When the eye catches a flicker of movement, the brain sends a message to the tongue. Calculations are instantaneous. The tongue targets the flicker, usually an insect, and the frog nabs his meal; but in this case it was the Lady Oo who had made a flicker, just behind her plum tree, to throw off the Mugwump's aim. It worked better than she ever hoped. In his fury, the bullfrog set a new distance record. The tongue shot past Atel and wrapped itself around the trunk of the plum tree, snagging securely on the stiff thorns. For a few moments, all of Nassump held its breath. The next moment the butterflies cheered, and chaos erupted.

The Greatest Power in Nassump was hung up, but his Fuzz weren't buying into defeat. Their only thoughts were revenge on the Oo, and un-hooking the tongue. Alarm pheromones wafted through the marsh air drawing patrols from everywhere. Hundreds of Fuzz attacked the Lady's island in waves as they arrived on the scene, kamikaze waves. Nearly all the first waves were attracted to the will-o-wisps and went into the water, there to flounder. A couple of Fuzz closed their eyes out of fear and did reach the island, landing in the plum tree just above the fixed tongue. They started smarting off immediately, threatening the butterflies, and then spotted the Oo herself watching them.

"Well! If it ain't the Babe!" said one, a low grade named Jag. "Looky, Sarge!"

"Yeah! She tops the most-wanted list, she does. Hey Babe! We'll give you a few minutes to pack and then you come with us!"

The Lady didn't deign to answer, just glanced at them with an air of dismissal.

"Snooty, eh?" said the sergeant. "Lucky for you, orders are not to touch - not till the Top Brass arrives".

"They got plans for you", snickered Jag. "The buzz is: You'll be joining your daughters on the chorus line".

"That's if you're a good girl. So be nice to the Commandant when he comes".

"He'll expect a big kiss!"

"Yeah! Pucker up, Babe!"

The Oo ignored it all, but she was worried about the assault. She had never seen the Fuzz so angry. Reinforcements were arriving constantly, recklessly launching themselves across the water. Several more closed their eyes out of fright and made it to shore by chance, landing in the rushes below. But her biggest worry was the waters; they were getting so full of thrashing, drowning Fuzz that it was covering up the lights, and still more Fuzz kept coming.

The Fuzzers in the tree saw it too and got cocky watching the show. They recognized a lot of squadrons by their wing markings, which varied somewhat.

"Hey! That's fat old Otho and the pickerel bay boys, ain't it?" said Jag. "Watch out, Otho - Oof!"

"Too bad", said the sergeant. "Oh! There's a flight from the Big Slough. I served there when I was just a dumb recruit".

Jag, a young recruit himself, gave the sarge a dirty look.

Down by the water several half-drowned survivors straggled ashore walking on the floating bodies of their fellow Fuzz. Jag and the sergeant called down, cheering them on. "Hurrah! Hurrah, boys! C'mon in!"

Some more did. Too many to ignore. Atel went down to deal with them. Then the water started moving. Not from struggling moths but something underneath. The fish had caught on to the feast and started to chow down. Word had spread underwater and more were coming up from the river. There were a few greedy slurps at first, and then the water started to splash and boil from big fish gobbling moths and little fish jumping out of the way.

The Commandant had to call off the assault. His Fuzz were plentiful, but not *that* plentiful, and some thought must be given to alternate plans if the Mugwump couldn't be got unstuck. Even as he watched, the water began to clear, and the will-o-wisps shined forth again. He quickly looked away to avoid the spell.

Jag and the sergeant also shielded their eyes, knowing it would be suicide to look; but as good soldiers, they broke off thorns and climbed down to pry the tongue loose. Alas, it wasn't long before they also were stuck, face first, on the gooey thing. And that, for now anyway, was the last of the invaders.

Across the way the Toadies all re-emerged, downright pleased with the new setup. Big Boy was in serious trouble obviously. The two lawyer Toadies with the most jewelry took temporary command and sequestered themselves out of earshot, debating the wisest course of action.

The Prosecutor was all for giving the Mugwump a nudge. "He's teetering now! Let's do it before the tongue stretches and he settles back".

"Not so fast", argued the defense attorney. "There's lots of fish tonight, but none big enough to eat him. The catfish *had* his supper, remember?"

"Let all the fish have a bite! We'll make it look like an accident".

"Whoa! This ain't some juvenile delinquent. We better be nice--for *now*. He still might get loose".

"Well, sure - if we give him enough time!"

"Whoa again! There's something else too. The *Fuzz*. This has to look good enough to fool them. We'll need them later when we take over".

"True. Good point. They're decent at security".

"Unless someone shines a light at 'em!"

The two shared a belly laugh at the failed assault and waddled back to their pals. Then the whole bunch waddled down to shore and made a big show of trying to push and pull the Mugwump safely back from the water. He couldn't answer questions very well, so they weren't sure if he was saying 'stop' or 'hop', 'yes' or 'less', 'no' or 'go'; so, they jerked him around pretty good before giving up the charade. It seemed to satisfy the Fuzz who crowded all the airspace (except above the water). Clearly, they weren't going to leave any time soon.

It held everyone's attention over in the plum tree too, whether it fooled them or not. Their main concern was the tongue coming loose and an enraged Mugwump sending more trouble, or even throwing caution away and coming himself. But the tongue held fast even when it made the tree sway. Things settled down after that. Atel took the butterflies along to pay a courtesy call on the Lady Oo since there seemed no chance of going anywhere else for the night. They could see her up near the top of the tree calmly surveying the recent battleground, speaking occasionally to a daughter well-concealed a little behind her.

When they arrived in her presence, she was regal and cool (almost as snooty as the Fritillary, Boca thought), and didn't speak even when Atel inquired about hospitality, but just nodded slightly. Their guide seemed perfectly satisfied with such an answer and went to scout the island, but the butterflies weren't satisfied at all. They had been thinking about the apparitions in the tunnels and wanted an explanation, fair and square. Yero piped up first, actually pointing a finger at the Lady.

"We know it wasn't really you back in the muskrat tunnels", she said, "But it must have been you giving directions! You sent us straight to jail! Why?"

The Oo was discomposed, almost scandalized to be bothered like this. "No matter!" she asserted imperiously, "The Fuzz would have caught you anyway".

"Maybe", said Boca. "But *you turned us in*!"

The Oo was shocked. She was used to her own daughters who listened and never spoke, never talked back. Her whole reign was based on obedience. Now *this*! A look of pain flashed across the Lady's brow, pain and exhaustion. "We have a deal..." she began. She disliked the word, found it painful to utter. *Very* painful. Too painful! Without warning, the Lady Oo toppled from her perch seriously ill and splashed into the bay below.

"Mother!" shouted the close daughter; but even as she spoke, a fish swallowed the Oo. The butterflies were flabbergasted but the daughter calmly ascended to the Royal perch and spoke. It was finally her turn.

"Don't feel bad", she said. "My mother lived past her time. She didn't show it, but she was thrilled to live long enough to see this". The daughter smiled at the Mugwump in his dilemma. "Her responsibility is now mine. I hope I can do as well".

"So, you're the Oo now?"

The daughter nodded. "We only live one year, fasting. I am the 18th Oo, but we pretend to be just one. Don't spread that around, Okay? The mystique helps in dealing with the Fuzz".

Yero nodded. "That's safe with us. We don't like them any better than you do. But what did your mother mean at the last? She started to talk about some kind of deal".

The New Oo looked sharply at the butterflies. "I might as well tell you", she replied after a moment. "Mother was about to anyway. The three of you were traded for one of us, even-up. A prisoner-exchange. The Fuzz allowed one of us to escape into the greater marsh without the Mugwump knowing about it, and you were delivered to them".

"Three of us? For just *one* of you? That's all you could *get*?" Yero was offended, but some questions shouldn't be asked. A lot of folks have been humbled to learn what they are worth on the open market.

"Value ebbs and flows with the tide", said the Oo, coldly calculating. "Another day I might hold out for two, if it makes you feel better". It didn't.

"All these generations around here", Yero grumbled quietly to Boca, "and they're all in some fix! I don't think Royals are very good at dealing".

"Maybe it works in reverse", whispered Boca. "She's smarter than Foppish, and he had 70, so maybe the less Royalty the better".

"Right. And none at *all* is best - like *us*. We need to do our own trading, Boca".

"Everyone should", said the Oo, overhearing. "If they *can*. But you might feel differently if it was your own sisters being enslaved".

"You can be proud of some that were taken", said Yero, more kindly. "We met one named Lulu who gave them a lot of trouble, right to the end".

The New Oo hung her head. "I am sorry to hear this. She was my close sister. I had hoped she escaped".

"She didn't, but she laughed right in the Mugwump's face and spilled some news to him. She started the whole riot over there".

"That would be Lulu. I hope she comes back".

"Well, I'm sorry. The Mugwump ate her".

"Her *spirit*, I meant. She is part of the Family Tree, more than ever now".

There was a murmur through the plum leaves like wind hurrying past, but when Yero looked the leaves never moved. She suddenly guessed that the plum itself was the Family Tree, and older generations were still very close.

"When I summon the will-o-wisps I will look for her among them", said the Oo. "She'll be the one who goes her own way".

"Is that the secret of them?"

"Your guide knows something about lights. I will say no more".

With that, aloofness came over her face, as though the cares of her new office had gripped her and she must see to them, ignoring all else. The butterflies had been lucky after a fashion. Only in the last hour of one Oo, or the first hours of the next, will they speak at all to strangers.

The butterflies went down to where Atel was roosting, bringing with them questions about light tricks and apparitions, only to find her also in an unresponsive mood. All they got out of her was a grumpy, "Tomorrow is another day".

***

'Tomorrow' arrived sooner than expected, long before sunrise. Their guide was calling to them: "Wake up, sleepyheads!"

There was urgency in her voice. They opened their eyes to a drippy, foggy, miserable pre-dawn. They hadn't gotten nearly enough sleep. Yero didn't budge until a cold dewdrop fell squarely on her back and trickled off all sides. She tried to shake herself and discovered dew had collected on her wings too, and that got in her eyes.

"...trouble! We'll have to move", Atel was saying. That got her attention. Trouble again? So soon? It wasn't fair!

"Black ants", Atel explained. "The kind that chew wood. They're coming across - scads of them - and I don't have decent light to work with".

They looked where she was pointing, to the Mugwump's tongue still stretched tautly over the water. The bullfrog's belly had lost its luster, but the will-o-wisps cast an aura. A long line of carpenter ants was making its way across the tongue 'bridge', heading straight for them. Each carried an egg, as usual with them when migrating. The line extended back to the Mugwump, down his chin and belly to the sandbar, and across the span of floating reeds to the muskrat's tunnel from which the ants emerged apparently without end.

The air was filled with the Fuzz who kept safely back from the water but now began to yak it up. It wasn't hard to guess they had something to do with this. The noise woke up the Toadies too, who poked their heads up out of the sand.

In the dim light Yero noticed caterpillars crawling toward the top of the plum tree, spiny green silk moth caterpillars, aware of the ants coming and trying to escape them. She thought them ugly except for the little red bristles that showed which end was front. Cute little eyebrows! One of them found itself at a dead end on the tip of a twig and reached up, trying to grab a loose end of cobweb just out of reach. "Forget it", Yero wanted to tell the caterpillar. "That's just a cobweb, not a spider web. It'll break." And that gave her an idea.

"Boca!" she called. He was huddled under a leaf against the drips. "Boca! Remember Poppy? Remember the spider webs and the 'toesie-talk'? Let's play some music for the ants!" She fluttered to a sturdy twig within reach of the tightrope tongue, but safely away from the sticky end. Boca followed, beginning to guess her plan.

She braced herself by a thorn and reached forward with one arm, grabbing as much tongue as she could and giving it a 'twang' like a guitar string. The 'string' was much too large for her hand but so taut that she did set off a small vibration. "Come on", she grinned. "Let's pick a tune!"

Working together with two strong butterfly arms, they could twang it enough to see results. The line of ants, over halfway across by now, paused in their advance.

Hey! It was fun. The activity shook loose a shower of drips down onto them and the musicians didn't even notice.

"Let's play a real tune", suggested Yero.

"We can try. Which one?"

"I don't know any ant-tunes, but how about 'Shoo-Fly'?"

The ants had started moving again, faster now. So would you if you were on a tightrope and jokesters were fiddling with the rope. Then the music resumed. To be critical, the musicians didn't carry their tune very well, but you'd never know from the way the ants started tap-dancing. The column halted again immediately. Ants have great balance, but the vibration was numbing their toes and driving them crazy.

Other folk also took notice of this. Over on the sandbar the Toadies guessed this latest Fuzzer plan wasn't going to work either and substituted their own, lapping up as many ants as possible while the buffet was in front of them.

The cloud of Fuzz saw problems too and furiously urged the ants onward but did nothing to support them. Yesterday's awful losses were still fresh in their minds. Oh, yes. Speaking of minds, the Mugwump was rapidly losing his. The vibration went right into his bones.,

Atel saw the strategy and paid the young musicians a visit. "I never saw an instrument like this", she said. "What do you call it?"

"It's our *Bullfrog Banjo*".

"Can I play? I know a tune".

"Sure. What's it called?"

"*Ants Alive.* Let me show you".

She hovered over the 'string', reaching down to pick away. Being larger and stronger, she really livened things up. In moments, the ants were dancing again and juggling the eggs.

"Can we play too?" asked Yero.

"By all means. Just keep back from the sticky end there. Let the Fuzzers play in that".

Jag and the sergeant, still alive, still glued face-first in the 'knot', were unable to move anything but their angry eyes. Yero turned away and ignored them.

"They don't appreciate the fine arts", she said.

"No rhythm", observed Boca.

But as the Two reached again for the Banjo string, several things happened nearly at once:

Atel picked a high note. Some of the ants lost their balance and tumbled off, leaving gaps in the line.

Due to the gaps, the vibration became irregular and finally intolerable for the Mugwump. He hopped forward into the water to stop the torment. The tongue drooped and fell slack. Ahhh! That felt better!

But not for long. The catfish, returning on his morning rounds seized his long-desired entree by the legs.

The Mugwump gasped mightily, sucking in his slack tongue. It broke off right next to the musicians and went *zing* back into his mouth, ants and all.

Then the catfish gulped as much bullfrog as possible, but this still left half an angry Mugwump sticking out.

***

They swam away like that, down the channel together, with the Mugwump pounding on the catfish's head. The Irresistible Mouth had met the Unswallowable Object.

The war petered out then. The Fuzz, totally deflated at the messy end of their god, began to disperse into the marsh to take up their old duties as police and customs agents out of habit. Across the way the Toadies inherited the sandbar, but the Fuzz didn't care, so the dancing girls flew off in all directions and escaped into the wide world.

The New Oo, with much less to worry about, found *something* to worry about and a few words to do it with. The slimy end of the tongue remained securely wrapped around her tree and she fussed about it no end. It was like a dirty collar! And gnats were on it! And it smelled! And it would be there until it rotted off! And---

"Might as well get used to it", said Atel brightly. "Think of it as a parting gift from the Mugwump: His apology tied up in a ribbon".

"And see?" added Yero, pointing to Jag and the sergeant. "It's got pretty bows, too".

***

They waited all day as the Fuzz slowly dispersed with many an angry glance in their direction. Plainly, the warrior moths hadn't forgotten them. Then they caught a bit of good luck.

A flight of migrating ducks arrived noisily, quacking their heads off as they came down through the fog to this little bay they remembered. It had a long reputation as a fine eatery with lots of small fish. In moments, all of them were heads down, rumps up. They found the fishing even better than they remembered.

After a while, when there were duck heads to talk to instead of just tail feathers, Atel asked them for an escort and they agreed, but only to the south edge of the marsh. There was another eatery there featuring salads. Wild celery and duck potatoes. After that, they had a long non-stop flight and couldn't be hindered by "qua-a-a-ack-qua-a-a-ack butterflies". Atel accepted gratefully and translated the language to Yero and Boca, who weren't fluent.

They were impressed with themselves. Wow! Invited to fly with swift waterfowl! They would go like the wind and prove worthy of such an offer. Yes! *Air it out!* Atel didn't have the heart to tell them what the long, drawn-out qua-a-a-acks really meant.

At nightfall the ducks took off suddenly, as ducks often do, and the Travelers followed as best they could. There was time for only one backward glance. Nassump looked much different now, with no lights on the sandbar. But something was there, in the prime spot where the Mugwump always sat. A younger bullfrog had moved in, smaller but large enough that the Toadies gave room. He tilted his head up and Yero thought he was looking at her, but he was only drawing a bead on an insect. His long tongue shot out, slapped back in again, and the first firefly of the evening disappeared from the air above Nassump.

Chapter 11

The Way South

"Don't dawdle!" urged Atel, breaking the last thread of fascination. "*Air it out!* - remember?"

They did. The butterflies never worked so hard or flew so straight. Even so, the ducks slacked off in the fog to avoid losing them though it isn't in their nature to do so. They relented because of the Fuzz who were everywhere, obviously up to no good. Ducks do have a good sense of right and wrong and are quick to rally around any who join their flight. So, they slowed a bit and maneuvered to keep the Travelers in the middle where they wouldn't be noticed, and after that the Fuzz lost interest - or simply lost them in the fog, which got thicker as they went on.

Mostly the butterflies navigated by the sound of the duck wings because they couldn't see anything either. Occasionally there were flickers below and Yero wondered if they might be apparitions, lost and wandering. The only other hint of marsh was a faint sheen off the larger waters, reflecting a few moonbeams that penetrated the fog. But poor visibility didn't bother the ducks. They knew exactly where they were going.

At last the mist began to thin. The outline of the full moon and some of the brighter stars showed through. They were nearing the southern extent of the marsh and it took on the same appearance as the northern side: A mess of reeds and swamp grass. Trash, mostly. No doubt full of tunnels and rodents. Yero breathed a sigh of relief when the ducks flew over that part and left it behind. Bluffs appeared up ahead of them and one last body of water, a shallow bay. Yero knew it was shallow because there were herons wading around a flat rock out in the middle of it. That's where the ducks put down, just nearby, and immediately went into their shameless feeding routine. A feast of tubers awaited them under the surface. Yero wanted to thank them - but how could she? It wouldn't be polite now. Boca just shook his head and looked away.

Atel was already trading traveler's gossip with the herons, a somewhat antisocial species thrown together here because of the local eatery and the fact that this was the only exposed rock in the whole muddy bay. They stalked about on their tall, bony legs, dipping long beaks into the water and keeping a close eye on the lone rock so as not to miss their turn at it.

The heron at the rock now the one Atel was trying to visit with - had a clam and was busy opening it. She smacked it down hard on the rock. Whack! It opened a crack, then closed tightly again.

"Shellfish!" said the heron in disgust. "I hate this".

Another heron spoke up. "If you can't do it, Edwinna, just admit it and let someone else have the rock".

Edwinna ignored her and grasped the clam securely in her beak, a little farther out this time for more leverage; then she wrenched her neck sideways and swung down with all her might. Crack! The clam split completely in half and the halves rolled like dinner plates off the rock into the water. Edwinna got lots of help then. She recovered the empty half herself and tossed it in disgust. The heron who was badgering her fished up the full half and stalked off with the prize. Edwinna just stood there, scandalized. "Well! I never...!" she began, but a third heron interrupted.

"Oh yes you *have*, Edwinna. You've done that. Don't get all innocent with us now".

Edwinna exhaled, appalled. "Well that's just wonderful, Tawilla! A robbery is committed and you're favoring the thief!"

"You'll have to move, Edwinna. Rules are, if you don't have a clam your turn at the rock is over".

"Don't talk to me about rules! She stole my clam!"

"It fell into the water. Anything in the water is finders/keepers. That's the rule."

"Well it *shouldn't* be the rule!" squawked Edwinna, and splashed water everywhere with her wings. Tawilla got it the worst but others got splattered too. Edwinna was aiming at everyone.

A splash-a-thon ensued but no one suffered any harm since water runs right off their backs. Everyone got to squawk and air their grievances and it turned into something like a group therapy session. They needed it. None of the herons were any too happy.

Atel had bolted from the water fight along with the butterflies but now she returned and tested Tawilla with a question or two.

"Any news from the south? We're going that way".

"You might think twice. We went once and came back".

"For the shellfish here?"

"Heavens, no! I feel like a common gull doing this -" (Here Tawilla felt something with her toes and stabbed down with her beak but came up with just an empty shell.) --"but the stupid clams *are* nutritious, and we need it. We're fattening up for an extra-long flight".

"Why such a long flight, if I may be so bold?"

"You sure are, for a wee little chirper! But you're flying *south*, I think I heard you say..."

"Yes".

"Yes. Well, it's dry. Real dry. The ponds and eateries we usually stop at are just mud. Dry mud. Except one".

"There's one good water hole?"

"*Was* one! But the *boys* muddied it up before we got there! How do you like *that*??"

"Well, I don't know what to say".

"Just watch what you *do* say, sister! They're still our boyfriends and don't forget it! I'm sure they're waiting for us somewhere".

"I'm sure they are. But how far does the dry go on, I wonder?"

"So do we! Then we eat some more, and the next day we do it again. But we'll have to try again soon. Winter is coming".

"It is. Will you all be flying together?"

As soon as she said it, Atel wished she hadn't. There was a very brief silence, and then the carping and nitpicking started up. Tawilla took it upon herself to loudly explain some aerodynamic problems this would expose.

"We can't fly the wedge like some do", she pointed out, "because of *irregular* body shapes. Just as example, Skirilla there is too skinny, Shiboola is too fat, and Edwinna flaps too much - both wing and beak".

Squawking and splashing re-commenced. Tawilla chuckled at what she'd started and stole a nice clam from someone in the melee. She stalked quickly to the rock, broke it open, and expertly plucked out the stubborn occupant, which she gulped.

"One sure thing", she added when things calmed down, "we *do* have a girl who would gladly bring up the rear and *stay* there--hey, Grossfuss?"

Everyone tittered except Grossfuss, which was just a nickname. The bird had extra-large feet and was embarrassed to lift them out of the water when walking like others did.

"Show 'em!" someone teased. "C'mon, Grossfuss, show us your big mudders!"

She did, then. She fetched up a gob of marsh muck and heaved it at the smart aleck. Most of it hit the mark. The dirtied one ran squawking in big circles trying to splash herself clean. Everyone else thought it was a good trick and Grossfuss suddenly found herself a favorite instead of a freak. The social order changes quickly with grumpy herons.

"One more question, if you don't mind", said Atel when the crowd settled down again. "How far did you go before you turned back?"

Tawilla shot the hummingbird a warning look. "Three days. Just the one mud hole in three days! And don't go a-blabbing about you-know-*what*!" Still cantankerous she eyed the butterflies, who had been well behaved through all this. "Three days is like three weeks for your minnies. They look like minnows with wings".

"Thank you, Miss Tawilla", answered Yero cheerfully. "We'll wait for you at the next waterhole".

"Don't dawdle", said Boca. He had been itching to use that phrase on somebody else.

That drew snickers throughout the group. Tawilla talked an awful lot and no one minded that she got sassed. Tawilla acted like it was nothing, just turned and showed her tail feathers--the usual fowl signal that a conversation was at an end.

The Travelers took the hint and left the herons behind, flying low under the thinning fog to the bluffs, rocky here also on the southern side but dotted with patches of fall asters that had taken root wherever a bit of shallow soil allowed. The blooms were drying up but there were so many to choose from that the Travelers made a decent meal.

The layer of fog settled while they ate, obscuring the herons somewhat but affording a good view of the sky and the first hint of sunrise. None of the Fuzz were around, possibly (as Atel guessed) because no travelers came up from the south in this season. But Boca figured the fish had eaten so many there were no longer enough to guard all the routes.

"We've probably opened up a major new passage", he declared, "and we should leave something here, so it gets named after us".

Yero readily agreed. "Sort of like they did up along the Rowah - but more praiseworthy".

"Do you have something in mind?" asked Atel.

Yero laughed. "I'd like to stretch the Mugwump's tongue all the way and tie it to these rocks so everyone could follow it. But, too bad. He got away".

"If you call that 'getting away'".

"What about our banjo music?" suggested Boca. "Could that guide Travelers like the fairy music?"

"No, it's lost. No one would trust it anyway".

"And we don't have esporellia to work with", sighed Yero. "We'll just have to make something with rocks". She looked around without much enthusiasm. Boca began rolling a pebble, but it was bigger than he was.

"Go ahead", suggested their guide. "We have a little time. You can build up your muscles and impress Tawilla if we see her again".

The butterflies went at the project slowly and made no reply.

"I'm going back a little way and get a nice, clean drink", Atel continued. "Better fill up, the way *she* talked". She left.

The butterflies decided to build individual markers, but not far apart. Progress was difficult and they needed breaks for refreshments. When Atel returned, they each had a small base of several pebbles pushed together.

"Oh, platforms!" said the hummingbird. "That's good".

"We expected you to be gone longer", said Yero. "We still have to build the big statues on top of this".

"Statues? Will that take long?"

"A while". Yero wiped her brow. "Longer if we have to do it all by ourselves". She plopped down for a bit of rest. Boca was already taking his break.

Atel said nothing, didn't do anything either. The Two took note and began to scale back their plans.

"Maybe we should just leave a note by these platforms", suggested Yero after a few minutes, "so each traveler could add one stone when they come by".

"I'd better leave a charm, so they look like you when they're finished", said Atel. "But I like the idea that others could put up a pebble and improve them. They need it".

"Yes, I doubt we'll be able to finish them before we leave".

"Time will tell. I'll just watch for a while. It'll be fun to see them take shape. I hope they turn out nicer than Gorda's".

"They'll be smaller", said Yero wearily. Both butterflies exhaled loudly and wistfully and went looking for smaller rocks.

"Something is upsetting the herons", said Atel after a few minutes. The two sculptors quickly stopped rock-picking, grateful for any distraction.

It was quite true. The herons were in a tizzy, stalking and milling around their rock. Will-o-wisps were dancing on it, causing the stir.

"Stand back now", warned the hummingbird. "Here they come".

The will-o-wisps floated off the rock, right through the gawking flock who stumbled all over trying to get out of the way. When a leg didn't move quickly enough the lights passed through it. That spooked the herons. Spookier yet, the lights looked exactly like the butterflies that had just sassed Tawilla, only bigger.

"Is that us?" marveled Yero. "Did you do that?"

"I did. We really don't have time for you to build proper stone statues, much as you'd like to..."

"No. We were beginning to think the same thing".

"...So I went back - quite a way, actually - to a pool where the lights bubble up, and had a word with them. Hush, now. I want to see if they do this right".

The will-o-wisps floated across the bay and up the hillside, right past the admiring butterflies, and took their places on the platforms prepared for them. They were good quality apparitions and they struck heroic poses showing the way south. The butterflies were thrilled!

Then they turned grandly and motioned to any wayfarers lost in the marsh: Come! This is the way! Thrilled!

Then they transformed into the simple rock totems the butterflies might have built given more time and assumed imbecilic expressions.

"Oh! We can't leave them like this," whispered Yero. "We would've done better than this!"

Atel might have smiled; it was hard to tell. She spoke softly to the totems. They improved their looks some, but not much.

"Is that the best you can do?"

"Probably. We're dealing with rocks here".

"But---"

"But wait. Have a little patience".

Soon the totems faded and winked out. "They're gone", said Atel. "They can't last long this far from the water".

To her mild surprise, both butterflies wanted them back in spite of the goofiness. "Travelers *could* follow them through the fog," marveled Boca. "We would be like lighthouses up here. Just so the dumb looks aren't lasting".

"I hoped you'd feel that way. More are coming. When they reached back and waved, they were signaling the next pair to start out. That's how I set it up. But I'm curious how silly the next ones get before they fade. It should be fun to watch".

The butterflies declined, preferring to leave right away, even as the next ones appeared down in the bay.

"It's funny how all these historical markers work out, isn't it?" said Yero later. "I'm glad folks will get some idea how much we did, but..."

"Yeah, I know what you mean", sighed Boca. "They could be better".

"That's how things usually work out", remarked Atel. "If you want something done *your* way you have to do it yourself".

They left the Great Marsh behind and this tale does not tell how many wandering Rasha La have since found their way through the fog by following the will-o-wisps. Doubtless some have. That tally is known only to the Keeper of the Halls of Waiting so we can only guess - unless someone finds the markers and counts the pebbles.

"That Tawilla", said Yero, changing the subject. "She talked like it was really dry where we're going. Is that a big deal?'

"It is for them. It may be for us too".

"I don't think herons would be happy unless they had enough water to splash in. Maybe that's what she meant. Not enough splashing water".

"She meant even *less*, I think. They always complain about their boyfriends but they're never far apart. If they are now, well, things must be serious".

"Butterflies don't need as much water as they do. We can get what we need from the dew if we have to".

"That may come in handy soon, but I'm not so easily refilled. Hummingbirds use up a lot of water, in case you didn't know. I can get by on the dew for a little while. But if it gets really dry, I may have to excuse myself to find a drink".

"We went down while you were gone and drank lots of water. It took time out of our work schedule, but this nectar around here is more like eating candy bars than sipping juice".

"Yes. It made me thirsty too, but we were lucky. In a day or so it will be dry and hard. We would have to unwrap the little candy bars and take them down to the heron's rock to crack them open".

Yero laughed. "We should have brought some along. I could ask Tawilla to break one open at the next pool. She's the best".

"But then she would steal it", said Boca.

"Maybe none of us will find water", warned Atel, "and the last thing we'll need is more sticky candy. Let's fly".

The morning and the land itself opened up beyond the marshes, opened up wide. The only trees for miles around were behind them, dotting the shorelines of the marsh. Brush and wild grasses now gave way to wheat fields. The endless wheat fields of the Great Plains stretched southward before them, broken only by the occasional imprints of men: Roads, mostly, as straight as sunbeams so men could hurry along on their business and hurry back again to the farmsteads that speckled the landscape. But a lot of these were deserted ghost farms now, with just a few remaining buildings in disrepair or ruin. Atel flew low over some of them as the afternoon grew warmer. The air was drier here than they were used to. It parched their throats.

"Why all the ramshackle places?" wondered Boca. "Don't men care?"

"They did, once", said Atel. "They came here long ago to grow the wheat and raise their families. The homesteads were small but well kept. Then the weather turned against them. The rains failed and the fields turned to dust. They lost everything and went away, and the places fell into ruin. There used to be more, but many were burned or buried, leaving only the windmills - *if* the wells were good. A lot of the windmills still stand. Like *that* one".

Their guide led them down to a tall metal skeleton in the middle of a vast wheat field. A few wind vanes still clung to the wheel assembly at the top, one of them by only a single bolt so it clattered as the big wheel slowly spun in the breeze. It took a decent breeze to spin the dilapidated wheel, but the big directional arrow was still attached, keeping the wheel angled correctly into the wind. The leathers were good, too, at the bottom of the well and no one had ever unhooked the pump jack, so while the wind blew the old mill still pumped a few drops of water into a catch-bowl hanging by a wire. The pipe from there to an old stock tank was gone so anything more than a half-inch deep dribbled out and was lost into a cavity in the ground, but the shallow bowl was a popular water hole. Atel stopped both spring and fall on her migratory routes, and a variety of other creatures made regular stops too because it was dependable. But Atel could see a change and also a need for caution - and held the butterflies back.

"What for?" objected Yero, a little put out. She was thirsty. So was Boca. They could all see a regular dribble into the bowl, even from a distance.

"There are feathers everywhere on the ground and a sparrow hawk perched up there below the wheel", pointed out Atel.

"So? We're not sparrows".

"I've noticed. You have no feathers to lose, but I have a few. Be patient. The water won't run out, although it's less than I remember. There used to be almost a steady stream, now just a dribble. I wonder if the old machinery is finally wearing out or..." She didn't finish her thought, but it was easy to guess.

"Is the ground drying up down under?" wondered Boca. As a typical boy who grubbed regularly in the dirt, his thoughts were closer to the water table than Yero's.

"I wonder about that after the news from the herons", said Atel. "But I wonder more about all the feathers here. It seems a lot for just one sparrow hawk, and they aren't all sparrow".

"Well, he won't dare eat the Rasha La, not if he knows what's good for him", said Yero. The dribbling water made tempting little splashes in the bowl that stoked her thirst.

"Just wait. I'm expecting trouble. Don't get caught in the middle of it".

"We can drink by turns while the others watch", insisted Yero stubbornly. "I'll drink first..."

A sparrow zipped in from somewhere and beat her to it; hard to say what species exactly, there are so many sparrow cousins, and that's lucky because predators find them tasty. The little hawk dived and grabbed the sparrow as it drank from the bowl. There was a flurry of feathers. When it cleared, the hawk was perched triumphantly on the rim clutching the sparrow down in the bowl with her other talon. The sparrow could only move its beak, which it did.

"Fat vulture! You don't need me. Let me go!"

"True, I don't", laughed the hawk. "Life is good! But a falcon never lets go his prey".

"Be the first, then! I'm just dry feathers and bones, nothing for a meal. I've been starving. There are no seeds this year, if you hadn't noticed".

"So sad. But I'm not buying it. I think you came to wash down your food, whatever it was". The sparrow hawk laughed at his own wit. He wasn't even hungry, just playing with his food. Life was indeed good for him these days. He had the best hunting perch ever. Sparrows and other small birds came from miles around to drink. He'd put off his own migration for weeks and was too lazy to go now - but who cared?

"What kind are you?" he asked, trying to work up some appetite. "What kind of sparrow? I like to compare tastes. You have that black stripe on your head there. I see that a lot. What's that for?"

"Grasshopper sparrow", said the other without thinking.

"Why, you little liar! Grasshoppers, is it? There's lots of those. I'll bet you're a juicy morsel!"

The sparrow regurgitated part of a 'hopper meal and spit it defiantly on the hawk's toes, knowing he was a goner anyway. It peeved the hawk who squeezed harder and maneuvered to rip the nervy sparrow's head off, but while he was preoccupied, he was himself caught by a larger bird in a flurry of shrieks and feathers.

When the flap settled, a pigeon hawk gripped the bowl rim with one talon and the smaller hawk with the other, rudely shoving him headfirst into the bowl. The little sparrow was lost underneath.

"Comrade, you've made a mistake!" came the little hawk's voice. "I'm a falcon too!"

That drew a "Bik! Bik! Bik!" of disdain. "No you're not! You're one of those little sparrow-chasers, not much more than a sparrow yourself".

A bubbling noise came from the bowl as the new King of the Rim pushed down hard to stifle any answer. He was pleased with his catch. All too often now he had to chase sparrows too. Old barns and the pigeons that nested in them were scarce nowadays. These 'baby-hawks' made a good substitute, although they could get mean with their beaks. But not this one. He'd got a good grip on its head. He shoved it down again into the shallow water to hear the amusing burbling noises. He was a bully and liked to bully his prey. Taunt them. Have some fun before dinner! He became aware of the Travelers watching from a little distance and bullied them too.

"If you're here for the water, forget it. It'll be a mess when I'm done!" But instead of eating, he just laughed some more, "Bik! Bikka-bik!" and shoved the sparrow hawk's head under again.

Atel, ever observant, answered politely, "We'll wait. We probably have more time than you do".

"What's that supposed to mean, pipsqueak?"

"Nothing. Just ignore us. We won't be any bother".

You already are! I didn't like what you said. Were you smarting off at me?"

"Oh, heavens no! I know my place. Please enjoy your meal".

That's what the pigeon hawk wanted: A weak, belly-crawling answer! "Bik! Bik! Bik!" He threw his head back to boast. The last thing he ever saw was a pair of talons much bigger than his own.

For the third time in a few minutes there was a flurry of feathers, a short scuffle, and a new King of the Bowl Rim, but this was a large prairie falcon and he hit hard. Ping! The hanger broke. The bowl crashed to the ground along with the struggling mass of birds. The sparrow, somehow still alive, escaped, but the new King gripped both smaller hawks mercilessly. He glared around without saying a word, then lifted off with his catch and flew away to have lunch and dessert somewhere in privacy. Probably the trip was short, but it was very noisy. The Travelers could hear both smaller hawks pleading and whining into the distance.

Boca whistled softly. "Wow. Falcons don't live very long, do they?"

"Two of them won't. I'm glad you witnessed it. It's a good lesson about water in the dry country where we're going. What did you learn from this?'

"I might as well say it", answered Boca immediately, "because Yero won't think of it".

"...And?"

"If you're gonna eat - eat! Don't talk".

For that bit of fun Boca got to keep watch while Yero and Atel satisfied all their thirst at the dripping spout. But he still figured it was worth it.

After the stop, they journeyed well into the evening. The weather had reversed completely since the marsh. The air - so much drier - was also much warmer. The wind had spun around to the southwest and the next day promised to be uncomfortably warm. If water was going to be scarce, Atel figured, they had better travel more at night and seek shade during the middle of the day; but although the sky was clear tonight without a single cloud, the stars were faint. It was the haze, the fine dust that gets up from very parched earth and lifts high into the atmosphere because there is no moisture to collect on it and bring it down as rain. So, the dust hangs there forming its own cloud and germs of drought attach to it. It would not do to travel all night in such haze, especially without rest. Atel called a halt when landmarks became hard to see.

The next morning got off under protest after a short night's sleep. They had perched on a weathervane atop a rusted-out cupula on an abandoned barn. All the shingles and boards were gone leaving the bare rafters and big wooden beams open to the weather. It was only the dry climate that had kept the framework from rotting away years earlier. It no longer provided shelter for birds to nest, or even for bats. Only a few wasp nests hung under the old eaves. That was one reason they perched where they did: Boca wanted to keep some distance from the bees; that, and a better whiff of the wind. Like most wild creatures, the hummingbird could smell any change coming in the weather and hoped for one soon. But the light of dawn broke rosy red through the same haze.

Atel tweaked the butterflies' antennae, her favorite way to awaken them.

"Up and at 'em, sleepyheads!"

They looked at her and grumbled, then looked at each other and scowled.

"What's for breakfast?" asked Yero, just to be contrary.

"Butterfly weed".

"Oh, great. We used to do flowers. Now it's weeds".

"Call it what you want, but there are blossoms. Come along".

Their guide had smelled them during the night on a variable breeze and been surprised. It was late for them; but they liked sand and dry ground, and maybe they were getting everything they wanted. She had gone to make sure of them before waking the butterflies and took them now directly to the plants, as if she knew every bit of ground for miles. Like the Oo, she knew that a bit of mystique polished her reputation.

The nectar was thick, which was to be expected, but the thirsty butterflies didn't mind. It was good! It was wet! Why didn't Atel join them?

"You are forgetting your peculiarity", she reminded them. "All butterfly weed is milkweed. This variety is different but still milkweed. You can use a re-charge of poison, I suppose. Everyone expects that. But the rest of us don't want any".

Boca laughed. "It's nice to have the reputation", he said. "I wish everyone could see us do it!" He sipped hard, then struck a macho pose and gargled. It was more reminder than their guide needed of her own thirst. It was shaping up to be a long morning.

The day warmed up quickly and they hurried on while morning lasted. Several times they swooped low to investigate old windmills and stock tanks, but they had all been properly shut down years before. Hawks - big or small - perched on these, too. Maybe there was no water but there were no trees either and the towers were still the best hunting posts. Mice were the usual prey here. The wheat had been short this season, cut close to the ground. The mice had little to hide in.

They came to a shallow valley with harvested fields on both sides of a streambed. It was only a dry run now, but it went generally southwest and they followed it to relieve the boredom of the flat country. There were abandoned homesteads, but here in the valley along the intermittent stream there were no windmills, just cisterns dug by hand to collect seep water from a shallow aquifer. The cisterns remained but were covered securely or filled in for safety reasons. Yero's patience was wearing thin again as they gave one of these a hasty look-over. It smelled of water but was covered with an iron plate and a huge rock on top of that.

"With never a thought for travelers!" she grumbled. "You'd think they might leave *some* opening".

"It would attract children", answered Atel. "They would drop things inside and lose them. Probably themselves".

They discovered another abandoned place by accident. There were no buildings or any remnant of foundations, only a cistern near the dry run. It was overgrown with brown weeds and grasses and they found it simply because they sought shade from the noonday sun. It had once been covered with wood, by the signs. That had rotted away and been replaced by a rusty sheet of roof tin. There were pinholes in it, but no other openings. There was shade under the grass, however, and the metal felt cool on their feet, so they took their break and Boca soon commenced to do exactly what their guide had predicted.

He found a pebble - a grain of sand, actually, from a heap that had drifted up alongside in some forgotten spring flood - and dropped it through a pinhole. He leaned forward to hear the splash, but it went 'thunk' instead. He dropped another one, 'thunk'. Yero dropped one too. 'Thunk'. Atel just looked the other way as they took turns: 'thunk', 'thunk', 'thunk', 'thunk', *'splash'*.

Splash? Yero grinned. Atel turned back. Boca dropped another to see if he could do it too. Sure enough: *'Splash'*. He shrugged, a bit puzzled. "It's water down there *now*".

"Through the same hole?" asked Atel.

The butterflies nodded. It was odd but true. Boca did it again. *'Splash'*. "All we need is a long straw", he said.

They examined the cistern cover more closely searching for a hole big enough to slip through but found nothing. The tin was nailed down solid on one end and the other was overgrown by grass. Sand

and dirt had filled up under the edges sealing it all the way around. There was no way in. The Two resumed their pebble dropping: 'splash', 'thunk', 'splash', 'thunk'. It got on Atel's nerves. She had intended to stay in the nice shade for several hours, but the whole while the butterflies would no doubt keep this up just to hear the splash. Hard to blame them, with nothing else to do; but the sound of water every few seconds rasped on her nerves. Eventually it rubbed them raw. She announced that she was going to scout for drinking water--"since all I get here is the noise, which doesn't moisten the tongue".

With that, she left. The butterflies watched her go but it didn't seem like a big deal. There were more pressing questions, like—"Did we try this hole yet?", and "What about this one?"

A pattern developed with the pebbles. If the first one down a hole splashed, the next one usually thunked, and vice-versa. But there were no other results, just 'thunk' or 'splash'. Eventually they lost interest.

The sun was pretty hot out on the tin anyway. The wind had got up and flipped the grass back. The best shade now was under the waving grasses on the overgrown end, so they moved over under those. It was cooler, but noisier. Something creaked and scraped every time the wind gusted and they almost skedaddled, worried that some large animal was close by. They should have. But curiosity led them instead further into the overhanging grass until Boca spotted the source of the noise. It was nothing dangerous, simply a loose flap of tin. A sheaf of grass had got caught under the flap or grown there. Gusts of wind caught the grass and levered up the loose tin. That was all. The edges of metal scraping each other made the noise.

"See?" said Boca, spotting the simple answer to the riddle. They watched for it to happen again. The next gust was a good one. The flap opened wide. Who could resist? They went in.

Light from the intermittent flap and pinholes in the cover gave some clue to the dank interior. The reservoir was well built, as country cisterns usually are, with walls made of whatever stones were handy but joined and plastered smooth with good mortar. The ceiling widened out below the cover to form a dome, and a much larger room than the cover hinted at from outside. The walls fell vertically from the round dome down to an irregular ledge, the outcropping of heavy stone footings upon which the walls rested. Water was invited to seep through the footings and collect in a pool available for use; and indeed, there was a pool of dark water rising almost up to the ledge.

Proof that the cistern had once been used hung from a rusty hook just below the cover: An old wooden draw-bucket still with its rope all coiled and stowed neatly inside the bucket.

The butterflies were not foolish. They flew around and around making sure there were no spiders, moths, bullfrogs, or anything alive at all. When they were satisfied, they settled down on the flat stone ledge to discuss their discovery.

"If we had time, Boca, we could turn this into a regular stop for travelers. They could bring honey and nectar and trade it for our water. We would have it made".

"Good idea. We could charge for fishing, too. I might even trade some water for a fishing pole".

"There you go again. But if we trade the water there won't be any place for the fish. There's no fish in here anyway".

"I wouldn't trade *all* the water, Yero. Anyhow, more would probably come in. I think that's how wells work".

"There might be fish after all", said Yero suddenly. "Look!"

Out in the middle there were ripples as if a fish had surfaced and gone back down. The ripples spread out and lapped below the ledge all around the pool. As they watched, the ripples petered out and the surface became smooth again. They peered closer and saw their reflections in the water - and then a wide mouth swallowed the reflections as it came right up at them.

"Alligators!" screamed Yero. The butterflies lifted off barely in time, saved by their own reflections, or the loss of them. The wide mouth burst out of the water and chomped down just where they had been sitting, chomped nothing, and then the rest of a disappointed monster heaved himself up onto the ledge with the ease of long practice.

It was a tiger salamander, a large specimen with oversized head and external gills, the result of constrained life and ancestry. He... (Yes, he was a male, like his two half-brothers who now crawled out of the dark pool also, taking their accustomed places opposite each other on the ledge.) ...He opened his mouth and hissed up at the butterflies, a hoarse, croaking noise: "H-a-a-a-k-k-k!" The half-brothers did likewise but their threats were directed as much at him, and each other, as at the lucky escapees circling above.

The real truth was, these were only ugly noises without literal meaning anymore. The tigers had lost their language during long years of isolation in the cistern. Lost their civilization too. Life had degenerated into 'everyone for themselves and watch out behind'.

It wasn't always so. Long ago by their own reckoning, these and others had made a nice living down here, back when the cover was open, up above. It had collapsed in the flood when the salamanders had been washed into the cistern. For years afterward food tumbled, fell, jumped, flew, and fluttered in for their dining pleasure. There were civilized rules and even young salamanders.

Then a demon came and nailed the tin cover on. That was years ago too, now. The lights went out. They didn't mind that so much, but the food chain stopped. Hunger set in and stayed. Tigers fortunately can get by without much for quite a while, and they had to. Only a few cave crawlies had to suffice for the whole extended family. Is it any wonder they eventually gobbled up their young? Of course not. And it was only a small step from that to eating each other, with the slowest being first to go. The population had fallen to these three misshapen old stags several years earlier and stalled out. There was enough subsistence to keep three alive: Tiny things oozed through the footing stones with the ebb and flow of groundwater, and the stags licked the stones clean - but only in their own areas and only with one eye on their half-brothers. Starvation still threatened.

Then tiny holes rusted through the tin cover. Light returned! With light a bit of algae began to grow, and they survived a while longer on that. Now *this!* The first real food in several years had fallen in. Things were looking up! As the tigers watched, the sight of real food stirred thought in their cold brains. They remembered something from long ago. A word: "Food!"

"Oo-o-ooth", said one of them, twisting his lips to make the word. A half-brother swung his head toward him, then away again, and made a better try at it.

"Foo-o-o-th".

"Hoo-o-o-d", said the third.

Yes, things were looking up indeed.

The tigers had been expecting something. The little pebbles had tipped them off. 'Hoo-o-o-d' (We shall name them by their own speech) had been basking in the tiny rays of light and got the first pebble 'thunk' on his head, and then several more until he tired of it and moved. But wherever Hoo-o-o-d went, more pebbles soon found him. He knew something was up there, and his half-brothers caught on too. They were dimwits in many ways but not about a potential meal; so, they set their ambushes under the water, each separately, and the food came! Hoo-o-o-d missed because he was too slow, but Oo-o-ooth and Foo-o-o-th licked out their forked tongues eagerly, hoping for their turn at it.

Unfortunately for the butterflies the wind had let up outside. The flap had shut and was likely to stay shut. They were locked in a cistern with monsters and no place to perch but a slippery wall. They shouted for help, but their guide had not yet returned. They tried to push open the tin flap, but butterflies aren't very good at that, and it was wet and slimy to touch anyway. They gave it up and perched there on the wall - or tried to. "This isn't going to work", said Yero with a hint of panic in her voice. Boca already knew. He, too, was slipping.

Oo-o-ooth reared up and tried to crawl the wall to reach him. The mortar was too smooth for that, but he flicked his long tongue to learn something of the flavor, repeating his new word. "Oo-o-o-o-o-th-h-h". His breath was sour.

"The bucket!" exclaimed Boca suddenly, surprised he hadn't thought of it sooner, but neither of them had dared take their eyes off the tigers. He didn't have to say it twice. They both alighted on the rim and found it slippery too, but wide and flat enough to provide safe footing. They breathed a sigh of relief and watched the 'alligators' creep back into their dark corners on the ledge. Soon the only movement below was a flicker of tongue now and again, sometimes up at them but more often left or right in the gloom, each half-brother making sure the others kept their distance.

"We're lucky", observed Yero, trembling a little as she realized just how lucky. "They aren't really alligators, I guess. If they had long mouths like alligators that first one would have got us".

"But he *did* get our reflections", said Boca. "He swallowed them. I don't like that".

"It doesn't matter. We'll get new ones".

"It does matter! Those are in his belly right now. It makes me uncomfortable thinking about it".

"It's silly to think about".

"It's not silly! Our *other half* went down his gullet, Yero!"

"I can't believe you're upset about this".

"You should be too! And he swallowed us from behind. That was a dirty trick. I feel like I'm missing something".

"You'll feel better when you see your next one".

"It won't be the same one. I wonder how many we're allowed?"

"Lots, I think. We leave them everywhere. The waters must be full of them".

"Well, good for them. At least they're free".

"How do you know? Maybe the fish eat them".

"Better than a monster. Who knows what else he's been eating? And we're squished in there with it!"

"Well, Boca, he'll be going you-know-what sooner or later, and then our reflections will be free again".

Boca scowled at the thought. "I'd rather he burped it up". He waved and jumped up and down to get the creature's attention and burped a small butterfly burp as a hint.

The tiger heard in the quiet cistern and took the noise as a challenge. "H-a-a-a-c-c-ch!"

The others echoed it back at him, at Boca, at each other. It got pretty noisy. Even Yero joined in. "Ha-a-a-ahh!" That surprised him. Yero usually didn't go in for gross stuff - and, phew! The smell!

"Yero! Don't! Your breath smells bad when you do that".

"It isn't her", said a new voice, expelling more sickly-sweet breath. "It's me".

They both turned to face the voice. It belonged to a snake curled up in the bucket, awakened now by the hubbub and trying to decide how grumpy he should be. He raised his head up to their level and studied them more closely.

"Okay, I take it back", said Boca. "Smells fine".

He stood his ground, as did Yero, partly because of the snake charm which affects everyone some, but more so because butterflies can easily sense the difference between mortal danger and something less. This was less, for now. The snake was just waking up and not hungry, having still a partial bellyful of mice and rats from the past evening. It was a bull snake and it had been *he* - and not any rope - coiled so neatly in the bucket all the while.

"That's nice", replied the snake. "At least we won't argue about bad breath then, ha-a-a-a-hh? Do you know why my breath is so nice..."? (He glanced down at the salamanders) ..."compared to theirs? Ha-a-a-a-hh?"

The butterflies shook their heads, stepping back from the breath.

"Because I only eat warm-blooded prey. Better for the digestion. You know. Rodents, birds, the occasional kitty cat or small dog. That sort of thing".

"Any insects?" inquired Yero.

"Sure, if I can't find a decent meal".

"I'm surprised. Someone as big as you? Bothering with insects? Seems like it would be a waste of your valuable time".

"It's still fun. I think of you as 'snacks', ha-a-a-ahh?"

"Do you eat *those* things?" Yero pointed downward, thinking it was time to change the subject, but the big snake drew a sharp breath, offended.

"Never! They're *cold*. You think I would eat *that*?" He rose up higher. His eyes came more fully awake.

"Gracious, no! Forgive me; I'm just learning this stuff. But where do you find your supper? There's nothing else in here".

"You must have guessed by now, ha-a-a-ahh? I go out through the same door you came in. The *only* door. I suppose the wind blew, ha-a-a-ahh? And you came in out of curiosity?"

"For the water, is all".

"Ha-a-ah...But still, through my secret door..."

The butterflies didn't answer.

"Ha-a-a-ahh! So now you *know* and would tell others. I can't let you leave now. You must realize that".

"It's shut so we're not leaving anyway," replied Yero. "Nothing to worry about".

"But I do worry. I can't let anyone know where I sleep! So, I'm going to eat you to keep you quiet, ha-a-a-ahh?"

"Why worry at all? You're so big no one could hurt you".

The bull snake thought about that. Yes, he was big. He could hang from the bucket and reach all the way down to the water for a drink, if he chose to, and he often did. The big lizards let him have plenty of room. He was master of the cistern, yes. But outside...well, there were rivals. He often wished to complain about them, but no one dared to listen. He studied the butterflies with his unblinking snake eyes. Why not complain to *them*, ha-a-a-ahh? Yes, why not? They weren't going anywhere.

"There are treacherous beasts out in the world..." he began, writhing a little, re-settling himself more comfortably in the bucket. He glanced at the tin cover, at the angle of the rays coming through the holes. Ha-a-ah. It was early, still early. No wonder he wasn't hungry yet. He never went hunting until near sundown. Usually after.

"Yes, there are barbaric warm-bloods", he mused. "Coyotes and pumas are the worst, curse them!" He explained that it was difficult to wrap around their sneaky necks, pointing out patiently to his guests that he was a 'constrictor', that he squeezed his prey to death. "I won't do that to you, though", he assured them. "When the time comes, I'll just swallow you, ha-a-a-ahh?"

"That'll be much nicer", agreed Yero politely.

"Good! We understand each other. I think anyone would rather be eaten by a sweet-mouthed snake than a foul-mouthed lizard, ha-a-a-ahh? I'm just *nicer* that way, and yet I get complaints! Most prey are quarrelsome about it".

"I can imagine. But going back to the pumas, what's a *puma*?"

Yero figured correctly that the only chance was to stall. Maybe the snake would go back to sleep, though it looked unlikely.

"It's a kitty cat, only bigger, ha-a-a-ahh? Like kitten is to you, a puma is to me. Not many of them, not many. Even less now – *augh, augh, augh!*" The bull snake made a choking noise that must have been laughter and went on to describe an amusing kill recently - a pair of puma kittens, nearby. He had seen the mother denning and bided his time, paying a visit when the mother went out to hunt. The new kitties were left all alone, ha-a-a-ahh? They had been so easy, so small. He had crushed them both at once. Somehow the dratted mother had tracked him back here, to the cistern, but the tin cover had confounded the crabby animal. "*Augh, augh, augh!* What a whiner she was! But her kitties didn't complain. They were warm and snug in someone's tummy again – *augh, augh, augh!* - it just wasn't their mommy's".

"Any...umm...digestive problems with that?" asked Boca.

"None at all. Should there be? Ha-a-a-ahh?"

"I don't know. It's just that...swallowing a whole kitten like that, and then another - bones and all - seems like trouble".

"*Augh, augh!* Silly, silly. No problem! Kittens in one end, hairballs out the other. Snakes have wonderful tummies. I swallowed a big owl once - claws and all. He thought it was going to be the other way around! *Augh! Augh! Augh!*"

The bull snake was interrupted just then by a commotion below. Two of the tigers were locked in battle. Oo-o-ooth and Hoo-o-o-d were thrashing about the pool in a circle. That is, they had gotten hold of each other's tails and were swallowing them while Foo-o-o-th watched impassively. The thought of food had become too much. When they saw the snake stealing it, they finally snapped. Already the tails had nearly disappeared, and the battle radius was shrinking.

The bull snake was only mildly interested. "It was bound to happen sooner or later", he yawned. "You might ask *them* about indigestion! *Augh, augh, augh!*"

Now the tigers were trying to swallow each other's hindquarters, but so full were their mouths that they were silent about it.

"It's getting trickier for your reflection to escape", whispered Yero in fascination. "Who knows how many tummies it will be inside of?"

"Too many", decided Boca. "I'm going to make a new one when we get out of here. In clean water".

"He says we're not leaving", reminded Yero.

The bull snake overheard. "Now, I never said that exactly, ha-a-a-ahh? Of course you'll leave. My bathroom is outside. *Augh, augh, augh!*"

"Tell us more about puma kittens", said Yero quickly. "What do they look like?"

"Ha-a-a-ahh? Kittens are kittens, that's all". He was getting restless. The afternoon was getting on. He was feeling the first tiny hints of an empty tummy. Hints that would take only tiny snacks to satisfy. Mmmm. His snake tongue licked out toward the butterflies tasting the smell of them. Mmmm!

"What did they *sound* like?" asked Yero, grasping at anything. "When you came for them, did they scream and fight?"

"Ha-a-a-ahh!" The bull snake liked that part. He settled back once more, remembering the fun. He couldn't hear very well, of course. Most snakes can't. But he felt the vibrations. Yes, they had whimpered and mewed pathetically, only spitting and biting when he squeezed them. He mimicked the mewing vibrations, his favorite, but the thought made him hungry. He raised himself up again, to strike and swallow his little snacks. But wait! A yummy vibration, just now! A kitten vibration, ha-a-a-ahh?

The butterflies heard it too. The sound of a frightened kitten mewing. Unmistakable. It came from outside. The Two had launched themselves toward the far wall, but the snake already disregarded them. There was better prey at hand! Softly and smoothly - so smoothly for a creature so large! - the big snake uncoiled himself up out of the bucket and made silently for the exit, using the shiny top of the hook for support. He carefully put his head out the flap and probed several times with his tongue.

Ha-a-a-ahh! There it was again. The kitty vibration! The whelp must be close, very close. What luck! But all caution was needed so it wouldn't take fright. He could taste the smell strongly now, with his head outside in the open air. It was very strong. *Too* strong! *Too strong?*

That wasn't the last thought that went through the bull snake's mind, but it was the last one fit to print. Something landed heavily next to him and seized his head between strong jaws. The mother Puma had got her revenge - or begun to. She knew who ate her babies and where he lived, but the serpent was hard to catch. She had come by regularly since then, hunting him, but always in vain - until she also heard the kitten not a minute ago. Well, that was her imagination. There was no kitten here - but look who was! She bit down hard on the skull and jerked his whole length out of the lair, tossing the body high in the air then pouncing on it when it fell, screaming with vengeance.

The Butterflies, Yero and Boca

It all happened way too fast. The tin flapped shut again with the butterflies still inside; but they heard enough uproar to guess most of the goings-on and heard the rest of the story from their guide who called to them through the tin cover. She had returned in time to figure a few things out and be of some help, as usual. It was she, naturally, who had made kitten noises a minute ago.

"Luckily, only a small noise was called for", she said. "It had to be small. I couldn't imitate a loud voice".

"Like the mother puma?" said Yero. "That must be her, isn't it? What's she doing to the snake?'

But Atel didn't answer. She had to leave in a hurry for some reason. There was sudden silence up above except for the padding feet of the big cat. Something was dumped *splat!* onto the tin cover and blood began to drip through the pinholes. Then the padding feet went away. After a minute Atel returned and explained, speaking as if she were holding her nose.

"The mother has separated the snake's head from the rest of him and tossed it here onto the cistern cover. The rest of the body she tore up and threw onto the owner's dung heap. When you get out of there you can inspect everything."

"Maybe Boca will. I've heard enough. What's the weather like? We need some wind to open the door".

"Nice and calm now, but a storm is gathering. I can feel it." The hummingbird smiled to herself and added, "It might be a few days. Is everything okay in there?'

"Just peachy", replied Yero, "if you don't count slime on everything and blood dripping. There's also alligators, and now it's getting boring".

"I'm so glad I asked. Remember down there: Patience is a virtue!"

There was no immediate answer. The Two had heard that one before. But what can you do in an old cistern to pass the time? They went down to see the salamanders. The smell of blood had got Foo-o-o-th into the water. He swam in frustrated circles licking at drips. Boca studied the action and concluded that fresh snake might work well on a fishhook. Why not? Foo-o-o-th wasn't all that different from a fish, except uglier.

Yero contemplated the other half-brothers, locked in their duel. It was still a draw, but their hindquarters had disappeared also by now.

"It gives a new meaning to the 'food chain', doesn't it?" she said. "But the lesson should be: If you have bad manners, you'll soon find yourself in a shrinking circle of friends".

They laughed and it wasn't as boring anymore, and then in the next moment the roof crashed in.

Mother puma returned one last time, still full of rage, and pounced on the snakehead. But she was a heavy animal. When she landed on the tin cover, it ripped loose and collapsed down inside - sheet metal, snakehead, puma and everything. The bucket broke off too and went down underneath it all, landing squarely on Foo-o-o-th and bringing an end to the salamander clan. The rest of the debris crashed into the water on top, except for the big cat who spun around in mid-air and rebounded off the debris, leaping up and out again while hardly getting wet. In just a few seconds, the demolition was complete, the cat was gone, and it was over.

Atel appeared in the big opening to survey the wreckage and spotted the butterflies clinging to the far wall and slipping. "Hello!" she called cheerfully. "Are you still bored?" They weren't, but for now they just shook their heads.

All's well that ends well, of course, and Atel finally got her drink which she hadn't found on her scouting trip. The butterflies drank a little, sparingly, near the ledge away from the mess.

"We'd better get on", said their guide shortly. "I need something to eat and I'm sure you do too. I don't suppose there was much to eat down here".

"Oh, lots!" said Yero. "But not civilized food".

The Two launched into an account about the salamanders and all the ugly things that happened, and possibly were still happening beneath the wreckage; but of course, the tin covered it all up. There was no evidence to show. Foo-o-o-th was dead under the bucket and his half-brothers, no doubt still cannibalizing each other, were quiet about it.

Their guide laughed, taking it only half seriously. "I don't doubt there are lizards in here that looked bigger in the dark", she said. "But a bull snake and a puma are enough trouble for one afternoon in an old cistern. I don't want any more".

The butterflies opened and shut their mouths silently, and then just left them shut. Their guide had a point, and the 'alligators' were pretty much a dead issue anyway.

They flew on for the rest of the hot late afternoon to make up some time. The shallow valley with its little dry run joined a wider valley with a bigger dry run. Their guide kept to a southwesterly course, flying low and close to the high ground on the western side to take advantage of the earliest shade, and hopefully any dew that might begin to collect in the shadier nooks; but when shade arrived, there was no dew. A dry north breeze got up instead.

Sagebrush took over the landscape and began to crowd out the grasses. It wasn't Atel's favorite shrub and the odor was part of the reason. The butterflies made faces too and turned their noses away from the strong, bitter smell. The lack of moisture and the sagebrush persuaded their guide to turn southeasterly.

"We've come too far west too soon", she announced. "We'll get all the sagebrush and desert we want later, so while there are still civilized lands to follow, we'll follow them".

They crossed the valley to the east side, then left it entirely and entered a region of flat fields separated by dry, meandering sloughs. The crop here was also wheat or had been. The dry sloughs were thick with cattails and tall reeds gone dormant or dead in the drought. Thousands of blackbirds, mostly, perched on the reeds now in the evening, waiting for dawn to resume their own journey south, but not waiting quietly. It seemed odd to Boca that there were so many other kinds of birds with them.

"What about 'birds of a feather', and all that?" he asked. "Are they going to argue all night in there?"

"Some will, because they're different. But they have a common purpose together. The bigger the flock, the safer they all feel. Maybe it improves their odds, who can say? But the flocks sure do attract predators. Every hawk, every owl, every carnivore for miles around is hunting, or will be tonight. Just be thankful. The flocks draw attention away from us".

They flew on. The sloughs fell behind as the earth healed its scars. Endless flat fields opened up before them again, separated only by an infrequent road or barbed wire fence. The wheat had been poor here. Parts of fields had been abandoned, not even harvested. A few were tilled and re-seeded for next year, but nothing had sprouted. An occasional milo field popped up, the drought-tolerant sorghum, but it hadn't done very well either. Still, Atel made straight for these hoping for aphids; yes, the tiny stalk drillers that suck out plant sap. But there weren't any. Patches had been abandoned in the milo too, but there was no sap in the shriveled stems for aphids to live on. There were only the grasshoppers who can live on no water at all (so they claim).

A new morning came. A bone-dry dawn. The sun jumped up eagerly to bake the earth all over again. The Travelers stopped by mid-morning to hide up under the eaves of a straw stack - an old stack put up back in the days of horse farming when the only big machines were the whistling, smoking steam engines and the threshing machines they pulled from field to field. The wheat was brought to a stationary thresher in those days and the plains were dotted by the straw piles left over. Cattle came then and ate into them when snow lay deep on the fields, sculpting the stacks into giant mushrooms, turning them into cheap barns really, with half-roofs all around and some shelter against the wind.

It looked risky to the butterflies. There were nest holes everywhere under the eaves where birds had tunneled into the straw, although the birds were gone now, in late autumn. Swallows had excavated most of the holes originally; but after them it might be home to anything from sparrows to snakes. With this in mind, their guide took a good whiff of every nest she could find. There were

243

snakes in two holes - or had been recently - lower down near the ground. She marked these with straws but didn't take any other special precautions. The butterflies decided to perch upside down, as butterflies sometimes do, and were in no danger out under the eaves of the stack. She herself chose a hole with a good view and explored it thoroughly. Then she perched on her doorstep and took a nap. Everyone napped.

They slept like babes until mid-afternoon when they were awakened by an ear-splitting noise that came from nowhere, apparently. Search as they might it remained a mystery. Finally, they resumed their naps and had just got back into pleasant dreams of honey and spring water when it happened again. This time Atel got a suspicion, a fairly accurate one after the second blast.

"We're sharing our hotel with an owl", she surmised. "You may as well go back to sleep if you can. I'll watch. Don't worry about missing anything. If it happens again, you'll wake up".

It wasn't very long. The butterflies hadn't even got back to sleep when the noise split the air a third time.

"Screeeeeee! Screeee! Screee! Scree!"

They all saw him. A small owl, much smaller than his voice, poked his angry face out of an upper hole in the straw stack trunk and shrieked his head off. Then he simply turned on his heels and walked back inside.

Atel went to the owl's hidey-hole and called to him. No answer. She called again, very nice. Still nothing.

"Very well!" she decided. "We'll wait for him. Nobody's getting any sleep anyway".

"What's his problem?" asked Yero.

"I'm not sure, except it's become our problem".

"Is it really an owl?" asked Boca doubtfully. "He didn't look big enough to carry off a skunk".

Atel laughed. "Like Kagu? No, that would take a Great Horned owl. This is a relative. A Screech owl, I believe".

"I believe it too. But how do you know it's a 'he'?"

"He's loud. That should be reason enough", declared Yero. "A girl would be more refined".

"Don't start with that," warned Atel. "I mean it! He's just small. The boys are smaller. That's how owls are. Shh! He'll be back pretty soon".

Almost on cue the screech owl came again, strutting and tilting side to side as he came. He looked even angrier this time. He stopped at the very brink, leaned out toward the sinking sun, and sounded off.

"Screeeeeee! Screeee! Screee! Scree!"

The butterflies plugged their ears. The little owl turned to go back inside. Atel tapped him on the shoulder.

"A word, please. You're keeping us awake".

The owl trotted inside as fast as his stubby legs could take him, to where it was darker. There he stopped and swiveled his head completely around to face them, keeping an inward bias with the rest of himself.

"You're early", Atel told him. "Look! The sun is still up".

"Not for long!" declared the owl. "I'll make it go away!"

"Fine. Can you do it with less noise?"

"Don't tell me my business! This is my job! I need to be loud! *Really* loud! So she *HEARS* me!"

"Oh, for Pete's sake!" exclaimed Yero. Boca just chuckled.

The owl looked at Yero, then back to Atel. "Who's he?"

"Not 'he'. He's a *she*. *SHE'S* a she!"

"You a guy too?"

"No! Now hold on, please! Why do you think we're boys?"

"You got good volume! Not like *her!*" He meant Boca. With that, he swiveled his head back inward and marched out of sight.

"It's late afternoon-ish", said Atel quickly. "I think we should move on. We need to..."

"We need to straighten him out!" shouted Boca.

"He called me a boy!" shouted Yero. "The moron!"

They huffed and puffed just like the owl. Atel saw nothing but trouble ahead.

"You need a plan", she suggested when there was a short pause. "You can't out-bluster him. You are way too small to beat him at his own game".

"But it's so unfair!" blustered Yero. "He says all those outrageous things and just walks away without letting us answer!"

"And he'll do it again", promised Atel. "He'll leave you just as mad every time if you don't wise up".

"No!" vowed Boca. "We'll get in the first licks next time!"

"Forget it! He's bigger and louder. You need to outsmart him".

The butterflies, sullen, said nothing.

"Try being *extra nice* - wait! Hold on! It's like this: He's young. He lives alone. He has rude habits, probably because no one has said a kind word to him since he left the nest, and maybe he was kicked out of that".

Atel wasn't finding any sympathy but at least the butterflies were thinking again. Yero, anyway.

"Why does he think I'm a boy? Just because I was loud?"

"Would you rather he called you a girl for that reason?"

"Any reason would be fine".

"I doubt it. What are you thinking, Boca?"

"He thinks I'm a wimp, that's what I think".

"Because he called you a girl?'

"What else? What is he - *blind?* I've got muscles!"

"Actually, he *is* somewhat blind in the daylight, so don't take that to heart. In the dark he would probably see his mistake".

"Then we'll wait until dark".

Atel rolled her eyes. Yero turned on Boca. "Are you calling me a *wimp*?"

Their guide stepped between them at that point. "Stature and toughness are not issues between butterflies", she lectured. "But they are with owls. The boys are smaller. Maybe that bothers this one. I'm sure there are good reasons to give him a break".

Just then the owl came marching back out and launched an encore at the setting sun. It was the loudest screech yet and he puffed up his feathers afterward. There! The stupid sun ought to hear *that* and vamoose! He was getting hungry and anxious for sundown. Oh, cripes. The vagrants were still hanging around! Didn't they have ears? The owl was surprised. He'd never had trouble getting rid of tramps before. He retreated a little way into his hole and swiveled his head to study them. They were getting on his nerves, interrupting his work! He turned about and marched out to the doorway to give them an extra blast.

"I just want to know", said Atel quickly before he could do it, "Are you one of those Great Horned owls we've heard about?"

Whoa! *What??* The little owl paused. "Maybe", he said gruffly. "Why do you ask?'

"You're so big! You're huge compared to me. And you have those horns."

Hey! This was more like it! The little owl raised himself up on tiptoes, so his horns brushed the ceiling of his tunnel, and laid it on thick: "I get asked that a lot. But if you can believe it the Great Horns are even bigger than I am".

"It's hard to! You're a boy then, I take it?"

The screecher was instantly suspicious. "Why? What made you say that?"

"Same reason. With a lot of folks, it's the boys who are biggest, so I just thought..."

"Ah!" The owl relaxed. "Good guess! Right on. But most of the boys aren't as tall as I am".

This was quite an exaggeration for the late fledgling he was, a candidate for smallest owl on the Great Plains. But be all that as it may, the screecher was talking nice now. It seemed like the right time to introduce everyone. To be polite, Atel asked the owl's name first.

"Screech!"

The Travelers were ready for it this time. In actual fact, his mother had named him "Peach" because he was a paler red than the other owlets. He hadn't liked the name and chose his own.

"Goodness! How *owlish!* I'm Atel, a lady hummingbird, naturally much smaller than yourself..."

Screech fluffed his feathers and nodded, very dignified.

"...and this is Yero, a girl butterfly, naturally smaller as well..."

"Pleased to meet you", said Yero, forcing a sweet smile like Atel had instructed. Screech mumbled something, hardly bothering to look.

"...and lastly, this is Boca, a noisy boy".

"Just watch your mouth! I'm no wimp!" shouted Boca, remembering to use the loud tone but forgetting everything else.

"You *are,* compared to me!" retorted the owl. "And you're last too! That means *least!*"

"Baloney. It doesn't mean anything!"

"Ha! It does! But with owls, it's best. I was last to hatch, and Mummer said, 'The last and the least are the most important. It will be your job every day to scare away *Ix!*'"

With that he took a deep breath and loosed another blast at the sun, now settling quite near the horizon - and marched importantly back inside.

"What was *that* about?" asked Boca in frustration.

"They never forget!" marveled Atel. "That's lucky for the rest of us if their story is true".

"Well? Who's *Ix*?"

"We know her as the sun, though she was once a great bird, mother to all the hunting hawks. But the night is ruled by Oolwa the moon, mother of owls. If I tell the story, you will understand him better, enough to get along maybe. I'm hoping he'll give us some advice about local water holes - maybe even supper. Does that interest you?"

— The Last and the Least —

In the Beginning when the earth was finished the Lord left his great birds: Oolwa, the moon, and Ix, the sun, to light the skies with their bright eyes, and watch over the lands night and day by turns while He went on to other works.

For a while they did as He intended and there was balance in nature, since they had each of them two bright eyes in the Beginning, and so the world was well lit. There were no shadows, no hidden places for mischief to hatch.

But there was rivalry between them. Before too long they began cheating on each other, wanting more than half the sky. Often, they flew ahead and appeared in the sky early, before it was their turn, or simply lingered in the sky after their turn was over.

They quarreled until a fight started - a battle that nearly ruined the skies of the world. In their fury each put out an eye of their enemy, and so the skies dimmed from what they should have been. Nature marched on, but differently in many small ways.

The mice were the biggest difference. Their natural enemies could no longer see them easily, so mice increased ten-fold, then a hundred-fold, and finally overran the earth.

About that time the Lord returned and was not pleased with the mess. He considered how to get things back into balance and decided to put the great birds to work for a while with some stones.

First, He directed them to make nests, each on their own opposite sides of the world. When this was done, he scooped up a variety of stones and put in Ix's nest, and another assortment in Oolwa's, with orders to sit on them and keep them warm.

"Waste of time!" protested the birds. "If mice have become a problem, let us hunt them! We'll fix that in a hurry".

"I doubt it", replied the Lord. "You'd start fighting again the moment I leave. Just sit on the rocks! One day they'll crack open and I'm hoping we'll have an answer to the mouse problem. In the meanwhile, I shall return each day to check the stones. I'll know if you've been sitting on them or not".

"How long must we sit?" they grumped.

"As long as it takes", replied the Lord.

Something in his tone persuaded them to behave, and in a few weeks the stones cracked and split open. A clutch of baby hawks hatched out under Ix, a brood of owlets under Oolwa, as many and as varied as the rocks. It came as a surprise to the unexpecting mothers and they might have abandoned the little ones to their fates - except they were so cute! Cute enough that the great birds stuck around and raised them. Then, again, the Lord returned, complimenting the mothers and excusing them from their chore.

"It's time for everyone to leave the nest", He informed them. "You mothers need to get back up into the skies. The mouse population has just gone crazy while you've been nesting. Say your goodbyes and I will see to the youngsters".

The great birds did so, and they behaved a little better afterward since they had family to worry about, but the Lord spoke to the fledglings and assigned them the task of hunting the mice. The clutch of hawks was given the daytime so Ix could watch over them; and since the Lord was in a hurry to get results, He spread them all around the earth without delay.

But the owls were given the night under Oolwa's eye and the Lord assigned the odd-looking bunch to various regions, each to a different place where their special talents would help most against the plundering mice: The snowy owl went to the far north, the burrowing owl to the south, the others to lands in-between. But the great horned owl, because he got along with everyone in the nest, was given to roam at will whenever Oolwa ruled the sky.

With that the Lord turned to leave and heard a noise behind Him, loud and insistent, and lo! There was still a fledgling remaining, a very small owl who had been overlooked.

"Well?" said the Lord doubtfully. "What are you good for?"

The runt rewarded Him with a screech many times his small size. The Lord was impressed and felt a little guilty too that the smallest one had almost been forgotten.

"I'll give you the most important task of all", He decided. "It will be your job every evening to remind Ix that her time is up. She'll hear you! And since you look like your big brother, the great horned fellow, you can hang out with him".

***

Atel finished the tale. The sun had set by now behind a hazy horizon, making a beautiful twilight. The butterflies watched it go down.

"Honestly", said Yero. "Do you think Screech had anything to do with that?"

"I have my doubts. A lot of folks do. But we aren't owls. We don't know their story like they do. They believe it. We all believe in the stories we grew up with, so who's to say? My advice is, don't laugh at any folklore. There's usually some truth behind it".

Screech came swaggering out to his doorstep. Ix was gone and he took full credit. He reared his head back and screeched at the sunset for good measure. The butterflies plugged their ears again. Atel looked away until it was over, but she complimented him.

"You did it!" she said. "Good job! Now what?"

"Breakfast". The owl began to make little snap and crackle noises thinking about it. He went back in and re-emerged with a favorite bone, working it around in his beak. It was too long to swallow, too thick to crack, but it was his habit to chew on one of these while he planned his hunting trip of the evening.

"Perhaps a cool drink somewhere...?" suggested Atel.

Screech nodded; mouth too busy to speak. He managed to snap the bone after all and busied himself with the marrow.

"My friends and I are thirsty", Atel continued. "Do you mind if we tag along for a drink? Water is hard to find these days".

The owl tried mightily to break the bone again, finally gave up and tossed the pieces overboard. There were quite a few such pieces strewn on the ground below. He looked both ways, as if someone might overhear a secret, and said quietly, "Not water. Not to drink. Apples! Do you like apples?"

"Love them! Will you take us there?"

"Sure!" Screech was more easy-going now that his chores were done. That's true of almost everyone, but especially screech owls and a few others whose work is so important. He took off and even looked back several times to be sure they were still following.

"I'd like to know how we're going to eat an apple", muttered Yero.

"Good question!" replied Atel. "How thirsty are you?"

"Pretty thirsty. I don't think there'll be dew tonight either".

"No, there won't. Too dry. Too warm. But we may get something out of the apples. Keep an open mind".

"That's still not an answer".

"I was getting to that, searching for words. Okay, I know how it is with butterflies. Drinking nectar, sipping water and all that. But now you'll have to learn to chew your food. We'll eat bugs".

Yero gasped, lost her rhythm and fell behind. Boca was more curious.

"We've never done that. What kind of bugs?" Butterfly teeth vary from negligible to insignificant and they know it. There are even jokes among them about their family name, and how they couldn't eat the butter out of it, to say nothing of the fly. But Boca, being a boy, had once pictured himself sitting down to such a meal, spreading the butter over the fly to make it smoother.

"Aphids, I hope", answered the hummingbird. "They'll be full of apple juice - sweet, like nectar. It'll be food and drink all in one handy snack".

"How big?"

"Very small. You can suck them up with your tongues".

"Like lumps? I've had lumpy nectar. It's not that bad".

"You'll do just fine. How about you, Yero?"

"No thank you. I'm not eating anything that moves".

"Aphids hardly move at all. You won't even notice".

"I would notice lumps. I would know they were sliding to their doom when I swallowed, and they would know it too. Would they scream?"

"I've never paid any attention".

"You've eaten them before?"

"Certainly; and a good many other insects too. It's all part of a well-rounded diet for hummingbirds".

Yero gagged involuntarily and fell back again, but quickly caught up. She didn't want to miss anything. If their guide ate insects - well, was anyone safe?

"What *kind* of insects?" she asked.

"Not butterflies, since you are obviously worried. Small bugs. Unfriendly types. Is that better?"

"Yes. What then? Hornets or spiders?"

"Spiders. Small ones. Bees are too big".

"You really eat spiders?"

"Yes. Little red ants too, and mosquitoes. Lots of mosquitoes and gnats".

Boca grinned. Yero at least didn't gag again, but her stomach rebelled philosophically.

"It seems so much like taking another life", she mumbled.

"Oh, it is. The whole world is that way, in case you hadn't noticed. Often there is no nectar, as you know. Sometimes there's no substitute. Then what? Nobody wants to sit down and starve. That's just silly. So, the Lord put in checks and balances, like the owls to eat the mice. I do my share too. I especially like to keep the gnats in check. They have a great tangy flavor".

"I guess I'm thankful someone eats the pesky ones".

"Don't be squeamish, Yero. If we find aphids, I want you to chow down".

"Chow...what?"

"*Swallow* the lumps. Chew if you have to".

"I want to see them first. Maybe ask---"

"Don't start with that! At least don't bother *me* with that. Anyway, you've eaten aphids before".

Yero didn't answer right away.

"You've had lumpy nectar, just like Boca. Some of the lumps were aphids. They're all over the flowers sometimes".

The owl slowed in the moonlight. The endless wheat fields were interrupted by another abandoned farmstead. No buildings or windmill remained. All had been bulldozed into a pit and covered over years earlier. A big windbreak had been ripped out too, but an orchard had been left.

Someone had kept it up until recently. The trees were well-pruned apples and plums, but the fruit was fallen and rotted on the ground except for one tree that held its apples. Some just do. There are stubborn ones that refuse to drop their fruit. This one refused to even drop its leaves. When that happens it isn't natural, and it wasn't natural here. The tree had been attacked by bugs as the apples were ripening, causing the leaves to malform and curl around the green fruit. As weeks went by the leaves turned brown and the apples did ripen, but all the stems held tight, so nothing fell. The rosy apple aphids were to blame, as Atel hoped, and they had now migrated from the leaves to the apples so thickly that the fruit appeared even redder than it really was.

Screech immediately attacked an apple like the Travelers only wished they could, taking big bites out of it. He wasn't here for the aphids or even the apples, just the juice. Everyone finds water somehow during a drought or they won't live to see the next one. So the owl chomped a fresh apple, but the Travelers prepared to dine on secondhand juice.

"Here we are!" said their guide cheerfully. "Find a place at the table". She, herself, didn't alight. Didn't have to. That's a nice part of being a hummingbird: You don't have to touch anything you don't want to. She busied herself licking up the bugs - just red specks really - that crowded on the apple, drilling through the skin in their slow way to draw out the juice. There were several ladybugs dining on the aphids too, and she gave them a nudge. They took the hint and flew off to another apple.

"Oh! They really *are* small, aren't they?" said Yero, relieved about that part at least.

Boca just nodded and found a place to land, a place for his feet without stepping on aphids. He studied the assigned meal and just went ahead and sucked up a plump aphid - partly out of curiosity, but mostly to awe Yero. In this, he was successful.

"What does it taste like?" she asked after a bit. "Does it move?"

Boca rolled it around in his mouth, thinking about it. He couldn't detect any struggle and said so. That was another relief to Yero. Then he bit down and popped the aphid. "Think of them as little grapes", he said. "Slurp the juice and spit out the skin".

Yero landed very carefully after several tries. "Will they crawl up my legs?" she asked suddenly. Boca shook his head, already popping his next 'grape'.

She wouldn't have done it except she was so thirsty, and the grape comparison helped. She did one, popping it right away so there would be no question of - well, she didn't want to feel it crawling around in there. Hey, it tasted like apple!

Things went better after that. "The second one is easier than the first", said Boca, and it was true. After a few each, it began to sound like kids popping bubblegum on their side of the apple. Over on her side the hummingbird just wolfed them down whole since she needed a lot more.

The owl was finished by now with his apple and ready for some nice warm mice. He flew to the tip top of the tree and hooted three times, testing the air, then screeched into the night and waggled both wings, bidding farewell. Away he went, and this tale doesn't tell if he survived the great drought, but it doesn't have to. Anyone can guess he'll be peachy fine. But down where the Travelers were, supper was about to be interrupted.

They came from all directions when they came, dozens of them, and surprised the butterflies: The dairy ants, coming for their aphid-cows. The Two just gawked as the ants quickly sorted through the aphids picking out the fattest and fullest for milking, and threw them over their shoulders, several to a bunch. The bloated aphids bounced and jiggled as the ants scurried over the apple looking for more. In almost no time they had grabbed up all the very nicest ones the butterflies had been eyeing.

"Hey!" shouted Boca, recovering from surprise. "Where are you going with our grapes?"

"This is *our* apple!" hollered Yero.

The ants ignored them. Boca reached quick as a thief and picked an aphid off one of the ants that was heading for the exit. All the ants caught on to that in an instant and approached him belligerently as a group. The one who had been robbed stood forth, hands out.

"Give!" he said. "Give back!" The message was strong, but the voice was so small that Boca didn't take it seriously. He sucked up his recovered aphid and spit the empty 'grape skin' back at the ant. This turned out to be a wrong message to send. The ants attacked and Boca got a toe bitten before he retreated into the air. Atel heard the disruption and came to see.

"They're taking our aphids!" said Yero indignantly, sounding like an entirely different girl.

"It's their work", said Atel. "There's no stopping ants".

"Eat them!"

"No. Too many. We'll just find another apple".

They went way to the top of the tree, thinking the ants might not go that far. Atel wasn't pleased at all when she heard the whole story.

"We'd better eat as fast as we can. You'll have a bad reputation now, Boca. And word gets around fast with ants".

"They started it".

"Not really. They've been tending these aphids for weeks, probably. They *own* them, I should say. They carry them back to their big ant nest somewhere. I almost feel sorry for these worker ants. They work like slaves except they seem to like the job. They're *all* girls, *all* work, *all* the time. 'Milk maids' describes them pretty well".

"They milk the aphids?'

"Back at the nest, sure. Then they bring the aphids back here to fatten up again".

"You mean we've been eating their little *cows*?" Yero was getting squeamish again. "So maybe some tiny baby ants won't get any milk? We shouldn't do that".

"Don't go soft on the dratted ants!" grumbled Boca, rubbing his wounded foot. Atel was wrapping it with a strand of spider web. It stung and Boca was putting up a fuss. The hummingbird explained that the sting would soon go away and the webbing would keep dirt out while the wound began to heal. The wound was small, in spite of all this to-do.

"Well, Boca, we *did* eat a lot of them", asserted Yero. She looked over the new apple. In the moonlight it appeared almost solid with aphids, including lots of fat ones. "I think we should leave these".

"Not me!" retorted Boca and went after them with a vengeance. So did Atel, fully expecting the milkmaids to arrive before long. Yero held back, debating the fairness issue.

"Let's do like this", suggested their guide. "Since there are lots of them here, we can safely have *some* and it will still leave plenty for the ants, don't you agree?"

Yero couldn't think of a good argument, surrounded by such a bounty. She reluctantly ate another, nagged by her thirst, but without any enthusiasm.

"We'll each have three", continued Atel, "and then look things over. If it seems thinned out, we'll stop".

That was very reasonable, so they did. Boca popped his loudly to take his mind off his sore foot. Yero was so slow they had to wait and nag her to finish. Then they took stock. It was impossible to count but even Yero had to admit she could see no difference. They did it again, and there was still no difference. For a final test, Yero determined to take hers all from one spot. But when she had done so - and called attention to the empty spot - it wasn't there anymore. Boca laughed and Atel continued to lap up supper. The proof was everywhere.

Yero stubbornly did it again, on her own, and this time kept her eye on the empty spot so she could call for witnesses; but even as she stared at it, the spot filled with miniature, pint-sized aphids.

"They split in half!" she marveled. "One of them turns into two!"

"Now you're getting it", replied Atel between slurps. "It's just their way of reproducing. See? There's as many as ever".

Yero had to admit it.

"Let's eat five", said Boca with his mouth full, and did so. It didn't matter how many they ate. There were always more. It was late in their season, the weather was perfect for them, and the aphids were on a rampage. In a few days, the apples would be shriveled and sucked dry like the leaves. Then the last baby aphids would sprout wings and fly off to make new mischief.

When the milkmaids arrived, the Travelers had gotten enough refreshments to go on with, and there really is no arguing with ants. It's either squash them or let them have their way, so it was time to leave. Boca voted to stay and mix it up but was overruled. He didn't like losing to girls.

"Especially girls with sissy names like 'milkmaids'?" teased Yero.

"I wouldn't call them sissies. They're tough, for girls".

"I'm glad to hear you admit it".

"I didn't admit much".

"You didn't have to. Most of us already know that girls are tough'.

"These were toe-biters, Yero! How tough is that?"

"Plenty tough, if you've ever smelled your own feet".

Boca gave it up. His foot was aching again. But another girl began to pester him even as they circled above the apple tree, waiting to set off on a course of Atel's choosing. It was a ladybird beetle. Yero recognized her from the first apple. She wanted to join them.

"Well, I doubt it", Yero had to inform her. She pointed to Atel high above, testing the winds. "I don't think our guide is counting on extras".

"I *really* doubt it", grumbled Boca. "We have enough girls".

"It's for my protection!" pleaded the ladybird. "Just a little way? It wouldn't have to be far".

"I'll ask", said Boca, unexpectedly reversing his attitude. "What's the danger?"

"It's these gangs - these new *gangs*!" replied the ladybug. "They get worse every year".

Boca smiled expansively. Yeah! This was more like it! This was how girls *ought* to act: A little frightened, a little helpless, in search of a hero. Yero stared at him as if he'd gone bonkers.

"I'll protect you!" he promised.

Yero gasped, "Boca! You didn't even ask!"

"Atel shouldn't mind. Not for just a little ways".

"Oh, thank you!" said the ladybird. "I needed someone with really big wings".

"That's me. You can relax now".

"Bless you! The gangs will be afraid of *you*! Your wings will totally bluff them out".

"Yeah. And behind that is a lot of muscle".

"Oh - I didn't mean *that*. If your wings don't bluff 'em, we're sunk. You look pretty soft".

Yero laughed. Atel came back down to report on weather conditions, which weren't improving.

"Still warm, still dry, still some kind of storm brewing. Who's this?"

"Nelli", volunteered the ladybird. "Thank you so much!"

Atel just smiled and looked to the butterflies for some explanation.

"Boca has already agreed to take her along and protect her--" began Yero.

" - only for a little ways", Boca ended lamely, but Yero cheerfully explained the details.

"It's not because he's strong or anything. She just thinks our big wings will bluff her enemies".

Nelli nodded eagerly. Surprisingly, their guide agreed. "We can use some good luck. Your family is known for it".

Nelli brightened. "Thank you! It *does* run in the family! But some worry that it's running low. The new gangs are just - "

"Excuse me!" Atel broke in. "We don't have time for the whole story. Night is getting on and so must we". She looked to the south. "We're going *that* direction. Does it suit you?"

It couldn't possibly have been better! But north, east, or west would've been just as good. Nelli really was in trouble, along with her entire family of native ladybird beetles. A new family of ladybugs had invaded the land, dirty ruffians and brawlers, larger than the natives but similar in appearance - so similar that the good ladybirds were being tarnished with a bad reputation.

"Nobody trusts ladybirds anymore", complained Nelli, trying to keep up and still pour out her story. "These gangs! They bite. They stink. They make a mess. Now everyone thinks we're *all* like that".

"I know them", replied Atel. "There's more white on their necks. I see a lot of them. They work in gangs?'

"Yes! The better to murder us! There aren't many of us left".

"Are they after you now?"

"Yes! Always! But that one promised to protect me." She meant Boca and was about to explain her reasons all over again. He fell back toward the rear.

"Fine, that's *fine*!" said Atel quickly. "I suppose you're migrating, aren't you? Where do the good ladybirds migrate to these days?"

"Into the mountains. We never used to. Too far! But we do now. The gangs haven't found us there yet. They're too stupid. They're *really* stupid!"

"That kind of talk might stretch your luck", cautioned Atel.

Nelli just laughed. "Not to worry! I have loads of luck. And they *are* stupid! They don't even know how to migrate. They go to the houses! Oh well - it gets them off our trail".

"They can follow your trail?"

"Sure. They stink, so when they find a trail that smells nice, they know it's us".

"Do they fly at night?"

"Yes, because we do. Oh, no - watch out!"

A loose gang of the invaders passed below without incident, until Nelli shouted at them. "Skinheads!"

Yero couldn't believe it. Boca could. Atel had to because the gang made a big U-turn, moonlight glinting off their hard shells, and came recklessly for Nelli until at the last moment they saw the butterflies and felt the breeze from Atel's wings. A few couldn't quite stop and careened past their very noses. As they swept through Nelli hurled more insults: "Softies! Knuckleheads!"

"This has to stop!" said Atel when the trouble had passed. "We'll escort you for a way, but only if you behave! You can't be taunting them".

"Not to worry," chirped Nelli. "I always do it".

"Why? It only makes them angrier. They'll rip you to pieces if they get their hands on you!"

"Ha! They never will. I'm too lucky!"

"No one is that lucky".

"I am! Count the spots". Nelli had six white spots on her shell, an unusually high number. She believed she was charmed with so many. And hadn't she got an escort now, too? How lucky was *that*! "All real ladybirds are lucky", she bragged. "The more spots, the better. Most have two, which makes me lucky times three!"

"Maybe it's true", whispered Boca. "More luck than brains. She'd be a goner by now if it wasn't true".

It definitely was true. Nelli proved it twice more in less than half an hour. She was having the time of her life, spoiling for trouble and looking for more. The gangs were scared of her new pals.

"Here they come again", she laughed. "Slap hands for luck!"

She exchanged high-fives with everyone, even Atel, but then pushed her luck too far by breaking formation and straying close to the gangs, the better to drive home more insults: "Stinkbugs! Dung Beetles! Ten of you couldn't catch me!" Maybe not, but about fifty of them could, and did.

There wasn't anything they could've done to save her, but it bothered Boca because he had given his pledge.

"You did the best you could", consoled Atel. "We all did. It would have worked, but she tempted fate. It's her fault, not ours".

"Her luck ran out, didn't it?"

"It did".

"Do you think she gave us some luck when we slapped hands?"

"I hope so. We can use it. But luck is a fickle thing. Don't ever plan on it, Boca. It won't come if you just sit and expect it. And sometimes when things are tough, consider yourself lucky that things aren't worse".

"That's not the kind of luck I had in mind. I was thinking of more cheerful stuff".

"Hard work and wise choices are the surest road to good luck. Anything else is wishful thinking".

Boca decided to leave it there. This was turning into a lecture on good behavior. His toe was still sore, and he didn't need any more reminders about choices. He slipped back and flew alongside Yero who was bringing up the rear.

"She's all business again", he grumbled.

"Well, that's why we hired her, I suppose".

"We *hired* her? But how will we ever pay her?'

"I've been thinking, Boca. We could be in charge of the good luck, so she doesn't have to worry about it. That's sort of like payment in kind".

"Yeah, I guess. She doesn't like to keep track of it anyway. She just said so".

"Okay, let's take on the job! Now - where do we stand? I think we've used up some luck that we started out with".

"For sure. But Atel just said that if we're wise, good luck will follow, so we're earning more all the time".

"Right. We'll add some back for that".

"And also some that must've rubbed off Nelli. I think she gave us everything she had left".

"I think so too. Quite a bit, maybe, because they're known for luck. Wow! It's a lot to keep track of, isn't it? And Atel has so many other worries. It'll help if we can lift *this* worry off her shoulders".

"That's good! We'll do the worrying! That means we aren't counting on luck, just letting it happen".

"Right. Like money going into our account that we don't even know about. But we can't let her know or she'll start worrying about *this*, too. You know *her*".

"Yeah. What do you think the balance shows right now, in our account?"

There was silence, and then more silence as they privately ticked off in their minds some close calls, unexpected meals, and narrow escapes.

"Well? What did you come up with?" said Boca after a while.

"I think - just to be safe - we should keep earning some".

Boca nodded wisely. "Funny how things turn out, isn't it? We hired her, but now we're working for her instead".

"Don't expect wages", grinned Yero. "But I suppose we could ask for tips".

"Oh no! That's why I dropped back here. She was giving me one tip after another. I'll do it for free".

Their underpaid guide did wonder for a moment what they were laughing at back there, but they never said anything about their new responsibility, because everyone knows you can jinx your luck by talking about it too much.

They made good time after that, stopping only for a short rest before midnight, and again in the wee hours to check for dew. There was none. The wind out of the southwest desert saw to that, growing gradually stronger as the fields faded away beneath them. Wheat, milo, even range pasture all took on the same scant, brown look. Almost nothing had sprouted this year, and what had sprouted never got tall. Most of these fields had been abandoned. It hadn't always been so. Straw and trash from earlier years was scattered here and there; but the new crop hadn't even got tall enough to cover the old. That proved fortunate when patches of the prickly pear were exposed in the moonlight. The small cactus was spreading, showing up in fields that hadn't been tilled in several years, trying to reclaim its old range. Atel flew low to investigate and found an armadillo working the patch, uprooting plants with his heavy claws and tearing apart the lower stems for the moist flesh inside. It's a hard living and not their favorite, but armadillos are well equipped, and well rewarded too, with a buffet of moths and other insects that come to the cactus.

Atel brought her own 'insects' to the refreshments, and the travelers were able to get water by licking inside the broken stems. It wasn't their favorite thing either, but it was water, and the butterflies were peeved when the armadillo decided they looked as edible as the next bug, and it became time to leave.

In the light of the setting moon, the hummingbird looked back more often now, not to check on the butterflies, but on the northern sky. A storm was following. That's what the south wind was hurrying to meet. A tall bank of clouds loomed there, already covering a third of the sky. But they were travelling nearly as fast as the clouds. If there was danger, it was yet a long way off.

Morning came, even dustier than the previous day because the breeze stirred it up. They kept on for a while in the daylight searching for better water, but without luck. The prickly pear juice would have to do until evening at least.

They had come to places now where farming had been unreliable in the best of times and no trace of old homesteads remained at all. Their guide hoped to find an abandoned prairie dog town, or failing that, at least some other hole in the ground to shelter from the sun, but there weren't many holes at all. It seemed the burrowing animals had gone away too, disgusted with the brick-hard dirt.

She finally settled for what there was - a patch of taller wheat stubble on a knoll open to the north so she could watch the clouds coming from that direction.

Even as they alighted on the tops of stubble Atel saw there might be trouble, but it was likely unavoidable in the area. Grasshoppers were there. Not all that many, but these were older ones, extra-large. They were eating away at the stubble in silence except for the busy chewing noises, each of them to their own stalk.

Part 3: Byways of the Butterfly

Grasshoppers don't talk like other folk, of course. They have a language of their own with sounds they make rubbing legs against wings, or whatever. Atel never understood it well and didn't much care to. She didn't trust them. They are strict plant eaters, which does help, but they're nasty about sharing their food, space, or anything else - especially with anyone who isn't a grasshopper.

The moment they landed big hoppers came up the stubble after them. Rather than resist and upset them even more she led the butterflies to shorter stubble out on the fringe of the patch. It didn't afford much shade but there were no grasshoppers.

"We aren't going to eat it anyway", she explained. "So let them have what they want".

The Two were not in the best of moods. It was hot already. It had been a long night. They were tired and thirsty, and this wasn't easy, trying to perch on the shady side of a stem. Boca gave it up and perched on top, but that was worse. The wheat had been cut with a serrated sickle that left a jagged edge. He couldn't find comfortable footing, kicked at it, and re-injured his sore toe. He climbed down to the ground for lack of any better idea and Yero joined him.

"This is no good", bellyached Yero. "There's no shade!" To be sure, it wasn't much. Only a thin picket fence pattern cast from the skinny stems. She glared over to where the big hoppers were hogging the thicker, taller stubble. "*They've* got shade", she griped. She got little sympathy.

"You can go back there if you want", Atel replied wearily, knowing they wouldn't. The big hoppers looked mean. Sure, they were vegetarians, but all that means out in the wild is, after they rip you up with their biting mouthparts, they don't eat the pieces, or if they do, they have a salad with it.

The butterflies grudgingly used the picket-shade to best advantage, folding their wings up so they almost fit into the slivers of shade. It did help a little. Then a quick gust of the south wind blew dust in their faces and they started crabbing about that.

Atel just let them crab. She wasn't as sympathetic as usual. She was more tired, more thirsty than they were. Hummingbirds use up lots of energy beating those wings, and a new worry was growing in her mind that the drought might be too big for them to cross. It could happen if old tales be true. She had half a mind to find suitable shelter and just wait for the storm to overtake them. It might mean hail or even snow this time of year, but there would be water or at least ice to chew. But the other half of her mind feared the storm. The clouds were darker than any she remembered.

She perched on the ground, not liking it. Hummingbirds are not ground dwellers except by necessity; but bare wheat stubble is nothing to perch on either. The dirt was already warm, disregarding the few slender shadows. She shuffled her feet, scratching to reach cooler dirt, and pondered what to do next. A younger, smaller hopper bounded into the stubble patch and landed nearby. It took one look at her and jumped further in. Two more arrived, even smaller, then another big one.

"Can't blame them for being hungry", she found herself thinking. Another small one arrived but bounced around the perimeter, looking for an empty spot. Atel followed it lazily with her eyes around to the north where the storm was building, nearer now, but just as dark and foreboding. The weather was different here than up north. Maybe the hoppers knew what was coming, but they weren't saying, at least not that she could understand. Another hopper bounded past - and suddenly a bad thought occurred, and she looked sharply again at the coming storm. It was impossible to guess - but if her suspicion was right, they needed to find a better place.

"Can you stay out of trouble if I scout for water?" she asked. The butterflies looked bored.

"Not much to do around here except get sunburn", answered Yero. Boca just mumbled.

Atel left fast. An instant later a big hopper landed *whump*, right where she had been. It glowered at Boca and bounded further inside where the big ones were. The action drew the butterflies out of their funk, and they noticed that the noises had become louder in the 'thicket'. The big ones were noisy about their eating habits, but there were other noises besides the snapping and munching. Some hoppers were loitering on the ground watching them and making the quivering musical sounds - first one hopper and then another.

"They're talking, I think", said Yero. Boca wasn't interested, but to Yero the music sounded like - what? Talk of some kind. She listened intently trying to guess what they might be saying, because they were talking about her and Boca. That was pretty obvious from their body language. Then she was interrupted in the middle of her thought when several groups of grasshoppers arrived all at once. Most were the larger, darker types who went straight for the tall, shadier interior, but several medium-sized hoppers took up residence out near the butterflies where there was yet room to spare.

These were lighter colored than the big ones and looked like identical quintuplets. All the hoppers looked pretty much alike, really, except the big ones were darker and had wings. The quints took only passing notice of Yero and Boca and went right into a stretching routine, extending one leg and then another. They went at it so slowly that Yero lost interest. The other hoppers were livelier and more musical.

She supposed it was the warmth of the day, but the hoppers seemed sociable. Every new arrival was greeted by the 'music', which was played by scratching legs across their fluted hind wings. The small hoppers without wings were dumb; that is, they made the same scratching movements, but without wings no sound came of it. Yero guessed they were practicing for when they grew up. There were lots of tones and actual tunes going around. Excitement. Energy. Almost a party atmosphere.

"Crack!"

The sharp noise drew her attention back to the stretching 'quints'. One had suffered a horrible accident and stood off by himself. His body had broken open, dark innards spilling out. Yero reached over and grabbed Boca's elbow.

"I don't know what happened but that one's a goner", she whispered.

Boca whistled softly at the ghastly injuries. They stared, unable to take their eyes off, waiting for the poor wretch to die, but he just stood there. His pals had backed away politely to give him room to keel over. Then it happened to another of them. "Crack!"

The butterflies saw it happen this time. The poor fellow staggered. Pieces actually flew from his body in some sort of exploding leprosy. Somehow, he stayed upright and appeared to still be alive.

"Crack! Crack… Crack!"

The last three succumbed to the epidemic, and it spread. The very noise seemed to be contagious, touching off more cases all over the stubble. Each fresh 'Crack!' sent shivers through Yero. Poor things! They were in such bad shape they couldn't even fall down. The original 'cracker' reached high with one leg, then another, in his final throes, out of his mind, trying to crawl out of his own stomach. It could only be described that way. Huge pieces of himself fell away, exposing more of the dark innards. Yuck! Gross. Yero looked away. Boca was fascinated. Presently he gave her an elbow.

"It's okay, I think. They're doing that thing with their skin. Dumping the old stuff off. Look - he's just fine".

Yero looked again. It was shocking, but true. It seemed impossible that the 'crackers' could survive such violence but there they stood, picking off loose pieces of themselves and tossing them into piles. The dark 'innards' spilling forth turned out to be newer versions of themselves, with wings, that could no longer fit inside and burst out from the pressure.

When they had thrown away most of their old selves, that was good enough for now. They ignored a few loose chunks still clinging to their backs or on their legs like tall boots, or even on their heads like helmet - unless the slag interfered with making the *music*. They seemed eager to 'talk', as Yero thought of it, obviously comparing notes about their new bodies, especially the wings which their old bodies had lacked. They reached up with their tall hind legs and strummed tunes with their toes across the rippled surface of the new wings.

Yes! Finally! The *wings*! This was their fifth or sixth and final molt, and they were perfectly tickled about it. Yero bent her mind to the music, imagining what they might be saying, and found she could guess some of it quite easily from the music itself and the way others reacted to it. This isn't surprising, really. Younger folk pick up languages quickly, and though they both would be insulted to hear it,

256

grasshoppers and butterflies are distant relatives - shirttail, yes, but still relatives. So Yero got a general idea pretty quickly and translated tidbits to Boca.

"They are thrilled with their new wings", she reported. "I probably shouldn't say 'new' because I think they knew 'about' them. Knew they had 'em inside, and stuff like that. But what thrills them most is, they can talk now in the way big hoppers do. Very proud, I think".

Boca picked up a piece of wheat straw, a stub an inch long, and held it like a musician would hold a guitar. There were parallel veins on the straw, and that's what got his attention. He nudged Yero.

"Watch. I'll talk to them".

He strummed the straw like they strummed their wings. His first tries were pathetic but soon he coaxed some noise from it. The entire patch of stubble hushed.

"They're all looking at us", Yero whispered.

"Good! I like an audience, you know".

"Yes, I know! But see? They think you're *talking*. I wish I knew what you just said".

When the hoppers had gotten over their surprise, they all started to answer at once. Yero was confused for a minute but then the general message became obvious.

"They think you're talking about the weather", she whispered. "Like you asked a question and now they're all giving their opinions".

"So? What's the forecast?"

"Shhh". Yero was learning as fast as she could but there was a lot of music all at once. "I think everyone has a different idea", she decided finally. "But they're expecting something big".

Boca glanced at the dark clouds, much closer now, advancing from the north. "Well, anyone can see that! I'll try again". He strummed his bit of straw vigorously, this time drawing much less reaction. Almost none. But the nearby 'crackers' were still watching. One of them stepped forth, a big chunk of old shell still covering his back and hanging crookedly off one wing. He made a short music, then turned away and showed his abdomen to them. The music was a little off because of the shell fragment, but Yero got the idea.

"He says you're stupid. He says it won't rain".

"Tell him he's stupid too, with that old shell hanging on him", replied Boca, and offered her the guitar.

"I'm not going to say that! I can't talk their language anyway. But now he thinks you've had too much sun".

"That part's true", chuckled Boca. "Let's work at this some more. Maybe we can earn some good luck for our guide".

Yero agreed. She picked out a fluted bit of straw and tried some hopper talk as quietly as she could. The 'crackers' watched without comment.

"Now I'll try to repeat one of their tunes", she whispered, and did her best. The same insulting 'cracker' spoke up but was polite to Yero. Even Boca could tell the difference.

"I guess I said that he has good, strong wings, and he thanked me for the compliment", said Yero. "He says we have pretty wings, but the wind will blow us...I'm not sure where".

The butterflies were catching on fast. Even Boca grasped some of the simpler tunes and learned to answer in a few notes that meant basically, "Oh, that's nice".

The 'crackers' took a liking to them for reasons that were hard to translate but had to do with just being present as they came out of their molt. Almost like blood brothers. They went so far as to open their semi-circle and allow the butterflies to join them but hanging out with grasshoppers - especially crowded grasshoppers - (A lot were arriving regularly now, hungry ones.) - does take a thick skin. They are blunt in their speech, not diplomatic at all. They expressed surprise that the butterflies had anything resembling a brain.

"Your kind are known to be idiots", said one. The others made a quick humming sound that indicated agreement.

"Why?" Yero was curious.

"Butterflies can't talk. You are the first we know of. He's still a half-idiot". That meant Boca, naturally. The others made the quick hum of agreement. Boca got it and fired off an angry reply.

"Stupid are looking you still dumb shell!" he strummed. His music was off, but the 'cracker' understood. He laughed too when he realized he still had a piece of old shell up on top. They all laughed as he tried to shed the chunk. The laughter came as a hearty exhale with rhythmic clicking noises in the mouth. Something only mildly amusing drew only a twittering rustle of wings. But it showed that grasshoppers could take it as well as dish it out.

"Where do you find water?" asked Yero, to change the subject. She expected - and hoped for - a simple answer but, alas, the 'crackers' didn't seem to understand. The music for 'rain' was as close as she could come to any understanding, but they didn't associate themselves with it at all. She endured a few 'stupid' comments too, before she guessed that a lot of these hoppers had never seen rain. They knew the music - she had learned it from them - but maybe it was only a tune passed down through generations. How do you explain water to those who have never felt it or splashed in it? She tried another tune with 'rain' in it. No reaction. She changed it slightly and tried again. On her third try, she struck a chord with the 'cracker'.

"Oh--the *dew*!" He corrected her tune, and everyone caught on. Sure, they all knew about dew. Very rare. There hadn't been any for many turns of the sun. So what? It didn't matter.

Didn't matter? Yero translated to Boca and they explained as best they could that butterflies die without at least some dew. How could grasshoppers not die from thirst?

The 'crackers' laughed. Ha-ha. They didn't need it. Didn't need rain either. So what? No need to die about it. Are thirsty? Breathe air. Just breathe the air!

They convinced the butterflies to try it, but all it gave them was parched throats. Yero pointed to the advancing storm and made music that she would wait for the rain.

More laughter. The 'crackers' even shook their heads for emphasis. No rain! The butterflies should get that out of their heads. But more and more hoppers were stealing glances at the storm too. They were well aware of it. They suddenly began a music together, almost like a vibration that went into the ground and spread out in all directions from the stubble patch, then rose quickly to a high pitch and disappeared. It didn't last long at all but had an obvious result. New hoppers bounded in faster than ever from - where? Somewhere with no food, apparently. These were gaunter, more famished. It was getting pretty crowded in the middle where the tall stubble had been. Actually, it wasn't tall anymore Yero noted with surprise. It was much shorter, and all the munching mouths were working outward from a bare spot where the tallest stuff had been just an hour before.

The 'crackers' were by now used to their new bodies and remembered they were hungry, which is their natural state. They began munching on stubble with both eyes on other munchers, afraid they might not get their share. They lost interest in talking.

Newcomers took up closer to the butterflies now, out near the edge of the patch unless they were very big or very gaunt. Then a really big one arrived in a giant leap and landed on Yero's shade-stubble, causing it to sway wildly. He commenced taking big bites from it. Her shade was about to be eaten up if she didn't do something about it but arguing didn't look like a good idea. He was the biggest hopper yet. She played a tune for him: "Where? Where did you come from?"

The big fellow stopped eating, surprised. Yero played more.

"How far? How far did you jump?"

It was a good question. The best she could've asked if she wanted him to stop eating and talk. Not that they can't do both at the same time but jumping is a source of pride with them and you'd better have time to listen if you *do* ask because they'll talk. Boast, more like it. They like an audience too, and butterflies are just right for that. Perfect, actually. Other hoppers interrupt, you see, to tell tall tales of their own.

"The last hop was best", the big fellow declared immediately, scratching away furiously on his fiddle-flank. He spoke fast and Yero had trouble keeping up, but he was describing in detail his last several hops, maybe more. Hoppers have fabulous eyes and memory for this since they must pick out good places to land, so by the time they get to be as old as this one they have memorized a lot of real estate - and told a lot of tall tales. To condense the stories (they *must* shorten them, or they will be interrupted) they have reduced flowery melodies for things like rocks and sand to simple tones, and often lump several yards of ground into a quick plural by adding a little 'click'. Like all other creatures on earth they've developed a slang dialect, not easy for strangers to follow.

Whump! Another big one landed in the dirt by the 'crackers', eyeing their stubble. It looked like trouble brewing but there was no time to think about it. Whump! Another landed on Boca's shade-stem and bit into it. Boca looked as if he might take issue.

"Wow! How far did *you* jump?" Yero asked quickly.

The new hopper glanced at the braggart eating up Yero's shade. He'd heard some of the braggadocio as he arrived and was calculating how tall to make his own story to top it. This is a normal urge, not unique to grasshoppers, but he overdid it. When he made his claim, the butterflies knew it must be wildly exaggerated because there were way too many of the plural 'clicks'. Even some of the nearby hoppers turned away and rudely waved their abdomens at the new braggart. There was some of the hopper laughter too, and the windbag decided to look for another stem and a more gullible audience.

He barely left and a new one landed to take his place, strumming a quick greeting (or warning) to another nearby. Yero wondered if this one might be a girl. They all looked the same, but some - like this one - had higher pitch. She took a chance and addressed the new arrival as a girl.

"Can girls hop as high as boys?"

"Sure, sure. Maybe higher - except for *I-Hop*, naturally. But these fellows here? Phfffft!"

That drew a sharp rebuke from Yero's hopper. He'd got back to eating and devoured several more inches of stem but stopped now and lectured the female arrogantly. Whoever *I-Hop* was, that's what *all* males were in his view, and the females should be grateful for such heroes.

There was selective laughter nearby. Yero guessed that the amused ones were the girls in the crowd. The big fellow got huffy about it. When he was upset, he ate until he felt better, and it didn't take long. He virtually swallowed the rest of the stem like a sword. Only the hammering of his mandibles proved that he actually chewed it.

"Who is *I-Hop*?" asked Yero.

There was a short silence. All who heard looked north to the menacing clouds before answering. Then, there was such a cacophony of answers that all detail was drowned out; but the general movement indicated that Mister I-Hop was well regarded.

The big hopper, still mad, still hungry, jumped recklessly into the middle of the patch, bumping others on landing. It was thick with hoppers in there now and the stubble was nearly all gone. Yero was amazed, and doubly so when she thought what the stale, dusty stuff must taste like, and what little food value could possibly be in it anyway, after bleaching out in the sun. But taste and food value don't matter much to those who are near starvation.

Still more hoppers arrived, bounding recklessly into the patch. These were smaller and even skinnier. They hadn't come any further maybe, but their speed out in the open would be less with shorter hops. None of them had wings, though some reminded Yero of the 'quints'--stiff and standoffish, as if they might crack apart too, the moment one looked the other way.

"What's going on?" whispered Yero. "Is this the only food left around here?"

"They sure act like it", answered Boca. "Let's fan our wings so they don't take us for something edible."

They backed away to be safer. Storm clouds had swallowed the sun anyway, so shade was everywhere. Another rush of hoppers arrived, the smallest ones yet. Yero felt sorry for them. They jumped bravely into the fray but there was little left to eat, and the big ones were quarrelling over that. It was getting rough in there. One of the little ones was trampled and disappeared behind a lot of big legs. The others jumped back out and bounced around the perimeter looking for scraps. There weren't any. Several hopped over to the butterflies out of curiosity and looked up with unblinking eyes. Yero played a tune for them.

"Are you hungry?"

The little ones hopped backward in unison, surprised at speech from an alien. But they understood. One or two lifted their legs and scratched at their smooth sides where fiddle-string wings might someday be. It made no sound at all. There they sat, pathetic.

It took several tries but Yero taught them to answer questions with a shake of the head, up or down, like real folks.

Was this the last food, this dusty straw? "Yes", came the answer. So, it was true. They had now reached the bone-dry heart of the drought. Nothing at all had taken root this year, or even several years running.

Did they expect to make many hops further, then, in search of food?

"No", came the answer, surprisingly.

Were they doomed to die right here?

"No", again. Yero doubted if they understood.

"How old are you? One molt?" Yero had to change her music several times before they caught on. Finally, when she was sure she had the music right otherwise, she busted her straw instrument over a knee at the end of the composition. Crack!

That did it. "Yes! Yes!" They understood. They were first molts and quite proud of the accomplishment. What's more, by their body language they wished they could eat her instrument. Yero broke the pieces again and passed them out.

Boca handed his over to her. "Take it", he said. "It wouldn't be right if you couldn't talk". Yero accepted with dignity and asked another question of the little hoppers: Were they the smallest?

"No". There were even smaller cousins - the nymphs.

"Still out there?" Yero waved at the dusty flatlands.

"Sure", came the casual answer.

Too bad for them. Mother Nature is harsh at times. At least out on the prairie everyone expects it. But time was running out fast for sad stories. The storm was rolling toward them from horizon to horizon. The butterflies began to worry about their guide. Where was she? Then the song commenced.

The swarm (by now) of hoppers was making a communal music. They had reduced the considerable patch of stubble to a few dirty stubs, too grimy even for a hopper to chew, and now beseeched the heavens with a prayer. That's what it sounded like, anyway. They all pitched in except the 'dumb' ones with no wings, who were now shunted outside the main swarm but still hung around.

But this music was more than a composition or even a concert. It was a symphony and Yero didn't understand a lot of it, but she caught on to the tone for 'I-Hop' early in the music and guessed that this was part of the story of their race. The hoppers seemed to think they had some sort of agreement with the Lord and were invoking what they called 'The Rule of One'. It was hypnotic and the butterflies were lulled into a dream world with the rest.

—I-Hop—

The story of the grasshoppers doesn't go all the way back to the Beginning like a lot of stories. In fact, most of the Green Earth had already been comfortably settled much as it is today. Nature had found a pretty comfortable balance. But the Lord's work is never done because we - *all* of His children - have minds of our own. That's how He wants it so we can learn and grow, but the lessons we learn aren't always the right ones, and growth is often in the wrong direction; so He set up experiments in the early Ages to correct a few things gone awry.

The beasts-who-ate-other-beasts had been too successful for one thing, and grass eaters had dwindled. Something more was needed to control the grass. A newer, *swifter* grass eater would help, He decided.

He set up a proving ground in a desert oasis, in the Dry Quarter of the earth. Here were lush grasslands, plenty of water, and the usual small animals; but the Lord introduced new varieties of antelope, very fleet afoot, to see if they would eat enough grass to be useful. He finished by ringing the oasis with sheer rock walls so the experiment couldn't get loose by accident.

A problem arose when the new antelope turned out to be finicky. They ate the new green shoots, but nothing else. They turned their dainty noses up at brown leftovers from the year before and this straw was choking out new growth. Something had to be found to eat the straw, and He introduced grasshoppers to do it - an ingenious idea provided they did what they were told. He created a goodly number of them, making them small so they could hide in the straw for protection, and had a word with them, revealing their purpose and the features of their new environment: The cozy grasslands, the waters, and the surrounding barrier walls.

"This is your world", He said.

The hoppers were only wingless nymphs and had no speech but one of them obviously wished to answer. The Lord showed how to make musical sounds by scratching on rough stems of the old grass and appointed this their language, to be understood by other creatures as well if they bothered to listen. The bold nymph 'spoke up' immediately.

"Do we get this world to ourselves?" His scratching was amateurish, but the Lord understood.

"No", He answered. "Snake is here, Mouse is here, and Frog is here. The big antelope are here also, to eat the grass. They like the fresh green shoots. You grasshoppers will eat the old straw".

"Oh. And what do Frog, and Snake and Mouse eat?"

"You, mostly. You will serve an extra purpose as a prey species since there are so many of you".

"Jimminy! We'll be wiped out in no time".

"No, no, no. The plan is, you'll increase so fast that you'll hardly notice some loss".

It didn't work out as planned because the nymphs were timid. They were tiny and knew they couldn't escape if a predator spotted them, so they hid in the straw hardly daring to move, eating very little.

When next the Lord looked, things had gotten worse instead of better. The antelope were unhappy because new growth was scarcer than ever, Frog and Mouse were hungry - having found the nymphs tasty but not very filling - and Snake, who couldn't see the little nymphs very well, was hunting Frog and Mouse instead.

"What gives?" asked the Lord when he found I-Hop, the bold nymph, hiding under the straw.

"We can't escape from anyone so we must hide", explained I-Hop. "Make us bigger".

There was some merit in the idea, so the Lord spoke a word and the nymphs molted into a larger size.

"How's that?" asked the Lord.

"Better, but it's a question of confidence, Sir. I can only speak for myself, but I would need to be much bigger still before I dare venture into the open".

After consideration, the Lord allowed half a dozen molts - at *most* - ignoring I-Hop who kept asking for more. The nymphs were confused with numbers, so it actually varied from four to as many as seven, but the molting proved to be a huge success. The hoppers gained all the confidence they needed and more. The whole ecosystem sprang to life and bustled with activity. The Lord was pleased and returned to His Great Works. It wasn't the first time He'd had a practical tip from little folk.

So, the experiment raced toward success. The big hoppers brashly hopped everywhere in broad daylight confident they could jump high enough to escape the predators. Snake, mouse and frog changed tactics and caught lots of them but as the Lord had predicted there was a baby boom and the hoppers hardly noticed some loss. Best of all, the antelope fulfilled their promise, gorging on the new grass and keeping it nicely under control.

When next the Lord checked it was good and He turned out most of the antelope to take their place in the greater world. Then the experiment was sort of put on the back burner and neglected, which led to mischief.

With less antelope in the oasis, some of the tender new grass went uneaten. Some hoppers took a liking to it, as they shouldn't, preferring it to the straw. I-Hop was the first of these and there were others. It led to a feeling of cockiness, of being upwardly mobile on the social ladder. I-Hop became a daredevil, a swashbuckler. He was the highest jumper of them all and it fed his ego. He wanted more.

"I will no longer be hunted!" he vowed one day. "I'm better than our enemies and I shall challenge each of them to a duel".

The straw reverberated with what could only be cheers as admiring hoppers scratched gleefully on the stems. The celebration was interrupted by an annoyed hiss when Snake appeared unexpectedly. The other hoppers bounded quickly to a safe distance, but not I-Hop.

"I accept", said Snake, who had heard the boast. "Duel to the death, I presume?"

"That's the idea", said I-Hop rashly. "Are you hungry?"

"Always. I did have some of you for breakfast, but you can be for lunch".

"Well, sorry. You're scheduled for last. Have patience".

"Who'sss firssst?" demanded Snake, beginning to drool and slur his words.

"Mouse. But listen, here's what I have in mind. You'll like it". He whispered the plan. Snake did like it and coiled himself on top of his usual sunning stone while I-Hop went off and challenged Mouse.

"Great! I'm famished!" responded the kangaroo mouse. "What kind of duel?"

"We jump over a big rock. Whoever jumps farthest wins".

"That's all? Then I eat you?"

"If you win, sure. If I win you must promise never to hunt me again".

"Lead the way", laughed Mouse.

The moment I-Hop turned away Mouse leaped for him, but I-Hop expected it and hopped quickly back to the rock, making sure it was close at the end. As they went over the top together, Snake struck upward, catching Mouse in mid-leap and swallowing him - also as I-Hop expected. He knew Snake would go for the bigger meal. I-Hop bowed to the cheers of his crowd.

Next was Frog: Bigger, stronger, a better leaper than Mouse, and every bit as treacherous. I-Hop bounded from one lily pad to another out to Frog's lair on the biggest pad of all. Frog was busily zapping mosquitoes.

"Want something bigger?" challenged I-Hop, skipping the niceties. "Catch me if you can!"

I-Hop turned and headed for shore and the sunning stone. He didn't have to synchronize this arrival - he barely got there alive. As they went over the top together Frog opened his mouth to eat him but was himself snatched and swallowed.

I-Hop was in his glory and his crowd was merry as crickets. He boasted that this victory also was well planned: He knew Snake would strike for the big frog - a much more worthwhile target.

"Wrong", interrupted Snake looking down at him, chin resting on the stone. "Our duel is next, so I knew I'd have you anyway. Go ahead. Jump whenever you're ready".

"That I will!" declared I-Hop. "But you must agree...in the unlikely event that you miss..."

"--*Very* unlikely".

"...Yes, but if you miss you must agree to swallow your own tail instead".

Snake readily agreed and coiled himself. I-Hop jumped. Snake struck upwards but being already heavy with Mouse and Frog came up short. Egads! How embarrassing! The crowd cheered wildly.

"Keep your promise!" insisted I-Hop.

Snake was mellow enough, with two big meals already, to humor the crowd. He took a length of tail into his mouth and spit it out again. Oops--wait a minute. He *tried* to spit it out and couldn't. Snake teeth curl backward to keep their prey from escaping. Each time he tried to spit he swallowed more of the tail. We'll leave him to his dilemma, probably to become the first of the mysterious 'hoop snakes' we've heard about.

I-Hop was a hero, entitled to seven wives, but he yearned to be a legendary folk hero. He gambled it all for more.

"I will out-jump the Bird", he announced one day.

This was ridiculous and met by stubborn silence. Everyone - even his seven wives - decided he had finally flipped his lid.

"Not just *any* bird, either", bragged I-Hop. "I will out-jump the Eagle!" A few hoppers stuck around to watch. Not many, but there were some witnesses. An eagle did take up the challenge and I-Hop leaped onto his back. The eagle flew higher and higher but couldn't shake him and was forced to carry him around the world. I-Hop saw everything and wanted it all.

"Take me up, way up!" he commanded, scratching out the words on a rough feather. "I wish to speak to the Lord".

The eagle went up as high as an eagle can fly, but it wasn't high enough to catch the Lord's eye. I-Hop jumped from there, even higher. Luckily, it was just high enough. The Lord noticed him. I-Hop waved urgently.

"Lord!" he thought (for he had nothing now to scratch on) "Lord, hear me before I fall!"

"What is it?" answered the Lord, hearing his thought, "I'm pretty busy".

"I've seen the world and I want to go there".

"Forget it. I'm keeping your bunch in the oasis. You could be trouble outside".

I-Hop wanted at least a chance at it. "If I can hop to the top of the walls will you let me leave?"

"No!"

Hang-time is limited, even for a springy fellow like I-Hop, so he began to fall.

"Lord, give me wings like the Bird", he pleaded, "or I'll surely die when I hit the ground".

The Lord hesitated. That was the last thing He wanted to grant, but He couldn't help admiring I-Hop's courage. He deliberately held up on the request to instill some fear in him; then, at the last moment granted I-Hop one extra molt, with wings, making sure I-Hop glided back into the Oasis.

"Now that you can fly, you are *forbidden* to fly out of there!" admonished the Lord. "Repeat that to me".

I-Hop did and bowed very nicely while he was at it. Nobody sasses the Lord - not even a legendary folk hero, for that is what he had become. He chose 27 wives, which is customary for a folk hero, and thought: What next?

I-Hop did stay in the Oasis for a while, but it's hard for a folk hero to settle down. He remembered that he wasn't forbidden to fly *within* the Oasis, so he did, which added even more to his renown and led to an interesting discovery: When the sun was high there were updrafts along the cliffs. All he need do was spread his wings and the thermals took him up - even above the walls. Oh, how he longed then for the outside world!

Now, beneath his folk hero image I-Hop had some low, lawyerly instincts. The more he thought about it, he saw where he could split hairs on the precise definition of 'flying', and escape without technically violating the Lord's wishes. Terms like 'soar', 'glide', and being 'buoyed up' came to mind.

But why escape and be alone? I-Hop decided to take several generations of family along to keep him company. They had all taken after him and inherited wings, adopting the more convenient grasshopper 'speech' still used today.

"Green grass!" promised I-Hop, and the new generations volunteered, because even brown grass was becoming scarce in the Oasis. With the demise of Mouse, Frog and Snake the hoppers had increased dramatically and competed with the antelope for what little forage was left.

Next day when the sun was high, I-Hop showed how it was done, jumping into the updraft and spreading his wings. Up, up he 'soared' and 'floated' over the cliffs, leading his clan to the Promised Land. It wasn't quite as advertised, being after all the Dry Quarter of the Earth, but if the grass was sparse, at least there was no end to the pasture.

For several years they chewed their way outward from the Oasis, becoming quite an army, until a year came without rain. They survived that too by eating absolutely everything. But the next year was just as dry and they dared not fly off in search of greener pastures lest they appear on the Lord's radar. Yes, they had laid low in their encroachment, but now I-Hop figured it was time to come clean with the Lord.

"Make us a great music", he told his following. "Sing a song of all our good intentions, all our trials and tribulations, in hopes the Lord hears and pities us in our need".

The Lord heard it - quite a racket from an unexpected direction. He recognized I-Hop, now in old age.

"You did it anyway, didn't you?" He scolded.

"Yes, Lord", admitted I-Hop. "But there were extenuating circumstances..." He went on with a list of excuses and loopholes while the Lord pondered the problem. The lawyer stuff irritated, but what could be done about lawyers? He ignored it for now. The big question was this horde of hoppers - *with* wings - totally out of control and expecting permission to keep going. What a mess!

Nevertheless, I-Hop's instinct was sound. This was the Lord of Light, not darkness. After a long, sobering lecture, He showed mercy. Yes, they could use their wings in great need, but *only* then. Only in the worst of times when the *last blade* of brown grass had been eaten - and then only *one hop* as far as they could fly without stopping. *And* they must ask permission each time, as they were doing now.

The hoppers quickly agreed. As luck would have it for them, a big wind came up, boosting them much further than the Lord probably expected. But He had left already, being busy as usual.

It's worked like that ever since. The hoppers do respect the rule, but the favorite trick is to ask permission in the face of a storm; and they take the noise of the wind to mean 'yes' because that's how they remember it.

***

The butterflies came out of the trance to see their storm nearly upon them. Thoughts blew through their minds: "A nasty one, but at least a drink" was quickly replaced by "If we survive it!" followed by "What *is* this? It sure isn't rain!"

It wasn't. It was one of the horrible dust storms that plague the Dry Quarter of the world when it gets *really* dry and becomes a playground of the Four Winds.

The crazy hoppers welcomed it. In the moments before the dust-wall struck they were a merry bunch, crouching to hop as high as possible at the right moment. They were well equipped to take the beating to come with their suits-of-armor, their hard, outer shells. Some would be smashed or buried under blowing dirt, but most would likely survive. They were I-Hop's descendants, a race of daredevils.

In the moments before it hit, desert voices spoke through the wind. The drought had awakened them, but the wind was their cat's paw, and they are the claws. A moaning, groaning noise descended upon the land. Hoarse, vengeful voices came for them.

Another voice, faint but much closer, jerked the butterflies back to reality. "The *Wust*", shouted their guide. "It's the *Desert Devils!* Let's go!"

They heard. Boca took off immediately. So did Yero, but a pathetic little nymph caught the corner of her eye, just now straggling in from open country to join his elders, the littlest one she had seen. An orphan! She grabbed it by the arm without really thinking and followed, with difficulty. Atel took notice and said something Yero couldn't hear. Then the storm hit.

Part 3: Byways of the Butterfly

They had just time to get ahead of the blasting sand to cleaner air where the surge actually helped them, like riding the crest on a breaking wave of water, and all they need do was surf the tumbling air with sand nipping at their heels. But if they faltered for even a moment, the wave would roll over them and crush them.

The nymph was a problem. What did Yero expect? It caused trouble with her aerodynamics just trying to hang on to the twerp who seemed to be having the time of his life, leaping forward repeatedly. He was imitating his elders behind them, the wingless ones who came leaping out of the churning mass like popcorn out of an open popper, sometimes only just missing the Travelers. The dust-wall immediately swallowed them again, but there seemed an endless number. The storm had swept up many swarms in its path.

Boca couldn't imagine what they got traction on to leap forward like that. Then one of the leapers did hit him from behind, just a smaller one but it knocked him off course for a moment and he guessed the answer: They were so thick in the churning dust that each one kicked off of the next. But there were other things in the rolling cloud too. Ugly sights. Dead or dying hoppers, wingless ones, came into view often. The butterflies quit looking back.

The full adults - the big, winged hoppers - were in the air above riding the gust front much like the Travelers, but up higher because of their style. They were not airfoils like the butterflies and had to beat their wings to stay airborne, perhaps lucky now to be starved and skinny.

As for Atel, she always beat her wings in a blur anyway. If the wind helped her, it wasn't apparent. She kept an eye on Yero and the 'orphan', ready to snatch the little thing in her beak if it caused too much trouble. It was on the verge of that now, kicking Yero in the side, trying to leap ahead. She pulled him up short each time and he fell back - only to kick off again. As miserable luck would have it, their arms and legs got tangled and the nymph kicked off her face instead. Yero got a foot in her eye, another in her ear, and let go of him in alarm. The nymph sailed diagonally forward, landing on Atel's back, and clung there - perfectly behaved, for whatever reason.

"Don't drop him!" Yero shouted. "He's an orphan".

The hummingbird, exasperated, had half a mind to swivel her head around and eat the little bozo. She didn't, expecting him to leap again soon like an idiot and be gone; but her body vibrated from her labor and that seemed to calm the thing. It stayed put.

The dust storm barreled southward with nothing to slow it. The prairie was flat in the middle of the storm where they were, so the center bulged forward and a lot of the cargo and passengers slipped off toward the flanks. But the prairie was wide, and the flanks stretched to the horizons. It was near evening and they were near exhaustion when they slipped off the edge into a barren, broken land, in the shadow of mountains, and were dumped like rubbish up against a fractured rock wall.

The wind didn't suddenly quit, mind you. It only tossed them there in a lull between strong gusts. More gusts blew by regularly, showering them with dirt and debris, including one very large, very dead grasshopper. They cowered against the rock lacking enough energy to find better shelter.

But not the nymph. He'd had a fun ride and now grew bored before the others had even caught their breath. He jumped off Atel's back, bounced curiously over to the big hopper carcass, and up onto the top like he was playing 'King on the Hill'. But he didn't keep the crown long. Even as Yero thought wearily about fetching him, a coachwhip got there first, appearing out of the dust and spotting the fresh corpse. Not sure if the big hopper was dead, the snake reversed itself in the blink of an eye and lashed out with its long tail, expertly smacking it with the whippy tip. Snap! It made a loud noise and sent the carcass rolling. The startled nymph jumped off but was ignored as the coachwhip set about swallowing its kill headfirst.

It happened before the exhausted Travellers could react, and their main thought was, "Well, that's lucky. It could've been us". But the danger was over for now, until the snake completed her swallow.

"If you're going to grab junior, do it now", advised Atel.

Yero fluttered over with an effort and took the orphan by the arm. He didn't resist. Who would, after seeing what he just saw? But the coachwhip hoped they would stick around and be dessert.

"Hey! Do'd leath tho fatht!" said the snake with her mouth full. "Leth' thalk".

"You want to talk?" asked Yero, guessing at the garbled words. "I don't think so. You'd eat us".

"Thure, thure", agreed the snake. "Bu' nod now. Nod yed".

"That's no comfort. How much can you eat anyway? That's a big hopper".

"I ea' lotth. *Big* thoood!"

"You shouldn't talk with your mouth full don't you know that? It's bad manners and hard to understand you".

The snake's eyes gleamed angrily. She said nothing more but worked all the harder at swallowing the hopper. However, the carcass had run into a snag. Due to talking-while-eating the food had got wedged sideways in the gullet. The coachwhip stretched her head forward and retched to clear the occluded passage. That didn't work and was very embarrassing. Snakes are famous for swallowing huge, ungainly prey. They take pride in it. Yikes! She hoped her sisters couldn't see her like this.

"That's better", encouraged Yero. "Just work at swallowing. Don't talk"

It was maddening for the snake. There were some choice things she wished to say! But the butterfly was right, much as that irked. She put her considerable muscles to the task again, but in vain. Her eyes began to water. Snakes aren't even supposed to do that.

Ridiculously, the nymph jumped onto the coachwhip's head. Yero went to fetch him and there they sat on the forehead, right between the eyes. Atel spoke up. She had seen it all and hadn't worried while the snake was ingesting, but this was getting out of hand.

"We need to leave", she ordered Yero. "Say goodbye".

Yero laughed, still a bit slaphappy from the storm. She somehow knew that she was safe for the moment. Boca joined her and stepped in the snake's eye. The coachwhip foolishly tried to curse and the carcass jammed into her windpipe. She gasped - to the extent she still could - and that got the dead hopper lodged in there for keeps. In her moment of mortal doubt the snake paused and the nymph jumped down onto her nose. Yero scolded and scooped him up on the fly. Boca followed and the whippy tail cracked only inches behind him. The coachwhip, dealing now with more pressing problems, almost killed them accidentally as she beat herself about the head in panic. She writhed and flopped against the rock wall making such a commotion that another meat-eater overheard. An odd bird came running and grabbed her, snapping her neck as unnecessarily as she had snapped the dead grasshopper, and disappeared with her so fast there was a dust trail. "That's more luck", thought Boca. "That might've been us too".

"What was that?" he asked.

"A *Roadrunner*, they're usually called", said Atel.

"Goofy name for a bird. Who calls them that?"

"The men who build the roads and drive their things, their automobiles on them. Roadrunners can't fly. They just run, very fast. Especially on the roads".

"As fast as the automobiles?"

"Maybe, but they run the roads mostly to pick up snakes that the autos run over. They eat snakes".

"I think it's the end of that food chain, then. The big hopper choked on the dust, the snake choked on the hopper, and now that bird will choke on the snake".

Atel shook her head. "No. She'll beat it till it's tender and probably rip it to pieces for her chicks".

"I hope she starts at the front then", said Yero, "so she sees how it choked. Then she'll warn the chicks against swallowing big chunks".

"Oh, don't worry about the chicks. They'll want the treats first anyway".

"Is there such a thing? We're talking about snakes".

"Sure there is: Whatever the snake ate that isn't digested yet. The 'treats' are nice and soft".

Yero looked away. Boca laughed. Their guide turned to the future, relieved to put the coachwhip behind. They had survived the dust storm, but that was all.

Let's go", she said. "We need shelter". They needed water too, especially the butterflies, but she didn't bring it up. The butterflies would soon enough. She herself had found a seep and got a drink while they were with the grasshoppers, but that bit of refreshment was many miles behind now. It had sustained her through the storm, but she was dehydrated again. The butterflies must be too. The next drink had better not be too far ahead.

Now, as if he understood the word 'go', the nymph went a-hopping along the rock face, around a corner and into a hole before Yero could stop him. Atel went in after and by the time the butterflies came inside she had explored the place a bit. It was roomy, most likely used for a den. The size of the hole suggested a coon or ringtail, or even a bobcat or small fox. But there was no scent of them and any signs outside were covered up or blown away.

"A snake has been here", she said. "Possibly the coachwhip, I don't know. Snakes smell a lot alike to me. There's an odd smell farther back that I don't like, maybe the toilet, but nothing I can see or hear in the dark back there. I think you should be okay for a few minutes if you stay near the door. I need to find water for us".

She left and Yero looked proudly at the nymph. "He *must* be good luck, Boca, to get us through the storm. What do you think?"

"Maybe, but I don't think it's his own luck. I think we're earning it for him. He's a terrible pain".

"Don't let him hear that! He might take a bad name to himself. Let's give him a nice one instead".

"I suppose you have one in mind".

"Yes. We've heard about I-Hop. That sounds so *hopperish*, doesn't it? I think they should all have names like that".

"How about 'Flip-flop' or 'Tip-top', or 'Lollipop'?"

"That's very nice, Boca, but I was thinking about 'B-Bop'".

"Okay, why?"

"It sounds like dance. I think B-Bop could dance if I showed him how. Is there anything we can play music on?"

"Nothing. Just sing to him".

"Oh, you know they need that scratchy stuff! See if you can find something to play on, will you? I want to teach him his name".

Boca grumbled and went out. The wind had pretty much died leaving a smattering of debris plastered against the rock wall and scattered about, but mostly just dirt and sand. No guitars that he could see. He heard some twangy sounds from inside and went back empty-handed just in time to see the nymph leap up and hit his head on the ceiling. He looked dazed when he landed. Yero had one hand on an old spider web along the wall and the other over her mouth.

"I shouldn't have done that", she kept saying. But when B-Bop straightened up, she smiled in relief. "Spider web scares them! Did you find an instrument?"

"No. We could try *that*, maybe".

'That' was a string of beads mostly buried in the sand near the doorway, seven or eight strung together in a loose row several inches long.

"I don't know", said Yero doubtfully. "What is it? Seed pods?"

"Of some kind, I guess. But now: Drums!"

Boca hopped from one bead to the next, kicking them as he went. They were hollow enough to resound, but at a higher pitch than he liked. Butterflies, in a few words, are more 'ping-ping' at drums than 'BOOM-BOOM!

"Sounds more like a xylophone", laughed Yero. "But see B-Bop? He likes it!"

He sure seemed to. Maybe it was the vibration in his toes more than the beat in the air, but he commenced to jig, first with one foot, then another, in a sort of soft-shoe routine. It needed some imagination to see a routine, and still more to match it to Boca's rhythm on the drums, but Yero imagined it.

"He only needs practice", she said. "Keep it up! I'll try to teach him a few moves".

Yero joined in, awkwardly. B-Bop was herky-jerky, and it was tricky to synchronize. When it proved impossible, she decided to invent grasshopper dance as she thought it should be.

"Do like this", she told the nymph, disregarding the language barrier. "I'll call this the 'Grass-Hop'. You can teach everyone when you grow up and do it on holidays".

Yero swayed gracefully one way, then the other, like a grasshopper on a tall stem in a light breeze. All hoppers should catch on to that, she figured, and B-Bop did, so she added a second movement, a climbing motion in time with the first. Climbing the stem! B-Bop watched and tried to imitate, but he hadn't any experience climbing stems in his young life. His version expressed itself in odd little hops. Yero didn't see much promise in this either. While Boca experimented and B-Bop reverted to his soft-shoe routine, Yero changed the choreography.

"We'll do the 'Ants-Prance'!" she said. "This should be good for picnics. No one wants ants crawling up their leg, so here's what to do about it". Yero imagined herself back at the apple tree - and here come the ants! She began a lively hip-hop on tiptoe to keep away from the imaginary ants. It was easy for Boca to accompany because it required mostly lack of rhythm. B-Bop caught on instantly and in no time was better than his teacher. Well, it's hard to out-hop a hopper.

But things happen when youngsters hop too much. B-Bop felt nature calling and stopped the Hop to make a new movement and a deposit on the floor of the cave. It wasn't - as they say - *messy*, being a bi-product of the drought, but it did smell. In surprise and disgust, Yero executed a backward 'moonwalk', holding her nose. Her student, ready now to resume dancing, watched closely.

Wouldn't you know? The nymph imitated her perfectly. Kids often pick up best on things they shouldn't. Boca started laughing, hardly able to play the drums.

"That's a serious mess!" shouted Yero. "Who knows how long Atel might be? Meanwhile, we're stuck here with the smell".

Boca didn't stop laughing but he changed the stomp to a somber, marching beat, with pauses for giggles. The student took the lead now with his own idea: When Boca took time out to laugh, B-Bop hopped gingerly up to the bad thing on the floor. When the marching beat resumed, he covered his nose and 'moonwalked' away again.

"We have a new dance, I guess", said Yero. "We might as well call this 'dirty dancing'".

She joined in and before long Boca had them both hopping curiously up to - then moonwalking back away from - the offending bit of lost luggage, doing the yo-yo in opposite directions. In the reverse Yero backed farther into the cave and B-Bop backed toward the entrance. It was fun, but Boca soon slowed down and the pauses became fewer and further apart. B-Bop went all the way out the door finally, and Yero disappeared back into the gloom of the cave, but she could be heard complaining about the smell back there too. That was the end of the fun for her and she came back to the main room. Just then something outside startled the nymph and he bounded back in.

Maybe it's just bad luck playing drums on old rattlesnake rattles. The previous owner of the rattles had been out of the den hunting all day and finally coaxed a rabbit into striking range where she sunk her fangs into the bunny's leg. The doomed creature had escaped and run some distance while the rattlesnake took time out to rest and congratulate herself. Soon the rabbit stopped due to trouble with his leg, then limped further and stopped again. The venom was beginning to tell, and the bunny knew he must find a safe place to hide up. Drowsiness was coming on. The bunny remembered a place nearby, a hole in the rocks where he could have refuge. With a great effort, he struggled to his feet and headed for the hole.

The rabbit is what B-Bop heard. Its head suddenly appeared in the doorway blocking out most of the light, then the whole animal squeezed inside - a tight fit. Its eyes were wild, its nose quivered, catching the same smell from the depths of the cave that had disgusted Yero a minute ago. The rabbit did an about-face and squeezed back into the doorway but could go no further. There it stuck and died, totally blocking the door except for tiny slivers of light from the setting sun that slipped between its wedged ears.

The butterflies had barely time to shrink against the wall and now wished they had made a dash for the door while it was still open. The few rays of light illuminated a narrow ledge high up on the low wall and they flew up to that. The ledge was roomy enough, up next to the ceiling, but still no higher than the top of the doorway. Yero called for the nymph but couldn't see him. Then another noise came from outside, a lisping voice.

The mother rattler was calling to her babies. She was as disgusted as anyone at the behavior of the rabbit in his final moments, blocking the dratted door. He'd done just a fine job of jamming himself in there! Now her babies were locked in the den and her outside.

She had borne her dozen offspring early that morning and gone for breakfast as hungry as a horse with room again for a big meal, but the blasted storm kept the usual prey hiding up all day until Lady Luck finally smiled and brought the bunny hopping along. She had teased him close with sweet words. That was half the fun, outwitting the stupid prey. Very satisfying. But who could foresee *this?* The blockhead had blocked the door! *Now* what?

She felt a twinge in her rattlesnake heart and called again to the 'Worms', her pet name for them. She hadn't formally met them yet, just birthed them, but they should be out of their birth-sacks by now. Rattlesnake babies are so eager they sometimes wiggle out of those even as they're being born and bite their dear Mum on the way out. Happened to herself once. Cute little hooligan, that one! As foul tempered as you could ask. Crawled directly out the door into the big world looking for someone else to sink his fangs into. It was a proud moment for a mother, but only a short moment. The running bird got him just outside the door. He should've waited for a bit of advice from his dear Mum.

That's all there was time for, usually. Just a bit of advice. But the cute little Worms were so busy biting each other and showing off their fangs it was hard to get their attention. In a day or two they would be gone anyway, but Dear Old Mum knew there was more to survival than just a quick strike and strong poison. She tried her best to pass on some wisdom.

She called to them again. No answer. Well, they probably couldn't hear with a stupid corpse in the doorway! Or more likely, they were playing back there - biting each other and denying it, telling their first little white lies. She smiled at the thought and hissed proudly. Little fibbers! They'd better get sneaky pretty quick. They would be fair game for herself one fine day, the moment they left home. Her motherly instincts stopped cold at the front door.

She got hold of a not-so-lucky rabbit's foot and tried to jerk the corpse out of the doorway but couldn't. She finally gave that up and began to swallow the leg. She was hungry, as we have learned, and sinking their teeth into the prey is not as risky for rattlesnakes as with ordinary snakes. If they can't swallow a whole creature, they simply squirt a few drops of venom and the mouthful rots off before too long.

Inside, the butterflies figured things out pretty quick. Mum's voice was muffled but obviously serpentine. They'd met enough snakes to recognize the language, and the smell too. Her odor found its way inside along with the rays of the setting sun. The smell from the back end of the cave was snake too, Yero now realized, but weaker and fainter, like most wild babies.

Noises came from back there now - not the usual slithering and rustling of snakes but more like the pitty-pat of animal feet. Suddenly B-Bop came into view and Yero called to him. He made a very big jump for a little nymph and landed almost on top of them, frightened at what was following. A stampede of something-or-others had pursued him. They all three leaned dangerously over the ledge to see what it was.

It was Mum's dozen 'Worms', of course. They had heard Mum. They had seen B-Bop. They had quit fighting and raced down the winding cave passage looking for someone to bite besides each other. It was the oddest stampede ever. They were sidewinders.

The whole bunch came down the tunnel crossways, reaching out laterally with first one part of their belly, then another, and pulling themselves sideways in stages. Rapid stages. So rapid it sounded like feet running down the tunnel but was instead the ploppity-plop-plop of snake bellies on the hard floor. They passed beneath the ledge, nipping away at other siblings who happened within reach and came up short at the big dead rabbit where they started milling and quarrelling.

It was a 'baker's dozen' actually - thirteen in all - and they were true sidewinders eager to get out and bake in the hot sun, or if it had gone down at least bake in the hot sand. That's one theory behind the odd propulsion: That they love the hot sand, but it would burn their hide if they slithered in it, so they do a dance to touch it as little as possible, like tiptoe-ing.

Mum was aware of them now with her mouth full so she couldn't 'coo', but they smelled her. They stopped quarrelling for a bit and called to her, trying to sound as sweet as possible since they needed help; each trying to sound more virtuous, more deserving of sympathy than the others. They were natural actors. It didn't fool their Mum one bit, but it spurred her sense of duty.

She withdrew from her bite. Her teeth were mostly into the fur as yet anyway. The babies must be named! It was the only formality in their culture and must not be neglected. It must be done properly, too. The names must be nice to match each little darling in their sweetest mood. There isn't much time. Young sidewinders are born with a limited supply of sweetness and need to save most of it for treachery later in life.

Mum announced the chore and waited, knowing it would be a little while before the 'Worms' settled on some pecking order. Judging by the noise it was clear they weren't using up any of their sweetness. She looked around suspiciously. The sun was down and the sunset fading, but a bright moon had already taken its place. She was not in the safest position here. Sidewinders - even a two and a half footer like herself - have enemies: The great owls, the running bird, and many furry animals including coyotes, bobcats and large weasels. They all know that sidewinder flesh is tasty if they can get past the fangs. Foxes are fond of saying it tastes 'like chicken'.

Inside, the Worms had bloodied each other some by now, but settled the order and recovered their sweetness. The first Worm spoke up, asking for a name and offering a nice word of thanks to the whole litter for voting her Number 1. It was a total lie and drew angry hisses. Mum smiled.

"You are *Honesty*", she announced proudly. It was from tradition like all their favorite names, to fool the prey.

"You are *Princess*", she told the second, also a female. Good names were occurring to her quickly now.

"You are: *Sweetness, Faith, Innocence, Credence...*" Mum paused a moment. #7 had apparently got a nasty wound in the tail and was grumpy from it. She heard him loudly complaining. His little voice was accusing.

"Patience!" counselled Mum, and on a whim decided that could be his name. The Worm didn't like it, but so what? He wouldn't be happy with anything right now.

"*Pleasance*", she pronounced, moving on. "*Trusty, Chastity, Precious, Angel, and Sincerely*. Now repeat them and smile your prettiest smiles. These are the innocent faces you must always show others, so they'll come *closer*". She laughed, a sound very similar to the bull snake in the cistern with a hint of lisp from the fangs, and resumed her bite on the rabbit's leg, greedily now - her maternal obligations more or less finished.

Inside, the Worms rehearsed like Mum told them:

"So pleased to meet you, Princess!"

"Delighted. You are such a gentleman!"

"Always. Did I mention my name? I am Sincerely, at your service".

"How sweet! And who is the handsome chap next to you?"

"This is Trusty, noble fellow. Trusty, please meet our Princess".

They rose up and bowed formally, fleetingly touching forked tongues. Only the best etiquette. It was the same all around, daintiness and courtesy. If there was any weak link in the decorum it was Patience, who had his reasons.

"How nice to see you, Patience!" others would say. "A shame about your poor tail. Surely it will heal over time"; or, "Dearheart, may justice be served to whoever did that!"

All twelve siblings offered their sympathy. Patience confined himself to one-word answers and watched for hints of guilt, occasionally twisting around to suck a bit of poison from the wound. The poison didn't affect him at all, but everyone's tastes slightly different and he was collecting clues.

Up on the ledge Yero was scandalized at the goings-on. "They're practicing up to be crooks and liars!" she whispered. "We should do something!"

"No - we shouldn't", said Boca. "Let them be".

"Well, I'm going to ask Atel to report them".

"To who? I doubt if there's any law around here".

"What about that Roadrunner?"

"There's an idea. But this bunch hasn't actually broken any laws yet, have they?"

"They're sure going to! First chance they get. If I was sheriff, I'd just hang them all at an early age!"

"Without a trial?"

"It should be a short one! When they commit their first crime, Boca, it'll probably be murder, and it might be us".

"Yeah, I've been thinking about that too. But at least we've still got your lucky charm".

They both looked over to where the ledge bulged out above the middle of the room. There was B-Bop in the spotlight of a moonbeam. He had recovered from his fright and was trying to attract the sidewinders' attention, clicking away with his mandibles. It worked all too well. The Worms looked up in surprise just in time to witness his little joke. Right there in the spotlight the nymph hoisted his abdomen at them and wagged it vigorously.

Everyone understands that insult. The bunch quit their polite talk and commenced a sideways pitter-patter to a point directly below. Confusion broke out. They all tried to coil and strike but there wasn't room for it in the confined space. It became a tangle, and someone nipped Patience again, but none of them could reach B-Bop up on the ledge. They settled into a group finally, coiled and watching, tongues flicking in and out. That's when they caught another scent - another two, actually - in addition to the nymph. Unfamiliar scents. They stretched their heads up toward the butterflies, licking at the new smells. The butterflies knew they were discovered so Yero stepped forth and introduced herself.

"Good evening Honorable Ones! I am Yero the butterfly, and this (she poked him) is Boca - also a butterfly. Do you have a question?"

The Worms were puzzled. They had absorbed a lot of their Mum's knowledge and reasoning power as she carried them. That's how it is with baby rattlers. They're born alive and ready to go with a well-developed brain. They have to be. But Mum had always ignored butterflies, so the Worms got no clue. They listened but didn't move an inch.

"We couldn't help overhearing", Yero went on, "and my, but you have such good manners! Such beautiful names!"

Who knows what goes on in the mind of a sidewinder? They remained silent, eyes on B-Bop, flickering now and again to Yero - all except Patience, who mostly watched out behind.

"Why don't you repeat your nice names?" suggested Yero, "That's a good way to start a relationship".

Silence. B-Bop figited. Yero went on quickly.

"Your Mum did say to put on your prettiest faces for strangers. You should do as she says".

There's something about the word 'Mum' in any language that will bring out better behavior. One of the Worms rose a little and bowed politely.

"My name is Honesty - 'Honey' for short".

Yero bowed in turn. So did Boca. B-Bop still fidgeted but nothing more.

Princess spoke up next, then Sweetness, then all the rest in the same order they had received their names. They were very polite, even Patience. Yero began to think all might be well.

Then Honey spoke up again with a hint of anxiety in her sweet voice: "We request that you hand over the little culprit for his punishment".

Yero bowed again, keeping up decorum, and gestured at B-Bop. "Is this the 'accused'?"

The Worms all shouted 'Yes!' at once.

"And what is the complaint against the accused?" Yero saw nothing else but to play for time. The Worms had time to kill too and caught on quickly to *due process*'.

"If you please", replied Honey, "the *accused* insulted us!"

"And what punishment do you have in mind?"

"We'll eat him. It's the natural law".

"That's very serious", observed Yero, bowing yet again. "We'll need to hold a trial. This will take time".

Sullen silence. Yero tried to explain the concept of fairness, which is utterly foreign to rattlesnakes. Several of the Worms got bored and went exploring along the walls looking for some stairway up to the ledge. They found none and failed miserably at climbing the wall.

"...So, we will call him the 'defendant' - not 'culprit'", Yero was saying now. "I will act as defense counsel and Boca here will be the Judge. Please address him as 'Your Honor'. Now, which of you wants to bring charges?"

All the heads rose up as if they were raising their hands. B-Bop promptly mooned them again and all the Worms spoke at once in outrage.

Judge Boca had seen it too out the corner of an eye but pretended not to. He waggled his wings and shouted, "Order in the Court!" but it was only time - several minutes of it - that finally calmed the snakes.

"Everyone will be allowed to speak in the proper order", said Judge Boca importantly. "Honey will testify first. State your complaint now, remembering your Mum's instructions".

"The defendant mocks us, Your Honor. He wags the unmentionable at us. Nobody gets away with that!"

"Overruled. The defendant already *did* get away with it, if true. Who's next?"

Princess was next: "The defendant did it again only a moment ago, Your Honor. You must have seen it!"

"Nope. Didn't see anything", ruled the Judge. "But let the record show: Second witness confirms the charge".

Yero began keeping score with scratches on the sandstone wall. "Next witness!" she called, acting as bailiff. The butterflies had learned a lot in Toady Court.

"My name is Sweetness, Your Honor, "and I can sugarcoat almost anything - but not *that!*"

"Let the record show--" Yero scratched another 'yea'.

"It's a capital offense", testified Faith, up next. "But eating a defendant in Court would be uncivil. Just expel him in our custody".

"I agree", said Innocence, "and let the record show that my pure heart was soiled by his actions. Expel the defendant!"

"My name is Credence", said the next Worm. "And believe me; I witnessed the offense *three times!* Look! There it is again!"

It was getting harder and harder to cover for B-Bop, who was in his glory. The butterflies could've used a real bailiff to keep order.

"Let the record show--" Yero scratched several 'yeas'.

Part 3: Byways of the Butterfly

B-Bop mooned Patience who was up next, and trouble came of it. Patience forgot about his own rear while accusing B-Bop of wagging his, and right during testimony several siblings sunk fangs into him again. He gasped and turned around, but siblings were crawling everywhere and the guilty had let go.

Boca declared a recess and the Worms demanded an explanation. When told it was a time to do nothing they jeered, "We're doing that already!"

Yero approached the Bench to suggest they just let the Worms stew, and the recess go on. Why not? Time was needed, maybe lots of time. There was no sign of their guide and it looked worrisome.

"All because of a fool rabbit!" she grumbled.

"Yeah. Atel will have to find someone to pull it loose. It has to be someone big enough to scare old Mum away too".

"Or *bad* enough. There must be skunks around. I bet even Mum would back up from a skunk".

"I hope it's not that, Yero. Just imagine one of them backing into the doorway to finish off these Worms".

***

Outside, Atel actually had returned, but was stumped. The predicament put all other troubles out of mind. She introduced herself to Mum and inquired about the situation.

"It looks like one of those old riddles", she observed when Mum declined to join the conversation. "Which came first: The stupid rabbit that got stuck in the hole? Or the stupid sidewinder who got stuck on the rabbit's leg?"

Mum glared. She had worked her teeth in deeply and released poison, but it would be several hours before the flesh weakened enough to pull the leg off and swallow it. In the meantime, she was hung up, unable to defend her honor or anything else.

"Lucky I came by", continued Atel, "so you don't have to suffer alone. I guess this is your den - and your little ankle-biters are locked inside?" It was easy to add up the clues now. "Let's see. You would've been hungry after giving birth, but your venom was weak from giving so much away to the babies? So the rabbit ran all the way to *here,* and got stuck, and by the signs you are unable to dislodge him". Atel shook her head, still stumped. There was nothing she could do here, alone.

"I'll go for help", she said sweetly. "Does that comfort you?"

***

Inside the den, Court resumed. The Worms had searched in vain for another exit and started to strike up at the ledge again, coming closer this time. Practice makes perfect.

"Court is back in session!" Boca announced imperiously. Who could say when he might get to be Judge again? He intended to make the most of it. He had to repeat it several times until the remaining witnesses lined up grudgingly. They hated this, but it was better than total boredom, and there was a chance of a snack if they played along and got the silly nymph.

"My name is Pleasance, and I wish to be a co-complainant", said the next Worm. They were really catching on now. Courtroom conduct is after all much like the fake courtesies their Mum had taught them. This bunch showed promise as future lawyers, and who's to say? Maybe some baby sidewinders eventually molt into them. The evolutionary path is certainly there, and it would fit together some missing links we've always wondered about.

"Go ahead", said Judge Boca.

"Well, laying aside his earlier rudeness, the defendant is mooning us even as I speak - *Look!*" It was impossible not to see this time. B-Bop was shameless.

"Don't matter", ruled the Judge. "The original complaint is all we're concerned with. Do you wish to speak to that?"

Pleasance flicked her tongue in frustration. "Yes, Your Honor. He did it then too".

273

Yero scratched another 'yea'. B-Bop went on waggling.

"Next!" called Boca.

"My name is Trusty, and if it please the Court..." (He described gas and other things that hadn't actually happened but would make the crime worse. Yero hoped the nymph wouldn't understand, lest he try these things out) ..."And so in conclusion I ask that the defendant be remanded to his victims. We will moon him as he mooned us, after which of course he will be set free".

"What a windbag", thought Yero, and marked another 'yea'.

"Next!"

"My name is Chastity, Your Honor, and I suffered emotional scars. I wish I could forget! Why would anyone do such a thing? Why can't we all just get along? Oh, boo hoo!"

Yero marked another 'yea' and scored Chastity an A- for her act. The crying was good for a snake, but of course, no tears.

"Next!"

"I am Precious, Your Honor". The Worm struck a pose, turning bashfully for best effect.

"Well?"

"I saw the deed, though my adoring siblings tried to shield me from it. They love me most, Your Honor, and my suffering makes the crime much worse".

Snakes can't roll their eyes either, or her siblings would have. Next to Patience, she was least liked. Another 'yea'.

"Next!"

"My name is Angel, Your Honor. I know sin when I see it and the defendant is full of it, as my siblings have testified; but they say nothing of their *own* sin, do they? I fear for the defendant's safety if they get hold of him! Grant custody instead to a pious soul like myself. Amen". As she postured, one of her siblings sinned again, nipping her tail. She turned, snapping and cursing.

"A fallen angel", thought Yero, and scratched a 'yea'. That left just Sincerely who had thought up a clever point of law.

"I move to allow the defendant his full rights, Your Honor. The accused deserves the right to confront his accusers face-to-face, nose-to-nose. Would you deny him this? Unfortunately, we are unable to approach him so you must send him down. Hopefully then, we can settle this out of court".

"Motion denied", ruled Judge Boca. "A motion must first have a second and secondly it must follow the first by less than two seconds or it shall be deemed a second first and not the first second".

Confusion. Even the Judge wasn't sure what he'd just said. But it sounded official, so the Worms made no protest. Boca snapped his fingers smartly and Yero marked up another 'yea'.

Now it was time to add up the totals. The snakes gathered close. Yero called out the marks and the Judge added them on his fingers and toes.

"Yeas, *thirteen*; Nays, *none*. Mistrial!" announced the Judge.

The Worms looked blankly at each other. *What?*

"The Court will not accept thirteen, which is an unlucky number", explained Boca. "We have to start over".

"*You* saw him do it! You *both* saw him do it!" hissed Honey. "That makes fifteen!"

"Out of order!" ruled Boca. "You'll have to bring a new complaint. Anyway, we're Officers of the Court. We can't be witnesses".

The verdict was poorly received. Forked tongues licked the air in the dim light. Decorum was about to be smashed. Then Honey saw a loophole.

"Twelve would be okay - is that what you're saying?"

There was no recourse. The Judge had to agree and issue an amendment to the verdict.

They all turned on Patience, every one of the virtuous bunch, slashed him wide-open and dragged the evidence out of sight.

"There are only twelve of us now", said Honey afterward, "and we have no more Patience".

Part 3: Byways of the Butterfly

They began building a snake-stack. First, one curled up into a tight coil, then another on top, then another on top of that, assisting each other very cooperatively. It wasn't important to them any longer who got to eat who. They wanted revenge! It didn't even take all twelve. Precious, at #10, climbed into range and struck immediately at B-Bop who took fright and leaped backward--only to rebound off the ceiling and into her mouth. Snap! No more B-Bop. However, Precious lost her balance from lunging and tipped the stack over. No matter. They began to rebuild promptly.

"We'll just have to fly and dodge the best we can", said Yero, "unless you can restore order in your Court!"

But the Judge was about to be impeached. That's what happens when you don't have any Todies.

***

A quarter mile away Atel was making acquaintance with a local resident, a reveler of sorts.

"Beg pardon", said the hummingbird. "Are you hungry?"

The roadrunner cocked an eye at her. It focused slowly. This was a different bird than the earlier one who had nabbed the coachwhip. That was a female; this was the male. Both look exactly the same to non-birds, but the next bird knows. They know from mannerisms even more than appearance. This bird seemed a bit down on his luck.

"What's it to you, pal?" he mumbled.

"I've spotted some nice snakes".

"What's your problem? Don't you think I eat?"

"I didn't say that. Of course you do. All birds eat".

"All right then, don't argue!"

"As I said, I can offer you some nice, fresh sidewinders. Or I can go offer them to someone else".

That jogged something in the bird's mind. He cocked his eye more sharply. It had been sagging.

"Some females pick on me for my habits..." he began, and actually crossed his legs and leaned on a bush. Clearly, he was about to launch into his life's story. Atel made as if to leave.

"I'm sorry", she said, "but I'm in a hurry. I'll find the *Correra* I saw earlier". Atel used the correct name so he knew what she meant.

"No! Hey - wait up! Don't tell her *nuthin!* She don't need to know where I am".

"Fine. I won't say a word about you. But I'll need her for the snakes".

"No! Forget her! *I'll* deal. I never said I wouldn't deal. I love deals! Whaddaya want for the snakes?"

Atel looked closely at him. He wore a red twist-tie for a bandana. His eyes came and went. He stumbled. His speech was a little off. "Are you drunk?" she asked.

"A little, sure! Is that a big deal to you?"

"It might be. Can you remember a deal? Can you walk without falling down?"

"Hoo, boy! You sound just like *her.* Sure, I kin do all that! What's the deal?"

"Good food. For free. Just follow me".

He did his best, but it wasn't very good starting out. If it were farther to go, Atel would've given up on him. He staggered. He went off track. There weren't many bushes in the area, but he hit one of them. Still, he was fast when he finally got his balance right. They arrived at the den pretty quickly. Kuri (his name) leaned against the rock wall, breathing hard.

"Out of shape?" asked Atel without much sympathy.

"A little, sure! Is that a big deal?"

"No, no. We're here! See? This is the Momma, and her little ones are inside - behind the rabbit".

Kuri squinted, blinked, and squinted again, wondering if he was drunker than he had thought. "That right there's a new one on me", he drawled. "Never seen nuthin' so dumb".

"That's what I thought too", said Atel. "As you can see (I hope) Mum has begun her last meal and can't spit it out, poor thing".

Mum glared helplessly. Kuri went on squinting, leaning close.

"If you would pester her a bit, perhaps she would summon her strength and pull the rabbit out of the hole..." spelled out Atel.

Kuri straightened up, offended. "Whaddaya think I am? A *girl*? Stand back, pal. Everything's comin' loose!"

He had sobered up a little and 'snaking' was his favorite sport. He checked his footing and probed Mum's tail with his sharp beak. Mum knew what was coming and tried to thrash her tail, but a Correra (even this one) was quicker than she was. He seized the tail, braced himself and pulled, all in one fluid motion. The rabbit came loose and Kuri went over backwards.

He bounced up instantly, but Mum was still chewing her drumstick. Good! She could wait. He took up position by the door and began collecting the Worms as they came out, pinching them behind the head and tossing them in a pile behind him. Atel counted ten, then hovered by the opening and called to the butterflies.

"Don't come in!" hollered Yero. "They're waiting just behind the door!"

"Oh ho! Back off, pal. I'll get 'em!" said Kuri.

"Or they'll get *you*!" said a sharp voice. "How drunk are you tonight?"

Her name - the bird they had seen earlier, the same one Kuri was avoiding - was Kira. She was tending to business and checking on this well-known den (Because *someone* had to! Someone who was *sober*!).

"I'll have you know..." Kuri began, puffing himself up. Egads! The injustice of it! For once, he had done a noble deed and she refused to see it!

"Sure! I know what *you* know: How many bottles are left, and how much is in them! Not much else! Let someone do this that's got her wits about her".

She didn't waste time, just popped her head in the doorway and nabbed one, and then the other in mid-air as they struck at her. She gathered the still-wiggling pair just by the necks and tossed them over her shoulder.

"Food for the children!" she snapped. "They must eat, remember? *Someone* must bring food!" It was all in a rush. Then she was gone.

Atel went inside, but Kuri, who didn't deserve it this time, went to work on old Mum to take out his frustrations. Very soon she was a thing of the past. Then the Travelers inside heard a *thump...thump...thump* on the wall. Roadrunners have a habit of tenderizing the big ones before they eat them. Kuri was out of shape, maybe, but he worked at it until she was extra-tender.

The butterflies first wanted to know what large animal Atel had hired to pull the rabbit out and were disappointed it was only a bird.

"'Only' is a fair description for some birds, but this one has his moments. Give him credit, okay? He doesn't get much". She described Kuri and his habits. "He's sobering up now. Be polite when I introduce you. He knows the whole area and may be able to help us. But what happened in here? Twelve little sidewinders! You were lucky".

"There were thirteen to begin with and their Mum gave them nice names", said Yero. "Much nicer than they deserved".

"We told them thirteen was an unlucky number", said Boca, "and it sure was for one of them. But it was almost as unlucky for us".

"Where's the nymph? Not so lucky?"

The butterflies looked at each other, not sure how much to say. No evidence remained of this scrape either.

"He teased the snakes", Yero finally blurted. "Like Poppy did to the spiders. We had to put him on trial, and Boca was Judge and gave him every chance, but he just wouldn't stop, and there was even a mistrial, but he was finally found guilty and executed. It was Precious who ate him, I think".

Atel smiled. She didn't doubt things had gotten dangerous, but it wasn't long since the Toads had put them all on trial, so a little imagination was to be expected. She shifted the subject a bit.

276

"About their names", she asked. "Did they sound extra-decent and honest?"

"Oh, she was the first one! *Honesty*. She liked to be called 'Honey'".

"There you are. That's sidewinders for you. They talk nice, just don't ever believe it".

"They're total liars!" exclaimed Boca. "And why do they crawl like that? It looks stupid".

"There are different theories, but I believe they're so crooked on the inside they can't even crawl straight on the outside".

"This bunch needed to be punished!" insisted Yero. "They took the law into their own hands. Well, into their mouths".

"Snakes always do. Some others do too, when the law fails. But there *is* law around here. That's what the roadrunners are for. They police the sidewinders".

"The poison would kill them, wouldn't it? They must be very brave".

"A little whacko, actually. There's an old saying: 'They are related to the Cuckoos, only more so'. Only a Cuckoo could straighten out a sidewinder. That's why they got the job".

"Wow. Why would anyone take a job like that? And who would ask them?"

"Who knows why, but someone *did* ask. Snakes were a problem right off the bat, when they slithered into the world. Surely the Lord must have been busy elsewhere. He doesn't like them either. Doubtless they crawled out of the darkness, but they would lie about it so don't bother asking. The Lord banished the worst of them to the Dry Quarter where they might cause less mischief and gave them rattles to wear as a warning to innocent folk. But crime prospers without a sheriff they say, so the Lord asked for volunteers. Only the Cuckoos showed interest. A lot of them couldn't fly anyway, so the open country was appealing. It was a good fit, and they were the only volunteers, so the deal was done and from all accounts the roadrunners have been pretty good country sheriffs".

***

The Travelers had to spend the night with no relief for their parched throats. Atel inquired about water, but Kuri only waved a wing into the breeze. He knew where to get a drink, sure! And he would show them in the morning! He strutted about and played with his limp sidewinder toys until all hours, still under the influence, but even he dozed off eventually.

The Travelers awoke at first light to a noise outside, the same *thump...thump...thump* of the evening before.

"Is he still at it?" marveled Boca. "Old Mum mustn't have any skin left".

But when they went out it wasn't Old Mum still getting beaten up. It was Kuri banging his own head against the rock, trying to dislodge the hangover pain.

"Kinda rough morning after?" inquired Atel.

"Oooohhhh". Kuri stopped pounding.

"What did you drink, anyway? It's hard enough to find water around here, to say nothing about alcohol".

"Beer", replied Kuri remorsefully. "I swear I'll never touch another drop".

"That would be wise. I'm sure *she* would be happy".

"Oooohhh! You don't know her! Harsh woman. I'm clearing out before she comes to give me the *lecture*". He wasn't ready to go anywhere just yet, though. He sat down on his rump and hung his head between his knees.

"Well, she'll be glad to hear you're swearing off".

There was silence for a few moments, and then Kuri said, "I say that every time. But this time I really mean it!"

"That's good", said Atel, but she shook her head doubtfully. "Drinking kills off brain cells, you know".

"Yeah, that's what *she* says".

"It leads to accidents too. I don't know if you remember that bush last night..."

"Ooohhh". Kuri waggled one wing at the memory. It was still a little sore from the mishap.

Atel ticked off: "Bad for relationships, family life goes downhill".

"Ooohhh - she's hard to get along with on her *good* days! That's why I *started* drinking".

"That's another sign of alcoholism, blaming it on someone else".

"Hey, pal! She's a little rough! You don't know what it's like being married to someone who kills rattlesnakes".

Atel laughed. "Okay! I'll give you that. But here we are at sunrise and you've already received your lecture. You're free to go! Will you do us a favor?"

"Sure! Whaddaya want?" Kuri sat up a little straighter. The headache was going away. The day seemed much brighter. It felt good to confess his sins and start over.

"We're very thirsty, and we need food".

Kuri waved proudly at the bush where he'd hung Mum's little 'worms' all in a row on a branch. "I was about to have breakfast anyway. Dig in!"

"We can't eat that", explained Atel. "We need nectar, or honey. But especially water".

"Sure! Okay, pal. I kin help, but not on an empty stomach. I kinda drank my supper last night. Need sumpthin' solid".

He gobbled down half a dozen young sidewinders but reluctantly left old Mum and her last four.

"*She'll* be back soon", he reasoned. "Won't be none too happy if I'm gone. I'll leave the rest for a peace offering".

"You're so romantic".

"Think so? Say, maybe you could put in a good word with her..."

"I don't think so. That's your job. I'm not getting into the middle of it".

"Sure, okay! I'll cool off the doll...tomorrow, maybe".

"Fine. That leaves today open then?"

"Sure. Look pal, I know the fella who runs the trading post. We'll get a drink there, no problem. He might have some honey too. He'll mix you a drink".

Atel considered for a moment, but even that was suddenly too long for the roadrunner, who began fidgeting.

"Is it very far?" she asked. "What kind of 'fella'?"

"Just back in the canyon. He's a pack-rat".

"A *trader rat?*"

"Sure. Hey - I gotta go! She'll be here soon. *Way* too soon!" He knocked his head against the rock in frustration. "I need time to think up pretty words, know whut I mean? Let's clear out".

Chapter 12

Home Sweet Home

Off he sped toward a narrow crack that opened southeastward from the tall mountains. It was farther away than it appeared, like all great wrinkles in the earth - farther, but not much wider as they drew near. The sheer canyon walls narrowed at the bottom leaving only enough room for a dry creek bed strewn with boulders and along the right-hand side an abandoned road, graded up originally from older rubble, now strewn with the rubble of more recent flash floods. It was a quaint 'scenic route', fallen into ruin since the new highway came through further north.

The debris were no great obstacle to a roadrunner and the party hardly slowed, making good headway around one great bend and then another, but then progress halted at the mouth of a side-canyon. Kuri was winded.

"We rest", he puffed. "Not long".

"Fine", said Atel. "But the butterflies need water soon. That is a serious concern".

"Sure, I get that. But I need cash".

"You need what?"

"Cash. Money! To *trade*".

"Water costs *money* there?"

"Yeah, sure. Is that a big deal?"

"I guess it is. We don't have any".

The roadrunner had a gleam in his eye. "I do. At least I know where to get it. Follow me".

He detoured into the side-canyon. It soon ended in a wall of rubble, but this wasn't the work of any flood. The old canyon walls had collapsed in some long-ago cataclysm now mostly weathered over.

Kuri hopped with renewed energy up the rubble wall on the western side, the side piled highest against the mountain by the ancient avalanche and stopped at a dark opening under an overhanging boulder.

"Here, pal!" he announced eagerly. "We go underground".

"That sounds like a very bad idea", objected Atel.

"Suit yerself. But I wouldn't mind a rearguard on the way back out".

"Good grief, what is it? Snakes again?"

"Sure. What's the big deal? You scared of shadows?"

"No, it just strikes me as a waste of time. Isn't there a creek or spring in one of these canyons?"

"Nope. They're all dry this time of year except one - and the Trader has it. You can hear it, but you can't see it. He sells water by the glass".

The cuckoo was obviously going in regardless. Atel resigned herself to follow. The butterflies were tired and content to wait outside until Kuri (already some distance into the broken passage) called back, "You'll see the bikers too".

What piques a butterfly's interest from one moment to the next? Maybe they don't even know; but now they just *had* to see! It wasn't 'bikers' that showed themselves first, however. It was snakes, as Kuri had promised.

Anyone with a nose for such things or an eye to the ground would realize what lay ahead even without a tipoff from the roadrunner. The downward-angling tunnel floor was smooth like a raceway from the buildup of shed skins, a moldering mess worn slick from the passage of serpentine bodies. They overtook a small grass snake on its way in, then a bigger one. Kuri ignored them and the tunnel was just high enough for the butterflies to stay up out of the way. At least to this point there was still light from the entrance and a few indirect beams through fractures above them. Another grass snake dangled several feet off the floor from one of these fractures, waving and squirming, trying to find bottom. Almost absent-mindedly, Kuri reached up with one foot as he passed by, yanking the reptile loose from its upper moorings and tossing it off to the side of a wider passageway up ahead. Yero winced at the ruthlessness and stole a peek as she passed by. Something writhed and contorted in the darkness. Boca must have seen it too. He was trying to get her attention. But silly Boca, he was looking in the wrong direction.

"Over here," Yero whispered. "Look over *here*".

"They're everywhere", came Atel's voice out of the gloom. "The snakes are hibernating".

Boca veered off to have a closer look, slowing the others to wait for him. He veered back, a little spooked. "They're awake!" he reported. "They're rolling like rope into big balls!" There was a low, rhythmic hiss in the room. He lowered his voice in alarm. "What are they saying?"

"Nothing", answered Atel. "Not one word. They're all asleep, or nearly so. The sound you hear is just snakeskins slipping past each other. They do it to stay warm as the temperature drops. Come, we mustn't waste time here. We could get lost if we fall too far behind the Cuckoo".

"Cuckoo is right!" whispered Yero, putting on a sudden burst of speed around another snake hanging from some hole in the ceiling. The 'danglers' were the worst.

"Snakes will get him someday when he's drunk", predicted Boca. "But that doesn't mean we'll live to see it".

"Just keep your wits about you", said Atel. "But these snakes here are no danger at all". She was doing something with a beam of light in the middle of the room, beginning to glow. It was a big room, they now saw, with a smooth, steeply sloped ceiling - a huge slab off the old mountain that had wedged against the lower canyon wall. The slab had cracked down the middle allowing a hairline sliver of sunshine from high above. In the dim curtain of light, the butterflies saw more than they cared to. Half a dozen large snake-balls and other smaller ones, glistening and changeable, rolled ponderously about. Yero could hardly believe her eyes.

"I didn't know there were so many snakes in the whole world", muttered Boca.

As they watched, two of the largest balls bumped and began to merge - or maybe they were becoming three balls. It was difficult to tell, but the effect was hypnotic. Boca began slipping into a trance, losing altitude. Yero shouted but he didn't hear. Then Atel pinched them both in the rear with her beak and urged them to hurry. Yero felt insulted.

"I'll remember *that*, Boca!" she sputtered. "You were falling for some snake-spell. You needed to be goosed! I didn't".

"Well, don't talk to me. Talk to our guide".

"She's already gone. Just don't stare anymore!"

"Sure, okay! You're right for once".

"*Once?*"

"Yeah. It was bound to happen sooner or later".

Yero opened her mouth...and just shut it again. They hurried after their guide who had disappeared into an exit at the far end of the 'Ballroom'. The mass of snakes, nearly all non-poisonous types, never even knew they passed through.

Into the exit they went, if it could be called that when it led further into the mountainside. Atel was waiting impatiently. She had brought along some light shimmering in her breast feathers. In the darkness ahead, it would be needed.

The passage floor returned now to the primitive rock with none of the shed skins. Plainly, the mass of snakes behind them came no further than the Ballroom, but something did. Atel read the signs as she hurried forward. There were droppings, most likely rat, fairly recent; and there were roadrunner tracks in the dust. But where was the roadrunner? They had lost him for the moment.

The passage became confused with loose rubble, then narrowed drastically and dived straight down through solid rock, and finally fractured rock with many fissures. Yero wondered how Kuri could have descended without falling, and how he could ever scramble up out again. Boca saw eyes in the fissures or thought he did. Then Atel's light disappeared below and the butterflies bumped into hard bottom. Kuri laughed, somewhere nearby.

"'Bout time! Took long enough. As I've always said, anyone's a fool to use wings! Legs are faster".

Yero opened her mouth to protest but shut it again without a word. She was bumping up against a natural law and there was only one solution: Allow plenty of room for the male ego but ignore it.

Kuri was in a fine mood, anxious to get on with his errand. By Atel's shimmer they saw open spaces ahead of them again, wedged over like the Ballroom by the same massive plate off the mountain. But here were no snake-balls, nor anything else in sight that slithered or scurried. This had obviously been a place of men. From the wedge-room, a wide passage led into the mountain - plainly the entrance to a mine - partly man-made, partly a natural cavern. The man-made evidence was provided by armored guards still reclining against the walls of the entranceway and lounging against quarried pillars within. But the armor was hollow. Even in the dim light that was easy to see.

"Empty. All empty", said Kuri. "Bikers from the desert. Bikers got trapped here".

"I don't think so", said Atel. "This is old".

"So? Bikers have always been around".

"There's some truth to that. Whoever they are, I guess they didn't have any way out. Have you looked?"

"Sure. No back door. No trap door. Nuthin'. Not even ghosts that I can tell. But we ain't alone. See? Over there!"

Atel shifted the angle of her shimmer. Dark forms scurried back out of the dim light. Rats. The common, bare-tail kind.

"That's not your trader friend".

"No". Kuri was suddenly serious. "Where there's rats there's rattlers. Let's get our cash and go".

"It sounds easy. Do the rats count it out?"

"Knock off the jokes. You ain't seen nuthin' yet. But you will!"

They passed the first 'sentries' and Yero wondered who they might have been. The suits of armor sat resting against the wall in almost lifelike poses. Some were full body suits with leg armor; some had only the torso armor as if they never had any legs. The odd, curved helmets were scattered. Most were on the floor, but some rested in the 'laps', as if the soldier/miners had lost their heads but meant to put them on again one day.

Narrow gauge wooden rails emerged from the interior of the mine, ending by the entrance in a loop complete with a track siding. Two wooden pushcarts with wooden wheels sat parked on the siding. Here were more suits of armor and pieces of native jewelry. Indians had been here also. The side-carts were full of ore. Kuri ignored all this.

Off to one side - *way* off, it seemed in the gloom - there was another light. It wasn't much more than Atel's, but it had once drawn a desperate crowd. That's where the roadrunner made for in haste.

The light was a tiny hole in the domed ceiling high above, and the ceiling was very high in that part where trapped men had once worked desperately to build a way out, throwing up a spiral ramp of rock toward the tantalizing speck of sunlight. Wooden mine supports had been robbed to construct scaffold and ladders on top of the ramp, but the effort had failed. The pencil of light proved too high. Stains on the ceiling showed that water had once trickled into the cavern through the hole. Meltwater off the mountain. But the earth had shrugged and changed shape, sealing the destiny of the miners. Now all that remained were the armored suits and a tragic tale, easy to read. Later, rats no doubt had seen to emptying out the armor. Yero tried not to think about that. Kuri changed the subject, quickly and cheerfully.

"See there? Money!" He bolted up the ramp and hopped up the latticework of scaffolding to the top where the workers had offered their treasure to the Lord in a final, desperate plea. He didn't hear them, and the Indian Gods had ignored them, having no use for such treasure; but the roadrunner gladly helped himself in their absence.

Two large wooden chests lay open in extravagant display of gold and silver, mostly coinage, doubtless smelted and minted from this very mine. The coins on top were tarnished from long exposure to the ghostly bit of light from an open sky so utterly out of reach. But rats had gnawed holes in the chests and Kuri knew how to wiggle shiny coins out the holes, like fishing into a vending machine change cup.

"Looky here!" he crowed, deftly plucking out a silver coin. Several extra coins followed, rolling and clattering down to the stone floor. "Ever seen anything brighter an' prettier?" He turned it slowly in Atel's light. It gleamed.

"Now looky here". He discarded the silver coin and pecked away in a rat hole in the other chest, actually sticking his head inside the hole to fetch out a small coin, a golden one. It gleamed in the light too, but less than the other because of the darker color. "See? Smaller, duller - anyone can tell it's cheaper - but this is what the Trader likes. He doesn't want the shiny ones. He's stupid that way. Can you carry some of this?"

He dug out more gold coins of different sizes, keeping only the smaller ones that fit nicely into his cheeks, and nearly got his head stuck in the hole when coins above collapsed into the empty corner. Kuri had indeed been here many times.

Boca immediately tried to lift a big coin and couldn't budge it. He couldn't budge a medium-size one either, and then found he couldn't even lift the small ones.

"Not worth your weight in gold, are you?" said Yero.

"I'll get it! Mind your own business!" replied Boca, rapidly falling under the spell of the metal. Gold is like that. It pulls everyone under its spell with time. Boca just happened to be easier than most.

"The problem..." Kuri was saying, as everyone tried to help (even Atel found herself 'helping' and able to carry a very small coin) ... "the problem is gettin' back out. The old mine shafts way back are a-hoppin' with rats and a'buzzin' with rattlers. Hear 'em? They let anyone in, but we'll have to fight our way back out. They're sick of eatin' each other, see? They want variety meats". He left it at that and kept stuffing his cheeks with coins.

Yero, slower to fall under the spell, listened up. The roadrunner was a veteran, attuned to these things, but she could hear it too now - a *rustling* - everywhere. She laid a hand on Boca's forearm, squeezing until he finally looked at her blankly.

"Rats are coming! Drop it. We have to go".

"Sure. Just a sec. I want to take this." However, the little coin was way too much.

Yero squeezed harder. "Drop it! Take some of *this*, if you want gold". Crumbles of the metal, wastage from the forging or just gnawed by rats, had spilled out with the coins. Yero picked up a piece and dropped it again. Oof! The stuff was heavier than it looked. She grabbed a tiny one and lifted off to see how it would go. It wasn't bad. Boca, with a fierce grin, took possession of the big piece she had dropped and barely got airborne.

By now the rat pack was all over the scaffold chattering about the nice, organic visitors. One attempted a flying leap, narrowly missing the sluggish Boca; but most of them went right for Kuri who withdrew to the top of a wooden pole and fended them off with his feet. After a minute of ferocious action, there was a disturbance below and the rats retreated down from the edifice, but not back to the old mine shafts where they came from. The entire colony of several hundred scrambled out the 'front door' and became quiet about it.

Kuri hopped down the stone rampway shouting, "Follow them!" But it came out completely garbled owing to his new gold dentures. He sounded more like a small trumpet player.

"Watch out below!" warned Atel. "Snake!"

"Let it ressst, sissster", came reply from below. "I've made my kill". Yellow eyes stared up at them. A large rattlesnake was already coiled there again after making a deadly strike. A few feet away a rat stumbled, trembling, and fell over. The rattler smiled sweetly, but the smile quickly stretched into a series of exercises to unhinge her jaws for the feast. Kuri tried to say something again but utterly failed.

"Ssstupid!" taunted the rattler, laughing in the peculiar manner of rattlesnakes, with the lisp. "The *sssiblings* will get you! The *sssiblings* will eat all of you!"

Kuri leaped right over her and made for the door, unknowingly swallowing a coin on the hard landing. That proved fortunate in the here and now, allowing him to speak more clearly. "Stay close to the rats!" he shouted. That was the secret to escaping alive, he had learned: Following hard on the heels of their scramble.

There was routine even here in the underworld. This was a very specialized ecosystem, totally self-contained except in winter when the masses of outside snakes came to hibernate in the Ballroom. That provided the bonus that kept the ecosystem going. That's where the rats were headed now at mid-morning (outside time) as they did every day during the hibernating months. All winter they would gorge on the sluggish snakes and grow fat, returning to nests in the old mine shafts to raise huge litters of pinkies. Later, during the warm months outside, there was little food to be had and rat life got secretive and ugly; but always there was a promise of the next snake-buffet. Their only serious issue was with the rattlesnakes.

These were western rattlers of a larger type than the sidewinders. They were the top predator and there were enough of them to threaten the existence of the rat colony. They naturally knew the routine as well as their prey and ambushed the rat horde in many places along the scramble path. The same principles worked for them: Lots of food = lots of young rattlers by the end of the 'fat' season. Then hunger set in. Rats became fewer and smarter, and the rattlers - loners that they are - gobbled down their own young, sometimes to the last hissing whelp in the pit, and so balance was achieved between these less than desirable species.

Kuri knew the last rats in the scramble were usually safe because the rattlers were impatient, selected over time to strike the first good target they saw. When he came through last, they had usually made their kill and ignored him. The first year they shied away from the snake-killing bird anyway, but over a season or two they came to realize he was less of a threat on the way out with his mouth full of coins, a weakness they seized upon because they hated him for insults and many injuries. It had got to where some even let the rats go by, now, hoping to strike at the 'Runner'.

Atel was first to recover from the temptation of the gold, but not before she had lugged the heavy coin in her claws all the way into the up passage. She went first, allowing the vermin some lead-time; then came the butterflies, with Kuri bringing up the rear. When she realized she couldn't even keep her head up she exclaimed something short and sweet and dropped the coin in disgust, which may have saved one of the others.

A rattler struck out at the coin from a crevice, snapping poisonous fangs down hard and accurately. In the blur of action, the only sound was the unlucky splintering of fangs on metal.

With an off-note hiss, the wounded one tried to withdraw back into her crevice. Her plan had been to wait for the 'Runner', which was easy in theory: Kuri's footpads were well known, and she felt his vibrations coming. But the *ssstupid coin* triggered her instinct! Now Kuri grabbed her with a claw as he passed by and ripped her out of her hidey-hole, twisting her neck out of habit.

After that, the vertical tunnel became chaotic. Atel was nearly snatched from behind in a clever double-bushwhack. She was hit a glancing blow and spun around like a top. In that instant, another sibling struck and might have finished the job, but her shimmering feathers illuminated other movements. Unable to zero in on a single motion the sibling struck empty air, overextended herself, and fell all the way to the bottom. With that, the worst was over. There were several more siblings along the way, but they were busily swallowing their rats.

The Ballroom was a very different place on the way out. Nobody likes snakes, maybe, but this struck Yero as unfair. The rats were ruthless and the snakes were helpless; but she did note in passing that they ate what they killed. It was survival of the ugliest and survival often is that way, out beyond the last Drive-Thru burger joints.

Boca thought it more like a 'war' and perched on a ledge to study it. At least, that's what he told Yero when she joined him. He was all pooped out from lugging his gold, more like it. She frowned at the sight below.

"I feel sorry for the snakes".

"I don't know why, Yero. Next summer they'll be outside eating mice and rats".

"Oh, I suppose. But will you answer me something?"

"Sure. Just don't be asking for my nugget. You dropped it. It's mine now".

Yero laughed. "You can have it. I'm not as rich as you are, but I'm not as tired either and it might be a long way yet to the Trading Post. No, I just wanted to ask: If there was nothing else, could you eat a snake? If you had teeth and everything?"

"Why not? It's just like aphids, only bigger".

"But...*raw* like that? It's so messy!"

"Yeah, I wouldn't eat it raw. But I wouldn't have to. I've got money now. I could hire servants to bring fresh nectar every day in a cup with my name on it".

"Now you're talking! I'd like that too".

"Well you can't, Yero. You don't have enough money".

Yero felt a twinge of envy bubble up but pushed it back down. "I never said I wanted *lots* of servants. One would do, if he was good. I would pay a little bit more for just one, and the best one would come to me first".

"They would *all* come for the big money and you would have to guess which ones were any good. You would guess wrong and I would still get the best ones - cheap".

"That's not true! What makes you think I would choose wrong?"

"Because you're a girl. You would just choose some handsome dude and he would turn out to be lazy. Girls aren't good at business".

"That's stupid! Anyway, you would probably hire pretty girls and they might be just as lazy. So there's no difference".

"Sure there is. I would hire 'em cheap - so who cares if some are duds?'

"They'll *all* be duds if they come cheap. That's why they're cheap!"

"Oh, Yero! Don't just lump off *all* of them that way. Maybe girls aren't as good at business, but some are bound to make fine servants".

"I never meant that! Where do you get *that*? Give me one example that girls aren't good at business - just one!"

"Sure. You've got that little tiny bit of gold. I've got a big nugget".

Yero sniffed. "This is more than enough. I'm not greedy".

"Wait till we get to the Trading Post. Then we'll see. Want another example?" The gold fever was gripping him.

"No. Let's go", replied Yero, trying to put an end to it; but Boca wasn't finished.

"Atel dumped her gold, but the roadrunner still has his mouthful!" Boca whinnied like a small horse with a big bag of oats. "See what I mean? Boys hang onto their money".

"It maybe saved your life when she dropped it! You saw what happened, didn't you?"

"The bottom line is, boys take care of business".

"I'm leaving!" Yero never looked back. If she had, she might have enjoyed watching Boca struggle to get airborne. He made it finally, and it's a good thing the rats were busy with their buffet and paid no attention, because he flew much lower than he should have.

With no further mishap, the party re-entered the outer world. It was pleasantly cool with bright sunshine and their spirits lifted. Yero even smiled, forgetting or forgiving - and why not? They had survived a danger. Now a quick trip up the canyon road for well-earned refreshments at the Trading

Post, maybe a tip about overnight accommodations and some neighborly advice for the next leg of the journey! And who could say? Maybe the next leg would be easier. Something more suitable for carefree butterflies! Such were her thoughts in the noonday sun.

Kuri was just as optimistic. He took seriously his promise to get the Travelers something to drink. The first coin was meant for that. The other coins would go for 'the usual'. Hey! Why not? He took a big risk helping out, didn't he? He was due some reward!

Atel had only one thought: "This better have been worth it!"

Not far up the road, around only a bend or two, the roadrunner called a halt - or held out one stubby wing in lieu of speech. In a handy nook in the rock wall he spit out several coins, counting them carefully: One, two, three. Then three more: Four, five, six. He worked his tongue around counting what was left. A puzzled look overtook him. He spit out the last three and scratched his head on the rock. It wasn't coming out right. He expected a remainder of four, not three.

"Look", whispered Yero. "A boy counting his money". She alighted on a stone next to Boca who had already done so. Yero thought it was a cute joke, but Boca was barely listening. He was puffing and trying to conceal it by waggling his wings.

"Sure is hot", he said.

"I don't think so".

"Well, Kuri had to take a break".

"He's just stashing coins. I think he swallowed one and doesn't remember it".

"Oh. Well, I think we should take regular breaks going up. The air gets thinner, you know".

"I hadn't noticed. Maybe I'm just in better shape."

Boca was being pushed into a corner and didn't have an answer, but was spared this time by the cuckoo, who finally guessed the truth and glanced cockeyed, suspiciously, at his own gizzard.

"Is there a problem?" inquired Atel. Kuri straightened up promptly.

"No! No problem at all, pal. Just leaving a few here for tomorrow. He popped three back into his mouth and started up the road, turning over ideas in his mind about salvaging the swallowed one - theories which this tale will not delve into.

"Time to go, Boca", said Yero sweetly. "Need any help?"

"What *for?* Just keep up yourself! That's all *you* have to worry about!"

A moment after she lifted off Boca managed it too, with a grunt. The gold felt heavier all the time.

"Did you say something?" asked Yero.

"I said 'Good!' It's good to get moving". Boca was having trouble with his altitude again.

"Are you flying down there for any special reason?"

"The air isn't so thin".

"That's a good reason, I guess. But I wish you wouldn't. It brings back memories of that gypsy moth. She was so *heavy*! I just kept sagging".

"Hmmpph".

"Oh, Boca! Now that you're rich you don't want to talk to ordinary folk?"

"Hmmmpphh!"

"Tell me if I'm wrong, but it seems like when folks get rich they don't live free and easy anymore. They're like, *weighted down* with worries. Have you ever noticed that?"

Here again Boca was spared when the road bent sharply back upon itself to begin a series of switchbacks up the steep mountainside. Kuri called a halt to catch his breath and point out the Trading Post high above, nestled into a cleft. Boca gratefully plopped down on a cable - all that remained of an old guard rail.

"Remember", puffed Kuri, "when we get there let *me* do the talking. I know how to bargain with him. I know his weaknesses".

"Like the coins?" asked Atel. "He's a sucker for the gold ones?"

"You betcha. Works for me too. Don't mention the big shiny ones, pal. He might change his mind".

Soon they set out again at a slower pace. The way was steep and Kuri was showing the effects of his summer-long binge. He hadn't done his running in the mornings, just slept off hangovers. He could only plod from one hairpin corner to the next and then lean on the rail for a while. Boca wasn't any better with his burden. He grew so irritable that Yero quit teasing him and fell into conversation with Atel during the lengthening breaks. She looked up, counted six or seven more switchbacks still to go, and sighed.

"At this rate it'll be dark before we get there".

"Yes. Just as well, probably".

"Oh? Is the place open after dark, do you think?'

"Certainly. These Trader Rats are mostly nocturnal. They're up all night".

"That's a relief. We're so slow! I don't know if you've noticed, but Boca is just as pooped as Kuri. Maybe worse".

"Yes, the gold. He's come under the spell".

"He'll never give it up. I think our journey is doomed".

"Oh, he'll give it up. Don't worry about that. The Trader Rat will get it one way or another".

"Is the Trader a guy? I think Boca would be too stubborn to do business with a girl".

"Yes. A guy, most likely. That's traditional with them".

"Atel...are boys better at business than girls? Boca thinks so".

The hummingbird chuckled. "Because he has a bigger piece of gold? Look at him. More money isn't always better, and boys aren't always better at business. However, they did get a head start, long ago. Boy Trader Rats were first. They began it".

"*Rats* started business?"

"Not ordinary rats. All they think about is their stomachs. Trader Rats, now - all *they* think about is business. By the way, don't call him a 'pack-rat' if you hope to trade. They consider it an insult. They're *Traders*".

"Are they rich?"

"Maybe. Some are I'm sure. They're experts at setting fair market value on things, so they've always run shops and stores. Some still do".

"Fair value sounds okay".

"Don't get your hopes up for bargains. You'll have to haggle".

"I guess that's okay too. But why did it start with boys - not girls? That part doesn't seem fair".

"Just the luck of the draw, the way I heard the story. It's a long story".

"Tell it so girls are the heroes and think up all the business stuff!"

"No. History is what it is. If it makes you feel better, I will venture girls could've done as well if the draw had been different. But it wasn't, and they didn't. Do you want to hear about the boy Trader Rats or not?"

Yero was spared a decision for the moment when Kuri roused himself and started up the next incline. Boca was able to follow, determined as ever. He watched Yero suspiciously out the corner of his eye. The party managed two more switchbacks, and then Kuri stopped again for 'just a minute'.

"I think we have time for the story", said Yero. "It would be good to know more about Trader Rats before we get there".

--The Trader Rats —

From the Beginning the Lord of Light found creation easier and more enjoyable than repair work later. Wear and tear on the universe was inevitable and He accepted it, but wear and tear on His creatures concerned Him. There was always some. This was owing to the darkness of course - that part of the universe that worked against Him, which would not accept the Light. The darkness touched everything and everyone at some point, and whatever it touched it tempted with bad behavior.

Part 3: Byways of the Butterfly

Everyone gave in to some small temptation and was promptly offered more. We all know how it works. Once bitten by such a snake it becomes a question of resistance to the venom. Most of His creatures did resist, but all had been bitten. Manners and good conduct had suffered. A lot of repair and especially *cleanup* was going to be necessary.

As the First Age of the world drew to a close, the Lord studied progress reports and turned a critical eye toward Earth - an especially messy planet by all accounts. It had been an Age of large inhabitants with large appetites - by itself no vice in a bountiful world - but the inhabitants had become slovenly. The earth stank of trampled food and much else. A cleanup crew was needed, and something needed to be done right away. For better or worse, the Lord decided on rats, lots of them.

He drew them forth from the slop and mess that was everywhere, and so gave them that much head start on the cleanup, though it may also have given them the wrong idea. But they thrived, and every Age since could probably be called the 'Age of Rats' if we gave them their due - which we won't, but they'll get it anyway if they outlast us, which they might - the dirty rats! They were easily tempted into mischief. The Second Age wasn't very old before rats themselves became a problem, making a lot more mess than they cleaned up.

There must be irritating moments in time even for the Almighty, when free creatures go wrong. What more can the Lord do than grant life, liberty and a chance at happiness? That's about it without interfering with the liberty part, the part that makes it worthwhile. So the common rats, given the noble purpose of cleaning up the earth proved anything but noble and the Lord approached the dilemma in His usual way, resolving to draw something good out of the bad - to repair the mischief of a wayward creature by bringing forth a better, more responsible relative. To this end, He created the janitor rat, a better cousin to set a good example. He drew forth the new rats - two brothers to begin with - out of the same mess but added a few of the better spices.

Now, the Lords' creatures are all brought forth with a good deal of common knowledge for their own protection - a fair understanding of the dangers that await them - and so most come forth quietly in a listening mode, pondering the wisdom they've just been granted. Not so the janitor rats.

They had already taken names to themselves: 'Eemert' and 'Fleemert'- and commenced a noisy argument. They detested their bare rat tails and offered them to each other in exchange for extra ears, teeth, some hair for their bare feet, anything at all. However, there were no bids. The market value of bare rat tails was zero; and as the Lord listened for a fleeting moment, it fell below zero. The noisy ones began offering their tails for "a song" and belted out just awful tunes they would take in trade.

"There!" said Eemert, following an ear-splitting squeak. "Just sing *that* and I'll give you my perfectly serviceable tail, in mint condition".

"Too much, too much", protested Fleemert. "But if you make *this* bit of everyday music you can have mine!" He turned around and lifted his rat tail and blew a tune out that end of himself.

There are some species and their sub-species that cannot be reasoned with politely. Everyone knows who they are, and of course the Creator met them first. The janitor rats wouldn't shut up and the Lord had to raise an eyebrow, putting them on 'pause', as it would come to be called in later Ages.

It had been such a rude, disrespectful get-go that the Lord looked into their hearts expecting to see shadow, but there was none. It was His own doing. In His eagerness to produce a better rat, He had granted them more pizzazz than necessary. Already their rat brains were hatching theories and novel ideas that would change the world. A quick peek into their minds confirmed this. Advanced concepts flowered there: 'Trade', and 'Money'.

The Almighty expected such things to gradually evolve in the world - but so soon? It wasn't necessary yet. Later, sure, when the earth became crowded, but there was still a comfortable niche for everyone. Every possible need of every creature had been put in their own back yard, so to speak, for the taking. There had been no report of shortages. So *business*, as it flowered in their rat brains, was premature.

The Lord rarely ever interfered 'down below', but the janitor rats weren't down below yet. There was still time to chasten them. He let His eyebrow fall part way. The rats awoke and immediately tried to resume haggling but realized they hadn't got their voices back and had to give it up.

"I've brought you into this world for a *purpose*", stated the Lord. "Are you ready to listen?"

The rats had lots to say but couldn't.

"I'll take that as a 'yes'", continued the Almighty. "Your noble calling will be janitorial work, tidying up the messes of the world - especially of the other rats. You will come to love your work".

The brothers felt a tug at their heartstrings. A sudden ambition to pick up and organize things entered into them. The Lord let His eyebrow fall the rest of the way. The rats regained speech and had discovered courtesy. They bobbed and bowed but were confused.

"If you please", they asked, "what do we do with all the garbage and junk we pick up?"

"Follow your instincts", replied the Lord. "Sort it into neat piles so it weathers away and returns to the earth".

But there was another instinct in the rats that simply wouldn't be suppressed. "What's in it for *us*?" they asked, bewildered.

"The satisfaction of a job well done, a beautiful world cleaned up, and the gratitude of everyone in it".

The rats were still bewildered. "That's a lot of work for just a pat on the back", said Eemert. "What else do we get?"

"Well, the trash is free", considered the Lord. "No one owns it. You may keep a few items that you fancy".

"Ah, that's more like it", said Eemert, bowing.

"One rat's junk might be the next rat's treasure", agreed Fleemert shrewdly.

The brothers grinned at each other.

"Your business is the garbage", reminded the Lord sternly. "Don't get any grand ideas".

"How could we?" they complained, "With tails like these? If we're to *be* good we ought to *look* good, too".

The Lord conceded the point and dressed them as they wished with furry white feet and bushy tails - which ought to help for sweeping and dusting as well.

The tails especially were a nice improvement and the rats fluffed and admired them until Eemert found he could fluff his tail a bit more than his brother and said so, adding that Fleemert's tail looked "cheap".

Without waiting for Fleemert's retort the Lord sent them both down to earth, hoping for the best. In light of the episode He brought forth fewer of their kind than originally planned, and though the janitors worked hard and packed away astounding amounts of garbage and trash, their numbers never increased much owing to their disagreeable, haggling nature. They only marginally improved the hygiene of the planet.

But like their cousins (what *is* it about rats?) they turned the world upside-down in unintended ways. It began with 'treasure hunting', or what is now called 'dumpster-diving'. In fairness, they did clean up after their messy cousins at first, but quickly learned the dirty rats' trash held nothing of value, certainly none of the shiny objects they looked for. They recognized value in these and collected small fortunes in gems and spare change from higher-class dumps. Then they turned to trade and found even bigger possibilities.

In truth, the Lord had provided for the *needs* of all creatures, but the new rats looked around and saw *wants*. Everyone had a few. It seemed obvious the world could be greatly improved with some salesmanship. Thus, swapping and deal-making came into being.

The new rats stepped up in class, calling themselves *Traders*, and introduced these ideas to other creatures of the Age. Business boomed from the start. Everyone wanted to deal. However, it led to some questionable transactions in the early years when swapping got out of hand. Creatures took to trading even their own body parts for others and the Trader rats took a commission on everything. Harpie eagles appeared, along with centaurs, sirens, mermaids, and all the other unlikely hybrids of folklore. The Trader rats became so rich they even bartered up fierce griffins to guard their treasure hoards.

Reports eventually reached the Lord of all this and He didn't like it, so these creatures mostly faded into history; but through the Ages the descendants of Eemert and Fleemert have always been the dominant Trader families, though they employed very different business models - models still widely copied today.

Eemert thought big. He built a large central place of business where the busiest pathways of the world came together, a sprawling nest and superstore complex that covered acres. He stocked a huge variety of merchandise and called it the 'E-Mart'. There was something to interest everyone and Eemert sold stuff at a discount to attract customers, but he had to sell a lot to cover his fixed costs.

Labor was expensive. The store was family run but he was divorced several times and didn't get along the kids, so he had to hire them. Advertising was expensive too, but 'specials' made the place a popular destination. Eemert was smart enough to be nice to ordinary customers, very pleasant. He collected a lot of addresses in casual conversation and sent sale flyers right to the customer's homes.

Fleemert was more of a gypsy, setting out his goods wherever he could drum up a crowd. His family turned into a network of peddlers, hucksters, vendors and brokers. Each had their own bag or small cart, but they had a grapevine connection with each other and could find anything a customer might want - new or used. They usually undersold Eemert because their fixed costs were low. Eemert dismissed these small operators, calling them 'Fleemert's flea-marts'; but he knew they took away a lot of business because his chief bean counter showed him the numbers.

All good things must come to an end of course, and the rise of humankind ended the Golden Age of the Trader Rats. Men call them simply 'pack-rats' nowadays for their quaint collections of shiny objects, and mistake their offices as just 'nests', not realizing the rats are still doing their best to pick up the mess and clutter of the world and turn it into profit.

Even their invention of free trade, which makes our crowded world tolerable, has been forgotten. Trader rats get no respect today - but if not for their hard bargaining over the Ages we still wouldn't know what things are worth.

***

Atel finished the tale outside the store while the roadrunner and Boca puffed and panted. The whole site wasn't much more than a wide spot in the road with most of that being a parking lot. Automobiles once pulled in and nosed their front bumpers up to a heavy log barricade there, at the very edge of the Lookout Point. Now the barricade was falling apart. Some timbers had tumbled off the edge. One that did remain supported Kuri and Boca. It wiggled from their huffing and puffing.

Across from the lot was the 'Trading Post': An abandoned gas station still in fair condition. A tin canopy sheltered pumps still labeled 'Regular' and 'Ethyl'. Beyond that the front door to the store stood open, hanging crookedly from one hinge. High above towered a sign proclaiming, 'Gas--Food--Cigarettes' in electric lights. Remarkably, several bulbs still worked.

It was an odd place for a gas station in the best of times, except for the scenic view, and of course the water. In the cleft behind the shack, spring water had once bubbled forth in a small waterfall that disappeared into the earth again not far below: A flash of precious water on the dry mountain. Years earlier the bubbling spring had been enclosed and put to work. It was harnessed to power a water wheel, which in turn ran a generator that still worked enough to light a few bulbs up on the sign and the chandelier in the main room of the station. A picture of the station from an earlier day dangled next to the front door, neatly framed, with 'HOME SWEET HOME in large letters across the bottom. A tag read: 'For Sale/$1.98'. An old prospector had built the place. He couldn't find gold but turned out to be a right clever inventor.

"Well?" said Atel presently. "Shall we go in?"

"Wait a sec, wait a sec", replied Kuri. He had caught his breath by now but held up. "Sun's settin'. He'll shoo the big lizard out".

Sure enough, in a few minutes there was a squeaking and chittering inside and a big Gila monster stalked out the door thrusting its head this way and that, probing the air with its tongue, followed closely by a chattering rodent ushering the lizard outside.

"Never liked that danged thing", said Kuri. "Can't trust 'em. Okay, let's go".

Kuri fairly pranced to the narrow porch and bounded up the short steps. He was full of energy now, already in animated conversation with the rodent - no doubt the Trader himself. Kuri waved a wing to beckon the Travellers. They all went in and found the store larger than it appeared from the outside. There was a little cashier's counter by the front door still with a cash register, now standing open and empty. Small shelves nearby were bare, except for dust. Empty cigar boxes and candy cartons littered the floor. The most valuable merchandise had obviously been rifled and stolen years before.

Past the cashier's desk, a luncheon bar with open kitchen extended into the hillside behind the wooden frame building. Back there in the 'grotto' at the end of the bar was the machinery that kept the lights working years after abandonment.

A thick metal shaft turned slowly there, supported by heavy bearings on the bar itself and by others embedded in masonry where the shaft reached through the wall. Water could be heard on the other side, splashing into the cups of the wheel, spinning it endlessly and turning the shaft. A roller chain coupled the shaft to a generator, which took up the whole back end of the kitchen aisle. It was geared down for low output and longevity and fed a gang of batteries arranged around it. The batteries had gone bad a while back and someone had jump-wired the output direct to the light circuits. Altogether, it was an ingenious do-it-yourself project and the works was left open on purpose for customers to admire.

The trader rat had no part in the actual construction, of course, but as current sole proprietor he liked to loiter on the bar near the operating machinery and lean on his Ferris Wheel as he welcomed customers.

Oh, yes. The Ferris Wheel. A word about that. The prospector would've quickly gone broke in his little country station in spite of free water and ambition simply because the county was 'dry', meaning rainfall was allowed but NO BOOZE. The only small stores that flourished found some way to sell bootleg liquor, which meant a risky cat-and-mouse game with the authorities. The prospector invented a way to fool the inspectors by building a scale model Ferris Wheel into the bar. Owing to its size (about six feet in diameter) and the necessity of aligning it with the power shaft, he had cut a gap in the top of the bar so that the top half of the wheel was above but the lower half rotated down underneath when it was engaged by a lever under the bar.

The inspectors never caught on that the decorative bucket seats were attached to extra-long chains that drooped way down to the cellar floor below where he kept bottles of moonshine and many cases of beer. The prospector trained a pack rat to roll whiskey bottles or cans of beer into the pretty seats so that, when it was called for, he simply engaged the lever and up came the illegal beverage.

The authorities knew he was up to something but never guessed the existence of the beer cellar, even though the trap door was right in the middle of the floor, because it was hidden by a cage and soiled newspapers spread underneath it. The Gila monster in it was a good tourist attraction, though a bit vicious, and kept the agents at bay. As for the pack rat, he learned the trade well, the whole business, and promoted himself to proprietor when the old prospector disappeared one day. Now he leaned an elbow on the Ferris Wheel and made a bit of small talk with Kuri. The roadrunner was his best customer.

"Yer lookin' good, old boy! What'll it be tonight? The usual?"

"Nope. Just want you to meet some friends of mine. They're thirsty. How 'bout a glass of plain water for thirsty travelers - on the house?"

The Trader laughed, a chitter that started in his nose and made his fat stomach quiver. Yero guessed it reached even his feet because he danced on his toes as if they tickled.

"On the house? The *poor house*, that's what this is. Times are tough, ol' boy. I'll starve if I cut prices any more".

"You'd charge beggars for water? Show some pity! They need a break".

"Sure they do. But I get sob stories all the time. Everyone wants a freebee".

"They're little bitty folks! Look at 'em! A few drops in a shot glass..."

"Yeah, yeah, and then it's a glass to wash when I'm busy. Time is money".

"You got time! Ain't no other customers".

So it went. Kuri did mean to help, but he enjoyed the haggling too. The Trader relished it even more. Obviously, it might go on for quite some time and the Travelers were parched.

"Is this enough for water?" said Yero, suddenly interrupting. She held out her tiny piece of gold.

"Maybe, kiddo. Lemme see!" The Trader snatched the proffered bit and scampered down behind the bar to examine it through reading glasses that had once fallen there. He wiped dust off one lens and scrutinized the gold from all angles, taking his time about it.

Atel flipped her beak in disgust as she surveyed the store. It was exactly what might be expected in such a run-down place, and worse. Dust was everywhere, thick dust in most places. There was a swept path from the cage to the door for the big lizard on his nightly excursions, a clean mirror on the kitchen shelf above the stove, and the bar was nicely wiped off. The trader did some cleaning. But other than that, Atel couldn't recall another place quite as dusty.

"Poor quality, Kiddo", declared the Trader. "Very small sample. D'ya have more?"

To Atel that signaled the start of bargaining. "The gold is good, as you well know - worth more than a few drops of water. We want sugar with it".

There was a lidded ceramic bowl on the shelf next to the mirror, with 'sugar' engraved in fancy script. It might have been empty, but the Trader's reaction said it wasn't. Atel pressed the point.

"If you would rather return the gold..."

"Here it is then". The rat offered it back, bluffing. He wanted to see if the newcomers had any more money. They were mighty thirsty, that's for sure. If they were holding anything back, a little bluff should flush it out.

"Look, pal", chirped Kuri, "If you want any profit you better grab it quick. I'm not hankerin' for any beer tonight, myself".

It threw the Trader off balance. He turned back to the roadrunner, keeping a grip on Yero's gold. "What's up? You swearing off?" He didn't believe it.

Kuri spit out a coin on the bar to talk easier. "The doll is on the warpath. I'm goin' on the wagon for a few weeks. Maybe I'll be back then, maybe not. She's really steamed". He scooped up the coin again.

The Trader hesitated. Kuri hadn't tried this ploy before, and he wasn't even bargaining for himself so it might be true. As the cuckoo scooped up his coins again the Trader made a quick decision.

"Sold!" he squeaked and put Yero's chip between his teeth for safekeeping. "One shot of Sweets coming up!" He jumped onto the shelf where the jiggers were lined up and reached for one.

"Not that glass!" objected Atel. "Let's have one that's upside down there. A clean one".

"Fussy, eh?" The Trader was insulted. "I would've rinsed it".

"Don't forget the sugar".

"Now don't you worry, girl! I can mix drinks in my sleep. Don't be tellin' me my business!" He paced belligerently on his hind legs, hands on hips, bushy tail wagging away, sweeping dust into the air and down onto the short-order grill. Then he spotted Boca's gold piece.

"By the way", he added, suddenly cordial again, "You might enjoy a few drops of the *good stuff* with that, eh? *He's* got money".

"No", said Atel firmly. "I'm in complete agreement with Mrs. Roadrunner. Liquor is the source of all evil".

"Oh. Teetotaler, eh? Whadda ya gonna do? Turn me in after I help you out?"

"No, again. Your business is your own. But I won't allow the butterflies to take up bad habits".

"Okay, okay. Don't be so touchy! I'm a poor Trader trying to make ends meet. It ain't easy, it ain't easy". He chattered and squeaked the whole while as he shoved the sugar lid ajar. He gave it an extra nudge and it fell clattering to the stovetop and then to the floor. There was white sugar in the bowl - a bit crusted, but he broke out a nice chunk and dumped into the glass. He hopped down to the stove and across a counter to the sink. There was a single faucet, still much used. It was simply a direct line through the wall into the cascading water. The trader filled the jigger and leaped nimbly over to the bar, setting it down in front of the newcomers - click! - with an air of much practice. He hovered hopefully for a while as Atel and Yero helped themselves. Boca looked away.

"Okay, eh? You like?" He hoped for a tip. One never knew about new customers. They were all suckers, some more than others. But these were still sober.

"Fine, thank you", said Atel politely. "We'll call you if we need something".

The Trader shrugged and turned to Kuri again, who looked willing now to re-think his vow. The cuckoo planted his big feet stubbornly on the bar ready to haggle, but his knees shook a little. He needed something to calm the shakes and the Trader saw it.

"Hair of the dog?" smiled the rat.

"Maybe", said Kuri, still nonchalant. "I ain't got much cash. It'll have to come cheap".

"You know how it works", laughed the Trader. "And I haven't eaten today. It won't be cheap!"

Kuri glared and the dickering began in earnest.

"Boca! Come and have some", urged Yero. "It isn't nectar, but it's wet and it's sweet". Atel had in fact pronounced it "too sweet" and was at the faucet helping herself to the drip while the Trader was busy with Kuri.

"I'll wait til you're done", muttered Boca. "I want to drink alone and have my gold with me. I can't leave it over here, unguarded".

"Oh, don't be silly! Just set it down. You can keep an eye on it. It's only inches away".

"I'm not taking a chance with this much gold. You're poor. You don't understand".

"Okay, fine. But listen, I'm sorry I teased you so much about it. I'll gladly guard it for you so you can get a drink".

"Oh, sure! *I* get a drink and *you'll* get my gold!"

"Don't talk like that. I don't even want it!"

"Yes, you do! Everyone does. You blew yours and now you're jealous".

"Good grief! I bought supper with mine and I'm offering to share it!"

"Easy come, easy go. That's how it is with girls. I knew you'd never hang onto it".

"Be a nincompoop then! I'll drink it myself. I did pay for it, after all".

"So what? I'll get a few drips out of the faucet, or find some way to get past that wall, or maybe even buy some of that 'good stuff' he talked about. That sounds pretty high-class. I'm high-class now".

"The way Atel talked that stuff is low-class. Just trouble".

"That's another thing, Yero. I think I can have a little extra fun now and *buy* my way out of trouble. Remember those Toady lawyers, when we were in jail? If we'd had money *then*, I think we could've bought our way out".

"We're not in trouble now. Why would you want to buy any?"

"For adventure. You poor folks, you don't have any imagination. That comes with wealth. I'm even thinking of going back for more gold. Just Kuri and me. Just boys next time!"

Boca's eyes gleamed. The fever had taken him over totally. Kuri's stash wasn't safe either. Boca was laying plans to raid it. He had even spied a safe nook along the road to stash his own 'nugget' while he carried out these plans. He stole a furtive glance at the roadrunner, wondering if the bird might be distracted enough in conversation that he, Boca, could slip away unnoticed right now and do the deed. His eyes glazed over thinking these thoughts.

Meanwhile the faucet stopped dripping and Atel returned, fed up with the dirty joint and the immoral atmosphere.

"I don't like it here", she declared. "I'm going to look for a more wholesome place to spend the night. Shouldn't be hard to find. What's your problem, Boca? Too tired to drink?"

Boca blinked stupidly, still scheming. He hadn't even heard.

"He'd rather sit there, thirsty, and hug his gold", explained Yero. "He doesn't trust me to watch it so he can drink".

"Don't take it personal", mumbled Boca. "I don't trust anyone".

Atel narrowed her eyes. His delirium was farther advanced than she expected. All the more reason to get him out of here, away from the rat and the roadrunner. She looked him straight in the eye. He looked away, very unlike Boca. That did it. She would find another place, come back and get them. As for the gold, if she had to wrestle it away from him, she would!

She left, but only Yero noticed. Boca had slipped back into his plots, gripping his precious nugget. Nearby, the haggling between Kuri and the Trader was taking a curious turn. The rat went over to the Ferris Wheel and climbed into one of the bucket seats. The big wheel jiggled up and down a bit as he upset the balance, but then stabilized motionless.

"Show me the money", the rat teased. "I know you've got enough. You wouldn't come without it".

Kuri appeared finally to capitulate, spitting two coins into the seat with him, adding some weight. This is how a fair price was arrived at. When the rat plus extra coins became heavy enough, the Ferris wheel moved, acting like a balance scale. The Trader and his coins went down one side and a can of beer came up opposite for the customer, who then rolled it out of the seat onto the bar. That allowed the Trader down below to get off, set aside the money, and roll another full can into the empty seat. He could then scamper back up the bucket chain without it turning and return to his business at the bar. He had always established the price of beer this way, but in his old age he was putting on weight and had to cheat.

While he stood innocently in his bucket, holding up his hands to show there was no hanky-panky, his toes gripped the seat and his bushy tail casually pressed down on the bar top so that more coins were needed - in this case, more than two, which *had* been the fair price all summer.

The rat laughed again, the same nasal chitter that made him dance. He had to grab the back rest to keep from tipping out of the bucket, but he didn't stop laughing until Kuri got mad and snatched his coins back, turning on his heel to stalk out.

"Hey! Where ya goin'? We almost got a deal here!"

"We ain't even close. Two coins shoulda done it. Grease your wheel, pal!" He kept heading for the door.

"Whoa, not so hasty! I'll sell you a different brand: 'Light' beer. Less weight".

"Been there. Done that. They all cost the same!" But he paused to argue.

"Whadda ya want? I should cry poorhouse tears?" protested the Trader. "I can't *give* the merchandise away!"

"The going price is two coins! *Two!*"

"Was. Times change".

"Before that it was *one!* And all the while, you've gotten fatter. It should take less now, not more!"

"What can I say? Beer takes on weight as it ages".

"Who says? You? I've had it, Rat. I can't afford this anymore!"

"C'mon, c'mon. You'll have the shakes all night. You need a drink".

Kuri frowned. The Trader smiled, but if he saw the inspiration in the bird's eye, he might not have. Kuri was finally guessing the trick.

"I know you've got more in your cheek", coaxed the rat. "C'mon, let's make a deal! You kin be drinkin' beer inside of a minute".

He enjoyed this. He even went and grabbed a bag of salted peanuts down behind the counter, as if it made no difference on the balance. Well, of course it didn't, so long as his tail kept things stabilized. "C'mon!" he teased. "Let's do it".

"Maybe so, lemme think! Go ahead and finish yer lunch, pal".

"Thank you, I will. Just don't expect charity. Business is business".

"Sure, pal. Lemme think".

The Trader finished his peanuts, licking the salt off his fingers. "Say, d'ya mind if I have a drink while I wait? Salted nuts, y'know". Kuri still procrastinated.

"Sure, pal. I'm still thinkin'".

The rat got a drink, shutting the faucet tight afterward. He returned with another bag of peanuts. Kuri let him munch.

"Well?" said the Trader presently. "Show me the money".

Kuri spit all three coins into the seat with him. The wheel budged as if to rotate down, and then stopped. The rat was pushing his luck. "Almost, not quite", he judged. "Ya' got any more?"

Kuri lost his patience. He had the shakes noticeably now and was itching to see his idea tested. With a lightning movement he jabbed sideways and neatly plucked Boca's little nugget out of his grip, tossing it into the bucket with the rest. The Trader, now satisfied he'd got all the money in the room, let go with his tail and the wheel spun quickly. The grinning rat disappeared into the cellar even as Boca went bananas.

While Boca fluttered wildly, trying to protest but failing at words - and Yero guarded him from stuffing himself down through the Ferris Wheel - it fetched up a can of beer on the other side and came to rest. Kuri strutted over, rolled it onto the bar with a practiced motion, and tipped it upright with one big foot. Like any veteran beer drinker, he hooked open the tab with a finger (well, a toe).

"Spooooffft!" Beer foamed out from the shook-up can. The roadrunner was ready for it, stuffing his thirsty beak into the hole. Very little spilled, disappointing several flies that suddenly turned up.

Nearby, Yero finally did the only thing she could think of, slapping the berserk Boca right across the face. Remarkably, it worked. He calmed down immediately and looked around. Amazingly, he wasn't angry anymore, didn't even realize that he'd been slapped. In fact, he had forgotten nearly everything. The gold craze had been lifted - and left him blank.

"I'm really thirsty, Yero", he said. "Tired too. Where are we?"

"We're at the Trading Post. Here. Have some of this. It's almost like nectar".

For a while Boca did nothing but drink and behave himself. Amnesia can be such a blessing sometimes.

And so - except for a few disappointed flies - everyone at the bar was happy, and happy customers should make a happy proprietor. So, what was keeping him from coming up to share the good cheer? To answer that we must slip into the cellar ourselves, showing patience while our eyes get used to the poor light. Ah! There is movement! Yes, the Trader has rolled a new can of beer into the bottom-most bucket seat and commenced to scamper up the chain. All appears well. Soon he will reach the bar and climb out onto it - but what is this? He's coming back down if our eyes don't deceive us. Yes, coming down quickly while the next can rotates up. The Trader has put on too much weight and become heavier than a can of beer. It was bound to happen and bound to manifest itself first down here in the cellar. But he had almost reached the top when the Ferris Wheel reversed, so that when he ended up on the bottom again a new can of beer appeared at the bar. Kuri, hoping for just such luck, rolled it safely onto the bar before the Trader collected his wits down below.

"Dratted bird!" the rat's voice snapped like a short circuit in the electric wiring. "Dratted bird! You owe me for that one. I'm puttin' it on your tab!"

Kuri was drinking out of the first can. He tilted his head back as birds do and swallowed a mouthful. "Baloney!" he belched. "The second one is on the house. I never ordered it".

The Trader became outraged, lost his temper and did it all over again with the same result. Kuri now had three beers for the price of one and the rat still sitting on the cellar floor.

"You better have tons of money!" came the rat's high-pitched voice from the depths. "Yer rackin' up a huge bill!"

"I don't owe nuthin'", giggled Kuri. He was feeling it by now after half a can. That's all he could get out of the pop-top hole so he popped the second can, "Spooofft!" and slurped the foam. "We'll call this 'Customer Appreciation Night'!" he called down. "'Bout time, too, after all the money I've spent here!"

There was silence in the cellar for a couple minutes. Then the trader offered a deal: "Hold the wheel so I can climb up and you can keep the extra beers".

"Not yet! I'm enjoyin' myself. We're havin' a party up here".

"The newcomers drinking too?" asked the rat, interested. The idea of 'separate tabs' occurred to him, but Kuri disappointed.

"Nah. Just m'self. And the flies, o'course. Should I charge *them* somethin'?"

There was no answer. After a bit, Kuri remembered his good manners and offered the butterflies some.

"No thank you", said Yero politely. "We don't do that".

"What is it?" Boca asked the roadrunner. "Is it food?" Yero shot him an angry look.

"Ya might say that. It's supper for me!" replied Kuri. "D'ya want some? Y'did chip in, after all".

"He doesn't want any!" Yero insisted. "And he doesn't remember the, ah...what you borrowed. I think he bumped his head".

"Sure, okay. That's no big deal. Tomorrow I'll be bumpin' my head on things too". He winked at Boca. "That's how to get rid of a hangover. You'll learn the tricks. Just stick with me. C'mon, have a swig!"

"Don't tempt him! He's not in his right mind just now".

"Neither am I", giggled Kuri. "That's no big deal either". He popped open the third can and stomped on the bar. "Hey! It's pretty quiet down there. What's up? Or maybe I should say, 'What *ain't* up?' Yee-ha! Here's a clue: It ain't you!"

It was great fun. This was the first time he ever had any advantage over the Trader. He stomped on the bar again.

"I'm runnin' short up here", he chirped. "Send up another free one!"

"Forget it. I'm not that big a fool".

"Yee-ha! Ya coulda fooled me!" Kuri thought that was the funniest yet. He'd never drunk so much beer in a short time and was getting tipsy. Usually he could only afford one, and when he couldn't get any more out the top, he tipped it over and slurped up as much as he could before it ran off the bar. But tonight he hadn't even done that yet. He giggled and stomped again.

"Have ya started yer diet yet? I'm doin' you a favor. It can't be healthy, carryin' all that extra weight".

"I've started. You will too, one day. You'll eat your own words!"

"Not today! Oh-dang!" Kuri had slurped all he could out of the last can. It was time to tip one of them over, always a sad moment. He knocked over the nearest one - splash! It ran toward the Ferris Wheel, spilling a little down that dribbled onto the Trader.

Yero expected a squeak of indignation from below but it came from the roadrunner instead. Kuri's wife had tracked him down and burst into the Trading Post. She got him by the comb with her beak and hustled him out. It happened so fast they raised dust off the floor.

The sudden exit left a hush in the room, or something near to it. Smaller noises became audible. The butterflies became aware of a buzzing up on the kitchen shelf. A cloud of flies was into the open sugar bowl making a mess, or maybe the swarm looked bigger with the mirror behind. Either way, the lights stayed on 24 hours here, and so did the houseflies. Several of them approached the shot glass where the butterflies perched. They milled around, making trial dashes at the sugar water. Yero flapped her wings vigorously to keep them away. Boca watched with interest, learning things. He had a lot of spare room for new knowledge now.

"Scram! Beat it! This is ours", Yero warned.

"Well, get a load of the Big Shot!" said one. "Hey, Big Shot! Don't be selfish! You don't need it all".

"You can have what's left after we leave, but not before", replied Yero. "I want to keep it clean". She knew enough about flies to be careful. Everyone does.

"Oh ho! 'Miss Goody-Goody', is it? Think you're better than everyone else?"

"I'm not going to argue. Just keep your feet out of our supper".

"What're we supposed to drink, then?" said another. "Beer?"

"If we get drunk it's your fault!" said the third fly.

They laughed as if they were tipsy already, but it was just a sugar high. They'd never had such a treat as the open sugar bowl and having stuffed themselves were now looking for something to wash it down. The three were regulars here and had 'shared' spilt beer with the roadrunner more than once. That's where they were headed next, but the sugar made for a festive atmosphere. An unexpected holiday for barflies.

That's what they were, of course, in a place like this. And to prove it they went right to the spilt beer and started sucking up brew and dropping 'specks' on the nice, clean bar top next to it.

Two of the three - boys, judging by their close-set eyes - were especially busy at it. They deposited their messy specks in long dotted lines. It disgusted Yero and she looked away, but Boca figured out they were competing with each other, marking out territories on the bar. He was impressed - not by their skill with geometric patterns, though that part deserved some regard - but with the sheer number of deposits. The flies were excrement machines! When they could dump no more, they buzzed back to the spilt beer and sucked up refills. Beer, seemingly, was the perfect food for such activity. It went right through them.

The boys staked out ambitious territories near the spilt suds but where they bordered, they left a narrow strip of 'no man's land'. This prevented actual fighting and, more importantly, allowed a walkway for the third barfly, a girl, to approach the beer in style, which she did as soon as the walk was ready.

"Hey", whispered Boca. "Check out the dame!"

Yero couldn't resist but soon wished she had. The 'dame', a middle-aged floozy named Lena, had all the right moves to impress the boys, Doo-Doo and Loo. All three had been married to other flies and divorced, or the barfly equivalent. They were seasoned veterans of the local social life. In fact, they were the oldest flies in the joint, very street-smart. This became obvious when others from the sugar bowl buzzed down for a drink. All the best real estate was taken, and they had to lick at corners or take the risky gamble of dropping into the pop-tops of the standing cans. There was lots of beer in those, but the flies weren't likely to get out again. Soon the cans were buzzing like little beehives.

But Doo-Doo, Loo and Lena ignored everyone else. Romance beckoned! Or at least, Lena did. She sashayed slowly down through the no man's path, neatly depositing her own specks, but careful not to step on any of the boys'. *Very* careful. With her wide-set eyes, she was able to keep track of both boys and their specks too, and not step into anyone's territory. She enjoyed flirting but had no intention of getting caught up in another *relationship* - Ugh! Her Ex had run out on her when she needed support, going into the egg-laying stage. The bum! No way was she doing that again! But she loved attention and she was getting it. Doo-Doo and Loo would do anything for a smile, and she was all smiles. Just to drive them crazy she tap-danced and sang:

"Piddy-paddy, Piddy-paddy,
Doo-de-*Doo*, *Doo*-de-*Doo*!
I love you!
...Or maybe *Loo*?
Coochie-coo?
I love *Loo* too!
Piddy-paddy, Piddy-paddy,
Who will be my sugar daddy?"

Both boys lit out for the sugar bowl without a second thought, fighting through the crowd to get some and bring back for the fair lady; but romance and property rights are fleeting in their world. In only a minute's absence, a number of other boys invaded the vacant territories and began sipping beer and even marking out lines of their own, while Lena took up with a group of younger dudes who gladly made room for her at the spill. Doo-Doo and Loo had a battle on their hands to reclaim even part of their properties; but when the young dudes figured out that Lena was a tease, they lost interest and she came sashaying back up the neutral lane to her old beaus. They were setting baits for her, placing the sugar grains just within their dotted lines, hoping she would step into their territories and reward them with a peck on the cheek. Even more than winning the 'dame', the boys wanted to beat each other.

But Lena hadn't been born yesterday and wasn't about to let the fun come to an end. She danced along admiring the baits without taking any, so the boys nudged the sugar closer to the lane. That's when Lena got a better look and turned her nose up in distaste.

"It's dirty!" she told Doo-Doo. "Goodness, what are they doing up there in the sugar bowl? I won't eat that!" Doo-Doo was crestfallen. Loo grinned and rolled his grain even closer. That was a mistake. He'd also been hiding the soiled side and now she saw it.

"Ick! Yours is dirty too! What did you bring me? Is this all I'm worth?"

The bachelors offered excuses. Yes, of course the sugar bowl had been clean when the Trader opened it. Fit for a Lady! They'd been first to get into it. The sugar was a bit spotty now, but this must be expected with all the flies. After all, hadn't they tainted it a bit themselves while they dined? Perhaps even Lena had done her bit? Ha- ha. Sure! In one end and out the other! Oh, the joy of being a fly at dinner! They could eat non-stop if they had something to wash it down.

Lena was only putting on airs. For everyday dining, flies aren't fussy. Everyone knows they'll eat the most disgusting entrees so long as they're organic, and if the food is respectable they'll make it disgusting with their juices. Then they slurp the resulting mess. In other words, if you want to keep your own appetite, don't study theirs.

But Lena declined, feigning lady-like notions, and headed for the beer again. The bachelors weren't about to let the sugar go to waste and did their thing, spitting all over it first. Yero tried not to gag. Even amnesiac Boca, watching with an open mind, thought it vulgar.

"That's filthy!" he hollered. "Don't you have any manners?"

The bachelors were genuinely surprised. Flies are well aware of their dirty reputations. They flaunt it, even use it to get food from squeamish humans who throw it away if they see a fly on it. But here they were eating sugar! Sweet sugar! Leaving flyspecks from sugar is considered very high class in their world.

"Are you talking to *us*?" asked Loo.

"Yeah, I don't see anyone else spitting all over their food".

"You a 'Goody-Goody' too?" jeered Doo-Doo.

"We'll call you mister stuck-up-know-it-all!" grinned Loo.

"Think you're better than us, boy?"

"*That* one sure does", hiccuped Loo. "She won't even look at us. Hey, you! Hey, Miss Goody-Goody! You're eatin' the very same sugar".

Yero spun around angrily. "No one pooped in ours!"

"You sure?" said Loo. "You been watchin' r-e-a-l close?"

Yero couldn't help glancing at the shot glass. That's what the bachelors were waiting for. They guffawed.

"Nothin's safe with flies around!" heckled Loo.

"Just stay back!"

"Sure, okay! But you ain't gonna make any friends actin' like that. Nobody likes a Goody-Goody".

Yero squirmed, feeling somehow in the wrong. "Look, I'm sorry if I insulted you, but don't get all worked up about it. We aren't staying long".

"That's what they all say when they come in", snickered Loo. "But we accept your apology. C'mon. Let's have a drink and start over".

Boca started to go. Yero grabbed his arm. "No!" she almost shouted. "We don't do that!"

Doo-Doo acted hurt. "I thought we were friends now and you weren't going to be 'uppity' anymore. But if you won't drink with the regulars it means you're stuck-up, girl! That ain't no virtue".

"I'm sorry. But we promised our guide we wouldn't drink".

"So? Where is she?"

"Gone for a minute. She'll be back".

"Well, this is your chance, Kiddo! Take some advice from a regular. Have a little fun while you can! What she don't know won't hurt her".

"We can't. Just go and have a good time".

"Suit yerself, Snoots. But yer welcome to join us if you ever lower yerself to mix with regular folk.".

The bachelors buzzed off to join Lena at the spill. She was flirting again with the younger crowd. Semi-juvenile dudes were clustered around. Lena was a 'looker', a party girl, and always drew a crowd. Doo-Doo and Loo buzzed the lads noisily and they dispersed. The three long-time regulars settled down to drink seriously. Back at the shot glass, Boca was totally at a loss.

"Who's our guide?" he asked. "What's a guide?"

"Oh, Boca! This is so sad. I might as well call you 'Dumb Boca'. You really don't remember?"

"No, but I'm learning a lot".

"That's what worries me. Our guide is a hummingbird named Atel. She is helping us through the wilderness".

"Is she snooty, like you?"

"No! I'm not either! Why do you say such a thing?"

"Because she doesn't want us to drink beer with our new friends. Neither do you".

"That's not 'snooty', Boca. It's just good sense. Our guide wants to keep us out of trouble".

"I don't remember any such orders. So why not have some fun?"

"Because it's dumb! Maybe you don't remember the roadrunner, but he got goofy from the beer. He got *drunk*. It's just lucky that his wife dragged him out of here".

"I don't know any roadrunner, and I don't know what a wife is either, but it must be some kind of party-pooper".

Yero threw up her hands. "Go ahead then, be a dummy! But sooner or later you'll know it was wrong".

"Oh, don't be a worrywart", said Boca expansively. "I'm bigger than they are, so when they've had too much, I'll see it and stop. Drinking is simple!"

Boca fluttered over to where the three regulars were drinking and asked to join them. By comparison, he was huge and most of the other flies skedaddled, but not the regulars.

"Well, I *never*..." Lena began, and promptly turned her charms on him. "And I thought you were stuck-up! Ooooh! Such a big, strong boy!" The bachelors just chuckled, knowing how this would end. It would be great sport.

But they underestimated Boca a little. He had a fair amount of experience himself, flirting with girls, and Lena loved it. In no time, he was slurping the beer and describing to Lena how pretty her eyes were.

The three regulars (Known locally as 'Doo-Doo, Loo and Lena, Knights and Lady of the Cantina') showed no signs yet of drunkenness. Some other flies did, probably the youngest ones just out of the pupa stage. Flies don't get drunk very easily because the alcohol doesn't stay with them long enough, but they delight in getting other folks drunk. Yero was a bummer, but this one showed promise. He was already slurring the letter 'S' after only a few guzzles.

Yero did her best to ignore it, deciding that since she couldn't stop it she wasn't going to care. She sipped some sugar water out of boredom. A noise of many flies taking off at once caused her to turn around.

Nothing had changed over Boca's way (not for the better, anyhow) but the regulars had gone quiet watching the kitchen shelf. A cloud of flies had suddenly exited the sugar bowl, which was starting to smoke. Yero looked closer in alarm but it wasn't actually smoke, just dust - whew! Then she got worried again. The bowl was becoming a magnet, somehow sucking up dust from the shelf where it lay an inch thick. That didn't look right at all. She went to collect Boca who hadn't noticed anything except that Lena had quit listening to his witty comments.

"Can you fly?" Yero asked him.

"Shure, but I'm not going anywhere. Thish ish fun! I'm a regular now. You should try some".

Yero directed his attention to the dust. "Look up there", she said. "The sugar bowl is going crazy! Can you see it? The flies are all watching it. It's making me nervous".

"Yeah, shure I can see. Someone's kicking up dust. Oh! I know why everyone's looking!" Boca grinned cockeyed, knowing the answer.

"Why?"

"There's *two* shhuugar bowls now. Shhpooky!"

"The beer has gotten in your eyes, Boca, There's just one".

Yero studied him critically as he squinted and blinked, cocking his head at different angles.

"Now itsh gone completely", he said, mystified.

It wasn't just the beer. Yero turned and saw it was true. A blob of dust had risen out of the bowl and spilled over the sides, like bread dough rising uncontrollably. Some force held it together and it was growing fast, drawing dust now from several feet away, but in an orderly fashion. A small dust devil had formed above the blob and was vacuuming the kitchenette area.

"She's coming back", said an admiring voice. It was Lena. The three regulars ignored all else and watched the show, bobbing their heads politely toward whatever-it-was, as if they had expected this.

"D'ya 'spose she'll give us our reward?" wondered Loo.

"She owes us!" said Doo-Doo. "But you never know".

"We'll remind her", said Lena. "I want something for all the hard work we've put in!"

"No lie. Partying ain't easy," said Loo. "And we done it all for her!"

The barflies laughed at their private joke, but the dust was getting bad in the room. The blob and even the dust devil were obscured. Dust was lifting off the floor now and cobwebs full of it were being sucked down from the ceiling corners.

"I'm outa here before I get sucked in!" said Lena. "I'm going to the nursery to check on the children". Off she went. The bachelors groaned. This was not their favorite pastime; but anyone could see Lena was right about getting sucked in. Away they went after her, as fast as they could fly.

The possibility dawned on Yero too. "Boca! We need to get behind our glass! Can you fly - or not?"

"I don't know why not! What kinda queshtion ish *that*?"

"You're *drunk*! I don't know *how* drunk. I don't want you flying off toward that dust thing by mistake".

Boca was insulted. "I can fly!" he insisted. "Don't be shilly!"

"Then follow me!" Yero had to work against the suction but landed on the safe side of the glass, breathing hard. She turned to watch Boca who was laboring, beginning to drift with the dust. He had proved he could fly but had no idea where he was going.

"*Here!*" Yero shouted at the top of her lungs. "*Here!*" Boca somehow zeroed in on her voice. That worked better than his visual piloting, but not much. He reached the glass in good shape, but crash-landed face-first into the sugar water. He thrashed mightily and got his face above water but failed miserably to extricate himself.

"Help me, Yero! What ish thish?"

"Our supper, ninny. I bought supper, even if you don't remember".

But he did. He suddenly remembered everything except Kuri snatching his nugget. The splash in the face jogged something, along with Yero's reference to...*money*. Boca suddenly realized he wasn't clutching his gold anymore. Panic welled up! *Okay, be calm!* It must've been lost just now in the water. He reached down and felt around blindly.

Yero thought he was drowning again and went to his assistance. She tugged hard at one antenna, hoping to get his nose up. He fought hard to stay down while he searched frantically for the precious gold. Aha! He found it, way at the bottom, and allowed Yero to pull him up. He opened his eyes and took stock: He was still mired in the sugar water, and he was drunk - a fact that was at last sinking in. But he had his gold! The panic went away. He turned and smiled at Yero. That surprised her. She let go and his face fell *splat*, back into the water.

"I'm sorry!" she shouted, grabbing the antenna again. It was difficult to hang on as Boca struggled, but up he came again finally. This time Yero braced herself and pulled until he could grab the rim of the glass before she let go.

"Thanksh!" said Boca, laughing and trying to bend the antennae straight with one hand. Dust flew past, buffeting his wings but it was easy to hang on with sticky hands.

"I'm glad you aren't mad", said Yero. "I'm sorry I had to pull so hard, but you wanted to go down instead of up".

"That wush on purpussh! I dropped my nugget, but I got it back. I remember shtuff now".

Yero studied his face. It was such a mess. Who could possibly guess what was going on inside?

"Do you remember Atel, and the journey?"

"Shure! Everything".

"And the Trader Rat? And Kuri bargaining with him?"

"Shure! Kuri gave up all his coins".

"But the Trader wanted more. Do you remember that part?"

"Nope. What happened?"

The Trader wanted *your* gold too, and Kuri snitched it from you".

"Nope!" said Boca proudly. "I've got it!"

That's a good place to leave Boca for now. He's happy, he's proud, and he'll have lots of problems soon enough. Right now, the dust storm drowned out any more talk. The whirlwind revved up and up until it had sucked up all the dust in the trading post - and then suddenly quit. All was silent. Nary a fly buzzed. Boca had shut his eyes to keep his head from spinning and kept them closed. Yero looked up to the sugar bowl. It was hidden. Something – *someone* - was sitting on it. A large, ugly woman sat there. The bowl was obscured by her plus-sized behind. Her legs dangled off the shelf, dirty feet overhanging the cooktop stove below. Yero noted oddly that the cobwebs had gone into a hairdo which somewhat relieved the ugliness of her face. She was staring directly at the butterflies as if they were the only other living creatures in the room. Perhaps they were. Certainly, no flies were anywhere to be seen. Any that hadn't fled must have been sucked up and become part of the woman. In fact, a fly crawled out her nose even as Yero watched. It irritated the woman. Or did it? At least she took her eyes off the butterflies.

She grunted something to the fly. Maybe it was just indigestion, but more flies now emerged from her nose and even her ears. She belched, emitting still more. She smiled at them as they flew happy little orbits around her head.

Yero dug a toe into Boca's side, then twice more before he opened his eyes. "Look", she said. "It's an old 'Dust Bag'!"

The woman heard that in the quiet room and squirmed on the shelf. It suddenly broke beneath her weight and everything on it came crashing down, old 'Dust Bag' included. The woman ended up standing shakily on the fry grill and a good bit of her outside layer flaked off from the shock, piling up an inch deep around her feet. That made her mad. She bent down and tried to sweep it up with her hands, recovering a small amount which she sprinkled on her shoulders. That improved her mood. Then she noticed the butterflies again and scowled. She detested anything pretty or colorful and started to take a quick step toward them but stopped abruptly as she realized where she was, still three feet above the floor.

"Tell me whush happening", whispered Boca. "I think I got dusht in my eyes".

"Mostly beer, I'm sure", amended Yero. "Can you see the old Bag at all? She's hard to describe".

"Oh yeah. Big blob like that - who could miss her? But she's all fuzzy".

"You're seeing pretty good. She's not stuck together all that well. When she moves fast, dust shakes off. Maybe we're lucky. You can't move at all, but at least she can't move very fast".

But she *could* move slowly. It occurred to the woman now that she had no clothes on, and she apparently recalled some manners from - when? A previous life probably. She reached out gingerly and took a large towel from the wall rack, a grey one that happened to be darkest, and very carefully put it around her.

That's when the regular barflies returned, all in fine spirits and smelling of manure from the Gila monster's dung heap out back. Please do not be offended, but the heap was the local nursery for all the cute little baby flies. The Three buzzed the woman from a safe distance for now, judging her mood. They hadn't lived so long by being foolish. Loo even fell back and sounded out the butterflies.

"That's our boss", he grinned. "Want we should introduce you?"

"No thank you", Yero declined politely. "We'll stay here".

"What's the matter? Ain't she friendly?"

"Not especially, no".

The regulars laughed. "She's her old self then", pronounced Lena. "She don't like no pretty dolls or dandies. You hurt her eyes. Oh-oh. The mirror!"

"Something wrong?" asked Yero.

But the barflies were already gone a-buzzing around the kitchenette, upset about the mirror. It had fallen off the shelf too and lay face down, smashed, next to the sugar bowl. They went to their 'boss' with the disturbing news but failed to get her attention. She had caught sight of the faucet and began edging toward it, ignoring them. She was surrounded by flies anyway which is natural for creatures like her. Yero called her a 'Dust Bag', and that was pretty close. They are properly known as 'Night Hags'.

This hag, like all new ones (or re-newed ones) was drawn to liquid. Being only a collection of dry dust, they desperately need to soak up some moisture and firm up or they'll never make their way in the world - and the sooner the better too, as Yero had seen, before they fall to pieces. She took baby steps across the grill and narrow counter to reach the sink, only to discover she couldn't safely bend far enough to reach the faucet handle. When she tried, dust broke loose off her middle, and though Yero thought the woman could afford some loss there, she didn't like it. What to do? Lacking any handy chair or stepstool the hag retraced her steps to where the fallen shelf lent itself as a slide. One end was still held up by a support bracket while the fallen end rested on the kitchen floor. It was her only chance at a normal life. A hag like herself could probably live on that countertop for years, but what fun is that? She edged into position, pausing only for a few second thoughts.

"Boca, I want you to try to fly", whispered Yero. "If you can, we'll head for the door. Do you see what she's up to?"

Boca squinted hard, and then closed his eyes again. "I can't see", he groaned. "I get dizzy when I try".

"Well, she wants to get down to the floor. She's going to slide down the broken shelf. If she makes it, I think she wants a drink first, and then she'll come for us. She doesn't like us. We need to get out of here. Can you fly or not?'

"Not if I open my eyes. I'll just get dizzy and crash".

"Try opening just one eye".

He thought about it. Thinking made him dizzy too, so he just did it. Ah, that was better. "I'm good", he said. "Tell me when".

"Just a sec - oh, my! There she goes!"

The hag slid down the board in fine shape and hit the floor walking to slow her momentum. She picked up scads of slivers in her feet from the broken board and never even noticed, but it was her agility that caught Yero's eye. Who could guess that such a creature would be nimble? It didn't bode well. The sink and faucet were at working level now. The hag bellied up and studied the faucet handle. Which way? There were no arrows.

Boca was trying to follow events with one eye like he was told, but Yero suddenly changed her mind. "Look the other way", she ordered quickly. "She's not decent from behind".

Indeed not. The towel was too short, and the Hag didn't bother about it. However, she had figured out the faucet enough to give it a try. She carefully grasped the handle between thumb and forefinger and attempted to turn it counterclockwise. Luckily for her it was the right direction. Unfortunately, her thumb and forefinger weren't up to the stress. They broke off and fell into the sink where they lay relatively undamaged. The hag flinched in surprise, shaking off another minor amount of dust, but showed excellent patience otherwise. After a few more moments of study she reached into the sink, carefully retrieved the lost digits, and stuck them back on in the 'up' position. They balanced nicely - but would they hold? She slowly lowered the hand. Bad luck! The dirty digits fell off again and this time shattered into dust. She cursed so loud she expelled more flies.

"Yikes!" chirped Yero. "My mistake, Boca! I should've told you to plug your ears instead! She's no lady. Okay, let's go".

"I can't. I'm stuck".

"You're just drunk. Try harder!"

"Have it your way. I'm drunk. But I'm stuck too".

The sugar water on the glass and all over Boca's body had thickened and gummed. He wasn't joking. He couldn't move. Worse yet, the regular barflies were talking to the hag again, bringing the beer to her attention, trying to cheer her up and curry favor. She promptly abandoned her lost parts and made her way around the bar to the public side, advancing toward the spilt beer and helpless Boca.

She bellied up to the bar next to them but ignored the butterflies for now, plopping her hands down in the spilt beer instead and closing her eyes in bliss. A slow smile misshaped her mouth - a mouth not designed for such a purpose - as the beer soaked into her palms and fingertips. A 'coo'-ing noise escaped from her, and a smell of naturally composting gasses as her body settled. The beer puddle was quickly sponged up, but the hag waited a minute or two for the liquid to soak way in and firm up her grippers. As she waited, her eyes re-opened and she scowled at the butterflies. It was a bad omen but definitely a more natural arrangement of her facial features.

There was nothing Yero could do except try to negotiate, so she introduced herself a few inches in front of the woman's nose. The hag never moved except her eyes, which brooded unblinking, like knotholes in a rotten tree.

"Your eyes are like knotholes..." Yero found herself saying.

"Like *what*?" The 'coo'-ing noises stopped as the hag stiffened.

"Knotholes", Yero said lamely. "But what I *meant* was: You look big and strong and *solid!* Like a tree!"

That was much better. The 'coo'-ing resumed. But the hag thought now to try out her improved grip, reaching for the shot glass and Boca.

"There's more beer in those cans!" said Yero quickly. "They're at least half full, and it's not any 'lite' beer either!"

"Beer", said the hag, trying out the word. She shifted her reaching fingers and laid them on the bar again, but it was dry. She felt tricked! She didn't understand beer cans. Her fingers strayed toward Boca once more.

Yero took a chance and landed on her nose, regaining her attention and directing it back to the beer, pushing temptation as bad as any barfly. She even flew to a can and pointed into the pop-top opening. "In here!" she urged. "Soaking wet beer! Makes you feel *good!* Gets into your *head!* C'mon, have a swig!"

Maybe the hag understood - or maybe there's just something about a can of beer that attracts characters like her. She reached for one, experimentally. Her grip closed comfortably around it, a sure sign of intemperance. She lifted it with great care. Up came the can with no problem but the hag didn't put it to her lips. Taking Yero's advice literally she raised it high over her head and tipped it. Glug, splash! The first gush landed in her hair, dead center on the noggin. Some ran off in little rivulets, eroding gullies down her cheeks, but the overall effect was moistening and beneficial. In a show of intelligence, or at least sobriety, the hag tilted the can less so that it only dripped - a pace that could fully soak into her cranium.

She closed her eyes once more in bliss. The unnatural smile returned, and also the release of compost gasses. The gasses tended to rise but not fast enough for poor Boca, unable to escape them down there. He twisted, turned, and tried to hold his breath, keeping his eyes shut tight. That was just as well. If he opened them, he would've seen he was in far worse danger than just gas. The hag hadn't forgotten him. Even now in her moment of content, her hand reached out slowly, blindly searching for him. Yero could only watch with dread.

Now the groping fingers found the glass, feeling all around it for exact position. The hag never opened her eyes. Didn't have to. She had a good mental picture of the glass and the butterfly there that needed pinching. Now her fingers confirmed the shape of the glass. She raised her hand a bit and went for the pinch. Unfortunately for Boca her aim was perfect. Fortunately, however, the pinching digits were the missing ones. Their stubs moved, sending a signal to her brain that all was working well but the missing pinchers saved Boca for the moment.

The whole while she dripped beer she kept pinching away at Boca, serene in the knowledge that she was smooshing him. She had a nasty mean streak. Yero could only hope she kept her eyes shut. Then the drip stopped. The can was empty. The hag stiffened at the change, but only slightly. She was mellowing out quickly. The beer soaking directly into her cranium was affecting her much faster than if she drank it. She liked the effect, and even stopped pinching at Boca. After a minute, she remembered there was another can near at hand and roused herself enough to locate it. She gripped it as comfortably as the other or thought she did. But the hand wasn't as steady as before. She tipped the can toward herself and it gurgled out splashing into her belly. She stepped back in surprise so that most of the beer ran over the edge and formed a large pool on the floor. Undaunted she stepped forward once again, putting her big feet right in the puddle. Getting a new grip on the can, she raised it overhead and enjoyed the last drops that way.

The overall effect was wonderfully relaxing and she settled together more, forcing release of extra gasses that overwhelmed the room and drifted out the door. The veteran barflies cruised blissfully about relishing the 'new hag' smell. Boca was overcome and fainted. Yero fled out the door for relief and met the Gila monster returning from his hunt. She landed right on his head and shouted something in his ear that angered him. Then he caught wind of the smell drifting out the door and that upset him even more. He charged in, head wagging, and stopped, baffled at the sight of the hag.

Some extra sense warned the woman and she turned to see what raised her hackles. Oh, just the stupid lizard. She had been aware of him over the years indirectly through the eyes of her pet flies and considered him no threat at all. Animal brain! He had no magic, only a big mouth. "Scram, idiot!" she barked.

The Gila monster hissed or snorted - an unintelligible sound. The hag underestimated him for lack of speech, and it's true they have none; but it's only because of their slobbery poison that slurs everything. They are very intelligent in their own way and quick to anger. He charged.

That's where he underestimated the hag. She did have magic of a crude sort. Night Hags dream it up in the long years of their hibernation, especially spells against other inhabitants of the house, in case they are needed when the hag reawakens. Yes! She had the perfect spell against a big mouth! It would be awkward though. Her feet were stuck in beer mud and she had to twist around to point her finger at the charging lizard (a good finger, this time). "Shut up!" she commanded.

Too bad she'd had so much beer. Her aim was unsteady. The spell whizzed past the Monster and attached itself to the cash register. Clang! The drawer slammed shut. The hag still had time to try again and did. "Shut up!' she hollered a second time, but her aim was no better than before. The spell missed and found the front door, hanging on its lone hinge. Bang! Tinkle, tinkle. The door shut squarely and broke out the window.

That was her last chance. Then the monster reached her and chomped her lower leg, taking out several inches of elevation. She dropped that much to one side, jarring her sensibilities, and before she could collect her thoughts he took an even bigger chunk out of the other leg. He was in no danger of choking on the dust because he gushed so much saliva. Then he really went to work, chomping her down to size chunk by chunk until all that remained was the beer-soaked top of her head and her cobweb hair. The monster walked away satisfied at that point, leaving those parts untouched. There are some things even a Gila monster won't put in their mouth. If any proof was needed that the hag was truly gone, the cash drawer popped ajar and the front door fell open again on its hinge. The Monster glanced at the unpredictable door and made a mental note to rip it off entirely. Maybe tomorrow. With that pleasant thought, he retired to his cage for a nice nap.

Down in the cellar the Trader was chittering and squeaking like crazy about what all was going on up there. Yero ignored him and rushed to see about Boca - stuck fast to the shot glass and miraculously alive - but pathetic. He was snoring, face down, tongue hanging out, and even the tongue was stuck to the glass.

"Not very pretty!" said a familiar voice behind her.

"Oh - Atel! I wish you were here a few minutes ago. We needed help".

"So I see. But together with the lizard you did fine! We won't count Boca in on that".

"No. He's stuck here. We'll have to un-stick him somehow".

"I think it best we do nothing for now. In the morning he'll wake up hung over. We'll melt him loose then and he can try Kuri's remedy, pounding his head. It'll be a lesson in the old school of hard knocks".

"He needs one. But to be fair he wasn't right in the head when he joined the boozers".

"Drunks are never right in the head", laughed Atel.

"I meant *before*. He went crazy over his gold, you know. Then Kuri snatched it and threw it in on a beer deal with the Trader! Boca totally lost it for a while".

"And for that we should just wink at his intemperance?"

"I don't know what that means. Is it like being tempted? Because the barflies really tempted him".

"All he had to do was say 'no'".

"It wasn't that easy. They said we were stuck-up, that we thought we were better than everyone else. It wasn't fair. I don't go around thinking like that".

"Sometimes you should".

"Really?"

"For sure! You darn well better aim higher than the bums of the world, and barflies are usually bums".

"Oh, thanks a lot! We don't have enough trouble already? Now we're bums too!" grumbled Lena, eavesdropping.

"You certainly are. But it's not a terminal condition. You can improve yourselves".

"We almost did! *She* came back. Our boss!" Lena waved at the heap of dust that had been the hag. "She would've taken over this joint. Big improvement".

"In what way?'

"Free beer, all day! She owed us. So much for *that* happy idea!"

"You must be one of her 'True Flies', her eyes and ears".

Lena backed off evasively. "I don't know nuthin'", she said.

The bachelors gallantly supported her. "We don't know nuthin' either", they said.

Atel laughed. "By your own admission then, there is room for improvement. You won't ever know nuthin' until you kick the habit. But at least now you can be free".

The regulars disappeared in a huff. Yero was glad to see them go. "Their boss was a really mean old Dust Bag!" she said. "Something happened in the sugar bowl after the Trader opened it, and there was a dust storm up there. When it cleared, she was sitting on it. She looked funny until she showed her bad side".

"That's all they have. There is no virtue about them. They're called 'Night Hags'. I smelled this one in the dust when we came in, and probably shouldn't have left you here. I know that now. It's unusual for one to awaken, but it does happen. Do you mind if I have a bit of your sugar water?"

"Be my guest. I'd love to finish it and get my money's worth. I've learned that much in this joint".

"That's a good lesson. Maybe this hasn't been a total loss".

"But we'll have to stay here for now, with 'stuck-up' Boca".

"Yes, maybe tomorrow night too. We'll just have to see how sick he is in the morning. But drop the nickname, even if it is clever. He won't be in a very good mood".

"I had a better one, even! He's been just inspiring them! Oh, well. I'll try to be helpful".

"Good girl! You can start right now by thinking up positive things to say. Boca will need them tomorrow".

"That sounds boring".

"Okay. How about a bedtime story then?"

"Sure. Which one?"

"About the Hags and where they come from".

"I don't think that would put me to sleep".

"Who can sleep anyway, with the Trader carrying on so?'

Yero laughed. "Okay. And if I'm still awake, I'll tell you how *he* got stuck down *there*. He deserves it".

—The Night Hags—

In the Beginning, according to witch-lore, the Lord of Light made the earth out of a spinning cloud of dust. Afterward there remained a lot of good quality dust circling above, so He encouraged His Artisans to take from it and add extra beautiful touches to the new planet, and this also was done.

"What shall we do with the rest, Lord?" they asked, for some low-quality dust was left over - grimy stuff they deemed too dirty to be of any virtue in a brand-new world.

The Lord sniffed it and made a face. "Just leave it there", He ordered. "You did well to sort that out".

So that was that, for an Age or more.

Some of the refuse drifted off into space but most of it hung there in the upper stratosphere, neither heavy enough to fall to earth nor light enough to be carried off by the solar wind. To this very day, there's a smuttysphere up there. Some now argue that we put it there ourselves, and no doubt we've added some to it, but most of the mess has been there from the Beginning.

Meanwhile, Ages passed splendidly on the clean earth below. Good folks with fine manners lived privileged lives in sanitary houses with spotless mirrors, exactly as the Lord intended.

But eventually (according to witch-lore) the spoiled people got what they deserved, and it was their own goody-goody thoughts wafting up that awakened the smuttysphere to thought of its own.

The thought was dark and resentful. Perhaps that's understandable: There it was in limbo, just a dirty layer of air circling helplessly beyond the reach of gravity, never to be anything more.

That's as far as things likely would have gone, except for the voices. The smuttysphere is close to the darkness up there, and the darkness always argues against the Lord of Light. The voices taunted the smuttysphere, stirring it up until bits began to clump together, growing layer by layer around a bad temper, a lot like hailstones. Thus, the first hags appeared and floated down to the surface of the earth.

Once started it has never stopped. They call themselves the 'Smuttsee' (rhymes with 'butt-see') and there seems no pattern at all to their appearance. New ones must be festering up there all the time and perhaps weather conditions below create a downdraft. No one really knows. But they're still coming, according to the old trappers of the far north who get the best view of a clear night sky. They say it's common to see a hag floating down. In more civilized regions, they're usually mistaken for weather balloons - as round and slow as they are - unless they pass across the moon. Then folks take notice! That's how the image of flying witches started. But new hags don't have brooms or umbrellas, or anything like that - just a hopelessly out-of-fashion covering that looks more like a diaper than a garment.

As they approach the surface, gravity grips them, puts pressure on their brain, and they fully awaken. The lower layers of atmosphere contain water vapor, which the hags crave to bind their flimsy dust bodies together. They have almost no navigation about them as they near the ground and quite a few fall *splash!* into deep water. So much for those. Of the ones that fall on land most do survive, retaining one main ambition after they've collected their wits, and perhaps a loose limb or two. They want revenge on this clean earth and its favored inhabitants.

They know instinctively where to go: To the places of men, the most favored creatures of all, whom the hags imitate in appearance. They know they must have shelter, or wind and rain will erode them, so they find homes, barns, and other buildings, the nicer and cleaner the better, and hibernate. They're tired. They usually enter a house at night and tour the place while it's asleep. The cleanliness angers them, steams them until they dry out and begin to crumble. The hag can feel it coming on. She opens all the doors and stands in a hallway. Then she takes a deep breath and pokes herself in the stomach. With a hollow *Pop,* she explodes, casting herself adrift throughout the house. The last thing she sees is spots dancing in front of her eyes. When the dust has all settled the spots are still dancing, at least two of them. These are her 'Hag-flies', what we call houseflies. That's her last dirty trick - releasing them from her eyes to be her lookouts and infect the house.

It's a girl and a boy, of course. At least one of each and the hag's thought is in them. They must be fruitful and multiply for many generations, usually, if she is to come back again. So, the Hag-flies search out garbage to lay eggs in. Most houses have some, so that's easy. But some houses don't. Some are too tidy. Does that save them?

No. In that case the Hag-flies search out a mirror when they get old (although any well-polished surface will do) and invite their reflections out into the room to take over. Then all *those* invite *theirs*...well, you get the picture. Emerging flies pause to plaster the mirror with a filthy speck, their mark of passage. So, the flyspecks on your mirrors are tally marks, really. Altogether, if you could ever count them, this is the number of 'True-Flies' (as they call themselves) which have patrolled the place over the years. True-Flies consider themselves a cut above lower class 'garbage-flies. Barflies are usually just garbage flies.

Over time however, the high class True-Flies - even the true mirror clones - tend to marry below their station and the line gets diluted. The hag's thought is weakened and forgotten. There must always be some 'True-Flies' to see and hear for her, so she knows when the time is right to pull herself together again. If they disappear, the hag can be swept out the door and the house actually cleaned up again.

—Stage 2 of a Hag—

Luckily for the world, most hags perish somehow, such as drowning, failure to gain entry to a nice home, or because their True-Flies fancy the garbage girls and forget their duty. But some hags do pull themselves together again from the dust, wiser in the ways of the world, totally bored from years of inactivity and anxious to re-enter our civilized society looking for mischief.

This is when they begin to pose a threat. They've thought up some tricks and minor magic by now to annoy the human race and have learned deception and disguise. But the big thing is they have a goal.

Oh, yes. Even the dumbest new hag floating down tonight knows what the Big Deal is: From their bitter race the Great Witches evolved, the Coven of Twelve. All hags hope to join someday, but it's tough. There are only twelve and they live practically forever. A hag - no matter how skilled she may become - cannot hope to be promoted until there's a vacancy. But at least it doesn't have to be a natural vacancy.

So, there are a fair number of these troublesome creatures circulating among us with time on their hands, causing problems. Almost none of them will ever join the Coven, but they're a pretty hardened group of their own and don't perish easily. It is these hags, especially, that are mistaken for real witches. They're fairly common, usually lazy, not always smart enough to keep secret, and thus there have been numerous references to witches throughout folklore, and even serious essays. Sir Isaac Newton himself postulated in the 17th century (at the age of four): 'A hag at rest tends to stay at rest'.

But a careful reading of folklore narratives reveals most stories to be only hag-encounters, the proof being that the witness lived to tell.

***

Yero was asleep by the time Atel ended the tale and Boca snored all the way through it. The Trader had finally piped down but certainly wasn't sleeping. Several times during the night the Ferris wheel sprang into motion and brought up a beer can as he tested his weight against it, but the beer quickly disappeared back down each time. The rat needed to lose a lot of weight and was determined not to lose another beer to any customers that still might be hanging around up there.

The only other disturbance was around midnight when the Gila monster awoke with hag-breath and dry mouth. He made his way outside, attacking the broken door in his cussed mood and breaking off the last hinge. It clattered onto the steps with a racket, waking everyone for a little while, even Boca. He struggled feebly to move, could not, and immediately went to sleep again. After that, even Atel dozed off for a while.

Long before sunrise, at the first hint of dawn through the open doorway, the barflies roused themselves piteously and began to move around with their hangovers. Yes, they could hold their liquor from long practice, but it still takes its toll the next morning. Lena eased into a soulful strain and the bachelors hummed the tune - also with much practice. All of them held their throbbing heads.

"Oh, woe!

I never touched no booze!
My momma knows it's true.
I got the Good Girl Blues...

Oh, yeah!
I've paid my dues!
Momma knows I paid my dues.
I ain't got much to lose--
Except the Good Girl Blues!"

They carried on mournfully until Atel decided it wasn't going to end any time soon. "The door is open", she advised. "Take it outside. We're trying to sleep".

"Oh, great. More goody-goody talk", moaned Lena. "Now we know where that butterfly gets it, the snooty one".

"You are correct. Here's some more good news: Us 'snooties' aren't hungover. We feel just dandy".

"Ugh! Save the sermon. We got enough troubles".

"Okay, no sermon. But your boss is gone for good. You ought to make plans. What will you do?"

There was a lot of mumbling and buzzy grumbling with a few sidelong glances toward the broken shelf.

"The mirror?" inquired Atel. "I can't help you there. I don't think it would work for you now, anyway. But at least you can live out your last days as decent ordinary flies. Is that so bad?"

"It's a lousy ending, to be thrown in with the rabble".

Well, look for a noble goal! Do some volunteer work. Warn the youngsters against drinking. Finish up on a high note!"

The barflies couldn't stand it and it hurt too much to argue. They retired to the far end of the bar.

"They're just like Kuri, aren't they?" said Yero, awake and feeling chipper. "Do you think they'll change their ways? I don't think Kuri will.

"Probably not. It's a tough habit to break. Best to not get started".

"Will Boca be a no-good drunk too, now?"

"Let's ask him. Mustn't be too gentle with these patients".

There's something about a first-time hangover that is extra-bad. Some would say the young reveler simply has no tolerance built up, that it won't be as bad the next time. That would be his drinking buddies giving him sympathy. Others have said it's a warning from the Angels. The message sure seemed to be reaching Boca, poor lad. He was sobered up. Sober, sick and sorry - and still stuck. Maybe the worst rookie hangover ever. Yero had so much good advice that Atel wasn't even needed and went to make a deal with the Trader.

"Are you down there?" she called. "I need some water".

"Where else? Sure, I'm down here! The Post is closed today".

"Well, let's open it. I know what your problem is. I think I can help".

"Is this the hummingbird I'm talkin' to?"

"Yes".

"Well, thank you kindly. Nice of you to offer. But the truth is, I'm just too fat. I overbalance this thing and you're too tiny to help".

"If I can slow the wheel so you can climb out, what's it worth?"

The rat calculated quietly. "Free water", he offered finally. "I ain't makin' no money down here. What's the plan?"

"Sugar water in the bearings. It'll take a while to harden and you can't move the wheel in the meantime. Have patience down there".

She dipped a beakful out of the jigger and dribbled it into one of the bearings, then some in the other. It needed almost all that was left of Yero's 'supper' to gum up both. Then she hovered close and fanned the mess with her wings to speed the gumming process. It took until noon, off and on, to be absolutely sure, and there was a huge lack of patience to deal with. Pack Rats have never been known for any, and Boca was feeling well enough now to panic in his sugar straitjacket.

"Isn't there *any* way to hurry?" he pleaded for the 20th time. Atel went to check the bearings, just to escape his whining. He was in good hands anyway. Yero was lecturing him.

"'All good things come to those who wait'", she quoted. "Remember that one? It really fits, doesn't it? So, a little extra delay won't hurt if you put it to good use. Think back once more. What brought you to this sorry state? Were you warned? If so, by who? Will you ever do it again? This is a pop-quiz, Boca, to see what you've learned. Atel will be asking later, I'm sure".

We must leave Yero's obedience class now because events are starting to move, even if Boca isn't. Atel gave the go-ahead at last and the Trader scrambled neatly up and out, hardly budging the wheel at all. However, in typical Trader fashion he now wanted to amend the deal on 'prior conditions'.

"First - before anything else! - I am owed for two cans of beer consumed but unpaid-for". He pointed to the empty cans.

"Forget it", said Atel. "Our deal is separate". She had expected something like this.

"The cuckoo was with your party. Everything goes on the party tab". The Trader grinned a toothy grin and added unfairly, "Also, my wheel is now stuck. My whole operation depends on it. Someone will have to pay for loss of income".

"Charge it all off against cleaning up your place. We got rid of your infestation. Did you know you had a hag?"

The rat looked around, surprised. Except for the hag-pile, the place was vacuumed and dusted. "That her?" he asked, peering down from the bar. "She just stumbled in one night and fell apart. It's been impossible to keep the place clean ever since. Okay, I'll call it square. What happened up here?"

Yero recounted how the hag came back to life only to leave it again, courtesy of the Gila monster.

The rat smiled. "So, he saved you? Then you owe *him*, and I do the collecting for him. We'll split the difference and say you still owe for one beer".

Atel said something about the "price of honesty going up".

"Bear in mind, too", added the rat, "that I'm the only one who can open the faucet".

"And I'm the only one who can fix the wheel", reminded Atel.

In the end, Atel won the argument. The wheel just had to be fixed. The Traders' bootleg business depended on it. He gave in and turned the faucet to a good drip so Atel could get her drink. After that, she melted Boca loose with pure water. Yero watched nervously as he pulled free of his gummy shackles and took to the air. Would he go looking for beer? He did not! Yero breathed a sigh of relief but their guide wasn't as charitable, studying him. He was still far from clean - and what was he clutching? Oof da!

"Just dump the fly poop", she scolded. "And - both of you! - take a shower under the drip".

Atel drew more water and began to rinse the bearings.

"*I* could've done *that*!" squeaked the rat.

"It'll take both of us. Spin the wheel as I drip water. It'll clean the gum out faster. And we'd better hurry or it'll start to rust".

They worked for some time while the butterflies dried themselves in a fresh breeze that blew in through the open door. Dust flew up from the hag-pile, but a lucky draft drew it mostly out the door. At last the wheel spun freely, and none too soon. The rat was exhausted.

"It's been an interesting visit", said Atel politely. "We'll be leaving now. Say hello to the cuckoo for us".

All the Trader could do was nod. His chittering tongue lolled helplessly. It isn't easy running a Trading Post, even if you're born for the job.

They had to fight their way out the door into another gust of wind and took shelter for the moment up under the eaves. The gust sucked out more of the hag-pile. In time to come the whole pile would blow out the door, plopped as it was on the near side of the bar, leaving only the beer-hardened footprints at the bottom. That would give rise to stories of 'Bigfoot' creatures among some locals. Others would laugh. No one would ever guess the truth.

"One moment", said Atel. "The Trader has caught his breath by now and is ready for final instructions".

She zipped back inside. He hadn't moved an inch. "By the way", said Atel, "You'll have to keep turning the wheel until the bearings are *dry*. Sugar water is bad, but even clean water will rust them if you just leave it".

The rat slumped.

"There's silver lining in every cloud", added the hummingbird brightly. "Think of all the weight you're losing!"

Chapter 13

Bats and Their Masters

"It's a Chinook wind off the high mountains", said Atel, returning to the partial shelter of the eaves. The soffit was loose and hung down so they could cling to a perch just up in the gap. Maybe there were dangers lurking in the dark attic behind; but if so, they had retreated from the draft into their own sheltered corners.

"It's from the north", observed Yero. "That's never a good sign, is it?"

"Not usually, but this isn't *her* wind. That's easy to tell. Notice the air? It's mild. These aren't her mountains".

"So, this is a friendly wind? It could be a lot friendlier!"

"It might let up. If it does, we're off. If not, we'll have to leave pretty soon anyway".

"If we lose our grip we'll be off even sooner", worried Yero; but since they didn't, she launched into an account of the hag pinching Boca with her missing fingers. It was funny since it ended well, but Boca felt like the butt of the joke.

"She probably just wanted to hold me up as a model", he said, trying to change the subject, "so she could tell her flies: 'Why can't you be handsome like this?'"

"Yeah, right", scoffed Yero. "More likely she would've said, 'See everyone? This is how drunk I want to get!' She gave it a try, too. But there wasn't enough beer left after you got done".

"I didn't drink that much! And I shouldn't be blamed so much either. It all happened when I wasn't right in the head".

Yero laughed. "You were off your rocker, that's for sure".

Boca suddenly turned grumpy. It's no fun having a fault, and everyone keeps pointing at it. Anyway, his head was far from right yet, with the hangover. "I'm going!" he said. And he did.

It wasn't a good time to go flying, but who knew when it would be? The others followed quickly, and the Chinook pushed them toward the canyon below. There, even stronger winds coming down the gorge hurtled them ahead, ejecting them out of the canyon mouth into the broken foothills.

A hummingbird alone might fight through such a wind, but butterflies can't. The Chinook blew directly across their line of travel, carrying them southeastward instead of true south, together with a dangerous mix of flying sand and grit. It showed no sign at all of diminishing. Atel decided to seek shelter and hope it would let up toward evening. If it did, they could set out again, correcting their course by the stars.

In answer to her hope a cave mouth soon beckoned - a group of cave openings, actually, on a sheer rock wall that nearly encircled a shallow valley. What could be more convenient? Obviously, humans had dwelt here in times gone by. The cave openings were chiseled and shaped nicely to appeal to the eye but were long-since abandoned. The old cliff dwellers had been gone for centuries. She checked the air in all the entrances and made faces.

"Bats", she announced. "Probably in all of these. Shouldn't be a problem for us if you can stand the smell. Can you?"

"I smell 'em", said Boca. "It's no worse than sidewinders".

"We've smelled a lot of bad smells since we took up with you", volunteered Yero. "One more shouldn't be any big deal"

"Good", answered their guide. "I'm glad you've been paying attention. The stink should be the worst of this danger. It's still midday. They don't awaken until near sundown".

With that they entered one of the caves, the biggest one, and found shelter from the stinging wind. The passage immediately turned right and fell back into shadow. Shelves and nooks had been cut into the walls near the front. All were empty, not counting grit from the weathering walls or dust deposited by passing storms. They settled down on a shelf with a smooth arch above, very smooth with no footholds. It was the only ceiling area not festooned with sleeping bats.

"There, now. Comfy? You can nap a bit if you like", whispered Atel. "I'll watch".

"I don't think so", replied Yero. "Who could sleep with all their racket?"

Indeed, the bats were noisy. Bats make an awful lot of noise in their sleep. Not enough to alarm big folk, maybe, but big folk don't understand the language and that's what all the noise is. Bats commonly talk in their sleep, though if you woke one up and said so they would probably deny it. They dream and the talk comes from that. With bats, there's just more of it and it's nastier.

Like other creatures of the darkness, their dreams would shock polite society. They dream mostly about pursuing prey, capturing it, and eating it, so smaller folk have come to understand the language out of self-defense, but it's difficult. Some of it is traditional words and some is just high-pitched pulses that big folk don't pick up, but little folk do. At point-blank range, the pulses can cause headaches and confusion, and a letdown of one's guard.

"Can you feel it?" grumbled Yero. "This won't be much rest".

"It's like woodpecker talk", said Boca. "The rat-tat-tat accent anyway. That one there - that closest one - I wish she would turn the other way. She sees us. I know she does because she's talking about us. Listen!"

It was true. Maybe the sleeping bat didn't actually see them, but she could smell and hear them. Butterflies of any kind aren't a common item on a night-bat's dinner menu, but they're not unknown. And butterfly smell is small-creature smell. The smell of prey.

"Don't get excited", said Atel calmly. "They *are* asleep, no matter what they may say aloud. Just ignore her. *You* turn the other way. That's easier".

"Easy for you to say", pointed out Yero. "I'm sure *you* could escape them".

"Probably. But these are likely dreaming about moths. Keep that happy thought and remember: They *are* asleep. Don't bother them and they'll sleep for hours yet. By then we should be long gone".

"I hope so. Where's our next stop? Do you know?"

"Certainly. A tall cactus, I hope. Do you know what that is?'

"Sure. All needles and pins. Why that?"

They hold water. I know a wren who lives in one, or used to, not too far from here. I'm going ahead to see if she's home and try to finagle an invitation for overnight. She's excitable and I think I should go alone first".

"And leave us here? With the bats?"

"You should be fine. If they do start waking up early, get into a crevice. See? Here are several. Choose the narrowest one you can slip into, and that should be too narrow for a big bat".

"Oh, so reassuring!"

"Good. I hoped you'd feel that way".

"I don't! I was joking. This looks like trouble, and we've gotten into trouble before when you left us alone".

"You have, and you've survived quite nicely! It helps if I don't always have to look behind, because a guide must also look to the future, to what comes *next*. That's where I'm going now. I'll be back. Remember the crevices!"

She left. The butterflies watched and put up with the smell for a while in silence. The wind whipped in and out but mostly in, so they knew the back passage led to others, and other cave mouths. That was a blessing, as most of the guano stink was carried back toward the interior. The stink was strong because it lay deep on the floor. It had been long since the cliff dwellers abandoned their digs.

"What I don't like", whispered Boca, "is they're mostly looking this way".

"I think so too. It's hard to tell except by their noses. Look at all those ugly noses!"

"Shh! Better not say that too loud if you know what I mean. But I never saw uglier ones. Faces either, for that matter".

"And now they're drooling. They're hungry! Let's pick out a safe crevice so it's handy".

There wasn't a perfect one that would hold both, so Boca gallantly offered the best one to Yero. "It was nice of you to buy supper", he said. "I didn't get much for my money". She graciously accepted, avoiding an argument. Boca was rarely remorseful about anything, but when he was, she knew enough to let him have his way.

The butterflies were right to worry about the signs, but wrong to feel like hunted game just yet. The bats looked to the entrance because of the wind. The Chinook was warming the cave air, energizing the whole colony. The drooling mouths were beginning to pant simply from the warmth. The weather had been cool, very cool. Migration time was at hand. These bats weren't hibernators - certainly not overwinter. They would go south, but after the recent cold spell they needed warm weather to really rouse them to leave. However, the butterflies were very much right about one thing: The bats were *hungry*. Hunting had been poor. So poor they even argued about it in their sleep.

A scuffle broke out in a cluster across the way. Conflicting impulses rang off in all directions. Voices were intermingled, accusing. A whole section of the roost stirred. The cluster itself, a dozen or more nearly grown pups, were having a simultaneous dream about the past night's hunt. There had been trouble and they were re-living it now. Courtesy had broken down during the hunt. Prey had been spotted and laid claim to, but no respect was given. All the pups went after the same moth. Scrapes and bruises had resulted, and the prey had escaped. 'Ka-Ka-Ka', the traditional law of the hunt, had been violated.

"I don't like moths, but I might've cheered for that one", whispered Yero. "Imagine being eaten in fifteen bites by fifteen different bats. He was lucky".

"It wasn't a boy", answered a cruel voice. A fully-grown bat suspended nearly above them performed a body bend and dropped guano to the floor below - splat! Then she looked right at Yero with her beady eyes. "Not a boy, no. It was a nice fat girl! The pups missed, but I didn't. She was decent food, nothing special. You're food too - but what kind? I like variety".

"First, tell us if you're asleep", said Yero nervously.

"I am. But with our kind there isn't much difference. I can hear you. I can smell you. I'll remember you when I wake up. I never forget food".

"There's no need to wake up. None at all! Maybe we could even make friends while you're asleep".

"That would be helpful. Then you wouldn't try to escape".

"You would eat your friends?"

"Naturally, if they're just food! I think you're lying anyway. Food always lies to save itself. Food has no honor".

"Do bats?"

"Of course!" The bat twisted irritably. "A great colony can only co-exist with honor! Do you dispute this?"

"No, no. Whatever you say! But that group over there a moment ago - you must've heard - -they were pointing fingers at each other".

"You are stupid, food. We have claws, not fingers, as you'll learn soon enough. As for those pups, they'll probably be culled anyway, so who cares?"

The butterflies looked at each other, wondering what that meant. They didn't ask.

"Better them than us, whatever it is", whispered Boca, but not quietly enough. The bat laughed in her sleep at a little joke.

"They'll be culled for food. You already *are* food, so there's no difference".

"Are you cannibals?" asked Yero, horrified.

The bat grew agitated, nearly awoke. She spoke to her neighbors and they didn't like what was said either. Yero tried to back away from the insult.

"Please, don't take us seriously! We're just food. We don't know anything".

"Ah! Well, at least you know your place! That's better. I like that in my food. I don't mind a little chitchat while I work up an appetite. Just don't get uppity".

"Sorry. I won't do it again. I was just wondering about those pups. Who eats them?"

A hush fell at the question. Yero wished she had just shut up, but the bat took no offense this time.

"*Goblins*, she said reverently. "They are our Masters! They make us fly. They keep us strong. They cull the weak. It's not for the strong to pity the weak!"

A rustling of wings awoke way back and worked forward all the way to the cave mouth. Then stone silence settled, but only for moments. Soon other noises came from way back. Voices. Disagreeable voices. Definitely not bats.

***

"Ouch! Blast it! I thought you crappy little sappers could see in the dark! Find us a higher ceiling, Stinky!"

"It's *Stanky*, sir. Sorry! A little 'oopsie' there. I hope yer noggin is okay?" This voice wasn't quite able to suppress its delight; anyone could tell - even the butterflies, who edged closer to their crevices nervously. What was this now? Goblins? And what did they eat besides bats?

"Just a little 'oopsie', hey?" replied the first voice, then suddenly changed the subject. "Ugh - *grotty!* The poop's over the top of my boots!"

The sapper giggled. "I could've told you that, sir. Take 'em off then. Go barefoot! That's what sappers do. We're sent down here all the time".

"Tunnel rat! You can polish my boots later! How's that sound?"

"In a pig's eye, Sergeant Hubbub, sir! Sappers don't pull that kind of duty. We're above that".

"Maybe. But you ain't above *much*, you little buggers! I might have a word with the Boss tonight. We go way back, me and him. I'll put the bug in his ear to send your lot and clean up under these roosts".

"Go ahead. It'll just be put off and forgotten. The poor sappers are overworked already, a'diggin' tunnels".

"You're behind schedule, that's all. Don't make excuses".

"Behind schedule?" Stanky spat into the muck. "And who writes up the schedules, I wonder? It's the Higher-ups, a-sittin' on their flabby rears doin' nuthin'. Anyone can make up a work schedule, but only the sappers do any work!"

Hubbub snorted, or maybe it was his laughter. "Not just anyone can write things up, Stinky! Take you little sappers, now. The way I hear it you don't even know your letters".

"That's where you're wrong, sir. We all know the first one. 'A' is for 'arse', and that's everyone above us, including you!"

There was a disturbance back in the darkness as the Sergeant got some poo in his face, and a sound of splashing and running feet.

"Easy, sir!" came the sapper's voice, a little panicky. "An accident! I stumbled. It was just 'splash-up'".

"Grr! You done it a'purpose! Wait till I get my mitts on you!"

"Hold up, sir! Easy now! We've come to the nursery. Mustn't scuffle and dirty the dishes! They wouldn't like that back at the kitchen".

The noise of the chase slowed and stopped, much closer now. The butterflies could see shapes moving in the gloom. Hubbub was breathing hard.

"Here they are sir, see 'em now?" Stanky was saved by the errand, but knew he'd better get more respectful. Fast. "We've been through most of 'em already, but these smaller ones still need the treatment".

"Yeah? Well, they're the best tender-treats anyway. Let's get started".

"Right. Well sir, I can't reach 'em. I'll have to hold the trays".

The sergeant grunted. "All right. Tell me which ones and how to go about it".

"Very good, sir! That group there, now..." (Stanky pointed out which were the youngest. It was easy to see the difference, even ignoring the smaller size. Their wings were pulled up too close and tight. On the roost, the good flyers had a relaxed look. Their wings looked much larger, especially longer.) "...about a dozen or more together. See 'em? Go ahead and pull their wings way out. Pull hard. If the skin stretches, they'll be okay, they'll fly. If not, pinch 'em and toss 'em on the tray".

He didn't say anything about the part where the pups are usually frightened into a bowel movement by this, but the Sergeant discovered that right away, being just underneath. He let loose a string of profanity and wiped his face.

"Sorry, sir", said Stanky. "They do that sometimes. If you'd rather, I'll stand on your shoulders and do it".

Sergeant Hubbub didn't bother to answer, just 'pinched' the guilty pup for the snack tray and went on to the next. It's a marvel, their ability to hang on, but their life depends on it. The pups know what to expect from gossip on the roost.

After the mishap with the first pup, Hubbub used a different criterion as to which ones needed culling. He dutifully (albeit more carefully) stretched out each pup and simply culled every one that pooped, skipping very few. In this way, the goblins worked through several young clusters and filled one tray very quickly. Stanky set it on a wide shelf.

"We won't have enough trays if you cull them all", he warned. "There's still quite a few to go over".

"So? I got an idea about that, if you can keep yer trap shut".

"Goodness me! Whatever could you be a-thinking of, sir?"

Hubbub licked his lips. "I'm a-thinking we'll have to eat our mistakes. D'ya like 'em raw?"

"Very good, sir! Same as 'rare', ain't it?"

They both laughed. That's goblins for you. If they aren't at each other's throats, they're probably breaking rules for mutual profit. The two launched into a bit of gluttony with enthusiasm. It was a lucky opportunity. The whole bat colony would soon be gone south and that would be the end of the hors d' oeuvres until next year.

"Reminds me of the old days when we rode dragons", mused Hubbub after a fair sampling of the finger food. "They used to treat us decent in the Dragoons. We had good grub and lots of it. Mind you, we earned it! Many a good lad was lost in the battles". He sighed, fingering a particularly horrible scar that ran up his neck past the remnant of an ear and disappeared under an oily thatch of grey hair. He was proud of his scars 'from the battles', never mentioning that most resulted from a drunken incident when he fell off his dragon. He gobbled down another 'cull' and continued. "We furnished prisoners for all the big Barbecues, o'course. Remember those? Your lot came to all the Barbecues, didn't you? Everyone else did".

"Just the off-duty lads. I went once".

"Just once? Ahhh! Don't give me the breeze! We barbecued all the time back then".

"*You* did. Not us. There's yer bleepin' schedules again, sir: 'The digging must go on!' That's orders. Always! So the sappers missed off most of your Barbecues".

"Shame. Bureaucratic bungling, I suppose. But hey, you et some hot off the coals *once*, then. Ever taste better meat?"

"We got cold sandwiches", said Stanky. "The meat was burnt".

"The chefs call that 'scorched': Black on the outside, bloody on the inside. Very popular right off the grill".

"Like I said, we got it cold".

"Pity. Your size is against you there. Bigger guys get ahead in the lines". Hubbub waxed philosophic. "Terrible blunder when they mustered out the Dragoons. Best outfit the army ever had! Now we're all infantry. No Barbecues. No fun. Times always change for the worse".

"Yeah, I'm sure it's quite a comedown from Royal Dragoons to plain dirt-grunts".

The sergeant grunted in displeasure. "Don't get cocky now and ruin my good mood! We're *grenadiers*. Say it!"

"Yes sir! Grenadiers, sir!"

"That's better. But you got a point. It's a step down from Dragonmaster. The Higher-ups blew that one".

"Headquarters didn't have much choice the way I heard it. Dragons are scarce nowadays".

"That's a fact. They all went off on their own, away north from this dratted civilization. I miss my beast, Torri-moto. All gas and smoke, he was! A right blabbermouth too, for a dragon. Ah, we had great fun a-burning and a-pillaging! Life was better in them days".

"Better for your lot. No difference for the sappers".

"Oh, let's have none of that, Stinky! It's only natural the Flyboys got first dibs at the meat. We risked everything to capture it! But there's always a trickle-down effect. If you didn't get your share at the tables, you were just too bashful".

"The problem was not enough places at the tables".

"Well, don't bellyache to me. Take it up with the Head Steward. Which reminds me - when are you sappers gonna bring in some red meat again? Some *manflesh,* like the Dragoons used to? Sure, you work hard diggin' yer tunnels, but you tunnel under chicken coops now and bring us chickens. Why not dig under a bunkhouse and grab some cowboys for an old-style Barbecue?"

"Ain't no bunkhouses anymore, sir. There's yer bleepin' civilization again. Times change, as you just said. So, we steal chickens. Don't complain. It's meat".

"It's a far cry from the good stuff, sapper! Listen, the Higher-ups want *red* meat for a change. Everyone does. Why not rustle up some cattle, at least? Beef is tasty!"

Stanky growled. "It sure is, sir! And perhaps you might fetch some yourself - you, and the other old Flyboys! You ain't done any real work in years".

"Oh, ho! So guarding Headquarters don't count, is that it? Or patrolling your tunnels every day? Sappers dig, we do security. We all got our jobs".

"All due respect, sir, that's a laugh! We go out, we work all day, and we come home late. We never see any of your lot. Where are they? Drinkin' and tossin' dice at headquarters, that's where!"

"So? No need to protect chicken thieves. They're a dime a dozen. Anyway, if you worked harder you wouldn't have to work late!"

"Maybe we won't work at all! How'd you like *them* bitters? There's talk in the tunnels about goin' on strike".

Hubbub snapped his teeth. "Pipsqueaks! You wouldn't dare."

"Ha! Tired of chicken salad, are you? Maybe the poor sappers'll get some respect when you've et *plain* salad for a month!"

"Says who? I want names!"

"I dunno nuthin'. It's just what I hear".

"Tight-lipped, eh? I could haul you up on charges, y'know. It might be fun watching Internal Affairs twist you into knots".

"All due respect again, sir, but they wouldn't get nuthin' outa me. It's the Rule, as you very well know".

This may come as a surprise to civilized folk, but goblins do have Rule of Law by which they abide. It's a very short list and the first rule is: 'Never rat out your pals!' Unlike human gangsters who swear by the same rule (but are known to blab), a goblin will never, ever squeal. They'll die first. So, Hubbub's threat was mostly hollow, and both knew it. But 'mostly' isn't 100%. Ordering a lesser goblin 'questioned' just for entertainment wasn't unusual. Both knew that too. It was a perfect setup for mutual blackmail.

"Don't quote me the Law!" retorted Hubbub. "It just strikes me that you'll live longer if I *don't* haul you up. But I might look the other way, sapper - for a price".

Stanky's eyes lit up. A deal was in the making. "Much as you're sick of 'em, sir, I know where there's lots of them chickens. I s'pose while they last, we could roast a few on the sly, eh? Say, ten for the Kitchens each day - and two for us?"

"Why not? I'm glad you see it my way. You can roast our first birds tomorrow at noon. Let me know when they're ready".

"Oh, they won't be ready until evening, sir".

"Why not? You're up and at it before daybreak and I'll be hungry by noon".

"I *used* to be up that early, sir, and off to a long day's labor. But that was before this deal. Now I'll be sleeping late too, if you don't mind".

"You little rat! You tryin' to shake me down?"

"Of course not, sir. I just figure you'll be happy with the extra grub, so I'll spend more time with our private Barbecues and a little less time diggin' tunnels".

"Just don't threaten me, sapper, or there'll be trouble".

"Never, sir! You're the sergeant". Stanky smiled graciously and slapped his forehead in salute. No way would he threaten a higher-up in so many words. That would be suicide. It was enough that Hubbub knew the underlying threat: The deal would fall through if he didn't offer something in return, and he would miss out on some great grub.

This is how goblins do business most of the time, and it makes a shamble out of their chain of command half the time, which is fortunate for the rest of the world all the time.

"Deal, then", grunted Hubbub. "Hey! Watch it, Stinky! You dropped one off the tray".

"No, sir. That one's always down there. He's a cripple".

"Well he's disgusting, all covered with muck. Give him the boot!"

Boot or no boot, Stanky let fly with a kick, sending the cripple and a shower of slop airborne toward the front door. Everything landed *splat, splat,* around the butterflies on the wall. The cripple was knocked out against the shelf and fell in a heap on the floor. He looked quite dead. The goblins laughed.

"Well, I s'pose..." said Hubbub, bestirring himself. "They'll be waiting on us back at the mess hall. They're gonna spice these up like 'hot wings', a big to-do of some kind. They never said what's the occasion".

"Didn't have to if you know your bats", shrugged Stanky. "It'll be the last appetizers of the season, I'm thinkin'. This lot won't be back, come morning. They'll be headin' south. I think they're starting to awaken right now".

It was true. As if to prove him right, the very first bat came flying past, heading out; but it was just one and no others followed yet. The goblins got busy filling up another tray. As they worked outward, they came into better view of the butterflies.

"Goblins are ugly", whispered Yero. "Do you think we're in any danger?"

"Ask *her*", said Boca. "The bat that's been talking".

Yero did, several times, but got no answer. All the bats were now in the slow process of awakening and coming out of their dreams. They spoke no more in their sleep.

"You're warm-blooded. You'll be finger-food too", said a voice below them. It was the mucky cripple, somehow still alive. The butterflies studied him in silence trying to figure out which end was what in the heap of bat parts and manure. The creature spoke again, and they saw his mouth move, but it exposed a nasty personality. The cripple was bitter.

"They take and eat whatever they want, idiots! Are you blind?" Surprised by the hostility the butterflies said nothing, so the cripple went on. "Oh, great. Two freaks that can't see past their noses, that's what I get when I need help". He began the labor of untangling his body from its heap. In a bit of good luck, he had landed in a spot where there was very little guano, so at least he wasn't mired in that too.

"We can see well enough", replied Boca. "Anyway, they kicked you. We didn't".

"Fine! D*on't* help then! Leave the cripple to his misery! Criminy, I can't believe I'm talking to the food. This is so dumb".

"We're not food yet, and we'll never be *your* food. What do you eat anyway, down in the muck?"

"None of your business!" The cripple scowled fiercely.

"Can you fly?" asked Yero more kindly. "You'll starve if you don't migrate with the others".

"*Can you fly?*" the cripple mimicked. "Do you think I'd be down here if I could fly? If you won't help, at least don't make fun of me!"

"Knock it off!" said Boca angrily. "You're too big for us to help and I'm not taking any blame for it".

"Might get your pretty wings dirty? And you'd have to touch my crippled body too? Well, don't bother! Everyone's a jerk!"

"Just so you know", informed Yero, "our wings are already dirty. We got splattered when they kicked you".

The cripple laughed so hard the sound waves fully awoke a bat just nearby who took off flying. All bats do their business in mid-air unless they're asleep on the roost, and this one - like the whole colony - was agitated. She dropped a load right on the cripple's nose that quieted him down. Other bats were awakening also, here and there, fleeing for the door. They all knew by now that these goblins weren't too fussy.

As for the goblins, they were nearly done with their errand. Only a few clusters of younger pups remained to sort through, the ones nearest the front door closer to the butterflies. But the ceiling was highest just there. Hubbub couldn't quite reach.

"Jump", urged Stanky. "We gotta hurry up".

Hubbub actually tried, but with poor results. Big goblins have a powerful, squat body type, not springy at all.

Stanky couldn't help laughing. "Try harder! Try *grunting*!" He knew it would irritate and it did. Hubbub stopped cold and gave him the evil eye. He backtracked quickly.

"Sorry, sir! I didn't mean it like *that,* sir. I know you're a Grenadier! Let me help. I'll stand on your shoulders".

"Not with those feet you don't. You're filthy".

"Then lift me up, sir, so I can reach 'em".

"Not that either. You'll wipe your feet on me. I know you will".

"Then we'll have to go back a bit short. They won't like it".

"Don't you worry, Stinky. We'll fill up the trays". Hubbub had the gleam in his eye again. "You're a sapper, see? Sappers dig. Sappers get dirty. Someone has to and it might as well be you pipsqueaks. You can't earn your keep any other way".

Stanky knew what was coming and started to back away but the muck slowed his feet and the sergeant got him by the arm.

"Down you go, sapper! That's a direct order. Get down on all fours!"

It was Hubbub's turn to smirk and snicker. Size and rank have advantages and bullies make full use of them. He meant to enjoy this and teach the sapper some respect. He was mildly surprised that 'Stinky' didn't protest, but what could he do? Nothing. The sergeant had the authority.

Stanky grumbled and made a fuss about getting into 'step-stool' position, scraping some manure aside. He was careful not to splatter the sergeant in the process, knowing he'd pay for it immediately. Finally, he was ready; but Hubbub wasn't happy with the spot.

"I need you a bit further this way", he ordered. "Don't complain, now! You'll be sleeping late tomorrow so you can spend all night washing up".

Stanky had to move over into deeper doo-doo. Hubbub put a big sloppy boot on his back and tested the step stool.

"Oops! Wrong. A bit further yet", he ordered, purely for fun.

"Just do it!" growled Stanky, unmoving.

"Just do it, *sir*", corrected Hubbub.

When the sapper had said it properly, and slapped his forehead in salute according to regulations, Hubbub stepped up with his tray - first on Stanky's head, pushing his face down into the glop, then finally up onto the back with both boots, which he promptly wiped off on the 'stool'.

"Can you reach 'em?" asked Stanky.

"Yeah, much better. Have patience down there. Don't move!"

But the sapper was all out of patience. "Can't hold any longer, sir!" he lied, and rolled suddenly sideways. Hubbub pitched forward helplessly and landed face-first in the stuff.

Stanky jumped up, dancing. "So sorry, sir!" he cackled. "So sorry! I'm headin' back with my tray. You can bring yours".

Quicker than you'd ever expect, the sergeant scrambled to his feet and gave chase, but the fates were against him. The roost was coming alive. Dozens and suddenly hundreds of bats took flight and headed for the exit. They could've missed Hubbub if he'd let them but he got upset, shouting and flailing his arms, while Stanky 'hugged the muck' down low and found less resistance. Soon thousands of bats were taking off and not even a powerful goblin like Hubbub could face them. He hunched down against the rush.

For the butterflies, it was worse. The horde was hungry and picked them up on radar even off to the side on their shelf. Several immediately made a pass at them, caught in the open.

"Face them! Be skinny!" said Boca. It was all they could do on a moment's notice, but it helped. They faded on the radar and were missed, but others came unseen out of the dark, only giving themselves away at the last instant when they opened their mouths and light gleamed off their teeth.

In a moment's respite the butterflies retreated to their crevices, backing into them as carefully as time allowed. Boca's chosen crack had been plugged by splatter and he had to take another, bigger and wider than he would've preferred but at least out of sight for now. After that, they just closed their eyes against the blur of wings and plugged their ears against the pounding sound waves.

When the rush slowed at last to just stragglers Boca opened his eyes in relief - and found himself staring into the face of a ravenous bat, the one who'd been talking in her sleep.

"Well! Looky what everyone else missed in their hurry!" she gloated. "Never get caught up in the nightly rush, I always say. Go slow and see what's been overlooked - like *you*, little one! Come to Mama!"

She stuck her head into the crevice as far as she could, chomping recklessly, trying to get a piece of Boca. All that saved him was her wide pug nose, the price bats pay for the benevolent stretching of the wings. Their noses are stubbed from that, and it gave Boca a quarter-inch margin of safety. That saved him for about three heartbeats, the time it took the bat to change tactics. She withdrew her head and folded one wing, then reached for him with the leading claw. Boca was at a dead end in the shallow crack. The powerful claw would obviously reach him. He closed his eyes.

But the rending claw didn't find him. There was a hideous squeak. Boca opened his eyes again and beheld a face even uglier than the bat's, if that could be possible. Sergeant Hubbub, scowling and growling, plastered with guano, had 'pinched' the bat and tossed her onto his dirty tray. He had recovered most of the spilled ones and they were a mess, but he still needed more.

"Thanks!" shouted Boca. "She was going to eat me!"

Hubbub peered into the crack in surprise. "What the devil are you doing in there?" he blurted. "This ain't no place for butterflies".

"The weather was bad, and we took shelter. But the bats woke up early. You saved me!"

"Never meant to! I don't give a rip about bugs. Who's 'we'?"

Yero leaned out and waved. "Do you eat butterflies?"

"Nah. Wings are dry and there ain't much else". He rubbed his nose at some half-remembered allergy, smearing the grime.

"We're poisonous too", warned Yero.

Hubbub actually laughed. "Don't count on that, little one! Goblins have cast-iron stomachs". Then he noticed the cripple. "Here, now! Who's this hiding in the muck again? You ain't been pinched yet, have you?"

He picked up the disagreeable thing. It promptly bit his finger and he dropped it. He tried to stomp on it, but the cripple was quick on the floor and scuttled behind him out of reach. That surprised Hubbub for a moment but he was determined. The bat wouldn't live long. Yero felt pity in spite of everything.

"You'll get sick if you eat that one!" she shouted. "He's a hunchback and missing a leg".

"I ain't gonna eat him - just kill him!" bellowed Hubbub.

"It's bad luck to kill a cripple!"

By unexpected chance, that worked. Without knowing, Yero had hit on a little-known weakness of goblindom: They are terribly superstitious. Being creatures of the dark they have no religion, so they fall back on pagan phobias. Luck - good and bad - figures into everything. But Hubbub thought about it and saw a loophole.

"Seems more like *good* luck for the cripple if I put 'im out of his misery", he decided.

"But what about *your* luck, sir? Pardon us for overhearing, but your luck sure went bad after the cripple was mistreated. It's bound to get worse if you kill him".

Hubbub twisted around to scowl at the creature. That did make sense when he thought about it. But payback came *first!* Payback means good luck to any goblin. With an oath, he kicked the thing into the air and off the ceiling, nearly sending him out the front door over the high ledge.

"There!" explained Hubbub, feeling much better. "The cripple is fine. I never killed him at all".

We must leave Sergeant Hubbub now, with his tray of mucky treats only half-full. Whether he went on to good luck or bad down in goblin town is not our affair, but you don't have to be a goblin to guess that bad luck usually follows a blunder.

Yero went to check on the cripple against Boca's advice. "Even if he's conscious he'll just be ornery", Boca warned, and he was right. The thing wasn't the least bit grateful.

"Beat it!" he sputtered at Yero. "Don't want any more of your help. I was doing fine till you butted in. Then he got mad".

"He was mad because you bit him. He would've killed you!"

"He wanted to pinch me anyway, Fancy-Pants, but he couldn't catch me! Then *you* butted in. Thanks a lot!"

"Say what you want, but I know he would've killed you. I talked him out of it".

"Yeah, I heard the ugly words: 'Cripple', 'Hunchback', 'Missing Leg'. Was that fun?"

"You're hopeless!" said Boca. "She's being nice and you're just a poop!"

"Jerk! What's it to you? Bug off, flutterbugs!" The cripple muttered an oath and scuttled back inside away from the open door. He moved more easily; his wings obviously more useful. They looked bigger now, longer anyway.

"Hey! You aren't hunched up anymore!" marveled Yero.

"I'm sore all over. Thanks for nothing!"

"I'm sorry, I really am. But I think that last kick stretched you out. Look at your wings! I bet you could fly now".

The cripple hunched back up reflexively.

"He needs it again", remarked Boca. "Another good one might fix his head too".

The cripple showed his fangs, leaving no doubt what he would do should opportunity arise. Yero ignored their quarrel.

"You just need to relax", she encouraged. "I think you could fly as well as anyone now. Stretch your wings again". But the cripple was stubborn.

"Can't! Never had the treatment. Don't mock me!"

"I won't".

"Why not? I'm missing a leg. You said so!"

"I won't talk about it anymore. But there's something about your nose..."

"Oh great. I'm a freak in ways I didn't even know of!"

"No. Your nose is just longer than the others'. It isn't smooshed back".

The cripple narrowed his beady eyes. "What's the joke?"

"No joke. Your nose is handsome compared to other bats. Do they fly into walls or what?"

There was a short burst of laughter, then silence. The cripple didn't know how to respond to a compliment. He reverted to mistrust and muttering.

"She asked you a polite question", prompted Boca. "Answer her! Why the long nose?"

"So I can root in the muck - is that what you want to hear? Butt out!" The beady eyes flashed, but he turned more politely to Yero. "I will talk to *you*. My nose is long because I never got the treatment. I was born with only one leg and couldn't hang on to the nursery ceiling, so goblins never stretched me and pulled back my nose. *That's* why I'm handsome". He gave Boca a superior smirk. "*Very* handsome, so I've been told".

"But you can't fly because you never tried, have you? You just like to play in the muck".

Boca had come closer to deliver the insult. Almost too close. The bat swung upward with a wing and a claw. It reached a long way, just missing him.

"His wings are fine", sneered Boca. "He's just lazy, like the gypsy".

"Oh, stay out of this!" scolded Yero. "That's not going to help! Can't you see? He's superstitious like Hubbub, that's all".

"He certainly is. Most bats are", said another voice. "And 'Hubbub' sounds goblin-ish. Have you met goblins?" It was Atel.

"Two of them!" answered Yero, all full of news. "And they didn't like each other! But now they're gone, and the bats are all gone, but this one is still here as he shouldn't be! He can't fly".

"Can't? Or won't?"

"That's just it. I think he could! I wish he'd try".

"What about it, bat? Can you spread your wings? The colony is probably gone until spring. Now is the time to follow them".

The cripple was tempted but saw only impossibilities. He pulled his wings more tightly about him and said nothing.

"We need to go", said Atel to the butterflies. "We have enough time to reach my friend's cactus before dark, but little to spare. She is brooding eggs and will not care to be disturbed late at night. This creature here can't overcome his superstition anyway. It's ages old".

"He should at least *try*. I like him". To prove her point Yero went down and hovered just above the cripple's nose - foolishly if she was wrong - but she knew he wouldn't try to hurt her. A kind word had closed the gap between them.

"Spread your wings as wide as you can", she urged. "Show me. Butterflies are experts on wings".

This time he did. He had never stretched them even when he had fallen, believing he couldn't. He was re-thinking that now and stretched hard, painfully hard. His joints were stiff, the wingskin encrusted with filth, but the picture looked very promising to Yero.

"I'm sure you can do it", she said. "Let's go to the door".

That part was easy. The cripple was very adept on the floor with two wings and a leg. But he was scared to approach the ledge. He had developed a fear of heights after his fall.

"Lucky for you", explained Yero, "This is a perfect place to get airborne. Just jump off and your flying instincts will take over. Your wings are fine".

He did his best, but it only amounted to creeping up to the edge and peeping over. It horrified him. The sheer wall fell thirty feet to the ground and that's all he could think about now that he saw it. He backed away, a little dizzy, and closed his eyes. Yero wasn't discouraged.

"You can do it even with your eyes closed", she suggested. "Just start sending out those sound waves and you'll know where to go. I think all bats do that".

"Don't know how! They teach that in nursery school. I dropped out of class". Sad but true. He had missed too much school in his young life and believed he could never catch up now.

Yero urged him on in every way she could think of, but it became time to leave. She said goodbye and expected the cripple to scuttle back inside but he crept forward again and peeked once more over the edge. It was still thirty feet down. He covered his handsome nose and retreated.

The Travelers left. Yero looked back several times until they were out of sight, hoping to see movement, but there was none. She and Boca had troubles of their own, too. They were slow, not very aerobatic; filthy, in a word. More like barn flies than butterflies. They needed to pick off the crud. Wings are very sensitive that way. Water or ice, or even ordinary dust will mess them up and make hard work of flying.

So, they spent some time on a prickly pear cactus and cleaned off their wings, wiping it on the needles. That is, Yero and Boca groomed each other and held their noses doing so while their guide perched upwind as lookout.

"I feel guilty now", Yero confessed. "I'm the one who told him his nose was handsome and now he's scared he'll hurt it. But it was so true! Have you ever studied bats up close, Atel?'

"Certainly. Most are born with ugly noses, but at least they outgrow it. With goblin bats it's the other way around. The babies are born cute - well, less *ugly* - and the noses are ruined later. It's a sure sign of goblins deeper inside the cave".

"You knew there were goblins in there?"

"Yes. They're mean, but no real threat to butterflies. The bats were the only danger and you had your safe crevices".

"*I* did", replied Yero. "But sergeant Hubbub saved Boca by accident". The butterflies told about Boca's narrow escape and the goblins going about their 'chores'.

"Exactly so", nodded Atel. "Goblins are farmers, you could say, and the bats are their livestock. Goblins did them a great favor once, teaching them to fly. All the servility and superstition comes from that".

"The wing-stretching, you mean? That's what the little goblin wanted, but Hubbub didn't care. He just wanted plenty of tender young bats for some feast. Why do bats put up with it? I think they could all fly without any help. They've got plenty of wingspan".

"You are correct, and a lot of bats discovered that as civilization advanced and goblins were pushed into remote areas. Most bats stayed where they were and found they could fly anyway. They had completely evolved.

Humans usually detest them, probably from ancient memories of their goblin masters; but for creatures of the dark, bats are surprisingly beneficial. They eat a lot of insects, begging your pardon".

"No need to", laughed Yero. "They call us 'food'. I don't think they know about our poison".

"They wouldn't. Butterflies are for the light; bats are for the dark. They wouldn't know. Wouldn't care either. Such creatures have strong stomachs".

"But why did they have to be taught to fly? It seems silly. Flying is natural for anyone with wings".

"A good question. The answer, according to old goblin tales, is that they were once mice. By the way, how are you coming there with your cleaning? Are you soon ready to go?"

"Not yet. My wings are fine, but Boca still smells pretty bad".

"So do you. If it's just the smell, we might as well go on. It'll hang with you for a while".

"There's *sticky* stuff in there yet. Tell us more about the mice".

The hummingbird sighed and resumed the history lesson:

—The Up-Lookers—

When mice appeared on earth, they naturally fell into two groups with different outlooks. Most were the Down-Looking type, content to live on the ground as the Lord intended, but some were not content. These were the Up-Lookers who saw a sky full of promise and felt it should've been promised to them. They complained - oh, they complained! But they were small - and their complaints were easy to ignore. The Lord didn't hear them and no one else cared. Then goblins got involved.

It all started because the Big Boss was hard to please in his dining room. This was the storied Urpgob, ruler of all the goblin bands in those days and a rough fellow to work for when he wasn't happy. The fare at his headquarters was pretty fancy, but never quite reached his expectations. This often put him out of sorts and the rank and file suffered for it.

It was the wine steward, they say, who came up with the idea of serving hors d'oeuvres with the wine. Quite a sophisticated idea in the crude goblin culture. But what delicacy to use? The Head Chef tried everything the sappers could trap, net, or grab, with mixed results. Mice, roasted with chestnuts, were Urpgob's favorite, but there were never enough.

Probably the poor sappers - out there grubbing for the Boss's treats - made a deal with the up-looking mice. It was a natural fit. Suitable caverns were set aside for the mice and the sappers stretched out their skin regularly until they could glide long distances just by spreading their limbs.

Some Up-Lookers were satisfied with that and escaped to become what we know as flying squirrels. But most were under the goblin spell by then. The sappers kept the bargain and stretched the mice every day as part of their chores, always keeping back a few for the Boss's table - those that weren't stretchable enough. The mice did their part by multiplying like mice do and embracing their changing bodies. In time the Up-Lookers learned to cling to the ceilings for ease of take-off (and to be up out of the droppings), and so their evolution became complete.

The goblins saw it coming, the day when their flying finger-food would no longer need them but weren't worried. The bond was solid by then. The flying mice were as superstitious as their masters, so it was only natural to leave the stretching and culling tradition in place. Permanent. The mice didn't mind. They were domesticated now. They had become bats.

***

Atel finished the story and urged the butterflies to hurry with their grooming. They looked clean but the stink remained, and they were convinced some pluckable yuk was in there too.

"You're as clean as you'll get without a bath", said Atel impatiently.

"Please", begged Yero. "It smells so bad. Just a few more minutes".

"How come they're called 'bats'?" asked Boca to gain time.

Atel thought a moment. "It's an old goblin expression meaning 'to blink', so I guess it's about their eyes. After living so long in the goblin caves the mice had changed in other ways too. They could no longer stand the bright sun. If they ventured outside in daylight they blinked, or 'batted' their eyes. It would be just like goblins to poke fun at their own pets that way. Their humor has a mean streak to it. At any rate they were creatures of the night from then on".

"They can have it", said Yero. "I like sunshine. I like basking in it. I like dilly-dallying and dawdling in it too".

"Don't forget lollygagging", grinned Boca.

"You're going to fit in perfectly where we're going!" replied their guide. "Just don't start until we get there".

Chapter 14

A One-Armed Bandit

"Great!" said Yero. "We've been hoping it gets easier. We need the rest".

"I suspected as much. What kind of holiday would you like? Just sitting around, being lazy? Soaking up a few rays of warm sunshine?"

"For sure! But you said the wren was...'fidgety', or something. That doesn't sound relaxing".

"She is. She's very nervous. All wrens are. But her cactus is one of the tall ones, the kind with arms, one of the laziest creatures ever on earth. They used to be called 'shams', and a group of them together called themselves the 'Shamash', back when they had voices. That's all ancient history too, now".

"Much, much better! That sounds peaceful".

"Maybe, maybe not. The cactus holds water, so it attracts other visitors too. Some aren't so nice".

"Like what?"

"Mice and bats, to name just two".

"But that's not fair! That's what we just escaped from!"

"There could also be lizards, woodpeckers or owls. It's always a gamble, sleeping in a tall cactus. But I was teasing about bats. They do come, but only for nectar in the spring".

"That helps. But it still sounds crowded".

"It can be. But for overnight guests there's an extra attraction: The music. Peaceful, background music. If you close your eyes, you can hear it. Maybe it's the plant growing, so slowly it sounds like a lullaby. Nothing at all like the great noises the Shamash made when they walked the earth".

"Cactuses walked?"

"These did. They were half-plant/half-animal. It's not unheard-of".

"You better tell us about them too, so we know which half to expect tonight".

Atel cast a wistful glance at the sinking sun and resigned herself to a later schedule.

—The Lazy Ones—

In earlier Ages when the Plant and Animal Kingdoms were still sorting themselves out there were a fair number of beings with claims to both Kingdoms. Most were carnivorous plant types, but there were others including the wood nymphs, the tribbits, and a few oddballs like the baby skunks who come from the kagnabag.

Time came for the hybrids to choose one Kingdom or the other, or to be outcast and shunned. A few, shackled by doubt, never did choose, and were relegated to remote parts of the world. Such were the Shamash: Huge man/tree creatures of North America, known from the northern hardwood forests where they first appeared. Their leaves were deciduous and grew thickly next to the trunk on tiny twigs. They had only a few short branches and appeared from a distance to be giant men with arms upraised.

The leaves were rectangular, which was unusual in any Age, and when they turned in the fall the *top* of the leaf might turn any color of the rainbow. Oddly, it was the *underside* of the leaves that were similar throughout the species, with exactly 13 different styles of spots and mottled markings. Every sham had some of each and leafed out a brand-new assortment every spring.

But oddities aside, they were chiefly known for their laziness - regardless of which Kingdom they should belong to - with only enough ambition to seek out sunny clearings where they could bask and tan their smooth, pale bark. They basked in small groups and were able to get nice tans because they picked off their leaves - picked them and played games with them like humans might get up a game of cards. They enjoyed gambling and their leaf-games were more difficult and lengthier than modern card games because they had hundreds of leaves and extra arms to play with. A single game might last all summer.

All was fine and pleasant with them in that season. Then winter came. The days shortened, the sun retreated into the far south, and their nice tans turned pale. They bellyached and bellowed about that, but the sun was way out of earshot, and if they blamed the North Wind she pelted them with ice and snow.

One miserable winter they bestirred themselves and followed the sun, coming at last to warm lands and balmy skies. There they settled, more or less, and immediately fell to bickering over the sunniest, most pleasant 'parlors' where they pursued their games of chance. Typically, these were sheltered nooks in the hills - quiet enough for their leaf-games, but wide open to the best rays of the sun - usually along streams where they could sponge up moisture and cool off their toes.

They put on a lot of flabby weight from the sponging, which made them even lazier, but it didn't matter because the Shamash absorbed most of their energy directly from the sun. They were grass-eaters on their animal side and did graze the stream banks a little each night to satisfy their small stomachs, but mostly in the nice climate they just worked on their tans and they gambled, which meant shuffling off to a neighbor's parlor, or having some friends over. This was a small concession to exercise but they dreaded it, so the more central parlors were best, and everyone wanted them. Since they were too lazy to fight over them, they thought up parlor games to win property from each other. It was the Shamash who invented most of our modern forms of gambling such as dice, shell games, and especially poker, blackjack and other cutthroat card games. But they never wagered on physical events. In fact, they seldom moved at all unless there was some easy profit in it. They lived a life of leisure.

Yet they were in danger. Looming above their idle culture was a threatening weather issue. The Great Southwest Desert was green in those days and the skies weren't always sunny. The summer monsoons blown up by the South Wind were common at any time of the year, which spelled trouble for the shams. Sometimes it rained for days. Sometimes it just stayed cloudy which was almost as bad because lack of sun weakened them. It was a serious nuisance, but they had their voices then - loud, *booming* voices - and they complained to the South Wind who was responsible for it all. She ignored them for a while, but it was very distracting. One day the South Wind paused and scolded them.

"Stop bothering me!" she lectured. "This is my job and you should be thankful for a bit of rain".

The Shamash changed the subject, now they had her attention, and listed all their gripes. The list was quite long because they didn't do any work and had extra time to think up gripes. The South Wind blew them all off except one - the ongoing cloudy weather. She tempered that a bit, knowing it could get a little dreary.

"As for the rest, have patience", she reassured them. "In an Age or so the weather will change. That's the long-range forecast".

This upset the Shamash all over again.

"We've gotta shorten that up", said a shook-up sham. "Give us your medium-range outlook - or better yet, something day-to-day".

"Dump the rain somewhere else", suggested another. "Take it over the mountains".

But the South Wind was impassive. "The rain falls where it falls", she replied. "It's too heavy to lift over the mountains".

"Take a holiday then", said still another. "Take a *long* holiday! You work too hard - and for what? Take some time off".

The Wind swirled irritably. "I wouldn't know how to do nothing!" she blustered.

"It's easy", laughed the shams. "Watch us!"

But the South Wind rebuffed them that day and just let the Shamash howl to the heavens. Great winds are supposed to remain above such bellyaching. Nevertheless, it wore her down over time and she agreed to a game of chance to settle the matter.

The Shamash suggested a shell game and a six-armed dealer set it up, putting a pebble under one of five shells and shuffling them a little, but not much. Which shell held the pebble? It looked easy. The South Wind guessed but guessed wrong. Sure enough, the dealer lifted another shell - and there it was! Okay, possibly the dealer cheated. Who's to say, Ages later? But it led to big changes in that part of the world. The South Wind found she enjoyed some time off and came less often, until finally she brought rain only in mid-summer. The land changed. The Great Desert emerged. The shams loved it but most other living things fled, those that could. Those that couldn't, withered.

The Shamash happily staked their claims to newly abandoned stream bank property, utterly indifferent to the exodus going on around them. The desert became theirs for a thousand years and they did nothing but play their games of chance. That much loafing isn't good for anyone and the South Wind turned into a bum too. Some years she napped and never came at all, which proved disastrous. Then the small streams and waterholes dried up and the fat shams shriveled. Their skin folded into creases and the leaf stems sharpened into thorns. They were forced to become nomadic searching for moisture. Since there was no longer water to be found on the surface, they had to reach deep into the ground with their toes for enough to stay alive. Thus, they became rooted in loose groups here and there. Forced at last to make a choice, they chose the Plant Kingdom. We know them today as saguaro cactus.

The other Winds stirred up the South Wind eventually and some weather returned to the region, but the desert is still there. Deserts are stubborn, more likely to grow than recede when the inhabitants take more than they give back. But the Shamash did contribute something unexpectedly valuable that has made the desert a big success in modern times. The urge to gamble is strong in the air and the human race enjoys it every bit as much as the old shams. Gambling is big business now and probably will be for the next thousand years - or until they run out of water like the shams did.

***

"Is that the only place to get water in a desert?" asked Yero when the hummingbird finished. "From cactus? It doesn't taste very good".

"It's the only sure place this time of year".

"I don't suppose even the big ones have faucets like the Trading Post, so how will we get past the needles?'

"Patience! Sooner or later, all will become clear. That's the forecast".

"I'm so glad I asked. But Atel--will you do just one more thing before we go on? Will you go back and make sure the cripple didn't jump after all and hurt himself? I'm worried".

The hummingbird did go, not very thrilled about it, and was no sooner gone than Yero turned and offered a wager to Boca.

"I bet he jumped".

"I doubt it, Yero. He was chicken".

"Let's make a bet".

"Why? We're only guessing anyway".

"Just to see who's right! Only one could be right".

"But we don't have money to gamble with, so what's the point?"

"We'll bet small favors. Like prizes".

"Oh. Like, if *I* win, I could make you shush up?"

"You won't win, but that's the idea. I say he jumped".

"You're on!"

"Good! It's a bet! Here's another one: I'll spread my wings a little - like this - and you try to guess how many cactus needles in this cluster behind me. Get it? If you guess, I'll hold my nose and clean your wings some more. Maybe I'll find the hidden poop that makes you smell so bad. If you guess wrong, you have to groom mine!"

"Yours need it just as bad, Yero! Don't pretend different".

"I know. I'm just teasing. But I think gambling sounds like fun! Those Shamash liked it".

"I dunno. You heard the story. It didn't end very well".

"Not for the shams, maybe. That's because they overdid it. But gambling is big business now! You heard that part, didn't you? If it was all *that* bad it wouldn't be allowed".

"To be honest, Yero, I'm sort of against bad habits right now, after what happened at the Trading Post".

"You should be. But you didn't let it become a habit, did you? That's the secret, see? We'll keep it innocent, just guessing cactus spines a few times, and then we'll probably never do it again. How many in the cluster?"

"Five. I can see the points sticking out past your wings".

"Ha! Seven. You missed two short ones - see? I win!"

It's fun to win and even more fun when you win a prize. Boca frowned, knowing he'd been snookered, but dutifully took up grooming Yero's wings again. Losing would've been easier if she was modest about winning, but she giggled to no end about it.

"There aren't any more stickies", said Boca presently. "It's just the fine dust and the smell. It should air out on the journey".

"Well, keep looking. You lost the bet".

"Yeah, but there has to be some time limit, and it's time. I really can't find any more lumps".

"Oh, okay. How about *this* cluster then?" She covered another group and grinned. "You can pay me with favors as I think them up".

But Boca demanded a turn. "Fair is fair", he insisted. "Now *you* have to guess! But our guide will be back soon and we'll be leaving, so if you *do* guess I'll fly right behind you, right in the bad smell. If you're wrong, *you* have to bring up the rear".

Yero smiled serenely. "Name any stakes you want", she said. "I'm on a winning streak".

Boca opened his wings and moved around a bit for confusion. He stopped in front of a cluster directly between Yero and the setting sun. "Okay, guess these!" he said.

"You can't do that! It's right into the glare!"

"I sure can. I just did. We have a bet and you're not getting out of it".

"Cheating isn't allowed!"

"I'm not cheating. There wasn't any rule about standing here or there".

"Well there should be! We need to have rules about what's fair and what isn't - and *that* isn't!"

"Too bad, Yero. There's no rule against it. We can make a rule for *next* time, so you can't do it on *your* turn. Do you want to?"

"You smelly thing! That's tricky!"

Boca laughed. "I do smell bad, don't I? But I'm not cheating. I'm playing by all the rules. It's not my fault there isn't any".

Atel returned in the middle of the argument and couldn't get a word in edgewise. She wasn't thrilled about this, either. Yero was insisting on 'two out of three' for such high stakes.

"That would bring some skill into it instead of just blind luck!" she declared, squinting into the sun.

"Sure, okay", Boca chuckled. "I don't want to hear any grumbling when you lose, but I think you better count on blind luck".

Yero squinted some more and found she could see the spines faintly through Boca's wings. The sun was still bright enough to shine through them. She counted ten, then recounted to be sure. Same result. "Ten", she announced correctly. Boca, baffled, was now behind one out of three.

"Now, mister 'blind luck', let's see you do it!" she said gleefully. "Close your eyes". She hopped to Boca's sunny side, folded both wings together to make them opaque, and shielded a small cluster of spines. "Okay, how many?"

Boca peered into the glare and looked away again. The glimpse hadn't revealed anything except the whole cluster had to be fairly small the way she was hiding it. That helped the odds.

"Five", he guessed again, hoping the second time was a charm. It was. Now Yero was baffled.

"Enough!" interrupted Atel. "I don't know what you're gambling over, but it can wait. You are both even-up and that's a good place to quit. We're in a hurry". The butterflies glowered at each other defiantly.

"In case you're still interested", she went on sternly to Yero, "The cripple is gone. I couldn't find him. Were you betting on that too?"

"A little", answered Yero sweetly. "More like just making a guess. Do you think he's okay?'

"No way of knowing. He wasn't lying injured below and I didn't see him inside either".

Yero let out a sigh of relief. "I sure wish him well anyway. He's had a hard life. Want to bet if we see him again?"

Atel looked sharply at her. "I don't gamble for amusement", she said severely. "Life is a gamble every day. That's all I need. By the way, what exactly were the stakes that you and Boca were risking? The 'two out of three' thing?"

The butterflies didn't want to admit that part, so their guide yawned and fluffed her feathers, making ready to rest, regardless of the hurry. Yero finally told all.

"I sort of played along as a lesson to Boca", she finished up innocently, "so he could suffer the consequences when he gambles and loses".

"She never thought she'd lose!" retorted Boca. "*That's* why she took the bet!"

"I see some good coming out of this," decided Atel. "Since you are even-up, you shall *both* have an opportunity to learn the consequences. Yero, you take the bad wake first. I think you started it. Away we go then. Follow Boca!" She took off, pausing only to be sure they followed in the correct order.

"Follow close!" insisted Boca. "Luckily we're going into the wind too, so you'll get everything you've got coming".

"I bet I can take it longer than you!" said Yero stubbornly.

"That's a bet! Don't be lagging now!"

So the Travelers made their way generally southward. To her credit, Yero hung tough, but it couldn't last long. Flying is work. It takes energy and especially good air. When she began to cough and wheeze, she fell behind. Boca whooped and whooped some more. Then he asked Atel to estimate how far they had come and keep track of it.

"Why? Are you betting on this too?"

"Just for 'funsies'".

"Okay. That's not as bad. Well! You've had your fun and now it's her turn".

Lucky for Boca, Yero had aired out her wings some so the vapor trail was weaker, but he had whooped too much a moment earlier and had to gulp air almost right away. There was controversy too when he accused Yero of adding to the smell, but he only wasted his breath doing so. Soon he also fell behind. The challenge was over. But who won?

"All things considered I have to give it to Yero", said the hummingbird. "By a nose".

Boca protested weakly. Atel laughed. "Oh, call it a tie! You both suffered through all that for nothing. Are you happy now?"

The miles melted away southward in perfect silence after that. The rocky hills gave way to other hills with sandy soils. They entered a desert where rocks had long ago weathered away but summer rains still supported life, mainly poor sagebrush and small cactus. The last bit of sundown slipped away. Darkness sprang into the sky rather suddenly. They weren't up north anymore where sunset lingers; and the evening was accompanied by clouds hurrying to meet them. The Great South Wind wasn't napping.

A storm was brewing, still many miles away. Now and again, lightning glimmered but the thunder was far off, only a distant rumble. Steering by glimmers that reflected off the clouds, they followed a shallow vale as it meandered through the hills. Here were rocks, some boulder-sized, scattered through a dry run where flash floods had rolled them down from the mountains. In ancient times, a reliable stream had filled the ditch seeking a way through the hills. Water usually finds a way, so they followed the old course, peering into the night around each new hill, expecting - what? Only their guide knew. Then a hillside came into view much different than any other.

When lightning lit up the sky ahead, they saw things - tall things - everywhere, waiting for them. It was a saguaro forest - a hundred or more - loosely grouped on both sides of a gully that ran up nearly to the top of the hill. They loomed so big, so bizarre in the intermittent light, that Yero wondered if it might be a mirage.

"They are! They aren't. They are! They aren't", she whispered as the skies flickered behind the giants. As if to settle the argument a huge bolt split the sky only a few miles away, lighting the hillside up like daytime. Yero cringed. Then night returned, quiet and peaceful. Yero relaxed again. Atel could be heard counting, "...thirteen... fourteen...fifteen"...*BOOM-BADOOM-BOOM!* The delayed thunder caught both butterflies by surprise, very loud in the desert hills.

"They *are!*" assured Atel. "Here be the tall Shamash, or what they've come to in this Age of the world. Say hello!"

The butterflies looked blankly at her. "Why?" asked Boca. "They're just plants".

"True, but we'll be needing one of them for shelter. Why not be polite from the start?"

"What's the use if they don't talk? Are they awake?"

"They once were. That should be reason enough for courtesy".

"It just seems silly", said Yero. "Like talking to the grass".

"You've made that mistake before, calling something 'grass' that wasn't".

"The tribbits? Did they tell you about *that*?"

"Certainly. The tribbits tell me everything whether I want to hear it or not. Especially the littlest one".

"He's stubborn, that one. Thinks he knows more than butterflies do. If I had time, I would've cured him of that!"

Atel laughed in the dark. "You would've wasted your time. But my point is, the Plant Kingdom is full of surprises. Even the grass awakens to rhythmic thought in the summer wind, and many plants in their own way have voices. The weather brings them out for those who bother to listen. So who can say about the saguaros? They *had* voices. *Big* voices. This is their land and I'm going to ask their leave". The hummingbird did so at the top of her lungs - not very impressive among the huge cactus - but startling to the butterflies who had never heard her full volume. "Some have said their hearing isn't so good, which is why they once had such booming voices. True or not, I want them to know we're here. This is no time to be bashful".

In awe, they made their way uphill through the grove of giants. The butterflies thought better of it then and offered greetings, feeling foolish about it.

"Why do some have one arm and others have five?" whispered Yero. Atel didn't answer so Boca did.

"Storms blew them off, probably". It was on his mind. The thunder thrilled him and he hoped for more. But the arms put Yero in mind of the old tale.

"I bet it was gambling, Boca, and that's the stakes they played for. Some families have extra arms now because their great-great-grandpas *won* them! And maybe some are short because *their* great-great grandpas lost an arm for cheating."

As they approached the upper reaches of the grove Atel made for the next-to-last saguaro, a little apart near the crest of the hill. It was less impressive than most.

"Either way, this one didn't come from the best of families, did it?" whispered Yero. Boca could only nod. The cactus was big but had only one arm, and that was crooked and puny.

"Hush!" whispered Atel sharply. "Right or wrong that sort of talk is rude! Curb your tongues! Wait here. I'll go first".

She returned quickly with a word to the wise. "We're welcome, I think. It's hard to tell when she's upset. Just don't ask questions. She stutters and it's not easy for her to answer".

Up, up they went to a hole well above the arm. A Flicker, probably, had excavated it and a variety of creatures had called it home over the years. Now a wren had it in her third year of occupancy, but for all her worries it must be wondered why she kept coming back. Still, she greeted them at the front door.

"H-h-h-h-h-hello! C-c-c'min!" She was a little house wren, not the much larger local type, and maybe that was the root of her troubles. The bigger cactus wrens can put up a stout defense against predators, of which there are many. The saguaros were the only tall things in the region, like lighthouses on a great sandy beach. Everyone saw them - nesters and nest-robbers alike - and visited them often. After the primary lure of water, the next attraction was usually eggs, which the nervous wren explained at length. She'd seen her share of troubles.

"Ev-ev-ev-everyone e-e-e-eats e-e-e-eggs!"

The interior was large with a spacious foyer and several holes leading to smaller rooms further within. The wren had her eggs in one of them, her third clutch of the season, and was frantic they would be plundered this very night or struck by lightning. In her panic, she went and sputtered a long curse from her doorway against whoever might be thinking such thoughts. Then she retired fretfully to warm her eggs in the right-hand room.

"Do you think that was smart?" Yero whispered softly.

"Not very", replied Boca. "That's like calling the animals".

Atel shook her head silently. She was watching the storm, closer now but weakening. Lightning still flashed and thunder roared, but less often. She was trying to set up a shimmer and having trouble about it in the intermittent light. "Hush!" she uttered impatiently. The butterfly jabber was messing up her spell.

Yero studied the room more closely when next the lightning flashed and felt sorry for the wren by what she saw. Lots of eggshell parts and pieces were scattered over the hard floor, obviously dragged out from an inner chamber and eaten here. There were several feasts' worth.

A steady, low shimmer enlightened the room. Their guide had succeeded, and it brought up questions.

"What did this? Who eats her eggs?" asked Yero.

"Mice, by the signs. One sign is their droppings. You're stepping on them". So was she, as she now saw. There was a flurry of wings as they all moved to cleaner spots. Most of the floor was clean, away from the eggshells. The wren did some tidying in quieter moments.

"If they raid her every time, why doesn't she move?"

"It's not so simple. This is a great nesting place, or should be, in a land without many good places. Now that she has it, she won't give it up. Too bad. There may be no happy ending for her. She's too small to win her battles. Let's hope she has none tonight. If the storm is done there will soon be hungry mouths prowling the area.

"How many eggs does she have?" asked Boca. He was trying to figure how many all the broken pieces added up to.

"Five or six usually. Less now, since it's way past the usual nesting season. I guess she's been robbed at least twice already this year".

The wren suddenly reappeared, angry at the world. She stalked to the door and issued more threats and warnings. If any evildoers hadn't heard the first time, they surely heard it now. Then she turned on her heel and scolded Atel: "P-p-p-put out the l-l-light! Th-th-they'll see it!"

Atel put it out in deference to their host. The night turned dark and the last rumble of thunder receded as the storm paused. Maybe it was all over, maybe just taking a deep breath. Storms don't rule the whole sky. Eventually they bump into winds unfriendly to them. But Boca missed the thunder, guessing it must be the Snogg and the Hoo as loud as it was. Atel had to disappoint him.

"Sorry, no. Thunder is a natural part of summer storms after the lightning. It's just louder here in saguaro country because their voices are added to it".

"And how is that, since they're plants now?"

"It echoes from long ago. Remember how the South Wind got hoodwinked in a shell game? She suspected cheating and paid the shams back with lightning. Things got ugly for a while.

***

The shams hated lightning anyway, being such tall targets. So a flash of lightning always guaranteed a roar of protest from the entire area, which in turn angered the South Wind who blew the noise right back at them. But when she began *aiming* at them and burning them up the roars doubled and trebled, especially at the point of the strike. Quite a few got toasted but they more than made up for the lost voices out of sheer fury. The South Wind saw then that she couldn't silence them and called for a parley.

She promised to quit hunting them, but of course lightning is natural in storms and everyone better just watch out below, so that's all she could promise.

The shams accepted this but reserved the right to curse as loud as ever if a bolt hit them - or even came close. The Shamash were still pretty numerous, so storms were twice as loud with roars of protest going *up* and coming right back *down* with the thunder. It still works that way in saguaro country because the lands were so charged with uproar that echoes remain, requiring only a shock to set them loose. The locals know this and just plug their ears.

***

Boca opened his mouth to ask another question but Atel raised a wing for silence. The storm remained quiet, quiet enough to hear other sounds in the dark. Something - or *things* - were scratching their way up the saguaro trunk.

The wren heard it too and rushed out of her nest hole in a panic to challenge whatever-it-was, tweeting threats toward the doorway much bigger than she could ever back up. She trembled, knowing what was coming. The scratching grew louder, like a rush of feet. It was more than one creature.

In moments mice appeared in the opening. The wren lost her nerve and escaped over their very noses, or rather their teeth as they snapped at her. She lost a few feathers but would live to nest again next year. As for her guests, their odds of survival dropped drastically.

These were grasshopper mice in their sandy color phase and the first three immediately stood up on hind legs to block any further escapes out the door. Their noses snuffled the air of the dark foyer for clues about occupancy. Not that any new smell might change their plundering plans, mind you. There were more than a dozen others behind them, and their kind are not vegetarians. They were quite willing to attack anything but puzzled for a moment about unfamiliar scents in the air. In their moment of hesitation, several things happened:

1) The butterflies took refuge in the empty room on the left side. 2) Lightning flashed one more time, presenting the hummingbird with a choice. She chose to set up a shimmer again on her breast and keep some light rather than risk all to blind a few mice - only to be overwhelmed by the rest. 3) Thunder arrived and the cactus shuddered. The mice in the doorway danced on tiptoes to keep their balance. One couldn't and fell out, but another leaped up to fill the empty spot. The thunder rumbled and echoed, finally fading away into vast canyons to the north.

When the cactus stopped trembling, Atel counted her blessings out of habit: The storm wasn't finished just yet, and the Travelers were still alive. Against that were arrayed a bloodthirsty mob and little room to maneuver. But her ghostly appearance proved another blessing, however fleeting. The leading invaders held up some moments longer, indecisive, drawing mocking comments from behind. Atel used the extra moments to fan dust and minor debris from a small area of the floor.

"Welcome to my parlor", she announced. "Do you have money? If not, what will you wager?" As she spoke, she rolled half-shells onto the clean area to set up a game. The mice looked at each other, incredulous. Then the whole mob laughed wickedly.

"Why gamble?" said one. "We have a sure thing!"

"Hurrah, boys!" shouted another. "It's warm blood for supper!"

The whole mob surged forward, pushed from behind, and our story would come to a sad end with this paragraph, but lightning flashed again, somewhere behind the clouds, a good bit of light when it was needed most. The hummingbird used it well, reflecting it into the faces of the attackers. All were blinded momentarily. Those in front suffered worse. The surge stalled and backed off. Three blind mice scrambled over their comrades and tumbled out the door in pain. The mob was a shamble for a few moments, but not much more than that. These were warriors, killers. They were famished, and they soon turned on their prey again; but this time they were wary.

"As I said, customers are welcome", repeated Atel. "But I will not tolerate hooligans. Are there any other hooligans?"

No one spoke up but hooligan eyes were fixed upon her, hooligan whiskers twitched angrily, and hooligan fangs drooled in anticipation.

"All right then", continued Atel calmly, "there will be order in the parlor. We will have a game of shells. Do you know the game?"

The mice didn't answer, just crept a small step closer. Atel used up what light she had in reserve to make a decent flash. It worked. The mob eased back again and stayed. It was all a gamble now. She had to play for time and just hope the storm would fire up again soon. Things were sure to get dicey but she might blind them all, even burn them, with a nearby strike.

"Don't know, do you?" she went on in the matter-of-fact tones of a professional dealer. "It's easy. I take one of your old droppings and put it under a shell..." (A muted gagging noise escaped one of the rooms and was noted by the mob.) ... "Just one, like this. Do you see? Then I move them around until you are confused. Like this".

Hummingbirds are very good with their beaks so Atel dragged this part out until the mob began inching forward again.

"There!" she said brightly. "Which shell holds the dropping?" All eyes riveted on the correct shell, but no one spoke.

"Of course, we must first set the stakes", Atel instructed them. "Since you have no money, why not wager your supper? Obviously, you wish to eat me and whatever else you find. Am I correct?"

"Yes! Yes!" The mice eagerly seconded that.

"Rules are - should you guess *wrong* - you must agree to leave immediately and not return!" Surly humor commenced. Atel continued: "On the other hand, if you guess *right*..."

"Yes! Yes! Yes!"

"Good! We have a wager. Who will make the choice?"

"ME!" shouted everyone. The whole mob pointed to the correct shell. There were by now more than a dozen crowded into the foyer, dancing on their hind legs and blocking most of the doorway. Then the storm flared again in the distance, some light filtered through the crowd - enough to flash back at them a little bit. They closed their eyes and slapped their heads in irritation. A dealer has to be stern.

"House rules are: All take a seat and mobs must appoint a spokesmouse", ruled Atel. "Sit down or you'll have to leave!"

It was pure bluff. If it didn't work, the game would end badly. But it did work. The mob had several tastes now of her medicine and wanted no more. They turned snappishly on each other, nipping and scratching. All sat down that could. A few remained standing by the walls and one or two were elbowed out to scramble among the spines. When the infighting was over one mouse stood forth: An old pockmarked veteran, very sly, looking to trade instead of gamble.

"This doesn't have to be *all*-or-*nothing*", he offered reasonably. "How did it ever come to that? Blame the hard desert life and set it aside. Let's start over, shall we?" He looked around threateningly at his pals who were creeping again. They stopped, fearing him as much as the hummingbird.

"Give us the eggs", he proposed. "That's all we expected and all we really want. Just that. You and the others go free".

"Thank you, but no", replied Atel, "The wren is a friend".

"You would defend her eggs?"

"I would", stated Atel flatly, knowing this would come down to a fight anyway.

"But why? Especially *these* eggs. As her friend, surely you must know we've robbed her twice already this year! She was foolish to try again, knowing we would come. The eggs are forfeit".

He had a point, but Atel declined the offer. "In all honesty", she said, "I don't trust you to keep your word".

The sly one looked hurt, a nice impression. "I'm saddened", he remarked, letting his whiskers droop. "I wasn't going to say anything about your shell game either, but now I must. I worry that you might cheat".

"No need to. The odds are 2-1 in my favor".

"Yet the stakes are high, and your cactus has but one arm. In these parts no one trusts a one-armed bandit, and the same goes for anyone in it".

"Tsk. It's the nature of gambling, isn't it? But we're at an impasse here. What else do you propose?"

"Shooter marbles. Five apiece in the circle, last marble wins".

"Later, maybe. Shells first".

"Of course. But since the odds are stacked, as you say, it's only fair to adjust the stakes".

"Suggest anything you like. It's still dealer's choice".

"If you win at shells we go on to marbles. If I win, we get our supper". The mob leered. The storm grew ever quieter, emitting just faint glimmers. Atel could only play for time, but a good dealer can usually keep the game going.

"Why not?" she replied. "But I'll shoot marbles my own way, if it comes to that".

"Why not? If we get that far". The spokesmouse showed his teeth. Without further ado, he pointed to the half-shell with the dropping under it. Everyone knew it including the dealer, but when she flipped over the shell - hey! It wasn't there. As the mob gaped in disbelief, she flipped over another - and there it was! There's no proof like real proof, the kind everyone can see, and the only risk was a bad after-taste for the dealer.

This did not sit well with the mob, but they were still very wary of the hummingbird's tricks. The sly one bowed graciously.

"By your leave?" he asked and stepped forward to scratch a rough circle on the floor. There were no real marbles so the match would be played with old droppings like many country games among rats and mice. They scatter these everywhere, even in their dining areas. They walk on them, nap on them - why not play games with them? Atel quickly selected the longest, oddest shaped ones within reach and a heavy round one for a shooter. So did the pockmarked one. They each tossed their five into the circle.

"I'll go first", declared Atel, "since you had your choice of shells". She expected and hoped for an argument to drag things out. The storm was still quiet, but she felt energy in the air and hoped it wasn't just the mob.

"Go ahead", shrugged the spokesmouse. "Fair is fair".

No delay there. Atel sucked up her 'shooter', rolled it back in her beak and blew it out like a bullet from a gun barrel. It struck an enemy marble and knocked it up and out, but the mouse blocked it with a foot and it bounced back in. The mob laughed. The sly one smirked.

"Wherever it ends up!" he jeered. "That's how we play it around here".

So it went. Atel had better aim, but the mouse was a better goalie, cheating like that on almost every shot. Naturally he won and an argument ensued. The mob insisted it was time for supper, Atel claimed the overall contest was a tie - one game each - and there must be a tiebreaker. She had absorbed enough glimmers to flare up her shimmer once or twice, enough to stall the mob for a little bit longer, but she had no answer when the sly one suggested 'Keepers' for the deciding game.

Sometimes called 'Blood Craps', this was related to a game of dice, although it would be played here using oblong droppings. The mention of it sent shivers of excitement through the mob. It always was for keeps in the most dreadful way. The mice rarely spoke of it, but many had played the game in winter, when prey was scarce and hunger had set in. Yes, when starvation loomed the mob turned on each other, but they were sporting about it. 'Keepers' was between two players. A mouse could challenge another to a duel with 'pointers', meaning long droppings. They faced off some distance apart and the challenged one got first crack, sending his pointer spinning on the floor toward the challenger. If the dropping came to rest pointing at his adversary, then that mouse was supper and the game was over. The mob enforced the rule. If the dropping pointed off to the side, the shooter 'crapped out', and the other player got a turn. It was gruesome, but it was how the mob survived cold winters that often settle into the desert, of which the sly one had seen several.

"Pick your 'pointer'", he sneered, taking up a nice specimen and testing the balance. "If you're frightened you may make your own. Some do". This brought laughter from the mob.

"I know the rules", replied Atel, who had indeed heard of the game. "I've been challenged, so I go first. As for the stakes, I'm not hungry. When I win, I'm going to burn your whiskers off - and then your tails".

The mouse just smiled. "I'm hungry if you aren't. Go!"

Atel had beginner's luck. Her spinner stopped at his feet pointing directly at him; but as it was coming to rest, he stepped to one side.

"Nice try!" he jeered. "A bit off, though. My turn!"

Atel expected as much but there was no use complaining. She needed some new light for any chance to really win and glanced in vain toward the doorway. If the storm was over and it came to it, she would retreat into the room with Yero and Boca for a last stand. But not yet.

The spokesmouse tossed his pointer with all the body english of a lifelong gambler. He was good at this. It was a big reason he had lived so long. But luck wasn't with him this night. Atel's light was fading and he missed seeing a small bump on the floor. His dropping skewed sideways and came to rest pointing exactly 90 degrees off - so bad he didn't even argue. Why should he? He knew he would have an ace on the next throw. Besides, he was beginning to suspect a weakness in his opponent. He couldn't quite put a finger on it, but the bird's light was inconsistent. Not that he would try to rush her (he would let the mob take its chances with that) but he sensed - what was it? *Fear* in the air?

Atel tried again and threw another pointer. This time the mouse didn't even bother to move.

"Too bad", he taunted. "It's pointing *between* my legs, missing both". The mob was emboldened now, their confidence growing by leaps. They inched forward, and Atel did nothing. They took another step. The sly one tossed his pointer carelessly, expecting the assault. He sniffed the air. Yes! The fear was very strong!

"Take her!" he shouted, and the mob lurched forward.

His only mistake was timing. The assault was a moment too late. The 'fear' he smelled was an electrical charge in the ground that now released as the storm fired up again. Lightning split the air above the hill and struck - not quite their cactus but the last, lonely saguaro just on the crest, exploding and frying it to a crisp. Spontaneously, the earth answered, sending the age-old protest upward and setting off a violent chain of events in their own cactus.

"Close your eyes!" shouted the spokesmouse. Some did, even as they rushed Atel, but it didn't help. The flash was so bright even she shut her eyes and her mirror worked by itself. Any mice that weren't blinded were burned severely, including the sly one. But other forces were at work too, beyond anyone's control.

The saguaro trembled and shook. An old memory awakened in its roots. For a brief time, the plant awoke to curse the lightning. But it had no mouth like the old Shamash, so the emotional pressure burst out through the middle room right past Atel. Water, pulp and noise spewed forth, blasting everything in its path out the door into the night. The whole mob, already in misery, was ejected to their fates. Atel backed into the left-hand room with the butterflies, laughing all the way.

"See what I can do?" she exclaimed. "Don't mess with me!"

The butterflies couldn't answer. The cactus was still throwing up and the return thunder shook the very hillside under them until the saguaro actually tilted forward in exhaustion.

When the uproar subsided, the Travelers ventured out and saw a gaping hole where the middle room had been. A small stream trickled out the wound and across the floor where the games had been played. The floor had been scoured and the water looked clean. The cactus was leaking from its brand-new mouth. They drank and pronounced it 'wet', but nothing better. The butterflies even had seconds while their guide went out for a minute, but the saguaro's sour mood was in it.

"We knew the blast was coming", said Yero when their guide returned. "These things do have inner voices but they sure aren't lullabies. It was mad. *Really* mad".

"At the storm? The lightning?"

"Something up there, for sure! It raised its arm and pointed - and then it cursed!" Yero held her ears to show what they had to do against the noise and the profanity.

"If you look outside", said Atel, "I think you'll find the arm exactly as it was".

"Well, if it never moved it sure meant to!"

"An old memory, then. Come! Let's see if the wren's eggs are unbroken".

There were three, a small clutch, but it was her third try after all. One was broken, but only because a chick was pecking its way out.

"What'll we do now?" wondered Yero. "What if she doesn't come back?'

"She will. She's stubborn down to her pinfeathers. We're staying the night anyway, so you'll see. But come with me. I want to show you what a close call we had".

The neighboring saguaro was unrecognizable, only half its original height and splintered. What remained was charred black and brown. All the sagebrush nearby was burnt to a crisp. One or two bushes were still burning, but the fires would soon die for lack of fuel here on the sparse windswept ridge. It didn't comfort Atel.

"The South Wind is still at war", she warned. "We may not be safe tonight after all".

"Why not?" asked Boca, watching the little fires dwindle.

"You're watching the wrong fire. Look to the south".

In the distance, a line of flames spread from hill to hill, still several miles away. The storm had brought no rain, only dry lightning, and started a big brush fire down thataway. Not satisfied with burning just one saguaro, the South Wind was pushing more flames toward the Grove of Giants.

"What will happen to the wren's cactus - *our* cactus - when that fire gets here?" asked Yero. "And the chicks are hatching!"

"The saguaros won't burn much with the water in them, but the smoke very well might be the end of the wren. That's if the fire reaches us. It may not. We'll keep watch".

There was nothing else but to do so. They perched in the new, larger doorway, and awaited the wren, swapping stories and questions. The butterflies wanted to hear in detail how Atel had cheated at shells. Yero especially was impressed.

"What did it taste like? I can't even imagine".

"I would hope not. Just imagine droppings the right size for your own mouth, then imagine any taste you want. If you're still curious, try a real one sometime!"

Boca was more interested in 'marbles', a game that could be played anywhere even by honest folk and wanted to learn the rules. The butterflies had overheard some of the cheating and now Boca looked for 'marbles' and asked questions. He got about as much answer as Yero.

"We just fired away by turns", Atel said irritably.

At that moment the wren came back, sparing their guide further irritation. As for the 'Keepers' game, she never spoke about that. The tradition of 'Blood Craps' is not a fit subject near bedtime.

The wren was more upset than ever, not less. The Travelers were blamed for wrecking the place and she chewed them out for minutes at a time. Twice she retired to her chicks (all were now hatched, by the sounds) only to come back out and add a few things. The stuttering added punch to her lecture, and she relished that. At last she stayed in her nest which was a relief. It's hard to take such a scolding when you don't deserve it, and the butterflies were under strict orders to take it.

"She'll feel different in a few days when she realizes she's rid of that mob of thieves", said Atel. "That is, if the wildfire doesn't sweep through tonight. Give her some slack. She has lots of troubles".

The fire was at the top of that list right now. It was definitely closer, pushed hard by the South Wind. It still stretched from horizon to horizon, with no end.

"I hope it wipes out all the mice out there", said Yero with feeling. "What is it with them? They're bloodthirsty! More like rats."

"Not the nicest kind, are they? They eat mostly grasshoppers, but anything with blood is on their menu. Can't really blame them for their diet. There isn't much vegetarian food in the desert except sagebrush, and you know what that smells like. It probably tastes even worse".

"Atel! They tried to murder and eat you for supper! Let's be mad at them! I hope they burn up like they deserve".

"Our mob *did* burn", said Atel. "That should please you. I was innocent in that, by the way. The lightning bolt burned them. I just reflected it in self-defense".

The butterflies laughed but Yero wasn't of a mind to let any mice off easy. She nursed her hope that fire would wipe them out until Atel had to disappoint her.

"It won't. They have burrows. They'll be fine. And that's a good thing, actually. Sometimes even the desert is overrun by grasshoppers or other pests. When that happens, the mice are heroes. Sorry, but a lot of villains are heroes sometimes".

"Oh, I get it. On their days off from grasshoppers they work at keeping wrens and butterflies and hummingbirds under control".

"Some of that might be useful. I find two butterflies are quite enough to look after. I can't imagine what I'd do with a thousand Yeros on one side and a thousand Bocas on the other".

"Your job would be easier. We already know so much! - then just multiply it out! We could offer good advice on everything".

"You already do. But imagine yourself arguing with a thousand Bocas. It might start a war".

"No. We wouldn't have to fight. A thousand Yeros could finally talk some sense into them".

"A thousand of you would make a lot of noise, that's for sure", commented Boca. "Even the South Wind would hear you".

"Oh, I hope so! I would lead all the Yeros and we would demand more rain and less lightning; and a nicer schedule too, with sunny mornings and calm breezes during our naps; also pretty sunsets and - gosh! - it'll be a big wish list".

"Here's something you should ask for", said Boca, waving generously at the blowout where the middle room had been. "You'll need a mouth like *that* to spout all your good advice".

"Oh, Boca! You shouldn't exaggerate".

"I'm not".

"But you are! That's too small. It'll have to be much bigger".

Chapter 15

The Sorrowful Skull

The fire line swept around a corner in the valley below and marched toward them, alternately clear and alarming then going nearly dark as wind patterns swirled in the changing land features, dragging the smoke back upon itself. All too soon wisps of that smoke pushed ahead and snaked up through the saguaro ravine right into their noses. Boca made a face and turned to Yero.

"Well? Give us your wisdom, O' Great Mouth. What now?"

"We ask our guide, of course".

"I thought you'd pass that off!" laughed Boca.

"Don't be silly! She sets fires all the time, so she knows about smoke".

"True", agreed their guide. "But the real issue here is the weather and the answer is simple: Check with the locals when in doubt. Move aside. Let the wren have some of this air".

They waited in silence until another finger of smoke found its way up the draw. This time it hung stubbornly in the air. Yero coughed and backed against the wall, covering her face. Boca was amused.

"It'll be worse if you get the mouth you wished for!" he chortled. Then he also fell to coughing.

Pretty soon smoke got into the wren's sanctum and she came storming out, scolding. But when she paused for breath and actually stuck her head out the door, she quieted right down. Yero hoped she had got smoke in her beak, and she did, but she got something else as well, something that put her in a better mood. Without another word and only a quick last look at the advancing flames, she flounced back into her hole and they saw no more of her.

"That's the local forecast", said Atel. "We'll stay. The wind will turn".

In spite of the forecast another wisp curled up the ravine toward them, even thicker this time. The butterflies closed their eyes and held their breath as long as they could. Atel watched them and smiled. After a minute Boca and then Yero gasped for air, expecting the worst. It didn't come. They opened their eyes. The wisp had dispersed outside.

"Not as bad?" asked Atel. "Lucky that time, but don't let your guard down. The weather is changing but a wildfire is a hard thing to stop".

It wasn't so much a change of wind, although the North Wind did come by later. Mostly, the South Wind had finally exhausted herself and abandoned the fire to burn on its own. As they watched, the leaping flames leaped less and less until they leaped no more. The fire still burned, still ate its way forward, but slowly and with less smoke. The cactus gained a reprieve, but the fire was far from out.

Atel and Boca tried to get some sleep. Yero stood watch, fascinated, giving regular updates about how close it was, how the fire line still stretched to the horizons, and especially comments about the wind, which was light and variable now but still occasionally from the south. She worried Boca until he kept watch with her while their guide retired to the last empty room to perch peacefully on an ingrown spine.

"We should get some sleep too", said Boca. "It's late".

"How can you even think about it?" replied Yero nervously. "The fire will probably come right through here while we sleep. We might breathe the smoke and never wake up!"

"Atel isn't worried".

"Can't stay awake, more likely. She's tuckered out from all that gambling, bless her. But this could be the biggest gamble of all! What are the odds we'll wake up alive?"

"Pretty good, I think. The wren isn't worried either".

"She's gambling too, just like Atel. And maybe the odds *are* good Boca, but there's always that one bad chance!" Yero shivered. "*Everything's* such a gamble around here! I just want to leave before we run out of luck".

"Yeah, you're probably right. I get antsy anyway, staying in one place. But we've had a good run of luck, haven't we?"

"Yes, and I think it's because we keep moving. Bad luck hasn't been able to catch up. But when I look down there at the fire - It's still coming, see? Slower, but it's still coming - I get the feeling *that* could be our bad luck, and all because we sat and waited".

"But where would we go? We'd have to go back in the direction we came. And if we're only a few steps ahead of the bad luck *now*, we shouldn't double back or we'll meet it".

"You are wise, Boca. It's no wonder you've come to be third officer of this company, after Atel and me".

Boca bowed solemnly. "That's just a sample. I'm fuller of wise stuff than anybody knows. Go ahead. Ask me something".

"What will happen if we get caught between the fire and the bad luck behind us?"

"Simple. We'll pop like pimples. You'll pop first because of your higher rank and fatter head that goes with it".

"I never knew wisdom was so simple! Maybe you deserve a promotion. You could be 'Third Officer in charge of simple stuff'. I'll speak to our guide about it sometime".

"This stuff is easy. Next, I will describe *you* in simple form. It won't take long".

"It shouldn't. You'll know you've got it right when all you see is correct answers. I have lots. And now I'm going to take one more chance after all and get some sleep".

"But what about the fire? Have you changed your mind?"

"Sure. Girls can do that. It's the simplest way to be right about everything at the end of the day".

It was a little while before Boca came up with a clever reply and by that time Yero was fast asleep. That irritated. He shook her a bit until she mumbled, and delivered the clever line anyway, knowing he wouldn't remember it in the morning. After that, he felt much better and slept peacefully, but Yero dreamed about the fire and had no peace at all.

In her dream, she watched the smoke and fire approaching and was aware of a relentless jabbering behind her: A collective noise of all the bad luck they had escaped from that wanted another crack at them. The jabbering took no visible shape but Yero recognized the voices of villains they had known, now hounding them again. In her dream, smoke spiraled up the cactus and filled the doorway. It went straight for her nose while behind her the jabbering came through the blowout and went right for her ears. Yero struggled, caught between overpowering forces. But it was too late! They had her now, squeezing mercilessly. She cried out but her voice was drowned by the jabbering! She awoke to find Boca shaking her.

"Wake up, pimple", he said. "It's time to leave".

"Don't call me that!"

"I didn't. You called yourself that".

"I did not!"

"Yeah, you did. Even Atel heard it. You were talking in your sleep. Are you sure you're okay? It sounded like someone 'popped' you".

"Someone will pop *you*!" Yero wound up but smoke got in her nose again. A fit of coughing released her from the temper.

"I *did* dream it", she admitted as it all came back to her. "Smoke was coming in the door and the bad luck was yammering behind me! I was caught in the middle. It was awful!" It was still awful, but it was only the wren scolding away. She had got a whiff of new smoke and stormed out of her nest yet again. Atel appeared in the doorway and called for them but the butterflies were already lifting off, wary of the wren in her bad mood.

The fire had actually advanced past them during the night, burning efficiently in the still air with very little smoke. It skipped around the immediate area, owing to the firebreak from the lightning bolt, but had scorched the bases of saguaros farther down the ravine. Shortly before dawn a North breeze had arrived, stopping the fire in its tracks. Now a gust front was coming through from that direction, blowing the last smoke back toward them with a cloud of ashes.

Wings can be so handy. The Travelers rose above the turbulence and settled back down again after it passed by to assess damages and to make a plan. The fire had blackened the entire valley in front of them. The shades of midnight could do no worse. On the higher, rockier ground were several spots less blackened and they made for the highest one, overlooking the bend of the valley. It was a gravelly site with a few shriveled blades of grass - brown in the morning sun from the fire that had eaten so close but skipped the outcropping in search of better fuel. Alone by itself in the gravel was one decent-sized white rock. Atel made for it absently, gazing beyond at the ruined landscape, and almost landed on a sharp corner of it before pulling up in surprise. It was a skull - obviously a cattle skull from the horn she had nearly landed on. The other horn was broken off near the base and missing. Empty eye sockets glared up at...who? The sun? The lucky living? Who cared? Atel did, but the butterflies didn't. They put down on the forehead and called her to join them.

"See? It's safe", Yero laughed. "Don't be superstitious".

"Superstition is against my rules. That's just ghastly. Come along. We'll find a nicer perch".

"But we need to brainstorm, don't we?" teased Boca. "This thing might be of some use".

"Another empty head won't help", sniffed their guide, and turned away to study the panorama. The entire valley below the bend was burned, as were the surrounding hills. From their lookout point no end appeared of the charred landscape. It had been a great fire, one of the biggest range fires in memory, and larger embers still smoldered as far as the eye could see.

"I will leave you to your brainstorming after all", Atel announced presently. "Perhaps the skull remembers water holes and a shortcut across the burn, but I doubt it. I'm going to have a look and try to learn the extent of this. It worries me".

"Go ahead", said Yero. "If any trouble comes along, we'll see it coming from here".

Their guide left and the butterflies warmed themselves in the morning sun. Yero was happy to leave their troubles behind, though she got some argument from Boca about that. He figured the short distance they'd come wasn't enough to throw off the bad luck, if any was pursuing them. But Yero danced out onto the good horn and explained it all in show-business terms.

"The distance shouldn't matter", she lectured. "We're like actors in a play, and the new act has already begun. This is just a short intermission and we should make use of it. By the way, Boca, I'm claiming this horn as my territory. We might have a long intermission - who knows? So we'll need rules. I want this side with the good horn to dance on. You don't dance anyway so you get that side".

"Just like that, huh? You claim it, so you get it?"

"Sure. That's what explorers do. We're the first butterflies to land here so we get to claim the territory and divide it up".

"How do you know we're the first?'

"I don't see any flags or markers".

"Maybe nobody cared. This thing is pretty worthless".

"You're probably right. But it's the location that's important. We can see almost everything in the world from here. It's the best spot on a great lookout point. I suppose other butterflies *have* landed here. Lots of creatures would, to get the best view. If they were smart they would've claimed it".

Yero was mostly right. It was a popular stop. Though only a few inches high, it was the highest point on the outcropping and attracted many birds and flying insects, but scavengers left it alone. It had obviously sat undisturbed for years, not worth gnawing.

Boca explored the side of the skull he was left with. There remained a short stub of horn about an inch long, rounded off as if the cow had lost it earlier in life. Next was an ear hole. He marched down the face past the big hollow eye socket to the longer holes that must have been the nose and tiptoed way out on a bony splinter to where most of the nose had collapsed into a cavity. Looking down from there he could see sharp teeth jutting upwards. The lower jaw was still attached, though mostly buried in gravel.

"Look", he chuckled. "The critter died with her mouth open, so we know for sure it was a cow".

"Oh, pooh-pooh! We knew that anyway from the small horns", said Yero, not bothering to take the bait. "Anyway, an open mouth doesn't mean anything. A boy would've been complaining to the very end".

"Hollering battle cries, more like it. But why would a big old cow end up here? I think a puma must've got her".

"I wouldn't be too sure. They drag off their kill, don't they?"

"Maybe he did. Maybe he dragged it here from somewhere else".

"But pumas have big teeth. Where are the bite marks?"

"Yeah, I don't see any. But what then? Her teeth look good, so she didn't die of old age".

"It could've been lightning, Boca, way up high like this. Just like what almost happened to us last night".

"Yeah. That would've fried her. But why is just the skull left and everything else is gone? Coyotes?"

"Probably. They crunch bones, don't they? For whatever's inside?"

"Yeah. But why not the skull too?"

"Nothing inside, I guess. If the cow had any brains she wouldn't have been up here in a storm".

Boca laughed. "That's good. Mystery solved!" Still, he walked back up to the forehead deep in thought, pondering the next mystery: The secret of the missing horn. But if he mentioned it to Yero, she wasn't interested. She was dancing.

"Figure it out yourself", she said, pausing gracefully on point. "It's on your side so it's your problem".

"But she was a girl. It must've been embarrassing when she was with the herd. Girls don't like to look mismatched".

"True. We do pay attention to our appearance. Boys should do more of that. Anyway, she probably lost it in a fight".

"I think so too. But not in her last fight. See? It's all worn and rounded off, what's left of it".

Yero stopped a moment. "So what? You're never going to find out".

"I know, but it makes me wonder. I wish she had a brain after all so I could ask her about it".

"Oh, ask anyway. Pretend she answers, if it'll make you happy. Pretend a whole conversation! Just don't bother me with that when I'm busy with this".

Boca did ask, speaking down into the ear hole. To his surprise, the skull answered.

"Don't know. Help me!"

Boca hesitated. The voice was clear enough, but he decided to ask once more before believing his ears. "Tell me again: How did you lose your horn?"

"Don't remember. *Help*".

Wow. Boca shook his head in amazement and tried another question. "If I call the other butterfly will you speak to her, so she believes this?"

"Yes. Need help. Need help!"

Boca interrupted Yero who was counting steps. Something in his voice got her attention.

"She talks! Ask a question in her ear over there".

Yero was *so* tempted to brush him off! But his tone indicated that he would keep it up. She sighed. Best to play along and just get it over with. All too soon their guide would return, and she wanted to get in some serious dance practice before they had to leave. Ballet is tricky even for butterflies, and the horn made a very nice stage runway. She sashayed quickly to a spot overlooking the ear hole, leaned over and immediately straightened up again, wrinkling her nose.

"You stink!" she declared. There was no answer. She cast a disgusted look at Boca, guessing that was his little joke - pathetic!

"You're bone-dry!" she scolded, in the general direction of the ear. "Why do you stink?"

The skull was silent. Yero turned away, irritated, to resume her practice.

"Rotting. Still rotting", came a belated reply from below. It was unclear which hole the voice came from, but it came from the skull and surprised Yero.

"Well, I'm sorry", she answered, "but you look way past that stage. What's left to rot in there?"

But the skull wasn't warmed up enough to make long answers yet, just repeated its plea: "Help me".

Yero glanced at Boca, totally amazed. But there was only one sensible answer.

"We can't help", she told the skull. "You're too far gone. It's time somebody told you that".

"Gone, yes. Forgetting too".

"Well, sure. You've got to expect that in your condition".

"Just tell us how you lost the horn", persisted Boca. "Was it in a fight?"

"Lost. Gone. Ears too", said the skull. "Can't hear much. Help me, please?"

Yero wasn't about to go near the smell again and said so, but the skull seemed to take no offense. "Please, just tell nice sounds you hear. I miss sounds".

The butterflies really would have helped, but the land was silent after the fire except for a light breeze. Boca tried to mimic that, but it was useless. The skull made no reply except for a rustling, creaking noise.

"What's going on in there?" called Boca. "You're making more noise than the whole desert".

The creaking stopped. Silence stretched on.

"I guess she's finally finished", said Yero. "Oh, well. We'll be leaving soon anyway".

That got a response: "No, please. We can talk!"

"What's the use? You can't keep up a conversation".

"Ask question. Ask about fight again".

"Okay", agreed Boca. "Did you lose your horn in a fight?"

"Yes". More creaking and rustling.

"I don't like that noise", said Yero. "It reminds me of spiders or something".

The noise stopped. "Big fight", said the skull.

"Who'd you fight with?" asked Boca.

"Bull. Another bull".

The butterflies looked at each other and laughed.

"Not funny! Bad, bad bullfight", insisted the skull.

"You're a cow", scoffed Boca, and the Two laughed some more.

"I have horns!"

"Sure, little cow horns. Not like a bull".

"You don't know!"

"Yes we do. We met a bull, or whatever, the other day. He was young and his horns were already bigger than yours".

"It's better to be a cow anyway", consoled Yero. "Brains are better than brawn".

Sullen silence. Obviously, the skull had a lot to re-learn. So would anyone trying to make a comeback from such a depleted condition. Yero went back to her dance practice but Boca, with time on his hands, tried to keep the conversation alive. He stayed well back from the ear, though. More and more stink came up out as if expressing the skull's foul mood.

And the skull *was* in a horrible mood. Or more accurately, the thing that lived under the skull was. Many such skulls are home to scorpions like this one. The skulls have a special attraction for them, and they seek out especially those of bulls, for reasons of their own. It's a deep insult to accuse them of hiding under a cow, but a common enough mistake since many range cows also have horns and the horns are all scorpions have to go by. But insulted or not, scorpions are always hot-headed and unreasonable. They never admit they're wrong, it doesn't occur to them. They only get mad. *Really* mad. That's their main talent, along with the stinger of course.

So the butterflies were in serious jeopardy though they couldn't see it, but the stink was actually a good omen. It meant the scorpion was molting just now and unable to attack. He had already climbed out of his old shell but the new one was still soft, and the molting juice made him stink. Another day he would have gone out and scurried around in the sunshine to dry off and toughen up the new shell, but not now. Not with skittish prey up there so temptingly close! He must bide his time, letting the armor firm up more slowly in shadow while somehow convincing the prey to stick around.

But his temper worked against him. A *cow*, they said! And *laughed* about it. Idiots! Imbeciles! The scorpion and the bull are *inseparable*. Everyone should know that! It made him hot, released more molting juice. That wasn't good. It kept the new shell soft. He must calm himself. Oh, yes - and *stretch*! - so the new joints didn't lock up. There were stories about lazy ones who ended up prisoners inside their own stiff shells. He stretched, but it made more of the squeaking, creaking noises.

"There it is again!" said Yero, stopping in her tracks. "That same weird noise. Did you hear it?"

"Yeah". Boca backed away from the ear. "Maybe we should just go", he said. "We don't have to go far".

The creaking stopped. "No", said the skull. "Don't go".

"Well, what's that noise?" demanded Yero. "Are you dangerous?"

"No, no. Just stomach growling. Hungry".

"That's not very comforting. Do you eat butterflies?"

"Please, no danger. Bulls eat grass".

"Maybe so", giggled Boca. "But what do cows eat?"

The stink increased. There was a long pause. Finally, "All cattle eat grass. Is there grass?"

"Not much. A few shriveled blades. Didn't you know there was a big fire?"

"No", lied the skull. "Nose not what it used to be".

"It burned through last night", said Boca. "You're lucky to be on this rocky spot or you'd be burnt up too".

"Please…show me grass."

"Why? You couldn't see it anyway".

"Let me try. Hold grass to my eyes".

"Oh, for Pete's sake!" said Yero. "This is getting dumb".

"Let me try…please?"

"Will the stink come up through your eyes too?" asked Yero. It was rude and Boca gave her a bit of a frown.

"No. Less now. Not to worry. So bring grass, please?"

"Oh, okay", said Boca. "We've got a little time". Yero's jaw dropped. He flew off to fetch some and she caught up, if only to admonish him.

"Don't be nutty! A skull can't see anything."

"How can you be sure until we try it? Who knows how long a spirit can linger if the bones are still there?"

"I'm not arguing about that part, only the stupid idea that a skull can *see*. Let's test the old bonehead".

They broke off short blades of the brown grass, brittle from the fire, and carried them back to the skull, alighting near the empty eye sockets. Laying aside the grass, they approached the holes and held up empty hands.

"Here is grass", bluffed Yero. "Are you happy now?"

There was a pause and more creaking as the scorpion stretched to peer up through the eye sockets.

"There it was again!" said Yero, backing away. "That noise spooks me". Boca backed off too.

The scorpion cursed under his breath and resolved to hold perfectly still until the prey got over their little fright. He could see well enough now, but he saw nothing.

"Please, no worry", he said in his nicest voice. "But I see nothing. No grass".

This wasn't what Yero expected but she tried again. "What about now?" she asked, without even approaching the eye socket.

The scorpion peered hard, confused. "No, so sorry. Sorry for friends who help. I see nothing".

Without a word, Yero picked up her grass and held it out. Boca did likewise.

"Yes!" said the skull immediately. "I remember now…valleys of grass. Ah, good old days". Nice words. As nice as he could make them. But behind them an awful tantrum was building. So! The clever prey had tried to trick him! It made him fume. More juice started to ooze. He calmed himself with the knowledge that he was much smarter than them, that his plan was still on track. He imagined eating them and that cooled him down nicely. Saliva drooled into his 'appetizer bowl', that part of his mouth that stuck way out, where the butterflies would soon be marinating. As he thought these happy thoughts and calmed down, his new shell commenced to dry again and smell better.

"Wish I could *smell* grass", the skull said wistfully.

"We can hold some to your nose", offered Boca. He was more than half convinced the skull had passed the test.

"Please, yes!" replied the skull gratefully. The scorpion was smart enough by now to stay put. He simply allowed a few moments for the dumb prey to put the grass to the nose as promised, then sighed blissfully: "Ah, sweet smell!" he bluffed. "Wish I could taste some".

That was his mistake. The butterflies had not put the grass to his nose after all, on a last lingering suspicion of Yero's. Boca whistled softly. Yero winked.

"I'm glad you like it", she said. "Here! Smell it again". And so saying, she tossed her blade away. So did Boca, in disgust.

"Mmmm…Good!" came the reply. "Put in mouth, please?"

"Not yet!" Yero advised the skull. "You aren't ready to eat anything yet. Your mouth must be terribly dry from standing open and the wind whistling through. You need to sniff the grass for a while and get some saliva back. We'll check from time to time and see if your mouth starts to water".

It was a huge disappointment to the scorpion. He was drooling like a drunk in his own mouth but there was no way to make the skull mouth drool, and that's where the butterflies must be lured so he could rush them. They were too quick to sting out in the open. A new plan was needed. He must stay calm and think!

"I'm going back dancing", came Yero's voice floating down, "but Boca will hold the grass for you. Does it still smell good?"

Boca waved an empty hand over the nose again, just for fun.

"Mmmm…Yes! Put in my mouth", said the skull hopefully.

"No, no, no", cautioned Boca. "Mustn't be impatient! You could choke on it if you rush things".

"So hungry! Let me try, please?"

"Sorry, but this is for your own good. When you can drool like a live cow - *then* we'll give you some. Can you?"

There was no answer. Boca went on diagnosing. "Can't spit? Tsk, tsk. Well, I won't be responsible for an accident. Just wait. It should rain by next spring. If we come back this way we'll try again, okay? Hang in there!"

What could the scorpion do? He figured the prey was onto him but couldn't be sure without moving over to the nose. That would surely spook them for good - especially the one that kept prancing off onto the horn. *That* racket was getting on his nerves! The activity was amplified by the hollow horn.

Up above, Yero had quit ballet in favor of tap-dance and was getting the hang of it nicely.

"Whistle me a tune, Boca", she called. "Or do a drumbeat, maybe. Yes, a *drumbeat!* This horn is like a drum anyway. I can hear an echo. Let's have some fun!"

It was getting to be more than the scorpion could stand. He was old, in his last instar, his last molt, a loner used to silence. He liked silence. It was easy on the nerves and worked well in his ambush style. He had no distracting mate or loutish offspring and he liked that too. Other scorpions rarely ventured to this barren point and most were scared off at the revolting sight of his double tail. Any who did come close he killed and ate. He seized on that happy thought to keep his sanity amid all the noise.

He'd been born deformed and held up as the butt of all jokes. The brood had tolerated him until the first molt, thinking that might fix him. It didn't so he was cast out, even as the family gathered for warmth in the face of winter. It only made him more clever and resourceful - more fierce! He'd been here a long time now and talked many a victim right into the mouth in broad daylight. But he preferred to go up after them when night fell. That's what he needed now - stalling tactics! But the noise was assaulting his thought. He could hardly think at all, and it was getting worse, not better.

They were putting on quite a show when Atel returned a little later. Yero tapped away in no particular rhythm and sang snatches of tunes while Boca pounded with a pebble, like a Hard Rock drummer - all this out near the tip of the hollow horn so every decibel they raised was magnified and sent into the skull. It had become unbearable, and doubly so when the scorpion realized he could no longer move - not even to turn his head away from the noise! He had stayed motionless too long. His new shell had hardened in place. All he could do was squeal piteously from inside of it. That part of the production puzzled Atel.

"Our band is pretty loose", explained Yero cheerfully. "Boca does instruments, I dance and sing a little, but most of the vocals are from down there. We're not sure who our friend is".

Atel ventured to an eye socket and peered down. The squealing at least stopped when the butterflies did. The hummingbird sneezed and backed away, shaking her head.

"Scorpion, by the smell. Molting, I think. Do you know how dangerous they are?"

"Sort of. He wanted to eat us, we're pretty sure of that".

"He certainly would have. Why did he join your band instead?"

The butterflies laughed and told her the details, especially the part about the grass.

"Well, let's see what we can see", suggested their guide. She hovered to get the right angle of sun and reflected light into the eye socket. The butterflies leaned close to look.

"It's just a crab", said Boca, a little disappointed.

Unblinking eyes betrayed the fury inside the creature. The eyes moved back and forth, focusing hatred on Yero, then Boca, ignoring Atel or unable to see her in the glare.

"No, it's a scorpion", said Atel. "They do look like crabs, don't they? But there's a difference". She shifted the light a bit. "See the tail? Oh, my!"

"Two tails?" said Boca in surprise.

"Yes. Unusual and even more dangerous. See the tips? The stingers? They're poison. This fellow could kill a coyote, not to mention butterflies".

"He has a lot to learn before he could do that. He must be pretty young".

Atel squinted into the hole, turning her light a bit. "No, not young. Quite old, I think. Just molted, as I thought. The old shell is at his feet. I do believe he's helpless, unable to move. Was he being quiet - so as not to alarm you?"

"I guess so", said Yero. "When he made noise it worried us, and then it would stop".

"He outsmarted himself then. He should have kept moving while the shell hardened. That's how it works with them".

"It wouldn't take much for this one to outsmart himself", said Boca. "He's pretty dumb. We knew that right away. He claimed this was the skull of a bull".

"He would. That's what they look for: The *Bull*. You've seen the Fish of Eternity. There's a Bull up there too, and a Scorpion. They're friends, those two, and their descendants here on earth feel the same bond".

"So now what? We have to watch out for mad bulls since we got the best of their little pal?"

"Watch out anyway! You've met a steer, so you know big cattle can be trouble. But they used to say that if you are ever at the mercy of a bull you might call for the Great Hunter, Orion. He's up there too, hunting the Bull of the heavens. I'll point them out tonight if the weather is clear".

"Show us the Scorpion too", said Boca eagerly. "He must be bigger than this little guy".

"This 'little guy' in his straitjacket is bigger than both of you put together".

"Except for his brain. If the one up in the sky is this dumb, he won't last long either".

Atel didn't say anything. She didn't have to. Someone else answered. The scorpion's eyes bulged at the insults and sharp, gaseous reports escaped every orifice.

"Is that part of their language?" asked Yero, startled. "What did he say?"

"I can only guess", laughed Atel. "He's quite a blowhard. But I advise you to leave *Big* Scorpio out of this. He's the Father of their race and quite beyond the two of you. Leave him to Orion. There is an old score yet to be settled between them".

"I didn't know constellations could move around up there", said Boca. "I thought they were just stuck in their places".

"They were, but they don't stay put. They move around a lot during the year. It must be expected from such a collection of egos."

Atel looked to the west. The sun was still high. She had in mind to wait until dark before beginning the long flight over the great burn. A lot of small prey had perished. The predator birds were hungry, and the Travelers would be easy to see in daylight, outlined against the charred landscape. There was time for a story.

— The Zodiac —

In the First Age of the World, even as the surface of the earth cooled and the Lord put things to His liking, native spirits stirred in the molten interior. Heat and pressure always stir up some sort of trouble. When the spirits heard echoes of activity above many found their way up to the surface. They were strong, born of the young earth itself, but jealous and mistrustful of each other.

Some of them liked the light of day and were decent enough. Some preferred the dark, and definitely were not. For all their powers they could easily have ruled the earth, but they wasted their time plotting against each other. No one paid them much attention until the first men appeared and were awed by them. Men called them gods, but they were *pagan* - being unrelated to the Lord of Light.

The pagan gods liked the flattery and took to hanging around early civilizations, especially near Mount Olympus during the early Greek period. They loafed mostly, accepting offerings and sacrifices and just soaking up the adulation of humankind; but the easygoing atmosphere on Olympus was soon to become stormy.

The gods began to quarrel over the plunder. They quarreled over everything else too, and when they tired of quarrelling with each other they assumed the shapes of animals, or heroes, to impress the human population and cause mischief.

The strongest of all the spirits, the pagan god that men called Zeus, sat atop Mount Olympus and watched with growing concern as the others terrorized the countryside just for fun, trying to out-do each other. He saw human civilization - the source of all the fun - crumbling and slipping away under the abuse. Something had to be done. He knew the other pagans well, knew which were strongest and did the most damage, and he summoned the nine worst to his mountaintop.

A tremendous argument broke out. Horrific storms gathered above the mountain, terrifying to humans below, but Zeus finally imposed an agreement. The nine would henceforth take turns with their mischief, one at a time. Zeus traced their favorite shapes in the stars: a ram, a bull, the mischievous twins, a crab, a lion, a scorpion, a centaur, a sea-goat, and the water boy. The greedy fishes, Kayla and Riba, were already up there tethered together as one, making ten in all.

"Up you go now to your places", commanded Zeus. "You will each get a whole month of the year to make trouble with no interference from me or the others. The sea-goat goes first".

"All well and good", bellowed Taurus the Bull, "But two months of the year will thus be wasted. Give them to me!"

Zeus ignored him and instead traced out two more constellations: A virtuous woman, and her scales of justice. "These are for the ninth and tenth months", he said. "Let the humans have a break during autumn for their harvest. They'll need it".

There was a lot of grumbling, but they all went to their places. It had to be like this and deep down everyone knew it. That should have been the end of any catastrophic trouble, but Orion - greatest hunter of them all - was skipped over and received no constellation. He took it as an insult.

"Why not me?" he demanded of Zeus. "I'm greater than any of them!"

"Because the villages need you to keep the monstrous beasts at bay", reminded Zeus. Orion was possibly the only pagan god who helped human civilization.

"But I am hunting the wild bull!"

"Good! There are dangerous ones near the villages even as we speak".

"Not *them!*" sneered the Great Hunter. "I'm bored with the little ones. Now I'm hunting *him!*" He thrust his sword skyward at Taurus in his new constellation.

"Well, you can't have him. It would mess up the arrangement. Hunt something else".

"I never give up the hunt! You know that".

"If you go up there, I'll see to it you never come back!" warned Zeus.

The warning was useless. Nothing ever swayed Orion from his chosen hunt. But when he went into the northern sky pursuing Taurus, Zeus lost his temper, so common with any of the pagan gods. He had a word with the Scorpion, and when Orion inevitably caught the Bull and raised his sword for the killing blow, Scorpio stung him on his heel.

Thus, Taurus was saved and is forever grateful to the Scorpion; which is why cattle skulls often lie undisturbed on the range, bleaching in the sun long after the rest of the carcass is devoured and gone. There is a charm on the skull, especially the ones with horns - a welcoming charm to nasty, stinging arthropods in the area searching for a hideout. It's the age-old bond between Taurus and Scorpio.

***

Atel paused with the story and checked the time. The sun was sinking toward the western horizon. Soon it would be time to go. The butterflies, especially Boca, weren't satisfied with the ending but Atel put him off.

"Later. When the stars are out. I'll show you more".

"At least tell us if he died from it. Did the Scorpion kill him?"

"Not yet. That's still up in the air".

"Yeah, right". Boca rolled up his eyes. "I know *that* part".

"I'm not making jokes on you. I meant the issue really isn't decided yet. We could say the same thing about *your* scorpion, except we know he's going to die in his stiff shell. The issue is *when*. It's not decent to leave him like this".

"He deserves it".

"I'm sure he does. However, starving takes a long time for a scorpion. It would be cruel. We should think of a quicker end".

"Now you're talking! What do you have in mind?"

"I thought you might strike up your band again and let him call in his own predators. There are some who eat scorpions".

"Good idea!" agreed Yero. "We'll give him one last thrill. He sure seemed to enjoy music".

The sun went down and shadow fell on the outcropping as the band sprang to life. The scorpion, overhearing all of this, was slow to contribute his vocal part but they coaxed it out of him; and when the shrieking started, he couldn't stop. The rest of the band broke up and waved goodbye.

They left none too soon. A falcon, diving in the twilight, pulled up at the last instant, realizing his prey was under the skull. The air force would have to find a different meal. No matter. Boca spotted the infantry coming up the hill from below. Mice, they looked like in the gathering dark. He was pretty sure he recognized one or two from the night before and had a comforting thought: If the scorpion could somehow get in a sting or two before the end, all would be perfect!

Their guide took them quickly up high after the close call with the falcon. The first stars were coming out and she took a bearing by them out of habit, though she didn't need it. The sunset still glowed in the west.

"How far now?" asked Yero after a little while.

"How far until what? The end of the burn?"

"First that, I guess. And then some milestones".

"We fly over the burn until we come to a river. That should be around midnight. We'll rest there, then follow the river south tomorrow, toward a larger river. We won't get there tomorrow, but that's just as well. We'll need more rest and some kind of plan to cross the second river".

"You make it sound difficult. What's hard about crossing a river?"

"Mosquitoes. Clouds of them sometimes".

"That would be a nuisance".

"More than a nuisance. There are two kinds of mosquitoes there: Some loyal to this side of the river, some to the far side, and they're at war. No one even remembers when it started".

"So? Let them fight. They won't even notice us then, when we cross".

"Sorry, but you can be sure they'll notice. That's what it's all about. Stopping travelers. Neither kind lets anyone cross without paying a toll, and the toll is figured in blood. That's what the mosquitoes want. We're small travelers. I don't think we could afford the toll".

Yero fell silent. Boca let it go too, for now. He was hoping for an end to the burn, a rest stop, and a chance to ply their guide with more questions about constellations. More than once he fell behind, peering up at the stars, and had to double-time it to catch up before she scolded him. A rest stop seemed the last thing on her mind right now. He glanced down to check out the burn and felt cheered. The land looked brighter! But only until his eyes adjusted from gazing at the stars. Then the land showed its true color again, still charred. In the distance, against the last glimmer of sunset, he could make out higher ground - a ridgeline, or maybe a chain of hills. The blackened earth stretched toward it unbroken. Boca turned again to the stars and the night sky, doubting that the burn would ever end.

But it did end at last. Lightning had struck a tree, one of several scattered cedars on the high ridgeline. That had set off the grass fire. Everything beyond the stricken tree was unburnt. As if she knew Boca's mind (which she did) Atel perched right on the blackened tree, on a crispy, surviving twig, and answered a few questions now that the hour was right.

"There's Orion", she said, tracing his belt and sword with a moonbeam. From that, the butterflies easily guessed the rest. The Great Hunter was almost directly overhead.

"And there is the scorpion who stung him, just peeking above the southern horizon. You'll have to use your imagination on this since only his nose and a foreleg or two are visible". She highlighted what there was, adding a few details to the nose that would be fresh in their minds.

"It's still hard to picture", said Yero. "If he would poke up a little farther so we could see his nasty eyes it would be easier".

"He won't dare. Not in winter while Orion is abroad hunting him. At least that's one side of the story, the one I favor".

"I believe it. It looks like he's hiding, afraid to come up".

"Yes, it does. But come next summer it'll be the other way around. Scorpio will be high in the sky, brandishing his stinger, and Orion will be running away, fleeing below the far horizon. That's how the scorpions will tell it. Unfortunately, that version's been repeated so often that a lot of folks believe it".

"Will it ever be settled?"

"Probably not - between *them* - but here on earth the score is tallied every day between men and scorpions. Both sides score a lot, but in this part of the world men always come out ahead. You know about the charm on the cattle skulls. Well, Orion set a charm to counter that. His charm gets into the heels of the cowboy boots and they've stomped out a lot of scorpions over the years".

Chapter 16

River Traffic

Southwest from their blackened tree a white ribbon gleamed in the moonlight - the first river, still some miles away. Their guide was very pleased to point it out.

"Anyone thirsty?" she asked.

She didn't have to ask twice, or even once. Since they left the scorpion to his fate she had been nagged with questions about water. They were all of them tired of sand, rocks, and cattle skulls. It was time for a change.

"By the way", she added brightly, "There is another large burn just across the river. We'll be venturing into that for breakfast".

Groans. This was unexpected and not taken as cheerfully as it was delivered. Boca especially was deflated.

"Let's just have water then", he grumbled. "Isn't there any nectar along the river?'

"Oh yes, but it's medicinal. Shall we do that first?"

More groans. "What's in the burn?" asked Yero. "Blackberries? Ash trees?"

"Clever, but wrong. We'll be looking for fireweed".

Yero made a face. "Are you kidding?"

"Not at all. Do you like spicy nectar?"

"You mean *hot*?"

Atel laughed. "It won't burn you. The nectar is just *spicy*-hot with extra flavor. We're far enough south now where a lot of food is spicier, even the nectar. You'll have to get used to it. Comes from the land, I suppose".

"If they named it for fire, maybe it *is* too hot".

"Actually, the name has nothing to do with the flavor. The plant just grows best after a wildfire. It's the first green thing that pops up through the ashes".

"Isn't there anything ordinary?" asked Boca. "Some plain mallasha, maybe?"

"No. Sorry. But downriver we might find monkey flower. You should feel at home among those".

"Oh, great. Maybe I'll try the medicine first".

"Good. That's best anyway. We'll have some *All-Heal* before the spicier food. Then we might not have to stop as often later, if you know what I mean".

The butterflies understood that and quit asking questions. The flight became much quieter. In the dark hour before dawn they came to a gorge. The moon had long gone, and a light fog hung over the shoreline and river hundreds of feet below, virtually straight down. Judging by a sheen off the fog, the river stretched nearly from canyon wall to canyon wall.

On a sunny day, the thermal updrafts could have been dangerous and maybe an impossible obstacle for butterflies, but on a cool, calm night the drafts worked to their advantage. They took a handy one down, almost like an elevator in a tall building, and 'stepped off' at the bottom. It was darker beneath the fog, but their guide was able to find the medicinal plant by its minty smell. There were a lot of them scattered along the narrow riverbank, still in flower though far from fresh. The butterflies dutifully took a dose and were relieved to find it wasn't bad, if you liked mint.

The plants were good cover too, so they rested and slept a little. They overslept a little, actually, but that was just as well. *All-Heal* needs time to take effect like any medicine, and when travelling in faraway lands one should thoroughly follow the directions.

It was near mid-morning when they stirred again - or rather, the honeybees roused them. These weren't the busy, suspicious ones they were familiar with but a new type, busy and belligerent. They excused themselves quickly and went across the river. It seemed luxurious, flying above all that water. Boca dipped low once, then again for a 'sip-on-the-go', until Atel saw him and chewed him out.

"The plan is to cross the river and have breakfast, not to *be* breakfast for some fish. Don't get close to the water!"

Boca pulled up quickly, collecting his wits. Of course their guide was right, but there were thousands of newly hatched fish flies everywhere, just above the water. That's what had lulled him into carelessness. It looked perfectly safe. The fish flies sure weren't worried.

Then, splashes everywhere! A school of fish did have lunch. The flies milled and fluttered but didn't rise up to any safe altitude. The fish gorged themselves, but when Boca looked back the flies were still there - as many as ever, like aphids - and still right on the water ready to serve themselves up to the next hungry school.

"They don't even care", he reported. "Do fish flies want to be eaten?"

"No. But they don't know how to defend themselves. They trust to safety in numbers like the bird flocks. Their odds are pretty good if they're normal. It's the ones that are slightly darker, or lighter, or maybe fly a little lower or slower that are most at risk. A fish will spot one that's different. That's why I chewed you out. You would've been the oddball in that bunch".

"*Oddball*", giggled Yero. "I like that. Can I call you that?"

"Go ahead, if you want to look different too".

"I already do, Boca. I'm the oddball who stayed up where it was safe".

Boca had to smile, and why not? They had at last put the desert behind with all its hardships. It was time for some good cheer.

When they approached the far shore there was only a poor gravel road and a few rank weeds between the water and the cliff, but breakfast awaited high above and once more their timing was right. The morning sun had warmed these western walls first and the daily updrafts were already commencing. They hopped on one and it took them most of the way up. The rest was easy. They soon reached the crest and found a much different landscape on this side of the river. A wildfire had swept to the very precipice the year before and stopped. The desert scrub and sagebrush were still blackened, but there were green patches here, there, and everywhere: The fireweed, whose seeds might lie dormant for years until awakened by a burn. Then they sprout immediately, beating everything else out of the ground. Many of their flower spikes were still active with blooms that varied in color from one plant to the next, and especially from one patch to the next.

"Help yourselves", said Atel. "All the colors are quite edible".

She went her way, to the reddish ones; the butterflies were tempted first by the orange. It was true about the spicy flavor.

"A little hot, isn't it?" said Yero immediately, and paused in case it got even hotter in the mouth. It didn't, but other spices emerged to the taste if the nectar was savored a bit before swallowing.

"Good", was Boca's only comment for some time.

It would've been better now had they not overslept. The belligerent bees were out in force and there was no sharing with them. They didn't even share among themselves but took a special dislike to the Travelers, hurling threats and brandishing stingers like the gunslingers who used to swagger about the Old Southwest territories. Nevertheless, the butterflies held their own long enough to taste the colors from yellow all the way to red - and found every shade different.

"They're a lot like real fire", decided Yero. "The yellower the color the milder the taste; the redder they are, the hotter".

"Yeah, and the bees like it hot if you've noticed. It matches their tempers".

"Time to go!" advised Atel, appearing suddenly with bees hot on her tail. She didn't pause because the bees didn't, but zipped way out over mid-canyon where her pursuers lost interest. That's where the butterflies caught up. She was debating, not answering questions, talking mostly to herself.

"We follow this river to the larger one", she was saying, drawing on memories of earlier years. This was not her usual migratory route. "I'm not sure what a safe altitude might be, or even if there is one. We'll go lower by stages and see where the trouble is, but I'd like to get pretty low, low enough to find any flowers that still linger along the shore. If we make good time, we might reach the big river in one day, two days more likely. Down we go then".

They descended from the clifftops a hundred feet, and Atel didn't like it. They were alone at that level and she could feel the eyes of falcons watching from their nests and perches along the rim. They drifted lower and ran into turbulence, a dangerous condition when unfamiliar with the local air. Lower still, they came out of the bumpy air into the zone of gulls who dominated the whole lower level, driving almost everyone else out by their numbers and their free-for-all style. Gulls aren't everywhere all the time, but when present they sure seem to be.

"We can navigate here", their guide decided. "These are Herring gulls, pretty rough and tumble, but they won't be after us. See? They prefer other food".

They made their way downriver without much trouble, zigzagging through the traffic. The gulls were after dead fish that had washed up on the banks, eating them and carrying them around. They paid no attention at all to the Travelers. There had been a die-off and hundreds of fish of all kinds were fouling the shore, rotting - a perfect banquet for the gulls. Some had eaten their fill and were playing with their food, dropping dead fish on the cormorants.

"I wish the gulls would eat them all!" said Yero, holding her nose. "Phew! The smell!"

"Oh, it's not that bad", said Atel. "We've smelled worse".

That's when the accident happened: A serious one that threw the entire journey into doubt. Atel was struck by a dropped fish. The gull never meant to hit her, but rather a grumpy cormorant further below perched on a floating log. It was a lucky deflection as the gull saw it: The rotted fish broke apart as it glanced off Atel and most of it did hit the cormorant as a result, scaring her and some others off the log. The way that worked out, ironically, was a bit of residual luck for the Travelers too.

But Atel was hurt and could barely flutter downward, steering a little with one wing. The butterflies tried to help but were no use at all, and she landed *thump!* - on the log. If it hadn't been there it would've been into the drink with her and fish food pretty quickly. As it was, she bounced and would've slid off anyway, but Boca pushed from below, Yero pulled from above, and they stopped her slide. That was the worst moment, but their guide was crippled in a most grotesque way. One side of the fishes' jawbone had broken off the skull and clenched itself on her left wing near the shoulder, as if the rotting fish meant to have her for a last meal but couldn't swallow her. The jawbone was as big as she was and that was probably lucky too. Her wing was solidly pinched between big teeth but not punctured. The worse thing was, the jaw was locked in a death grip.

"I don't think it's broken", said the hummingbird, "but it hurts when I try to move".

"What are you going to do?" asked Yero. This sort of thing wasn't in the plan at all. A guide just *has* to be okay.

"I don't know", said Atel simply. "For now, let's be thankful the log was here". She grimaced, twisting a little this way and that, trying to find a looser hold. There was none. The butterflies could only look on feeling useless and helpless.

Their log was a smallish one, as logs go. Cottonwood, possibly, although the bark was gone so it was hard to say. It was about six feet long and maybe a foot and a half across, broken off from a larger trunk somewhere upstream. Cracks ran the entire length giving the impression the thing might split apart at any moment. One crack opened so deeply that water welled up in it, adding to the uneasiness. That water was the level of the river, so the log was more underwater than above and reasonably stable, but there was no avoiding the cormorant poop which was smeared everywhere. It got on their hands and feet, and especially all over their guide and the rogue jawbone. But the log was home, for now.

"How far could we go on this thing?" asked Yero. "Not counting any worse luck?"

"If it doesn't run aground, we could float all the way to the big river", reckoned Atel. "That is, if we aren't kicked off the log by cormorants, or something else. Mosquitoes will be out tonight too. There's a lot of traffic on the river".

"We'll just have to stay here until we find someone to help you".

"That's not realistic, Yero. Trouble will find us. When it happens, I'll give you last-minute instructions and we'll split. I don't have to go all the way with you. You've learned a lot".

"But what about you? We're not going to leave you like this".

"No matter how bad you smell", added Boca.

Atel had to laugh. It hurt. "I did say we've smelled worse, didn't I? Maybe I tempted fate".

"Well, here we are anyway", said Yero. "And this is the smelliest place ever. About the only good thing might be, things can't get any worse".

But they did. Misery can always get worse. The log lurched and threatened to roll as a turtle climbed aboard, a basking turtle with red coloring behind the ears. It was followed by another, then a couple more. They were very familiar with the log, well acquainted with the easiest place to board, which happened to be up at the bow end. As each turtle boarded, the earlier arrivals were obliged to move down and make room. Most weren't very large, being about a foot long and less than that in width, and they were efficient about occupying space, which still left the Travelers some room near the stern. Yero found herself estimating the remaining space and dividing it by an average turtle shell, but then another clambered aboard and she had to refigure.

"I don't like this", she whispered to Boca. "How many turtles do you think are in the river?"

"Too many. They'll push us right off the end".

Yero glanced at Atel who was only half-awake now, fighting pain and fatigue, and resolved to negotiate on her behalf. She flew up atop the nearest turtle shell. He (or she) was half-asleep also, head and neck lolling out, resting on the log. Only the bow-facing eye remained open a slit.

"Good morning!" Yero hailed as cheerfully as she could, being careful to stand back a bit. The stern-facing eye opened a slit also, but the head didn't budge. There was no reply.

"Good morning!" Yero persisted. "I want to be polite, so - if you please - are you a boy or a girl?"

The turtle yawned slowly. "Who wants to know?"

"Yero of the Rasha La. A butterfly. A *girl* butterfly".

"Well girl butterfly, if you have to ask then you've insulted me. Do you imagine any *boy* could have such a beautiful shell?"

"Oh, never! Please don't think that. It's very elegant! Also, quite large. With some folks, the boys are bigger than the girls, so I was confused".

That helped a little. The turtle's stern-facing eye closed again. "In our kind the girls are bigger", she remarked, "so as to accommodate all the beautiful designs. The biggest girl is therefore the most beautiful too. That would be *me*".

"Ah! So that's how it works. Well, it's true. You're the biggest so far".

The suspicious eye re-opened. "*So far?* Is that what you said? Are you expecting to see bigger girls?"

"No, no! You'll surely take the prize! The others aren't even close".

"I know; but we're only a few yet. Wait til we're all here. I'll still be the biggest! You'll see".

"Umm...how many are there?"

"Lots. There isn't room on this log, even when we stack up".

"Oh my! I was hoping there might be room for three small passengers. We don't take up much space".

"You'll have to defend your spot like everyone else. Someone is always coming on board, so then everyone slides down to make room. When there's no more room at the end, it's up to the last turtle to hold on or fall off. I'll hold on, as big and beautiful as I am, so the next turtle will have to climb up top and start a second row. There won't be room for you, that's for sure. No offense, but I'll push you off the end".

As if to punctuate the point, another turtle clambered aboard up front, then another. A good deal of bumping and shoving ensued with many a 'Slide down, please', and 'Excuse me'. When everyone got settled at last, the bottom row was full. There was only a bare inch left un-shoved, and Boca had to brace Atel from rolling off that.

"Do you mind if we perch on your shell?" asked Yero quickly. "To admire it? We're small, so it will take three of us to admire all of it".

The turtle was agreeable. No, she didn't mind three little hitchhikers up there, all singing her praises. Soon enough on a nice day like this, turtles would be stacked up, jostling her, and offering no compliments. Turtles don't praise each other, as a rule.

It was one thing to get permission, however, and a whole other thing to get their guide up on top. She couldn't help at all, even by flapping her good wing. That just annoyed the turtle and impeded the butterflies trying to help. In the end, it was the indented designs on the shell that made the difference, as Atel was able to gain footholds and be of some assistance that way; but once on top, Boca (pushing from below) actually rolled her over onto her back. There she lay speechless, looking up at the open sky where she ought to be.

"Now you've done it", exclaimed Yero. "She's upside-down! She might not be able to roll over again".

It was unfortunate she said it so loud. That's a taboo subject with such reptilians. All turtles have a deep-rooted, genetic fear of this. All of these (there were seven or eight by now) came fully alert, heads up, necks stretching this way and that, questioning and arguing. They weren't able to reach any conclusion because the questions had to be passed down the line from one to the next. By the time a question reached the far end it had changed a lot, and by the time an answer returned it bore no relation to the original question. To complicate things further, some turtles faced one way, some the other, so that it quickly turned into back door gossip. Yero's turtle had raised the alarm but by the time her outburst made the whole circuit it sounded more like someone had died. "Kaput" was the word they used. Gossip put this unfortunate individual somewhere in their midst, but no one knew where. Yero could only bite her lip as the turtles became more alarmed each time the story went around the grapevine.

Things only calmed down when more came aboard and went up to the second deck. The earlier ones lost their train of thought when new ones stomped and bumped around on top of them. A smaller one shoved the travelers rudely aside and claimed the last spot in the row. They had to cling to the edge of their shell as best they could. Boca braced himself underneath and kept Atel from tumbling off while Yero flew up to ask permission of the new turtle - a younger, more sociable male. She hit it right off. Sure, they could sit up on top! He wouldn't mind someone to visit with. Everyone else was dozing off in the warm sun. He couldn't guarantee the place very long, though. More turtles would be boarding soon. It was prime basking time.

Yero and Boca teamed up once more and were able to shove their guide up the shallower slope of this smaller shell, but she ended up on her back again. Yero knew by now to keep quiet about it, but Boca didn't, and set off the grapevine once more.

"Upside-down! Someone's upside-down!" Yero could hear the babble making its way to the other end, then coming back. This time it changed into something more logical: More turtles were coming *up*, so everyone had to move *down!* Their young turtle stretched his rubberneck to count the newcomers but there weren't any. He bumped his neighbor roughly.

"False alarm! Pass it on".

His message went face-to-face first and that went well, but then face-to-tail, and so became confused. The next thing Yero heard was turtle #3 in the top row breaking wind, and everyone after that did the same thing. The truth is, a lot of turtle chain-messages retrograde into this sort of thing.

Maybe the word 'pass' triggers the reaction. Whatever, they do need the release, and before you criticize them please bear in mind their diet which includes the bloated carp, already producing gas under the hot sun. Yes, smile along with them! It's quite healthful and well-accepted on the river, and the only backdraft to really worry about is that predators might hear the barrel organ playing.

"This is not going to end well", predicted Atel, breaking her silence. "Anyone should see that. I know this kind of turtle. They're skittish. When startled, they slide into the water in the blink of an eye, and it happens a lot. Don't get trampled--"

Then it *did* happen. There was a sudden rush of new turtles scrambling aboard over the top of everyone, and a second later a huge alligator-like head burst out of the depths lunging for the turtle pile with open jaws. Turtles slid off in all directions as the creature snatched the largest one and flopped right on top of the log with it. The butterflies instinctively lifted off avoiding many collisions as the big body of the alligator - now looking more like a fish - rocked the whole log, actually splitting it in half along the major crack. With a final spray of water from its flopping tail, the thing disappeared again into the murky deep. No more turtles. No more log. No more Atel! The butterflies began searching desperately all around the split log. There was no sign at all, not even a feather.

"She's gone!" shouted Boca. "*Now* what?"

"I don't know!" uttered Yero. "She was so *right* about everything. Even her last words - remember? She *said* this wouldn't end well!"

"It didn't either", said a voice above them. "Not for one of the turtles anyway, and certainly not for our log. We might as well go on without it".

"Atel! What happened?"

"I thought up a few more last words. Your training isn't over yet". She laughed and did a few tricks in the air to show that she was rid of the jawbone. She had been bowled over and dumped into the water.

"All I remember is a turtle shell coming at me sideways like a saucer", she explained. "I think it smacked the jawbone at the hinge, popping it open. I'm still not sure and I don't much care. I'm fine now".

"It didn't seem right anyway", marveled Boca. "You'll never end up as fish bait".

"I hope not! But *you* still might. Come! Get up from the water. There are more hungry fish!"

"Yes, yes, but what was *that* thing? Was it an alligator?"

"Partly. And part fish too".

"That doesn't sound right".

"It's not. It's another problem left behind by the old pagan gods".

"A fish story? Boca will like this one", laughed Yero.

"Not the usual kind. I'll tell it on the go. We've lost some time".

"Are all the old tales true? Or do you only tell the true ones?"

"I tell them exactly as I heard them. If everyone did, we wouldn't have to guess, would we? Remember that when you re-tell them. As to the *level* of truth, I'm sure it varies with the age of the story. But there's some truth to all of them and *all* truth to some of them. It's the listener's job to use proper judgement".

"We'll do fine, then. Good judgement is one of our strong points".

"It certainly was today! Tomorrow..."

The butterflies let the pause end without comment.

"Naturally, Zeus comes into this story too", Atel began...

—The Unnaturals—

After Zeus dispatched the most troublesome of his kind to their constellations, he expected his job to get easier, but it didn't. The dispute with Orion was only the beginning.

Part 3: Byways of the Butterfly

Quite a few lesser gods still loafed about Olympus causing minor mischief. They might never have amounted to much but when they saw the Big Villains 'glorified' in the heavens they thought, 'Why not us too?', and re-doubled their mischief. Worse yet, another major figure had been left out and didn't like it. Things were about to get tough again for the young human race.

The first sign of trouble was drought. Zeus turned from the business with Orion only to see the rivers drying up. It was the Waterboy's month to play in the sky and he chose to withhold the water purely to irritate Neptune, ruler of the oceans.

These rivals had never cooperated as they should, each claiming ownership of all the waters. One had to go, and Zeus had stuck the Waterboy into a constellation because he was a brat - constantly teasing Neptune, spilling too much water into the rivers or too little. Now he was at it again – but *under Zeus' protection*, as Neptune saw it, and the ruler of the oceans went rogue.

He had always favored the shape of a giant arising from the ocean depths, but now he took the form of a sea serpent to feast on sailors and wreck their ships. He sank a whole armada that dared to sail against him and gorged on the mariners. Seafaring and trade came to an abrupt halt.

Zeus, master of thunderbolts, shot a hole in the Waterboy's pail, thereby restoring the plumbing of the world; but what to do about Neptune, who had been a friend?

"Be yourself again and all is forgiven", Zeus offered.

"Kick the brat out of his constellation and give it to me", replied Neptune.

"No. I want him where he is. The boy is worse than you are".

"That so? Maybe you haven't been watching".

"Oh, I saw. That was horrible! But I need your help so I'm giving you another chance".

"I'll think about it".

Unfortunately for this world, Neptune had come to enjoy being a monster. It sure beat the dull old days of 'managing the waters' that Zeus had put him to. Ugh! That was boring.

"Last chance, Old Pal", warned Zeus one day.

Neptune didn't even answer. He was playing sea serpent again, just now stretching his great neck hundreds of feet above the waves to threaten a boat. In a fit of anger, Zeus loosed a mighty thunderbolt and blasted the serpent to bits.

***

"That's *it?*" blurted Boca when Atel stopped there.

"Isn't that enough?"

"No! You never said where the alligator thing came from".

"Correct. I decided to make a nice, clean ending so the two of you don't have nightmares".

"Well, the sea serpent blew up! How clean is that?"

"It was very, very messy. You really want to hear more?"

Boca nodded eagerly. Yero narrowed her eyes a little but stuck close.

"Okay. It didn't work out as Zeus expected. Sea serpents are like giant worms. When you cut a worm in half you just might get two worms, as you've heard. That's what happened to the serpent Neptune, only there were lots of pieces. Thousands of pieces. All the pieces knew better than to grow back into serpents that Zeus would recognize, so they grew back into other ugly things that we know today. Some bigger pieces grew into octopus and giant squid, some into creatures that are better left to the dark regions of the deep. The smaller pieces became sea snakes and poison jellyfish. The pieces that were struck directly by the bolt became electric eels, the smallest bits turned into lampreys and leeches".

"And? What about the alligator thing?"

"That was accidental. The blast melted some things together that were never meant to be, and the true fish of the sea knew them when they saw them. They laughed at the alligator/fish and ridiculed them. 'Alligator Gar' they're called today. The true fish hounded them out of the oceans and chased them into freshwater rivers. The banishment made the Gar bitter and mean, and they're still out for revenge. Many a true fish has since paid for the deeds of their ancestors".

"Turtles too", added Boca when the hummingbird said no more.

"Yes, turtles too. But to be fair, all big fish eat little fish when they can. Even the Gar should have a right to lunch".

"As long as it isn't us".

"It's up to you to avoid that".

"Yeah. Well, that reminds me - we haven't eaten since, gosh, I don't know how long!"

"Only a few hours. That's not too bad for butterflies".

"Yeah, but we had to leave lunch early, if you remember".

"Well, we'll be coming to the monkey flowers soon. Let's get down along the shore so we don't miss them".

The dining area turned out to be casual with a 'hold your nose' ambiance so common on the fringes of human civilization. The plants grew around a marshy inlet where spring seepage oozed from a fold in the canyon wall. The shoreline widened below that point, allowing a dirt road to come up along the water from somewhere downriver. A vehicle had recently made a turn-around where the road ended, discharging garbage. This was common practice, obviously: Black plastic bags, a dozen or more, clung to the shoulder of the roadway. Others had tumbled down the short slope and rested partly in the water. Some had burst open from the tumble; some had been ripped apart by animals - a typical rural dump complete with several old tires and assorted cans, bottles, used diapers and construction scrap. The protective inlet made for calm water and plenty of time for the mess to stew. It smelled. Their guide led the way to the furthest flowers out on the fringe, but these were still only a beer can toss from the mess. The flowers were busy with all kinds of insects.

"Must be good if everyone's here", said Yero. "Are these the little 'monkeys' then?" She was joking, but a mosquito (most of the little 'monkeys' were mosquitoes) reacted angrily.

"Look who's talkin'! Look in the water, bimbo. See the monkey? You're the monkey!"

"I didn't ask your opinion, shrimp! What are you, anyway?"

"Mosquitoes, bimbo. But don't be sissy and panic. We don't bite".

"That's not what I've heard".

"So? We can't help stories that go around". The mosquito growled at her. The other 'monkeys' laughed.

Yero backed away and went to warn Boca, but he'd already bickered with them too. Together they approached Atel who was taking over a blossom from several skeeters, actually fanning them with her wings until they left, none too happy about it.

"Aren't you worried?" asked Yero. "They admit they're mosquitoes".

"They are, but they're boys. The boys aren't vampires".

"And we just take their *word* for that?"

"A good question. They do look the same, boys or girls, but the boys really don't bite, and the girls don't bother with nectar. We're safe here by the flowers".

The butterflies went off looking for blossoms without buddies, but they were hard to find. The best situation was a nice flower with only two mosquitoes crawling on it.

"I'm hungry", said Boca impatiently. "I'm going in".

"Oh, sure! And what about hygiene?" warned Yero. "Where were these two before they came here?"

Boca shrugged. "Some stuff can't be helped", he said, and muscled his way in. Yero reluctantly landed next to him. The mosquitoes backed off but hovered close by.

"Hoo! You stink", said one.

"So does *that* one!" said the other, pointing at Boca. "Whatta you bums been into?"

"I beg your pardon!" said Yero in surprise.

"Too late for that", declared the first. "You've already stunk up the joint".

"I don't...!" began Yero.

"You sure did! Now it's all over the flower, bimbo".

"Flies smell like that! Do you eat poop too? Like flies?"

The mosquitoes left in disgust. Boca laughed and hooted. "Well? You never answered them. Do you?" Before she could slap at him, he quickly reminded her where they just came from. "We *do* stink pretty bad, Yero! We're just used to it by now. Remember what was all over the log?"

It's not easy for a pretty girl butterfly to admit that much, but Yero faced up to it on one condition. "None of this *ever* gets out to anyone else, Boca! Do you swear? Anyhow, you're worse than I am".

"Okay. I swear sometimes anyway. But listen, I'm not going to wash up. I think we've stumbled into a lucky plan".

"We didn't stumble, Boca. We stepped right in it. You even sat down".

"Yeah, but did you see how the mosquitoes reacted? The bird poop can be our repellent! The mosquitoes won't even come close. Atel will love this idea".

"I doubt it. And now that I'm reminded, I can't stand the smell of me either. It's worse than bat manure".

"Oh, you're just jealous because a girl would never think up such a great plan".

"You're right about that. A girl never would! Because it's a dumb idea. It won't work".

"Why not?"

"Because it's a poopy plan".

"You can't brush it off that easy. Give me a reason".

"Okay. A girl *didn't* think of it, so that's proof enough there's something wrong with it".

"Oh, yeah? I have another great idea too!"

Yero just glared. Boca laughed. "Let's eat", he suggested.

There was no more argument. The monkey flower is rich in nectar, and either luck or their body odor did keep the mosquitoes at bay.

"So, what do you think?" asked Boca a while later when they had all finished lunch. He had put the 'repellent' question to their guide earlier and she had put him off politely, not wanting to be distracted during mealtime.

"Let's try it", she said now.

Yero's mouth fell. Boca's went way up.

"I had the same experience", she went on. "Mosquitoes don't seem to like cormorant poop. Who could blame them? Remember though, we're dealing here with the boys and they're not after blood. The girls might react differently. But we can easily try the idea by doing nothing. If it doesn't help, we'll wash off".

"Where are the girls anyway?" asked Yero. "Or aren't there many?"

"There's lots. As many as the boys, I'm sure. They'll be over by the garbage. During the warm part of the day they're usually near the nursery. They have some fondness for their little wigglers in the water. That would be the soiled water in the mess over there - or if there's any water in the old tires".

Yero squinted. "What about that crowd by the rotten fruit?"

"Boys again", said Atel with hardly a glance. There was quite a swarm of them around a bag that had split open, gorging on the overripe apples and spoiled veggies. "Remember, the girls don't like sweets. They want blood. They'll be out hunting after sundown when warm-blooded folks are easy to spot in the cool air".

"And what do boy mosquitoes do? Are they just bums?"

"Pretty much. Freeloaders and playboys. But I suspect they scout out victims for the girls. Just don't trust any mosquitoes after dark. You'll learn ways to tell the difference. One is, the girls do all the biting and the boys do all the talking. I call 'em the Bloods and the Pips".

It was late in the afternoon already, and even as they talked the sun sank behind the western canyon wall, plunging the dump into shadow. Almost instantly a couple mosquitoes zoomed up to chitchat, then backed off a bit.

"Hey! We're having a little party later", said one.

"We're inviting a few close friends", said the other.

They both grinned. It reminded Yero of the barflies. "We've got fermented apples", they said.

"Thanks anyway", replied Atel. "We're just leaving".

"Leaving? What's the hurry? You'll miss all the fun!"

"There'll be live entertainment! Some of the lads are getting funny already". So were these two. One made a show of holding his nose. The other giggled.

"Don't worry about your body odor", he said. "Everything stinks over there!"

"I'm sure it'll be loads of fun. Ask someone else", said Atel. She left, followed quickly by the butterflies. The 'Pips' followed for a bit, offering extra temptations before giving it up. A little later they might've persisted, but it was already enough to make the Travelers uneasy.

"What'll we do later if our repellent doesn't work?" asked Yero. "Will they be everywhere?"

"There'll be some, but it shouldn't be too bad. This river is faster and cleaner. Not too marshy or swampy. As I said, it's the big water where I expect serious trouble".

"And will we get there tonight?"

"One river at a time, please. Let's not get ahead of ourselves! No, we won't".

"So we'll spend the night here, somewhere?"

"Yes. We'll take precautions, but it's a good opportunity to test Boca's theory".

"That's a polite word for it. What if we get bit anyway?"

"It'll swell up and itch".

"Yes, but what if one bite is *too much?*"

"Let's hope we don't find that out. But I have a plan and a backup plan. We'll have to deal with the mosquitoes somehow".

A couple more Pips came by. One whistled at Yero and approached with a leer on his face.

"Hey, doll! Got the time of day?"

"Not for you. I don't go for Pips".

"Ooo! Feisty, hey? I like it! C'mon. Let's rub noses".

"Okay, if it'll make you happy".

The Pip winked at his buddy and zoomed in. Coming from upwind, he didn't know until he was very close.

"Ee-ewww!" he said then. "You stink! I thought you were a nice girl".

"I am, underneath. C'mon now." Yero pushed her nose at him but he skedaddled with his buddy. "Come back soon!" she called after them. Boca laughed at her.

"Yeah--*Come back and rub noses!* Yero rubbed noses with a Pip!"

"We never touched! That was just to get rid of him."

"I wonder. Better wipe your nose! A pip like that might've had —."

Yero flicked something off her foot that struck his cheek. Atel jumped between them.

"Cool it! Here comes plan #1."

It was the log again, or the largest half of it. Now it floated more like a boat, flat side up. It was unoccupied, but obviously cormorants had used it again during the afternoon as a roost and a bathroom. The new deck-face was all slop except for a clean white egg, apparently abandoned, that perched ridiculously an inch above the mess on an upraised knot. There it sat, pointy end up, big end sitting in the knothole, as if waiting to be painted by some artist. Somehow, the slop-artist cormorants had failed to color it.

"It's our 'biffy boat'", said Atel, quite pleased. "I hoped we might find it in this shape". She alighted on a dry splinter and stepped gingerly down onto the greasy deck. "Don't be prissy now", she called to the butterflies. "This might actually work. Do some body painting". She showed how to take a birdbath, buzzing her wings fast and splattering the runny stuff all over herself.

"Let's do it", grinned Boca. "Don't forget, it's my idea!"

"Don't worry", answered Yero. "I won't forget *this*". But to her credit, she jumped right in and even dabbed some on her wings. Some places on the uneven deck the mess was over her knees--or would've been, but she avoided those. Boca didn't and soon looked far worse, but to a Pip both would surely smell the same.

"What if we don't see any mosquitoes now?" said Yero, having second thoughts. "I would hate to think I did this for nothing!"

"Don't worry. We will, here on the water. Soon, too. The air is getting cooler already. Can you feel it?"

"Yes. Makes me wish I was dry---"

"Sea serpent!" whispered Boca urgently.

A large head had emerged silently from the water and moved up along the log, eyeing the egg on its perch. When it was in position, it squared up to the log, but then shrank back nearly underwater as if giving up on the idea. It hadn't. In a sudden rush, the head lunged up and forward on a thick, rubbery neck to grab the egg. The beak-like mouth didn't quite get it but knocked it off its perch. It rolled back and forth on the slimy deck as the log rocked from the assault.

"Turtle!" said Atel in some alarm. "Snapper! We surely didn't need a snapper. They're nothing but trouble!"

The creature didn't give up and now attempted to climb aboard from the port side, causing all kinds of hurly-burly. It finally got its front half aboard and the egg rolled obediently toward the still-open mouth, but that was only the beginning as the rolling egg proved elusive. It took several minutes of this commotion before the snapper secured its meal, and then the beak chomped too vigorously. Half of the scrambled contents squirted out the sides as the beak clamped shut. The snapper noticed the spillage and went after that too, twisting sideways and scooping it up like raw omelet with cormorant sauce.

It wasn't a big meal for such a large snapper - a female in this case – more likely just a bit of dessert following some other main course. But it put her in a nappy mood. She stretched her forelegs out and hooked the starboard side of the deck with big claws. This apparently balanced out her back half that was still underwater and she relaxed. Her head and neck oozed forward out of the shell and rested on the log. She closed her eyes blissfully, but her omelet leftovers attracted others. Pips, a dozen or more, had smelled fresh egg and now circled around the mess trying to decide if anything was edible.

The snapper opened her mouth, probably in a dream. She always opened her mouth underwater when lying in wait, fishing, on the bottom. Her 'lure', a tongue-like muscle, wiggled provocatively and attracted the Pips' curiosity. The lure was meant for bigger prey deep underwater, but it wiggled nicely in the open air too. The Pips clustered around it curiously, not quite landing, then high-tailed it to wherever Pips go.

Atel knew where that would be. They were off to find their girlfriends and curry favor with news of an easy victim nearby. They would soon return with the girls. It would be an opportunity to test Boca's theory and she explained to the butterflies what she expected.

"Come", she said. "Let's perch right on the turtle's beak and see what happens when the Bloods arrive". She glanced at Boca. "Still confident?"

He was, until they actually landed on the snapper's beak. In war, it's different up on the front line, in the dead of night, knowing the enemy is coming.

"There are useful things to know about hungry mosquitoes..." Atel whispered, and then stopped to listen before continuing..."They make a *humming* noise when they fly - the *Pips* do - but the *Bloods* sound different. They *whine*. Listen for that when they come so you'll always recognize it. That's important. Also, on the chance that our repellent isn't effective, here are some other tips: 1) Hold your breath if you can. They zero in when you exhale. 2) Don't move. Hold still! They don't see all that well, but they spot movement and go for it. 3) Don't sweat. Most butterflies don't anyway. If you do - don't! Any questions?"

There wasn't time for any. An obvious humming noise reached their ears that turned into more of a telltale whine as it drew closer. Dozens of mosquitoes, hundreds, converged on the log. Yero could hear the Pips shouting directions to the wiggling tongue, as if the girls needed any. They didn't. The tongue was so tempting, so defenseless! It was new to them, though. Even the eldest Bloods, crones more than a month old, had never seen such a thing before. They hovered, hesitating for a few moments, probably confused by the turtle's recent meal which still dribbled out the corners of her beak. Then the turtle exhaled noisily, and they lost all restraint. In they went, almost the whole lot of them, most landing successfully and stabbing the tongue simultaneously.

It was a new experience for the turtle too, who seldom napped out of water and left her mouth closed when she did. The lure was meant for fish down below, not this. It was automatic. The softest touch set off the trap and hers had a hair-trigger. Now the powerful jaws snapped shut. She stirred a little, wondering drowsily if she had caught something, then went back to sleep when she didn't feel anything solid. The trap stayed shut on the Bloods. They got their drink, but it was their last. Boca grinned and pumped his fist.

Unfortunately, there were other Bloods around, and still more arriving, who saw his movement. They zipped in near to the Travelers and detected warm exhale mixed with strong undesirable odors. Possibly they would have wandered off and Boca's theory proved correct, but he wanted the last word.

"You wanna bite me, don't you?" he jeered. "But you can't get past the smell!"

No one was ever bitten more swiftly by a mosquito and deserved it. A Blood nailed him from behind on the rump even as he taunted the other in front of him. Boca was fast too, spinning around before she drew much blood, whacking her loose from her bite and smacking another who was trying to slip in from the side. Yero joined the fight and Atel tried to organize a hasty retreat. Things were getting serious fast.

"This way! Into the shell for now! Hurry!"

Dozens of mosquitoes went after them. The butterflies' natural reaction was to flap their wings madly and get away, but they were hemmed in by the crowd of Bloods who darted in from all directions. In the melee, Yero heard their guide shouting repeatedly, "The shell! Into the turtle shell!" Yero grabbed hold of Boca by a hind leg and pulled him in that direction. Any port looks good in a storm, as they say, and the young sailors saw one: A gap above the snapper's neck, under the shell. But it was closing.

The turtle was awakening from all the commotion, opening one eye and raising her head. Without another thought, Yero slid underneath the heavy shell, half-leading, half-dragging Boca. It must have tickled because the turtle raised her head a little higher. The gap shut. The butterflies were locked inside with little room to move. From the darkness came the unmistakable humm of a mosquito, but it was lower pitched. A *whine*. A Blood had got inside with them. She laughed now.

"I smell you", she said.

The butterflies shrank closer together for self-defense. Their wings brushed the low ceiling of the shell and speckles of esporellia fell off. It's a peculiar property of the stardust that it sparkles in free fall, as if remembering the fireworks it came from. For a moment, the two were revealed.

"I see you!" said the mosquito gleefully.

The esporellia went out on the wet turtle floor. The butterflies said nothing, even held their breath, but they couldn't hold it for long.

"I smell *both* of you", said the mosquito, now very confident. "You smell sweet underneath the slop. Dumb of you to perch under the dirty birds".

The taunting irritated Boca. "You're all talk", he said. "Just talk! Or you'd be after us right now".

"We'll see about that! My sister got you, didn't she?" The Blood laughed again. "I recognize your voice. You've been bitten already".

Boca didn't have to be reminded. It hurt. He could already feel it swelling. "She didn't even draw blood!" he said bravely.

"Maybe, maybe not. At least you got your injection. She gave you some virus or other. Pretty soon you'll slow down and it'll be easy to suck your blood. I'll wait".

"I hope your sister did draw blood", retorted Boca. "We're poisonous! She'll die from it. She gets the booby prize!"

"Big deal. We only live until we lay our eggs anyway. That won't stop us".

"Well, something is. Either you're afraid of the smell or you're afraid of us. Which is it?"

The whine of mosquito wings almost turned to a hum, then subsided as the Blood decided to save her energy until she was free. The fact is, she was caught by both rear legs in a pinch when the turtle raised her head. Mosquitoes are clever at sneaking inside where they shouldn't, but this one didn't make it all the way in. No matter. Not yet. Mosquitoes have surprising patience for creatures that live only a few weeks, and they're very cunning in close quarters. She knew exactly how she was pinched and fully expected the turtle to lower her head again, freeing her. Then the smart-mouth butterfly would get it. For now, she kept talking to maintain contact with her victims, to know exactly where they were in the dark.

The bird-poop thing puzzled her and would have fooled her if the blabby one hadn't spoken up. Did butterflies eat manure - or what? Was that the poison they referred to? It didn't frighten her, but it disgusted her, and a certain Pip would hear about it next time he came smiling around. He hadn't mentioned *that!* She was supposed to poke her nose through *that* to get at the blood underneath? The jerk! But she would. As soon as chance allowed. She craved the blood.

"How bad is it?" whispered Yero. She was holding Boca's hand and his grip kept tightening.

"It stings and it itches, and it's swelling. What a dirty fighter - to stab someone like that! They didn't get you, huh?"

"No. I don't think they noticed me until the free-for-all started".

"I was pretty dumb, wasn't I? Now we'll never know if this repellent works or not. Are you mad at me?"

"No. I would be if I had got bitten, but this way it's almost a relief. Now we can wash the stuff off".

"Yeah. Listen, Yero. It really itches and I can't reach it. Will you scratch it for me?"

Yero scowled in the dark. "Where, exactly?"

"Here". Boca grabbed her hand and directed it back behind him. She realized where this was going and pulled away.

"No! Find yourself a stick or something!"

"Ohhh! There's no sticks in here and it's driving me crazy!"

"Too bad. It's not my fault. Work up some self-control, like you should've had when you smarted off".

Boca moaned and groped in the dark for something to use. His hand fell upon something. A hair bristle? No, it was something buried in the turtle's neck. There was a metal ring and even a length of stiff rope tied to the ring. His hand followed the rope and found the frayed end. He reached behind with that to scratch, but the rope was too short. He gave a good pull on it. The rope came up enough to reach where it was sorely needed. Ohhh, it felt good! He was mildly surprised at his own strength. The turtle's entire neck came up when he jerked. Whatever! At least he could *scratch!* He waggled the frayed end across the swelling bite. Ahhh!

As for the mosquito, her hopes were dashed when the turtle's neck came up again. The big snapper had begun to nod off, her head starting to droop. The Blood felt the pinch ease up on her legs as the neck sagged down away from the shell. Saliva - their infectious type that causes a bite to swell - filled her mouth in anticipation. But when her hopes were highest the dratted turtlehead jerked back up, pinching her legs even tighter.

For her part, the snapper was cursed with a fishhook. Some unlucky fisherman had snagged her behind the neck while casting for trout. His line wouldn't budge, and he figured the hook was caught behind a rock down below. He rowed his boat right above it and pulled hard. It came, but not all the way to the surface. Out of curiosity, he followed the line down with his hand, thinking it might be a branch. That's when the snapper bit him. He jerked away, only losing two fingers. Unfortunately for the angry turtle the line sheared off too, leaving the hook still buried on top of her neck. The point and the barbs were very sharp and ever since when she moved her neck it irritated. She was paranoid about it and Boca's little tug grated her nerves.

Under her shell, Boca relaxed and almost smiled. Ohhh, it felt good to scratch! Maybe it was done itching. He let up on the rope. Yero heard him sigh blissfully and hoped the same thing. Enough trouble about *that*!

The mosquito had nearly lost her lower legs when the turtle jerked up, but now the head drooped slowly again, easing the pain. Whew! Enough of *that* already!

Meanwhile the turtle slipped into a recurring nightmare. She opened her eyes and mouth, expecting to see the fisherman's hand. She was of a mind to get the rest of his fingers. When the hand wasn't there and the tension lessened, the dream went away, but she left her snapper trap open. The lure went into action again, pretty in pink, as her head dropped slowly and the pinched mosquito resumed thoughts of escape and revenge.

But - too bad for her - Boca's bite began to itch again. Arghh! It was intolerable. At least now he could do something about it. He tried to scratch with the frayed rope, but again it didn't reach. Oh, yeah. Stupid rope was too short! He jerked hard on the ring and set off another chain of events.

Every time the mosquito's legs were pinched, they numbed more until she just assumed she was still caught even when they pinched off. Outside, things weren't going any better for the Bloods. None could resist the snapper's breath or her wiggler. At each chain of events, more went for the bait and were swallowed. Even a big turtle like this should have felt the bites - at least the sum total of them - but she gave no sign. Several hundred mosquito bites on the tongue affected her no more than a spoonful of good chili. Soon there were no more Bloods and the Pips went back to find new girlfriends at the old garbage dump.

Atel had gone there too, on a critical errand. It is a serious thing for someone the size of a butterfly to suffer such a bite, even without losing much blood. The mosquito saliva goes in before any blood comes out. It's very dirty and toxic, even epidemic. Boca needed treatment and the only thing Atel knew of nearby that might help was back at the spoiling fruit and vegetables. She remembered smelling onions.

The mosquitoes were all but gone when she got there, and a skunk was rooting through the produce. The Bloods had gone after him in droves when he arrived, but he wanted to stay, and skunks usually get what they want. The place stunk before; now it reeked. A few Bloods were toughing it out, trying to get at his nose or tongue. The hummingbird made short work of them as a favor, being sure the skunk saw her do it. Then she addressed him courteously.

"Good evening! Would you be kind enough to dig out an onion for me?"

"No. Make my eyes sore". Unfortunately, it was a typical 'leave me alone' type of skunk.

"That's understandable", said Atel agreeably. "What's your favorite thing? Apples? Carrots?"

"Melons, no seeds".

"Ah! You have refined taste. Have you found any?"

"One. Spoiled. Everything here - spoiled!"

"There's better fruit underneath".

"Where?"

It was a tough question. All the bags were torn open now. Atel tried to judge where the onion smell might have come from earlier but had no idea. "Right about here", she lied.

"You don't sound sure!"

The skunk was right. She had a hard time telling a lie. Now she added to it. "Right *here!* Way at the bottom".

The skunk looked doubtful and sniffed the spot suspiciously. He finally began digging. Produce rolled and tumbled into the water. An onion or two came up and rolled. They hit the water too but Atel went for them when they bobbed up. One was just mush but the other was fresher. Better yet, the skunk had scratched it with his claws. She took a deep breath, stabbed at the cut and came away with a nice sliver of strong onion flesh. Behind her, the skunk grunted with pleasure as he recovered a cantaloupe. That helped. Atel shucked off the guilt that was nagging her. She hadn't told a lie after all!

But guilt returned as she searched downriver for the log. She worried that she had been gone too long. Maybe *way* too long. The butterflies had gotten safely under the turtle shell, but a lot of things might have happened since, mostly bad. Her only optimism sprang from a growing confidence in their style: Silly one minute but practical the next. She pinned her hopes on something practical this time. But where was the log? A thin overcast had dimmed the starlight and her eyes watered from the onion. She missed the log and passed by.

Inside the turtle shell meanwhile, Boca's itch was just steadily getting worse. He had jerked the rope half-a-dozen times already and felt the urge coming on again. The snapper kept her head halfway now, expecting another sharp tug. She was more than half awake and the thought was growing that the pains might go away if she went down and buried herself in the mud. That was her comfort zone when things bothered her.

Boca grabbed for the ring to jerk it and felt Yero's hand on his arm. "Don't!" she whispered. "They say scratching only makes it worse".

"I don't care! It's unbearable anyway".

"Boca! At least *try* not to! Maybe you haven't noticed but every time you do it, the turtle gets upset and jerks her head up. While you're scratching and getting relief, I'm getting worried".

"Ohh! Yero, you don't know what you're asking!"

"Yes I do. I've had itches before".

"Not like this one!"

"Settle down! What I'm trying to tell you is, *let her sleep!* What do you think will happen to us if she decides to go back down where she came from?"

Poor Boca! We must leave him to his dilemma because someone else was even more desperate. The pinched Blood overheard and panicked. She didn't want to drown! She hadn't got her blood meal yet, nor laid her eggs. Now her life might end in failure. It was just too horrible! She cranked up her wings to a whine, determined to pull herself free, and discovered she was already free. Oh, joy! She immediately mounted a frontal assault on the butterflies, who fought back with fisticuffs. It was a blessing for Boca, taking his mind off the itch and his fingers off the rope, but very frustrating for the angry Blood. Skeeters aren't the best fighters in the insect world. Their specialty is doing their dirty work on the sly when the victim is distracted. This one charged in headfirst and got punched in the face. It was a standoff, but both sides were losing.

They were losing because the turtle had decided to dive. She raised her head high and turned to see where she was. Oh, yes. She remembered now. Her tail end still drooped in the water. All she need do was let go of the log and slide off backwards. Simple. But what was this? A little bird fluttered around her beak. Okay. If the bird wanted to be eaten, fine. She put her head down again, opened her trap and wiggled her lure.

The little bird ignored the bait and flew up along the fat neck to where a gap had re-opened under the shell. She poked her head inside.

The Butterflies, Yero and Boca

"Atel!" shouted Yero. "We're fighting a crazy mosquito!"

The hummingbird mumbled unintelligibly and backed away, looking for a safe place to set the onion. A moment later the Blood came flying out past her, beaten and looking for an easier victim. Sure enough, the wiggling lure caught her eye as she went past. She made a U-turn and went straight for it, hitting it drill-first as deep as a mosquito can pierce. Snap! The beak shut. The turtle couldn't taste a single mosquito, was disappointed, and slipped off the log. Slooosh! Water surged under the shell. The butterflies floated out with the backwash onto the sloppy deck where their guide awaited them, there to drip and shiver in the night air. Esporellia sheds water very well, but the water cools it. Only tomorrow's sun would re-warm them.

As the adrenaline wore off, Boca felt weak and chilled. The only warm spot was the bite which was starting to burn. The itch was acting up again too, worse than ever. He ripped up a tiny sliver of wood to scratch it. This also was too short, but he contorted himself enough to do the job. "Ahh". He relaxed. That's when Atel swabbed the wound with onion.

"Ohhhh - thanks! That feels cool", said Boca without looking. Then it got warm again. Then it really started to burn, and at this stage we may as well leave him and join his companions who were sporting better attitudes. Atel was very relieved to see the butterflies hadn't lost their dust in the adventure.

"But *next* time", she suggested," - whatever your next predicament might be - just commence your escape a little sooner!"

"A good idea", agreed Yero. "I'll bring that up at our next meeting. Boca and I always discuss your advice at our next meeting".

"I'm so pleased. Do you follow it in the meantime?"

"Oh, yes. Even though it's temporary, we follow it to the very last letter".

"My advice is temporary?"

"Sure. Then we vote and make it permanent at our meeting - except if something really unusual happens - or maybe if..."

"...If you have a better idea?"

"Something like that. In emergencies, there isn't enough time to check back through the records, so we have to think up stuff on our own. But sooner or later we vote on everything".

"I see. How much of my advice is made permanent, eventually?"

"Well, Boca would be the one to ask. He's supposed to take notes while I do most of the talking. Would you like to attend a meeting sometime?"

"I'd like that. I didn't know what I was missing".

"We haven't invited you because you're always busy guiding and thinking up still more advice".

"I do keep busy. Will you invite me to the next one?"

Yero glanced at Boca. He seemed unlikely to attend. His focus was very localized. "I will", she said firmly. "We need to have a meeting right now, don't you think?"

"Yes. How do we start? Should I ask permission to speak?"

Yero laughed. "The meeting is now in order! I'll be the Chairman because I'm used to it, but we're pretty informal. Please feel free to open the discussion".

"Thank you, Madame Chairman. Do you have an agenda for tonight's meeting?"

"A what? You mean stuff to talk about?"

"Yes. A list, beginning with the most important".

"For sure! Three things. First, what about Boca? Is he going to be okay? It's not just the itching. He's slowing down".

"He has a fever. The bite is infected, like all mosquito bites. The onion will burn out a lot of it, but I expect him to be weak for a few days, even at best. I don't think he'll be able to fly".

"That's the second thing. What if he can't?"

"I don't know yet. It just depends. I have an idea for follow-up treatment, but I need reed herb, or the juice from the plant. It used to grow in great patches in the shallows of the big river downstream".

"Where the really big mosquito swarm is waiting for us?"

"Yes. That water has to be crossed anyway. But Boca must be in shape to defend himself first".

"Couldn't you just carry him across?"

"No. It would slow me down and there would be problems if it came to a fight, which it surely would. For the two of you I think we'll have to come up with a trick to make the crossing. Maybe as stowaways".

"On what? We can't steer the log, and I don't think turtles are for hire".

"Nevertheless, I have something like that in mind. Definitely not turtles, though. What is the third item on the agenda?"

"Food. Where do we eat next? I've worked up an appetite".

"Beyond the big river, I'm sorry to say. Unless we get lucky".

"Fooey! As Madame Chairman I expected better".

"Then I move to adjourn and bring your expectations down to normal".

"Normal is still pretty high, but I'll second the motion. Everyone in favor say 'aye'".

A vote was taken. The meeting was adjourned. Rest was needed for the day ahead, and Boca couldn't get any. Besides the itch and the weakness, he had muscle aches, and he complained about all of this. Atel swabbed the last bit of onion over the bite and worked the juice in deep. That really upset Boca, and no one got any sleep afterwards. Yero had pity, finally and scratched his infernal itch for him - with a long wooden sliver. But at least there were no more mosquitoes that night. They had reached a no-man's land of sorts where the mosquitoes of either river seldom ventured.

They stayed on the log because of Boca's condition. Luck was with them through dawn and a bright sunrise. Atel focused the first clear rays on the wound to cauterize the edges and prevent it from spreading. Unfortunately, the festering center had to be left open to drain. Okay, let's admit the festering smelled, too, and Boca didn't appreciate it when Yero told him so.

It had been an eventful night; but if nights are busy on the river, days are even busier. The morning was still young and fresh when a bomb fell from the sky and hit the log hard. It was a clam and it was a dud. It didn't break open as the gull intended, but surely would've been the end of any small folk it might have struck. It bounced twice and came to rest near the stern, somehow staying on the log. The gull followed it down and landed immediately, rolling the clam over and inspecting it, obviously not pleased. He looked around, hoping no other gulls had noticed the failed attempt. Good! None that he could see.

"That was dumb", said Atel. "Dumb and dangerous".

The gull had noticed the little Travelers but disregarded them. He wasn't mean or hurtful, understand. Just a typical gull, and gulls have no consideration for others – not even their own kind - so don't expect any.

"So? Scram! Or the next one lands on you".

"The next one will be this one again, and it won't open then either".

The gull was amazed at Atel. What a little babbler! She couldn't roll a clam but here she was, giving out advice! And before he could put her in her itty-bitty place she offered some more.

"The log is just wood. It's a soft landing. Drop your stupid clam on a rock if you want to break it open!"

The gull gaped. Wow! Didn't that beat all! Sounded like his dear mummsy, *that* did! She was full of advice, dear old mummsy was. So full and so sure of everything that he had set out to do things different just to show her! His first notion was to leave the nest early. That worked great. She never gave any more advice, which suited him fine. Unfortunately, she never gave him any more food either, so he had to scrounge in the dumpsters. He saw other gulls drop clams on the rocks and set out to prove *them* wrong too! He hadn't found anything else that worked though, and they laughed at him. That rankled. He *so* hated to be proved wrong! Now this sassy little hummer had proved him wrong, the squirt! Well, he wasn't about to admit it.

"This is just target practice," he lied. "Why? What did you think?"

"Oh, target practice. Then I take back what I said. Good shot!"

"Want to see it again?" The gull was absurdly pleased. All his life he had the urge to boast but nothing to boast about, so no one ever paid attention.

"Yes, I'd love to! But you must admit this log is a big target. Could you hit something smaller?"

"Sure, sure. The bounce is tricky, though. Don't wanna lose my clam".

"Why? I thought they were common. Are they hard to find around here?"

"Not for me! Why? What did you think?"

"Uh, nothing. I was just noticing that plastic jug floating over there and wondered...never mind. It's your clam".

"Don't think I can hit it, do you? Well I can, but it wouldn't break open anyway and I would lose it". He didn't mention that he had already made that mistake.

Several more gulls flew down and landed, attracted by the fat clam. They were all larger than the first gull and knew him.

"Yuk-yuk! You're nuttier than ever", snickered one. "Talk to yourself now, do you?"

"I wasn't talking to myself! I was talking to this little bird". The small gull didn't like the new ones. Atel made plans quickly. The newcomers were obviously going to be trouble.

"*Real* gulls don't talk to itty-bitty birds", chuckled the second one.

"Oh, I don't know!" yuckled the third. "We're talking to *him*, aren't we?"

They laughed and tried to steal his clam, but the small gull was expecting thievery and escaped with it. That produced another round of guffaws as the bullies enjoyed their prank. Now they strutted around the log bragging about the property they had taken over: "Hiyah, hiyah! Yuk-yuk-yuk-yuckle!" Which translated as near as Atel could figure it: "We own this place! It belongs to the biggest, strongest, blah, blah, blah!" She turned to Yero.

"Help Boca up onto my back. We're leaving right now".

Luckily, the bully gulls ignored them, which is unusual for gulls. These pigs of the sky will eat almost anything whether it moves or not, but just now they were playing Bigshot. Bigshots don't bother with small treats, only big ones. And these Bigshots were about to be rewarded. The small gull had positioned himself at altitude and was focusing his bombsight on the log. Hmm. Which of his tormenters should he aim for? It was hard to decide, but then the bullies clustered together at the stern watching something in the water. He dropped the clam.

The hummingbird had lifted off moments earlier, Yero riding on her back with Boca to keep him from falling. Atel cocked an eye skyward, knowing what was about to happen. She had to smile. The little gull was pretty good. The clam hit one of the bullies right on the head, then glanced sideways and raked a sharp edge across another's cheek, drawing blood. For good measure, it landed on the toes of the third one and jarred open. The bullies skedaddled in a panic. "Gah! Gah! Gah!" Their calls weren't boasting now.

Atel landed on the plastic jug that had been bobbing along to starboard. It was a gas jug, wedged into a protective metal base that rode below water and kept the jug upright. How it came to be in the river could probably be explained by human parents with small children on camping trips. Now it served as an oil tanker, half full of a fuel/oil mix plus some river water that occasionally sloshed into the open cap. This made for a nice ballast and kept the jug stable. The raised handle served as a bridge for the vessel with handholds on the middle seam. Here the three sat, keeping Boca between them, watching the bully gulls dwindle into the distance.

Over on the log, the small gull landed to reclaim his clam and was thrilled to find it open a crack. With beak and one toe he forced it open enough to pluck out the stubborn occupant and do lunch. Yuckle, yuckle! He spotted the Travelers and strutted proudly.

"Good shot, hey? Did you see?"

"Excellent", shouted Atel. "But it still wouldn't be open if it hit the wood".

"I wasn't aiming for the log".

"I know", laughed Atel. "They had it coming!"

"Jerks. Hiyah! Hiyah! They steal my clams".

"Where do you get them? Downriver?"

"Sure. Rats dig them; we steal them. Yuk, Yuk".

"Muskrats?"

"Rats! A rat is a rat! They're all rats. Anything else you want to know about rats?"

"What do they eat if you steal their clams?"

"Grass. Tall grass. Veggies. Yuck!"

The conversation came to a sudden end as a turtle clambered aboard the log. It tilted, bumped a rock, and turned toward shore where it was slowed by an eddy and then snagged by water clover in the shallows. The gull didn't care for the company or the becalmed boat and took off. The Travelers passed leisurely by in the current, what little current remained.

The river slowed down and got deeper here in its lower reaches. The big river had become a reservoir in modern times and backed up into all its tributaries. Midday found them stalled within sight of the confluence as a light south breeze neutralized the weak current of their tributary.

"Are we there yet?" asked Boca. He was feeling a little better and noticing his surroundings again.

"If you mean the big river, no. We're just sitting here at the moment", replied Atel.

"And now we're riding on garbage."

"No, again. We're better than that. This is trash".

Boca started to laugh, then stopped and groaned.

"Stiff and sore? Or just a poor joke?"

"Stiff and sore. Not as sick though".

"Let's see the wound again".

Boca painstakingly turned his rump to be inspected. Yero looked away and fluttered a few inches to the far end of the handle. The movement drew the attention of a large fish that leaped out of the water, twisted sideways trying to snatch the dodging Yero and smacked broadside into the jug, bowling it over and submerging it entirely. In the moments before it bobbed up again, both butterflies disappeared underwater.

Atel buzzed the area frantically. The only sound was a glug-glug of water entering the mouth of the jug between burps of escaping air and fuel. Then the jug uprighted and the butterflies reappeared bracing themselves inside the hole of the jug handle. Yero had ducked behind the handle and dragged Boca down with her as the fish went over the top. Both came up smelling of the fuel mix and Yero was more concerned about that than the near calamity.

"Don't wash it off!" said Atel quickly when Yero began working at it. "Just don't! It's only another smell, and you'll get used to it. But mosquitoes don't like oil. This might be another bit of luck".

"Like the poo-bath? Why does our good luck always have to stink?" grumbled Yero. "And where did that fish go?"

"I don't know, but we shouldn't have been perched on top where he could see us. Stay where you are. We can't let that happen again or our oil tanker will sink. We took on a lot of water".

"But if it doesn't sink, why not just ride it all the way across? We could laugh at the mosquitoes".

"The wind is against us, and the current would be as unpredictable as the fish. Meanwhile, we're becalmed. I'm going to look for that 'grass' the gull talked about. If it's reed grass the sap has an anti-toxin that would help Boca. *Stay down* while I'm gone. Don't make a silhouette!"

It became tempting. The top offered a better grip and a better breeze. The hole in the handle was just awkward in every way, and the fuel smell hung in there with them. A half-hour passed and Atel didn't return. The south breeze petered out and they floated downstream again with the current and so drifted into the big water, making a left turn at the confluence to meander along the north shore of the reservoir. Here also were barren cliffs but clefts soon appeared in the sheer rock, then narrow gorges widening into ravines. The river cliffs shrank into ordinary hills, opening into shallow bays between them. There was no trouble with mosquitoes though there were lots of them in the air, probably Pips. Fish jumped at all kinds of insects and gulls flapped about, but everyone ignored the butterflies. It was a chance to rest.

The sun was sinking when their guide reappeared with a mouthful of reed herb juice and hurriedly applied it to Boca's wound, then gargled with lake water.

"Bitter!" she spouted, shaking her head and spraying water. "It had better be worth it. How are you doing?"

"Better", answered the patient. He had been laughing at her along with Yero. "Not sick anymore. Just stiff and weak. Don't think I could fly much".

"That's the last thing you should be doing anyway, with evening coming on. I mentioned the 'tolls', I believe".

The butterflies nodded a little nervously.

"Yes. As I said, there are two types of mosquitoes native to this water: One kind on this side, a different kind on the far southern shore. They're very territorial and don't like each other. Both sides charge a toll coming or going, so most travelers get bit at least twice.

A strict border is enforced down the middle of the water during the daytime; but at night it's harder to patrol, and lots of southern mosquitoes slip across to this side looking for blood. Maybe it's better hunting here, I don't know. But the bottom line is: Day *or* night, the patrols are almost impossible to avoid".

"Why don't they bite each other and leave the rest of us alone?" asked Yero.

"They do fight, but not over skeeter blood. They want something better. Something warmer".

"How did they get started on blood, anyway? It seems so...*wrong*! And where did they come from? The same place as the snakes?"

"No. They were an afterthought to creation, the way I heard it. To fill a lingering need. But they weren't vampires in their beginning".

—The Bloods and the Pips—

As the first Age of the World drew to a close, the Lord of Light took a hard look at earth and decided it was finished. There was a place for every living thing, and everything had found its place. It pleased Him, but even the Lord appreciates a compliment occasionally, and like anyone else He sometimes must fish for it.

"Well?" He said. "It looks complete. What do you think?"

His assistants, the Artisans of Evermore, had done a fair amount of the detail work and were well qualified to answer. They offered up polite comments ranging from 'Good' and 'Pretty good' to 'Nice' and 'Okay'.

"That's *it*?" said the Lord. "But what could be better? It's well-populated and everything is nicely balanced".

"Oh, yes. Very nice. Nearly perfect, we think".

The Lord sighed. "Okay, what's missing?"

"There's a lot of foul water. Stinky sloughs and bogs. Almost nothing lives there. We suggest a clean-up crew. Some species to recycle the dirty water".

"That's the last detail then? Nothing else?"

"The planet should run by itself then".

So, the Lord filled the dirty waters with mosquitoes, a tiny garbage-disposal species to live on impurities and help clean it up. He made lots of them since they were helpless in the water and many would themselves be eaten. When He deemed there were enough to survive and prosper, He spoke to them, explaining their purpose.

"You are mosquitoes, recyclers of the fetid waters. Your task is important to the greater world. Be content in that knowledge".

They were a simple underwater species with no speech or sense of community, but they squirmed uncomfortably at this fate and came together as a race. The Lord felt their resistance.

"I sympathize if you don't like your place", He said, "but it's the only place left. Do the best you can".

He turned to leave, and the unhappy squirming commenced again, just enough to give him pause. He gazed upon the dirty waters and had pity.

"I'll grant you an extra life-stage", He decided. "A short one. For a few days at the end of your time, you may take to the clean air. How does that sound? Better?"

Much better. Everyone needs a bit of hope. The mosquitoes settled into their work and everything went peachy until the first generation took flight. Then the plan fell apart.

The boys learned that nectar, tree sap or anything with sugar tasted much better than swamp water. They became a bother for bees who called them 'pipsqueaks', or just 'Pips', because they weren't much at fighting.

The girls were worse trouble. They picked fights with larger insects and learned to bite them on the sly and drink blood, which was very much against the Lord's rules. *Wicked,* they were called. The girls laughed at the criticism, declaring it was no sin to rise from humble beginnings, and took the name *Bloods* to themselves.

But the habit *was* wicked and led to the discovery of a most unholy trick. When they drew blood, they left their own foul saliva. The exchange strengthened them and weakened their victim. After enough bites, they learned they could take possession of the victim, even trade places. They became vampires.

The thrill of taking over larger insects proved disappointing, however. These were all prey species themselves, and so the vampire chain stalled. What they really needed - what they *thirsted* for - was to take over a higher life form with few natural enemies. They found it first in bats, but the step-up in class didn't happen for a long time.

Bats eat just scads of insects, as you probably know, and their favorite is mosquitoes. Bats were the scourge and terror of all winged mosquitoes for several Ages until an inquisitive Blood overcame fear and figured out that bats themselves might be vulnerable in their roosts.

No other Blood would go with her, so she went alone to a great hollow tree one morning when the bats had returned for their long daily nap. She entered and bit the nearest one, drinking as much as she could and trading her infectious juices. She returned every morning for the rest of her life - almost two weeks - to the same victim. She was getting very old for a mosquito but the fresh blood kept her strong, and so her power increased over the animal. One day the changeover happened: Her spirit entered the bat and the bat's weakened spirit fell into the mosquito and died.

She napped the rest of the day and went out in the evening with the other bats for their usual supper - mosquitoes. Mmmm! Good! She spoke to some of them first, thinking they would do what she did, but they were frightened - an inferior race, nothing more. So? She ate the cowards and enjoyed it. Over time, a few good girls did take heed and followed her example, taking over other bats, and so the gang grew; but it grew too slowly for her liking. Then she found a shortcut. When she drank blood from *other bats,* it worked in an unexpected way: They turned into vampires on their own from the exchange of fluids.

After that, the whole bat colony was turned into vampires in just a few weeks and she was queen. But even vampires get old and die if they can't get enough fresh young blood, and there wasn't enough locally. The colony dispersed, to the misfortune of the world. The queen and some of her favorites took to preying on humans in a remote country called Transylvania. She herself took over the first human, a prince of the Royal Family no less, and assumed his name: *Prince Vlad*, in time to come better known as *Dracula.*

***

"Never heard of him", said Yero. "He couldn't have been too important".

Atel laughed. "He's long gone. And he would just die anyway if he heard that!"

"So... would our mosquitoes be his descendants or his ancestors?"

"Good question. Ancestors, I guess, because vampires didn't have children. Didn't need them since they lived practically forever in their own nasty way".

"Ugh! Somebody should *do* something about them. They should be wiped out!"

"Some brave souls did do something. I think all the vampires are gone now, except for stories that live on. Folks learned to fight them using symbols of the Light. Holy water and crosses were good weapons against them".

"They died from that?"

"They couldn't stand up to them. Old tales tell about finishing them off with sharp wooden stakes, and I think that's what happened. Warriors of the church destroyed them".

"Here come some of their ancestors now", warned Boca. "We should have wooden stakes".

"Time to begin plan #2. Climb aboard if you can. Help him if he can't, Yero".

Boca did it by himself, barely, and they abandoned the oil tanker. Atel headed straight for shore and turned east along a rocky beach. A lot of mosquitoes were out already, and the butterflies eyed them with new disgust. Then their guide slowed and dropped closer to the ground. They had come to lush vegetation, fresh and green, waving in the light breeze.

"Don't get excited now", warned the hummingbird. "I need one of these".

She skimmed close to the waving plants and snatched something in her beak, something that wiggled wildly. In the brief moment before she resumed altitude the butterflies saw what made the plants move. It wasn't a breeze at all. That had calmed entirely. It was armyworms - thousands of small green caterpillars eating their way along the shore, consuming everything that grew there. Yero fluttered up instinctively to escape the sight. Boca hung on, fascinated by the worm in Atel's beak. It was caught by the front end, seemingly, and curled its rear up repeatedly, trying to escape. It had red and blue stripes and when it curled into a U-shape Yero couldn't help thinking of candy canes. She choked back something from her stomach, and it made her eyes water. She heard Atel mumbling and flew closer to hear in case it was important, but it was worm garbled. She couldn't make it out. But Boca could.

"She says climb back on. We're going to visit a spider".

They followed the shoreline past several small inlets until they came to a larger one, a shallow bay that had been a farming area before the reservoir. Now it was grown up in reeds, a lush expanse of them with watery channels throughout; but the entrance to the bay was a single channel only a few feet wide next to shore.

Here Atel put down on a small mossy pad several feet above the shoreline and knocked on the ground as best one can with a wiggle-worm in one's knocker.

A hinged door flipped up. A husky brown spider popped out quick as a flash, grabbed the armyworm, and swiftly set about wrapping it with webbing. Atel remained motionless and the butterflies were only too happy to do the same. The spider wasn't much more than their own size but obviously much stronger. It had no trouble at all with the struggling worm. When it had the thing restrained, the spider dragged it into the trapdoor, beginning its feast on the go even as they watched. Unbelievably, their guide followed.

The tunnel went straight down as usual with trapdoor spiders, wide, but not quite wide enough for hummingbird wings. They all half-scrambled, half-tumbled down into the dark. The spider watched as they fell past his anteroom, a little side chamber just under the door. Here he spent most of his time, either eating a visitor or listening for the next one to knock. He stared as they passed by.

Part 3: Byways of the Butterfly

Their descent slowed a couple feet down where the tunnel bent toward the bay, and they rolled to a halt on a nearly level floor where the tunnel came to a dead end.

Atel recovered quickly and put a shoulder to the dead end. It gave way, hinged on top. The bottom swung outward. Here was another mossy pad, the spider's lower porch next to the water. He caught an occasional visitor down here too, but mostly this was his dump where he flipped garbage into the channel. Not everything made it into the water. Yero saw remnants of other dinner wraps out there and lots of dung pellets. Atel let the door swing slowly shut again and found the spider's peephole, which she set about enlarging.

The excitement and adrenaline calmed for a minute and Yero became aware of a bigger stench and unsure footing, even here where the floor was flat. It was tricky to step anywhere without slipping on rolling marbles. Then she realized what the marbles must be and stopped moving around. Boca figured it out too.

"We've landed in his bathroom", he complained to Atel. "How about opening up again and let's have some fresh air".

"Sorry, no. Two reasons: The spider likes it shut, and it keeps the mosquitoes out. But I'm glad to hear the smell bothers you. It means you're getting better. Your senses are returning to normal".

"I'm not so sure", said Yero, smiling in the dark. "He was pretty happy with all that slop back on the log. Who's to say what's normal for Boca?"

"Hush!" said Atel quickly. The spider can hear us. Let him think about the meal he has now, not the next one! I have a deal with him but I'm not sure how long he'll honor it when he's finished the worm. For now we're safe, and we can watch through the peephole for your ride".

"Our *what?*"

"You'll be crossing the big water by muskrat. Soon, I hope".

A vision of the tail and hindquarters of such an animal forced itself into Yero's mind. That was the only part she had ever dealt with and didn't want any more. Now they would risk a whole animal? "You'd better explain", she said.

"Yes. Pay attention, please. There are also two types of *muskrats* here: The usual, smaller type (I'm sure you remember) and a new, larger type that has moved in recently. Both types use the reeds for food, and also to build their mounds, their houses, along the shore. All the best reed beds are in the bays along this side, the north side. The smaller muskrats used to live here, but they've been pushed out by the larger ones and must build somewhere else. That's okay. There are plenty of shallows in this whole upper end of the reservoir, especially over on the south side, yonder. However, reeds don't grow there. The smaller rats have learned to dig plain holes in the bank but they like the old mounds much better, so they come over at night to steal the reeds from under the big rats' noses. They swim right past here, lots of them, going in and out of this bay. As soon as a likely rat comes out with a bunch of reeds, you'll hop on. With luck, you'll go straight across and your troubles will be over".

The butterflies looked doubtfully at each other, then back at their guide.

"How do we know which ones are going all the way across and which are going somewhere else?" asked Boca.

"There's no way to be absolutely sure. You know by now there aren't many sure things. But clues are everywhere. From these we can reckon a course of events. Are you with me?"

"We're stuck here with you", Yero grumbled. "What clues?"

"First we'll look for sun-bleaching on their fur. That's simple enough. Those who come from furthest away must travel in daytime, to complete the long trips. So, the more sun-bleaching on their foreheads, the better".

The butterflies still looked skeptical. Atel continued.

"Size is another good clue. The smaller the 'rat the farther it's probably been pushed away. We'll hold out for a runt". She paused for questions. There still weren't any, so she went on. "The final clue would be the size of the load. If they come from way off, I'm sure they'll want to haul a big, worthwhile load". Atel finished and looked out the peephole. Yero scowled as she added it all up.

"Okay. So, we watch for a sunburnt shrimp stealing more reeds than she can possibly make off with? Is that it?"

The hummingbird nodded seriously. "Yes. Put all your hopes in the most hopeless. It's the smart move here".

There was silence, but only for a moment. Then they laughed, all three of them. It broke the tension. Atel left it at that, but she was serious about every detail and the butterflies knew it. For a while no one spoke. In the silence, Yero became aware of an annoying, liquiddy sound like someone finishing off a milkshake with a straw. Then it dawned on her it was the spider slurping his supper up above. She began to imagine what it was like for the armyworm, and then stopped herself. It wasn't easy to stay stopped.

"I feel bad for that worm", she whispered finally. "The worm is paying the price of the bargain, isn't it? The price for us being safe here?"

"Certainly. Don't count much on safety, though. We'll see about that pretty soon, unless a likely 'rat comes by".

"But we *owe* something, and we can't ever pay the worm back".

"Look, I'll handle the guilt since it was my idea".

"But you did it for *us. We* should feel the guilt! I don't think you'll feel much, if you'll excuse me for saying".

"You've got that right. I won't. It's one thing to have civilized rules within your own kind, or between friendly kinds like us, but that's about it out here. You know it. Anyway, they're not called armyworms for nothing. There are thousands of them, all marching hard for the best food up front. There's hardly even time for school or the young ones will fall behind in the march, so it's just a few minutes of 'armygarten' class, and they only teach two things: *Eat!* And, *Don't be surprised if you're eaten!*"

"Wow! That's tough. Is it really true?"

"I just made that up, but it's pretty close. They're almost as bad as gypsy moth caterpillars, but they eat up fields instead of forests. I wish I had brought two instead of one".

Yero didn't have to ask what she meant. The slurping noises above were sounding more and more like air in the straw. She changed the subject.

"Why will we be any safer on a muskrat? Won't the mosquitoes just go after her and find us?"

"They don't bother the 'rats. Muskrats have oily skin and fur to shed water. The skeeters don't like that kind of oil either".

"You seem to have thought of everything, but I'm still glad you're going with us".

"I'm not".

That got Boca's attention. "You're not?"

"No. I'm flying over on my own". She smiled sweetly. "Much easier. Not as messy".

Now Boca frowned. "Suppose we do get across safely, how will we find each other?"

"The weather is good. I'll look for you in the morning. Stretch your wings, Boca. Could you fly now if you had to?"

Boca stretched slowly. It hurt at first. Then most of the pain went away, but he felt weak. He had gotten out of shape. His energy had gone into mending the wound. But his courage was returning fast.

"I can fly!" he declared. "You'll see when it's time to board the barge".

Brave talk, thought Atel. But exactly what she was hoping for. She took a turn at the peephole. A muskrat was going past, going into the bay. The wrong direction. She became aware of a faint, creepsy noise up the tunnel. The spider had finished his meal and must be coming to thank her! Ha-ha. She smiled grimly at the private joke and moved toward the rear.

"Take over the watch", she directed. "But block the door open first! Let's have some light! Our host is coming to chat".

Trapdoor spiders are strong. *Very* strong. However, butterflies are no weaklings. They pushed the big door open enough to jam a fat spider-marble into the crack. Light from the sunset glared into the tunnel past them, past the hummingbird, and surprised the spider with his eyes wide open. He paused, blinded for a moment.

"I guess you're worried about the door", Atel said to him. "Don't worry. We'll shut it when we leave".

"Ahhh. Nice, nice..." The spider squinted, regaining some of the lost vision, and groped tentatively with a powerful limb, leaving no doubt of his intentions regardless of the polite tone. He wasn't overly hungry now but remembered times when he was -like earlier, when he had made the deal. Well, that was *then*. *This* was now! The deal had expired when he finished the worm. Now a bigger meal beckoned. Here was his chance to live the good life for a few days! He groped farther, touched a feather. That was a mistake.

Light gathered instantly to the bird and leaped off her breast in a flash. The spider's eyes suffered some damage and he withdrew the probing arm - his favorite, strongest arm - to cover his eyes. He backed off.

"Here comes one", whispered Boca, on lookout duty. "Going in, though; but here's another, much smaller. Going in, too..." He kept up a steady chatter. The evening run was beginning but the traffic was all the wrong direction so far.

Back in the shadows, the spider took his arm away experimentally. Ahh! Darkness had returned. Much, much better! He knew every inch of his lair by feel and by memory. He hoped it would stay dark. It gave him the advantage. He crept forward again by fractions, reaching out for the prey. Blinding light flashed again but this time it didn't bother his eyes at all. He had got his wish about darkness but didn't yet realize he was blind. He groped and felt feathers again!

Guessing what was up, Atel adjusted her mirror to focus tightly on the groping arm near the claw, hoping it was sensitive there. It was. The spider hissed dreadfully and backed clumsily away, spitting on the burn. Ghahhh! The good arm! It was seriously injured but his anger rapidly overcame the pain. He took a sharp breath, readying another attack. Outside, the sunset was fading quickly.

"Another 'rat in. Another. One more..." Boca droned on, boring himself and worrying Atel. Then, "Here comes one out! Can't see how big. She's pushing so much stuff".

"We're going", said Atel. "I'll get the door".

Several things happened quickly. The spider rushed forward, groping with his weaker left arm, getting a momentary grip on one of the hummingbird's big wing feathers. Had he been naturally left-handed he might have hurt her badly, but he seldom used that arm. When she pecked him, he lost his grip. She flung herself sideways at the door and barged it wide open. The butterflies - also pushing on it - tumbled out in a heap with their guide on top of them. Behind, the door slammed shut from gravity but not before a spider wasp darted inside. If their spider wanted more fight, he would soon have it.

The Travelers got airborne before they hit the water and Atel breezed off the nearest mosquitoes. Yero landed neatly between the ears of the outgoing 'rat, but Boca didn't quite make it and splashed into the channel.

Yero yelled to starboard, toward the splash. The muskrat swerved nervously to port, bringing her tail and trailing payload of reed stems right over the top of Boca, or would have, but he grabbed hold of the scaly tail. It brought him perfectly upright when it twisted rudder-like, and he tiptoed along it onto the hindquarters of the rodent. Atel dipped one wing in acknowledgement and took off; but as she disappeared into the sky there was an incident down on the water. A big 'rat, one of the new types, caught up to their 'rat and confiscated her cargo. The small 'rat, terrified, dived to escape the confrontation. Yero bailed out in the spray of water and Boca bailed too, as best he could. But luck was still with them. Another outgoing 'rat was squeezing past the mess and both made a safe landing on her. That's where their luck ended. A group of Pips attracted to the activity had spotted the boarding party and came in for a closer look.

"Ahoy mates!" they called. "What's up down there?"

"Or maybe we should ask, 'Why aren't you up *here*'?"

"You do fly, don't you?"

"That's what wings are for."

"Oh my! We hope you aren't trying to skip the toll!"

They all laughed, several hundred of them, so loud that it caused a change of pitch in the general hum. Very insulting.

"Suck pond scum!" responded Boca. "We know you're harmless".

"Oo! Hear that, boys?" said one and came in real close, almost to Boca's nose. "You'll regret that", he gloated. "Everyone pays the toll! It's our job to make sure – *oh, phew!"* He backed hurriedly away, suddenly not sure what he was dealing with. Hard to blame him. Besides other smells, the butterflies now stank of trapdoor spider, or at least spider sewage. The Pip melted back into the crowd and their hum took on a lower tone. Several more dared to approach and Boca wafted the smell at them too.

"Yeah! Come in closer!" he blustered, playing it up. "We're spiders and we collect tolls too! Who's first?"

None dared. The Pips were confused, but Pips aren't dumb. Soon they withdrew, leaving spotters to follow and send reports. Someone would pay a toll before the night was over.

"How about that?" chuckled Boca, down on the 'rat-barge. "Turns out I was right after all. Poop wins! The secret is finding the right stuff".

"Maybe. But those were all Pips, by the sound. And there must be more we can do for protection than just sit here and stink. I don't like this. We're right out in the open".

It was too true. They were perched on the 'rat's neck, well behind the ears. The animal's fur was slicked down, offering no concealment at all. Further back the rear half of the 'rat was underwater. No help there. Off to port floated a loose bundle of long reeds trailing back from the 'rat's mouth where she clenched the bundled ends. The reeds rolled and flopped whenever she moved her head. No safe hiding place there either. Yero thought harder. The lack of cover had to be dealt with. Surely the Pips were rounding up their girlfriends to return and collect the toll. There were hundreds of Pips; there would be just scads of Bloods. The smell might help, but it would never stop a whole swarm.

"Keep watch so we aren't caught by surprise", she told Boca. "I'm going to have some girl talk up front".

"Go for it, Yero. She has her mouth full so you can do most of the talking. But don't scare her. I'm not sure how far I can fly".

That was no problem at all. The muskrat didn't fear insects or even notice them usually. In fact, Yero had a bit of a time getting the 'rat's attention, finally jumping right onto her nose.

"Hi! I hope you don't mind me being here, but I need your advice. Just wiggle your nose if you want me to leave". The only answer was an irritable cross-eyed look. Yero continued.

"My name is Yero, a girl butterfly just happening by, and I was enchanted by the color of your fur. It sparkles! What do you do to it? What's your beauty secret?"

As soon as she asked, she remembered the creature had her mouth full and wished she hadn't, but the muskrat answered out the side of her mouth.

"Live a clean life, sister!"

"Oh". This wasn't what Yero expected, but the muskrat went on.

"Living a clean life means not stepping in *it* somewhere and then stepping on someone else's *nose* - get it?"

"Pardon me!" Yero retreated, embarrassed, to a more considerate perch on the reeds. "Is this acceptable?"

"A little better. I do appreciate that you like my fur".

"Love it! Especially over your forehead. *Very* pretty. Unusual color. Do you tint it?"

"You might say. It's from hard work, actually".

"Well, I haven't seen it before. The lighter tone will be popular around here when others see it".

The 'rat seemed to chuckle. "They might want it, but they'll never have it! They live too close".

"I don't understand..."

"It's sun-tint, sister! I'm from the far side. It's a long trip and *he* doesn't help!"

"Oh, I see...umm...do you ever style it?"

"No. None of us do anything special. We just go with the natural look. The water ruins anything else".

"Too bad. Guys do like a new look once in a while".

"Think so? Mine's never said anything, but I think he likes the tint".

"I'm sure he does. They'll speak up if they don't".

That seemed to please the lady 'rat. She was lost in her own thoughts for a while. Then she asked the question Yero was hoping for.

"Could anything be done, do you think, that water wouldn't ruin?"

"I'm not sure, but we could style it right now while it's damp, and it would at least look pretty when you get home".

"Let's do it! How do we start?"

"It's always best to stand it up straight to begin with..."

"That's easy. Step back!" She shook her head as vigorously as possible without losing her reeds. Yero had just time to get out of the way. Boca, tired again and drifting to sleep on the job was awakened by the shower.

"That's perfect!" said Yero, returning to her conversation. I can style it for you now, if you like".

"You can? Great! Can you make it curl?"

"I'll try. It looks nice around the eyes already, and we can't improve the tint up on top. I wouldn't do anything with that. How about behind the ears and around the back? The longer stuff curls better".

"Oh. Well, dear me! I'm not sure! Just do what you think is best, I suppose".

Yero wasted no time - not on any styling but on sizing up the new defensive possibilities. The 'rat's hair stood up almost like a porcupine's, the bristles stiff enough for a barricade - or would be when they dried. She waded into them. They reached the top of her wings. Perfect! Then she checked for bugs. There were no lice, no mites, nothing. This lady had hygiene. Yero felt a pang of guilt, wishing she really could give her a hairdo. She never meant to and now it was bothering her. Well, she could try! She motioned to Boca and he joined her, a little grumpy from his latest shower.

"I don't think I smell as bad anymore", he said.

"Worse things could happen. Look - help me, will you? I promised her a hairdo. Let's try to do some curls. Grab a hair at the top, swing down and hold it for a little while. We'll do a few curls close together, enough to make it show".

Boca had no talent at all as a hairdresser, but it was good physical therapy and he worked out most of the remaining stiffness. Yero went up front again and told little white lies about the curls until she felt such a scoundrel that she offered to fix a pretty ribbon on top.

"We can't fake *that*," protested Boca when she told him. "She'll see herself in the water!" He had gotten his natural strength back and was getting sick of the girl stuff.

"We'll use a long leaf off the reeds! I see a loose one".

It wasn't actually loose, only loos-*er*. It took both of them to tear it off, and one on each end to carry it across the water to the muskrat's topknot. The leaf wasn't supple like a ribbon should be, but they managed a couple of loops, wedging the loose ends between stiff hairs. One loop dangled almost to her nose. She loved it when she saw her reflection.

"We're going behind again", said Yero, feeling a lot more honest. "Just call if you need anything".

"We're the ones that'll be needing something", advised Boca when they were hidden in the nape as deep as they could get. "The Pips have been coming and going in shifts. They know we're still here. You know what *that* means".

"We'll just have to count on our repellents. We've got a new one that might help. Can you smell her body oil?"

"Yeah, but I wish I hadn't dared them now".

"It wouldn't matter. They're just jerks. Do you hear something?"

Boca didn't answer. Didn't have to. A swarm of Bloods arrived all excited. The butterflies, now they understood mosquitoes, looked at their abdomens with dread to see if any were bloated with blood. None were. The Bloods were all after *theirs*, and the hiding place didn't fool them at all.

"Come out, come out, wherever you are!" they mocked.

"You haven't paid the toll, so they tell us!"

"You wouldn't skip the toll, would you?"

"It's just friendly give-and-take".

"You give. We take!"

They didn't laugh at their little jokes. The female of the species has no sense of humor. No time for it.

"You just want us because we're a higher life-form!" shouted Yero.

That gave them pause for a short moment because they didn't know what she was talking about. For all their meanness, these were just run-of-the-mill mosquitoes with no such ambitions. They lacked that one in a zillion mosquito brain, but their brains were excellent otherwise. They smelled blood and knew they needed it for their eggs. If that wasn't enough, the Pips closed in too, now, to incite the girls and watch the fun.

"Don't worry about the smell", shouted one Pip when a couple girls did wrinkle their noses. "They're just dirty. Take 'em! They're helpless!"

"Think again!" replied Boca. "We're muskrats. Smell the oil?""

That only brought them closer to check it out.

"Nice try, dearie", said one.

"I smell spider too, but you aren't spiders", said another.

"Bird smell too, but you aren't birds".

The various repellents made them cautious, but the preliminaries were nearly over. They were pumping themselves up for a sudden assault.

"Let's make crosses", whispered Boca. "Remember the story?"

"With what?" Yero couldn't take her eyes off the nearest Blood.

"This!" Boca grabbed a muskrat hair. The tip was dry and weathered enough to snap off. It was like a short pole for a butterfly. He broke another and held them up like a cross. Yero got the idea and did it too. It didn't work. The nearest Blood attacked, followed by all of them.

"Wooden stakes!" hollered Boca. "Use 'em for that!"

Yero already was. The Bloods did understand stakes; a lot of their victims fight if they know what's happening. But Bloods are grim to the death even if it's their own.

No, the stakes didn't stop them, but the dratted butterflies were difficult to get at in the tall hair. The bristles were like pikes, stabbing at their faces.

Boca jabbed his stake right into the first Blood's eye. Not a stake in the heart maybe, but it took the fight out of her. Several others quickly took her place, but they were crowded, bumping wings as they tried to bore in. They stabbed, and the stiletto mouthparts were deflected by hairs, but as the fight heated up the smell of butterfly rose into the air. Both had scratches. Blood! A female mosquito can smell blood and the breath of the owner from a ridiculous distance. Up close like this it drove them into a frenzy, but their frenzy worked against them in close quarters. Many poked their eyes out on the bristles, while the butterflies also took a toll.

But clouds of them were arriving. The Pips had spread the alert far and wide. Defense quickly became impossible. Every Blood in the upper reaches of the reservoir descended upon them, sucking up the available oxygen. The butterflies sagged under the pressure, still fighting but with less room, less and less air. With a last gasp, Yero shoved her stake clear up the needle nose of a hungry Blood. It stuck there. The Blood pulled out of the fight and another needle nose jabbed at them. Boca broke that nose half off with his stake. Then suffocation took hold and all they could do was wave tall hairs in the faces of their enemies - until shapes even darker than the mosquito cloud swooped into the battle. Bats had come.

***

It's a fair bet out in the wild, when a nasty, ravening crowd gathers, that their own predators will find them. The zodiac is still up there after all, with the fair-minded woman and her scales of justice. Maybe that's her job. She can't see all the wrongs from her constellation, but when she does see one the Nasties usually get what they deserve.

Anyway, that's what happened to the Bloods that night. Some great cave disgorged its swarm of bats. Probably the reservoir was their favorite hunting ground anyway and this sort of thing was the reason why. The bats gorged themselves, flying through the mosquito cloud with their mouths open. The Bloods tried to disperse but they aren't fast enough to escape bats. The larger battle lifted up and away. Oxygen returned on the water. The butterflies found breath and recovered. The muskrat swam on oblivious to it all, hoping *he* would notice her new look.

***

"So - which vampires do you like better?" inquired Boca after a few minutes. "Bats, who would swallow us whole, or the mosquitoes who only want a little drink?"

"Bats. I know they didn't mean to save us, but they did. And our friend might be with them".

"*Your* friend. But I hope he didn't eat the one you shoved your stake up. I saw that. She would be hard to swallow".

"It should be safe enough. I shoved it *way* up".

Boca laughed. "We better break off more stakes. We aren't across the water yet".

"For sure. But maybe things will be better when we *do* get there, Boca. Atel talked like it's a dividing line somehow. Maybe things will be different on the other side".

"Bound to be. I'm hoping for more food! And I hope she can *find* us. I expect you've noticed it's clouded over".

"I have. And have you noticed the mess around here? She won't impress *him* looking like this. We need to do some housecleaning".

There were bits and pieces of mosquito wings dangling everywhere like clothes hung up to dry. At their feet were scattered body parts and several dead mosquitoes. They threw everything overboard before it started to smell, out of respect for the lady who hosted the battle.

Fog or a light mist began to come down, very light but distracting. Every little pit or pat reminded them of mosquitoes and kept them on edge. That was good because a few Bloods did return, one or two at a time, and they found trouble instead of easy pickings. They didn't swarm up again, maybe because of the weather or maybe there weren't that many left, but there was no rest for weary butterflies.

The South shore appeared faintly through the mist. Muskrat mounds loomed here and there, mostly old ones but also some just under construction. Their 'rat made for one of these and Yero got another idea.

"Is that yours?" she asked, venturing up front again.

"Yes. It's not much yet, but it's home".

"Is *he* there now?"

"He'd better be! He's been working on our underwater entrance. Don't tell anyone about that, by the way. It's a secret".

"I promise. Here, let me adjust your ribbon a bit".

The lady 'rat paused. Yero pretended to fuss over the ribbon while she studied the mound. There didn't appear to be any entrance above water.

"There! It's nice now. But if you dive it'll mess up".

"Oh! I hadn't thought of that". She shifted gears mentally. "I'll go in the back side instead. That's not finished either, and I'll surprise him when he comes up!"

"Good idea. That way we can fix up your ears too. We'll give you earrings".

"*Earrings*? Well...I don't know! Are they pretty? Can I see them first?"

"Close your eyes".

She got Boca – very much against his wishes - to dangle below one ear while she dangled under the other. "Okay, you can look. What do you think?"

The 'rat admired her reflection. Yero turned a little, very slowly. Boca contributed mostly by turning his sourpuss expression to the rear.

"Let's do it!" decided the 'rat. She parked her cargo along the back wall and slipped in through the unfinished gap. The interior was mostly dry floor built above the water level with a puddle down in one corner. That was the secret entrance, and from the jiggle and ripple of the water it was evident that *he* was working down there. He seemed to know (married couples just know) that she had returned and came up to greet her.

"Surprise!" she sang out, turning her head proudly one way, then the other.

Like a lot of husbands, he didn't know what to say. If he'd had any hint she was going to do a makeover he would've had some answer ready, but he hadn't. Did she expect compliments - or sympathy? The grass looked like it must've been put there on purpose. As for the butterflies??? "Oooooooohh!" he said, hoping it could be taken either way.

"He likes it!" she whispered to Yero and giggled ridiculously.

He figured he must've scored and grinned with relief. "That's nice, honey. What's for supper?"

She slumped in disappointment. "*What's for supper!?* I make myself pretty just for you and all I get is, '*What's for supper*'!?? Rustle up your own grub, buster! And what are you going to do about that hole in the wall? Anyone could walk in. *Anyone!*"

He slunk out the back way and went to work chewing some of the new reeds into shorter lengths. She cast an angry look after him but didn't remove her ribbon. She would give him another chance later to make up to her. She paced the floor flicking bits of dirt, some of them imaginary, into the water. The butterflies excused themselves and went outside. "We'll come back later", said Yero. "When he's had time to think about it".

"Sure! Fine! He won't notice one way or the other!" she barked.

They slipped out. Boca went to the top of the mound to keep watch. Yero went to have a word with 'him'. He was sticking reeds into some mud that he had plopped at the base of the gap.

"You messed up in there", she advised him. "But I can help you fix things up".

He kept working but peeked inside to see where she was. "What happened in there?" he whispered.

Yero filled him in on some things any husband should know about ladies dressing up, and some proper things to say, and the proper time to say them. That gave him something to chew on besides the reeds, and she went up to see Boca.

"I'm with *him*", said Boca after she told him about it. "Who even knows what girls want?"

"How can you say that? I just told you!"

"Yeah, but when they pop a surprise like that---"

"It's simple, Boca! They're hoping you'll like it - *whatever* it is! When in doubt, smile and nod your head".

Boca smiled and bobbed his head like a jack-in-the-box.

"That's good", commented Yero. "You should do that more often".

He kept it up like the village idiot.

"You might make some girl happy yet, Boca. I didn't think you had it in you".

"I'm practicing. It takes muscles I didn't know I had".

"Well, I'm proud. But I actually came to ask your advice".

"That don't surprise me. When girls are stumped, they come to us".

"Oh - quit it, please! I'm trying to make peace between them so we can spend the night inside".

"I'm with *you*, now", said Boca, suddenly serious. "There's lots of Bloods around, higher up. Hear 'em? I think they're confused in the drizzle, but they'll find us if it quits".

Yero nodded. "Look, I'll teach him a little more charm. When he's ready, I'll call you. Just be prepared to be a pretty earring again, okay?"

Boca turned away and resumed watch. It was unlikely their guide would find them during the night but that's mostly what he was watching for, regardless of mosquitoes. Now the weather was turning to fog, collecting on his antennae and running down into his eyes. He imagined Atel, perching somewhere on shore with drizzle dripping into her eyes too. Oh well, at least they had made the crossing and tomorrow was another day. He made a mental note to wake up early, or at least wake up Yero. One of them ought to be here in plain sight when morning came. Cripes! Another cold drop ran down into his eye, blurring his vision. The stupid dew seemed attracted to the little knobs on the end of the antennae where they were most sensitive. The cold water felt even colder and dulled his other senses. Someone tapped his shoulder.

"Remember me?"

It was a Blood from the fight, the one with her nose partly broken off. Half of it was gone but her stiletto stuck out like a stabbing tongue. She sneered in her moment of triumph now, instead of stabbing. With no weapon at hand Boca just took a wild swing. He missed owing to blurred vision but splattered her face with dew.

"Here I come!" he hollered and made a dash for Yero. Together they backed into the small opening still remaining. 'He' kept right on working, plopping the last scoop of mud almost in their faces as they retreated into the cozy room, but not before they saw other Bloods circling with Broken Nose. Tomorrow there would be a grudge fight.

The husband finished his work (Good enough for now, he figured. She'll want it changed anyway!), and summoned the courage to go in. At least he had some good tips on what to say - *if* she had gotten over her temper.

He entered through the secret underwater entrance, the only entrance now, and the dratted, unfinished thing collapsed behind him. That surely was a bad omen. But when he surfaced, breaking water in the little pool, there she was, waiting and smiling. The silly grass was still looped on her forehead and the butterflies perched on her ears as ridiculous as before. He took a deep breath and whistled.

"Ah, my sweet Mucky-Muck! A ribbon in your hair? It's beautiful!" She purred. So far, so good! He knew he was on a roll. "Earrings too? You pretty little Clam Digger - you don't need makeup! You're already the loveliest girl on the lake! But I'm glad you did it".

Yero was thrilled. He remembered everything! His lady was even more thrilled. The bum finally appreciated her! She didn't say much but fished out some very choice tender bits of reed stem from her stash, and a fresh clam she had stowed away in case he ever deserved it. The rest of the evening passed blissfully. He cleaned up spilled mud from his work and used it to smooth the interior walls while she puttered about planning a nursery. Yero's work was well done and the butterflies stayed the night, but each awoke several times in the darkness, wondering how they would ever get out of there.

Part 4
The Lure of the Dragon Range

Synopsis

Wherein the monarchs lose their guide and fall into the company of the fairies Peco, Pio and Obobo – uncouth, unkempt fellows who strongly disapprove of girls that speak their minds but willingly lead the butterflies deep into Mexico, knowing that their own enemies – ghost warriors of the 14th and 15th centuries – gladly await them.

Yes, tomorrow is nothing if not perilous. But in the meantime, there is a new social order to get used to. Yero, as the only girl, finds herself an outcast within the company while Boca is heartily welcomed by the macho band. This is unfair but the fellows don't listen to complaints. She will have to earn their respect. No worries there; Yero will shatter the barriers. But *Manino*, winter home of the monarchs, will present greater problems if the butterflies ever get that far. Bad weather has gripped the mountains and jealousy has divided the Roost.

"Just don't expect paradise", they are warned. "It's cold up there right now. That's one thing, but not the only thing".

Chapter 17

South of The Border

Morning was announced by a scratching at the door that brought the muskrats awake in alarm and set them scurrying in circles trying to figure it out. There was no door of course, but someone was trying to make one right through the living room wall. Muck-plaster flaked off. Chunks crumbled and fell in onto the floor. The 'rats backed nervously away until they were perched on the last edge of dry floor, tails down in the pool behind. A big chunk fell in and a pointy nose poked through the small hole, sniffing the air inside. Hardly pausing, the nose pushed in further and sniffed again. A mouth shoved its way in and revealed - not muskrat teeth - but a more carnivorous set. Whoever owned them surely intended to eat the 'rats, but all they did was crouch, trembling. Yero flew over to 'him' and shouted in his face.

"Get her out of here!"

It didn't register at all. The 'rats just stared, frozen. More plaster crumbled away. A whole leering face appeared. The eyes tried to focus, adjusting to the dim light.

"The secret door!" Yero yelled. That seemed to register. He issued some sort of warning whistle - maybe too late now - and slid into the pool. She followed. Moments later the mink busted through entirely, bounded across the floor and followed after. The butterflies didn't see them again, but if the happy couple managed to escape it was due to the lazy husband and his blocked underwater entrance. Doubtless they broke *out*; but if it had been finished the mink would've come *in* that way, cornering the 'rats. That's what usually happens. So, 'Survival of the Fittest' doesn't always mean the swiftest or smartest. Sometimes it's just the luckiest.

Yero turned to Boca. "I saved them!" she said proudly. "What have you done today?"

"I've found a way out. But I don't want all the credit. That mink can have some. Do you think it'll come back?"

"For us? It sure might, if it misses *them*. Let's leave".

"Yeah. I don't want to be trapped in here by a gang of grudgy mosquitoes either. But let's not rush out without weapons. Old Broken Nose is probably waiting. Here's some good stakes".

There was a fine selection on the floor. They chose long, stiff guard hairs, the kind they had used in the big fight. Yero left hers long like a spear, Boca broke his in half for clubs, and they went out.

The weather was still miserable, foggy, and dreary. Even thicker than the night before. The mosquitoes were gone, but the butterflies couldn't see three feet past their noses, to say nothing of picking out the shoreline several hundred feet away.

"At least we know which direction it is", recalled Yero. "I remember the breeze was behind us all the way across the lake, and it still is. The shore is right over there". She pointed confidently into the murk.

"Unless the wind changed, Yero. Then we could get lost".

"That's a good point. Let's see. We went in the back side - the side toward shore - and that's where she parked the reeds, remember? Let's find those".

Even that was a bit of trouble in the fog, and they learned nothing fluttering about the mound. 'He' had used up the reeds, and the mound was wet and dripping all the way around. There was no telling which was back or front, older or newer. Everything looked the same except for the hole torn open by the mink. That was their only clue and they weren't quite sure what direction it faced.

"The fog is getting worse, not better", said Yero in frustration. "Let's just go with the wind! We'll start at the top of the mound again and put the breeze at our backs".

"I don't think so, Yero. The breeze has been shifting around even while we've been out here. Haven't you noticed?"

She hadn't and didn't much care to hear about it. "Let's at least try this, Boca! I'll *look* downwind and see how it *feels*. A girl can tell a lot from that".

"That kind of sense isn't weather sense".

She did it anyway and argued until a shift of the light breeze brushed her face and surprised her. That finally settled the matter.

"We might as well wait it out", she admitted. "You're right. There's no telling which way to go".

"There sure is!" said a nasal voice just behind her. "You never quit yakking, so we just follow your breath!" Broken Nose burst out of the mist with her mob.

"You should talk, *Stubby!*" Yero shot back and threw her spear in the general direction. Boca grabbed her and they took off into the fog with their mouths shut. That helped against the Bloods, and also against further argument, but it was entirely the wrong direction. They curved gradually in circles and lazy-8's until both were quite sure they were lost, and it was time to risk some discussion.

"We should've seen the shore by now", ventured Yero. "We must be going the wrong way".

"I guess so, but there wasn't much choice".

"At least it's simpler now. There's nothing to land on so we'll just keep going. Got any better ideas?"

"No, except I'm really hungry. Too bad muskrats don't keep some treats around the house for guests, like honeybees do".

"Maybe they do, but not for butterflies. She probably has a pantry full of all the choicest tidbits a muskrat could want".

"Yeah, muskrat food. I guess they don't entertain butterflies too often".

"No. Probably just neighbors. Or maybe the in-laws come over a lot. His family, I'm thinking about". Yero laughed. "'He' probably has brothers that don't know any more about ladies than he does".

"So? I could still picture them all shucking clams and throwing the shells into the water, having a good time".

"Oh, I doubt that. She probably serves up the old reed stems that are turning brown. That's good enough for brothers-in-law".

"Oh yeah? Well, if it's free they'll probably eat it. But if it's brown they'll spit the stale husks all over the floor".

Yero frowned. "They'd better clean that up afterward".

"Why? That's what the hostess is for. The sisters-in-law could help. All they do is talk about ribbons and earrings anyway".

"You're wrong, Boca. These girls would be back in the pantry having fresh green shoots after they served the garbage to the bums".

"That would be a low-down trick. Boys deserve better".

"Some do. But yours were spitting all over the floor!"

"Boys have to spit somewhere, Yero. Anyway, I think 'he' would know about the good stuff in the pantry".

"Not if she fixes all the meals. Anyway, 'he's probably okay with feeding the stale stuff to the family freeloaders".

Boca laughed at that. "Maybe it goes around and round. Maybe everyone saves up stuff that should be thrown out, just to feed the un-favorite guests".

"Yes. And the best part for *her* is, they might not come back as often".

Boca thought about that. It seemed all too real. "I bet that does happen", he said finally. "But it's not the way it should be. Would you do that if it was your in-laws?"

"I would never marry into a family of bums".

"That's easy to say. What if you never met them first?"

"I'd probably serve them what they liked, if they were at all polite about it. I'll share with anyone who has manners. It's just that some boys are so gross!"

383

The Butterflies, Yero and Boca

They fell silent and flew on, hoping luck would find them. The morning didn't get much brighter, the fog showed little sign of lifting, but some variable breezes found their way through it. Boca realized again that he was hungry, and an unexpected whiff of fresher air gave him a sudden craving. A treat was somewhere near, and he worried that someone else would get it first.

"Yero", he said anxiously, "If you find a fat, juicy nightcrawler, will you share it with me?"

She looked at him as if he'd turned into one himself. "You can have the whole slimy thing! Where did *that* come from?"

The breeze, and the craving, passed. Boca shook his head to clear it. "I don't know", he said, embarrassed. "Just forget it".

Yero laughed. "I won't forget that! Any special size or flavor? What's your favorite?"

"Oh, knock it off, will you? I don't know what came over me".

"When did you start eating them? If I only knew! I've seen some pretty interesting ones".

"I said knock it off!"

"You asked for it! Don't get mad at me".

Boca had put a little distance between them and it worried Yero. It wouldn't do to become separated. She opened her mouth to call to him just as a little breeze came to her, the subtlest of breezes, with a whiff of her most favorite food.

"Boca!" she hollered. "Come quick! There's a delicious white grub around here somewhere!"

That did it. Boca figured she was rubbing it in and moved away. Yero didn't even notice. She was following her nose eagerly, expecting to find the delicacy at any moment. Instead, she found a shift in the air currents and came to her senses, remembering everything. Her stomach revolted. When she recovered from that she called to Boca, but he was out of earshot. She was alone.

Things can always get worse, as we have seen, but more often when things look most hopeless, they've hit rock bottom and will improve if you don't give up. The air was freshening, after all, (even clearing out nicely from the nearby shore, if the butterflies only knew) and though they were separated in the fog the breeze suddenly offered up a tempting new aroma for both of them to savor.

Did their favorite foods used to be nightcrawlers and white grubs? Not anymore! Both butterflies drooled at a new promised treat - scurrying mice! - and followed the scent unexpectedly out of the fog. In fact, they had meandered near the clearing edge all morning. Now they popped out into the open some distance apart in full view of the nearby shore, saw each other, and raced jealously toward the same prize. They met just above the water about as far as a fishhook, line, and bobber can be cast from shore, and settled onto the bobber eyeing each other belligerently, ready to fight over the mice.

They would have to fight more than just each other. The bobber was homemade, just a forked stick tied on a line above a bare hook. The little stick wobbled from the butterflies bouncing on it, making ripples on the calm water like a bullseye target, and that's what the big fishes zeroed in on.

There were only two fish in the bay and they were very big, having eaten all the smaller fish. There was little else to eat and they were always hungry, but stubbornness kept them there. Both claimed the bay for their own, neither would surrender it to the other, so it had come to this. However, of late there were promising signs. Snacks were beckoning! Often, they smelled their favorite foods somewhere very close. But all they had found so far was the bare hook.

Of course, really big fish know about hooks. They don't grow so big without being hooked a few times and learning to spit the hook out. Many fishermen had tried their skill in the bay, for the lunkers were known to lurk here, and poor luck to all of them. The big fish could spot a hook no matter how cleverly camouflaged. But *this* hook was different. When it plopped into the water, they felt themselves lured close by illusions. Very realistic. One after another, as many likely baits as the fisherman could think up appeared on the hook, sorely tempting the big fish.

Sorely - but not quite! This duel had been going on for several days and the fish were winning - or at least not losing. When the water was calm, the fisherman could see them: Nose to nose on opposite sides of the hook; interested, but not enough to bite. Then the fisherman, a boy with a sombrero, would toss another pinch of dust into the breeze. Some drifted into the fog today, but most settled on the water and collected near the bobber, and especially around the hook. There it lingered, calling the fishes to come taste whatever choice bait the boy might imagine next. It was fairy magic, but so far it hadn't worked. Not even his latest idea, squiggling mice, could trip their triggers. The boy watched them edge closer, then back away and begin to swim off. He was about to give up and fish somewhere else when he saw the butterflies arrive. What happened next would later be described as 'beginner's luck' by Boca, who modestly claimed only half the credit for himself.

The butterflies themselves proved to be the bait that the big bass couldn't resist, perched so conveniently on the bobber. Both fish exploded upward to get them, one from each side. Just as they broke water the boy jerked on the hand line, tilting the stick with its perching butterflies to the side. Barely in time! The lunkers, mouths agape, crashed head-on where the butterflies had been a moment earlier. Smack! They knocked each other unconscious. However, having swallowed air instead of butterflies they floated there on the surface, hook and line actually lying on top of one of them. The boy squinted and saw possibilities.

"Put the hook in his mouth!" he hollered.

A splash of water had brought the butterflies back to their senses. "Who's he talking to? Us?" muttered Yero. But Boca had already sprung into action. This was his chance! He knew what to do. He planted himself atop the big fish and tugged at the hook, almost losing it in his enthusiasm. He slid the sharp point behind the lip and waved to the fisherman who was leaning way out, trying to see.

"Now! Pull!" shouted Boca, waving excitedly.

The boy couldn't hear at such a distance but there was no mistaking the signals. He snugged up the line expertly and jerked hard, setting the hook. The fish awoke and flopped in panic. Boca avoided the thrashing tail and crowed in triumph, "Hey! Look! I *caught* him!"

That was premature. The fish was as big as the boy and it became a tug of war, one on each end. The butterflies went ashore to offer help and perched on the boy's shoulders. Boca, especially, was full of help.

"Keep the line tight. Don't let him spit it!"

The boy didn't answer. It was all he could do to keep from being pulled into the bay. He dug his bare heels in, but it wasn't enough. The simple hand line allowed the fish good leverage. As a last resort, the boy heaved back mightily and caught the line behind a stump. That helped, but just then Broken Nose and her mob showed up.

For a split-second the Bloods were undecided. Revenge was on their minds; but when they saw the veins standing out on the struggling fisherman's neck, they couldn't resist. Most of them landed there right away. Yero shouted into the boy's ear, "Mosquitoes! On your neck!"

Without thinking, he swatted with one hand and got them all except Broken Nose herself, but the line slipped in his other hand and the fish got what it desperately needed - some slack. The boy grabbed hold again with his swatting hand but not before the bass leaped high out of the water to spit out the hook. That's when Boca landed boldly on the fluttering line and took up a smidgen of slack. Remarkably, it helped. The fish stayed hooked and croaked a word that fish say when they are very, very upset. After that, the battle on the water wasn't much in doubt, but the battle over the boy's neck still raged.

Broken Nose was wild to make someone pay and darted back and forth looking for an opening. Butterfly or boy? She couldn't decide, and it gave Yero time to grab an end of curly hair to defend herself with. The mosquito decided on Yero but when she darted in, she rammed headfirst into the stiff hair, impaling herself. She struggled, and in the heat of battle Yero pulled the hair out by the roots to be rid of the dratted creature. The boy yelped, but this time he kept both hands on the line, giving Yero only a quick irritated look. In a few minutes, the fish tired out and the boy turned and climbed the bank with the line over his shoulder, hauling the catch up onto shore. He sat down huffing and puffing, still keeping the line tight, but it was over. He looked gratefully at Boca.

"Way to go, *you*! I don't suppose you eat fish?"

"No thank you. I am Boca of the---"

"*Rasha La.* Si, El Boca. I've been waiting for you! And the other is...?" He jerked a thumb.

"Yero. She fought the mosquitoes while we fought the fish; but then, we can't all be great fishermen".

The boy seemed still a little annoyed. "Right. Girls get caught up in the small stuff. I suppose they *mean* well".

Yero opened her mouth and shut it again. What could she say? It was so unfair!

"I'm Peco", he continued, "and I've been waiting for both of you. A little favor for Her Ladyship, your guide. But why wait and do nothing? I've been after these fish for days".

Here, close-up, the butterflies saw he wasn't young. The eyes hinted of more years, and especially the whiskers; but he was every bit as spry as a boy.

"The other fish is just as big", said Boca, hoping for more action.

"Si, but for another day", replied Peco. He winked. "The *percas*, they almost got you, didn't they? That surprised me. Now I know the right bait to use!"

Yero gasped. "You would use *us*?"

"No, silly girl! I will 'cast the earth'. Throw *dust*. The fish will *think* it's you. An old fisherman's trick".

"Dust?" said Boca, impressed. "You can do that with dust? Will you teach me?"

Peco laughed. He pulled a sharp knife out of a sheath at his belt and began to clean the bass. "You are way too young", he replied. "It takes many years".

"Out there..." Boca waved toward the receding fog..."I wanted to eat nightcrawlers. She wanted to eat grubs. Was that your dust at work too?"

"Si. Today I am casting for bass *and* butterflies, but a poor morning to cast the earth. Too damp. I'm surprised it found you".

"You should be on the other end sometime", replied Yero. "You could learn what it's like to *eat* grubs. Yuck! I could actually taste them".

"Silly girl, I *do* know. Some days there are no fish, no nicer things, but we must eat, si? Grubs are good, fried in snake oil. That's what you tasted".

Yero remembered and felt queasy again. She tried not to think about it, but nightcrawlers waved, and mice danced on a dinner plate in her mind.

"You can call it a 'boy' thing if you want", Peco went on. "We're all boys, me and the fellows. I know girls have weak stomachs".

Yero didn't feel like talking any more, but Boca was very interested. Nightcrawlers, Peco confided, were good chocolate-covered, or with bacon. But he didn't eat mice. None of the 'fellows' did. "I just imagine them running and wiggling, eh? That's good enough to catch most fish. I don't know the taste".

He didn't fillet the bass but was deft with the knife, quickly cleaning out the innards and rinsing the fish - not with lake water but from a small freshet trickling down the hill. He left the head and tail on, making no secret that he wanted to show off the whole thing to the 'fellows'. Flies and a few local mosquitoes were attracted to the fish or maybe the fisherman, only to be disappointed. Peco simply pointed a gnarly finger at the peskiest ones and they fell to the ground and stayed there, though still alive.

But if the plan was to take the huge fish to wherever the 'fellows' were--*how*? Yero saw no wagon, nor any pack animal. Then in about two seconds, the mystery was solved. Peco hooked his fingers behind the gills, hoisted the bass up onto one shoulder and started up the steep bank with hardly a grunt, barely disturbing brush and bramble. He reached the crest of the hill well ahead of the butterflies and looked back impatiently. "You coming?"

When they caught up they beheld a wide expanse of flat, scrubby bench-land, miles of it, stretching off in the distance toward grayish hills far to the south. "We go there", he said pointing to the gray hills. "Try to keep up".

Before they could smile at his little joke, the butterflies fell behind again. It was startling how fast the little guy moved, burdened with the fish and camping gear, and even burlap bags, stuffed and tied shut, hanging from his belt. He talked as he hurried along, never looking back except to cast a pinch of dust occasionally to disguise his tracks. Just keep up! No excuses! However, he did answer questions when the butterflies learned to match his pace.

Yes, 'Her Ladyship' was well known to Peco and 'the fellows'. She had asked a favor. Would they watch for a couple of stragglers? She had business elsewhere and couldn't be here in the morning. Si, sure. Why not? They had helped in this business before. "Little people helping little people", he joked. It was a hobby of theirs. There were always 'stragglers' late in the year, usually in need of a meal and some good advice. Very different otherwise though, the Rasha La. Unpredictable bunch. Peco had never met any before who knew about fishing, his own favorite sport.

"Now we're *stragglers*", whispered Yero peevishly. "I hope he at least means boys too, and not just the girls". Boca barely heard, maybe didn't. He was admiring his big fish.

Already they were approaching the gray hills and finding them much greener than they looked from a distance. Greener, but less inviting. The greenish hue was from small leaves on trees, now losing some color at this late date. The gray shade was from thin peels on the coarse bark. These were the nicer parts of the thorn trees that now blocked their way. The hills were infested with thickets of Catclaw Acacia, impenetrable to humans and most respectable animals.

Peco made straight for the worst thicket on the dead run, taking hat in hand at the last moment and plunging right in. He disappeared. There was a yelp and he stepped back out, a bit embarrassed. "Una de gato!" he warned. "Watch the catclaws". Then he plunged in again, and no more yelps.

Yero couldn't believe her eyes. How did he do it? There was no path whatsoever, but the thorny branches opened and bent away to make room for him. Well, one hadn't - but the rest did. Plainly, they expected him and were accommodating. Yero thought it amazing but not Peco. He stopped some distance inside to pluck out the disobedient spine from his cheek, obviously disappointed in himself. He whispered to the thorn and tossed it back into the thicket. "I'm slipping", he apologized.

That was the only accident. After that, the branches were quicker to open and even seemed aware that Peco had brought guests, so the way lingered open for the butterflies too. But as they passed by, every menacing branch recoiled shut behind them, snagging other branches and tangling impossibly, leaving no trace of their passage.

They came to a Fairy Haunt, an open space under the thorn canopy about a half-dozen strides across as a large man would step it off, and as high as that man might reach to a coverlet of upper branches. These let the morning sun through but were trained to stay up out of the way of the little people who trained them. Peco picked up a last handful of dirt and cast it over the path behind. It seemed overdone to Yero as she watched the last branches slap together obliterating the path anyway.

The floor was dirt, strewn lightly with peels of bark and wood chips. There was a fire pit in the exact center ringed with stones. A fire was burning there with a low blue flame and no smoke at all. A spit was rigged above the fire resting on wooden posts at each end. Drooping from the otherwise well-behaved ceiling was a prickly branch long enough to catch fire in the pit if it drooped any farther.

"Up and at 'em, fellows!" hollered Peco. "Fix that roof before it burns up".

The 'fellows' were sprawled lazily on the floor, sombreros over their eyes in the mid-morning, warming their feet by the fire. The feet were shoeless like Peco's - two of them slightly smaller, two much larger - well calloused below and insulated on top with curly black hair. All four feet sprang up immediately and supported their owners in an effort to push the branch up with poles and tangle it with other branches to keep it there.

The bigger feet reclined again then and stretched out toward the fire. They belonged to Obobo, a fairy like Peco but taller and much larger, especially around the middle. "You'll have to move the pit if it keeps doing that", he yawned.

The other feet belonged to Pio, a skinny, nervous fairy, quicker to action and (he felt, anyway) quicker of wit. "Let's move it *now*", he insisted. "I don't fancy moving camp in a panic when the roof goes up in smoke". Pio was the smallest of the fellows, and the last. In fact, there were no other fairies for hundreds of miles, so far as they knew.

"After breakfast!" suggested Peco. "The bass is fresh, but it ain't getting any fresher".

He held it up with both hands. Full-length it was longer than he was tall by a foot - even a big foot like Obobo's. "New record for me," he bragged, "which makes it a record for any of us". Pio nodded approvingly. Obobo scowled.

"But I only claim part of the credit", Peco went on. "The rest goes to El Boca here! He actually hooked the bass and kept the line tight when I was distracted".

That made the others gape a moment, then set them laughing and joking, recalling other exaggerated 'fish stories' while they spitted the fish and got it roasting over the fire. So, Boca's claim didn't officially make it into the records, being taken with a grain of salt as they say. Nevertheless, he was a boy, and Peco vouched for him and that won him plenty of respect.

As for Yero, she introduced herself after a while and was ignored for her trouble. She repeated it but stirred no interest whatsoever.

"What kind of place *is* this?" she said finally. "Don't you talk to girls?"

That got a response from Obobo, none too polite. He stood up and put big hands on his wide hips. "Girls don't count for much", he declared. "You're the only one anyway, and a wee little one at that".

Yero bristled. "As a guest I should be allowed to ask a question!"

"Polite guests don't".

"I'm as polite as you are! It doesn't take much".

Obobo thought about that, rubbing his chin whiskers.

"Let her have the question", chirped Pio. "Maybe then she'll settle down".

Yero jumped at her chance. "What *are* you anyway? Are you the boy fairies we've heard about?"

"That's two questions", said Obobo obstinately.

"Just one, actually", said Pio, not really taking Yero's side but nitpicking the 'big fellow', as he loved to do.

"You stay out of this!" warned Obobo.

"Can't. She's my guest too".

Peco interrupted. Someone had to. "Turn the fish!" he shouted.

That got the fellows scrambling. The unwritten rule was, if you don't catch it or gather it you better help cook it, or you don't get any. Pio and especially Obobo turned all their attention to the spit.

"We've been called a lot of things", answered Peco while they worked. "Around these parts we're called *Duendes*".

"I was hoping you were the boy fairies", said Yero, disappointed.

"Sure, we *are* fairy folk. That name goes back to the Old World before we scattered. A lot of us came here then, across the water. New places, new names. That's a long time ago too, now. We've been here quite a while".

"Then this is wonderful!" exclaimed Yero. "The Lost Boy Fairies! How many are left, do you think? In all?"

"What business is that of yours?" demanded Obobo, overhearing.

"I just want to know if there'll be a boy for every girl fairy when you get back together again".

Obobo growled like a bear and busied himself with the spit. The fish didn't need turning but he turned it anyway, muttering darkly about 'girls' and 'piping down'.

Pio grinned and spit into the coals. "Sounds just like Her Ladyship, don't she?"

"She's their guide", said Peco. "Last night she asked me to help round these two up, with fog coming on and all".

"That figures", grunted Obobo. He turned and planted himself with hands on hips again, his lecturing posture. "See here, Zero! It's none of your affair! There *were* girls of our race once, but they're *gone*, and that's the *end* of it! I don't want to hear no more!"

"No need to bluster", said Pio calmly. "Anyway, her name is 'Yero', I believe. But what I'm wondering is, where is Her Ladyship? The fog's lifted. The sun's shining. She knows where our camp is".

"She had business and wanted us to take them", answered Peco. "That's all she said".

"She'll turn up sooner or later", predicted Obobo. "She always does. In the meantime, we can babysit. We're not going anywhere while the fishing is good". He licked his lips and turned the spit again. Pio wagged a finger and tut-tutted.

"Now, now! That's rude, 'Bo! I'm sure they've been through a lot. They ain't babies either - especially El Boca. That was pretty good, him hooking the big bass!"

It was more than Yero could stand, especially when 'El Boca' grinned and settled down on Peco's shoulder. She went and perched on a thorn where the morning sun filtered through, there to warm herself and ignore everything else.

Boca took up the story and volunteered a first-hand account of his part in the battle. Yero couldn't ignore that, and fumed. The story had grown. Fish stories have to, of course, to keep up with other fish stories. The record books are skeptical, but otherwise it's generally accepted that fish do grow after they're caught. Some grow a lot.

He joined her after a while, feeling rather important, like one of the 'fellows'. "You should've stuck around", he said. "We were swapping stories. It was fun".

"Yes, I heard. You might have mentioned that I fought off the mosquitoes for him".

"I didn't want to bring it up, Yero. Peco almost lost the bass over *that* bit. We were just lucky I kept the line tight".

That did it. She bumped him off the spike. "Go hang out with your pals", she snapped. "You're all a bunch of liars anyway!"

"Yero, that's not fair. These are great stories!"

"So what! Nobody's being fair to me".

"Oh, you're just jealous. You should take up fishing sometime. Then you could tell stories too".

Boca left with a big grin and re-joined the fellows. Pio and Peco were fussing over the disobedient branch. It had come loose again and swung down, nearly knocking over the spit. They tried the usual magic, as on other days, with little result. It did lift back up if they pointed at it sternly enough, but it had a very short memory. Since the magic failed, they were reduced to common drudgery - propping it up with the poles. They were put out and argued about it. They had done such chores with magic for ages and it was a bother to do them any other way.

Obobo paid no attention. He was the Head Chef today. But while he basted and seasoned (and sampled) the fish he found time to set out a bit of rare acacia honey in a small dish - a bottle cap, actually - for the butterflies. He was a blusterer, but deep inside his fat stomach he had a guilty feeling. Perhaps he *had* been a trifle rude. He set the treat off to one side, toward Yero's roost.

"You ain't had breakfast, have you?" he asked Boca. "Didn't think so. Make sure *she* gets some".

Yero was very agreeable to the honey, and semi-agreeable to the peace offering. She perched on the bottle cap with her back to Obobo. When she sampled the honey, her mood improved even more.

"Oh, Boca! This is special. It must be from the thorn trees. I smelled an aroma in them right away, underneath the ugliness. The bees have captured it!"

He tried some. It was almost pure white in appearance. "Hits the spot", he agreed. "I don't get much aroma, though. Just the taste".

"It's subtle, delicate. Maybe you would have to be a girl to appreciate it".

"I guess. I never said girls didn't have some talents".

"Let's not get into that again. I'm still mad about that!"

"Okay, let's just eat. Who knows when the next meal will be? I hardly remember the last one".

"Same here. And the air is changing again - do you feel it? No more sunshine today, I'm thinking".

"Come and get it!" Obobo announced to the fellows. "You've been working like carpenters; you must've worked up an appetite". He chuckled a little. It was meant as an insult and they knew it.

"Cork the bottle!" muttered Pio. "If you think you could do any better, show us!"

Obobo dismissed the idea with a wave of his hand. "No time for it. The fish is done to perfection. Grab the other end and we'll lift it off!"

They wrapped handkerchiefs around the hot iron and lifted spit and fish together off the fire-- laying it on a bed of sticks to cool, and also to serve as a table.

"Eat hearty, boys", said Obobo. "I should be the chef every day. You'll never taste better".

They dug in with nary a glance at the skies. Clouds had arrived and were thickening. Anyone could see that rain was likely, but the boys seemed unconcerned. They peeled the skin off the fish, calloused fingers rolling it back, then spit on their hot fingertips and licked them while the fish cooled a bit. Pio stuck a finger into the ground and flipped open a dugout pantry. There were ceramic plates, cups, real silverware, a small hand towel and a box of extra spices. He passed out the cups and everyone filled them from a jug of water that Obobo had been sipping on. At least it looked like water, thought Yero, but who could say with these boys?

Everything else was left in the pantry. Obobo had got out the salt & pepper earlier and now the fish had cooled a little the fellows went after it with their fingers, spilling nothing but racing to get their fair share. They had huge appetites and reduced the first side to bare bones in no time at all, then flipped the carcass over and started on the second half. In spite of their full mouths, they kept up a steady chatter centering on the quality of the fish and especially the flavor - or lack of it.

"You never salted it!" declared Peco almost immediately.

Obobo shook a big finger at him. "I did salt it! Give it more if you want. Don't crab".

"I'll crab if I want. You're the cook! You *know* I like more salt. We *all* like more salt than we used to".

"Well, the salt's wet. It won't shake out. Whose fault is that?" He shook his finger again.

"Yours! *Both* of yours." griped Peco. "You should've set it by the fire while I was out a-catchin' your breakfast".

"Now, now", said Pio, "I recall the salt sat out yesterday in the fog. That's when we were fishing, and *you* were napping".

"You never caught anything either".

"What's that got to do with the salt?'

"Nuthin', I guess, since there wasn't any fish to put it on! Just pass me the shaker".

"Don't use it all. You know we're running short".

"Skip it then! Pass the pepper instead. This fish needs something".

"It's not the fish", said Pio. "It's you. It's *all* of us these days. You know that".

"I know you keep *saying* it. Just pass the pepper!"

"Don't blame me, old friend". Pio turned to the big chef who was grabbing more than his share of fish while the others argued. "You're no better, 'Bo! And don't point your big finger at us!"

Obobo had way too much mouthful to answer but shook a fat finger at both of them. It was all very enjoyable until he got a cold drip of water - splat! - on his nose.

A light rain had started to fall, dripping through the 'roof' in several places, mostly around the unruly branch. Several drips hit the fire and sizzled in the coals. Then a second one hit Obobo on the forehead as he stuffed the last of the fish into his big mouth, closing it with some difficulty. He watched cross-eyed as the new drip trickled down and joined the earlier one on his nose, which then became too big and fell off onto his stomach. That was annoying. He buttoned his shirt but felt too lazy to move. Then a third drop hit his ear.

Peco grinned at him and then he got dripped on too. It was very unsettling. Each drop was an affront to their expertise, their mastery of nature and their surroundings. Big people call it magic but little people--fairy folk of all kinds--usually don't. To them it's skill, an acquired influence over natural things. And Pio was right, their skill was less than it once was. In another Age, the rain never would have leaked in. Every drop would have found a leaf or twig, trickled along the branch back to the trunks, and so on down the walls of the haunt and drained obediently away. It didn't matter in the old days if there were gaps in the roof, or even half-open to the sky. The rain never dripped in on them. Now it did.

Obobo reached out and caught a drop on the back of his hand. He licked it off and spit it out. "Tastes dirty. Like bathwater".

"You're just guessing", said Pio. "You never take one".

Obobo ignored that. "Where are we going to sleep?" he wondered.

"There's plenty of dry spots", observed Pio. "It's not leaking everywhere".

"But it'll turn to mud".

They all thought about that for a minute or two. Then Pio stood up, studying the roof. "Let's try and fix it again", he said. "All together".

It didn't help much. They concentrated on the leaky spots, pointing accusingly in silence. The drips always stopped for a few minutes. A couple seemed to be fixed; but the others resumed leaking all too soon. And more started up.

The butterflies had been quiet, as guests should be who've been served a rare and delicious meal. But the weather was easy to read. It was turning into an all-day drizzle. Since Atel hadn't found them, she wouldn't find them today. Maybe not even tomorrow. By then there would surely be a mess and a whole lot of quarrelling in the haunt. Housekeeping came to Yero's mind.

"How many cups do you have?" she asked politely, but so loud she couldn't be ignored. "Put a cup or saucepan under each drip. There'll be less mud".

"I was about to suggest that", said Pio quickly. "Counting drips and so forth. So, we'll call it my idea".

"Fine. Girls just have a knack for comfort, that's all. So, I spoke up".

"Well, I'm surprised you had a reason. From what I've heard, girls just *talk*".

"We do, when we have something important to say. A dry floor is important, so a girl might talk about that".

"Okay! It's been discussed. Now you can hush".

"The more you say it, the less hush you'll probably get", warned Boca. "That's just the way she is".

Pio frowned but took the advice, since it was from El Boca. The boys got busy with cups and several saucepans and kettles. It was enough to catch all the biggest leaks. Then they settled themselves by the fire, got out chewing tobacco, and stuffed pinches into their lower lips. They favored the fine grind in the little round cans and never missed their chew after a good meal. All was well again as they spit contentedly into the fire.

Nevertheless, Yero took a pessimistic view. "This won't work later", she whispered to Boca. "Look at the layout. There aren't enough good places to sleep even now, and more leaks might start".

"Let them figure it out. We're guests, remember?"

"I *do* know how to be polite, Boca! We've been guests at a lot of places. What are you worried about?"

"These fellows are *macho*. Don't push it".

"So? What does that mean?"

The Butterflies, Yero and Boca

"It's like: Girls, just stand back! We'll call you if we need you".

"That's dumb. Is that how boys are?"

"Some are. If they *are*, you better back off".

"Like 'hush'? Well, piffle to that! A guest should never be bashful with a good suggestion. Not if it's a good one. So I'll keep thinking".

"Just don't upset the hosts, Yero".

"Don't worry. They're just boys. I know how to talk to boys".

"I'm a boy, and you get on my nerves sometimes".

"Well, I have to correct you in a *hurry* sometimes, so that can't be helped. But here there's no rush. I'll take my time and say all the right things. Relax!"

For a while, everyone did that. No new leaks appeared, no new arguments started up, no new suggestions came to Yero's mind. Obobo even took an afternoon nap. It was break time. But when he began to snore intolerably, activity picked up around him. Someone finally poked him in the ribs and that stopped the snoring, but he woke up grumpy, and when 'Bo was grumpy everyone might as well get to work. The break was over.

That was just as well. Regardless of the weather chores must be done and done according to their daily job rotation. Obobo the Chief Chef had little to do, since no pots or pans had been used in the cooking. He just set the spit back over the fire to sterilize and otherwise made a show of stoking the embers to look busy.

Peco pitched in to help with the fish carcass even though he didn't strictly have to, since Pio was Housekeeper for the day. Together they folded the skin back over the fish bones as if folding a blanket and carried the works outside to dispose of it.

Boca thanked Obobo for the honey and apologized that they were unable to finish it. "We have big appetites for our kind", Boca assured him, "but nothing like yours". 'Bo just laughed and licked out the bottle cap, then put it back on the 'clean water jug' where it belonged.

The butterflies retired up under the roof for a nap of their own, clinging to the dry underside of a leaf, but sleep eluded them. The constant drips and splashes were never in rhythm, always out of tune. Then Obobo fed a few sticks onto the fire, sticks from the 'breakfast table' with grease on them. They flared and wisps of grease smoke curled up into their noses, until they finally moved to the drooping branch, which had sagged again offering a perch below the smoke layer.

The others returned later with muddy feet. One kept the entrance open while the other grabbed up a handful of dry dirt from the floor and tossed it out, hoping to cover their tracks. It just disappeared into the drizzle and the gathering gloom.

"A lot of good that'll do!" barked Obobo. "I hope you two didn't tramp all over the hills".

"We went quite a ways", said Pio defiantly. "I don't dump garbage right outside the door and you better not either".

"Well, don't track your mud inside. Kick it off!"

"Yes, yes. We already did. Anyway, *I'm* Housekeeper today, so it's none of your business!"

"The Housekeeper better start emptying some of these pans before they run over".

Pio said something under his breath and turned to the job. Two small saucepans were already full. He carefully picked them up and made his way slowly to the lowest corner of the room where he tossed the water through the thorn wall. That's what he had in mind anyway, but the waterproof spell was in good repair on the wall, so it just splashed and ran down, making a pool in the corner. He said something else under his breath, put the pans back where they had been, and reached for a cup that was nearly full, accidentally kicking over another behind him.

"Tsk! What a mess!" remarked Obobo. "You better figure out a system with that. I don't want you spilling water on me tonight when I'm sleeping". He tossed another greasy stick on the fire. It flared up, flickering brightly against the walls. Grease smoke formed a light haze around the ceiling.

"Hey! Keep the fire down!" said Pio. "It's getting dark outside. No telling who might see it".

Something did see it and was attracted to the light, or so Boca thought for a moment. He nudged Yero and pointed to the wall. The fire flared again and they both saw it - eyes shining just outside. More than one animal. Then the eyes disappeared.

"Is it wolves, I wonder?" whispered Boca. "What did you see?"

"I don't know. Sort of...*creepier* than that. We'd better say something".

"I don't think we have to. They saw it too. Look".

The fellows went on arguing as if nothing was amiss, but they clearly kept an eye on that wall and the other walls too, shifting casually in position to do so. Obobo didn't put any more sticks on for a while and it didn't happen again throughout the dreary evening. The haze cleared out and the butterflies finally did get some sleep but awoke later to the same bickering.

Tending the drip pans was becoming a bother. Pio got no help but did receive lots of advice, and more leaks had indeed started. More than there were cups and pans for. He had so far been able to double-up with the large pans where drips were close together; but it was a thankless job and he wasn't keen on keeping it up all night by himself.

"We're going to take watches", he announced. "You both better study up and remember where the leaks are. I'll take a watch too, but I'm not doing all of it".

"Nuts to that", replied Peco. "I'm the Hunter today, and it's still today".

"Then go hunt something! There's nothing left for supper".

"Is too. I gathered these".

He untied a bag at his belt and emptied out a pile of lumpy roots, potatoes of some kind that grew wild in the region but resembled civilized potatoes only by having eyes. The variety was purple in color and extra lumpy, but they were delicious. The fellows dug them wherever they found them, always replanting a few eyes. If history was rewritten correctly, boy fairies should get credit for spreading the roots all up and down the Americas long ago through their trade with the people of the high Andes. It was a nice pile and Peco expected compliments, but he didn't get any. Obobo was out of sorts and Pio just scowled, so Peco did too.

"I'll take a watch, but no housekeeping!" he declared.

"You'll both help or you'll both get wet!"

"Quit bellyaching", grumbled Obobo. "Do I grumble about my work? No!"

"Why would you? Half the time you don't do it!"

'Bo got a mischievous gleam in his eye. "All day long I've been Chef and done everything I'm supposed to. Argue that now!"

"So far, yes. You did roast a tasty fish. But what have you done about supper? Those taters will help, but what're you gonna fix alongside?"

"Nothing. Taters are a meal in themselves, and we'll eat 'em raw. They're good raw". His eyes twinkled. "So there! Clear me a place to stretch out. My work is done and I've a mind to warm my toes by the fire".

That was the last straw. The quarrel turned nasty - and the language too. That was bad enough, but then Obobo overturned the biggest drip pan while trying to get comfortable. It was full (or had been) and it all ran into the fire pit and drowned it. All three boys leaped into action to save a few coals but failed. It made a lot of smoke too, and the butterflies had to move to a low wall where they clung nervously, worried about eyes and animals on the other side.

Seeing all was hopeless, Obobo laid back down, adjusting his sombrero over his face and shoulders to keep the drips out.

"Fire is the Housekeeper's job", came his voice from under the hat. "You're it today, Pio! Make us a new one".

The Housekeeper picked up another full pan and might've dumped it on the big fellow, but Yero somehow got his attention and offered another domestic tip.

"If you can't keep a house tidy, it's probably too big", she suggested. "Can you pull this place *in* some? Make it smaller? The leaky holes might not leak as much".

Pio blinked, and took the idea for his own. "I was coming around to that", he said thoughtfully. "Yes, that's my plan. We'll tighten things up, and that should solve the underlying problem in the overhead". He grinned proudly. By golly, it sounded clever! Besides, it gave him a good reason to do *this:* He kicked Obobo in the rump. "Everyone up!" he shouted. "We're going to try something new and it'll take all three of us".

He explained the plan, expecting argument, but there was none. The theory was sound. Even Obobo thought it worth a try. But they didn't do it forthwith. It was a new trick and involved living trees, while their traditional skills were better with metal and stone. It was 800 years since they were driven out of their underground halls and had to adopt new ways in the outer world, but they still weren't all that comfortable with 'Green Magic', as they called it.

So they were hesitant, but soon devised a typically macho plan. They would order all the trees around the circle to pull their opposites toward them, a simple matter of muscle. It failed horribly. The stronger ones pulled the weaker ones right into the room, and the tugging didn't quit. The boys reversed the spell before someone got hurt and asked the trees instead to just lean in toward the center.

They did so, quite obediently, but the interwoven ceiling was now so tangled and matted that it simply sagged. All the drips ran to the middle and trickled in a stream down into the fire pit, overflowing it and flooding the area where Obobo liked to sleep.

"Do something!" he shouted at Pio. "It's not working!"

"It was her idea!" Pio shouted back, jerking a thumb at Yero.

"That's not what I heard!" barked Obobo and pointed an angry finger up at the tangle. "Just get back the way you were!" he hollered, but the trees did nothing. He cussed them roundly.

They didn't like that. The trees stiffened, pulling the ceiling too tight and tearing off twigs. Drips commenced right above him and found ways to get under his hat and down his neck. New drips appeared everywhere, far too many for their drip pans.

"'Bo, now you just apologize!" said Peco sternly.

Obobo actually took hat in hand and bent down on one knee, speaking under his breath to keep the others from hearing. He must have been truly sorry because the trees accepted it. The ceiling relaxed a bit. The dripping lessened.

Pio leaned toward Yero and whispered so only she could hear, "If you have any more bright ideas, keep 'em to yourself!"

"I do! I know how you could stay dry. Want to hear it?"

Poor fellow. Now his curiosity was up. "Okay, quietly".

"Wear raincoats".

"You're a real wise guy, for a girl!"

"I'm not joking. See all the leaves? Braid them into coats. That's what girl fairies do when it rains". She bit her tongue, worried she had said too much. She certainly had.

"Baloney to *that*! We don't wear girl's clothes and we don't need any more girls' help! Our sombreros will keep us dry".

All in a huff, he squatted down near Obobo who was trying to get underneath his hat too. He was bigger than the hat, so it was impossible. When he leaned forward a cold drip landed on his lower back and found a crevice down there, but when he leaned back to prevent that his legs got wet up front. He had to choose, so he leaned back. That brought the drowned fire pit into view and prompted him to comment about the housekeeping.

Peco announced he was going night fishing since he was wet anyway and headed out. Maybe he was, and maybe he wasn't. Peco just got tired of arguing sooner than the others. He wasn't gone ten minutes when he hustled back inside, all jittery, tall ears flipping this way and that like a wild animal. "They're out there!" he said.

All bickering ceased. Pio got busy trying to make a new fire while the others peered into the gloom, standing guard against - whatever it was. He quickly bailed out the pit with a cup. The charred wood was soaked and had to go, but he had dry wood, some - if it was still dry. He kept a few sticks and extra matches in another cubby near the dishes and got them out now. Water had gotten at the sticks a little, but they could be shaved. The worse problem was the matches were damp and he wasted several in discovering this. He threw up his hands and cussed, very unlike him. It must've been serious because the others noticed, and they cussed too.

"We can help with the matches," whispered Yero, "but you better suggest it, Boca. They'll listen to you". He nodded and went to have a word with Pio, who laid down two sticks right away and placed the last matches across them. Boca waved to Yero and together they fluttered just above the matches in hopes of fanning them dry. Urgency was in the air but if the Butterflies inquired who 'they' were, outside, Pio was tight-lipped.

"If we get a fire, you'll see", was all he would say.

"And if we don't?"

"You'll see then, too".

In a few minutes, he tried a match. It sparked but failed. Obobo kicked mud at the wall in irritation. It splattered all about.

"Just don't hit the dry kindling", warned Peco, "or we'll send you out to parley".

"They don't parley. You know that".

"Sure, but some good might still come of it".

"Yeah? Well, keep it to yourself!"

Peco couldn't. "If they get *you*, I'm sure it's all they could carry. The rest of us could escape".

Peco grinned in the dark. Obobo knew he was smiling and wound up to kick more mud, but a match flared up behind him. Pio put it carefully to the shaved wood. It caught slowly, illuminating only itself. Even so, it reflected off things outside the walls, things moving about.

A breeze like a puff of air came through the walls unexpectedly, causing the baby flames to go out. Obobo threw mud in the direction it came from. Pio shielded the remaining bit of coals and blew softly on them. The flames revived. All three boys got down close now and protected the fire, adding shavings bit by bit until it looked able to burn on its own. At that point, Obobo busted a couple of greasy sticks over his knee and stacked them around the pit like a teepee. In a minute, the flames licked the grease and flared up, revealing the menace.

All around the walls were fierce, painted warriors of some tribe, milling and searching for an opening, some even reaching through the gaps. Their eyes reflected blood red in the firelight. But no one spoke, inside or out, until Peco said low and urgently, "More wood!"

The warriors didn't like being seen, or maybe they just didn't like the bright light, but they began to pull back right away. The fire hadn't gotten much bigger before they were gone.

Yero let out her breath, unaware she had been holding it. So did Boca. "Wow", she breathed, "I thought all the cowboy and Indian wars were over with!"

In the absolute quiet Pio overheard and turned to them where they perched up under the ceiling. "Come down by us", he said. "There'll be no war tonight after all, not while the fire is burning". A lot of tension evaporated, but the butterflies did take up a perch on one end of the spit, in the best light where it seemed safest.

"...and speaking of fire", Pio was saying now, "We owe some thanks to El Boca here. It was his idea how to dry the matches".

For the next few minutes it was all, "Good job!" and "Quick thinking in the pinch, lad!" Boca was embarrassed and answered only, "Aw, it wasn't much", which only brought more praise for the modesty. There was little for Yero but to look away and wait for it all to subside. Finally it did, and the snuffboxes came out. They unwound with a chew and spit from time to time, but at the walls now, not into the fire as before. Other than that, they acted as if the crisis never happened.

Yero finally whispered irritably, "Boca, you let them drop the subject! I want to know who those warriors were!"

"I don't think they want to talk about it, Yero".

"Well, piffle to that too! It looked serious".

"Okay. But let *me* do the asking, don't butt in".

Pio was willing to talk a little and it wasn't comforting. The 'warriors' were ghosts of long ago - the fabled Jaguar warriors of the old Aztec empire. They ruled the Ghost Realm in this part of the world. Pio left it at that, which did not satisfy the listeners.

"So, what's their problem?" asked Yero. "They sure didn't look friendly".

Pio frowned into the fire. "No. Quite the opposite. Their problem is *us*, a big part of it anyway". He glanced up at the butterflies before continuing. "I suppose -if you're going to travel with us - you ought to know about their grudge because you'll be in danger too". The others nodded silently and let Pio talk, but he hesitated.

"Just spill the gory details", prompted Boca. "We know there's some in all the old tales".

"Yes, there is. However, this old tale wants come *back*. To rise up from the grave. Do you handle fear well?"

"Okay, I guess. There usually isn't time to sit and think about it".

"As I expected, El Boca. What about *her*?"

The doubt was obvious. The others glanced up. Boca answered quickly before Yero could let fly.

"She is brave. As brave as you could ask for".

Coming from Boca it seemed to satisfy them perfectly. There was an unexpected side-benefit too. The fairies' opinion of her, and courtesy toward her, went up noticeably after that.

Pio studied the fire for a while, nodding in thought, putting the right words together. "They don't want to kill us, understand - nor *you* either - but something worse. They wish to capture us and drag us into their world for their masters to play with. I speak of their High Priests. They want victims again for sacrifice, now more than ever".

He stopped again at that point and the butterflies didn't ask for more but changed the subject to something more practical.

"You said we might be travelling with you", put in Yero. "Why? And where is Atel? Do you know anything more?"

Neither Pio nor Obobo knew anything, and Peco could only repeat what he had said earlier. Atel had found him in the gathering fog, given him an errand, and went off toward the south. Who could say where? He couldn't.

South sounded promising to the butterflies. "We're going that way too", said Yero. "Which way are you going?"

Obobo answered as he broke another greasy stick into pieces and leaned them against the new fire. "We're going with you, at least until she turns up. We know where you're going".

"It's nice of you to offer", responded Boca. "But we don't expect help from everyone".

"Good. A lot of folks wouldn't anyway. But the fellows and me are in the business, you might say. We've done it before".

"But why?" asked Yero again. "We know Atel is hard to ignore, but you have your own troubles with those Jaguars. There's no need to risk more on our account".

"But there *is* a need", answered Pio quietly. "A need for all Ages. You were children of the Big People, but the Priests were cruel to children of all kinds. One of their gods - the rain god, Tialoc - demanded the tears of children in payment for rain, or so the Priests claimed; but in their cold hearts they just enjoyed the tears. That was the evil our people found here in the upper world, after we were driven out from our halls. It made us mad. We stole a child appointed for sacrifice, and then another, and another, and spirited them off to be adopted by tribes in the north. The Priests didn't figure out right away who was cheating them, but when they did it was war. It still is. That's why their warriors were here tonight".

"But if they're in the 'Ghost Realm', they must have died. What good is any sacrifice to them now?"

"They wish to return to this world, but they need *life* to do so. They'll take it wherever they can get it, but they especially want *ours*, for revenge, and *yours* - children of all races - because yours is the purest".

"Why don't they just grab anyone? They looked pretty strong".

"They can't touch most folks outside their realm; but some are at risk. We are, because we're so few now. The earth is forgetting us. We're losing our shadows. We have one foot in their world already, you might say. So do the Rasha La".

"But we have fire", said Boca hopefully. "They didn't like that".

"They sure don't. Fire, and the light of day! Both pierce them like spears and they flee back to their own world. They can't take us here if we have enough light".

"We're lucky then", said Yero. "We've had Atel, and light is a specialty of hers. And you fellows have the same skill".

"Not the same. We do it the old-fashioned way", laughed Obobo. "We'll need plenty of matches if we're going south. The Jaguars are strong down that way".

"Which reminds me", said Pio. "We're short on matches".

"We'll borrow some", said Peco. "We need snuff too. I'm about out". He grinned at the butterflies. "The Big Folk have always been generous to us - more than they'll ever know".

"You steal things?"

No, no! I didn't mean that. We *trade* for supplies. We'll leave something of value along the way, don't fret".

Yero decided the less she knew the better and steered the subject back to the journey again. "Do you know the way to Manino? It's a very long ways yet, we think".

"Yes. A long way. To where all the monarchs go. But for now, while Her Ladyship may yet return, we'll take it one day at a time. We have 'safe' camps all up and down this land. We'll make for the first one and go from there. But after this business tonight - who knows what's safe?"

They all fell silent with plenty to think about. It was well into the evening now and the drizzle persisted. The ceiling sprang more leaks. It was shot after being jerked around so much. The fellows had to settle for places with less drips than others and kept their bare toes to the fire. Worse, the dry firewood stack - small to begin with - was getting scant. Peco finally said the obvious.

"Let it burn low. It has to last the night. They might still be out there".

The butterflies went up under the leaves again; but for the boys a wet, miserable night stretched before them. They all tried the same trick, using their sombreros for umbrellas. It was better than nothing, but not much. The grumbling soon started up and got steadily louder.

"What do you think?" whispered Yero. "Should I suggest raincoats again? I don't want to listen to this all night".

"Well, don't talk to Pio about it. You know what he'll say".

"He'll hear it anyway. They're all cozied up to the fire there".

"*I* could suggest it, Yero, and they might do it. But you'd have to come with me and teach them how. I don't know the first thing about braiding".

They went down and after a bit of chitchat Boca brought up the subject. Pio was instantly suspicious.

"Did she put you up to this?" he asked Boca. "Sounds like the girly clothes again".

Obobo broke in, to Boca's relief. "What's all that? Just let him talk!"

"It's *her* idea!" said Pio contemptuously. "Braiding leaves into rain-*dresses*!"

"Rain-*gear!*" corrected Yero

"*Dresses!*" insisted Pio. "Baloney to that! You might as well ask cowboys to wear skirts".

That rang a bell in Yero's mind. She whispered quickly in Boca's ear. He smiled.

"Why not make *chaps*?" he suggested. "Like the cowboys wore. They wore 'em all the time to protect their legs. Kept 'em dry too".

"Well...that's...entirely different", drawled Obobo, thinking his way through it as he spoke and seeing nothing sissy. Peco agreed.

"I say we try it. It's El Boca's idea, after all".

Even Pio finally agreed since the others did.

"Lay it on us", said Obobo. "How do we make 'em?"

El Boca grandly turned it all over to Yero. "I never bothered to learn the craft", he declared. "Girls are best at that stuff. Boys just *wear* 'em!"

It was a stroke of inspiration, a thought the boys had never thought before: Let the girls do it! Now, that had appeal! Boy fairies are rough and tumble, but they have to mend their own clothes. In the sacks they all had at their belts were little sewing kits, among other things. It was a subject they didn't talk about much.

"Go ahead then, little sister", chortled Pio. "Make me some chaps!"

"Be realistic, mister", replied Yero, taking over. "If I were your size I could, but I'm not. I'll explain about braiding and weaving, and you can take it from there. You'll be working with those leaves". She indicated the ceiling canopy. "Once you catch on to the weave it'll go pretty fast".

A breeze shook the canopy enough to dislodge a shower of drips. If the boys had any lingering doubts, that erased them. They hung on every word as she spelled it out. Then, as with 'tightening up the haunt' earlier, things slowed way down while they debated the idea and nitpicked it. Were there enough leaves? They hemmed, hawed, and asked Yero to repeat the part about 'overlapping'. Also, there was the question of new leaks. More rain would surely drip through when the leaves were gone. And, finally, *fair shares* of the leaves. Pio and Peco expected one/third each, but Obobo was bigger than both of them put together and wouldn't stand for it. Boca saw a simple solution.

"Do like the cowboys do", he proposed. "Whoever is fastest, wins! Get ready, get set..."

"Whoa! Hold on a minute, lad", said Pio. "The leaves ain't green anymore. Will they lay flat? Let her explain that part. Then, anything goes".

Yero patiently did. Leaf weaving is tricky, especially late in the season when they crisp and turn color. But the drizzle would help to soften them. The most important thing was the tips had to point down to shed water. "And don't break off the stems!" she warned. "They bind it all together".

There was more, but the boys quit listening. Fairy folk are quick to action when they think they know it all, and they usually do. They didn't survive all those Ages by being slowcoaches. The fellows turned on their heels and pointed up at the leaves they wanted to start with - Peco with his right hand and Pio with his left, but Obobo used both hands.

The leaves responded with an instant rustle, detaching themselves from their twigs and fluttering down to join others already spiraling around the boy's legs. Round and round they spiraled, laying on row upon row of leaf plating. The smaller fellows caught on to Obobo and started using both arms as well, but he had already moved on to using all of his fingers and even thumbs. Suddenly it was over, and the big fellow had won. His 'chaps' came clear up onto his waist (With Obobo this was an approximate level, hard to define.) but the others had done well enough. They sat down now on one-legged stools, feet to the fire, doubting all of this. But it worked, and their hats protected the rest of them. The rain did drip everywhere now, so they put their few dry things under pots and pans, threw a stick or two on the fire and an old coat over the last of the wood, and relaxed. Things were good enough.

They had thoughtfully left several leaves up where the butterflies liked to perch, and now in a mellow mood they sent their compliments up to El Boca for the fine, practical plan. Boca accepted them with no modesty at all; and if Yero frowned, he pointed out that it was best to leave success alone.

"We don't want them asking any more questions, do we? They'd rip 'em off in a minute if they knew they were wearing girl's tights".

"They're not girl's tights!"

"It's all how they see it. If they ever got the idea..."

"Who's going to tell them? You?"

"Shh. Your voice carries when you're upset. Just admit I saved the day tonight and congratulate me! They already have".

"Okay. I suppose that's where they get the 'El' for your new name: 'El Brainy'".

"Sure. Or even 'El Genius'".

"Or maybe smart-'El'-ick".

El Boca just smiled and closed his eyes. Everyone got some sleep after that. Toward morning the light rain stopped, and a dry southwest wind pushed the fog down off the hills and across the water. It was a chill wind and a few flurries greeted them with the light of day, disappointing to butterflies who had thought they were too far south now to be bothered by snow.

"We get it once in a while", noted Pio. "Nothing like up in the mountains..." (He waved vaguely toward the south) "...but sometimes up to our ankles. We don't like it. Hard to cover our tracks".

But this was only flurries and soon gave way to clearing skies and a welcome sun. There was no sign of Atel, but the boys decided to wait a while for her, and also for the ground to dry and firm up a bit. Mud was as bad as snow for leaving tracks, as difficult to cover over, and there were many reasons besides ghost warriors to stay unnoticed in the 'Big People's' world, especially when they needed to borrow a few supplies. They were low on almost everything and would need to visit civilized places to trade. Obobo waved open the doorway and looked critically at the tracks the others had left.

"This mess will have to be cleaned up", he admonished. "I can't imagine why you left it like that".

"It was mud, if you don't remember", replied Pio. "But we might as well shut this camp down for good. *They* know about it. It's not safe anymore".

Peco was against this with the other big bass still uncaught, but he was outvoted.

"There's good fishing anywhere if you're the great fisherman you claim to be", said Obobo. "Anyhow, we can make another camp somewhere else in these hills. Thickets are everywhere".

"How might that go, I wonder?" said Peco. "We can't even keep this one in good shape. I doubt if we could train a new one".

That notion was pooh-poohed as the others set about packing up their things. "Regardless", overruled Pio," this place looks too much like a hideout now, and someone could stumble onto it any time. It needs to go back natural".

"Try it then", said Peco.

The others harrumphed and started pointing and waving casually. It should have been easy to reverse the spell. It's much easier to cancel one than set one up. But nothing much happened. The thorn trees, stretched and tangled as they were, couldn't relax.

Peco just laughed. "Might as well keep it", he said. "They'll untangle themselves by the time we get back up this way".

"*If* we do", said Obobo. "But at least let's clean it up so there's nothing tell-tale; and *you two* will have to get rid of your tracks out there! You left a lot of work for yourselves. Where did you dump the garbage, anyway?"

"Far enough so coyotes wouldn't show up at the door!" Pio shot back.

"Now, now! Don't get testy. You made the mess. Just fix it".

"Well, they meant to wait a while anyway", observed Yero, watching from up above. "So it can't be said they're wasting time".

Boca could only agree. "Too bad they don't have wings like the girls. There wouldn't be any tracks to worry about".

"Maybe they *do*, somewhere. Remember the story?"

"That didn't sound too hopeful".

"No. I wonder if it's true?"

"Shh". Boca noticed the boys were looking at them. Pio had overheard.

"That would be Her Ladyship again, I suppose?" he said stiffly. "Just don't believe everything you hear - especially *girl-talk!*" Clearly, the subject was closed.

The fellows resumed cleanup and soon the Haunt looked wild and untended. No big person would raise even an eyebrow (should one ever crawl back that far) but Obobo was fussy about wood chips and a few ashes that had drifted out of the pit. Finally, there was only the fire to dispose of, but the coals were still burning. 'Bo was Housekeeper today and chose to stay and be sure it burned out while the others went to rake over their tracks. By manual labor, of course.

The butterflies went down by Obobo and made an apology for 'talking out of turn'. He accepted it gruffly, but did get out the little jar of honey again and re-filled the bottle cap.

"Here, now. Have a bit of breakfast", he said more sociably. You've probably missed more meals lately than I have". He patted his belly.

The butterflies didn't have to be told twice. Boca dug right in, but Yero luxuriated in the fragrance first.

"Something in the aroma uplifts the spirits", she told Obobo. "Someone should make a perfume with this. Girls would go crazy about it".

He looked surprised, then frowned. "There you go again!" he growled. "Just keep it down. I'm busy!"

"Not that busy!" She flew up by his nose. "As long as I'm with you'll have to put up with *some* girl stuff. I *am* a girl. Anyway, I like you fellows".

Obobo didn't know how to answer. Finally, he said, "We've had girls before, of your kind. It's no big deal".

"Did you listen to any of them?"

"Not a one".

"Just as I thought, so I'll give you some advice".

Obobo was getting edgy fast. Yero hurried on. "You'll find it easier to get along if you *pretend* to hear, even if you aren't really listening. A lot of boys solve the problem that way".

This wasn't what Obobo expected. It made sense. "That little tip might come in useful", he admitted.

"See? Girls can be practical too, when you least expect it". She paused as Obobo relaxed and even smiled, then went on. "By the way, you'd look a lot better if you covered up your belly-button".

Fortunately, the other boys chose that moment to return, looking ragged and tired.

"We're done", said Pio. "But I see you haven't done anything".

"That's where you're wrong!" shot back Obobo. "I've been figuring stuff out".

"Yeah? Like what?"

"None 'o your business! And look at your chaps - all torn to pieces! We need some new clothes". He pulled his shirt down as best he could and spun around in a huff to see about the fire.

Pio looked to the butterflies in bewilderment, jerking a thumb at Obobo. "What's with him?"

"Shirt's too small", said Yero.

Pio looked at Peco, who just shrugged. There were a few sticks of firewood yet to be gotten rid of and they picked those up while 'Bo carefully swept the last ashes into the pit - except a pinch or two - and rolled the stones away haphazardly except one large flat one. He set that on top of the pit, covering it nicely, and pointed a big finger at it. Finally, he tossed the handful of ashes up through the bare branches where the morning breeze caught them and carried the little cloud into the open sky. The boys all watched a moment as it drifted away, an old custom when breaking camp. It was forgotten now, but 'casting the ashes' hearkened back to a time when the girls were still down here on the green earth, and the boys sometimes did look for them. If any girls had been nearby within memory the trees remembered, and the ashes showed their silhouettes as it drifted away. That part was forgotten now, but the custom remained. Now it was done 'for luck', or simply to see which way the wind was blowing, since the acacia fires themselves gave off almost no smoke.

Yero watched longer than the boys and was amazed to see not one but several female shapes appear, girls with long hair and wings. Just a fleeting glimpse. Then they fell apart. But when she spoke of it excitedly, the boys laughed.

"You can read anything you want into smoke and ashes", joked Pio. "Flim-flam artists make a nice living at that kind of trickery".

The boys no longer remembered, but the Acacia did. The girls came here often in bygone days - not for the honey, but for the ingredients of a most rare perfume. Yero guessed right away. A lot of girls would. But for the boys, the most important things on their minds right now were matches, clothes, groceries - and especially, *snuff*.

Peco led the way out, being best at opening the path. Pio went next to widen the way, then the butterflies, and Obobo brought up the rear with a branch to rake over their new tracks wherever they showed in the still-soft ground. He hadn't volunteered but wasn't given any choice. He sweated at the job, looking mostly back at his work and depending on the others to make the path wide enough. A loose branch did rake him now and then, but he never cussed. He just pulled his shirt down and his pants up and kept working.

Yero was still amazed at the girls that appeared in the ashes. "I *did* see them", she whispered seriously. "Three or four of them with long, pretty hair".

"Or you imagined it", answered Boca.

"I can't believe you missed it! They were all in a circle, talking".

"Okay, now I'm starting to believe it".

"Stop it, Boca! You *do* want them to get together again one day, don't you? Be serious now".

"I guess so, but I'll leave all that to the boys".

"Well! That's just it! It's been up to them for Ages and they haven't done a thing. They need a push!"

"You do it then. You're good at that. I have something more important in mind".

"What could be more important than a legendary romance?"

"I want to try some of that snuff, Yero. It looks pretty good".

That's where the conversation broke off. For a while, the only familiar sounds were an occasional muffled oath up front and Obobo laboring behind them. The thorn branches made surprisingly little noise parting. Behind Obobo, though, they slapped together again and didn't care how they did it. Sometimes it was startling, like antlers clashing together. Sometimes it was quieter and 'Bo took the opportunity to loudly complain about 'tracks from last night' that hadn't got brushed out. The boys up front weren't having any sympathy but his racket worried them, and they slowed the pace. That suited Obobo better and Yero guessed that was his real intention.

As they climbed higher into the hills, the thickets reluctantly yielded to grassy clearings where the ground was dry. The boys up front called a halt at the first one. "We dumped the garbage here", said Pio, waving a hand at a lot of trampled grass. There was no sign of the fish carcass, but many animals had been there. Obobo heaved a sigh of relief, flung his raking branch back into the thicket and sat down exhausted. It took a while for him to catch his breath.

"You *did* leave tracks!" he said when he could. "You might've dumped it sooner!"

"*You* might have", replied Pio. "And look what might have followed you home!" The animals had torn the place up fighting over the scraps. Coyotes had been there, a whole pack by the signs, and some larger animal as well.

"Anyway", said Peco, "it was raining. We figured the rain would wash away our trail".

"Well, it worked out swell, didn't it? You skipped back for a nice after-dinner chew, and old 'Bo fixed your mess today!"

"I wouldn't mind a chew right *now*", responded Peco, "and I ain't got any left". None of them did.

The quarrelling stopped for a common purpose. Like most tobacco users, they were rarely without any, and not for long. As soon as old 'Bo was rested they struck out again but now they made better time, reaching the ridge of the highest hill in the area late in the afternoon. It was more hospitable with no thorn trees, but cold and windy. There was a lower elevation, a saddleback, across the ridge that offered some protection against the wind. The boys made directly for it and plopped their gear down as if they'd been there many times. The only other feature on the ridge was an irregular line of huge barrel cactus along the highest ground. They looked tired - leaning, almost tipping down the hillside toward the south.

It was a good lookout point and while everyone rested, Yero and Boca took in the view. To the north from where they had come were lower hills and the great reservoir lake stretching across the horizon. To the south, which seemed of more interest to the cactus and the fairies, were other hills dotted with farmsteads, and a small village in the valley just below. The sun, near setting now, illuminated much higher elevations beyond, but it was the village that most interested the boys.

"We're going shopping", they announced. "You stay here. Is there anything you want from the store?"

"Nothing for me", said Yero primly. "But Boca wants a can of snuff".

The boys chuckled and hooted. "Not a whole can!" Boca protested. "I just want a pinch. All boys should at least try it, I think".

"They usually do whether they should or not", laughed Pio. "We're getting some anyway, so we'll see about that later".

They made ready to travel light, leaving behind all their heavy gear down in the saddleback. Nearby, in the very lowest spot, lay a large flat rock. Together they turned the rock over, exposing a well-used fire pit with old ashes. From his bag, Peco fished out the leftover acacia firewood and stacked it neatly but made no fire.

"For later" he told the butterflies. "When we have something to roast".

At the setting of the sun, in the shadows of the big cactus, the boys set aside their sombreros and scraped up handfuls of the local earth which they cast over their gear. It was dry up here after a day of wind, and the dust worked quickly. Yero blinked and blinked again. So did Boca. The campsite had disappeared. The saddleback looked exactly as it had when they arrived. Satisfied with that, the boys cast a few pinches at each other, and they disappeared too.

"A bag", said Pio's voice. "Grab an empty bag".

A moment later there was a low, thumping sound and a minor cuss word. Obobo had stubbed his toe on the rock. This was followed by muffled laughter.

"Maybe you're not losing your magic after all", came Peco's merry voice. "That was just clumsy".

Without a sound an empty sack appeared - pulled out of a larger, invisible one. It swung an arc through the air, obviously aiming at something but missing. Then it disappeared too.

"All right then", said Obobo's voice gruffly. "Off we go. Watch your own step, smarty!"

There was no more talk after that, nor any noise at all, and the butterflies correctly guessed the fellows were really gone.

"No use following them anyway", said Boca. "We wouldn't see what they were doing".

"Just as well!" concluded Yero. "Maybe they do leave 'equal value' in trade, and maybe they don't. This way, we can *say* they do".

Very good! This is the correct attitude if you ever happen to travel with boys like these. It's wise not to follow too closely when they're foraging. You won't see anything anyway. If you hear a dog barking that would be about all, and the dog will stop when they cast a pinch of earth in its direction

- earth that smells like pork chops or mutton. That will keep any dog occupied while the boys visit the grocery or dry goods stores.

The boys knew all the villages quite well, and a lot of farms too, with their chicken coops and milking barns. About the only places safe from them would be any place a girl might shop - or liquor cabinets. Fairies learned their lesson about liquor Ages ago and haven't forgotten it. On this particular night they shopped here, there, and everywhere. They had a long list.

While they did not always leave the same 'value' in the strict sense of the word, they at least left something of equal weight, or size, or maybe age: 'Comparable worth' in a broader sense. Rocks might be left in place of chickens, for example. Or a jug of water where there had been milk. Or perhaps an empty snuff can in place of a full one. So, strictly speaking they are not thieves. They take only what they need and often return at night to work off a debt doing odd chores that clearly need doing, like washing a dirty window or watering your plants. Before you judge too harshly, at least consider their poor circumstance. It's true they once had heaps of treasure, but they lost it long ago. Now they live meagerly in the wild, perhaps the poorest of us all. So, if you stroll out to your garden one morning and are surprised to see a whole row of carrots dug up and missing, don't be overly alarmed. If it was fairies, they'll return and make things somewhat right. They're good people. If it was rabbits on the other hand, just get that fence up and quit complaining.

Their last stop was a farm place where Obobo did indeed leave rocks, pound for pound, for two fat hens while Pio went into the barn and skimmed cream off the top of a ten-gallon milk can. He re-filled the can with water and was about to leave when the barn cat started mewing loudly, seeing the ladle in action and smelling the cream. He smelled the fairy too and expected to be fed, and his mewling was likely to wake up the house if he didn't get it. Peco and Obobo came running from the hen house in alarm.

"Just give him some!" whispered Peco. "Here! I'll do it".

While the cat was being fed, Obobo poked around the milk house. They had picked up a treat for El Boca but nothing yet for Yero. He opened a cabinet and found veterinary supplies. A smallish bottle caught his eye between the wound dressings and the injectable medicines. He pulled it out.

"Okay, let's go", Pio called.

"Just a minute! I might take this perfume along for the girl".

Pio looked baffled.

"It says it's 'minty', but I don't have anything to trade. Hey! Put the cat in the cabinet! That's close enough value, and then he won't follow us either".

Pio shook his head about it but went ahead and locked the cat in the cabinet. They opened the door to leave and were greeted by several other cats. The word was getting around fast. These were even louder so Pio reluctantly poured them some of the cream. "There. Let's scram now!" he whispered, but it was too late. Cats were arriving from everywhere, homing in on the mewling and doing a whole lot more of their own. Pio grabbed an old hubcap that hung on the side of a shed and poured all the borrowed cream into it. There would be none after all for their coffee.

They left the farm and tried to skirt the village on the way back, but cats appeared, waiting for them at the city limits. After that, it was a costly retreat all the way up the hill. Every cat in town had heard about the free food and it simply wouldn't do to lead them back to camp. The boys had to give away all the fresh rolls, the bread and cheese, even the baloney - everything except the chickens still clucking away in the sack.

The butterflies heard them coming. There was no mistaking Obobo laboring up a steep slope and the others kept up a crabby grumble. All the mixed noises surmounted the ridgetop and settled into the camp like a small weather disturbance. The boys, nearly invisible still, even after losing some dust, recovered their sombreros and put them back on against the cool breeze. It looked ridiculous: Three hats bobbing in mid-air, arguing which one was most to blame for things gone wrong.

"And the hats most likely the only ones not guilty of something", observed Yero critically.

A match was struck. The hats busied themselves making a fire. In the glow, familiar faces could be guessed at. Then a handkerchief came out and wiped the sweat from Obobo's forehead and face. Presto! There he was, from the neck and up.

"Wipe off your sourpusses!" he growled at the other hats. "I like to see who I'm arguing with!"

More handkerchiefs appeared and got busy, exposing Pio and Peco, but just their faces. Peco had no ears but seemed able to hear well enough and didn't like what he was hearing. Obobo was blaming him for causing all the misfortunes.

"You should never have fed that first cat", he groused. "If you just left her complain the others wouldn't have come".

"Why didn't you say so then?"

"Because you're too stubborn to argue with!"

"That never stopped you before".

It was all a bit confusing to the butterflies but seemingly a lot of loot - or rather, 'borrowed goods' - had been squandered. That much was clear.

"Just so they haven't lost the rest of themselves too", whispered Boca, only half joking.

"Cross fingers on that", replied Yero. "But you know what? They could make an honest living renting themselves out like this for Halloween. Pumpkin heads with sombreros!"

"Shh. They're grumpy enough already. But see? They didn't lose everything".

Peco's face looked into the shopping sack and unseen arms produced blue-jeans bibbed overalls. He held them up to admire, then with no thought for modesty he pulled down his own pants, chaps and all, and nothing dusted underneath. The whole rear area, especially the white cheeks, stood out brightly in the firelight. Obobo's head jumped up and he grabbed out another pair of overalls to cover Peco.

"That's embarrassing!" he scolded. "We've got mixed company here. Go over behind the cactus and clean up a little while you're at it!"

Since it was on his mind Obobo dusted off his own arms and shirt the best he could, dug out the biggest pair of overalls, and headed for the biggest cactus. Pio decided to do the same.

"Wow!" whispered Boca. "You really spooked these guys! I doubt if they ever went behind a cactus before in their whole lives".

"To dress, you mean?"

"Or anything else! They're roughnecks!" There was too much admiration in his voice to please Yero.

"Sometimes I worry that you want to be a roughneck too".

"Sure! Why not? This is the country for it. Like the old cowboys!"

"Here come the cowboys".

They were completely visible now, looking more like suburban gardeners in their spanking new dungarees with creases. And they were nearly too late to save their supper. One chicken had already wiggled out of the sack and the other stuck its head out. Peco grabbed that one by the neck but the other made a break for it - dodging here, there, and back between their legs. Pio dived for it and missed, and then Obobo dived. He caught the bird but there was a sound of glass breaking underneath him. He scrambled to his feet, worried, and watched a wet spot on the bib pocket spread all down the front.

Whatever it was, the chicken didn't like it and tried to escape. Obobo just stopped and began plucking broken glass out of the pocket. Peco moved in quickly to grab the chicken before it got away. In this he was successful, but it left him without a free hand to hold his nose.

"Phew!" he muttered and backed away.

Pio took a sniff and laughed, "Is that the 'minty' perfume? You read the label too fast, 'Bo. It's *liniment*. Liniment is for horses".

The strong veterinary odor overspread the campsite. The butterflies got a good whiff and retreated.

"She doesn't like it, 'Bo!" cackled Pio. "Hey, little sister - it was supposed to be for you!"

Obobo stood dumbfounded at the turn of events. The other boys made a comedy of fanning the fumes away.

"You should've put it on sooner, when the first cat showed up!" giggled Peco. "Then we wouldn't have had any trouble at all!"

That's when Obobo came to life and went for his throat. Peco ducked around the fire to escape and 'Bo stomped off into the darkness without another word, which did help, but a lot of the smell lingered and likely would all evening.

"Well, the fun's over", said Pio, doing his best to get serious. "He'll be mad and hungry as a bear when he comes back. Let's butcher them hens".

Peco made as if he was about to wring their necks right on the spot (which he was), and Yero gasped.

"Don't do that! Can't you just eat the eggs every day?"

"And carry live chickens around in the sack?" said Peco in astonishment. "No! And we ain't going to lead 'em around on little ropes, neither".

"But you were going to hurt them!"

"Nah! They'll be croaked before they feel a thing".

"Don't you have anything else to cook?"

"This is *it*!" declared Pio. "It's all we've got and we're gonna *roast* 'em!"

"But---"

"But *nothing*! We'll butcher 'em where you don't have to watch".

"We'll save a "cluck" for you", laughed Peco. He went off with the hens and Pio followed.

Boca flew after them. "I don't mind!" he said in his best roughneck voice. "Are you going to have snuff too?'

"We're chewing right now", said Pio, and spat expertly into the brush. "Want to try some?"

"Yeah! For sure. I don't want to miss my chance".

"Have you tried it before?" Boca shook his head. "I didn't think so. Tell you what. It might make you sick the first time, especially on an empty stomach. We always have a pinch after supper. You can try it then".

Boca was thrilled, not disappointed. He had worried they might not consider him *macho* enough: Too small, too young, too whatever. Now he pictured himself spitting tobacco juice like an old pro, like Pio! He made a mental note to do it in front of Yero. Yeah, bring it on! El Boca was ready for anything! Except the very next thing.

It happened so fast El Boca didn't faint until afterward. Peco wrung the neck of one hen and stretched it out so Pio could whack it off with a hatchet. El Boca's eyes bulged in surprise. Then the boys quickly repeated it with the other hen. El Boca fell to the ground where they had to let him lie while they finished the job and washed up in a trickling spring some ways down the side of the hill. Next thing El Boca knew, Pio was shaking his leg to revive him.

"You must've taken a bump on the noggin somehow", said Pio. "You've been out for a while". He was back in his old clothes, as was Peco. The new dungarees had gone back in the bag, for special occasions.

"Yeah, I guess so. Not sure what happened". He wished he had some excuse for fainting. Then he felt his head. There *was* a bump. Whew! He rubbed it so they noticed, and felt courage returning.

"And here's the hens, all ready for the fire!" said Peco proudly. He held them out for El Boca to see close-up.

The Butterflies, Yero and Boca

Boca couldn't find any words but at least didn't shrink away. The hens were dressed out whole, very nicely, just like you might purchase at a popular meat counter. Nothing wrong with that! El Boca felt tough again.

Back at camp, they found it deserted. Yero had gone off to perch on a barrel cactus in protest, and of Obobo there was no sign. The boys had no actual spit but simply skewered the birds with long sticks and began roasting them like wieners, propping the stick over a stone and holding the bottom end down with one foot. El Boca sat on Peco's shoulder and studied their spitting techniques - which were very different - so he could decide whom to copy.

Pio spat more often and more accurately. He sucked on his tobacco all the time and shot small wads by pointing his lips at the target, sticking them out like a gun barrel, and expelling the juice with a charge of compressed air. It made a very cool sound and a quick sizzle when it hit the fire.

Peco spat less often, much less; but when he got around to it, he launched a gob so big it fell apart and sizzled like multiple fireworks in the coals. He did it entirely with his lip muscles and made very little noise doing it. The only tip-off was, he leaned forward so it didn't run down his chin, but some always did anyway. It was much less stylish, but he actually quelled the fire right where it landed. That bugged Pio since it was always aimed at his coals, cooling them and maybe adding unwanted flavor to the meat. Understand, please, that tobacco chewers love their tobacco, but they like regular food to eat.

Obobo returned presently, minus the new overalls. The smell of roasting chicken brought him in. He had on his old clothes but still reeked of liniment. He took a seat on the ground opposite the others and glared, daring them to say anything. They only smiled, and when he took exception to that, they just claimed to be glad he was back.

"And the butterflies?" he demanded, determined to find some fault, "Have you offered them any supper yet?" Well, no. They hadn't.

Aha! So there! 'Bo felt better. "*No?* Well, don't trouble yourselves. I'll fix something!" He stood up and called to Yero. "Here, now! There's a bit of this honey left yet". He dug into his personal sack and found the little jar. That did convince Yero to unbend her stiff neck and come, but neither she nor Boca could stand the smell very long. They backed away pretty soon, at a loss how to be polite about it.

"Not very hungry?" said Obobo in surprise. Then he caught on when the other boys grinned and pointed at him. It cost them. 'Bo pulled out his knife and reached across the fire mighty quick for such a big fellow. He stabbed Peco's chicken right off the stick, all nicely browned and done. "Who's laughing now?" he growled and stomped off into the night with his prize.

So, in the end everyone had a nice supper and finished with about the same share as if they had all sat down together. In the afterglow, Pio and Peco put their feet up on stones near the embers and picked their teeth with small chicken bones. It was time for a chew. Peco took out his new can, rapped it smartly with his knuckles, then opened it and took a pinch, which he tucked neatly between cheek and gum, savoring the flavor with his tongue. Pio did the same, and then offered the open can toward the butterflies nearby, much to El Boca's delight. He flew over right away and Yero followed, determined to talk him out of it.

"Now, there's two ways of doing it", explained Pio. "Regular users either put it in their cheeks, like we're doing, or sniff it up their nose. Both are perfectly acceptable, being only a matter of preference. Which would you like to try?"

Yero interrupted with a barrage of warnings about 'dirty habits' and 'turning into a junkie'. El Boca barely heard. He *so* wanted to do it! But now, with Pio actually holding the open can out to him, he couldn't decide which method. He hadn't expected choices. Pio began to withdraw the offering. Yero cheered!

"Wait!" exclaimed El Boca. "I'll try both!"

Pio's eyebrows went up a little at that, but Peco just launched a load of tobacco juice at the embers and grinned. "Let 'im", he said.

Yero flew off to the cactus again in disgust, but El Boca perched on the lip of the can. He studied the contents eagerly but with very little knowledge.

"How much?" he asked.

"If I were you? First time? Just a tiny bit", advised Pio. Peco nodded at this nugget of wisdom, spilling some juice.

El Boca dug a hand into the tobacco, feeling the texture. It was slightly damp and finely ground, which was a relief. As a butterfly, he didn't have room for a whole lot. He went ahead and did it quickly, stuffing a couple grains into his mouth with one hand and another up his nose with the other. He sniffed hard. For a fleeting moment he was glad he did it. "Wow! What a wild ride!" he thought. Then the ride spun out of control. As he told Yero days later, "The top of my head blew off and I felt my brains popping like popcorn. I have no idea how it got back on again. Do you?" "Yes, I saw it all", Yero would answer. "Do you remember when Peco undressed and showed us his white cheeks? Well, he's the one who caught the top of your head and set it back on. Then he squeezed you between those white cheeks to hold everything in place until it stayed, like clamping something with glue".

But all that would sort itself out later. For now, El Boca was caught up in a fit of sneezing. You would think the first frenzied sneezes would dislodge a foreign object and expel it, and probably this did happen. But that leaves no reason for the dozens and dozens of sneezes that followed, unless it might be the nose punishing the rest of the body for being so dumb.

At last the spasms passed, and peace returned to Boca's body, but with it came a nagging thought: What about the snuff in his mouth? It was gone. He dearly hoped he hadn't swallowed it. But of course he had, and soon the expelling of *that* commenced.

Obobo heard the miserable racket and returned to camp. Yero held her breath as best she could and told him everything. He was a little sympathetic, but not a lot. "Same thing happened to me once", he recalled. "It's sort of a 'rite-of-passage for young lads".

The boys kept a few embers going all night but otherwise posted no watch. The saddleback hid the fire from all but the birds, who know better than to bother the fairies. No Jaguars popped up, no other surprises, and everyone except Boca got a good night's sleep.

***

As was their custom on the trail the boys stirred long before dawn, rustling up a pot of black coffee and a dab of acacia honey for their guests. Yero had a fine appetite, and also ate Boca's share without feeling guilty at all. There was the usual amount of early-morning crabbiness among the fellows, but no arguments, nor any talk at all about where they were headed next.

"Which way from here?" Yero finally asked as the fellows poured water on the coals and flopped the big rock over again, covering all traces. Pio pointed to the barrel cacti, all bent over toward the south.

"They point the way", he said. "Always have".

"Oh! Did you do that? Bend them over for a trail marker?" Yero had been curious. Boca too, before the stomach flu.

"No, no. They don't mind very well. Cactus has a mind of its own".

"So they just grew that way?"

"Not that either, little sister".

Pio paused a moment and Yero became aware of the other fellows casting disapproving looks at him. Obobo wagged a big finger.

"They have enough worries already", he cautioned.

"The question deserves an answer", said Pio stubbornly. "He's gone anyway".

"Suit yourself if you know everything", replied Obobo. "We're off to scout ahead". He and Peco, minus packs and gear, slipped away quietly into the pre-dawn.

The Butterflies, Yero and Boca

Boca, still awake, still in misery, fell to retching again - the empty, useless kind. He was bent over, nose almost to the ground on which he squatted. That was good. He would have fallen from any higher perch.

"So, what's the answer?" asked Yero, returning to the question, ever more curious. "I was thinking they might have gotten sick like Boca at one time and couldn't ever straighten up again".

Pio smiled at that and stooped down a moment. "You'll be fine", he encouraged the afflicted one. "Next time it won't hit you near as hard". Boca just moaned.

"No, it wasn't any illness", Pio resumed. "Nor old age, nor anything natural. A dragon came through here long ago on his way south and blew them down in a rush of wind. Nothing can withstand a dragon, underground or above".

"A *dragon*! You don't mean that. They aren't real".

"All *too* real, unfortunately for fairies. This dragon brought our ruin. There were a lot of us still in those days, and the mighty Jaguar warriors were just a wandering tribe. But they curried favor with the dragon - the *Feathered Serpent* they called him - and together they plundered us. With the stolen riches, the Tribe built a great empire, great and cruel.

We were a small nation ourselves then, in our underground realm. Miners mostly, with a knack for finding silver and gold. I won't bore you with the details, but dragons lust for that and the Tribe knew our ways. In a wicked bargain, they set the dragon upon us and shared the spoils. We were doomed. We had no way to fight a dragon. It was soon over, and we were scattered, we who survived. We still don't know who or how many".

"That's terrible! So why are we *following* him?"

"He's gone, just a memory now. But after he finished with us, he turned on the Tribe".

"Good! They deserved it".

"They sure did. But the Priests fed him and tamed him for a while. That was the start of their bloody religion. They sacrificed living people to the beast".

"I hope he ate some of those Jaguars, then. Is that how they died?"

"Sorry, no. It was they who captured prisoners from other tribes, or even took from their own, for dragon fodder. The Jaguars were privileged and untouchable until eventually the dragon turned on *them* too and became our friend. Strange are the tides of war! And that's enough for now. We'll be off as soon as the others return. Do you think El Boca can fly?"

El Boca had at last slipped into merciful sleep and was beginning to snore. Yero fluttered down and unmercifully woke him up again.

"How ya feelin'?" she asked cheerfully.

Boca lifted his head, dropped it again and moaned. Yero went back up. "Hopeless", she reported.

The others returned almost silently and took up their gear.

"Any trouble with cats?" asked Pio.

Peco chuckled. Obobo pretended not to hear. "A couple showed up", reported Peco. "They skedaddled when they smelt 'Pretty Boy' here. Cats won't bother us today".

"It's doing some good", growled Obobo.

Pio turned serious. "Beyond the town, then? What's it like?"

"Even with an early start we likely won't make the island tonight", said Obobo.

"We did last time".

"Well, we ain't getting any younger. But that's not the reason. The bridge is washed out. There's been a flood again".

"Oh, great. And the boat? The little ferryboat? Which side?"

"The other side, as usual. Same little bell on this side. Same little bandido running his same little racket".

"Drat!"

"Don't drat at us. It ain't our fault".

"Sorry. I only meant - why just *him*? There's money in that ferrying! You'd think someone would set up next to him".

"Well, they haven't. And I don't think we've got enough money".

Obobo had the only purse. The boys seldom needed cash. He dumped the contents into his big paw, and they all counted eleven pesos. Too little, for sure.

"Couldn't you swim?" asked Yero. "Or float a log, or a raft?"

That bugged them. They looked at her irritably and reminded themselves that she was just a girl who didn't know much.

"We don't swim", said Pio impatiently.

Other than their stature, it's about the only shortcoming of the boy fairies: Fear of water, especially deep water. Even after centuries up under the sun where streams and ponds are common these three might wade ankle-deep if they could see the bottom, but that's about it. They're not like the girls that way. Never were.

To her credit, Yero kept mum this time about 'wings'. To Boca's credit...well, he had nothing to his credit right now. That would take time.

Chapter 18

Islands in The Sky

"Off we go then", said Obobo. He slipped a fat finger under Boca somehow and got him up onto his shoulder. El Boca's feet scrabbled feebly to hang on and Yero was told to watch him, which she did, but she refused to touch him. They followed a circuitous path down the hill, different from the last - always different from the last so no trodden path would ever lead the curious to the campsite. Dawn was breaking when they reached the outskirts of the village once more. Obobo stayed with the butterflies while the others slipped into town on an errand.

"Where are they going this time? To the bank?" asked Yero. A worry had been growing in her. Court experience had taught her about 'accessories to a crime'.

"Don't fret, they're not after money!" replied Obobo curtly. "We don't 'borrow' money. Not from honest folk, anyway". He was insulted and his tone left no room for further questions.

"The clinic", said a weak voice. It was Boca. "Pio said...to get something for my tummy".

That sounded like a fool's hope but Yero was relieved to see any sign of recovery. It signaled that he might be a smidgen *cleaner*. She reached *way* out and patted his head.

They did return with tummy medicine from the clinic, and a lot more. They had crutches, a white cane, tape and gauze - even an arm sling. Obobo smiled approvingly. Pio pulled out a small bottle of pink liquid and poured some in a plastic spoon for Boca.

"Drink up!" he ordered. "It'll do you good".

"And *this* is for you!" said Obobo meaningfully. He reached down as if to pet a couple yowling, begging cats that had followed out of town. They caught his veterinary scent and bolted.

Boca sipped a little and kept it down. He even perked up for a minute, enough to be curious as the boys all tried out the crutches and joked about them, but it was a short minute. Then he conked out again as they headed off down a public road, deserted at this hour. Obobo put the butterflies under his hat and the crutches on his shoulder and jogged with the fellows to make up some time.

The river came into view off to their right and the road ran next to it down to the bridge a mile below the town. There were signs of a recent flood everywhere. Brush had been flattened and washed into piles. A huge log had ended up across the road and been cut to allow traffic. The ugly tinsel of Big People's trash was snagged and hanging in low branches everywhere. The river had receded a week ago or more, back into its channel, but the water was still high and swift. There was a bridge across, or had been, but the area was poor and remote; few highway funds ever made it this far back into the hills, so the bridge was wooden and temporary, lasting only from one flood to the next.

When the bridge was out, Allandro set up his ferry service. He was clever enough to ferry police and a few local officials free, and in return they discouraged any competition, so he set his fees very high and got away with it - or even higher, if he thought the customer had the money.

The valley floor was still in shadow when they came to the last bend and saw the bridge, or what was left of it. The drive approaches and abutments remained, along with exposed pilings amidstream, but the spans were gone. A short walk path led down to the water's edge where a pole had been set up supporting a bell and chain. When the ferryboat was on the far shore customers had to ring the bell for service. It was always on the far shore because that's where Allandro lived and slept in a homemade shack. He was snoozing now. 'Rush hour' didn't start until later.

The fellows stopped just behind the bend and fixed themselves up. It was pathetic. They wrapped gauze around Obobo's knees, and he took the crutches. Pio got the arm sling and a head bandage, especially puffy around the jaw, and Peco got dark glasses and the cane. It was 'Bo first, then Pio, then the blind one last, hanging on to Pio's belt as they hobbled down the path and rang the bell.

Part 4: The Lure of the Dragon Range

A lad of about eleven or twelve years popped out of the shack rubbing his eyes and hiked down by the abutment yonder where a rowboat was tied. He peered across at them - a distance of about thirty paces had it been dry land.

"How many?" he hollered.

"Three. Patients from the Free Clinic", answered Obobo.

The lad was clearly disappointed. "Got any money?"

"A little, very little. We hoped for charity. We aren't well, not well at all".

The lad was unmoved. "How much you got?"

"Eleven pesos. It's all we have for food".

"That's not enough anyway. Go downriver ten miles. You might get across at Fifty/Fifty Ford. Or you might not. Adios!"

"You would turn away the injured? The blind?"

"Sure. Anyone without money", laughed the lad. But he didn't walk away just yet. "What's in the sacks?"

"Our contaminated clothes. To be burned in the hills".

Allandro decided this deserved a closer look. He jumped into his boat and paddled expertly across, putting into the calm eddy behind the abutment, but not quite ashore in case a fast getaway was called for. Even at this distance, he got a whiff of Obobo.

"Oh, man! Smells like horse liniment! Whadda they give you that for?"

"Bursitis. Gout. Lumbago. I got all of them". Slowly, obviously in pain, Obobo opened the purse so the lad could see as he emptied the contents onto his palm. Eleven pesos.

"I'll take one across for that".

Obobo slowly put the coins back in the purse. "No, we need each other for support. It wouldn't do to be separated". He turned and explained to the others. Pio couldn't seem to hear through the bandages. The blind one appeared to be deaf as well. The three re-formed the rag-tag chain and set off, stumbling up the walk, dragging their sacks.

Allandro studied that last part closely. The bags looked promising. "Wait!" he called. "Show me the old clothes".

Obobo opened his sack and displayed some rags on top. The lad wrinkled his nose and pointed to the others.

"Let's see theirs. You beggars must have something of value!"

Obobo reluctantly pulled them open. Right on top were the brand-new dungarees. Allandro grinned and stood in the boat for a better look. "Old stuff, huh? I'll take those for your fare, plus the pesos".

He beached the boat and waited for them to climb in but only Pio boarded at first, very slowly and unsteadily. Obobo was hampered by the crutches, not knowing what to do about them, and the blind one could only stand helplessly waiting for a hand.

Allandro mumbled a grown-up curse and climbed out to help - at least to toss the bags aboard. The overalls were good quality, expensive! This was going to be a moneymaker. Finally, Obobo managed to climb in, terribly clumsy with the crutches, and turned to help his blind friend, but Peco had started walking the wrong direction. Allandro lost patience and grabbed him, giving him a rude shove toward the boat, just as Peco hoped. It gave him a running start and he leaped aboard, landing safely on the floor as Obobo shoved off hard with a crutch. Allandro stood there like a fool as the boat jumped out into the current. The fairies laughed hilariously and waved their sombreros, calling him a 'cub' and a 'pup'. Boca awoke and grabbed what hair there was to hang on to. Yero took to the air. The lad shook his fist and proved as fluent in profanity as any old-timer. Then the fellows realized they were headed - not across - but downriver. Fast. And they knew nothing about oars.

Obobo and Pio just froze and were useless. Peco, the best fisherman, was a little better around water. Yero rode on the brim of his hat and tried to tell him about the oars, but he grabbed a crutch instead and tried to pole with it, losing it almost immediately in the fast water. He finally took up an oar at her urging when it looked like the boat was turning back to Allandro's side (and him keeping pace along shore), but he tried to use it as a brake. By dumb luck, it behaved like a rudder instead. Peco caught on and was eventually able to beach the boat in a snag on the far shore, where a tree had fallen into the water. He tied up there and the boys crawled on hands and knees along the tree trunk to dry ground. Once there, they recovered their courage instantly and hurried to get off the road, which is what they found themselves on again. The road had resumed on this side of the river. It was full morning now, traffic would soon be moving, and they'd had enough of the Big People for one day, especially the twelve-year-olds.

Peco flung the dark glasses and cane into the river and led the way into the brush. Only when they had put several hills behind did they finally take a break.

"You've followed a blind guide long enough", joked Peco. "One of you can break trail for a while".

Obobo wiped his brow and lifted his hat, allowing El Boca to hop down to his shoulder for better air. 'Bo smiled and complimented the 'guide'. "You did right well for a blind fellow! What's your secret?"

"I was to the clinic. Didn't even need an appointment".

"And that toothache, Pio? You in less pain now, I hope?"

"Much less. They must've put me under. I don't remember nothing".

"What about the broken arm?"

"Just needed exercise, I guess. How about you, 'Bo? What was that ailment again? *Lumbergout*?"

"Ha-ha. Just hope you never get it! It's hard to pronounce".

They had been cheated by young Allandro twice before and thoroughly enjoyed this. Obobo guffawed and slapped his knees that had been so 'inflamed'.

"Best of all, though", Pio remarked, "is how you faked that horse liniment, 'Bo. How'd you turn that trick?"

Only two out of three thought that was funny. Obobo straightened up without a word and took the lead as Peco had suggested, leaving the others to catch up.

The brush was different here than back at the Haunt, yet much the same. Here were mesquite thorn trees instead of the cat's claw, taller but still small as trees go. The thorns were just as sharp, just as many, but lacked the nasty hook. Overall (or underall, as fairy folk go) it was less dense and tangled and responded more readily to their wishes. A lot of the trees still held their fruit, their bean pods, which the boys obviously coveted, having missed breakfast. But the pods were stubborn and clung to their twigs with strong stems, only wiggling when the fellows pointed fingers at them. They would have to climb a tree.

They had done so on other trips through here, but the boys differed from the girls as climbers too, being less nimble in the greenery. So, they watched for a suitable tree and presently came to one: Less twiggy and more open inside, with plenty of ripe pods way out on the ends of the branches. Surprisingly, Obobo and not one of the smaller fairies unslung his gear and prepared to do the climbing, setting Boca carefully on a low twig. He clambered easily up into the branches for a fellow his size, but then closed his eyes. Wiggling branches made the boys almost as nervous as water. Nevertheless, he tiptoed out along a branch - steadying himself with another - until the branch sagged under his weight. At that point, he re-opened his eyes and inched farther until the pods drooped close to the ground where the others could pick them. They would've done more branches but 'Bo got a thorn in his heel, yelped, and fell off the branch, which was only a foot off the ground by then anyway. He suffered no further injury, but breakfast had to be put off while they extracted the broken thorn.

He needed help doing it because of the awkward location, and it was a tossup who complained more: Obobo with the wound, or Peco with his knife, having to put up with the smell of Obobo's feet. It bled plenty and Peco pronounced that 'good', but they had used up all the bandages back at the ferry so antiseptic would have to suffice, and it stung. Yero couldn't read the label very well on the small bottle, but it looked more like t-e-q-u-i-l-a than a-n-t-i-s-e-p-t-i-c. Still, all was well when it ended well, and Pio served breakfast.

The pods had to be sliced open, a small matter, but the next step surprised the butterflies. Pio shucked out the beans and threw them away. It was the spongy inside surface that made the boys drool. They turned the pods inside out and gnawed the stuff like frosting off a cake.

"Sweet", said Pio after a few pods, and offered one to the butterflies. "A favorite of ours. We sometimes live on it for days at a time".

"Thank you very much", said Yero politely. "But we can't gnaw like you can".

"Oh, I forget that. Here, I'll squeeze you a little". He squished the pod hard and got no real juice but a wet coating at the edges, enough to taste. Boca tried it first since he had the emptiest stomach, and just kept tasting. Yero liked it too.

Peco got on Obobo's shoulders and picked a good many more pods, but the boys were in a hurry and stowed them for the trail. They weren't happy with the chances of reaching their destination before dark. 'The island', was all they said about it, and moved out at a brisk pace. There was no account taken for Obobo's sore foot and he didn't ask for any. Fairy boys can ignore a lot of pain when they have to, and they'll tell you that's another difference from the girls (if you bother to listen). It might be so, or it might be that all fairies are very quick healers because they have to be.

"I haven't seen any water", whispered Yero after a while, "so we aren't even close to the island. How're you doing?"

Boca just nodded, flying next to her again. The Rasha La are fast healers too.

***

The hills gave way to larger, ever-steeper ones, always with a narrow valley or deep gully between them. Oak trees appeared between the groves of mesquite and there were cool springs in the deeper gullies, but they barely paused at these and gnawed the rest of the pods on the march, bypassing even the easiest climbing trees now in favor of speed. At every clearing Yero watched for a lake or river but there were none. Privately she had doubts about the direction they were going.

"Wouldn't you think we should seek lower ground?" she whispered. "That's where islands *are*, down on the water somewhere".

"Why don't you ask them?"

"They'll probably have some simple answer and I would be embarrassed".

"So what? I've been embarrassed plenty and they haven't kicked me out of the gang".

"Well! They excuse you for anything because you're a boy!"

"Being a boy isn't always so wonderful. I had to try that snuff and look what happened".

"You didn't *have* to!"

"Yero, you don't get it. All boys have to do stuff like that. We're protecting the girls. We make those mistakes, so you don't need to".

It must have been comforting to be in the company of such heroes, but Yero didn't say anything.

They went through one last very deep gully, almost a canyon, and climbed again, higher than before. They came to a different kind of mesquite - a little shorter and thornier maybe, but the main difference was the pods, which were twisted and corkscrewed. Here the fellows took a break and picked a lot of the odd-shaped things, making a pile on the ground. Peco cast a pinch of dust on them and Yero expected them to open and the beans to pop out, but it wasn't dramatic at all. The magic simply relaxed the twist so they could be stretched out and sliced open. Obobo squeezed the very first one for the butterflies and then the fellows went to work on the pile with gusto.

Maybe there was more juice in these, or maybe Obobo just squeezed harder, but there was lots of the honey-sap and this was even sweeter. Yero had her fill after a few minutes and went up above the thorn canopy to have a look around. Just as she thought, their direction of travel would take them nowhere but up, though clouds obscured the view.

A pair of juvenile Viceroys happened by and made a U-turn when they saw her, cruising past a second time for a better look. They dipped their wings and made a third pass, close up.

"Hey, doll-face! What's happening?" said one.

"Hey, shorty. Nothing's happening with you!"

The Viceroys laughed and whistled.

"Do you live around here?" asked Yero, just to be polite.

"Sure. This is our home", said one.

"At least we *have* a home", said the other. "That's more than you can say!"

They laughed at their wit and flew off. Yero went back down, disgusted. The fairies were done with lunch and ready to take a chew. Peco looked purposely over at Boca, but he was looking the other way, pretending to study something. Yero joined him.

"Smarties upstairs", she fumed, and told him about the Viceroys, especially their parting remark. That hurt.

"I dunno", said Boca. "There isn't any help for it. Anyway, we find a different home every night, don't we? It's risky, but I kind of like the adventure. Did you tell them to shove a thorn up their—"

"Boca! No! You've been around these fellows too long".

"Ha! That's where you're wrong. They're full of good ideas that I haven't even tried yet. The trick is to pick up the habits that work best for you. Some don't".

"So I've noticed".

Boca laughed. "Yeah, tobacco didn't work. But *cussing*, now! Cussing might be just the right habit for me, but I haven't decided to take it up for sure. I'm still listening".

Yero turned away, at a loss for words. The boys slung on their gear. "Let's get a move on!" said Obobo. "We need to reach the clouds before dark". They had picked a lot more pods while she was upstairs, and his sack was bulging with them. Fine. But where was the water? Where was the island? She finally asked.

"Don't worry. You'll see", said Obobo.

That was all. Nothing! Then they were off again, putting the mesquite behind and climbing higher into stands of oak and even pine. By degrees, without realizing, they entered a layer of cloud. A thin mist gradually surrounded them, limiting visibility. It energized the boys and they redoubled their pace. The butterflies labored to keep up.

The mist thickened more and Obobo, the rear guard, looked back regularly to be sure they followed. Finally, he stopped and collected them on his arm, then set off at a run. The oak forest blurred, becoming all pine as the mist closed in around them, and Yero suddenly guessed the mist *was* the clouds; it's what they were made of.

It grew dark within the cloud and the butterflies felt Obobo waving away branches that only he could see. Drips splattered them. Then, almost suddenly, the light came back. It wasn't night after all, not yet. There was the sun to the west, still setting. They had come out above the clouds, above the trees too. It was colder. 'Bo climbed on toward a crest where Pio and Peco stood waiting. In a minute they reached the summit.

"We're on top of a mountain!" said Yero in amazement.

"We call it an island", said Pio. "An island in the sky. See? There is another."

All the world appeared white, a vast sea of cloud stretching to the horizons, but they were on higher ground above the sea. To the southeast across the 'sea' was indeed another island, and possibly more, fading into the distance.

The boys went to the highest ground while it was still light and marked the exact direction of the next 'island', to get a bearing. Once they got a feel for it, they never strayed their course through the wilderness along the way.

"We might as well get a fire going", said Obobo then. "It should be safe enough back around the north side".

They retraced their steps a little way and scrambled down into a fissure - the deepest of several ancient fissures that split the mountaintop - and found a nice shelter from the icy breeze.

"Any wood left?" asked Obobo. "There should be".

There was. Peco drew forth a bundle of sticks from a cleft where they had been stashed another time and remained undisturbed. The same could not be said for another cache nearby, an expected store of food.

"Drat!" exclaimed Pio. "Animals got into the freezer".

Here on the north face there was ice year around in the deepest clefts. Long ago, the fairies had carved out a niche in it to keep perishable items fresh indefinitely. At each visit they would thaw and use up the old food, replenishing the 'freezer' with something new. They did put the usual spell on the niche so it looked like the rest of the ice, but it wasn't sure protection against a keen nose - or heavy claws.

"Bear, I'm sure", reported Pio. "Honey and jelly are gone". He held up small, empty jars and shreds of metal lids that had been chewed off and scowled at a chewed biscuit lying on the ground.

"Anything left at all?" asked Obobo.

Pio peered in, but the cubby was a mess of snow and ice chunks. He reached in, fumbling around with bare fingers, and found something. His face lit up. "My bread!" he said happily.

The others groaned. Pio fancied himself a baker but nobody else did. He did know the basics well enough and produced baked goods, but not the kind that people called for. His were a bit 'crusty', to say no more. He had stashed a batch of his finest biscuits here the last time up - being encouraged by the others at the time - and here they still were with hardly a scratch on them. What luck! It was a baker's dozen and he dug them out now, one after another, as pretty as the day he baked them. He picked up the chewed one too and studied it with new interest.

"Even this would still be good inside", he predicted.

"Only because the bear couldn't bite into it", mumbled Peco.

"What did you say?"

Peco turned away and bit his lip. "A *lucky thing* the bear didn't bite into it", he answered.

"Yes, it *is* lucky! These are very nutritious. Whole grain".

"Fix the spell and put 'em away for next time", suggested Obobo. "We've got all the mesquite fruit to eat".

"No! Biscuits should be eaten fresh".

"Well, they're not fresh. They're a year old".

"Fresh *frozen*! These are perfectly preserved. They'll thaw out nicely. Peco, what are you waiting for? Let's have a fire!"

The others knew better than to argue about his baked goods. Their strategy was simply to keep the baking to a minimum, throwing up objections such as 'lack of proper firewood', 'lack of ingredients', 'spoilt' ingredients, or 'bakery smell in the wind'. Failing that, they tried to excuse themselves from the tasting later with sudden 'toothaches', 'sore throats', or even just 'dirty hands'. They had learned how to kick Pio's little wood stove at the right moment to make the 'chef-d'oeuvre' fall, although they quit that when Pio insisted they eat the solid bread-cakes anyway. Pio even began toting his stove on the trail to distant campsites, but his career as a master baker suffered a setback when a big rock rolled down the hill one night and crushed the stove. Owing to that natural disaster they had been free for months from Pio's 'armadillo' bread - until now.

Peco went ahead and made a nice fire. Obobo scavenged some windswept grasses to sleep on later, and Pio stacked his biscuits carefully by the fire to thaw, safely back far enough so no accident could happen.

"Well, they'll never thaw like that", remarked Obobo. "You have to put 'em closer".

"No. If they're slow about it, we'll just have 'em for breakfast instead".

"They won't be thawed then either. It takes a while to warm a rock clear through. Now, don't get mad! They're frozen hard as rocks. You can't argue that".

He couldn't, but it got his suspicions up. No way would he push them closer now.

"'Bo is right", put in Peco. "They'll never thaw, not that far away. Anyhow, the wood is short. It'll be an Indian fire tonight. We'll all have to get close to be warmed clear through".

Yes, fairies joke about that like anyone else. It's in contrast to 'White Man's fire', which is too hot and burns your face, while your rear is still freezing. There's a traditional 'Fairy' campfire as well. The size varies but gives off almost no telltale smoke and burns up completely.

The others ignored Pio and broke out the mesquite pods. Obobo squeezed one again for the butterflies and (after quietly nudging the biscuits a few inches toward the fire) Pio eagerly joined them. The boys were hungry but proved they could gnaw the juicy pods without a pause in the conversation. However, all the water had been drunk on the march and there would be no early morning coffee unless they melted ice, so Peco got busy with that. Then at last they relaxed with their tobacco in the afterglow of a journey well begun, and Yero saw a chance to ask a question or two.

"There's still no sign of Atel", she ventured, "but she could find us here if anyone could, don't you think?"

"She will, if she's anywhere near", answered Pio. Yero was encouraged. The boys were getting used to a girl grabbing her share of the conversation.

"And if she doesn't? What next?"

"She has till morning, so don't get antsy, little sister". They had all taken to calling her this since they decided they were stuck with her.

"But suppose she doesn't by *then*. Will we be off to that next 'island', as you call them?"

"Yes, if you have to know. Counting this one there are three in all, before the Long Mountains. We'll be island-hopping for a few days".

"And then what?"

Pio glanced up at her in irritation, perched next to Boca on Obobo's hat brim. "You don't need to know that yet, so pipe down. I'm trying to enjoy my chew".

He clammed up except to spit his tobacco juice. Yero persuaded Boca to ask the same question, just generally, to whoever felt like answering. Finally, Obobo did. He was in a mellow mood by now with his own chew, toes wiggling contentedly by the fire, and he launched into a rambling answer.

Nothing was decided yet, or could be, except the plan to set out for the second 'island' in the morning, and even that depended on what might happen overnight. The main goal was Manino, but anything could happen from one minute to the next. The butterflies' whole journey must've been like that anyway, wasn't it? So, no big deal. If they wanted his best guess, he didn't expect to see 'Her Ladyship' again on this trip. Not any time soon, for sure. If she was gone, she meant to be gone.

"So, you're *stuck* with us?" asked Yero.

"More like you're stuck with *us*", chuckled Obobo. "*She's* the best. We've got troubles of our own, and you've landed in the middle of them".

"Those Jaguars?"

"For sure. It throws everything into doubt. We'll go from one island to the next, keeping our eyes open. If we get as far as the Long Mountains, we'll have to choose one side or the other, going south. The Rasha La always take the eastern side. Less harsh, more food, especially water. It's the route we favor too, with a string of safe camps we used to use. But we don't trust much of anything right now.

The western side would likely be safer from our enemies, but the ordinary dangers are unknown. It's a wilderness we aren't familiar with". Obobo glowered at the fire. "The Jaguars will be waiting somewhere, though. They want what we have. They won't rest until they get it". He dipped into his snuff can again and chuckled suddenly. "Their masters wouldn't permit them to rest anyway - but *I'm* going to!" And with that he leaned back very comfortably.

For his part, El Boca had decided to let such things take their course. The question bugging him was: When would Obobo spit? He couldn't recall seeing this and dearly wished to. He had decided to take up spitting, if not actual tobacco chewing, and was pursuing the study. Pio and Peco were good role models but he suspected Big 'Bo might show them both up. Finally, he asked Obobo to do it.

"I don't spit", said the big fellow. "I swallow the juice".

"Oh", said Boca. His stomach suddenly felt funny. "I think I'll cozy up to the fire", he managed to say, and fluttered down to perch on the biscuits. Yero joined him there.

"I'm glad you've sworn off tobacco", she began and then wished she hadn't said the 'S' word, but Boca didn't seem to notice. He just nodded absently and closed his eyes. Yero changed the subject and continued quickly, worried that he might fall asleep. She had things on her mind.

"We're really lucky, Boca! These fellows have scores to settle with - gosh! - *lots* of old enemies down south, but I doubt they ever would've set out unless Atel asked them to - unless *we* showed up - don't you think?" She made sure Boca nodded again to show that he was listening.

"It's a different kind of journey, on the ground like this, and I think our chances are good with these fellows, but I miss Atel. I'm worried those Jaguars got her".

That roused Boca a little. "How? They can't fly".

"Who knows what they can do? Especially in the dark? They're ghosts and they can reach through to this side. You heard that part".

"You're worried over nothing. They're scared of fire and she would figure some way to fry 'em. Forget it".

Okay. I'll quit talking about it anyway. But speaking of fire puts me in mind of these biscuits. My feet are like ice from this one. They aren't thawing at all".

"Tell Pio, then".

"Oh, no! I'm not getting into the middle of *that*".

She didn't have to. Peco said something more. Then Obobo, then Peco again. Pio finally turned the biscuits so the other side faced the little fire.

"That won't do nothing", scoffed Peco. "Turn 'em all you want! They're just too far back!"

Pio finally relented and pushed them close enough to end the bickering, which also suited the butterflies perfectly, and the fellows settled down then to get some sleep. Yero talked on and the bread warmed enough so a wisp of bread smell, pleasant even to the butterflies, reached Pio's nose as he slept (and snored, like the others). His nose and lips twitched eagerly between snores, but he kept on snoring. They all did. It got so loud the butterflies had to shout at each other.

"I'm sure Pio wouldn't listen", said Yero, "but I think I know why his crust gets so hard. I think he bakes it too long. You should tell him".

"No, Yero. He would guess you put me up to it. Besides, you could be wrong".

"If I'm off, it's only by a few degrees".

"Ha-ha. Maybe so, but I'm serious. It could be he's just putting something on them that he shouldn't".

"That's called 'basting'. Anything else you need to know?"

"Ha-ha. Okay, what did he baste these with?'

"Different things", replied Yero, enjoying the moment. "If he's as good a baker as he thinks he is, it would be something the bread would *like* to be covered with, like butter or honey. Maybe even caramel if he had some on hand".

"What if he didn't have those on hand? What if he put something on that the bread didn't like? I bet the bread would form a hard shell to protect itself".

"But a good baker would never do such a thing!"

"Pio might. He chews tobacco".

"What are you saying, Boca?" Yero suddenly felt uncomfortable standing on the biscuit.

"He probably spit on the biscuits to brown them. Snuff is brown".

Yero bailed off the biscuit and landed on Obobo's hat, wiping her feet. El Boca followed and thought he saw Obobo open one eye, just a crack. Or maybe not. But an accident occurred then. Obobo rolled over in his sleep and an errant foot pushed the whole pile of biscuits into the fire. It made no noise, and no one woke up. The butterflies were alarmed and Yero said they had better wake Pio, but that didn't happen either. In the middle of a snore, Obobo reached up in his sleep and curled his hat brim so they were folded inside. 'Bo slept that way for the rest of the night and the butterflies finally drifted off too.

Pio awoke first in the pre-dawn. The coals were nearly out. He fumbled around for a mesquite stick to stoke them but looked quickly back at the coals. His biscuits - they were gone! Burnt down to little embers, except three, and those were smoldering! He cursed loud enough that it awoke everyone, but no one was close enough to be obviously guilty.

"What's the matter?" asked Peco. He looked genuinely surprised. Pio looked hard at Obobo who was yawning and shaking his head in sympathy.

"It was you!" hissed Pio.

"Now don't go accusing people", replied 'Bo. "It was you who set 'em too close, and then went to sleep and left 'em there".

Pio opened his mouth to answer, then remembered the smoldering ones and turned to save them, scraping off ashes and a few hot coals. "I'll keep *these*", he vowed, "and enjoy a nice breakfast later when no one else does!"

The others did a decent job of looking disappointed and busied themselves making coffee and burying the ashes and coals afterward. Pio was right about one thing. There was no more food except his burnt biscuits, and the mesquite groves with their delicious pods were all behind them now. But the thought of food recalled past trips to mind as they sipped their coffee, and a new catchword came up: 'Agave', some sort of food plant in the wild. Neither Peco nor Obobo looked overly concerned about starving to death. Pio finally sat down with them and took the last of the coffee with the grounds and gnawed a biscuit while the others reviewed what they remembered of the trail ahead.

There was a big river between this mountain and the next, but the bridge was modern and likely in fine shape. No worries there. On the other hand, the valleys were increasingly populated with the Big People and they would need to take extra care, especially after the trouble with Allandro. He would've squealed no doubt, and the police would be on the lookout. The boys filled a small box with dust, just in case, and slung on their gear once more.

The way down the mountain should have been faster, but boy fairies are rather like bears in steep terrain. They find it easier to go up than down. Then a problem arose with the expected food source. They found agave plants among the trees but they had clearly been harvested by the Big People, obviously for the bulb - the fat core of the plant where the juice was. The juice when boiled down made a delicious caramelly syrup popular in these parts. Also, when refined a bit further, it was the basic ingredient of an alcoholic drink even more popular. It was mostly for the latter purpose that men scoured the hills for it.

About mid-morning, the party neared the river and populated areas, and was forced, like water down a funnel, into the common traffic as all roads joined into one big thoroughfare heading for the bridge. It was all manageable. They had crossed the bridge before in broad daylight. But there were risks. Among so many Big People they much preferred to simply dust themselves and slip through unseen, avoiding the usual curiosity about their ears and hairy feet. They sometimes wore simple disguises, but today - after the ferry business - it seemed extra-wise to stay unnoticed. A small problem came up about that. The dust they had brought didn't match the local dirt very well, or the pavement either. However, pedestrian traffic was heavy, and their faint outlines should be lost in all the motion. A second risk was just bad luck: There was roadwork on the bridge. It was down to one lane, and a police officer was stationed there directing traffic. The fairies did what they could, dusting themselves and their gear, and waited in the ditch for some pause in the traffic, but it never came.

Part 4: The Lure of the Dragon Range

"We don't have all day", grunted Obobo finally. He climbed up onto the highway and everyone followed, including two stray dogs. Vehicle traffic at least wasn't dangerous today. People walked everywhere, even in the traffic lanes, taking advantage of the slow work-zone speed limit with the policeman enforcing it. Drivers honked their horns and steered impatiently around pedestrians but the fairies, now trailed by half a dozen curious dogs, had no trouble picking their way through until they approached the bridge and its walkway.

Luckily, a pedestrian detour walk, a narrow one with a single board railing, had been attached to the side of the bridge during the project, but it was crowded. The town was large, partly on one side of the river, partly on the other, and the bridge was crowded almost all the time. There was no help for it. The fellows (with about ten dogs behind them now) ducked onto the walkway and dodged Big People as best they could, removing their sombreros at the last moment to avoid bumping anyone. All might have gone well had not the mayor come along on his golf cart at the wrong moment.

Traffic unfortunately had jammed on the bridge despite the officer's best efforts, and the mayor - not used to waiting on anyone - turned his cart onto the walkway and laid on the horn, stampeding pedestrians back toward the fairies. One of them, a frightened lady already fingering her prayer beads, spotted the boys' undusted ears and the tops of their heads right in front of her. She screamed and pointed. The policeman blew his whistle and approached the disturbance. The mayor speeded up in frustration. Everyone and every dog jumped the curb onto the bridge proper as the mayor sped by. The policeman saluted and someone else screamed, just behind him.

Exactly where he had stood all morning at his post was now a circle of dogs, some barking and some wagging their tails, all looking toward the center. Worse yet, the fairies' camouflage failed somewhat against the fresh blacktop. It was bizarre. Everyone pointed and shouted.

"It's the ferry thieves!" hollered the policeman. "Stop them!"

Yes, the fairies rhymed with their own crime. They could smile about that later. Just now, a whole lot of unfriendly hands were grabbing for them.

"Feed the dogs!" shouted Peco and cast some 'bait' into the air. It was meant for the dogs, but everyone likes pork chops. A riot ensued. The butterflies, tagging along safely above the fray, lost all track of their friends. The dogs went crazy searching for mouthwatering chops that must be right under their noses. Grabbing hands grabbed nothing as grabbers struggled to keep their feet in the melee, except one man who got hold of Obobo's hat and a large woman who got hold of his buttocks. The hat lost its dust, became visible, and remains a mystery to this day; but the other thing drew a loud protest, and the entire affair was eventually accepted as a 'Duende' sighting. These are common in that part of the world, but it might have been the only genuine one in years.

There were other minor bumps and collisions but the fairies escaped, crawling under a truck and scampering off the bridge and up the road into a canyon beyond city limits, but it would be hours before the traffic jam was unsnarled and the bridge thoroughly inspected and declared safe. Meanwhile, varying accounts of the incident spread through both sides of town and the citizenry went on alert, taking up everything from arms and crucifixes to garlic and mirrors. The siren sounded and church bells rang. Just around the first hill beyond the town, the fairies sat down off the road and laughed until their ribs began to ache and they remembered they'd had no breakfast.

"The sad part is, we won't be borrowing any groceries there today", said Obobo. "Or anything else either", he added regretfully, squinting at the sun and rubbing the top of his head. The curly hair was thinning noticeably up there, thin enough to sunburn. He dusted himself off while he was at it. They all did. Half their dust had been lost anyway.

"No fresh groceries", agreed Peco. "But there might be *other* groceries to be had, if you remember". Pio made a face. They all knew what Peco meant. The town dump.

They had visited it before, naturally. Some folks throw away valuable stuff in case you didn't know. Everyone likes to rifle through a dump, and these fellows had picked through many. But this dump, just outside a prosperous town, was usually rewarding. It was only a little way further up the road where the canyon floor widened out. A bulldozer had cleared quite an expanse, years earlier, and still remained parked nearby to bury the trash and garbage periodically. Luckily for 'treasure hunters' (several were picking through the piles already when the fairies arrived) nothing had been buried for weeks, or even months. A shiny, newer pickup was backed up to the heap and a respectable-looking man was tossing his bags of trash off the tailgate. He cast disapproving looks at the rag-tag treasure hunters who gathered round with interest, only waiting for the gentleman to leave before tearing into his personal stuff. That's how it works. Your trash belongs to everyone as soon as it hits the ground, so don't leave your name on anything.

The gentleman left and the treasure hunters moved in. The fairies arrived and detoured around them to the far end. Obobo felt a pang of envy as one of the 'thrift shoppers' hoisted a large sweatshirt with only a few stains. But the boys soon found their own treasures.

Very early in the mornings the big bakery hauled out their old, stale goods and dumped them way in back where the boys knew to look. There was a trove today, quite a pile of pastries and baked goods - maybe not 'bakery' fresh, but 'fresh to the dump'. Peco chased off a couple rats with a stick and the boys commenced to fill up their sacks. Even Pio liked the pastries, but he turned a professional nose up at the bread, calling it 'boughten'.

The bakery goods turned out to be the only thing of value today. Obobo did dig out some old clothes but they were the kind that should be burned. He tore off a piece of one rag to wrap his balding head against the sun, and then it was time to leave. A municipal trash truck was coming up the road piled high with who-knows-what, and a small caravan of treasure hunters was following it. The fairies took their leave privately, up a dry run toward the head of the canyon, the direction they wanted to go anyway.

It was all uphill from there. The next mountain had exposed 'roots' like a tree: Long, wooded ridges leading up to and buttressing the tall peak from all sides. They found a well-worn trail when they got to the nearest ridgeline and the fairies studied it closely before following it. Animals of many kinds had recently been on the pathway, but there was no large carnivore sign of recent evidence. The party struck off up the long incline, spread out somewhat so their eyes and ears weren't confused by each other. Peco, the best woodsman, led the way up ahead with Pio as rear guard. The main reason for this arrangement was Obobo's snacking which held a lot of his attention but shouldn't matter if he was in the middle. At his invitation, the butterflies rode on his shoulders again and tried to eat some jelly from a roll. It was a gentlemanly offer and tasted good, but they could only lick at it. It was pretty hardened.

They decided instead to forage in the open woods and found mallasha - or a close cousin - on the dry slopes, especially in the more open spots. It didn't resemble the usual variety except for the attractive smell. The flowers were white for one thing, the leaves more like grass; but the taste was very familiar. For several minutes they busied themselves trying every blossom on a number of plants.

"I've been worried about our poison", Yero confessed. "It must be getting weak. It's a long time since we've had this".

"Maybe it won't help. It's white, like it has nothing in it".

"I think it does. I think I can taste the poison. It's the last bit in each blossom that isn't as sweet".

"That's just moth spit. It's heavier and goes down---"

"Boca! You know I don't like that talk!"

"Sorry. Really, this time. I don't want to spoil a feast".

"Thank you. But there might be something else to worry about. If the mallasha is all white down this way, will we fade?"

"You mean our orange color?"

"Yes. And maybe more than that. Like the fellows".

"What about them?"

"They're fading. Not very much, but sometimes their fingers or their noses are fuzzy, even when they aren't trying to disappear".

"That's just dirt, Yero".

"Maybe, but the girls had trouble with fuzziness too, remember? And the fellows grumble about 'slipping'. That's the same as fading".

"Well, we won't fade. Our color is burnt in, remember?"

"That's on the outside. What if we fade on the inside? Those Jaguars saw us. I know they did. I don't want to make it easier for them".

"Well, I'm just going to eat all I can. It's bound to help. The more we eat the stronger we'll be, if nothing else".

"I guess that's true. Until we get too fat".

"If you do, you can wear Obobo's hand-me-downs".

Yero laughed. "He'll soon have some. He's eating himself out of his clothes as we speak".

"Yeah. But he's eating on the go, when I think about it. They were all going pretty fast. We better go too".

They went, not without a few last sips, and found they were quite a way behind. The ridge was reasonably straight and the path clearly visible up ahead but empty except for a shadow, a fast cloud maybe, and that was fleeting. They hurried for a while - a gear that most people never see in butterflies - knowing they must be gaining, but all they saw up ahead was the shadow again.

"What is that?" whispered Yero. "It's following the trail".

"Can't tell. Looked brown".

"I thought so too. Let's go faster".

They caught up to the shadow as it caught up to the fairies. Obobo was taking a turn at rear guard, still nibbling more and guarding less than he should. He never heard the puma behind him. As it crouched to leap for him, three things happened in rapid order:

1) Yero and Boca dodged in front of the puma's face as he leaped, and...

2) ...he knocked them silly and out of the way, which threw off his leap somewhat, so...

3) ...as Obobo reached down to dig out another sweet roll the cat sailed past him ripping off his head scarf, but not his head. The puma spun in mid-air, screaming, and landed in front of him ready to pounce again.

Fairies have nothing in their bag of tricks to tame a bloodthirsty mountain lion. They have to do it the old-fashioned way, but at least there were three of them and only one lion. As the big cat crouched to spring, Peco grabbed his tail and cut off the tip with his knife. The cat spun around spitting and screaming, and Obobo grabbed the tail and cut off a few more inches. When the cat spun to face *him*, Pio had a go with his knife, leaving now less than half the original length.

The butterflies recovered and re-entered the fray just as the beast turned to face the smaller fairies again. But he was learning from his mistakes. He only faked at them and spun back to go for Obobo. It might have worked but he got the annoying butterflies in his face a second time. He stopped and swatted at them fiercely with a paw, and that was his last mistake. Pio and Peco whacked his tail down to the nub. That was enough for the mighty lion. He whined in pain, knowing something shameful had happened back there, but was too panic-stricken to check it out. With a tremendous leap, and one more after that, he was gone.

"I saw it all!" shouted Peco and ran to see about the butterflies. El Boca was already upright, bruised but nothing broken. Yero hadn't been as lucky, obviously. One wing was bent back at an unnatural angle.

"The cat might've got you, 'Bo", said Pio, "but the kids got in his face".

'Bo picked them both up with a finger and looked to Yero's injury. It wasn't an open wound, and that was something, but it was serious. Something broken, that looked obvious. She said it didn't hurt as bad if she didn't move it, so she just held it crooked.

"I don't know what to do", she said matter-of-factly. "I'll only be a burden now".

"A small one, as burdens go", said Obobo, raising them up to eye level. "I'll carry both of you for now. That's the least I can do".

"Might work to everyone's advantage", decided Pio. "That's his favorite snacking hand. A little less of that won't hurt".

Everyone smiled a bit, even Yero; but there was a lot to think about. None of the boys was really a small animal doctor, to say nothing about butterflies. They gathered up their gear, some of it blood-spattered. Peco kept the end of the tail with the tuft on it for a souvenir. They left the other pieces in a pile on the path for anyone to see and puzzle about.

"He can have them back for all I care", said Pio. But I doubt if he'll come looking anytime soon".

They moved up the trail, this time with Obobo in the middle again. The ridge steepened as it approached the mountain proper and they caught glimpses of higher elevations through the trees.

Yero was having regrets. She'd been struck by a claw and wished now that she had avoided it.

"I saw it coming and dodged", she whispered to Boca. "But I dodged right into the next one. If I could do it over, I'm sure I could miss them both".

"I did miss them, or they missed me", said Boca. "But only by accident. The paw hit me in the behind".

"That's good. You need more spankings anyway".

That's as far as she ventured into self-pity. Butterflies and other creatures of the wild don't go in for that much. It doesn't help. As a rule, survival is up to them alone. If they have friends who'll slow down to their speed, they consider themselves lucky. Yero considered herself doubly lucky.

***

The ridge broadened and merged with the mountain about halfway to the summit. The well-worn path melted away and they picked out their own, bearing toward the right, the western slope. It was drier on that side even coming up the ridge, and that was the favored habitat of the white mallasha. Obobo picked sprigs of it for them as they climbed, even digging up a whole plant for later, with a big root-ball so it wouldn't wilt right away; and he entertained them with old tales and glimpses of history.

"This was our 'sentinel mountain'", he said. "Our watchtower, in the days when we helped kids escape north. A fair number of us had regrouped by that time and at least one was always on duty up there..." (he waved toward the summit, still high above) "...to watch for signals. Our brothers down south kidnapped the condemned youngsters and ran the biggest risks, but we all had a turn at that, and everyone helped with the long escape route. There were lookouts on other mountains too, down that way, all of us watching for signals. The guides used mirrors and when a signal came, we sent a relief party to guide the next leg of the route. Everything depended on vigilance. We never replied with our own mirror, lest it be seen by our enemies".

The others called a halt near a water seep to fill canteens and grab a bite of lunch. Most of the good stuff was in Obobo's sack and he had to give up some of his sweet rolls. Yero requested some of the hard jelly, the darkest variety, and employed it like a sucker. Boca dunked his and slurped off the water. He wasn't admitting to Yero's theory about fading, but he took the dark jelly too.

Then they were off again, up an ever-steeper incline. The trees - all pines at this altitude - became shorter and sparser until there was nothing but a few ground-hugging junipers. The soil itself, which had been interspersed with boulders, became just bare rock interspersed with the boulders.

As the sun sank toward the horizon they struck the summit path, a well-worn trail zigzagging upwards through the stones. It was used by weekend climbers now, especially in summer: Big People who had no idea how old the path was and climbed just for fun. Who else but the Big People would beat such a path to the top of an inhospitable peak, just to casually mention it over cocktails?

Part 4: The Lure of the Dragon Range

It looked anything but inviting. The cold wind picked up in the open and the butterflies could see snow on the ground up ahead. Obobo offered to go back with them to the shelter of trees while the others went up and got a bearing on the next day's march, but butterflies are curious. Who wouldn't be, now? With the tiptop of a mountain so near? They politely declined. Boca even took to the air again to show his toughness.

They came to the snow and saw that it was old and hard, left over from the year before. Sometimes that happened, some years it all melted. There were tracks in it, but nothing recent, all blurred by melting and re-freezing. The path disappeared but it no longer mattered. The top was almost in view, hidden above a ring of jagged rocks. But when they reached them, they saw that the rocks encircled the summit like a primitive balustrade and actually marked the highest ground since it fell away inside to form a shallow depression: A small, natural bowl filled half with water, half with ice. It bubbled a little on the melted side giving off wisps of vapor, but Boca paused at the balustrade to take in the spectacular view. The sky was clear for many miles and the next goal glittered in the distance: The third island in the sky. The entire mountain was visible, though the lower reaches were swathed in shadow, but the summit caught the setting sun and was so bright it seemed separate, not even connected to the mountain underneath.

Meanwhile, the fairies had proceeded down to water's edge and around to a point facing directly south. From there the stone ring appeared more enclosed above them, less open and 'picketty'. If one used imagination there were steps up to likely lookout points through the gaps, but the boys climbed instead to a blind spot behind a large stone face. Pio stuck his hand into a crack and felt around a bit. A hidden hatch swung open like a cupboard door, enabling him to look through a hole - a peephole aimed at the next mountain almost like a telescope. He took his bearing and while the others were doing the same, he opened another cupboard door and looked through another peephole, this one aimed more to the southeast, toward a more distant mountain. Then the others did. Obobo let the butterflies have a look.

"Did someone stand here all day long?" asked Yero.

"No", said Obobo. "Too boring. It would lead to laziness and neglect. We scanned every hour on the hour while the sun was up".

"Did you ever see signals?"

"Sure, a few times. We all did. We watched by turns".

"The wood is gone", reported Peco, digging through crusted snow in a nook.

"Let's go get some", said Pio. "It'll be nice here tonight with the little steamer going".

The 'little steamer' was upwind of Obobo and his little passengers, between them and the other fellows, and smelled bad; but the butterflies jumped to a wrong conclusion about the source of the smell.

"I don't know what else they ate", Yero whispered, "but sweet rolls shouldn't do that, should they?"

"No, or we'd have it too, from the jelly".

"It might be from the excitement with that puma. But that's excusable".

"We should excuse them anyway, I think".

"It would be easier if we were out of their wind".

"Oh, Yero. Let it go. It's a cool *macho* thing! I'd like to do it like *they* do it".

Yero turned away and took a short breath, not bothering to waste it in reply. Boca was good enough at that already, she felt, without trying any harder.

"It's just another fun habit", he mused. "One of those things that's called a *bad* habit by those who can't do it very well". He tried it now, with some success. Yero was caught off guard and tried to fan the bad air away using her injured side without thinking. She grunted from the pain.

"Oops! Oh--I'm sorry! I won't do that again".

"Yes you will. Just don't do it on *purpose,* that's all I ask".

"I'll make sure it's downwind. I really am sorry! But I need the practice. It's macho, and if they do it I should too".

"Macho stuff doesn't impress girls, you know. Not *that* kind, anyway".

"That's not the point, Yero. Boys just gotta do what we gotta do".

"That doesn't make any sense. Where do you get *that* from?"

"The first boy. Or maybe the second. I doubt if it went past that. Boys will be boys - that's all you need to know".

Yero suddenly realized that Pio and Peco had gone for firewood several minutes earlier and couldn't be blamed anymore. "It can't be them after all!" she said. "But if they aren't blowing gas, who is?"

Obobo had done his best to ignore this conversation but now he chuckled and walked around to the other side of the pool.

"Here now - is this better?" he asked. "It's the little hot spring that's getting into your noses". He held them down for a close look, upwind. The bubbles came up from a hole at the bottom of the pool. "It was more active years ago", said Obobo. "Dangerous, even. Now it's doing good to melt even this much ice. Some years when there hasn't been much snow the pool is dry, and the 'bubbler' is just a steam vent. So you see, El Boca, you're giving the fellows more credit than they deserve".

The fellows returned with wood and also juniper boughs to sleep on - no featherbeds, those - and all three began making up their beds while the light was still good.

"Did you hear?" Boca whispered, gazing upon his new heroes. "He talked about *credit*, so gas must be a big-time habit! This is exciting".

"It's even worse when you put it that way! But some good could still come if you give up a worse habit in favor of it. Like *cussing*".

"No. I'm sure it all works together. When we make a really cool noise there must be special words for a victory yell".

Yero tapped as hard as she could with her good side to get Obobo's attention. "Put me somewhere away from *him*", she requested.

"I have just the right job for him anyway", said Obobo, who had picked up plenty of the conversation. He opened his sack and propped it open near the edge of the warmest water, but upwind of the bubbler. He laid the whole mallasha plant inside the sack and set the butterflies down next to the still-fresh blossoms. Yero, of course, could only go to a few of the lowest ones, being unable to climb with her injury, but 'Bo had foreseen this handicap.

"Remember how I went out on the mesquite branches and bent them down?" he asked El Boca. "Yes? Well, that's your job now. Be a good fellow and bend them all down to her level".

"All of them?"

"Yes. She needs the energy now. Later, I'll see about some sweet roll jelly for you. It's getting stale, but that's probably better for making gas".

And so El Boca was re-introduced to humility, which is the opposite of macho and almost as common, though boys don't talk about that part. As a rule of thumb, the higher you climb up the macho ladder, the more humiliating it is on the way down.

The poolside proved a good place to camp even with a cold breeze, thanks to the 'balustrade' that kept most of it out, allowing for a cozy camp down in the bowl. Night fell, but the boys didn't make a fire just yet. Pio had an idea how to improve the stale bakery goods.

He put everything, including his last damaged biscuits, into a gunnysack, tied it to the end of a stout pole, and hung it out over the pool. The air grew chill with the evening and the warm water gave off steam, warming the baked goods and softening them. When Pio took them off and served supper the rolls were almost like new, and his culinary reputation went up. As a peace offering, the other fellows scraped jelly off a few sweet rolls and gave him to put on his biscuits, which had softened considerably. But they were content to let him work at those by himself.

Maybe it was just the air, but Yero also was struck by inspiration. She had sipped pretty much the whole bouquet dry (as Boca bent stem after stem and worried that the fairies were using up all the jelly). She needed it all, but it was enough. Now to do something about her aches and pains!

"You've been very nice, Boca", she said. "I just need one more thing. It hurts when I yell very loud, so will you ask Obobo to lean down where I can talk to him?"

She requested a raft, when she got his attention, to float on the warm water and try to relax her knotted, injured muscles. Obobo guessed right away what she meant and broke off a wide chunk of wood and launched it, setting her up as captain of the vessel but keeping one eye on her.

She closed her eyes and the raft drifted slowly in the warm water. It was wonderful, except when she drifted into the southern quadrant, into the sulphur stink. Then Obobo reached out with Pio's pole and pushed the ship clear of the bad weather. Yero lost track of time, but not of the soothing feeling. Her injury did improve, and this shouldn't be wondered at in the fog of a hot springs mineral pool. Many Big People will swear to the same healing properties, but there are limits. Something broken or damaged would require more than mineral steam to repair it. It would take time.

The boys finally made a small fire down in the hollow and got out their tobacco. Boca declined their offer again, with the handy excuse that he was still working on his hard jelly. When that was gone, he excused himself to check on Yero and flew off to join her on the cruise ship.

"Permission to come aboard, Captain", he requested, and saluted smartly.

"Permission granted, sailor. You can wash the deck".

"Aye, aye! As soon as I'm back on duty, sir. I'm off right now".

Yero laughed, and it hurt less than it did before. "I guess you've done enough duty for one day, sailor. At ease!"

"Thanks. How you feeling? You're all wet".

"A lot better. Not joking. But I still can't move my wing or right arm. I can't tell if it's broken or what, but something's really wrong in there".

Boca felt bad and wished a lot of things, but the truth couldn't be changed. "It's funny how things work out, isn't it?" he finally said. "We might never have gotten this far without these guys, and then you never would've got hurt if we were alone, but now that you *are* hurt, we wouldn't stand a chance without them".

"Yes. I think we did some good too. You poked that puma right in the eye. I saw you".

Boca blushed. "I didn't mean to. He more or less rammed into my foot".

"Well, I think it was brave. It made him blink, and I think it threw him off".

"Maybe a little. But the fellows are tough, aren't they? No magic at all. They just whupped him hand-to-hand".

It was a comforting thought, and a comfortable perch. The wind had calmed, and the bad smell floated straight up and away. The butterflies could scarcely be faulted for drifting into slumber or the fairies either, after a hard day's journey. Tomorrow would be another day and that was soon enough to take up the errand again. But around the witching hour, Yero awoke to unmistakable sounds of fighting. Boca was already awake.

Cloud and mist had overspread the mountaintop shutting out the starlight and the crescent moon. From out of the darkness came shouts - *battle cries* - and the groans of the wounded in their agony. The fighting was outside the balustrade somewhere and going away, down toward the tree line judging by the sounds. But the combat was mortal. People were dying.

"We're in for it!" whispered Boca. "I'm sure it's those Jaguars".

"We've got to warn the fellows!"

"It's too late, Yero. They're out there already! I heard Obobo yelling and cursing".

The cruise ship bumped shore on its leisurely tour, startling them, and Yero wrinkled her nose suspiciously, peering into the shoreline.

"I smell Obobo's feet", she said matter-of-factly. "He's right here!"

They had bumped into his hairy toes. Now, as their thoughts shifted, they still heard sounds of battle but Obobo's snoring was mixed in with it, and Peco's snoring too. And Pio's. Boca flew into the mist guided by the snoring and landed on Obobo's nose. That by itself didn't awaken the big fellow, but a sharp tug on his nose hair did. He woke up grumpy.

"What the devil! Oh - it's you! Well? *What*?"

"Just *listen*, that's what! They're fighting outside! It's an awful battle!"

Obobo calmed down enough to listen. He heard the fighting as well as Boca, but made no move to sit up, lost in thought.

"It's an echo", he said finally. "The earth remembers both the good and the bad. There was a battle here once".

"I heard *you* out there! That's what woke me up". Boca became aware that the others had woken up also and lay quietly, listening to the past. At last, Obobo stirred and sat up. He reached down and plucked Yero's cruise ship out of the water, setting it on his lap.

"What you hear now happened hundreds of years ago", he said. "It's over. There's no danger tonight that we know of". He lay back again and stared up at the darkness as if he still didn't believe it. "We were overrun," he murmured.

He fell silent. The sounds of battle faded away down the mountainside. Pio took up the tale.

"We asked for trouble when we challenged such a powerful Tribe", he began, "and troubles we got. But they made mistakes too. They had Emperors, but the real power was with the Priests, the top ones, who worshipped innocent blood. That part angered even the dragon. When they brought him a child for breakfast, he ate the servers and turned the child over to us. He did that more than a few times. Dragons do like kids, if not much else. That marked the end of their alliance".

"With some help from him we drove the Priests crazy, but over a century or two they found ways to get at us, to spy us out. One by one they learned our Haunts and outposts, and the Jaguars came. Sometimes they surprised us and there was battle, our few against their many. That's what happened here. We lost two fine lads captured that night and couldn't free them". Pio hung his head. "I told you what happens. No need to repeat it".

"They were at the peak of their power then, arrogant and cruel, spilling blood purely for entertainment. No one could challenge them, or so they thought. Then the Spanish came with guns and horses and ended their fun. They gave the Priests a chance to renounce the butchery - the human sacrifice and other horrible sins. Far better than they deserved! When they wouldn't, they were put to death and that was reckoned to be the end of the evil. But it didn't end. It was only banished to the Ghost Realm".

"From which it could return" reminded Obobo. "All too easily. Our three lives might be enough to renew the top Priests, so we avoid their warriors at all costs. But enough about all that! On a happier note, keep in mind they can't abide fire - and we have a nice one here tonight! While it burns you can have pleasant dreams". He smiled and re-launched Yero's ship into the mineral bath and put extra wood on the fire. The juniper crackled and flared, and all the unpleasantness ran away into hiding.

Next morning Peco was up earliest, as usual on the trail, stomping around and stoking the coals. The clouds were dank and thick, and there was nothing left for breakfast except the coffee, although it sounded like he was preparing a whole meal the way he rattled the pot and the lid. No one could sleep and everyone finally got up, which is exactly what he had in mind. Getting the day going this way always put him in a good mood and the others in a grumpy one. But they were always a little grumpy when he made coffee, no matter what time of day.

Peco liked it scalding hot and made it to suit himself. He liked it extra-strong too, which was sure to bother today since there was no milk or cream, or even sugar. The others poured their own cups and made faces about it. Pio added water from his canteen to thin the brew. It got too cold and he had to add hot coffee, but that was too strong again. He tinkered with the blend several times and finally just drank it cold, grounds and all. Peco never bothered with the little basket so the grounds went right into the cups along with the coffee. Obobo frowned and spit out the grounds. He made a point to spit each one separately and Peco made it a point not to notice any of them. He finished his own cup with a satisfied slurp to show how much he liked it.

The butterflies were served up a bit of hardened jelly on a saucer and Peco dribbled boiling water on top to soften it. It was good. Boca felt the energy and wished for sunshine to fly in. He looked up and was encouraged. Either dawn was breaking or the clouds were thinning. He flew up a little way and popped right out above it. The sky was clear for miles. What little cloud remained had settled into the bowl. Even the jagged stone ring was in the clear. He went back down with the good news, but it didn't impress anyone.

"The cloud comes from that", said Peco casually, pointing to the warm pool steaming in the cold air. Boca felt a little silly but went on to report that the sun was just coming up, and that was well received. There is something about sunrise that always lifts the spirits of free people.

Obobo lifted Captain Yero carefully off her ship and set her on his big toe near the embers, to dry off. It was necessary and kind and she found that by facing the coals and leaning forward the warmth came up past her and carried Obobo's foot odor away. That lifted her spirits too and she answered all their concerned questions with, "Yes, much better, thank you".

They all of them went up to the rim while the embers cooled, to take in the sunrise and see what could be seen. The chief interest was the next mountain, that being the last 'Island in the Sky', and also the northern reaches of the Long Mountains beyond: An unbroken chain stretching hundreds of miles southward toward the old Aztec empire. A long day's march lay ahead, at least as difficult as the day before. The last 'island' was yet quite distant.

"Like old times", said Pio wistfully as the sun rose above the eastern horizon. "This was the first hour of watch", he explained to the butterflies. "The first check of the day". He went up to the hidden doors and opened them, sighting first toward the next 'island', then through the long-range peephole to an old outpost far beyond. Peco went next while Obobo waited with the butterflies.

"What do you look for?" asked Boca. "What were the signals?"

"Just flashes of light in a sequence. A code that no one else would understand. The most important signals concerned the 'runaways'. The Priests called them that rather than admit they were being stolen. But other messages were important too, and we did flash messages back from here at great need, using the bored holes to aim precisely".

Peco had his turn and shrugged. Obobo went last and voiced the old refrain, "All quiet on the southern front".

The butterflies had to look too, naturally. All was hazy through the long-range hole, but the nearer mountain was clear.

"Oh, there it is", said Yero. "I see it". Boca did too.

Obobo smiled to himself, holding the two of them to the hole on his finger. It isn't hard to see a mountain on a clear day. The butterflies peered intently, counting aloud.

"There are three runaways to pick up", reported Yero finally.

The fairies paused what they were doing and looked at her.

"Aha! And how do you arrive at this number?" asked Pio.

"The signals. We counted three flashes".

The boys took turns again at the peephole but saw nothing.

"False signals", declared Pio. "Random reflections. It happens. There's a lot of quartz on that mountain".

"Maybe someone is inviting three to lunch", said Obobo, making light of it. "I'll go with the kids".

"You better go alone, with your appetite".

They laughed a little and made ready to march, slinging on their gear and gathering up any bit of sign, even the juniper mats. The local fog had cleared and they scattered the campfire ashes to the wind (Yero watched as always now, but there were no girl fairies). Then they loitered, making small talk. They adjusted a strap here, a belt there, and mostly watched the sky. An hour passed and that was their main concern. They all had one last peep at the next mountain, on the hour, but saw nothing. Obobo let the butterflies look again, out of curiosity, but they saw nothing more either.

The day's march began by re-tracing their steps down to the timberline where they scattered the juniper mats. From there they skirted around to the south face looking for an old route through the thicket, and so down the mountain. They found it right away or seemed to think so. Obobo pointed it out to the butterflies. The 'entrance' was nothing but a mess of stunted juniper - in other words a typical fairy trail, meaning no trail at all unless *they* passed through, and then it shut again behind them.

Obobo took up the rear, shielding Yero from the raspy branches with his free hand, leaving the trail blazing to the others up front. The boughs scratched him, but they weren't mesquite or acacia, and he was remarkably moderate in his reaction. Boca rode with Yero on his finger through the worst of it, on her advice. She was big on caution now and even Obobo was reluctant to argue.

There were a surprising number of birds in the juniper thickets, chiefly scrub jays and their antagonists the thrashers, who mimic them for fun, but there were also red towhees, odd sparrows and one bushtit who peered at them out of the top of her sack-nest. All were eating the blue juniper berries that hung ripe and thick on the branches, but the hungry fairies ignored the fruit. "Too many seeds", sniffed Pio.

Morning passed as they descended into a more hospitable pinery and the mixed forest below that, following a spur ridge similar to yesterday's. The trees were shorter, the brush scrubbier on this sunbaked side of the mountain.

The butterflies grew hungry. Yero could only imagine how hungry the fairies must be, but the only hint they gave was pausing to collect nectar from a good-sized agave plant that had been missed by hunters, hurriedly trimming off the top stalk and pouring the juice into a canteen. Then they went on even faster until they reached the lowlands - another valley between mountains, but narrower than yesterday's and seemingly unpopulated. There was no town, no proper road, not even a regular stream. The only tall trees were cottonwoods and a few large willows. Most of the willows were a smaller type that sprouted on sandy drifts and the bare banks of a dry run. The flood had swept through here too and the wreckage and mess seemed even worse on the narrower valley floor. It was a jumble to get through, but the boys didn't mean to go all the way across just yet. They took their break at the dry run. Pio and Obobo got busy making a fire and Peco untangled his fishing line.

The flood had left pools of water that stood for days or weeks. The deeper ones persisted year-around like ponds, varying in size. These held fish, chiefly trout.

Peco wound the line neatly around one arm, running a little whetstone along the hook to sharpen the point, then made his way leisurely to the largest pool, turning over a few rocks and chunks of driftwood to see what the best local bait might be today but didn't actually collect any.

Pio and Obobo put the agave juice in a fry pan and set it directly on the fire when the coals were hot. Before long, the juice warmed and gave off a sweet, almost candy smell that interested the butterflies. It was partly meant for them, partly for the boys, but the main course for the fairies was still swimming around, not biting yet.

Peco stood in the shallows casting 'bait' to them as best he could, imitating every worm, grub or beetle he had found near the water, without so much as a nibble. The other fellows grew impatient and hollered useful comments over in his direction: "The day isn't getting any younger - was he aware of that?" and, "The coals were ready five minutes ago!" Things a fisherman needs to know when he's having no luck.

When he realized they were expected to wait also, so everyone could eat together, Boca wandered over to see what could be keeping Peco and found him frustrated with the sand, which was all there was to cast. It cast a weak 'lure'. At the moment, he was imitating a little red worm.

"Did you try a butterfly?" asked Boca.

"Yeah, that too".

"A Rasha La? That really worked on the bass".

"No!" Peco was embarrassed. "I joked about that, but I wouldn't actually---ouch!"

He splashed to shore and reached down to feel the back of his leg where something had bitten him. It was a leech, and it was still there, trying to attach itself deeper. It was slippery and hard to get ahold of and had a suction mouth on its tail too so that it tried to bite Peco's fingers with that while it burrowed in with the front end. Peco grabbed sand, using it to grip the slimy thing, and pulled it off with an audible 'pop'. He tried to throw it away and couldn't. It kept latching on to his fingers.

"The hook!" shouted Boca. "Put him on the hook!"

Peco grasped the idea right away and plunged the hook with pleasure through the fattest part. The leech let go everything else and tried to chew the hook.

"Fish him!" said Boca. "Try the live bait".

Peco thought about it for a moment. "I haven't used anything but artificials in years", he said. "But what's to lose?"

That's what the trout wanted. Live bait. Soon Peco was hauling them in faster than he could put them on a stringer, or the long stick he used for one, and hiked back to camp with a nice limit of trout. (Fairies do observe 'angling limits' like everyone else, but as with campfires there are different kinds: The traditional Indian limit is however many will bite, because there were always more fish than Indians in the old days. Peco stopped at whatever the fellows could eat for lunch, plus salting a few down for a late supper on the trail. The 'white man's limit' can be found somewhere in the updated book of fishing regulations among the plethora of restrictions, warnings and *fines*. Just read the book before you leave home, mister!)

Pio and Obobo had sharpened skewer-sticks and the fellows were soon roasting trout over the fire. The agave juice was cooled and Obobo dipped out a spoonful for the butterflies, knowing they would like it because it turns into an amber syrup if cooked properly, sweeter even than honey with a bit of caramel flavor. It was a hit.

Peco gave a lot of credit to El Boca for the live bait idea, freely admitting that it saved the day. Boca was rather expected to take a bow, but he gave the credit back to Peco, pointing out that he hadn't done any actual work.

"What's with you?" asked Yero privately. "Going modest?"

"On that I am. He would've stabbed it with the hook pretty soon anyway, just to get rid of it; and once it was on the hook, the rest would've come easy. Just be glad butterflies don't swim, Yero. We'd never get one of those things off".

There was a renewed sense of urgency when they finally set off again. Lunch had run late and they meant to make up some time; yet every step brought them closer to a mountaintop under suspicion. The fairies hadn't spoken about it aloud, but they did whisper. They had never whispered before about anything, and Obobo was tight-lipped. "We'll see tonight", was all they got out of him.

Once again, they found themselves marching steeply uphill as the afternoon wore on. There were no spurs or ridges leading up to this mountain, or even real foothills. Those at least were usually wooded; this mountain was mostly bare, devoid of any leafy plants. "If it was a dog", Yero found herself thinking, "we'd call it hairless". And that is what nature had populated the mountain with - hairless creatures. There were numerous snakes, horned toads, scurrying lizards, even an armadillo.

The afternoon grew warm for the time of year, and even warmer as they climbed past the last scrub ground cover halfway to the summit. Above that were only small cacti, the chubby hedgehog type and the smaller, even nastier pincushion variety; but the dominant feature of the mountainside was the rock, the loose rock that slipped away under their feet without warning, making them stumble among the cactus. There was no recognizable path at all, and they left none behind them except the shifting shale and grit.

The Butterflies, Yero and Boca

It was true, what the fairies said about quartz. It was everywhere, glinting in their eyes till they squinted, embedded in the great limestone uplift that had created the mountain ages earlier. Only the north face and the south were accessible at all. East and west were nearly sheer cliffs, home only to buzzards.

The going was slow with frequent stops to pluck out cactus spines, or just to cuss at them. The sun was hot, the rock was hot, and the sweat dripped off the fairies' noses. Obobo, without a sombrero and rather overweight, dripped a lot, and Yero had a day's adventure just dodging drips as he held her close to shelter her from the glare.

It had to be this way: A push for the summit before dark while they could at least see the poor footing, a push made more difficult by the firewood they carried along. But they did make it and paused a moment to catch their breath.

The butterflies had expected something more dramatic and were disappointed at first glance. It was nothing more than a flat skyway, a narrow windswept ridge distinguishable only by its slabwork form of geology. Over time, wind had eroded away the softer stone leaving a short stairway of hard slabs leading to the actual skyway. The boys climbed the tall steps with some difficulty, leaning to their right into a strong westerly wind. El Boca might have been blown away but Obobo collected him at the last moment on his finger with Yero and shielded them both behind his stomach.

Other than the assaulting wind they met no trouble nor saw any sign of it; but then, the wind left no traces on the skyway except old cracks in the hard surface, and these were well known to the fairies. Now in the last hour of watch Pio and Peco took their places on the proper cracks and Obobo sighted by the longitude they formed, picking out the correct peak in the Long Mountain chain that divided the lands to the south. In the last blustery minutes before sundown, they all watched for a signal, however unlikely, and saw none. When the last rays winked out, they gathered in a group along the eastern edge and drew upon some magic, pointing to the very precipice at their feet. A guard-rail should have been conjured up there, Yero thought, as the rock fell away hundreds of feet nearly straight down, but that wasn't what the fairies were looking for. Reality shifted a few feet below Yero's nose, and her nose twitched in surprise as a stairway appeared leading down alongside the cliff. It was narrow and showed damage, hewn long ago with pickaxe and chisel, but concealed with a simple spell. Yero remembered Obobo climbing awkwardly in the tree and wondered if the stair was safe for him, but if she asked, the wind blew her voice away. Moments later, she was glad no one heard. The boys bounded down the stair as easily as mountain sheep. Rock is their element, underground or above.

They descended ninety-nine steps, a lucky number in the old days, to a hard sandstone landing below the limestone layers. A narrow ledge ran from there along the natural curvatures of the cliff to a large alcove, shallow and exposed but featuring a habitable ledge wide enough for the party with all their gear, quarried back enough in the middle to afford space for a campfire. But even here on the sheltered side of the ridge the wind swirled and bothered, tossing sand and driving in the chill. Pio and Peco got a flame going with perseverance and more matches than they could afford while the butterflies perched on a shelf in the deepest part of the alcove.

Well, almost the deepest part. A crack led a bit further into the sandstone wall, narrow and pinching, too small to be of any use, but as the butterflies discovered right away, big enough to be a problem. A draft came out of it with occasional spits of sand.

"It's the other side of the ridge weathering through", explained Pio when they mentioned it. "We noticed the draft a few years ago". He frowned. "It seems to be getting worse. Bound to happen, I suppose. The prevailing wind blows against the other side". He jerked a disapproving thumb toward the crack and beyond - and was answered by a shower of sand from 'beyond'.

It was a wind tunnel or archway in the making. As geology moves this was moving fast, owing to the configuration of the opposite cliff face. The west wind set up a swirl there, a vortex, when it blew really hard. Bits of the sandstone were dislodged and caught up in the vortex, and by their action more bits were dislodged. On a wild night like tonight, the vortex became a natural sandblaster and an irritation. The fellows didn't like it one bit, remembering the labor that went into building the stair and alcove.

But other than that, things were tolerable. The fire was going nicely, and they had plenty of wood. The boys had salted fish for supper and there was wholesome agave syrup for the butterflies, so let the wind howl! It would be just one drafty night. In a few years, this would be shelter no more, but tonight it still was. The fairies tended the fire while the moon rose above them and debated the next day's journey until it disappeared behind the cliff. Then everyone slept as best they could, but the boys kept watch by turns and fed the fire regularly.

Maybe it was a trick of the wind. It certainly calmed down for a while on the other side, from a howl to a soothing distant wail; and Obobo fell asleep on watch, as he never had before.

The wind seemed to know it when he nodded off and came back up stronger than ever - but more on the other side and less on theirs. It was the butterflies who finally woke up to an increased draft through the crack. They moved along their ledge a foot or two out to the end and huddled in the dark. It didn't help, and they were pelted with sand more and more often.

"This is no good", said Boca. "Maybe the fellows could stuff some old rags in there, do you think?"

Yero certainly agreed, but pointed to them, all asleep. "They're the ones who need sleep the most. We'd better tough it out, at least for a while".

They tried, but it was impossible. Butterflies are not built to withstand sandstorms, and it was worsening. Then Boca noticed the fire, or what remained of it, and both butterflies became aware of a smell, familiar yet elusive, as if from far away. A new gust came through the crack and sprayed more sand onto the coals, and they suddenly realized what was happening to the fire. Boca flew to Obobo and scratched his nose to bring him around.

Like a wild animal, he understood everything in an instant and shook the others awake. Pio went to stuff a rag in the hole while Obobo shielded the fire and Peco salvaged what coals he could, carefully scraping back the pile of sand; for it *was* a pile, a neat drift right over the fire and nowhere else. That bit was well noted by all.

The wind shrieked its displeasure at Pio's rag and spit it back at him. It took an old pants and some underwear of Obobo's, jammed in with sticks of firewood to plug the gap and thwart the wind for the moment. That still left the smell that had obviously come through the hole with the wind. It lingered in the calmer air and everyone knew what it was, even the butterflies recognized it by now.

"Those Jaguars", said Yero, speaking for all of them. "It smelled just the same that night in the rain".

No one else spoke or needed to. Pio went to work pounding the firewood sticks tighter into the gap. Peco blew softly on the remaining coals to coax a better fire. Obobo watched the stairway in the darkness and Boca circled outside the alcove helping with sentry duty. The wind died down considerably as if aware of its sudden impotence, which was probably why Boca felt grit land on his back that he wouldn't have noticed a minute earlier. He looked up instinctively. Jaguar warriors were standing on the skyway in a long line, looking down.

"Peco! Hurry!" he shouted as loud as he could. The Jaguars heard him. Some kicked rock chips down at them. One shouted something in their strange tongue. They all laughed at that. The talker - a chieftain of sorts in elaborate warrior garb - shook his club and advanced down the stairway followed by the rest.

If they hadn't stood gloating up there, they might've had the fairies by surprise. Others have made the same mistake. He wasn't halfway down when Obobo drew a burning stick from the fire and went to meet him. Then Peco grabbed a torch too, and that turned the tide. The ghost warriors could do things with sand and gravel here, closer to their old center of power, but still couldn't stand up to fire in their faces. They retreated back toward the darkness, cursing their weakness.

The rest of the night two of the fellows stood guard while the other slept - one at the fire, the other at the top of the stair, but there was no more fighting, no more wind or sand.

By first light they were all stirring, even the butterflies. No one had much rest, and no one was looking for more. Everyone wanted to get moving and leave the mountain behind. Peco might even have forgone his coffee, but habits are habits and it was agreed that coffee would help since they had slept poorly. That's when they discovered the coffee, the syrup, the last of the salted fish and all the spices had been blown over the edge during the affair, lost in the rocks hundreds of feet below. That was that, for any breakfast. Faces sagged.

"We have syrup at least", said Yero brightly. "Right here". She had asked for 'seconds' at suppertime, and Obobo had left the bottle on the ledge. Now they divided it five ways, more or less, and it lifted their spirits. Then they double-checked the other gear and seemed to have everything - except Obobo's pants and underwear, of course, jammed into the gap. They tried to get them out, but the sticks had simply been pounded in too hard. Anyone could see that except 'Bo.

"Just leave them", Pio finally told him. "They're rags anyway. We're lucky they were big enough to plug the gap".

"Oh, sure! But what if they were yours?" growled Obobo. "How would you like to leave *your* underwear around for anyone to see?"

"Don't worry", grinned Peco. "No one will ever guess they're yours. They'll think the underwear belonged to one of the *really* Big People".

Peco didn't expect it, but Obobo saw wisdom in this. "If you think about it", he considered, "there's two good reasons right there to carry a few extra inches around my belt line". No one offered rebuttal.

The wind had reversed overnight and was now gusting from the east as if trying to repair its behavior of the night before. They would've swept their ashes off the ledge anyway, but a gust did it for them now and it got into their eyes. It was time to leave quickly before an accident happened. They paused only to conceal the stairway behind them and take a second bearing on the next signal mountain because they intended now to avoid it, along with all paths east of the Long Mountains. There was morbid curiosity too. The sun was rising and the first hour of watch approached, as of old. They waited the extra minutes to have a look and were rewarded with doubt. There were flashes, a whole familiar series as if friends were still there. They were marked. All cheerfulness vanished.

"It's *them*", Obobo said finally when Yero pressed him for his thoughts. "They're trying to lead us into some trap or other. So, it's the western side for us, and hope to put them off our scent. If we disappear, they may think we've gone back north. That is our hope".

Chapter 19

The Roads Less Travelled

The way down the mountain was as treacherous as the way up with loose rock and stub cactus; except today when the fairies slipped, they got needles in their backsides instead of their knees. Boca had to assist in this by hovering back there and giving directions so that the fellows could pluck out their own thorns. They weren't about to pluck out each other's.

"I don't think I was meant to be a doctor - or even one of those animal vets", he confided to Yero. "At least, I would specialize in some parts higher up, if you know what I mean".

Mercifully, the descent was shorter than the climb. Ridges branched out from this southern face in great curves, south and east. All the first morning they followed one conveniently southward, the direction they wanted to go, through wild, unpopulated country. There was some agave and they cooked down a pan of syrup at lunchtime. That was it for grub and it was enough to go on with, but the lack of coffee was wearing on the boys. They chewed tobacco more often, overworking one habit to make up for the loss of another, until the tobacco ran low.

"Grub. Matches. Salt & pepper. What else?" Peco ticked off shortages and started a list.

"Put down underwear", commented Pio. "*Extra*-extra-large". In their present mood it was meant to needle, not humor, and in this he was successful. Obobo's fuse was short right now.

"Make that half a dozen pairs", he growled. "I'll stuff the extras in your mouth!"

So it went all morning until the ridges bent east toward the northernmost peaks of the Long Mountains, the very peaks they intended to avoid. There was no choice but to veer right and cross the cordillera country the hard way, one ridge and valley at a time. There were nettles throughout most of these woods, beginning to turn brown but still a nuisance. In their grumpy moods, the fairies didn't bother to wave off such smaller stuff so by the time they reached the top of the fourth ridge they were itchy besides everything else, but an answer to their problems presented itself.

In the valley below was a small country store alongside a dirt road. As far as they could see up and down the road there was no traffic, not even afoot. The boys scratched their itches and discussed the opportunity. The store was open; at least, a woman appeared on the porch and began beating out a rug. However, in such a small store, in broad daylight and no other customers, 'borrowing' was a bad idea. They still had only their 11 pesos to spend so that wasn't an option either - and don't bother asking for credit.

"We'll have to work it off", said Obobo, stating the obvious. "She must have odd jobs". Most of them did. This was nothing new to the fairies. "We'll do like usual", 'Bo added. "I'll be the Dad; you're the 'teenage kids'".

This never sat well with Pio and Peco, but it was the only logical way, and even so Obobo was a tad short to pass off as a big person. Pio took the butterflies under his hat and they went down. 'Bo hailed the lady from across the road.

"Any work here? We'll work for food".

"Not much. You don't look like you could do much anyway!" she shouted back in a shrill voice and went back inside with her rug and slammed the door.

It didn't discourage Obobo at all. He marched right across to the porch and knocked on the door with the 'kids' tagging along behind.

"That you again, you bums?" came the shrill voice. "Scram if you don't have money".

"Don't be stubborn, woman!" replied Obobo. "We'll scrub floors, patch shingles..."

"Don't need any!"

"...chop wood", added 'Bo, eyeing a paltry little pile next to the steps.

There were footsteps. The door opened a few inches. A severe little woman shorter than Obobo stuck her chin out and looked over the group. Peco and Pio tried to hide behind 'Daddy'.

"Waddaya want?"

"One or two small grocery items. Camping supplies".

She sniffed and wrinkled her nose. "You've been camping too long already, but that's none of my business. Groceries are! *What* groceries?"

Obobo passed along the list Peco had written down, not noticing he had added a few things to it. The woman's eyes squinted, and then bulged.

"A whole winter's worth of firewood won't cover this!" she yelped. "Where've you been? Prices have gone up in twenty years!"

Obobo grabbed the list back and studied it. "We don't need all this", he growled. "The kids made a wish list, I see!" He reached behind and swatted at them, knocking Peco's hat off. It rolled off the porch and him after it, sputtering and cussing.

The woman put hands on hips, offended. "Well! I never! What kind of father would teach a dear child to swear?"

"I didn't have to teach him. He picked it up on his own".

Peco recovered his hat and dusted it off. He spat tobacco juice out into the road and stomped back up the steps holding the sombrero with both hands. The woman was scandalized.

"He *chews* too? You allow him to chew *tobacco*? What about the other boy?" She whipped reading glasses out of her apron and leaned forward for a good look at Pio. "Sure! He's got tobacco juice on his chin as well!"

Obobo opened his palms and appealed soulfully to the heavens. "Raised without a mother", he groaned. "Blame it on that. They lacked a mother's gentle touch. It's been hard for me".

"Hogwash! You should've straightened them out long ago. They're not babies anymore. Egads! They're half-bald! They've got whiskers!"

"Premature aging. It runs in the family. Very sad, very embarrassing. That's why I keep 'em out in the hills".

That tweaked a sympathetic chord. She herself had turned gray before her time (in her opinion). It had made her 'a bit snappish', as she called it. No, she wasn't easy to get along with, never had been and she knew it, but it was just exasperation with the miserable quality of menfolk in the area! Still, she knew it was bad for business and couldn't afford to drive away customers - even these barter-boys. Plus, dry firewood always sells. She calculated quickly. Most of the old windbreak behind the store was dead and could be turned into profit. Haggling points came to mind and she scowled sharply.

"D'you trust the brats with an axe?" she inquired.

Obobo snorted. "Why not? If they lose a finger, it's their own. They've been taught".

The 'brats' had their hatchets out already, fingering the edges and scowling back at her as if measuring her neck.

"Ill-tempered things!" she mumbled to herself. Well, no matter. She would deal with the fat old man and it was up to him to control the brats. "Follow me", she ordered. "Don't spit on the porch - and don't step on the flowers!"

It was a mystery what she meant by that last. If there were any flowers they sure weren't blooming. Obobo decided the less said the better and just tried to step where she did. She pointed out the trees to cut and where to stack the split wood. Her terms were simple: She would check back later and decide how far they had gotten down the shopping list. With a final disapproving look at the brats, she went back into the store.

As soon as she left, Peco had a few choice words for 'Daddy', who reveled in the role, although he pretended not to. 'Daddy' acted surprised and drew the butterflies out from under Pio's sombrero to hold as a buffer. "Come, come now", he replied innocently, "it *had* to look realistic. And I couldn't swat

Pio with the kids, now could I?" Yero detected the glee in his voice. So did Peco. But it was time to get to work.

The old woman never imagined. She was astounded an hour later when she came out again. The old man and his brats had already turned half the dead trees into a large stack of firewood - a good three cords or more - using just their hatchets and the woman's rusty crosscut saw she had left back there and forgotten. They had only just sat down on the stumps to hone their hatchets, and that's what she harped on immediately.

"You won't earn any groceries sitting down!" she scolded. "Did you cut the tree just for the chair?"

"Women!" scoffed Obobo. "You don't see nuthin' when you don't want to. Look at your wood pile!"

"I saw the pile - it must be easier than I thought! I don't need to give as much credit if it's *that* easy." She licked a pencil and proceeded to make corrections on the list.

"Let's see if I have this right", drawled Obobo. "Since we split so much already, you think you can drive a harder bargain now?"

The woman's jaw dropped. "Well! I *never, ever*! That's like saying I cheated. Did you say that?"

"No, ma'am. You just miscalculated. Gimme me the list".

The woman paused. This wasn't quite as simple as she thought. The dolt had a little bit on the ball. The thought brought out the 'snappishness' in her and she thrust the list at him angrily. She had circled about a dozen items earlier, and then crossed them all off a moment ago except 'matches' and 'salt & pepper'.

"That's how it stands right now!" she shrilled. She dug out these items from an apron pocket and handed them to Obobo. "You've earned this much! They're the small size I expect you'll want for hiking and camping".

Obobo tut-tutted. "Oh, dear. The boys won't like this. They figured we'd earned the whole list by now. Well, they can't read. I'll try to explain".

"Yes, you'd better wise them up. I won't be ripped off by little urchins out of the backwoods!" She turned on her heel, quite satisfied with the outcome. She was very much used to getting her way.

"Sorry, lads", she heard Obobo quietly breaking the news to the brats as she walked away. "She won't pay a fair wage so you might have to ransack the store and take what you want, like you usually do, and then burn the place down. I don't know what to say. You boys decide".

That brought the woman back, faking sympathy. "I've changed my mind", she said, squeezing out a tear. "I love the children. Always have. Never could walk away from a child in need. Here! Give me the list back". She highlighted most of the crossed-off items and even added 'candy'. "There, now. Is that better? If you finish the job, you'll get the whole list. But give the boys a well-earned break and I'll go fix lunch for everyone". She walked back to the store as calmly as possible and got right on the telephone.

Behind the store, the fairies went back to work except Obobo, who made sure Yero was safely out of the way on a stump and asked a favor of Boca before he rejoined the others. They all expected trouble.

Then wood chips flew. In spite of their size, boy fairies are exceptionally strong and slow to tire. Even in this day and age, when they no longer wield a hammer and pickaxe regularly, they can still do the work of two or three big people. As Yero watched in awe (and dodged a chip or two), a whole tree was reduced to stove-sized chunks and added to the pile, and then another tree. Granted, it was poplar--a fast-growing type that makes a quick windbreak and then dies, but the trees were over thirty feet tall. Another tree followed before Boca returned, alighting by Yero to avoid the flying chips. He didn't bring good news.

"She grabbed her phone as soon as she was inside", he said. "I tried to read her lips but - I dunno - I think she called the cops".

"That's nasty! The fellows are keeping their bargain".

"She doesn't care. I have to warn them".

They expected it but it didn't make them any happier, and Boca was able to take note of one or two new words he hadn't heard before. They kept working anyway, guessing that any police officer must be quite a few miles from this little backwater. But in that they were wrong.

Phones are wireless now. Even in a valley like this there is some reception if the cell tower is situated properly. It was, and the new constable of the village to the south happened to be driving on the road, exploring the limits of his new jurisdiction. He was only minutes away when his official cell phone rang. That by itself was a thrill. His first official communication on his first day of duty! He turned on the flashers and flipped through his pocketbook of regulations to double-check the protocol. This was his first job and he intended to follow the rules precisely. He answered the phone.

"Si, this is Mobile-1, Constable Seso speaking. Go ahead, base".

There was a pause. The veteran secretary on the phone was the only other employee at the small-town jail. "Yeah, well this is Bebe. You out north somewhere?"

The young constable frowned and made a mental note to remind Adjutant Ms. Bebe Robozo about telephone protocol. He noted the trip odometer. "I am at kilometer 10.2, northbound. Do you copy?"

"Yeah. Listen, the old woman at the store thinks she's in danger again. Some old coot must've winked at her. Better check it out". She hung up.

The constable's frown deepened. Adjutant Robozo was making light of crimes with whole sections devoted to them in the manual - sections with *footnotes*! He'd better have a word with her about *that* too - WHOA!!! The old '58 Chevy veered into the ditch and bounced along until he wrestled the wheel and got back up onto the road. Stupid cell phones! Distracting. He hit the gas again to get up to the correct speed limit and felt around for his official constable hat on the floorboards. Ah, there it was. He put it back on and hit the siren. He'd never been up to the store but the wall map at the jail showed the road with kilometer marks. He knew he was getting close.

The old woman heard the siren and marched out to witness the arrests. She shook her fist at the old man and his brats who were just finishing up, tossing the last chunks onto what had become a huge pile. Good! So much the better! She would get it all for free now.

For their part, the fairies had no intention of going anywhere. They had done all the work and were determined to get paid.

All eyes fixed on the last, blind corner of the road where the siren promised a police car would soon appear - and suddenly did, sliding sideways to a stop exactly crossways in the road a few feet short of the store parking lot. The constable stepped out, dashing in his new uniform, and leafed through the pocket manual as the woman hurried toward him.

"This is a 'Roadblock, escaped criminal'", he announced, reading aloud a short sub-section. He also took time to make an entry in the logbook.

"There they are!" squealed the woman. "Arrest them!" The fairies stood leaning against the woodpile, arms folded, calmly sizing up the situation.

The constable stepped back to the vehicle and peered in at the trip odometer. It read precisely 17km. He pursed his lips, took out the tire iron and scratched a line across the road, allowing barely enough room to open the driver's door, not one inch more.

"That is the limit of my jurisdiction, ma'am", he declared. "I can't arrest them unless they come across". He snapped to attention, saluted smartly, and assumed the parade-rest position guarding the line.

"Idiot!" the woman shouted. "If you can't do it, call for some policeman who can!"

The constable was unmoved. "If you will please step across the line, I can take your statement according to Section 29, paragraph 12".

She stepped across the line, all right, and launched a tirade with rude gestures. The constable blew his whistle.

"You are disturbing the peace, ma'am. This is your first warning under section 7, sub-section 4". For a minute the woman was speechless. Obobo walked over at that point with the rag-tag brats in tow and offered to "make a statement in the defense".

The constable looked it up. Yes, there it was in section 29, paragraph 3! He flipped on a small tape recorder, identifying himself, the time, and a brief rundown of the situation. "Speak slow and clear", he ordered. "Start *now*". He pressed the button.

For Obobo (or any fairy), this was easy. In all their long history on earth fairies have dealt with lots of policemen - some rough, some rougher - but all of them tougher than this young constable. 'Bo explained the bargain, showing the shopping list with its markings and pointing out the impressive new stack of firewood. He even pledged that although it was a barter agreement, they fully intended to report fair value on their tax returns. It was a lengthy statement but that was allowed under paragraph 4, and he stretched it out as far as he could just to tweak the woman's nerves while the 'brats' grinned at her.

But the woman, no fool, saw an infraction as she awaited her turn. As Obobo finally finished and folded his arms, the constable turned back to her.

"Arrest them *now*!" she squealed. "They're across the line!"

They were and made no move to step back. The constable held up a hand for order and informed her that according to section 1, subtitle nine, he lacked 'probable cause'. "I have no evidence they've done anything wrong", he stated. "If you wish to make a complaint, then that could be construed as evidence provided it's written and notarized according to section 19; however, I am not a notary, so we'll have to tape it for now. Do you wish to record a complaint?"

The woman certainly did. As soon as the constable did the intro, she grabbed the recorder and shouted her name into it, but that's all the space that was left on the tape. Click! The recorder shut off. The constable took it back and turned to leave, feeling his work was done.

"Put in another tape!" insisted the woman. But that was out of the question. The constable only carried one tape, pursuant to Constabulary office memo#11.

"You may come down to the office and file your complaint there if you wish", he offered. "Please call Adjutant Robozo first to set up an appointment".

"But what about these bums? You can't let them go!"

"Sorry. There's nothing to hold them on under section 1. They recorded a complete, official statement. You didn't. There's no probable cause".

"But the tape ran out!"

"You may file a complaint about that too if you wish, under section 3. As an impartial officer of the law, however, I advise you to get a lawyer. Your case is so weak the respondents may wind up collecting damages - section 31, last paragraph".

She leaped up to grab his ears and tried to bite his nose. The constable slapped the cuffs on and read her rights under the Preamble to Section 1, page 1, then locked her in the cage, which served as a back seat. He turned the old cruiser around, taking care not to inch past the line, and headed south with his prisoner, lights flashing and siren howling.

"Oh, goody!" said the brats. "Let's go shopping, Daddy!"

Obobo grinned. "I'm sure she's got money in her apron. We'd better hurry in case she decides to part with some".

He went to collect the butterflies who doubtless had a list of their own. "We're getting a fair deal after all", he told them. "She's letting us have the run of the store".

The meat and dairy cases were small, just milk, butter and cheese, and a few cured meats like ham and bacon; but the bakery was excellent. Customers came from quite a way and put up with the shrewish woman for her delicious breaded doughnuts and the fabulous variety of pies and frosted cakes.

"Now I know why she's so crotchety", marveled Yero. "She puts all her sweetness into this! Bring that cherry one and the blueberry too. They have soft jelly".

The fairies were happy to oblige. There were take-out boxes enough for almost everything. Boca found honey on the shelves and that filled out the butterflies' list, but the boys kept on shopping and filled their bags. They found spices to replace nearly everything that was lost over the cliff, plus three different brands of coffee and large boxes of matches. There were clothes in the dry-goods section that looked about the right size and Obobo picked out a big sombrero. The only disappointment was tobacco. She didn't stock the little snuff cans they liked, so they had to settle for plug tobacco. But all in all, they hadn't had such a shopping spree in years and lost track of the time.

***

Meanwhile down south, as the police cruiser pulled up to the jail, the woman quieted down back in the cage and counted her money. She was hauled inside and Bebe opened the lone cell. The woman took one look and made an offer they couldn't refuse: A whole week's salary for both. Bebe took the young constable aside for a moment. He was indignant until Bebe told him about section X, where officers of the law could personally accept money for 'good and proper reasons'.

"It's well-known among veterans", she explained. "They don't even bother to put it in the manual anymore".

"But what constitutes a 'good and proper reason?" asked the constable, still with misgivings.

"Oh, she could get released on good behavior for example. Was she any trouble on the way down?"

"It was just awful! I couldn't believe the abusive language".

"Forget that then. But listen, she has the best little bakery I know of. She needs to get back to it. A lot of people depend on it! Let's just say the money is for a ride back up. You'll be doing community service".

That made sense to the constable. The whole job was beginning to make more sense. So *that's* why the pay was so poor! They expected officers to make it up in tips, like waiters and waitresses! A thought struck him, and he asked if she would throw in a dozen doughnuts. That was no problem. She expected it. They *all* wanted doughnuts!

"You're going to make a fine constable, just fine!" said adjutant Robozo.

On a hunch, he put the old woman in the cage again to keep her away from the gas pedal and was glad he did. She urged all speed, but he stubbornly refused to exceed the posted limit. Then she offered an extra dozen doughnuts and he felt that elevated her request to 'good and proper'. He hit the gas pedal hard and licked his lips but forgot to turn on the siren.

So it happened that the fairies, just now leaving the country store with sacks so full they bounced along the ground, never heard the cruiser until it swerved around the last corner and went into another slide right at them in the middle of the road. The constable was groping for the emergency brake and never saw them, but the woman did. She shrieked so loud it hurt his ears and he turned to chew her out before even coming to a full stop.

"There they are - right there!" she shrieked. "Stealing everything!"

That last part was debatable. But they certainly were there, tossing road dust at each other and fading fast. By the time the constable turned around they were gone. The woman screamed in panic.

"Let me *out!*"

He did, gladly, reminding her politely about the doughnuts; but she began acting nutty. She ran into the road grabbing at - what? There was nothing there! Ridiculously, she seemed to think she had ahold of something. She braced her feet and called for help.

"Stop them! *Arrest* them, you idiot!"

The constable shook his head sadly, for more than one reason. The woman was herself the idiot. That was clear. She fit the description of a psychotic under section 24. Even worse, he saw the promised doughnuts slipping away. That part angered him. He put in a call to the next police jurisdiction to the north and reported the lunatic who was now sitting on her behind shaking her fist at - what? Things only a lunatic can see. He tried to get her attention one last time and got a clue to her bizarre behavior: She flashed a gang signal at him as she marched off toward her store. That left only a monarch butterfly fluttering above the road. "Late for those, isn't it?" he found himself thinking. Then he turned the cruiser around once more and headed south.

At the neighboring police station to the north, the secretary passed along the message. "The old woman down at the store is acting up again. You going down?"

"Nah, let her cool off for a while", replied the portly constable. "But I might go down later for some doughnuts".

***

Snap! "Ouch!"

The young constable might have heard those two sounds while the woman was struggling on the road, but he hadn't been listening. The first was the sound Obobo's underwear made when the woman lost her grip on the elastic, the next sound was Obobo's reaction. It was all Boca had to go by, trying to follow the fairies into the woods. They didn't want to be followed so they were careful about tracks and very gentle with the undergrowth. When he got close enough, he heard muffled puffing but saw nothing except fleeting shadows. Even Yero had got a good coating of dust and then 'Bo had stuck her under his new hat.

The fairies made a big U-turn in the steep woods to throw off pursuit and re-crossed the road below the store into an open field, then up the next ridge to a clearing at the top where men had cut timber. There were flat stumps and new grass, a perfect place for a picnic. But it would be a picnic in the dark. Night was gathering fast.

"For tonight at least, we'd better stay out of sight", said Obobo's voice.

"'Brats' shouldn't be seen or heard anyway", said Pio's voice.

Everyone had a good laugh and at no one's expense. Truth be told, the firewood would fetch more than the woman lost to their shopping spree. 'Bo set Yero on a stump and at her request carefully blew the dust off her, enough so she looked butterfly-ish again to a casual observer. But Boca wasn't casual. He noted the wing, which still hung crookedly and asked about it. It was "fine", and didn't hurt unless she moved it, and that's all she would say except to change the subject to supper.

That was a popular idea all around. Unseen bags opened up and revealed their contents to the rising moon. A cherry pie, a chocolate one, and an angel food cake selected themselves and leaped out into mid-air where they turned and tilted and began to vanish bite by bite. A piece of cherry pie went and sat on a nearby stump next to the butterflies. When the pastries were gone, something containing water was passed around. Slurps and gulps replaced the munching and snacking noises, only to be followed by long, drawn-out belches. A big plug of tobacco appeared and unwrapped itself on one end, then jumped around a semi-circle in panic losing part of itself at every stop, and finally dived into a small container that quickly shut. Quiet returned, and all that remained of the picnic feast was the butterflies on their stump sipping on the syrupy filling of their pie.

The fairies camped right there and slept on the grass. It was better than a lot of camps even without fire, and they planned to camp without that for several nights at least. They would have to avoid the Big People's police for a while, but they were only a nuisance; and now, in the dark without fire, the real enemy seemed uncomfortably close again.

It was remindful of a winter evening, too. They weren't up in the tall mountains where winter had already settled in at higher elevations, but the cold reached down into these foothills at night. It wouldn't freeze here, maybe, but the butterflies were glad for the energy food. It kept them warm on the inside while their worn esporellia tried to warm the outside. In the moonlight, they could see matted spots on the grass around them where they guessed the fairies must be sleeping, or their gear was piled. Then one by one, the fellows began snoring and it was easier to guess what was where, and who was who.

"I think that's Pio right there", said Yero. "He smacks his lips. And that's Peco - the one that whistles".

"Anyway, *that's* Obobo", said Boca. "He's loudest, and I can't always tell if it's snoring or whatever".

They laughed and recalled the tribbits snoring in the afternoon sunshine; a long time ago, it seemed now.

"Yesac snored a lot like Obobo, now that I think about it", giggled Yero. "Not as loud because he isn't as big, but it was confusing in the same way".

They laughed some more, and life was pretty good in spite of the chill and the ghost warriors, and even a crooked wing, when there were more cheerful things to think about. They talked about Manino for the umpteenth time, guessing as always what it would be like, because no one ever told them that part.

"It'll be crowded", predicted Yero. "I'm sure there's thousands of monarchs, maybe millions, and everyone distant cousins of each other. Some are probably distant cousins of ours too".

"If everyone's related there's bound to be trouble", said Boca. "Cousins don't always get along the best".

"True. They're probably just like us and we argue whenever you're being ridiculous".

"Boys do a lot of heroic stuff, Yero. When you don't understand it, just give us some slack".

"You're lucky there. Girls are very forgiving. If they're bribed".

"Yeah? Like how?"

"With things like comfort and safety. If Manino is what it *should* be, girls will be allowed the best perches and the sweetest nectar".

"If it's crowded there might not be enough nectar".

"There's bound to be, Boca. Everything must be pretty good or there'd be no reason to go back, year after year".

Boca didn't answer right away. "I hope we find out together", he finally whispered. "And I hope the fellows don't dust you anymore. It was lonesome without you".

For a while, they just sipped cherry syrup and listened to the fairies snore.

"I'll take first watch", Yero said, when it got even louder. "Someone has to watch. The fellows might be hidden from searching eyes but not any ears".

They each took a watch and when it was Yero's turn again, Boca didn't have the heart to awaken her. She was twisted to one side with her cheek resting on her crooked wing, sleeping very soundly. It was easy to guess that she needed the rest, that her injury sapped her strength.

The moon had gone down in the west and the breeze had calmed to nothing. In the quiet Boca realized that the fairies had quit snoring. That was a blessing. And what was the point of keeping watch if they were quiet? He couldn't think of any and fell asleep too but didn't sleep well. He entered a bad dream, then left it, then entered it again. Each time it was the same: He was on watch and smelled the strange, wild odor of the Jaguar warriors. They were nearby, searching. Then he saw them, and they saw him too, and came for him with their clubs and hideous war paint! But he wasn't able to raise the alarm; wasn't able to move, or even speak! The smell was overpowering. When they reached for him, he did scream but his voice was weak and made no sound. Then the Jaguars shook him. They wouldn't quit shaking him!

"Boca! Enough! We're all awake and it's only a skunk!"

It was Yero, but she didn't understand! Then he awoke completely and realized he was still shouting. His voice did work, all too well. He had even awakened the fairies and they were up and moving away by the sound of their voices. Then the skunk smell hit him and the dream was forgotten. The butterflies held their noses as a big skunk waddled right past their stump and continued on. She'd had a bit of fright upwind and sprayed whatever it was. Now she was escaping at a leisurely pace, surrounded by her own nasty cloud as it drifted slowly away.

It was first light anyway and a coffee pot would soon have been rattling around on its own with no visible means of support. Peco would have risked a very small fire in the light of dawn. They all would, for coffee, but not now. The boys had gotten the grub sacks out of the skunk's path but everything else had got tainted. The smell clung to their clothes, their gear, the butterflies' wings, even their leftover pie. They couldn't break camp fast enough in search of better air, but El Boca was considered a minor hero for raising the alarm in time to save the food from being tainted. Only Yero seemed to have noticed that he'd been shouting 'Club! Club!' not 'Grub!'

The fairies' voices led the way downhill and then uphill again to the next cross-ridge. A breeze came up with the sun and everyone appreciated that to air the stink out of their clothes. Boca flew well above, only too happy to air out his wings. By the next hill, the boys felt they could stand themselves long enough to have coffee and soon a fire sprang up, attended only by a pair of monarchs on a low branch--or so it appeared to a vulture circling around the ridge. The vulture was surprised to see a coffee pot jump out from nowhere, fill itself with water, and take a seat on the hot coals. Sweet rolls and doughnuts materialized, and a piece of pie landed on the branch next to the butterflies, who seemed totally unsurprised and started eating. The vulture turned his beak up in disgust. It was all very curious but not appetizing to any self-respecting vulture. He veered off in search of tastier food.

The land changed during the morning as they went forward. The ridge country ended, and they entered a region of more rounded hills with fewer cliffs and escarpments. This was foothill country proper to the Long Mountains. The first tall peak, already behind to their northeast, had been bypassed. Others were now in view, east and southeast. They had gotten to the western side of the chain successfully, into unfamiliar country, and planned simply to keep the high peaks to their left and travel southward. But the woods were dry here in the lower hills. They came across no springs or seeps and were forced gradually to their left and upward in search of water. That evening they camped early near the top of a tall hill in the shelter of thick pines and made their small fire before night fell so that only coals remained after dark.

The fairies were losing their camouflage gradually and Boca could make out noses and fingers, especially Obobo's finger where Yero paced back and forth. They weren't happy about the dust or the lack of it or anything else about it. They simply felt dirty and itchy. Even boy fairies get enough dirt sometimes.

The following day was much the same. The dry woods yielded no food or drink. They hadn't counted on that and hadn't rationed the baked goods at all. Now they would have to. Around the noon hour, they stopped near an outlook point for lunch and sent Peco ahead to scout. Pio and Obobo took inventory of the remaining goods, laying them all out on a shelf of rock next to the trail. There was much less than expected and they quarreled about it. Obobo was always to blame for this sort of thing and grumpy when it was pointed out. He scratched behind his neck and shook a canteen. It was empty and there was grumbling about that too. The butterflies, perched on a piecrust, expected this new round of crankiness. It had been several days since the last one and the fellows didn't take to adversity very sweetly.

At that moment, Peco returned with news of water. Lots of it. There was a large stream in the valley below. The downside to the news was, it was *way* down below. Steeply downhill. The three all went to the lookout while the butterflies stayed with the pie. This was the blueberry one with their very favorite jelly filling (of the moment).

The fairies returned shortly in much better moods. They were going down for a bath. The butterflies were to stay and guard the food from flies and pesky bugs, of which there weren't many on such a cool afternoon at the edge of winter. The boys left behind most of their gear taking only snacks, the canteens, and the dirty clothes on their backs, and headed downhill whistling and chuckling. "Keep a good watch, El Boca!" they called back, and that was all.

Yero laughed. "El Boca!" she mimicked. "What are you going to do if a squirrel comes, or even a mouse?'

"You might be surprised, Yero. If nothing else, I can go get the fellows".

"What about flies? Can you shoo them all by yourself? Because there's one right there".

Boca might have ignored just one, except it landed on their pie and had dirty feet. Anyone could see that. He hopped over to have a word with the smutty thing.

"This is *our* food", he said in his best official tone. "So just beat it!"

The fly lifted his mouth out of the mess he was making long enough to say something incoherent. It could have been a strange accent or maybe just too much food in his mouth, but the tone was very negative.

Then another fly landed, and a third. They were just as rude. He tried frightening them, flapping his wings, but they didn't shoo at all. He finally jostled one of them enough to get a scuffle going and the scuzzy thing wiped its mouth on his leg, and then laughed about it.

"Gross!" said Yero when he showed her. "But you have to do something, or they'll spoil the food. Look at them all!"

There were a dozen by now, and more were arriving. "Don't worry, I'll think of something", replied Boca. "It's my job".

The one that wiped its mouth flew over and landed right in front of Boca. "You're nuthin!" it sneered, and spit into the jelly where they were eating.

They say a fly's eye can spot trouble from a thousand angles, but that's only if they're paying attention. A small grey flycatcher swooped in from a surprising angle and snatched the fly right off the pie, and when the others fled she snatched a lot of them too, right out of the air. Then she perched in a branch nearby to wait for more. Boca suddenly was a big success.

"What do you say now?" he asked Yero.

"That the bird did it, not you".

"That's not the way to look at it. I was given a charge which is now fulfilled. All's well that ends well!"

"I suppose so. Maybe a lot of heroes start out that way".

"Why not? Even heroes can't always make things happen. Sometimes they just happen".

"They do and it's called luck".

"So? Even if a hero was only lucky, he's still a hero".

"Okay, you're right", laughed Yero. "And I wish you lots of luck. We still haven't had the squirrel yet, or the mouse".

It was fun to be on the winning side, no matter how, and the butterflies made good use of the extended lunchtime. Boca even fetched pine needles and stuck them in to mark the dirty spots where the flies had been, so the fairies could throw those bits away when they returned. Then he just took a perch next to Yero and felt important. Everything had been thought of, obviously. Except one thing.

It wasn't a mouse or squirrel that was about to walk in on them, but something bigger. They heard it coming from a distance and wondered what it was. It came straight for them following a promising scent on the trail: The scent of sugar doughnuts and pastries. Bears are renowned for their sweet tooth. He was a black bear, a large specimen, a true King of the Mountains, and very much used to getting anything he wanted. He'd been following the sugar scent - and the 'hombre' scent with it - for the last hour, wondering how dangerous the hombres were. Now he came lumbering into view at a great pace, seeing no hombres. He stood up to the rock ledge on his hind legs and began shoveling goodies into his mouth with both paws, beginning at the opposite end of the buffet from the butterflies.

Yero decided right away to bail out and clambered down off the piecrust. At the speed he was gobbling, who knew? He might not even notice a butterfly in his pie.

The bear had a clever way with doughnuts, hooking them one at a time with a claw and flipping them toward his mouth. The mouth handled it from there, snagging them on the fly and wolfing them down whole. The sweet rolls quickly followed and Boca thought, "Why even eat sweets if you hardly taste them?" But when the bear got to the cake (only an angel food cake was left) his lack of manners worked against him. It was soft and fell apart when he grabbed, and he smeared the whole ledge trying to pick up the pieces. He solved that by licking everything right off the rock, then turned his attention to the blueberry pie, the last item on the menu.

The bear had consumed considerable bulk by now and took a moment to lick his paws and their claws while he cocked his head, sizing up the pie. That's when Boca decided to caution him about what the flies had done. It was the decent thing to do. The bear took notice of him but disregarded the warning.

"That's nothing", he rumbled, and proved it by gobbling up every smidge, although he did spit out the crust. Then he noticed Yero also, and actually grinned.

"*Muchas*", he said. "You are *muchas*. I don't eat muchas".

Since he was acting civilized, they introduced themselves. But the bear was more interested in someone else. He knew the sweets had come to his woods by way of 'hombres'. He smelled them, and now that the sugar lust was wearing off, he was nervous. Where were they? Had the muchas seen *hombres*?

"Sure", answered Yero. "They're our guides. They'll be very angry with you for eating all their food".

"Do they carry *armas*?" The bear's unease was growing fast.

"I don't know what that is, but the other day they cut the tail off an angry puma, so just watch out for your own tail".

The bear laughed, or maybe he growled. The butterflies didn't know much about bears, so it was only a guess, but his whole body shook and the great muscles quivered. "Big talk from little muchas", he remarked. "Tell your guides I'm no pussycat but the King of the Mountains! Tell them that". His tail twitched a little, but he put it out of mind by standing tall and threatening and gnashing his teeth loudly. It was an old habit of his which basically meant 'I am Oso! I take what I want! Get used to it'. He turned and stumbled over a sack that was hard to see, spilling things out of it. Only one thing caught his eye - a honey jar. He fumbled with it, somehow unscrewing the cover, and licked out the contents with his tongue. Then he waddled off, already beginning to think about the next meal. He was fattening up for winter - for hibernation in the high mountains - and he was greedy.

Boca flew after him, hoping for *some* little thing - almost *anything* - to put a better face on the mess when the fairies returned. His watch had turned into shambles.

"I think you should at least say *Thank You*", he suggested. "There might be less trouble later".

The bear snapped at him playfully. He'd never met such sassy muchas. "Sure", he rumbled. "Tell them it's my treat next time".

"That'll help!" said Boca. "Have a nice day".

"I don't see why not! It's been great so far." With that, he stood up, sniffed the air, and trundled off into the woods. The muchas were forgotten.

El Boca went down and broke the bad news to the fairies. He did lose a little shine off his reputation, but very little. They had brought the crackers and cold cuts down with them and at least had a nice lunch after their baths. The loss would be made up somehow. It wasn't the first time a bear had robbed them. All the way back up the fellows traded bear stories - recent and ancient - all of them horrifying.

They were pleasantly surprised to find the bear hadn't rummaged the rest of their gear, and Pio held up a bag of flour, untouched. He estimated that he could replace almost all the lost bakery goods. No one replied to that.

They moved on in decent spirits. A bath will do that for anyone, and the dirtier you are the more it refreshes. So there were even smiles and a joke or two, and a bounce in their step. For Yero, a better-smelling Obobo was almost as good as taking a bath herself.

It turned into a perfect afternoon on their side of the mountains. The sun warmed the western slopes and the breeze smelled good. They appreciated the dry woods that day because it clearly wasn't as nice on the other side. All day they heard distant thunder as storms moving in off the ocean spent themselves on the eastern side, unable to cross the great divide except for a few harmless wisps. It was so nice they marched on even after sunset in the light of a nearly full moon, climbing gradually higher on the slopes. Then the nice evening was shattered when the sound of large animals fighting rent the air up ahead in the woods.

"Bear!" said Pio. "Puma!" said Peco, and they argued quietly while the savage fight went on. Eventually it ended, or at least the racket died down, and it was decided not to venture further until morning but to make a fire in case one of the beasts approached. Supper was frugal. They had one ring of baloney left and roasted that over the fire like a big hot dog, eating it along with the last of the crackers but one. That served as a plate for the butterflies, and enough honey was salvaged from the licked-out honey jar to make a meal for them. It was meant kindly and they accepted it politely and ate it, but they closed their eyes and ate fast.

They didn't post a watch other than their usual practice of sleeping near the fire with a few long sticks of wood at hand. Whenever one of the fairies awoke during the night, he poked a new stick into the embers to light and went back to sleep with a finger on the other end, should a torch be needed. But it wasn't. Morning came and a grey sky greeted them. Clouds had finally crossed the mountains, but they had dumped their rain and now held only dreariness. Breakfast was simple: One dry dinner roll and a few odds & ends of cold cuts were all that remained to go with Peco's strong coffee, and that was the last of the groceries.

Pio dug out a little rubber pouch and unzipped it to leaf through his recipe cards. There weren't very many and all the recipes called for yeast, which presented a problem. His old yeast was 'dead', or so weak it might as well be; and the store had been out of that. Still, an idea occurred, and a smile spread across his face. "Flapjacks!" he announced happily. "We can have flapjacks for days with all this flour!"

"And what might we put on them?" asked Obobo.

There was no satisfactory answer to that. The flapjacks would have to wait. Anyway, they had eaten well for days. If they had slim pickings for the next few, so what? They would grumble, but that sort of thing is understood out in the wild. They weren't overly concerned. What they did worry about is what they worried about all night: The fighting animals. Were they still nearby? The path ahead led directly toward last night's uproar. They proceeded with caution through a gully and up the other side, then past a grove of tall pines, and then...

They stopped to marvel at the sight. The fight had produced a winner and a loser, if you could call it that. Both were still locked together. *Caught together,* actually. A great black bear, very much alive, and a full-grown puma, very much dead, were each caught by the leg in the jaws of the same trap, and the heavy metal trap chained to a tree. The bear was the same one the butterflies had made acquaintance with, and when he saw the fairies he quit biting at the trap and sat down *plop,* directly on his tail.

The fairies saw instantly that the bear was no threat if they kept their distance and took time out to laugh at him in his misery.

"Is this the great 'Oso' you talked about?" said Obobo to the butterflies. "The King of the Mountains?"

"I think so", replied Boca.

"Ask him. Ask him if he's the Pastry King".

"No need to ask", growled the bear. "I know the muchas".

"Thievery didn't pay, did it?" scolded Pio. "It led to this".

"You set up the buffet", shrugged the bear. "I just ate it".

"And what did you fight about here? Did you steal his supper too?"

A hint of a grin flickered across the bear's face. "No. Check out the cat's tail".

There was none, only a scab. It was the lion they had fought, now come to an unhappy end.

"Amusing, isn't it?" said the bear. "*A puma without a tail is just a bobcat*. That's what I told him".

The fairies laughed with him, having even less sympathy for the big cat. Peco showed the souvenir tuft and they laughed some more, but the bear squirmed uncomfortably.

"How did it come to this?" asked Obobo. "What happened with the trap?"

The bear described the fight, pleased with himself despite deep scratches across his nose. It was pure bad luck that some hombre had set a trap here, but at least he hadn't stepped in it alone and the puma left free to tease him. Grrrr! Just thinking about *that* set off another fit of temper. Oso grabbed the dead cat in his jaws and shook it violently. That was a mistake. The trap jerked his foot. He threw the carcass down so hard it bounced.

The fairies backed away from the wild action, making a slow detour to go on their way.

"Don't blame us", said Pio. "We hoped to get revenge on you, but we don't use that kind of trap. It belongs to the Big People, the Big Hombres".

The bear wrinkled his nose. "What *are* you, anyway? Your scent isn't the same as hombres. It's new to me".

"Call us 'little people'. That's close enough. But we'd better leave now. We avoid the Big Hombres too, and they'll be coming to check their traps".

"They'll kill me, you know that", said the bear. "Help me to get loose".

"We don't trust you. We can fight a puma, but not a bear. Not one as big as you".

The sound of a diesel engine came from somewhere down the canyon. No one spoke. No one had to. It was likely the trappers.

Boca broke the silence, shouting to make the bear hear him. "You said it would be 'your treat next time', remember? We need food. What can you find for us?"

Oso perked up. "*Honey*! I'll get you *honey*. Where are you going?"

"All the way south along the mountains", said Pio. "But why should we trust you? You might eat one of us if you don't find honey".

The engine noise grew louder. An hombre could be heard yelling, still down the canyon, but closer. Also, a dog.

"Let the muchas decide", said the bear suddenly. "Why not? They know me".

There was a pause as the fairies looked to the butterflies.

"He told us he didn't eat *muchas*", said Yero. "That was nice. And he could have swatted us for arguing, but he didn't".

"Fair enough", said Obobo. "But what's the deal with the honey? Is it wild?"

"Naturally", said the bear. "In honey trees. That's where it always is".

"Maybe you can find it, but what about the bees? The bees will sting us".

"No worries, no worries! You'll get honey - no stings". The bear kept one ear trained toward the canyon road. His time was running out.

The fairies looked skeptical but finally Obobo jerked a thumb at the heavy trap. Peco pulled out his hatchet and advanced toward the bear. So did Pio. Yero was aghast. "Don't fight!" she started to shout, but they weren't about to, and the bear knew it. They used one hatchet to pound on the other, wedging the trap open a crack, and then pried the crack a little wider. It was enough and the bear didn't waste his chance. He jerked hard. Out came the paw and the hatchets too, everything except the puma's leg. The bear landed in a heap, bounced back up and limped away on three legs at a great pace off the trail and into the deep woods. The fairies followed.

He led them higher up, right to the timberline, before stopping to lick his injured paw. There were no bee trees at this altitude, and he didn't pretend there were. He only wanted to be near the cold rocks if the hombres trailed him with dogs, thinking his scent would be harder to follow. But the sounds drifting up from below signaled luck was still with him. The trappers were pleased with the puma hide and continued on their trapline, never guessing the whole story.

Pio got out the first aid kit and had a look at the paw. It was ugly. The skin was ripped up pretty badly, not even counting trouble that might come from being pinched for hours. He opened the kit and it was almost empty. There was one needle, a bit of fine suture thread and part of the bottle of antiseptic.

"This might sting a little", he said and emptied the bottle, working it deep into the gashes with his fingers. The bear took it well, but he would not move an inch until the trappers and their dogs returned and drove off again. Who could blame him? But it was boring for everyone else. Then the bear fell asleep and started snoring as only a fat bear can snore.

"It's a lot to put up with for a little honey", grumbled Peco.

"You just wait! It'll taste scrumptious on my flapjacks", said Pio.

"*If* he finds some, and *if* we get any of it, and *if* your flapjacks can be chewed, and *if* the bear doesn't eat them first, and *if*..."

"Hold on now! *If* you don't want any, I *will* give them to the bear! He'd eat 'em".

Peco turned away, signaling he might not be that stubborn.

"The bear's a little fussy", said Boca, sticking his nose into the middle of it. "He spit out the pie crust".

"First of all, my flapjacks will be soft, *not* crusty", lectured Pio. "Second of all, it's a fact that black bears will eat almost anything that fits into their mouths when they're hungry. That's how the Lord made them, and I've never seen any reason to doubt the story".

"Tell us!" requested Yero. "Atel always told us the stories".

This was unexpected. The fairies had heard each other's stories so many times they didn't even bring them up anymore. Obobo set the butterflies down and wandered off in one direction, Peco in another, bored in advance. "Just don't encourage him too much", hinted Peco. "We gotta leave soon".

"Ignore them", advised Pio. "My stories are all true. They don't change with every telling".

"Or get any better, either", Obobo called back. "But never mind. I'll correct a few things later".

Pio scowled in both directions at once, if that's possible, and began in a voice loud enough so they had to hear it.

—The Honey Bears—

In the Beginning, after the Lord made the land and the sea and the sky, He named the eagle 'King of the Skies', and the lion 'King of the Lands'. They tolerated each other and didn't care who might end up being King under the Sea, an issue that hadn't been settled yet. Thus, order was established in the animal kingdom and the Lord left to continue His works in the heavens. But when He checked back one fine morning, He discovered the lions had been lazy. They hadn't budged from where they were before - in the nicer, warmer parts of the world. They had kept order only locally. Elsewhere, there was disorder. Another King was obviously needed.

That morning the Lord took ice and snow and made from it the great white bears of the north. In the afternoon of the day, He took boulders from the high mountains and made from them the great brown bears, very large animals like their white cousins.

But altogether these were still few, so He worked through the night with whatever was at hand and made a great many smaller bears to roam the rest of the world, and these took on the color of the night in which they were made.

Part 4: The Lure of the Dragon Range

The white bears were satisfied because they were given all the seals to eat. The brown bears were pleased because they were given the moose and the elk. The black bears weren't special in any way, so they were given nothing special for food.

"Are we to be just scavengers?" they asked.

"Yes", answered the Lord as He turned to leave. "There's edible food everywhere. Clean it up".

It was pretty deflating.

"What about dessert?" growled one. "How about a special *dessert* at least?"

The Lord reflected a moment. What was the harm? He turned back. "You can have the honey", He replied. "If you can get past the bees".

***

"That's the part I'm worried about", said Yero when Pio finished. "We got some honey once, but we had to be *very* polite. I just don't think the bear has it in him".

"No, he doesn't", said Pio. "Honey bears aren't polite at all. But you'll see. He'll still get it".

"You never told the part about how they almost put the bees out of business", said 'Bo, returning now. He'd been listening, bent on correcting Pio on something. He collected the butterflies on his finger again to 'finish out' the story.

"I was coming to that!" said Pio angrily, but Obobo ignored him and launched into his amendment:

***

The great brown bears had so much game that they all grew fat by autumn, so fat it made them sleepy. They found dens under the ice and deep mountain snow and slept through the winter. They still do, and it's a lucky thing because life is tougher in winter, but that's not why they do it. They do it because of *nibbana*, the bliss they enter in the long sleep. Once they've done it, they'll go to any lengths to do it again, and mothers teach this to their cubs. However, it doesn't work if they aren't fat enough. The blissful dreams don't come. That was a problem for ordinary black bears.

Maybe there was less food where they lived; or maybe there were just too many of them. But they didn't get fat enough and the dreams didn't come very often, until a wise old sow figured out the answer.

They all remembered the old promise of honey, but few ever got past the bee stings. The old sow learned that if she waited until she was almost too fat to climb the bee tree, the stings didn't get through the fat. She couldn't even feel them, except a few on the nose. She also learned that's what put on the necessary extra pounds: Lots of dessert! She taught her cubs and the word spread. Black bears, too, found *nibbana*.

That's when problems arose. Black bears ate all the honey in late autumn when it was too late to make more. The hives died off. Bee trees became scarce. Lucky for the bees, that's about the time Big People appeared who hunted and trapped the bears.

***

"That's how it stands now", said Obobo, finishing up his addendum. "Things got balanced out. The bees returned from near extinction, but it's a fact the Big People have been tough on the bears".

"...Unless you consider their garbage", put in Peco, who now arrived in time to add his own postscript. Fairies love to get one-up on each other.

"Leave it to you to bring that up", grunted Obobo.

"Don't give me that!" laughed Peco. "You could've been born a bear yourself the way you root through a dump".

Obobo put his nose up and would have stomped off with the butterflies, but they wanted to hear more. They were dumpster-divers too, at heart.

"There's just less food to be had in the wild nowadays", Peco explained. "And less room to roam, too. It all adds up to less bears, especially less *fat* ones. *Nibbana* would have been lost to black bears again except for an unexpected gift from their mortal enemies: Big People's garbage. The Big People dump out enough food to feed half the animal kingdom, and that's what a lot of bears fatten up on now".

"Well!" said Yero after a pause. "I feel I've learned a lot about bears, but I can't help wondering...how would *he* tell it?" She looked at their bear, who had quit snoring but was still plainly asleep.

He was slowly awakening but still in a light slumber, the state where a lot of wild animals hear and smell things. "They got it pretty close", said the bear suddenly, licking his lips and nose. "These little people are like bears with scraggly fur". He rolled over and snored a few more notes, then sat up quickly on his rear and licked the sore foot. The drowsiness vanished from his eyes and he looked around. "I haven't talked in my sleep, have I?"

Without waiting for an answer, he got up and took a few steps, and then a lumbering bound. "Much better!" he said and headed south. He did limp, but it hardly slowed him down. All that afternoon and into the evening he led them in search of honey trees, mostly because of his promise but also because he himself had reached such a stage of rotundity that he craved desserts. He visited half a dozen trees that he knew of, but all showed signs that other hive robbers had been there first, and they had been. All he got was a stung nose and swarms of angry honeybees chasing him off through the woods.

That was his plan, when he got a good tree. He would rile up the hive and draw them off so the fairies could climb and get the honeycombs. That was good enough for young bear cubs who didn't mind a few stings, but the fairies weren't too keen and didn't complain when the bear found no good trees that day.

That evening Pio made the fire and got out his flapjack recipe. The bear didn't like fire and went off into the woods. Peco made coffee and they all got something fancy to go with it when Pio produced sugar packets and little cups of artificial cream he'd borrowed from the store lunch counter and saved back "for when we've got nothing else".

Boca asked for coffee like the fellows and they gave him a little, straight black with sugar. Yero was quite satisfied with just sugar-water. The most pleasant minutes of the day passed while Pio reviewed his recipe.

"Well, I'll have to substitute", he announced finally. "It calls for eggs and we don't have any". He dug through the grub sacks and found a squeeze bottle of mayonnaise. "This'll do", he decided. "It's got eggs in it and should whip up about the same way". He emptied most of the flour into a bowl and squeezed all the mayonnaise onto it, then referred back to the recipe. "*Milk*, it says. I'll substitute some of these creamer cups". He emptied six or seven into the bowl. "*Oil*". He did have cooking oil and poured some on. "Let's see: *Cream of tartar,* yes; *Vanilla,* yes; *Salt,* yes; *Baking soda,* yes; *Cinnamon*--why not? And *yeast* of course. Well, it's weak. I'll put all of it in". He added water last, stirred everything up nicely and set it near the fire to rise.

Then he leaned back on a tree root and reminisced about the good old days when he had been 'Chief Assistant Chef of the Halls' - the upper, habitable parts of the old gold mines.

"We had regular kitchens then", he said. "Two, for the different shifts. I was usually in charge of the Night Kitchen, myself". Pio stretched out his arms and cracked his knuckles for emphasis.

"I remember well", said Obobo. "I saw you leaning back like that many times".

"The posture comes from being important and overseeing everything", Pio explained to the butterflies. "Sometimes the help gets the wrong impression".

"There was a long waiting list to get on day shift", put in Peco, "so miners could eat in the other kitchen".

"Pay no attention", said Pio grandly. "It's an old tradition to complain about cafeteria food no matter how good it is. It was pretty fancy fare, truth be told. We never had to substitute in those days. The cupboards and pantries were always full".

"That's where we came in", Obobo interrupted again. "We were traders, me and Peco. Traders kept the shelves stocked and made the cook's job easy".

"Not as easy as trading", maintained Pio. "What could be easier than trading gold for ordinary goods?"

"It *was* easy at first", agreed Obobo " - ignoring the long trips and heavy packs. But the tribes learned fast and figured out pretty quick that we couldn't eat our gold. The bargaining got tough all too soon, especially with one tribe. I think you can guess which one".

"The one with the Jaguars?" guessed Yero.

The boys nodded silently. Peco stoked the fire. "I wouldn't mind a peep at the old 'Digs'", he said. "We'll be just passing by, not that far off".

It was on all their minds. It always was, just under the surface. They hadn't sunk a mineshaft in centuries, but gold and jewels still came into their dreams.

"How far from here?" asked Boca, who had also dreamed of gold.

"A week or two, it all depends", said Obobo. "Are you okay?"

"Sure. I think so. Why?"

"Your eyes are twice as big as they were. Um...how much coffee did you drink?"

"I dunno. Some".

Obobo reached the butterflies out on his finger so the others could have a look at El Boca. They laughed.

"El Boca can have first watch", suggested Peco.

"Probably second watch too", said Pio.

"He might still be awake to see you make flapjacks in the morning", said Obobo. "It'll take that long for your batter to raise".

It was the yeast not doing its job. Pio was half-expecting it. "No matter!" he declared. "It'll be *flat*-jacks instead and they'll taste just as good. We'll re-heat 'em tomorrow and have honey on 'em! Now where's that green willow?"

Peco reluctantly fetched willow sticks they had cut down by the water and laid two across the hot coals to set the fry pan on. For 'gourmet' cooking Pio didn't want the pan right on the fire. He spooned the first batter on, four small dollops in the pan. The others couldn't bear to watch and went to get a little sleep some distance away, but Peco was bothered by the willow smoke and made a mental note. Yero also went to sleep and dreamed about pancakes with faces, but El Boca never slept a wink.

It was the bear who roused the camp in the morning, eager for honey. The fire had burnt out, so he ventured close enough to flip the smaller fairies over and Obobo up onto his rear end. The butterflies had perched for the night atop the not-too-tall stack of flatjacks and he nosed them too, surprised that Boca was awake so early. Then he backed away, having got a whiff of the stack.

"That'll stunt your growth", he growled.

Pio glowered at him and carefully put the flatjacks in a sack all by themselves. He slung it over his shoulder with a muffled grunt and trudged after the bear who was already on the move. Maybe the flatjacks did lack something, he admitted to himself, but they would make up for it with durability!

Coffee had to be skipped to keep up with the bear, and the one who needed it most now was Boca, who fell asleep on Obobo's finger not twenty feet down the trail. He could've used another shot of Peco's Best.

The bear smelled out more honey trees that day, a long day on the mountain slopes toward the south, but none were worthwhile. All had been robbed in recent weeks and that spelled trouble, even if they had begun new combs. These were all the new bees now, the angry type. They were angry enough when first robbed, downright dangerous the second time. However, near sundown he found what bears think of as *their* gold mine: A huge oak, very hollow from the ground up. Some ambitious woodpecker had made a row of holes right up the trunk at one time and these were the major entrances. Honeycomb actually bulged out from some of them. Perfect! But what about the bees?

The butterflies were set down at a safe distance, El Boca still asleep and Yero to keep watch, while the gang of thieves held a pow-wow. Mostly the bear did the talking, but Peco had his own plan as well; so, as darkness gathered and all the worker bees returned and settled down, the fairies lit a small fire next to the hollow base. When it got going, they added damp grass and some of the green willow. Soon smoke curled around the trunk and up through the trunk itself.

"I'm not going up through that!" declared the bear. "What's the big idea?"

"An old hombre trick", grinned Peco. "The bees'll be sick for a while and we can help ourselves to the goodies. See now? I'll steer all the smoke inside". He leaned branches against the trunk and hung his jacket over them. It wasn't perfect, but in the light of the fire they could see smoke coming out the woodpecker holes. All at once, the bear grasped the idea and started to climb. So did Pio and Peco, while 'Bo tended the fire.

The fairies had brought several kettles and 'Bo tossed them up one at a time to the others. The bear filled them all. The bees stung him when he reached in for comb after comb, but if you've ever seen a bearpaw you'll know it barely tickled him. Some of the combs were nurseries and he threw those away, but most were the very best honey. He gorged himself.

Finally, the bear called a halt, figuring the hive needed what was left for the winter, and the gang climbed back down no worse for the wear.

"Just one more thing", said the bear. "We need to put some distance between us and the tree. They'll be out looking early in the morning. I'd rather not be found".

The fairies got lids on the kettles, collected the butterflies and their gear and put out the fire, only to have trouble with the bear. He had fallen asleep waiting for them.

Maybe it was the smoke. He had breathed it most and was least accustomed to it. But they couldn't rouse him, and it got a little worrisome. Peco noticed a grin slowly spreading across the bear's face and wondered aloud if he might be slipping into the 'bliss'. That was especially worrisome, and they tried harder, pulling and poking at him with no success.

Peco tried speaking quietly into his ear, calling to him. The grin faded but that was all. The other fellows tried too but got no response. They had begun to shrug their shoulders about it all when Yero asked to try it. Obobo smiled indulgently and held her close enough to say something. Whatever it was, the bear came fully awake in moments and scrambled to his feet, glowering at everyone. Then the mood passed as he gathered his wits.

"Off we go then!" he growled.

Everyone had gotten a bit nervous about the bees, so they put a lot of distance behind. A whole mountain peak passed by to their left, bathed in moonlight, before they camped near another good hive. The bear had found his way to an old favorite tree and thought they should do that for breakfast. They all fell asleep without even a fire or any talk about supper. That happens when you snack on sweets all evening.

Except for El Boca, of course, who wasn't tired. His days and nights were all turned around and he bothered Yero with small talk until she got cross with him, and he realized others weren't as wide-awake as he was. But there was one last question that baffled him: "What did you say in his ear that woke him up like that?"

Yero yawned. "I just said his tail was sticking up and the fellows were going to cut it off".

Boca dreamed about that and a grin spread across his face too, almost like the bear. *Nibbana* means different things to different folks.

The sun was up when he awoke. The bear was gone somewhere, and the fairies were gathered around a small fire. Pio was re-heating his flatjacks and extolling their virtues. There was no mannerly way out of it, so the others held forth their plates and received their 'ration' of one, as Pio put it. He warned that they might have to ration these out for days to come, so they 'dursent get greedy' about it.

Peco spread honey with his hunting knife and tried cutting a bite with his fork. No luck there, but he did get it cut with the knife. The next hurdle was to chew it, but it was too rubbery. He finally washed the piece down with water and set out to cut smaller pieces.

Obobo kept spreading his honey, over and over, while he watched Peco's plight. He sighed. Pio's cooking was living up to its reputation. He set the butterflies down a little enviously with their plain honey and began sawing his cakes into small pieces too. "Yes, I agree", he said. "We'd best ration them. It wouldn't be wise to eat them all at once".

As for the bear, Pio didn't offer, and the bear didn't ask for any.

They worked the same smoky trick on the nearby tree after breakfast, with decent results for the time of day. The bees were already active and only the bear dared climb up with so many buzzing around. They slung two kettles around his neck and he did all the work, mostly stuffing his mouth but scraping some into the kettles too. Then the bees chased him down. He came on drowsy again but only when they were safely down the trail. The bear was expecting it this time. His speech became slurred and rumbly, but they seemed to be approaching his home, his *ajero* is what he called it. Soon he ambled off the trail and up the steep slope like a typical bear, without any goodbyes, shaking his drooping head and licking the last honey from his cheeks.

The fairies waved after him but didn't stop. They never took many breaks on the road anyway, and now the lure of their own ancient home stirred them. With the honey and no need to sit down to eat (except when Pio insisted on 'rations') they marched steadily, at as good a pace as caution would allow, and approached the southern end of the Long Mountains by the evening of the fourth day after the last bee tree. They made camp on the southwestern shoulder of the last mountain peak, a good vantage point to plan the next day's march. The fairies were in fine spirits, very pleased to have come to the last mountain; yet everywhere Yero looked were more mountain peaks in the distance.

Chapter 20

The Roads More Travelled

"More mountains?" asked Yero. "Is that all there *is* in this land?"

"No, and yes", replied Obobo. "There's a wide civilized expanse to cross first, and *then* more mountains". He waved west/southwest toward distant peaks still illuminated by the setting sun. "There is the *Dragon Range,* so named for the beast you've heard about. It was called that for a hundred years after he was gone, and then another hundred because the volcanic fires and the old dragon tales fit together so well. But that's all forgotten now. Men have their own names for things".

"When did dragons come into the story anyway? The Big Story, I mean. Did the Lord put them here?"

"Again, yes and no. The way we heard it, He put the old ones out *there*..." (Obobo waved toward the stars) "...but the young ones turned up *here* on their own".

"There must be more to that story", prompted Boca. "Dragons are pretty awesome".

"Words just fall short. And we only know of the really big ones from old tales".

"There was a purpose for them", asserted Pio, taking over the story. "The Lord *always* has a purpose".

"So does Pio", Obobo informed the butterflies. "He fancies himself as the storyteller. Let him tell it then".

So, he did.

—THE *DIRE-AGON*—

When Creation began to take shape the Lord summoned helpers from the Light to polish the rough edges of His new universe. These were the Artisans of Evermore, as you've heard: A dozen or more ladies with thread and needles, a cosmic sewing circle to follow Him, knitting together loose ends and stitching extra beauty into His works when He must move on to new ones.

They were perfectly true to His thought until they became so skilled at their job that they drifted into thoughts of their own, and one thought above all occurred to them that the Lord didn't expect: They were unhappy with His stars, with His pure white light. It had become boring.

"What could be better?" asked the Lord impatiently. "White is the opposite of darkness".

"We'd like *color,* if you please. Something prettier to work with".

"Okay. Light the stars yourselves, then. Put in any color you like - but keep up! Don't fall behind about it".

This wasn't what they had in mind. Fire was supposed to be *His* work. The ladies didn't like it.

"We don't want to *start* the fires", they replied. "We only want more beauty in them. There are natural colors within Your white, Lord. Let them out. Let us decorate with them!"

The Lord paused to consider this. The Artisans were fabulously helpful, and He knew they did their best work when they were happy. The solution that occurred to Him put this somewhat at risk. Oh, well. He had to keep His eye on the Big Picture. Some risk along the way was inevitable.

He made up His mind and summoned spirits from the ether - untamed spirits that had no purpose yet except their own. There were seven in total, loyal neither to darkness nor light but only to themselves, and they answered the summons grudgingly.

"We hear you", they growled.

"I have a gift for you and a job I think you'll like. Interested?"

"Maybe. Right now, we have an arrangement with the darkness that suits us. What's your deal?"

"Fire. Watch this!" The Lord gave a little demonstration to capture their interest. It didn't take much. Then He explained what was needed. "You will be the fire-starters, each with a different color. The Artisans here will fill in the details if you agree to help".

The spirits readily agreed. There isn't much mischief one can do out in the darkness and they too were bored. "Count us in", they said. "This might be fun".

The Lord allowed them fully into the light then, and they were revealed. The ladies were aghast. "They're ugly!"

But ugliness and beauty are different things from different angles. The Lord looked at the enormous flying creatures and was optimistic they could do the job. He gave them fire: To each, one color of the spectrum, and put them straight to work.

"Remember, the ladies are in charge", He emphasized. "Do what they say! Any questions?"

There were none. There never would be any. These were the titanic dragons of yore - capable of melting icy comets, of firing up new stars with their breath; monsters that could blot out the sun with their great wings. The Artisans didn't like them, and the feeling was mutual, but there's no denying they put color into the heavens.

So, the First Age of the World passed, and with it the largest works of creation. The breathtaking pace slowed down, though it never actually stopped, or ever will. Stars burn out and new ones need lighting up even today, but there is less and less work for the Seven. They lost interest in the new, calmer heavens and sort of faded away. The Artisans politely suggested an out-of-the-way place to spend their retirement, *very* out-of-the-way.

***

(Pio paused to chuckle at this part, and Obobo jumped back in to finish the story.)

"It's been an Age or two without much news of them. Maybe they took the ladies' advice, maybe not. But that part of the sky became known as *Draco* - the dragon - and was said to be the direction from which the lesser dragons came that have plagued the earth in our own Age. Sons and daughters, no doubt. They appeared on earth first in the far north and were called *Agon* for their fire: The *Dire-Agon*. The name was soon shortened up to *Dragon*. It's a mighty history and likely not over".

***

"That's all very well to talk about", put in Peco, "but their downfall here on earth wasn't so high and mighty. Tell about their garbage dumps".

"I left that for you again".

"Well, it's true. Their messy habits worked against them. In every Age there are a few heroes brave enough to battle even dragons. When a hero arose, he found it easy to locate the beasts from the smell of their garbage. Dragons are gluttons and slobs, and most of them dumped their waste right out the front door - down a mountainside, usually". Peco paused and scowled at Obobo. "It's a good lesson for anyone", he added meaningfully.

***

Obobo ignored him. Meteor showers had begun above, easy to see in the December sky and quite close at this altitude. From lower elevations, these falling stars seem to wink out, but most simply break up into esporellia, too small to see from a distance. Obobo held Yero up to catch some and Boca caught a lot and shared it, enough to replenish their color and with it their good cheer and curiosity. Yero asked a question that had been bugging her.

"We aren't going *into* the Dragon Mountains, are we? Even if the dragon is gone it still sounds risky".

The Butterflies, Yero and Boca

"Yes. We are. It draws us more and more. And it's the last leg of your journey also, the way to Manino".

"We're that close?"

"Oh, I didn't mean it quite that way. Manino is well up in the Dragon Range, still a few hundred miles from here as the Yankees measure it".

"I guess that'll work for us", said Yero. "We're Yankees too. We just go south for the winter".

***

They made no fire that night, or even any silhouette against the high mountain skyline that might attract attention, but laid plans to cross a wide river and well-populated lowlands that separated the great mountain ranges. If all went well, they intended to cross the river over a railway bridge, on a freight train, disguised as migrants. It had to be disguise. They didn't dare dust themselves now, so close to the old stronghold of their enemies. When the sun rose, they would need substance and good shadows or risked being seen by the wrong eyes. "Get some rest", advised Pio. "It's up early for us or we'll miss the train".

Before pre-dawn, the fairies were stirring and arguing in the dark. Pio insisted on passing out cold flatjacks and spread the ration of honey on them himself so the others would think twice before tossing them in the dark. The coffee was cold too, leftover from yesterday, but still welcome. Boca requested 'just a spot' to go with his honey.

"I want to be at my best", he said when Yero thought it foolish.

"You're getting into 'uppers' and 'downers'", she informed him. "Didn't you ever hear of that? You get 'up' from the coffee and that's okay, but when it wears off you come back 'down', and then some. The next step is 'down and *out*'".

"Not for me, Yero. Not if I can get refills".

Peco laughed and assured Yero they would get him 'off the stuff' in time so he would sleep at night. With that, the boys gathered up their gear and headed down the slopes toward the river and the rail sidings where the freight cars were parked in rows.

Dawn was in the sky when they got to the yard. An engine blared somewhere up ahead near the bridge. The engineer laid on the horn longer than necessary, drawing rough profanity from the yard laborers. The fairies wore their sombreros and long jackets with the collars up, very natural in the chill air. They were spotted right away.

"You there! You three! What're you up to?" shouted an assistant foreman. Migrants were a pain in the neck! No food, no money, no brains whatsoever around rail cars - and if one of them got hurt it would be himself getting chewed out for it.

"Passing through, just passing through!" Obobo shouted back.

The assistant foreman came running. Passing through? Yeah, sure. That's what they all said. The yard workers used to kick them out, but it got to be so many they helped them now. Helped them on their *way*, that is. As he got closer, he realized they weren't much more than kids. A big fat boy and his little brothers. Mierda de toro! The migrant problem was getting worse.

"Here!" he shouted. "Get in this car if you're going north! No? Then get in that one over on the next siding. You'll be hooked up and out of here by noon, maybe sooner if the engineer quits playing with his horn!"

It may sound too good to be true, but it happens in railyards all over Mexico these days. Usually it involves a small shakedown. It just happened to be free today, at this busy hour.

They climbed up into the car and found it already half-full of migrant passengers. They pulled in their chin whiskers the best they could and claimed the last empty corner for their own. Every eye in the car followed them, which always happens, but even more so with these pitiable muchachos with no shoes. A kindly mujir came over to check on them. Obobo tipped his hat politely. Underneath were the butterflies sitting in the large bald spot. "Boo!" said Boca. Obobo pulled his hat down quickly but the woman had seen all she cared to and returned to her group.

"On the run from some institution, I'm afraid", she whispered. "Not right in the head".

"Now you've done it, silly goose!" said Yero. "That's what comes from all that coffee".

Boca couldn't answer. He was still laughing.

The big door was slid shut. A back-up bell started dinging way up ahead and the engine came toward them making crashing noises like a chain automobile accident. Bang! Chung! Chunk! Presently their car took a jolt, and the next one. A whole series of loose cars were hooked together - and then sat still.

After a while, everyone gave up on the idea of starting out. A while after that the door slid open again and a pair of young bandidos climbed in, toughs wearing their caps at odd angles. They pointed their switchblades around the car and decided to rob the fairies first, the smallest group with the biggest bags.

It was dim in that corner but light enough to see the hatchets and hunting knives when the fairies opened their jackets. If that wasn't enough to discourage the bandidos, the fairies snarled like animals. The toughs backed off but didn't leave. Next, they accosted the kindly mujir and her group, who quickly opened their bags and let the bandidos rifle through them. That bothered the fairies.

Obobo took off his hat, set the butterflies on it, and moved toward the trouble with Pio and Peco right alongside. The toughs waved their knives, but it didn't matter. In a fight, fairies are like wild animals, stronger than most Big People despite their size, and much faster. All at once, the bandidos found themselves flying out the door and landing headfirst in the slag and cinders. The fairies retired to their corner with all eyes upon them once more.

The kindly mujir approached again - though not as closely - to offer her thanks and tell them about a nice orphanage where they might turn themselves in. The runaway life was no good, she advised them. "Why, once they clean you up, who knows? (She shuddered a bit) Someone might adopt you! Would you like references? I'll be glad to introduce you".

At that point the assistant foreman cursed them for opening the door and slid it shut again. The kindly mujir cursed back as good as any yard worker before she caught her tongue. She hobbled back to her group, determined to try again later. The 'orphanage' paid hundreds of pesos for the cutest, marketable toddlers; maybe 25 for the less marketable ones. She did the math quickly: 75 pesos! Possibly extra for the cutlery.

Her plan never came to fruition. The train finally moved forward and others in the mujir's little gang of traffickers discouraged her. Lucky for them. They might've been the next ones flying out the door if the fairies smelled that kind of rat.

The train, nearly a hundred cars altogether, gathered speed enough to manage the ramp and bridge. Once across it turned left to follow the river for a little way, and then bent towards the great populous regions southeastward of the mountains. The fairies had no knowledge of the route but it was plainly south, and they intended to go west. They picked up their stuff, slid open the door a bit and disembarked. "That's the trouble with kids nowadays", said the kindly mujir. "Uncontrollable!"

There were bumps and bruises. Even fairies can't tumble onto cinders and just laugh about it. Obobo's hat was knocked off and Boca went somersaulting, but Yero hung on to 'Bo's ear and escaped further injury.

From there they fell in line and trudged along a busy road all morning like typical migrants in search of work. The road took them up onto a broad, uneven plateau, the next leg of the journey. It would be perhaps a two-day's march across that to reach an arm of the great Dragon Range that thrust northwards, interrupting civilized lands. It was on the northeastern slopes of this arm where the old fairy 'Digs' used to be, of which the boys hoped to find some remnant. Owing to the natural mountain slope the main entrance and several side entrances to the *Commons* had opened to the east and were always open. There had never been any need to close them until the treachery of the Tribe and the coming of the dragon.

The beast had loosed avalanches, covering them all except the front one which he used. Later, the earth swallowed that too. Surely it remained that way: Out of sight, out of mind, out of history. The fellows had never gone back to disturb bad memories. Now they planned to. There was talk of light shafts and ventilating shafts, possibly still serviceable; but mostly the talk was of a 'north' entrance, lesser used in the old days.

Memories of those places had become a bit hazy, but the roads of the plateau were quite familiar. This was a 'cut-across' for the monarchs also, and the fellows knew the migratory route well from having guided occasional stragglers for half an age.

There would be several main roads to cross, along with two smaller rivers that couldn't be waded. All these ran diagonally southeast toward the populous regions - the ancient capital of their enemies. It was a great city now, proud of its archeological digs. Pyramids had been rehabilitated, temples restored, even sacrificial altars unearthed and put on display. All these things should have remained buried forever until the end of time but had been brought back up into the light of day. Because of this, things the earth had been well rid of stirred again in the underworld.

However, there are other worries more immediate to wayfarers on the roads. The Highway Police stopped the fairies. The patrol truck turned on its flashers and pulled up alongside as they trudged along the gravel shoulder. There were two officers and the one not driving leaned out the window, studying them through his sunglasses. "Looking for work?" he asked.

"Si", answered Obobo wearily. "Know of any?"

"They need help at the Mayor's hacienda over in our Home Municipality. You three might be just what the Lady is looking for". He waved toward the west.

"We're going that way anyhow", hinted Pio. "It would be easier to ride".

The officers were friendly and even invited the 'migrants' to sit in the back seat with belts on like respectable passengers, not in the cage that was bolted to the open box in the rear. Luck was with them, especially the fairies in their own personal quest. The officers steered generally northwest, exactly the direction toward their old mines, if it came to that.

But for now, reality intervened. They were given a few tips about their destination. They would be employed at a spacious mansion with extensive grounds. The Mayor of the Municipality was very rich, very important, but they wouldn't see much of him. He was always at City Hall. It was his wife, the Senora de la Grassa, who ran the hacienda, and she would speak to them upon arrival.

So, a trip of two or three days became instead a matter of that many hours, even accounting for braking and cornering on zig-zag roads, because they made very good time on the straightaways. *Very* good. Who was going to stop them?

Their city turned out to be in the lowest northeastern foothills of the Dragon Range, perhaps even in the vicinity of the old Digs, though it was hard to see much from the back seat of the patrol. What's more certain was, they had likely avoided plenty of trouble on the open road and were much nearer both of their goals. They could cut this job offer short, decline in any number of ways, and set out on the last legs. The Highway Police dropped them off near the big gates with a few words through an intercom and left. The fairies walked up to the gates and rang the bell, just for fun.

Obobo lifted his hat to give the butterflies some fresh air and a peek into the grounds. It was beautifully landscaped and there were hummingbirds at several pretty feeders. He pulled his hat down again just when it was interesting, as the guards came out of the shack.

They were uniformed city police. The Honorable Mayor, patron of the huge estate, could easily afford private security, but - well, that's how this stuff works in politics. The bigger the politician, the bigger the perks, and Mayor de la Grassa was very large in all aspects (except height).

The Senora was even shorter (barely over four feet) but broadly impressive and imposing in every other way, as should be expected of such an important woman in city society. But she was sensitive about her height. She wore elevator shoes to appear taller in public but took them off at home because they hurt her feet, and the servants - all somewhat taller than herself but the shortest she could find - hurt her pride. But now! What was *this?* She peeped through the silk curtains of the master bedroom (an entire upper floor) and smiled at the sight of Peco and Pio, if not Obobo, as they were escorted around to the servant's entrance. She must get a closer look, but it appeared as if she had just got some new house servants! She put on white gloves and a business face and hurried down to 'Receiving'.

The butler had them all lined up when she got there, and she could hardly contain her glee. They were a good half-inch shorter than herself - the smaller ones. But they were terrible otherwise: Seedy, grungy ragamuffins. The butler barked at them to remove their hats and bow to the Lady, which they did, awkwardly, and the Senora saw something that clinched the deal.

"Do you always keep butterflies under your hat?" she asked. "It must be stuffy for the poor things!" Without waiting for an answer, she snapped her fingers and a maid appeared from the kitchen. "A cake platter with refreshments for these Monarchs", she ordered. The maid disappeared. The Senora assumed the air of an army officer and inspected the new troops.

The maid returned with a platter on a pedestal and two tiny saucers of instant hummingbird nectar. Boca took the hint right away and went to sample it, but it had an off taste and he quietly spit it back out. Obobo set Yero next to him and the Senora's eyes narrowed.

"Oh, dear! This one isn't right", she said, "but nourishment should help. Put them in the kitchen where it's warmer!" She smiled beautifully after the butterflies, and then turned critically back to the fairies. "Clean them up and show them to me again!" she snapped at the butler.

It all happened fast. The fairies were led in one direction, the butterflies went another; but all seemed well enough for the moment. The butler led the boys to the men-servant's lavatory and lockers and pointed to the shower and soap.

"That's first for you. Put your dirty things in a locker. I shall return with suitable apparel".

They were treated to something new: Hacienda showers had warm water. The novelty kept their interest although they ignored the soap. The butler returned and laid out underwear, white suits, and ties. That was disgusting, but a little later he brought in a barber and a manicurist. All the long hair and whiskers would have to go, he informed them, but the manicurist would only do their hands. The Senora thought their wooly toes were cute.

Not a chance of this happening, you say? You are correct. Fairies will not go so far as to actually join the Big People's civilization. They politely declined the job offer and proceeded to undress and put their own clothes back on. The butler departed in haste.

Meanwhile in the kitchen the Senora was leaning close to the cake pedestal, quite concerned. The butterflies seemed to have no appetites! Could the nectar be stale? She snapped her fingers again. "Some fresh nectar here! Bring them into my study as soon as they've eaten - and get a lid on that!"

The maid followed orders, setting a pretty glass dome on top that matched the pedestal. She blushed and looked away from the butterflies.

"Something isn't right about this", said Boca. Yero felt the same. They didn't even sample the new 'fresh' nectar but dawdled over it to gain time, wondering where the fellows might be. Then the Senora shouted from the other room. It was hard to hear through the glass. The maid hoisted the cake platter, cover and all, and marched slowly into that room. Through the glass, Yero and Boca saw horrible things. The Senora had a hobby. She collected specimens.

All the walls were a display of flying insects. There was every kind known to the area, all stuck through with pins into the quaint knotty pine boards. One whole wall was devoted to moths, another to bees and wasps, still another to insects that hatched in the soil, or in water, and one wall - the longest one - to butterflies, with dozens of Rasha La prominently featured. If that weren't enough, stuffed (or simply dried) hummingbirds were suspended from the ceiling in carefree flying poses. All the insects were given active poses; or maybe they just died that way, Yero suddenly realized, when the pins were stuck through them.

"Now I know why all the hummingbird feeders down on the grounds", Boca whispered. "I hate to think what's in that nectar".

"I hate to think what's in *ours*".

The Senora assumed they had drunk some and was getting impatient, but the maid suggested "just a little more time to let it take effect". There was common sense to this. If the maid had to go in after them with a tweezers there would be rips and tears, possibly ruined specimens; however, the Senora wasn't concerned with "the crooked wing...just the good one".

All this macabre talk by Big People with no thought for who's listening goes to the heart of their ignorance about the Rasha La, who do indeed hear and understand. No one guesses that part and sometimes it works in favor of the butterflies. Here, that was yet to be determined.

Back at the servant's quarters the fairies were dressed again and got their gear together just in time to meet the police guards in the hallway. They had their handcuffs out and ready. They probably should've had their guns out instead, but that would be a matter for some Board of Inquiry to sort out later. As a result, the police guards ended up handcuffed to a toilet stall and the fairies went looking for their friends, hoping it wasn't too late. In the Senora's study, it was about to be.

"I'm a busy woman", said the Senora curtly. "I want to pin them *now!*" She thrust a large tweezer at the maid. "I don't want both. Just the good one. Toss the other in the garbage disposal". She pressed the tweezer firmly into the maid's hand and proceeded to her 'butterfly wall' to choose a nice spot and pick out a pretty pin.

A minute later, she turned to see what was keeping the maid and saw her still standing there with the tweezer, staring at the butterflies through the glass. "Do it or you're fired!" threatened Madame de la Grassa.

"Yes, Senora", answered the maid. She lifted the lid - then stumbled and flipped lid, pedestal, butterflies and all off the table. Everything crashed to the floor and smashed. Boca was hit in the head by a saucer and fluttered aimlessly trying to gather his wits.

"I saw that! You did that on purpose!" bellowed the Senora, grabbing a large butterfly net. She advanced sputtering and swinging the net at Boca but the maid blocked he - feet firmly planted, arms folded.

"No more! That's *it!*" declared the maid and wrestled the net away. She then brought it down on top of the most important woman in city society, all the way to her ankles, and held her there.

That's what Boca saw when his eyes re-focused. The Senora was screaming and struggling. But someone else was shouting too. What was that about? Then Yero's face appeared in front of him. *She* was shouting. He remembered her injury. Of course! She must be hurt even worse now! But somehow, they still had to escape. "Hang onto my legs!" he shouted back. "I'll carry you!"

"Wake up, ninny! I'm flying, can't you see? It's better".

The fairies found them like that and helped the maid march the Senora into a small closet, still wearing her net. They locked the door behind her.

"I'm leaving too!" vowed the maid. "Uno momento!" She fetched two small jelly cartons like those that restaurants serve with toast and gave to the fairies. "Something nicer for the *mariposas!*" She left her bonnet, apron and pretty shoes on the floor and slipped into the old sneakers and heavy shawl that she came to work in. "Straight out the front door!" she directed. "I don't see anyone at the gate".

The guards were of course otherwise occupied at their toilet stall, so the getaway was easy out to the street; but soon enough - all *too* soon maybe - they and the Senora would be rescued and the wrath of the Law would roar through the city searching for the desperados. It would be swift and merciless. Against that, all anyone can do is run for it. The maid said not to worry about her, she had lots of friends. We can only take her word and wish her well. The fairies had no friends and their best hope was to make for the hills; but how? They didn't dare dust themselves, and such a large police department would have dogs anyway to sniff them out - but how else to drop out of sight?

"There!" said Peco. "We'll go where the water goes".

'There' was a cast iron grate by the curb, in a low spot where storm water ran down the street and poured into, to be discharged somewhere outside city limits into a lake or reservoir. Peco lifted off the grate.

"Good idea", said Obobo. "But how big is it?"

"Can't tell. You better go first. If you get through, we all will".

"What if I get stuck?"

"No one escapes. You're blocking the way".

"Fair enough. But in case the worst happens I want to know *now* how our little sister finds herself up in the air again, flying with two good wings!"

Yero just smiled and shook her head. "I don't know. The maid shoved everything off the table, and I went down with the lid. A broken piece came up and hit me. Whacked something back in place, I guess. Isn't that nice? It doesn't even hurt".

The fairies laughed and Yero's reputation went up very close to El Boca's. But happy moments are fleeting and this one was shattered by a bellow from the mansion. The Senora had got out of her closet somehow and there would be the devil to pay for this. Obobo didn't even look back, just squeezed in headfirst. His muffled shouts sounded upbeat. There was room. Peco went next.

"Don't come with us", Pio instructed the butterflies. "This is easy for fairies. We're used to tunnels. But it's no place for you. Find the outlet - where it dumps. It'll be in the valley. Meet us there!" He went in and pulled over the grate, not a minute too soon. Sirens could be heard from several directions. The butterflies decided to perch for a bit in the palms shading the gate, and watch. It was quite a show.

The Senora burst out the front door and down the wide marble steps. She threw herself on the walk a moment before the first vehicle pulled up - a television news crew. As they hustled up the walk, she raised herself 'painfully' but with all dignity and calculation, flaunting a bruised cheek toward the camera, and told a harrowing story, perfectly concise for the leading segment of the evening news.

Si! Desperadoes had broken in and overpowered the guards! Terrorized the servants! The devil only knew what other calamities would have befallen had she not driven them off! She brandished the butterfly net with which she had beaten and chased them. Si! *Chased* them! Until she had collapsed here in exhaustion.

It was a great performance by a great socialite and certainly would have led the news that evening except there was better footage yet to come. Police cars were now arriving helter-skelter and a big fire truck came careening in too fast for the corner. It swerved off the pavement taking out traffic signs and – spectacularly - a fire hydrant, the only one in the area, put there specially to protect the hacienda. A geyser shot up higher than the palms and gushed continuously, soaking everything in a half-block area and pouring down the street. Luckily there was a storm sewer so most of the water went into that, but the butterflies had to move fast to escape the spray.

"And the fellows better move it, too!" said Yero.

It seemed sensible to follow the water downhill, but the sewer grate was so thirsty very little got past. They decided to simply follow the parade of vehicles beating a retreat from the gusher. The parade soon crossed a bridge over a dry run, and the butterflies turned and followed that. It was easy from there. The arroyo went right through the center of town, gradually widening. It sprouted levees, a chain link fence, and guardrails along one side near the municipal government buildings. The other side was bare dirt banks and poor residential: The barrio bajos. From their altitude, a lake could already be seen in the distance and they reached it with no further mishap. They searched the brushy shore but couldn't find the fairies, nor any culvert or sewer outlet, but they wouldn't have long to wait.

The fairies had already put a lot of sewer main behind when the first trickle of water caught up to them. They had come to a 'T' in the main and sat there debating which way. That's another thing about slope. It's not easy to feel in the dark. Water always tells so they felt lucky when it came, but surprised. There hadn't been a cloud in the sky that they remembered.

"Just so this isn't regular sewer too, and someone flushed a stool", said Pio.

"The last stool I saw was out of reach", commented 'Bo. "Those boys could maybe stretch and flush it with a toe, but they'll never get close enough to sit down".

The fairies laughed and crawled to the right where the water was going, first Peco, then Pio, then Obobo who laughed longest at his own joke. Sometimes little things... (Okay, let's not call Obobo's backside 'little'. It would soon get lots of credit for being big.) ...*some* things make all the difference. Good fortune put him last now, and his big behind last of all. The water flow rapidly increased. The fairies scrambled fast, but not fast enough. They were only halfway to the lake when they were suddenly overtaken by a flood. They would have drowned but the water couldn't get past Obobo very well. Pressure built up behind him, big time. He felt himself slipping on the smooth floor.

"I can't hold it anymore!" he shouted.

Pio, just ahead, heard him and wondered what he meant. He soon found out.

Like slugs plugging a garden hose, they suddenly lost traction and shot forward from the water pressure. The second leg of the sewer trip was quick. In less than a minute they shot out the discharge about six feet above the water - or where the water level usually was but wasn't this year due to dry weather. They landed in a heap on the shore, still gripping their bags, with water gushing around them; then realized they were clear, and could breathe, and scrambled up out of the effluent.

The discharge made quite a stir and froth when it hit the lake water and the butterflies found them there but veered off to go see prettier sights. "The fellows are getting into worse trouble all the time", worried Yero. "Now they could be charged with skinny-dipping".

The fellows had unabashedly stripped and were hanging their wet things on bushes to dry in the last hour of sunshine. The hydrant water had flushed out a lot of mud and they were rinsing everything off in the shallows, including themselves. Other than the clothes and their metal gear, the only salvageable items were matches and Pio's recipe cards. He had these items in a plastic bag sealed tightly shut. But everything edible or chewable was lost.

By good fortune the lake was deserted. No doubt the regular sewer did discharge into it too, somewhere. The algae hinted at that and there were no fishermen. No one would look for them here, but up in the city sirens squealed constantly. The search was on.

As night fell, searchlights came on all around the city. That was a good sign. The desperadoes were reckoned to be still holed up in town. And why not? Roadblocks had gone up in minutes and police dogs had picked up no scent around the city limits. Loudspeaker trucks cruised the streets exhorting the guilty ones to give themselves up in exchange for leniency, and a National Guard helicopter was on its way. The whole effort was aimed at the poorest barrios where the desperados were sure to be hiding, and local television covered it all live - mostly featuring the de la Grassas who were thrilled with the publicity.

When it was dark enough the fairies got a bearing from the stars and set out west/northwest, giving the city a wide berth, climbing well into the foothills as the curfew siren blared behind them. There, they finally took a rest and swapped stories about the caper. The butterflies of course had no idea how close their friends had come to being domesticated, but the fellows told all.

"Yeah, we put on the fancy clothes", Obobo admitted, "to play for time. We thought we might have to take the jobs after all, to find you. We didn't expect the maid to come up a hero. I hope they don't catch her".

The chauvinists allowed a moment of silence in her honor, which surprised Yero. She started to say something, but Pio brushed it off. "It happens - even with *girls*", he said. "There's Her Ladyship of course, and *you've* sure surprised us. Leave it at that".

Boca was glad the barber didn't get his way. He'd been thinking of trying to grow a beard himself, over the winter.

"Ha! The *barber*!" grunted Obobo. "Just an itchy scissors finger, that's all *he* was. And a girl came to 'do our nails'. Not joking! I don't know how the Big People can have any fun. They spend most of their time staying clean".

"The fairy girls wouldn't mind if you cleaned up", replied Yero, exasperated.

'Bo snorted. "If they want us, they'll have to come down in the mud and get us!"

The fellows all thought that was hilarious, but it got worse. They followed up with a few rude exhaust noises and laughed at that wit too. Yero fluttered off to a nearby bush to be by herself for a while. Introducing the boys to even the *simplest* nice things was *s-o-o-o* difficult!

Perhaps she was too tough on them. Boys often make jokes when they know they're walking into danger, just to ease the tension. Afterward, all is forgotten as if it never happened. Obobo had forgotten already and came to fetch her.

"Come on, little sister", he said. "We need you to make plans".

In the light of the moon rising over the foothills they talked about the way ahead, or maybe two ways: One for the fairies, and one for the Rasha La now that Yero was back in shape.

"The North Entrance - the back door to our old Digs - is not far up in the hills ahead", explained Pio. "We think we can reach it before morning if we march through the night. But the memory is old and lands change. It might be buried. Still, we wish to find it if we can, and see if the way is open. But it will only delay your own journey".

"Your Manino isn't far now", continued Obobo. "Perhaps two days - one with us to our back door, another after that to go higher up into the mountain forests".

"We'll be taking our own risks if we go inside", warned Peco. "Extra risks that you don't need. We think you should go your own way, if we *do* find an entrance".

The butterflies whispered together for a bit.

"We want to go with, if you'll let us", said Yero. "We think we can do more good than bad".

"Skill like that should be put to use!" laughed Obobo. He stood up and pointed to his right shoulder. "If the way is open, it'll be dark inside. Too dark to fly. You can sit *here*. When you do good, it will lift the shoulder. When you do bad, you'll slide to the other side. If you do anything foolish, you'll fall off and we'll leave you there. Any questions?"

"Just bring up the rear", suggested Yero, "so no one steps on us".

Chapter 21

The Commons

They set out again in good spirits. The better outfits usually do. But the hills were a mess, having been logged and re-logged. At least there were narrow paths where firewood gatherers came and went, but as they climbed further into the mess, the paths petered out, to be replaced by sticker weeds of many kinds. These had lived their useful lives and died, now to become the parasites of the woods, and since they were dead, they didn't respond to the fairies' wishes. So, the boys got stickered up thoroughly and were no happier about it than your dog would be. Yero and Boca flew above it all and never lost their good spirits.

"Look to the bright side", Yero called down. "It's almost like you dusted yourselves. If anyone comes along, they'll never notice you".

"Make yourselves useful!" suggested Pio. "Scout us out a better path! Don't get lost".

"We won't", said Boca seriously. "We'll hear the cussing".

The butterflies departed at that point and it worked out well. The boys' testy replies faded away quickly, and nicer going was indeed just ahead, but some distance off to the side: A shallow valley that might well have been missed, a hollow with no stickers at all, just short grasses and tussocks. They returned quickly with the good news.

"Must be a sink", said Peco. "Was there water?"

"A little, in the middle. It reflected in the moonlight", reported Yero.

"There's rabbits", said Boca. "Little ones, all over the place".

Well now! *Conejos!* If there was a more favorite menu item for the fairies, it could only be fish. Visions of rabbit feasts sprang to mind. They liked it grilled, fried, baked, roasted, smoked, simmered, and of course re-heated. They especially liked rabbit stew but didn't have the ingredients just now.

"*Small* ones, you say?" asked Peco. "No big ones?"

"I should have said, small ones and *smaller* ones", replied Boca.

"No matter. Just show the way!"

There was no more cussing, no more stumbling or bumbling. The hollow was indeed a 'sink': A sunken, bowl-shaped area where water collected and couldn't run off. The ground was of porous volcanic origin and the water gradually seeped away. Now in the dry season it was almost empty, allowing extra room for multiplying bunnies.

The smaller fairies crept in and hid in the tussocks while Obobo worked the outer edges. It wasn't a large sink, only a hectare or two, but there were more rabbits than they had ever seen in one place. More than there should have been. Except for the tussocks, the grass was cropped nearly to the roots and hungry rabbits were hopping everywhere, making it easy to catch them barehanded.

They throttled three or four apiece in only a few minutes and the hunt was over. The fairies stood up and showed off their catch and bunnies ran for cover in all directions - more than before, you might say - but that's asking a lot even of bunnies. So, the catching was easy, but now what? They weren't about to light a fire and knew better than to eat rabbits raw. They each gathered their clutch in one hand and set out again.

"That maid saved us from being pinned but we sure pinned those bunnies, didn't we?" whispered Boca.

Yero looked at him sharply, startled. "Oh, knock it off", she said. "It's survival for whoever can find their supper out here. You know that".

"Yeah, but it's so soon after our lucky break I can't help but compare it".

"I should be arguing *your* side and you should be arguing mine. That's what usually happens".

462

Boca hardly heard her in his funk. "They whistled high-pitched when they were caught", he pined. "*I* might've sounded like that when she stuck pins in me".

"No way, Boca. You would've used cuss words on her".

That jerked Boca out of it. There was a pause, then: "I missed my chance! I should've done that anyway!"

"It wouldn't have bothered me that time. She was killing us just for fun or would have. And she used dirty tricks".

"Yeah. I think I'll have some rabbit stew after all".

"You're back to normal. Let's not fall behind".

From there the woods opened up more. It hadn't been logged in some years and oak trees were again reaching up, shading out some of the stickers and brush, so the party made good progress for a while. Then it reverted to brush. This changed back and forth several times as they climbed higher through different tracts with different owners. But it was still moonlit night when the fairies reckoned by the higher peaks and major land features that they were near their back entrance, or the wreckage of it. The land had changed. There was a dam and reservoir in the valley below and the big woods was gone. A fresh road led through the area to logging activity higher up. It was a young wood now, a relic of what once was.

The fairies were undecided about where exactly to search. They remembered a cliff face veiled by great trees, but the rock face was missing if this was the right spot. It was decided that Obobo should wait with the butterflies while the others investigated further.

They left and Obobo offered to open the last jelly cup, but the butterflies declined. "We'll wait and eat with you fellows", said Yero. "You-know-who wants to try some rabbit. When are you going to cook them anyway?"

"If we find the door, we'll make a small fire inside, away from prying eyes. I hope they find it. The conejos need to be cleaned up". He peered around more keenly now as the pre-dawn appeared in the east. "This doesn't look at all like what we remember, but it feels right in *here*". He thumped his big chest.

At that moment, a growling and snapping of teeth erupted some ways ahead, followed by ominous barks.

"Wolf!" shouted Obobo and lit out straight for the noise. The butterflies followed. They met the others warily retreating. They had disturbed the animal.

"We found the door, but it's caved in along with the rest of the cliff", reported Pio. "Earthquake, I suppose, at one time or another. There *is* a way through the rubble into the passage, but she's guarding it". He jerked a peeved thumb behind him. The wolf had followed them out beyond the rubble and stood there gnashing her teeth.

The fairies approached close enough to parley. They knew enough of the language to deal if the wolf was interested, and had a lot to bargain with, but they quickly learned who had leverage. The she-wolf had pups. They were in the passage. She would die fighting if she had to and someone else would likely get hurt too.

Her hackles were way up. This was her den! Four years, and never been disturbed - until now! Did the little people want *in*? Well! The little people had conejos. She smelled them. How many? How fresh?

When the fairies finally waved for the butterflies to come on ahead, they had given all their breakfast away - traded it for safe passage. The wolf called her pups out and they tore into the feast. The fairies trudged past without so much as a glance, determined not to give her any extra satisfaction, but she laughed at them anyway - a yip, yipping noise that quickly reached high-pitch. Then she howled at the moon in her triumph.

"Mutts!" mumbled Obobo. "Nothing but trouble for fairy folk".

Little wonder her den was never troubled. The entrance looked outwardly like a dead end, but crevices in the rubble led to a bigger passage plainly dug with pick and shovel. Pio risked a match and shielded it against a warm draft coming from within. The light revealed a mess on the floor. The she-wolf was clever. She disposed of bones further into the passage instead of outside where a hunter or trapper might see them. The bone pile was the pup's potty too, the draft told them that even without a light.

What Pio was looking for was their names, and others, carved into the walls near the old door. The graffiti of all who worked on the tunnel. But the names were now part of the rubble--along with a map of the passages ahead, also carved into the wall. Pio regretted the loss of the roadmap with its precise measurements and coordinates. They could have used a refresher for the dark way ahead.

"Shouldn't need it", grunted Obobo. "We all know it's basically straight with some side-passages. The only other tunnels were straight up - air ducts and a light shaft or two, if they're still open".

"We'll probably bypass the New Digs then, the Silverlode. I wouldn't have minded a peep down there".

"Let it go. Just take care you don't stumble into the Deeps".

"Peco should've kept his walking cane. But he can lead anyway, to start out. How much stuff do we need to carry? I expect we'll have to come back out the same way we're going in".

Peco was already shedding his stickered-up things and putting on others. He kept only his hatchet and hunting knife, stuffing his hat and other gear into bags and cinching them up against curious wolf-pups. On second thought, he cast local 'dirt' over them, commanding everything to smell like the mess on the floor. The others did likewise.

Pio lit another match to see a bit further inside and found better news. The narrow-gauge rail track remained in good shape, at least here, on this end. The rails were hewn oak, worn but not rotted. The warm draft was responsible for that, drying the inevitable ceiling drips. The crossties were also oak, spaced exactly 24 inches on center. This was traditional with the boy fairies anywhere in the world. It was the length of one *pace* as an average boy would step it off, and they all learned to step it precisely. It enabled them to walk almost any distance in their dark tunnels and know where they were without a torch. It doesn't take many torches to foul the air in a mine, air ducts or no air ducts.

Yero and Boca took their place on Obobo's right shoulder as the match died out. The fairies stepped onto the tracks and set out at a good clip between the rails as if it was still their second nature.

"Did you haul gold out on this railroad?" asked Boca. "You must have had heaps!" Greed was already tempting him.

Obobo chuckled, answering quietly so as not to mess up the others who were counting paces. "We didn't haul any gold at all on this line. It was laid as part of the 'back door' project. It's a long tunnel to dig - and what to do with all the earth? So this line, with two pushcarts, carried excavated dirt and rock back away from the miners. It slopes a little downhill as we go in, so full loads were easier to push. Mind you, we dug from the inside out. The door was meant to be secret. We couldn't very well have huge piles of tailings outside, and everyone watching us dig".

"Then where did it all go?"

"Into the *Deeps*. You'll see if we get that far".

They marched in the dark for what seemed like hours to Yero, with less and less talk. What could be worth talking about anyway, in such uninterrupted monotony? Then there was an interruption.

"Stop", said Pio up front. "I hear water".

There was a trickle, just ahead. They advanced slowly until Peco reported a drip on his nose. A match flared briefly, showing the water problem. It came mostly from one area on the ceiling, maybe under some new sink in the mountains above. There were a lot of drips. Many had formed stalactites, some over a foot long that Obobo surely would have bumped his head on. The whole floor was wet, and water trickled down the incline. The rails and ties were rotted away and gone leaving only the tarnished brass nails, green in the match light.

"Mind the nails", said Peco, taking the lead again. He had the toughest leathery feet of them all. Regardless of nails, they splashed along at the same pace, passing by several side passages known only by a cool draft and a sense of void at their elbows. A few hundred more paces brought them under another drippy shower. Then the floor abruptly dried up. Pio lit another match. A wide door yawned open to their right. The water all followed a worn channel into it, down an incline into a cavernous space that could only be guessed at. A pool reflected up at them.

"The Silverlode", murmured Pio. "Drowned. There was a light shaft here, too, in the old days".

This did not augur well, but at least there was no temptation to explore it. They went on and the wood rails resumed on the dry floor. That was much appreciated in the dark. The warm draft felt gradually warmer in their faces and presently a hissing sound came from up ahead, then quit, then hissed again a minute later. The fairies stopped and compared memories, but they had no recollection of this. They went ahead more cautiously.

As they advanced, a dim light appeared down the tunnel - regularly, like the hissing. In fact, it glowed most of the time *except* during the hissing. This was also a mystery to them. They knew they were approaching the *Deeps* where there had also been a light shaft, but that let in light from above, from the sun and sky. Not like this light.

The tunnel opened up somewhat and the light grew. Clearly, they were entering a much larger cavern. The crossties became loose and wobbly under their feet and they had to step off the track. The rails themselves, solid brass here in this old high-traffic area, were stretched tight and raised, suspended above the old rail bed. It soon became obvious why. Thirty or forty paces downslope a fissure split the floor of the great hall, for that's what it was: A huge cavern - partly natural, partly hewn and sculpted with a vaulted ceiling. The fissure extended indefinitely left and right, and the light came up out of it. Straight ahead, across the fissure, the suspended rails continued into another cavern. The fairies paused at the unexpected sight and that saved them. Suddenly the hissing noise awoke in the deeps and a geyser of steam and boiling water shot up, engulfing the bare brass rails where they suspended across the chasm. The pause became a halt. Things were vastly different here than the fellows remembered.

They recognized the fissure, all right, but it had been dark and silent, just a great stress crack under the mountains. There were many such under the Dragon Range, some deeper than others, some longer, all formed by immense volcanic force. Some cracks healed themselves over time, drawing metal-bearing quartzes from the surrounding walls to fill the void, forming veins of precious elements: *Ores*, the Big People called them. The fairies had excavated fabulous quantities of gold ore, nearly pure, from this very fissure in the old days when it was quiet. This was the *Deeps Mine*, source of much of the fairies' legendary wealth.

It was narrow then, the fissure was. Right here had been the widest gap, about five or six paces. Arched bridges had been built for rail and foot traffic. The stone abutments remained, mortared solidly to the precipice, but the spans were gone, lost to the depths when some bygone shock jerked the fissure wider, allowing molten lava to well up below. That was the source of light and cause of the steam. Water seeps had always percolated down into the great hall. Very useful, once. Now, when they trickled into the fissure, the fire below hurled them back up in steam.

"Well? Do we go back?" asked Yero, but Obobo didn't hear. The fairies were already debating steam intervals and especially the sturdiness of the suspended brass rails, stretched and lifted across the void but still holding. The rails beckoned them like tightropes. Pio and Peco sat down well back from the edge and began to time the intervals, hoping for a pattern. Obobo spoke with the butterflies.

"Since you are determined to be useful, I have a job for you", he said. "It would help if you scouted beyond the gorge; following the rail as far as any light reaches. The passage is winding because it is natural. The incline will steepen. The rail comes to an end and a curving stair will commence - or it did in those days. It used to rise exactly 499 steps to the upper halls - *The Commons*. That was our living quarters and place of commerce. When the dragon came, we were forced down here and he destroyed the upper stairs, blocking any escape, or so he thought". Obobo smiled grimly. "See if the way is open. If it's not, we won't attempt the crossing here".

The butterflies went after the next surge subsided and entered the winding way. There was reflective quartz in the walls so when the fissure glowed, the light leaped ahead by tiny mirrors around many curves, and they were able to explore all the way to the railhead, or where it was buried. Everywhere great chunks of the ceiling had broken and smashed onto the floor or into the walls. Fractures split the walls. Little of the great stair was recognizable. Then the light dimmed behind them once more as the fissure steamed and they debated how much farther to explore.

"We better go until we can't see anything at all, until it gets pitch dark", said Boca. "They mean to go on if they can".

"Yes, they do. I wonder what they hope to find?"

"Gold. What else?"

"I don't think gold draws them like that anymore".

"Maybe it should, Yero. They could use the money". An odd look flickered across Boca's face.

"Don't go getting nutty again, Boca. They said it was gone! Anyway, our job is just to scout. Let's go".

They explored up the ruined staircase until it ended, and a hallway commenced - or used to. Now it was only a wall of rubble. Then the light faded away again for a time, and darkness closed around them. The destruction of the dragon was incredible. All the rock was scorched and blackened. But quaking and shaking over centuries had settled the rubble somewhat, leaving gaps and voids up near the original ceiling. When dim light returned, they entered those and saw new light up ahead, but sensed something else in the air, too. Something familiar. They paused to make sure.

"Do you smell it?" asked Yero. Boca nodded without a word. It was faint but unmistakable: The scent of the Jaguars. They went back with this unsettling news, but it only made the fairies grimmer and more determined.

"We hadn't figured on them", said Pio. "The Front entrance and the side doors were all buried, as we said, so I don't know how they would have gotten in. Maybe the scent is from long ago and still lingers. But they would delight in rummaging the old bones". The thought put fire into their eyes, and they lined up to attempt a single file crossing when the timing was right.

When the steam erupted again and subsided, Peco in front began to count, allowing a little time for the rails to cool but only a little. The timeline didn't allow for much. Then he took off along the rail like a squirrel on a branch. He did a skip-step over the Deeps and made it look easy. Pio studied his movements to judge how hot the rails must be and attempted it next with the same good results; then Obobo went.

He did very well until he reached the midpoint when his weight caused a few spikes to pull loose back along the track somewhere, and the rail itself to suddenly sag a bit. He threw out an arm but couldn't quite steady himself until the butterflies jumped out and alighted on his fingertips, adding their bulk to the balance. Maybe that was the difference, or maybe it was just Obobo sharply inhaling at the sudden turn of events, but he caught himself and went on. Moments later, he was far enough along and jumped for it, beating the next eruption by moments.

They followed the winding way, pausing during the steam events, picking their way through the wreckage when the glow returned, and presently found themselves studying the same new light beyond the rubble wall.

"Light shafts into the Commons", guessed Pio immediately. "At least one must still be open. So, the dragon didn't mind a bit of light".

"Or a vent", suggested Peco. "Maybe sometimes even dragons get their fill of smoke".

"Anyway, the light is good. The Commons should be safe for now", Pio explained to the butterflies. "If our enemies have been here recently it would've been at night and it's not much past mid-afternoon by my reckoning".

With that, they began to dig and pry and shove rubble aside to widen the hole. It was marvelous, their ease with stone; but after all, these were three of the very miners who excavated the Digs long ago.

The dragon had meant the passage to be shut forever, that was obvious. It was jammed solid for several hundred paces or had been before the rubble settled, and the work was on hands and knees to begin with. But after some heavy labor they found easier going and even places where they could walk upright. There was only one glitch when Obobo bumped a knee in his hurry and yelled so loud that dust and rock chips fell onto his head. Everyone hushed. Even Obobo was embarrassed. But nothing came of it, and presently they clambered down into an expansive hall lit by four overlapping beams of sunlight. It was real sunlight from angled shafts bored up toward a single opening somewhere on the mountainside. This was the heart of the *Commons*, the main dining hall and gathering place of bygone days, but the lighting was the only recognizable feature from those days.

All around and piled high against the walls was the rubbish and refuse of the dragon: Charred and smashed trappings of the prior inhabitants, and the bones of many feasts. The center of the room where he had slept on his treasure heap was bare. The treasure had been looted from the original looter. Straight ahead on the far side of the hall a wide passage, almost a concourse, had once led up to the front entrance, but no more. A quake had brought down the roof there, and part of the mountainside on top of it, but the fairies hadn't come to stare at that. There was an adjacent room to one side, still with a doorway into it, and that's where they went.

The doorway had been 'widened', to put it nicely, by the dragon. This had been the main treasury, now empty except for the inevitable rubble. One whole section of the ceiling had caved in violently, sending rock tumbling and crashing into all the walls. The light in here was dim but Pio saw something interesting right away.

"The lockbox. It's open".

A niche in the wall had been smashed by flying rock, a spell of concealment wrecked along with it. Remnants of stone doors hung on twisted hinges. Peco reached in and pulled out a burlap bag from a box that balanced on the edge of the sill. Inside was a large gem, pale except for tiny lights that sparkled deep within. It was the 'Fairystone', the oracle of their race, the main reason they had come today. They bowed their heads in respect to the Lord whose gift it once was, but only for a moment.

"Let's have a peep, then", said Pio, holding it toward the better light in the doorway. Everyone crowded closely to see the magic, the butterflies too. It didn't take long. The twinkling lights faded and were replaced by painted faces of Jaguar warriors, staring out at them. Obobo cussed. They all did.

"What's that about?" asked Boca nervously.

"It's our future", said Pio grimly, "but we knew that part! We hoped to see something new. Something *better!*"

There would be nothing else, obviously. The picture didn't change except for the faces, as if all the Jaguars in the Shadow Realm wanted to see the fairies in their disappointment.

"Put it back, or better yet throw it away!" muttered Obobo. "It's showed nothing but doom ever since we came to these shores".

Pio wrapped it again, but while they grumbled about it, Yero found a small tray on the floor, partly covered by rock and dust. A jewelry box. It still held some rings, and more were scattered about the floor. Obobo took notice.

"Here now, little sister. What've you found there?" He picked up a ring and blew the dust off. It was gold with a diamond inset. He held it to the light. "Well, well. I had almost forgotten. Looky here, fellows! Do you remember this one?" He laughed and tried another, then handed them to the others.

"It doesn't matter now", he explained to Yero, "but we made these for the girls. We each made one". He sighed. "They refused them, of course". Maybe so, but he took a knee and began gathering them up. Pio and Peco helped. Yero was thrilled.

"What do you see through them?"

In answer, Obobo held one up for her to look through. A girl was inside the ring. Not just a picture, but a real girl by all appearances. She smiled and seemed aware of Yero. Then the light faded and the girl with it. They all looked to the door to see what happened to the light. It wasn't streaming down the shafts anymore. A storm had come up in the mountains, very dark, and blotted out the sun. In the next moment, ugly laughter arose out in the Commons and ghost warriors crowded the doorway.

"Where are your shadows now?" taunted one, the same chief who had been on the windswept ridge. "Where is your fire?"

Pio struck a match - but what could they burn? He reached for the burlap bag, but the chief waved an arm. Cold air blew out the match. Violence erupted, an unequal battle with the fairies at the disadvantage. The Jaguars were strong here - not the full strength of flesh and blood, but near to it - and there were many of them. The butterflies, overlooked, did the only thing they could. They went up near the ceiling and hoped for the best, and for a time it sounded like it might yet happen. Boca even found himself wondering what happens to ghost warriors who die again. Some did suffer that fate, whatever it might be; but superior numbers took a toll. The tide of battle turned. Powerless to help, unwilling to just wait for the end, the butterflies went into the Commons as the din of battle diminished behind them.

The Jaguars had come down the light shafts by rope ladders when the storm hit. Somehow, they knew that the fairies were here or soon would be. Their victory yells rang out now into the Commons. It was over. Once again, the butterflies had lost their best friends.

Or maybe not. Not dead, at least. Short minutes later the fairies were dragged out, struggling and gagged, trussed with many windings of rope. They were being taken alive, hauled up the shafts with rope by more warriors above, and then off into the stormy night without delay, for night had come.

The butterflies followed as best they could by the lightning flashes until the heaviest part of the storm moved on and a cold rain lingered. Late at night, the darkness stopped them somewhere in the foothills. Boca took it very badly.

"We'll have to look for the trail in the morning", said Yero. "There's nothing else we can do".

"But the rain is washing out the tracks, Yero - if they even *do* leave tracks!"

"They don't", came a voice out of the darkness. "But it doesn't matter. I know where they're going".

It was Atel, but she wasn't welcomed as politely as she might have been.

"If you *know*, why did you let them be taken captive?" demanded Boca unreasonably. "You could've made the difference!"

"I don't think so, from the signs. But I wasn't there. I'm late, and it hasn't been easy catching up".

"Where *have* you been?" asked Yero. "We've been worried!"

"Helping others who need it. You two are quite capable now".

"Not enough!" exclaimed Boca. "But we're still going to try!"

"Certainly! Just as I expected. However, I'll take up the pursuit now. I have a separate errand for you that could make all the difference".

"Nuts to that!" protested Boca. "We're not going to quit!"

"Of course not! The fellows need *lots* of help, and I want you to get it for them! I want you to fly faster than you've *ever* flown! But in a different direction".

"Just point him then", laughed Yero. "He's ready".

"Unfortunately, that will have to wait until morning. You can't navigate at night under these clouds. As to the errand, listen closely: There is a mountain, old but still hot inside. A dragon sleeps there. I need you to wake him".

That got their attention. "You must be joking", said Yero.

"No, no time for jokes", answered the hummingbird, but she would say no more until they found a decent place to spend the night, a scraggly bush clinging under an outcropping of rock.

"The dragon perished long ago", she explained to them. "He died, but his spirit hibernates up there in the heat vents".

"If it's the fairies' dragon, we've heard about him", said Boca.

"They've told you? That's good. How much?"

"Everything, I guess. Except what happened to him. I don't think they knew for sure".

"He was killed. The Spanish Conquistadores killed him for his treasure. They had guns, something new then. His spirit found refuge in an old volcano. He finds the heat comforting. It renews him to some extent. I've seen him. He talks in his sleep. He hates the Jaguar Tribe. He might help us if he can be roused".

"It sounds pretty risky", said Yero. "Can a ghost dragon breathe fire?"

"I certainly hope so. I'm counting on it".

"Then shouldn't you come with us?"

"No time for it. Not for me. At first light, I'll point out the mountain and then I'll be off to the New City to await the Jaguars - and battle. But tomorrow night I'll need a *heavyweight* on my side, or our friends will be sacrificed at the ruins of the old Templo Mayor, a shrine with a terrible history. Did the fairies tell you about the old Priests?'

"Enough". Yero shivered. "They steal life".

"Yes. We can't let that begin again. There is misery enough in this world without the return of their bloody practice. But I'll need help. *Big* help. I figure if anyone can rouse a dragon it just might be the Rasha La".

"That's way more than I expected", replied Yero, yawning in spite of herself. "I have no idea how to shake a dragon".

Chapter 22

The Templo Mayor

With that, Yero fell asleep, followed immediately by Boca. Atel watched over them as long as she could. In slumber, their spirits appeared to her as the children of men they had been, and she marveled again at the unlikely toughness of the young. Then she too fell into a deep sleep.

After all, what is the measure of a long, hard day? Is it the tally of work and sweat, or worry, or even enemies met in battle? Or just the soundness of sleep that comes after? Because by the last measure the day had been very long, and morning came too soon. At first light, the butterflies awoke to the hum of the hummingbird's wings.

"Good morning little ones!" she said cheerfully. "Sleep well?"

She was answered mostly with mumbles and bleary eyes.

"There's no breakfast, I'm afraid. We'll just have to scrounge up something on our separate ways. I'm going *that* way (she indicated southeast) to the New City where the ruins are. Your dragon is *there* (she pointed southwest at a snow-covered mountain), in a fumarole vent in the crater wall. The whole crater is open to the east where you can enter below the snow line. You will see two lakes. Look to the far western end of the larger lake, to the crater walls above it. Watch for a whiff of steam in the cold air, or smoke when the dragon clears his throat. That will be the right opening. Any questions?"

"How do we wake him, then? Knock on his nose?"

"Definitely *not!* But that might be a safe place to perch in case of, umm...'hiccups', shall we say? I'm serious about this! If we are all very lucky, he will be talkative in his sleep, and you can *coax* him awake".

"Does he have a name?" asked Yero.

"Several that he doesn't like but one that he does. He calls himself *Volcan*".

They wished each other luck and went their ways without small talk. All morning the butterflies barely spoke except to discuss their route. Near midday, they found breakfast in the form of an agave plant under the pines, more brown than green. A tree branch had fallen in the storm, crushing the stem but splitting open the base. The nectar was diluted with rainwater and a fat pincers bug was not happy to share with them. Their mountain, still distant, appeared somewhat larger but no closer. As they sipped the boggy mixture the bug suddenly charged and pinched Boca painfully from behind, and that spelled the end of any breakfast. They took off with Boca lagging, feeling down behind for any bleeding wound, but it was just a bad pinch. Yero wasn't as sympathetic as she might have been when he finally caught up.

"Honestly, we'll have to do better than *that,* dealing with the dragon! Atel would laugh at us".

"We'll do better. The bigger they are, the easier it should be".

"That's a nice way to look at it. Do you have any reason?"

"We can sit on the dragon's nose and be safe from his teeth. It doesn't work that way with nipper bugs".

"What about his fire?"

"Same thing, I'm sure. He won't shoot at himself".

"Good thinking, Boca. I'll let you handle everything today".

"I'll get us there, Yero. You do the talking".

"But he's a boy, like the fairies. What if he doesn't take me seriously?"

"Shouldn't matter. You're good at bugging people. Just keep at it until he wakes up. Then blame it on those Jaguars".

"He won't see any Jaguars, Boca. He'll see us".

"You'll think of something. I'll get us there. That's my job".

Boca was as good as his word and took the lead the rest of the day. They bypassed a large city and made for the eastern reaches of the mountain. It was close enough now to see big features and looked from the north more like a mountain range than a single mountain, for there was no major central peak like most volcanoes. Still, all the high elevations were white with snow.

Late in the afternoon, later than they had hoped, they came around the eastern side where it gapped wide open allowing much lower, warmer access. On some frightful day long ago an explosion had blown away the entire peak and eastern shoulder of the mountain, leaving an exposed crater, now partly filled with water. A large pool and a smaller one.

"The lakes", noted Boca. "We take the big one. So far, so good!"

Whether because of lower elevation or the fires beneath the mountain, the water was unfrozen and washed vigorously against the far shore from a strong wind coming through the gap behind them. Whitecaps dashed onto the rocks and sprayed their foam into the air. The butterflies had a job just to avoid being slapped against the crater wall themselves but managed to explore the wall all the way along the shore and back again. There were a number of fissures, but it was impossible to say what might be steam and what was just splashing water and foam. Evening was falling. Shadow from the crater wall already covered most of the lake.

"Again!" insisted Boca. "But this time we'll go into each one and smell the air".

The same stink blew out from each of the first seven fumaroles: Warm, wet, rotten egg smell. No draft at all escaped the eighth and last; there were no rotten eggs, but the smell was still bad.

"This is it", declared Boca. "The only one that's different".

They entered and found themselves in a rough, circular passage corkscrewing down into darkness. After several twists, all light disappeared and wind - or rather, the sound of wind - came to them from vents somewhere below. They drew closer together and their slight sheen of esporellia was enough to guard against bumping into the walls. Then a fiery glow appeared. The wind gusted and fire issued like a blowtorch directly below them, receding to hot coals as the wind let up.

It was the dragon of course, breathing in his sleep. They could only guess at the rest of his bulk in the darkness, but the nose showed up gloriously with every breath. Yero found herself thinking, "He *does* breathe fire! Atel will be so pleased!"

Then the beast shifted, and a crack of light appeared alongside his belly. A draft of air came up past him, stuffy and rank. The dragon was sprawled over the very crack of the fumarole enjoying the heat, and another thought occurred to Yero: "He's more than a ghost if he can plug that hole".

Indeed, he was. A good bit more, owing to the heat, but not yet fully alive. Real live dragons - the few that still survive - make their homes only in the very far north now. The rest were killed and exist only in the ghost realm - or like this, if they were lucky enough to find a hotspot and lie up in hibernation. Then, over time, the heat adds something back and they become more aware. But remembrance comes with it of their downfall, so most are content to remain this way. It's a rare thing now when a hibernating dragon bestirs and arises. Unheard of in recent history.

Yero landed forthwith on his nose, to the rear of the active nostrils, and Boca beside her. The massive body trembled at the touch. Loose rocks tumbled into the crack and rattled far below. Flame flickered upward and caught the dragon's eye, for he had opened it a slit. His awareness extended itself out to the end of his nose where he saw the butterflies. He studied them in silence, allowing memory to catch up, but drew a blank. Later, perhaps, he might speak if the little winged things jogged a memory. For now, he couldn't place them anywhere and speaking was a bother. He hadn't actually spoken to anyone in centuries. He closed his eye again and toyed with the thought of blasting carbon out of his lungs but discarded the thought lazily. That was a bother too.

"It's your turn", whispered Boca. "Say something".

Yero folded her arms, very businesslike. "Sir--" she began - but was interrupted by a snort and blast of fire.

The Butterflies, Yero and Boca

"Not *sir*", whispered Boca. "Don't say that! It probably reminds him of the soldiers who, umm... you know what I mean!"

Yero took another breath when the fire died down and tried again: "Your Excellency---" But this was interrupted as fearsomely as the other.

"Not that either!" whispered Boca. "That's for Kings or Queens".

"*You* do it then! I can't think of anything when he's like this!"

"Oh, no! You're the talker. You can do it".

A bit frightened, a bit angry, Yero marched up and looked straight into the eye, which had re-opened just a crack. "Volcan! We're here to ask your help".

This went over better but still poorly. Volcan closed his eye. "Go away", he rumbled. Nevertheless, behind the closed eye memories were starting to come together, though he gave no outward sign.

Yero took advantage of the lull to keep talking, laying out the whole desperate situation. There was no indication that the beast heard - or cared a whit if he did hear. She spoke of Atel and the fairies, giving their names and bits and pieces she knew of the old days when the dragon and fairies together had cheated the priests of their young victims. She harped on the Priests a lot, about how they planned to return and take up where they left off. Night came outside and deepened, and there was no further sign of any kind that the dragon was even awake. When she could think of nothing else Yero finally said, "The High Priests laughed when you died. Do you know what they said?"

A lot of things suddenly came together in the dragon's mind. He opened both eyes a slit and focused on the butterflies. Yero went and said something directly into his ear and his eyes opened wide.

Atel never saw the fairies all that day, nor did she expect to. They had been dragged into the Ghost Realm, which is the opposite of ours. *They* have the night shift; the Living have the day. The Jaguars would have hustled until dawn with all speed. That wouldn't have brought them to the Templo Mayor, by her reckoning, but close. Close enough to resume the march in the evening and arrive at the Blood Altar before midnight. That was the hour she feared most, but any hour of night put her at a disadvantage. She would need a light source - a good one - or the fight would end badly. Just now, late in the afternoon, the sky was clear. There would be a good moon if it stayed clear - enough light to put up some resistance.

She approached the New City in amazement. She rarely came this way. It had certainly grown in a hundred years, sprawling into huge areas of old wilderness. The people were beyond count - all born now with some hope of a long, happy life. Quite an improvement over the bad old days when the High Priests butchered so many, even of their own.

The city was grown so huge that night was already falling by the time she found the old ruins. An overcast or smog had settled in, but there were good city lights around the historic area. They would have to do. She swooped to investigate. The lower parts of the Templo Mayor had indeed been uncovered, exposing steep stairs and remnants of the sacrificial platform. She had never seen the temple, but it was easy to recognize from stories the fairies told. It was the centerpiece of the ruins, but by no means all. There were remnants of other structures as well, including even a cleared and restored ball field and what might have been the temple of the Priesthood. She took up a perch to observe the area and waited; but for a while, nothing happened except the city lights winked out one at a time as midnight drew near, until there were not enough for her liking. But things would get worse.

Later, the High Priests appeared as dark forms arising from the ruins of their temple, exactly as Atel expected. What she didn't expect was, they remained simply moving shapes, poorly defined. They stayed within the Ghost Realm. That wasn't good. The city lights would be very dim on their side. She had counted on them coming out and performing their cruel ceremony in the living light.

Light she could use! They were very strong here, strong enough to cross over and do what they wanted, but they were being cautious.

They were waiting; and what they were waiting for now appeared, also on the ghost side. Jaguar warriors - lots of them - approached, moving along the tourist walkways toward the shadowy Priests who were by now on the Templo Mayor itself. The Jaguars, a bit easier to see in their bright paint, surrounded three shrouded figures roped together, doubtless the fairies. But what lifted the hummingbird's spirits were the burdens they were forced to carry. Each had a heavy bundle of firewood strapped on their backs, and it was real wood. That and the ropes were the only things not faint or fuzzy.

They would be sacrificed to Huehueteotl, their old god of fire; but it would be a real fire, to burn what needed to be burned and complete the sorcery.

The ceremonial fireplace had been destroyed by the Conquistadores, but no matter. The Jaguars unstrapped the firewood bundles all in a heap near the sacrificial stone, or what would serve as one, and used the fairies' own matches to light the fire. Atel waited. The fire must be big, the brighter the better for her purposes - unless the Priests got impatient and she had to act sooner. She reminded herself now in passing that it was not permitted for her or any fairy to cross of free will into the ghost world, but she meant to come back. She would break the rule and worry about it later.

When the fire got lively enough, a Priest with a ceremonial knife cut Obobo loose from the others, leaving his arms and legs still trussed. The Tribe knew from bitter experience how strong fairies are. Next, four Jaguars grabbed and tried to lay him belly up on a bench. Atel crossed over and burned the Priest with the knife. Violence erupted around Obobo, who had sense enough to hold still for Atel's mirror. She burned him too but burned the ropes more, enough that he ripped his arms loose and knocked the surprised warriors sprawling. As he worked frantically on his lower bonds, Atel shifted her beam to the next trouble spot. A second Priest had grabbed the knife and went for Pio and Peco, still trussed together and pinned on their backs by several warriors. Atel concentrated on the knife hand but it was a moving target.

The Priest drew the knife back for a mortal thrust but had to pause for better aim because Peco was also a moving target. That pause was enough. Atel's beam settled squarely on the knife hand. The Priest screamed and dropped the weapon. It clattered into the pile-up and into Pio's grasp, who never took his eyes off it. After that bit of luck, things got easier. Obobo was loose and grabbed a burning stick. Atel, with all the firelight to work with, got into everyone's eyes while the smaller fairies cut themselves loose. It was a more even fight after that. The fairies backed against the fire and Atel above them while the Jaguars circled, looking for an opening, and the Priests shouted at them from outside the circle. Here at the center of their old power they didn't mind fire at all, but the mirror was too much and their flesh was real enough to be burned.

That was the good part. On the bad side, the fairies couldn't hope to escape. There were many Jaguars, more than a hundred. They had taken the fairies once and they knew they could do it again here. Not while the fire burned brightly, maybe, but it would soon die down. They already had it figured out. They backed off and fell at ease, talking idly and paying little attention to the 'prisoners' for now.

A Priest - the first to be burned - came forward as the warriors made way for him. He stood tall and shouted things at the fairies, amusing things by the reaction of the Jaguars. He had another knife and made gestures with it. His crowd thought that was even more amusing.

"Anyone could guess that part", said Atel. "What else is he saying?"

"Just what we already know", Obobo answered. "Soon the fire will die, and they'll have their way with us. He's right about the fire, more's the pity, but not about playing with us. We have a knife too, and we'll take our own lives before *they* get 'em".

"Don't talk that way. Not yet!"

"Just letting you know, Your Ladyship. Promise one thing if it comes to that?"

"Like what?"

"They'll be horribly disappointed if they lose us. Laugh at them!"

Half an hour passed, then another. The fire became like an hourglass, running out. The Jaguars began a cat-and-mouse game, edging in when the fire burned low, edging back when the fairies stoked it. When all the unburnt ends but two had been fed into the embers the warriors started circling again, taunting the fairies who faced them with only a knife and two torches - until with a rush of wind everyone's plans blew away.

The dragon came.

***

The High Priests shrank into the midst of their warriors for protection as he circled low, but he saw them. He would've incinerated them, and everyone else too, except for the interference of a pesky hummingbird who clung to the bridge of his nose, shouting that she had a better idea.

"No, Volcan - no! Three are *fairies*! Spare those!"

What is it today? the dragon thought. *Always someone on my nose!* He ignored her and focused on the Priests. That's what he came for - to *eat* them! He landed heavily among the Jaguars, crushing several who were slow to move, and reached for their masters who were screaming orders to the warriors.

"*They* die too!" one Priest shouted to the dragon. "Your dirty conspirators die first!" The Jaguars advanced on the fairies in a phalanx of spears. Death hung in the balance.

Conspirators? That jogged more memories. He looked again. The fairies *were* familiar. He *did* remember them. *Well? So what! He was hot!* He kept reaching. Then the bird on his nose had an inspiration.

"Let them play ball!" she shouted. "In the arena! Jaguars against the fairies! You eat the losers".

Well, now!

Dragons do exactly as they please when they're hot and this one was hungry for revenge; but there's a sporting side to them too, when they hold most of the aces. Volcan knew he could pick and choose - so why not have a little entertainment before supper? He remembered the sport, played with a rubber ball. The Old Tribe played it all the time. Sometimes even Kings and Emperors challenged each other with their kingdoms and their own lives at stake. *Yes! Why not have some fun?* He threw back his head and laughed, spouting fire into the sky.

"*PLAY BALL!*" he roared. "*THREE AGAINST THREE! I GET THE LOSERS!*"

It went without saying that he would referee as well, but the idea was welcomed by both sides. Weapons slowly lowered. There was a lot of grinning and cockiness among the Jaguars as the crowd split and moved to the arena, but the Priests themselves were under no illusions. Everything still depended on the whim of the dragon.

The first rule of the game was: All wagers must be paid! But if Volcan was going to eat only the losers, the Priests saw a sure way to save themselves and quickly picked a team from the Jaguars, veterans and experts in the sport who should win easily; and if they lost - so what?

The fairies had played the game too, especially Obobo and Peco on their trade routes back in the day, but mostly for the novelty.

"Nice of you to get us out of a jam", grumbled Obobo. "But this ain't a whole lot more promising".

"You're welcome", replied the hummingbird. "Better do some warm-ups".

The old arena had been excavated in fine condition except for seating areas that were mostly missing. It had a level, narrow floor about twenty paces wide (by fairy measure) and about twice that in length, with steeply sloping walls on either side and a half-court line extending up one sidewall to a stone goal with a round hole in it. The game rules were simple: 1) Keep the ball in the air by striking it with any part of the body except arms or legs. 2) Return it across the line and into the ground for points as in volleyball, and to keep the serve. 3) To win the game with one shot, send the ball through the goal for ten points. The ball itself was rubber and heavy enough to cause injury, but there was no allowance for this. No excuses. Several balls were obtained from the tourist display and warm-ups commenced, but the dragon called a foul on the Jaguars at that point and stopped everything.

It was his intention to devour the High Priests *first*, following the match, and have the losing team for dessert. But he liked his food warm and they were cold, like everything in the Ghost Realm - so without bothering about protocol he ordered them personally to warm up and play.

The fairies breathed a sigh of relief. For their opponents, it was a blow. The Priests were fat - good to bounce a ball off, but slow to the ball. They hadn't played since taking up their ceremonial knives and their skills had slipped. But their Order had no honor. The referee would have work to do.

Volcan knew all this and reveled in it. Dragons, when awake, insist on taking an active part in everything. He ordered the field cleared of all but the contestants - scorching a few slowpokes to make his point - and awarded the ball to the fairies first, as visitors, drawing a few scowls from the crowd.

The fairies put Obobo in the middle where he could return a lot of volleys, being biggest and strongest, with the others as setup players on each side. To start, Pio tossed the ball up where 'Bo could easily whack it with his hip, and the game was on. Unfortunately, Obobo was badly out of practice and sent the ball directly to the center Priest who turned casually and made the return volley with a rear end even bigger than 'Bo's. The Priests had shed all their feathery paraphernalia and moved more quickly without it. Whether by luck or skill it was a good shot, low in front of Peco, but he dived and managed to save it off his back. He bounced it several times that way and got it up nicely for Obobo who almost missed the ball, bumping it just enough to drop it on the line.

"POINT TO THE VISITORS!" ruled the dragon. The Priests and their crowd protested hotly. Volcan answered with fire, singing a lot of bangs and locks in the gallery. It never pays to argue with the referee. Play resumed with the fairies holding serve.

This time Peco tossed the ball and 'Bo struck it well, but the center Priest anticipated and blocked the serve back at him and into the ground, backing across the center line to do so. Atel protested but was drowned out by the cheers of the Jaguars. Volcan let it pass. Now it was the Priest's turn to serve.

The right wing simply tossed the ball at the center's rump - poised just above the line - and it glanced down onto the fairies' side. Tie game! The Priests laughed. Then the left wing did it. There seemed no defense for it. 2-1, Priests. The crowd was enjoying themselves now. The right wing went for it again, but this time 'Bo was ready.

Timing it perfectly he rushed backward and slammed into the center rump to rump, which was legal because the Priest's rump was sticking well over the line. The ball squirted up, bounced off the sidewall and down at Pio, who simply caught it on his back and let it roll off across the line. Fairies' serve!

By now Obobo was getting the hang of aiming and found he could hit the gaps quicker than the fat Priests could fill them. The fairies scored three quick points and the Priests were pooping out. The fairies' athleticism was starting to tell. On the next serve, the center Priest simply walked across the line and blocked the ball with his hands. The dragon called a foul and a free shot.

Obobo took his stance and Peco flipped the ball. Smack! It sailed true and would likely have gone through the goal, but a Jaguar reached down with his war club and swatted it away. While Peco stood waiting for a foul to be called the ball landed in his area. Volcan winked at the interference. *"HOME SERVE!"* he ruled. He wasn't going to let the fun end so quickly. The Priests pulled off another of their 'derriere-drops' while the fairies protested. *"HOME POINT!"* ruled the referee.

The Priests were pooped, but not dumb. They wised up and stayed away from Obobo, picking on Pio mostly. The Three would rush either him or Peco as a group and do their little trick. When the smaller fairy dived and saved it, the wings stepped across the line to block the referee's view and the center just grabbed the ball and slammed it down hard on the fairy. Pio was seriously hurt, unable to continue, and Peco was knocked out cold. Volcan leaned one way and another for a better view but allowed play to continue. While Peco lay unconscious, the Priests quickly lined up over him to do it again. Obobo lost his temper and stepped across far enough to take a good swing, knocking the center flat onto his back

"*FOUL!*" roared the dragon but ruled the unconscious Priest must take the free shot. Volcan was enjoying himself immensely.

The center staggered up, unable to see clearly, but still got the ball up onto the wall. From there it took several unexpected bounces on the way down. Peco was awake again but not seeing too clearly either and he missed saving it. Still 'Home' ball.

The Priests kept up their bullying tactics. Why not? Pio lay injured and Peco was knocked silly again. Even Obobo had bruises from the heavy ball. When the score reached 9-4 against them and the dragon seemed indifferent to the cheating, Obobo stepped across and levelled another Priest - this time the right wing. The center backed away, but the left wing swung wildly in retaliation, missing Obobo entirely.

"*FOUL!*" roared the dragon, but to everyone's surprise, he awarded the free shot to the fairies. He winked at Atel as the gallery erupted in protest. "*That's what always happens*", he confided. "*Referees miss the first punch but call the guy who retaliates*".

Volcan had to get a little rough to restore order but eventually the fairies got their free shot. Peco tossed it up because Pio couldn't and Obobo hit another good shot. An excellent shot. The Jaguars were ready for it, of course, and several war clubs reached out to bat the ball away, but Vulcan was ready too. He blasted the Jaguars, charring several and setting fire to the ball, which continued right through the goal. Visitors win!

But no!

"*TIE GAME!*" ruled the dragon. "*NOW - SUDDEN DEATH! CHOOSE YOUR WEAPONS*".

He ordered the Jaguars to toss down knives and war clubs, which they did, but all to the Priests. Volcan didn't interfere, leaving it to the fairies to think of something, and allowing the Priests to 'warm up' some more. Pio still was unable to help, but Peco was. He went to the burning game ball at midfield and kicked it into the Priests who stood in a group choosing ceremonial knives. It knocked one down and spooked the others. Obobo grabbed up a war club. 'Sudden Death' didn't last long after that. The High Priests were great at murdering people forcibly held down but weren't much in a fair fight. Volcan stopped it before the end and snatched up the Priests for his own style of sudden death, being careful to chew his food well before swallowing. The Jaguars pressed in to do battle, those who had spears, but the spears simply glanced off Volcan's thick hide. If they wanted to do real harm, they might have thrown them at the fairies, but they missed that chance too, and then their chances ran out.

As each priest went down the hatch the Jaguars lost courage. When the third was swallowed, Volcan reached for them next and they scattered, melting away into the ruins, into their underworld. The Priests no longer held their loyalty.

Of course, it wasn't the end of the underworld. It never is. A bad chapter was closed but the voices of darkness are sure to find new listeners. One day, ghost warriors will come again. But not for a while.

The fairies were awfully beaten up and grumpy. Obobo even picked an argument with Volcan.

"You should've called more fouls!" he barked, jerking an angry thumb toward Pio, still flat on his back. But the dragon was playful and jolly in victory and brushed it off.

"*THAT'S NOTHING*", he rumbled. "*BUMPS AND BRUISES! ANYWAY, I THINK I ARRIVED IN THE NICK OF TIME.*"

The heat of battle cooled enough for this to sink in. Obobo bowed in deference and offered compliments. So did Peco. Even Pio raised an arm in agreement. Volcan was insulted.

"*SKIP THE FLATTERY!*" he growled. "*THE PRIESTS USED TO DO THAT*". Then he surprised them, calling them by their right names, and turned to Atel. "*BRASSY LITTLE THING, AREN*"*T YOU?*

BUT YOU FELL IN WITH DECENT COMPANY. I WOULD'VE EATEN THE PRIESTS BACK IN THE OLD DAYS, BUT THEY USED TO DELIVER EASY MEALS TO MY DEN".

Perhaps it occurred to him at this point that his 'den' had been the Fairy Commons before that. Whatever, Volcan seemed slightly embarrassed. He belched and picked his teeth with a spear. Dragons are invaluable friends on their good days, but most days aren't so good.

"Where will you go?" asked Atel. "They say there are dragons still in the far north. I daresay you're hot enough again to join them".

Volcan wasn't interested. He felt chilled after his meal. The Priests - even warmed up as they were - still were like cold cuts. And he didn't like the modern world, now that he looked out at it. He and all of them were still in the Ghost Realm but the city showed through well enough. He wanted no part of men and missed his comfortable fumarole. With the typical unpredictable nature of his kind he suddenly roared, blasting fire through to the living side and scorching the entire ball field.

"THERE! LET MEN FIGURE THAT OUT!" he snorted and launched into the living sky.

Atel followed through the opening to go find the butterflies. The fairies hurried across to catch the early morning sun. It's cold on the spirit side for the living, and though the earth was slowly forgetting them they weren't forgotten yet. The sun felt good.

Chapter 23

Escape to Manino

Now that the worst was over, Atel's thoughts were turning to the fabulous nectars in her own winter gardens far to the south, but she wanted to say goodbye to the butterflies, and had a question that needed to be asked. By chance or fate, she met them just outside the city.

"Ahoy, little ones!" she called from a distance. "You are going the wrong way if you expect to find Manino".

The butterflies laughed. "We don't worry about such things", answered Yero. "That's for our guides to keep track of".

"Then you're going the right way after all", smiled Atel. "The fellows are straight ahead, more or less. I think they would be interested in journeying back with you, at least as far as their 'Old Digs'. Manino is near there, did you know?"

"Yes. Somewhere higher up, from what they told us. Are you leaving, then?'

"I am. I need the rest".

"We don't know how we can ever thank you".

"Then I'll tell you. Finish out your journey. Do what you can when you get there. There is trouble even in paradise".

"What does that mean?"

"Don't expect paradise, that's all. It's cold up there now. That's one thing, but not the only thing".

"Do you have to be so realistic? We're setting out to be cheerful today".

"You usually do. It's the guide's job to temper that a bit".

"Since you're leaving, we'll ignore that", laughed Boca. "But what about the dragon? We think he just passed us going the other way, unless it was an airplane. Did he find you, then?"

"He certainly did. The fairies will tell you everything. But I'm curious. How did you wake him? What did you say that riled him so?"

Yero was bashful about this. "I made something up", she said. "He was going back to sleep, so I told him the Priests laughed when he was killed. That shook him up some".

"Well? 'Some' isn't 'a lot'".

"I told him they said, *Good! We won't have to kiss the lizard anymore!*"

Atel laughed like she hadn't in months. "*Lizard*, huh? I love it! *That* would fire up a dragon".

She gave them directions and said goodbye. The butterflies hurried on. Morning was upon the city. The fairies needed to leave quickly. They should have left the area earlier, but who would expect the police before 7:00 AM?

It was the green-uniformed Tourist Police, two of them patrolling on horseback. Young senior corporal Honero and a junior corporal were the lowest ranks at their precinct, which explains why they were out on patrol. They were also decent fellows, which explains why they had been assigned to the Tourist Police. They were trotting along the adjacent city street when they noticed the fairies on the walk path in the historic site, and reined in. The senior corporal hailed them from a distance.

"Attencion touristas! This site doesn't open until 9:00 AM. What are you doing in there?"

When the fairies didn't answer right away, the corporals trotted right up to them along the walkway. The fellows were a sorry sight, tattered and bruised.

"Have you been assaulted?" asked the senior corporal in surprise.

"Si", answered Obobo, seizing on the idea. "We were set upon by the gangs and beaten". Obobo offered Pio as clear evidence. "They dragged us in here...and robbed us, too", he added as an afterthought.

The senior corporal noticed the scorched arena, still smelling of combustion. "Mio dios! Did you do that?"

"Please, sir. How could we? We can barely walk".

It worked. Both officers were genuinely moved. "You're lucky to be alive!" marveled the senior corporal. "The gangs are brutal". Obobo simply nodded. The smaller fairies just shivered.

"We're going to take you in for medical attention and some clothes", decided the officer. "You can call home from there".

Obobo tried to decline but the senior corporal wouldn't hear of it. "We'll need to take your statement anyway", he explained, "to get an investigation going. You can look through mugshots while we shuffle the papers. Climb on!"

There was just no way to refuse. The walkways were swept daily so there was no dust to work with and the officers really wanted to help. Obobo was nearly as tall as the senior corporal and able to climb up behind him. Peco and especially Pio needed assistance but were duly horsed - one behind the junior corporal, one ahead of him - and they headed for the sector station some blocks off from the busier streets.

It wasn't a large police station at all, just a small building in two parts, with offices up front and stables in the rear. It had a hitching rail out front for horses and that's where they tied up when they arrived. The officers dismounted and assisted the victims into the front office. The First Sergeant in charge hardly bothered to look, just pushed a form toward them as he was putting on his coat.

"Get their stuff down; you know the drill", he said. "I'm knocking off early. It's Christmas, day after tomorrow. Cover for me".

Out he went, which meant the senior corporal was stuck in the office for the day, responsible for patrols. He sent the junior corporal back out and ushered the victims into the interrogation room, settling them in chairs as comfortably as possible. He called for the cook to see to their wounds and serve breakfast while he dug up some clothes. This is what he envisioned the Tourist Police to be all about. He would soon learn a different job description, but for now the fairies couldn't have fallen into a better situation.

He discovered whole boxes of obsolete uniforms, scheduled to be burned. The Ministry was big on uniforms if not pay, and often commissioned natty little design tweaks. Naturally, the old uniforms must be burned - what else? He found a uniform for Obobo without much trouble. The best he could do for the others were oversized but gratefully accepted. Next came paperwork and routine questions.

"Names, please".

"Torres", answered Obobo readily. "We are Fathers Obobo, Pio and Peco of the Torres Missions".

"Home address?"

"We have none. Our Order requires lifelong pilgrimage".

"I suppose you have no phone then?"

"No, there is no need. In our work, we seek out lost souls and speak only to The Almighty".

"How much money or valuables did they take from you? We have a very small charitable fund for indigents..."

"The children's food allowance will be sorely missed", replied Obobo sadly. "There were 70 pesos, for baby formula".

"Also, the simple gold crosses", lamented Pio. "The Mission's only material possessions".

"They stole the alms" bewailed Peco. "And the cup too! We must pray they needed it".

They might have talked the senior corporal out of the entire fund, but it was destined to go to another - another *three*, actually - who trotted up on horses at that very moment.

One was known to the senior corporal: The Commandant of Tourist Police, resplendent in his decorated uniform. The others were from Ministry Headquarters: An Inspector and his accountant, obviously uncomfortable on horseback. Senior corporal Honero took one look out the window and cursed under his breath, understanding better now why the First Sergeant had vamoosed. He rushed the victims out the back door with their unauthorized uniforms and ran to greet the Delegation, but the Commandante threw the door open without knocking and marched right in, demanding to see the First Sergeant. He had to settle for a corporal, which didn't help his mood any. He was under pressure from the Ministry.

"Where is the staff?" he demanded. "We send a lot of paychecks down here! Where are the people?"

"There is only myself at the moment, sir. And of course, our award-winning cook..." Everyone knew about the Commandante who ate free everywhere, especially at the best restaurants.

"Well, get me some breakfast then! In the meantime, these gentlemen have some questions and concerns. Get your books out".

Get your books out? The senior corporal had never been allowed to see those. He didn't know where to look. He could only point to the duty desk. "Everything should be in there - or in the file cabinet", he stammered.

The Inspector riffled efficiently through the drawers. He pulled out records of tickets and fines and a box of petty cash - the 'indigent fund' - handing that to the accountant who emptied it into his coat pocket without bothering to count it. He flipped through pages of several ledgers and slammed them shut impatiently.

"That's just the fines you *record*", he snapped. "Where's the rest? Who keeps the *bite*?"

The senior corporal wished he were somewhere else. They marched him into the interrogation room and demanded to know who was skimming the money because their kickback had stopped coming in.

"We expect ten percent of *everything!*" the Inspector shouted at him. "We know you're biting the tourists! You just aren't sending in our share! We're going to withhold half your pay for a while to get things moving again".

The senior corporal clung to one happy thought: If he could somehow satisfy these Big Shots and see them off, the real trouble would end up in the laps of the station sergeants (there were four, all taking a few unofficial days off) where it belonged. He promised the Ministry vultures anything, just to get them into the dining room with the Commandante. The cook took it from there and brought out the tequila right away. Eventually the questioning subsided, and the senior corporal was relegated to server duty.

Out on the street meanwhile, police routine went on as usual. Three uniformed Tourist Police appeared and mounted their steeds - or tried to. The opportunity and temptation proved irresistible to the fairies. Why not ride out of town? However, first things must come first. The oversize clothes were manageable, but the tall boots were an absolute hindrance. Corporal Honero had insisted on boots and they would need them now for appearance, but they came way up to the rump on the smaller fairies. They couldn't bend their legs. Obobo lifted them enough to swing a leg over the saddle, but then the stirrups were too long. He finally jammed the boots into the stirrups and the smaller fairies just dangled their feet into the tops.

So, the Official Delegation lost their horses, but it would be at least an hour before the problem was discovered. The fairies regretted that the good corporal would catch heat for it, but it didn't end up that way. As it turned out, it was the good corporal who noticed the steeds missing. He called the Judiciary Police about it before he said anything to his guests. The Judiciary bunch weren't under the Ministry and would enjoy this case - especially the tequila aspect during duty hours. Senior corporal Honero hung up the duty phone and hurried to pour another stiff round, courtesy of Sector Station 7.

By now the odd little tourist police were many blocks away catching on to horseback duty very well. The Station was of course situated on a bicycle route - a network of narrow streets and paths reserved for bikes and pedestrians - so horse patrols were a common sight. The route was so well marked that even these raw recruits were able to follow, and since the precinct was in the northern part of the city, they figured to escape the busier parts of town by midday. It looked easy, but they didn't account for tourists with cameras.

Part 4: The Lure of the Dragon Range

The route was designed to bring tourists together with greenery and various small attractions. There were benches and fountains at likely spots where visitors would have their cameras out, and the picturesque mounted police were a favorite subject. All through the noon hour it was stop and go.

Sometimes it was easy, a matter of waving as they trotted past. Sometimes they were obliged to stop a minute, and that wasn't much hassle. But sometimes the tourists were full of ideas. Could the officers arrange the horses in a semi-circle? Could they wave their caps? Dismount? Dismount and salute? That would be so cool! They were saved the first time by Peco's horse who took the idle opportunity to dump a pile of horse-apples in the midst of the photographers. The charm faded and that crowd dispersed. One offended lady even gave chase demanding to know why police officers - 'of all people' - couldn't control that sort of thing'!

The second incident was trickier. There were the usual requests, all manageable. Then someone asked for their Station telephone number to call and pass along compliments. Obobo declined but it was mistaken for modesty, prompting insistent requests. Then someone noticed that Pio's legs looked twice as long as they should be in the boots and people started to stare.

Luckily, that's when the butterflies caught up to them. They had missed the fairies at the ruins but noticed a lot of activity at the police station. From what they overheard it wasn't hard to guess their friends' plans. Now they got in front of the cameras where they couldn't be missed.

"Monarchs!" someone shouted. "From the Preserve!"

Pio and Peco backed their horses up slowly as the photogenic monarchs fluttered and danced in the air, perfect from every camera angle. Some in the crowd didn't know anything about monarchs and others did. "Oh, yes", someone explained. "The pretty things come all the way down from the U.S., even Canada. They spend the winter in the 'Preserve', up in the mountains".

"Too bad about the snow", said someone else. "Did you hear about the snow?"

Obobo reached his hand out. The monarchs landed on his finger. Amazing! More pictures! More pictures!

"Don't waste any more time than you have to", advised Yero. "They're after you".

'Bo smiled to the crowd and moved his arm around slowly, graciously, just a bit longer, then put on a stern police air. "We are taking these endangered species into custody, to be returned to the Preserve", he announced. "Poor things must be hungry". It got the desired reaction. Tourists offered pop, candy bars, even yogurt. "No, none of that. Nothing chocolate or carbonated. Nothing diet. Anyone have honey?"

Someone offered a breakfast syrup packet, which Obobo accepted. Then it was time to leave. Bicycle police were approaching with their whiny sirens going. The fairies lit out at a gallop. Peco and Pio both lost their tall boots and reins and just hung on to the pommels as Obobo led the way and the butterflies kept a lookout to the rear. When the cycle cops got close 'Bo did the only thing he could, reining his horse off the path, over a low fence and through the pretty green border into thick brush and sharp rocks. The Parks Department believed in leaving things 'natural'.

A helicopter came over quite low, so they left the horses, rolled up their trouser legs and went ahead on foot. The helicopter circled ominously, following them; but there was no dirt or dust to cast with, only rocks. Then they emerged from the brush belt into - of all things - a golf course, near the 18th hole. The helicopter landed by the clubhouse and an angry Commandante of Tourist Police emerged along with some sort of S.W.A.T. team.

A foursome was putting out on the green and a small crowd stood by - some watching the golfers, some watching the helicopter, even a few looking curiously at what must be uniformed groundskeepers emerging from the rough.

It didn't look like any race, but it was. The nervous golfers called everything a 'gimme' and headed for the clubhouse; the Commandante shouted through a bullhorn as the S.W.A.T. team surrounded the green; the little groundskeepers walked very businesslike to a big sand trap and went to work. Two grabbed rakes and stood downwind while the other tossed scoops of sand upwind and gave directions. That was Peco of course, but he was talking to the sand. It was windy here in the open and the finer sand got all over the groundskeepers. They faded and soon disappeared entirely. Butterflies that had been hanging around apparently got bored and went away also.

We will leave this puzzle for the Big People, along with the scorched ball field and a few other things. It's their world now. If they can't figure it out, they can always file it under *Strange but True*, where a lot of things end up that were once common knowledge.

Beyond the golf course was a major thoroughfare and a traffic jam in the outbound lanes. It was Friday and people were leaving for the weekend, or trying to, and Peco noticed an empty logging truck among the stop-and-go vehicles. They made for it and climbed aboard between the heavy side stakes, settling themselves under the shadow of the tall hydraulic log grapple. The jam stayed jammed for some time as always on Friday afternoons, but they hardly noticed. Everyone had news and questions. Boca had been surprised to see his buddies in uniform and relieved to learn it was only temporary.

"You'd have to swear off all your bad habits, wouldn't you?" he asked. "Police are supposed to be well-behaved. Did they warn you about that?"

"We didn't get into background checks", chuckled Pio. "We didn't have time and they didn't either. But I think we could've fit in just fine, if the stirrups were a little higher".

Yero laughed. "It's a shame you had to quit the job so soon. You were such crowd-pleasers! But I suppose it was boring after the dragon and all".

"It was. Surprised us, that did. Last night we thought more police were *needed* around here, but maybe not".

Everyone laughed again, and then Boca wanted a full description of the ball game, especially 'sudden death'. "Volcan wouldn't have let you lose, would he?"

The fairies scowled and shook their heads slowly. Pio checked his bruises. "No, he wouldn't have", said Obobo after a minute. "But he made sure to push it to the limit. Rough fellow - even as a friend! But we were doomed without him. Things look a lot brighter today I don't mind saying".

"We figured you'd head back north to your Digs", said Yero. "Are you?"

"We are. A lot's happened. We wouldn't mind another peep at the stone now".

"And maybe find your old rings?"

The fairies just laughed and Yero suddenly felt more like a 'Good Old Boy' than a girl. She was finally 'in', and not so sure that she liked it. But Pio teased her out of the mood.

"You never give up do you, little sister? - Oh, good! The jam is moving". It was. At last! The truck lurched.

"That's a good way to change the subject", said Yero.

"Then we'll change it again. Are you off to your Manino now? You might think twice. All that rain would've turned to snow higher up. It can't be good up there".

"Then we'll need dinner first. Why not open that syrup?"

Why not indeed? It had been forgotten in the rush, but now it was nicely warmed up in Obobo's pocket. The conversation continued but the butterflies dropped out of it to enjoy their meal, maybe their last for...who knew? It didn't sound promising.

Traffic picked up. There were more stop-and-goes but no more real delay. The fairies' spirits picked up too as they rumbled through the northern suburbs into open country beyond, working northwest in a direct reverse of their forced march with the Jaguars. Their future, whatever remained of it on the green earth, was opening up in front of them. A centuries-old threat was removed. Plans and ideas long out of mind were occurring to them. The butterflies listened with mixed feelings, wondering what their tomorrow would bring.

"The driver is probably heading where you want to go, near enough", said Pio after a while. "Logging goes on up there, in spite of some restrictions. When he stops for fuel, we'll be off on our way and you can follow him up. We'd rather you come with us to see the stone again, but it's your choice".

The truck did stop for fuel and the fairies got off. It was getting late in the afternoon and the Digs weren't far away. Not far at all. The butterflies decided to tag along for practical reasons: Night was nearing, and it was already cold, even here. The weather promised to be clear in the morning. They could get an early start then.

There were also un-practical reasons: Boca was just not quite ready to bid his macho pals goodbye, and Yero did want another peep into the stone.

They found the light shafts just about dark with ropes still dangling down into them. The old spell of concealment had worn away through years of sunshine but the 'window' itself was in fine shape, situated atop a solid dome of rock. Pio and Obobo gathered firewood and threw down the shafts. It wasn't especially warm in the Commons this time of year and they intended to spend a comfortable evening. They shinnied down the ropes to make a fire while Peco, who was best at it, repaired the spell temporarily and then joined them.

There had always been a roaring fireplace in the Commons during mealtimes, especially in winter, and the smoke went up the 'chimney' shaft to be erased by the spell on its way out. The dragon had cleared the fireplace away, but they built their fire where it would have been and soon had a cheery atmosphere. There was a bit of leftover supper for the butterflies but nothing for the fairies, who didn't seem to mind at all.

"For tonight let's just be happy, all of us", said Pio. "Tomorrow is soon enough to look at the stone".

"And the rings", reminded Yero.

"Sure. Just for you, little sister", shrugged Obobo. "But the stone is what we've come for. It should show a different picture now. If it shows better days ahead, we might look for our brothers again after all this time. It's been most of an Age since fairies had much to look forward to".

The fellows talked far into the night, but the butterflies drifted into slumber. Yero slept well but Boca dreamed of their journey's end. In his dream, they searched for Manino all through the pine forests, but when they found it they were turned away. He awakened angry from the dream and saw the fire, and Yero, and their friends, and realized it was only a dream; but when he nodded off again the dream returned. When Yero shook him in the morning, he was cross and felt like he had no rest at all.

"Wake up, sleepyhead! They're getting out the stone. Hurry!"

They reached the old Treasury in time to see Peco lift the Fairystone and hold it out toward them, toward the morning light in the doorway behind them, and look into it. He dropped the stone and turned away blushing. Pio caught it in mid-air and had a look too, just as Yero arrived to peek over his shoulder.

A fair-haired lass looked out to see who was watching her. She smiled. Pio winked at her but seemed totally at a loss for words. Maybe that was best. She smiled again. He handed the stone off to Obobo.

"Who was she?" asked Yero, but Pio didn't answer. He and Peco were trying to look over 'Bo's big shoulder. A cheerful red-haired lass, size medium-large, looked out curiously. Obobo grinned and smarted off like the roughneck he was: "Hey, babe! Where've you been all my life?" Irritation flickered across her pretty features and the lass turned away with a few choice words for 'Bo.

"What did she say?" asked Pio, but Obobo frowned and shrugged his shoulders.

"Couldn't tell", he said. "Sound don't come through very good".

Pio laughed. Peco grinned and jabbed Obobo in the ribs.

"Is that your future?" asked Yero.

Pio rubbed his hands together nervously, pretending they were cold. "Who knows? 'Bout *time* the babes turned up again, though!"

Boca alighted on Obobo's shoulder. "Will it tell *our* fortune?" he asked. "Can we look?"

It could. Already the image was shifting, turning mostly white. No one looked out this time. It was just a glimpse in the distance of a grove of fir trees in the mountains, branches drooping from the weight of snow.

"That's the place!" exclaimed Boca. "I dreamed of it last night". He turned to Yero. "They don't want us. They won't take us in".

"Oh, no!" said Yero in alarm. "We have to go!"

It was better this way. There's never enough time for good-byes when friends will likely never see each other again. The butterflies waved and were off, up the light shafts and into the cold morning outside.

"You're worrying me now", said Yero. "Snow would be bad enough and we don't even know that for sure. Maybe you just had a nightmare".

"Maybe. But there was snow in it, and you saw the stone. I don't think it ever lies".

They retraced their way to the Truckstop and followed that road up into the pine forests - or what remained of them. A lot of patches were logged off although many showed re-growth. The loggers were always blamed. All the fingers pointed at them. But these men had families and needed work. And where did all the wood go? Everyone shares in that. But this was not yet Manino. That was more remote, further off the beaten path.

All morning they climbed, following the good road until it petered out at the last village and they flew on into the wilderness. The pines were mixed now with a type of fir at this elevation. There were still clear-cut patches, but not as many. Everywhere was snow. It wasn't unheard-of in these mountains; but the amount and the deep cold afterward were rare.

Around midday, Boca saw in the distance what he was looking for: A tall stand of the firs nestled into the slopes, thicker than the surrounding forest, for all the world like the picture in the Fairystone. Boca knew it twice already. It was the same place in his dream.

"There it is!" he said. "Follow me".

He was not mistaken. As they drew close, he led the way down into the firs searching for the Multitudes, but the grove was larger than it appeared from a distance. They saw no one for a while, only branches heavy with snow. Then, "There!" said Yero. Up ahead they caught glimpses of orange mixed with the green and white. They flew toward the color.

"Parada! Stop!" called a voice unexpectedly. A lone monarch scrutinized them from her perch. Whether by design or chance, the sun warmed her there and she was active. "*Comun* or *Realeza*?" she demanded.

"Beg your pardon?" said Yero.

"Oh, Northerners. I mean, are you one of *Us* - or are you *Royals*?"

"We didn't know there were differences. You can see we're monarchs".

"Yeah, sure - but what's in your *head*, Sweetie? Are you one of *us*, or are you *Estallados*, the starry-eyed ones? They have their own roost".

"I know there are other generations. I didn't know it made any difference".

"Sure! There it is! *Other* generations, you *say*. *Lesser* generations is what you mean! You are Royals. I can tell every time".

"Let's just ignore her", said Boca. "She's in a bad mood".

"Go ahead then. You won't find any welcome. We don't like snobs".

"I'm starting to think it's the other way around", replied Yero. "We didn't bring any chip on our shoulders, but you sure have one".

"Wrong again, Sweetie. It's the Royals who bring an attitude. You think you're special".

"Think what you want. We're going to have a look".

They went in, Boca leading the way. The orange was dazzling in the sunshine, great orange clusters. A few branches sagged from the weight of snow, but most were drooping with masses of monarchs huddling against the winter weather. But all beauty evaporated after the first glance. There was a constant flutter of them to the snowy floor, like autumn leaves. The dazzling brightness of the roost was due in large part to frost on the clusters. The monarchs were dying in the cold.

"Let's leave", said Boca. "Atel was right. This isn't any paradise".

Yero nodded. They left the way they came. The sentry laughed at them on the way out. "Not welcome? I told you so!" Yero stopped a moment.

"Do you know they're dying?" she asked.

"Some are", admitted the sentry. "And some will recover in the sunshine. It's none of your business. We don't need advice from Realezas!"

"Do you mind telling us where the Royals are?'

"That's no secret. They have segregated themselves".

"And? Where are they segregated to?"

"Higher up - what else? Realezas *always* want to be higher up!"

They left, glad to be rid of her. The trees thinned out uphill except one small grove near the Big Roost. Boca went for that and struck orange in the middle of it, but this was different. There were no clusters and far fewer butterflies, but from a distance almost as much orange. These monarchs were spread out everywhere catching the afternoon sun - far fewer, but still some thousands of them. They went to search for a good perch, but monarchs hailed them from a nearby branch and room was made.

"Got the boot, did you?" asked someone. "Welcome to 'Rejects Roost'". That brought good-natured laughter.

"Thank you", said Yero. "No, we sure weren't welcome down there. They call us 'Royals'. What's that about?"

"You have esporellia on your wings. *Real* esporellia, like us. Maybe they're jealous, I don't know. Anyway - Hi! I'm Nagge".

"Pleased to meet you. I'm Yero and he's Boca. We've just arrived".

"Merry Christmas Eve, then! Other than that, your timing couldn't be worse. It's the worst weather of the journey for most of us. The local talk is, it's never been so cold".

"That sounds like our reception down there, though maybe I shouldn't talk. We've only spoken with a lookout sentry".

"You're lucky then. I arrived early when everyone was active. It hurts when they *all* tell you to beat it".

Yero shivered, more from the ugly truth than the weather.

"What's this 'us against them' stuff?" asked Boca. "How far back does that go?'

"Who knows? Nobody knows", said Nagge. "Maybe a long time. Maybe years".

"Maybe it's just the rule now, and they don't even remember why", ventured Yero. "But they're dying. Have you seen it lately?"

Nagge had and didn't much care to see it again. "They don't want us, and it hurts to look", she said. "The worst part is the sadness. They know what's happening to them. We feel it out here at night. It's a shame because we're cousins, or our kids would be next year. So much for that happy idea".

The afternoon stayed cold, but also calm and sunny. Everyone in the roost became active. Quite a few took to the air within the small grove. Others basked on fir needles. Here in this more exposed roost wind had blown most of the snow off the branches and the sun melted the rest, allowing the sunbathing that looked so lazy but was so serious. When the sun shines, all monarchs soak it up; but when night falls, the earthly generations cool off far too quickly in winter weather. Not so the Rasha La. Their esporellia holds the heat longer - sometimes for days. It's stardust, after all, and so they survive nights like this. In happier times, the Rasha La brought extra warmth to the Big Roost. Everyone's chances were a little better in the cold.

The afternoon was nice enough for lots of talk. Everyone had a story, a harrowing adventure. No two were alike except the choice they made and the fiery journey down to earth when they earned their esporellia. Some of the liveliest talk was about that.

"I thought it was like the biggest water slide ever", said Boca, "but with fire instead of water".

"Or a zip line with open ends", laughed Ava, a girl from the 'burbs'.

"For me it was more like a rodeo", said Iago, a boy from the *high plains*. "Have you ever ridden a runaway horse? Bareback?"

"Ours was like a burning bungee jump from somewhere out past the moon", offered a girl from *out east*. "Except we just stepped off at the bottom".

"That's another thing", said Nagge. "We didn't get any instructions about going back up. Did you?" Yero shook her head. Everyone did.

"We lost good friends on the journey", said someone. "They went back the hard way".

"We lost some too", said a boy named Trebo. "I hope they get another chance. But it was all about *getting here*, not what comes after".

"We figure the job isn't over", said Yero. "We think it goes on all winter and maybe up north again in the spring".

"That's what we think too", said Nagge. "How do you think it ends?"

"The hard way probably. That's not as scary anymore. Or maybe - if we're lucky - we'll just topple over from old age".

"I'll take old age", said a boy from *'way'* up north. "I'll need that long to get home again".

"I'll take it too, if I have a choice", said a girl from *the lake country*. "But I don't want to get old and *fat!*"

"I wouldn't mind that", said Jayd, a boy from *the hood*. "It would mean there's plenty to eat. Sometimes where I come from, there isn't".

"I always figured *old* was when you get married", said someone else.

No one spoke for a while after that until Elle, a girl from *down on the farm* asked, "Did they talk to any of you about that?" Everyone nodded. "I don't know what they told you", Elle continued, "but I don't think we're supposed to marry each other".

"We're not", agreed Nagge. "They told us that too. We're supposed to fit in with all the generations. But how do we do that when they hate us?'

"How do we do that if they all die?" asked Yero.

"Never happen", said Rehta, a girl from *the big city*. "Some always survive, that's what I've heard. It's not that big a deal".

"It would be if you were one of them".

"Well, I'm not. And I won't take the blame for it".

"Me either. That's just silly. But I'd still help them if I could".

"Sure, I guess I would too. But Nagge's right. They hate us and there's no getting around it".

"'Getting around it' is like going in circles. We should do something more direct".

"There's been plenty of direct talk", reminded Nagge. "You've heard some. Talk is hopeless".

"I wasn't thinking about *talk*".

"What then?" laughed Rehta. "We should charge the Big Roost?"

"Sort of. If it gets really cold tonight, we could give them a gift".

It got quiet for a while again. Finally, Boca broke the silence.

"That would be a big one".

Everyone knew what he meant. The idea went through the roost in whispers. No one wanted to talk about it while the sun was shining, but in twos and threes throughout the afternoon quite a few ventured into the Big Roost out of curiosity and came back silent. It was quiet over there. A few monarchs fluttered around, those that caught the sun just right on the outside of the clusters; a few scowls greeted them and a few catcalls, but not many. The Big Roost was weakening.

To chase the depression away some of the Rasha La decided to have Christmas early, and it was a popular idea. The first thing always is to decorate a tree and they naturally went for the biggest one with the sunniest exposure, decorating it with themselves, each showing their best side toward the